Love and Samsāra

Love and Samsāra

EUSEBIO L. RODRIGUES

Washington, DC

Library of Congress Control Number: 2007929774
ISBN 9780979448812 hardcover (alk. paper)
ISBN 9780979448881 paperback (alk. paper)

 An imprint of New Academia Publishing, LLC
PO Box 27420, Washington DC 20028-7420

 info@newacademia.com
www.newacademia.com

Sounsar
Chearuch re dissancho

This world
It's of only four days

Goan folksong

the multiple meanings of *saṃsāra*

the "great ocean" is saṃsāra, says Śankara.
going or wandering through, undergoing transmigration, course,
passage, passing through a succession of states, transmigration,
metempsychosis, circuit of mundane existence, the world, secular
life, worldly illusion.

God is Love

1 JOHN 4

List of Illustrations

The Gujarat Coast   1
Diu Island   13
The African Coast   41
"Salve Rainha"   192
The West Coast of India   245
Goa Island   535

Maps by Ali Abedin
"Salve Rainha" is a painting by Lazaro Luis, 1563

ONE

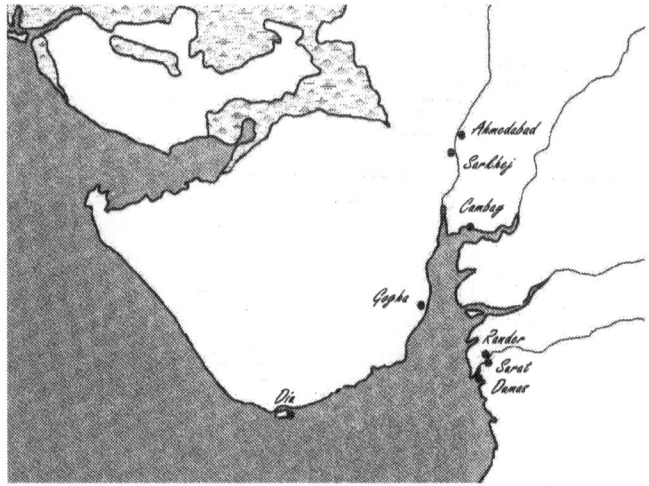

*E*arly May, 1509, Evening
A cave on Diu promontory
I begin writing

I do not know why I am writing this, nor do I know to whom I'm writing. Beloved, I cannot yet set your name down on this paper, but I will, soon, soon. In the old days I wrote only when I needed to write. I used to write down detailed reports with occasional sketch maps about my voyages for traders and *shahbandars*. Or else, I would set down for my fellow navigators clean cold facts they could memorize with ease about that vast stretch of the world that I thought I knew as it were my salt toughened palm.

From behind me comes the faint human hum of Diu town, the only place I know to which I belong. But there, beyond, growls that savage beast that I now know can never really be tamed. Why do I use such a strange expression for the sea when I could use images from the Arabian and Persian poets who disliked the sea? An unstable element, they claimed, that unlike land can never be conquered. What I feel driven to write now is not poetry but the truth. Not really the truth, but a truthtry to understand my shattered world. Do not write poetry, my hakim had often warned me. For you, he had said, writing your story will be a form of healing.

For a month now I have been coming every day to this blackrock promontory when the sun is low and no longer burns my face, and when the wind turns around and a breeze blows soft from the west. It was my friend, Malik Aiyaz, who made me accompany him every day to this commanding spot after our defeat.

I don't want to brood about what happened, Malik Aiyaz told me, I want to understand why it happened.

Why, why, Malik Aiyaz would ask, looking bitterly at the broken *sankalkot* lying lifeless in the bluegreen water, and then he would shake his fist at the smashed little seafort across the channel. He would look down at the jagged cave openings that ring the bluff in a half curve, and shake his head at the smashed remains of the Ottoman guns.

Why, why, he asked me again, why did those guns not keep the Portuguese out of my beloved Diu.

He would pace up and down in this cave where I now sit, then pause a moment to place his hand upon the barrel of the cannon.

Why, oh why did Straighthitter have to crack at the breech end, Malik Aiyaz would say, stroking the cannon as if it were alive.

I would keep quiet. An Ottoman gunner from Bandar-i-Turk had told me that the siege gun had been made of wrought iron that had rusted because of the monsoon winds.

He would say, don't offer me the usual consolation about kismet, that what is written, is written. Help me understand, Ahmad my friend, Malik Aiyaz would say.

And then he would ride off on his horse. And I would walk back to my house in the swiftly gathering darkness.

Why, why, asks Malik Aiyaz.

I too want answers to other painful questions that do not seem to trouble Malik Aiyaz. My friend wants to know why a handful of Portuguese could defeat the combined might of his people, of the Mamluks of Egypt and Syria, and of the Zamorin of Calicut. He is a practical man, a lovable human being, too, and he wants to understand his defeat so that the next time the Portuguese come he'll be victorious again as he was at Chaul last year in March 1508, when he defeated Dom Lourenço de Almeida and the Portuguese fleet.

We had thousands of fighters here in Diu, Malik Aiyaz kept on repeating to me, a hundred ships and *fustas*. Our combined guns numbered fiftyfive. We had the *sankalkot*. I had thought no ship could smash through that chain.

He pointed to the sagging chain, now strung once again across the harbor entrance, and shook his head, trying to understand his defeat.

The Mamluk fleet with its guns and *maonas* was considered invincible, Malik Aiyaz said, it was the most powerful sea force ever seen on the Bahr-i-Hind. It was led by Amir Hussein Kurdi, he said, the most skillful of the admirals of the Mamluk Sultan of Egypt. Young Salman Rais also was there, the Turcoman corsair sent by the Ottoman ruler to help the Mamluks.

Malik Aiyaz still does not understand naval fighting. Perhaps he cannot. He is a commander of land armies. He does not belong to the world of the sea and of ships as I did. He does not realize that what we both had watched, standing that February morning on this blackrock Diu promontory, was not just a battle but a prevision of disaster.

João has told me that there are different modes of seeing.

The moment of change is never quite visible, João had continued, cryptically.

What Malik Aiyaz saw from this promontory was not what I saw.

What Malik Aiyaz had seen, spread out here in front of Diu harbor that early morning of February the 3rd, just three months ago, were two powerful naval forces that met in battle in our Indian Ocean.

The Mamluk *maonas* and war galleys had come down slowly from Suez, a port at the head of the Red Sea in Egypt. They had stopped at Jiddah, the port for Mecca. They had then sailed warily through the narrow gullet that is the Red Sea, and rounded the strait of Bab el Mandab. They had then traveled past Aden and, because they were oared Mediterranean galleys with lateen sails that didn't dare venture on the heavy seas of the Bahr-i-Hind, had hugged the coastline till they reached Chaul on the west coast of India where they had attacked the Portuguese fleet and killed its commander Dom Lourenço de Almeida in March 1508. They had then come back to Diu to celebrate their victory. A year later, on February 3, 1509, they awaited the Portuguese fleet led by the viceroy Dom Francisco de Almeida, who came from the Portuguese headquarters in Cochin in South India to destroy the Mamluk ships at Diu and avenge the death of his only son, whom he loved very much.

Huddled together, their sterns backed towards the shoreline below, with protective netting hanging from their mast tops, cannon fixed on their prows, level and pointing straight, the Mamluk *maonas* and war galleys awaited the Portuguese attack. Large Gujarati oceangoing dhows, each armed with two or three small guns, lay concealed within the inlet bend beyond the *sankalkot*, waiting to surprise the enemy. Innumerable Calicut *paraos* swarmed unsteadily together along the southern shore like angry black bees.

How, Malik Aiyaz asked me, how could just seventeen Portuguese ships, twelve big and five small, prevail against such a circling wall of our ships and guns.

Malik Aiyaz couldn't see what I had seen as we both looked down from the blackrock promontory.

What I had seen on that February 3rd morning was not just a naval battle.

I had looked down and I had seen two worlds meeting head on. I saw the old world that I had lived in clash with the new. It was a savage encounter. I looked down and I saw two naval powers confront each other. The semicircle of Portuguese ships became a concentrated explosive whirl. I heard the controlled thunder of their powerful guns. What I really saw down there from the promontory was a powerful enemy fleet, armed with a new technique of sea fighting, bearing down on us.

Five of the Ottoman siege guns thundered at the Portuguese ships down below. But the Portuguese ships were not damaged at all. The five cave openings erupted into flame, for the guns had exploded killing our gunners. Malik Aiyaz could no longer depend on his siege artillery for support from land. The small guns of the Gujarati dhows, occasionally used to repel sea pirates, were no match against Portuguese cannon. Majestic when sailing before the wind, the dhows now looked like hens huddled together for protection. The black Calicut *paraos* were armed with bowmen. The stately *maonas* from Suez, their oars at rest now, their large lateen sails furled, thought they were still in the eastern Mediterranean. They relied on defense strategies used on an inland sea by slow moving galleys. They expected the Portuguese to use tactics of ramming and boarding. That's why the *maonas* had deployed netting from the mast tops. They were prepared for hand to hand fighting. Passively they awaited the attack, taunting the Portuguese as cowards with trumpets and drums, with shouts and yells.

The Portuguese had a different plan of action. Their tactics were new, put together for attack not on an inland sea with fitful winds like the Mediterranean, but on the oceansea. They ignored the taunts hurled from the *maonas*, ignored the carelessly aimed shots fired from the Ottoman prow guns by gunners who did not take into account the roll and dip of the seawaves. The Portuguese waited patiently for the noontime shift from a land to a sea breeze. For the dense smoke of the Portuguese guns would clear from their ships and drift towards the enemy ships to blind their gunners. Then the Portuguese ships swung in to attack, using sails that could be turned around to harness the blowing sea winds. They mounted an attack of broadside quickfiring guns, placed low in order to send shots skimming over the water. They pounced, weaving between the anchored *maonas*, attacking from all sides, especially from the rear to avoid the stationary prow guns. They had worked out earlier how long it took for the enemy gunners to reload. Each ship captain targeted a *maona* to bombard and destroy.

A well directed cannon shot blew out the seafort's iron pillar to which the *sankalkot* was attached. Then the smaller Portuguese ships proceeded cautiously into the inlet where they attacked the Gujarati ships at close range. They did not need to bombard the Calicut *paraos*. They used swivel guns mounted at rail height. Chain shot and scatter shot wreaked havoc, for they could not miss that swarming cluster of black boats.

By evening the terrifying display of Portuguese power had ended.

Corpses and broken planks, severed arms and legs, torn banners and flags and sails choked Diu channel so that it was difficult for the tide to move in. Malik Aiyaz ordered his forces to stop fighting. Several white flags were raised. He sent his envoy, Sidi Ali, to negotiate terms of surrender and promised to deliver to the Portuguese Viceroy, Dom Francisco de Almeida, the ten hostages we had taken at Chaul in 1508. Malik Aiyaz even invited the Viceroy to land in Diu so that the keys of the city could be presented to him in a formal ceremony as an acknowledgment of submission. But the Viceroy, suspecting a trap and knowing that Portuguese power was strong on the sea and weak on land, shrewdly refused Malik Aiyaz's offer and returned in triumph to Cochin bombarding Muslim portcities all along the coast.

The setting sun transformed the sea, red already with blood, into a dazzling red.

Then night fell sudden and black, and all was quiet.

Malik Aiyaz does not know what I am slowly beginning to realize now as I keep staring from this blackrock promontory at the sea below. That what I had witnessed, three months ago, was not just a savage encounter but also an event that has confirmed my growing fears that the Portuguese and their black ships are not just pirates but invaders who will change our world forever. My fears had begun as a slight premonition, eleven years ago, in 1498, when I saw the ships of Vasco da Gama and Paulo da Gama drop anchor in Malindi bay. The ships then were a black blur against the rapidly setting sun. And suddenly it was night.

I keep staring at the swirling currents of change in the sea below and I keep wondering why they are invisible to Malik Aiyaz. Perhaps the words on this paper will make them visible. Perhaps I am writing to tell my friend Malik Aiyaz that the movement of power is wavelike, that it goes up and then has to come down. Perhaps I want to make the entry of the Portuguese into the Bahr-i-Hind visible to my friend. Visible to myself too, so that we can understand the swift rise of the Portuguese to power. I have to make my own buried past visible too. For myself. For the two stories are connected and I am the only one who can put them together.

I need to explain myself to my self. Explain, that's the wrong verb.

One must accept things, Usha had said.

Usha accepted *samsāra*. Love, too.

There, my Usha, I have at last set down what I have not uttered for years, your name. I am beginning to tell our story. What I am writing is an act of love, this pen, like a *linga*, making its mark on this virgin white paper.

Love doesn't need words, you had said once as we sat with our arms around each other on Lamu beach in East Africa looking at the Bahr-i-Hind.

But I do, my Usha. I do need a bridge of words now to tell our love and to cross the silence of time, that destroyer of the past.

Stop, stop, Ahmad ibn Madjid, don't indulge in these flights of fancy. Just set down cold facts.

That's the voice of the cynic within me.

Thank you, my cynic, I reply, I will.

Being possessed by an intense need to discharge a coiled pressure within me, I told Abdul yesterday, the 8th of May, to buy the finest Ahmedabadi paper, white as cotton but rough textured because of the sand of the Sabarmati river, and to place a stool and a small table in the cave next to Straighthitter.

Today, May 9th, 1509, I walked from my house to the promontory, and viewed the familiar scene. Some fishing boats came swinging in to Bandar-i-Turk as graceful as a flight of white butterflies. The sea gulls that had been mewling and circling obliquely overhead sped straight in the direction of the boats. They would wait patiently at the promontory for the fish filled boats to return, and would fly in a circle and complain if I usurped their place.

My friend João, who sometimes accompanies me to the promontory, does not like them.

A seagull, he says, is half vulture, half dove.

But João, the seagull is not fierce, I tell him.

I don't care, João says, it doesn't belong to the sea or to the land. It's an inbetween, a hybrid. Like you, João would roar, especially when he was drunk.

And then he would yoke strange images together. João's observations, odd but somehow relevant, tend to jump into my mind at sudden moments. He is more than a friend. He is a part of me.

Jan Mirza, formerly João Machado of Lisbon, now a citizen of Diu, knows that he doesn't belong anywhere. The seagull can move between land and sea, but poor João cannot go back either to his country or to his religion. He is a *degredado*, a convict banished from Portugal, and because he had abandoned Christianity and turned Muslim, and adopted Jan Mirza as his name, he would be imprisoned and hanged by the Portuguese if he returned to them. I have a matter of fact approach to seagulls. They would tell me that my ship was approaching land and that it was the end of my voyage. For me their cries were of welcome.

With their cries as omens I walked down the six steps into the cool of the cave. It was dark at first. But Abdul had placed my stool just right so that the sunlight fell exactly on my teak table, my favorite, with the top unpolished, its grain visible. From here I can look straight down on the Panikot, for Straighthitter could be trained on the middle of the channel between the seafort and the mainland.

Malik Aiyaz, who loves his Diu even more than I do, had planned very carefully. He had got together the best metalworkers from Ajmer, and they had forged a chain so strong that two elephants with the chain tied to their legs and prodded on by their mahouts in opposite directions could not break it. He had an iron pillar driven deep into the bowels of Panikot and had wrapped several rounds of chain around the largest boulder on the other side so that no dhow could get into the harbor. With great difficulty he had imported six great Ottoman siege guns from Suez, dynamited caves in the cliffs around the harbor, and set the guns in place so that they could blast out any ships that tried to sail in. Malik Aiyaz had tried to make sure that no pirates, specially the neighboring Sankhodaris, could penetrate his territory from the sea.

Sitting here now, looking directly at that wounded snake of a *sankalkot*, I bethink myself though I know that brooding will not help me understand the past.

But can one ever understand the past, asks my cynic.

I want to know who I was to know who I am, I tell my cynic.

Does it really matter, the voice of my cynic continues.

Yes, I want to reply to him, but am unable to. I keep silent.

Writing is a form of action. Perhaps this act of writing will allow me to define myself, I tell myself.

Why do I need defining. I only want to be loved as Usha loved me. Our love in 1497 had brought our world into being. Then, one day, in Anegundi, five years ago, in 1505, our world was shattered. One of the murderers hit Usha on the mouth to prevent her from calling out for help. Two of them held me down and gagged me. I saw blood drip from the beloved mouth on to the intertwined hands she placed on her stomach to protect our baby. They pushed me into a gunnysack, dragged me over rocks and stones, flung me into a bullock cart and then hurled my body into a ditch beyond Anegundi. The other two must have then killed Usha and our baby within her, and Layla too.

After the hakim rescued me from the ditch, he took me to a Golla village hut where he treated my wounds with herbal poultices and gave me *neem* water and rice*canji* to drink. It took me three months to be able to walk. My hakim asked me what I planned to do after I recovered from my wounds.

I dont know, I said.

I have to travel north, my hakim said, to heal the sick of other villages.

I was silent for a long while.

It was a problem. My hakim hadn't asked, and I hadn't told him how I came to lie wounded in the ditch. Nor did I tell him about my total despair. I was so sure that Usha and our baby, and Layla were dead that I didn't want to return to Anegundi to find out. I couldn't speak any South Indian language and I did not want to go back to the Jain temple to find out from her uncle if they were really dead. Perhaps the uncle would not break his vow of silence. Perhaps I was afraid of facing the truth.

I stood silent before my hakim not knowing what to say.

Come, my hakim said, come with me until you can decide what to do.

For five years now I have lived in a numb state beyond despair. For five long years I've locked our story tight within myself. I told it to no one. Not to my hakim. Not to my friend, João. Not even to my self. Now I am driven to gather together the pieces of our shattered world in order to recreate it.

The act of writing will heal you, my hakim had said.

Hence these words on paper.

I was born some thousand miles away from here, in Julfar opposite Hormuz. The announcer on formal occasions adds al-Julfari to my long ancestral name. But Julfar is not my home. I don't remember my mother at all. She is a name that my father and grandfather occasionally mentioned. For me she is like fragrant incense that lingers in the folds of clothes washed and stored away. My grandfather and my father took me away with them when they were *rubbans* who piloted merchant ships through the Red Sea. I was only twelve then but my father wanted me to continue the hereditary calling.

I came to know, young as I was, the small world of the Red Sea with the Straits of Bab el Mandeb at its southern end and Suez at its head. Suez then was a small barren port not the naval dockyard they tell me it has become today. It had nothing, no wood, no copper, no iron, no cloth for sails, no provisions. Everything had to be camelbacked from Cairo. At twelve I learned how to steer through the narrow gullet of the Red Sea, how never to sail at night because of the many shoals, and I learned also to take into account the shifting crosswinds and the many deeps and reefs that made the Red Sea so dangerous for large ships.

I used to be proud of my piloting skills, proud also of my tribal group. My name really is Shihab al-Din Ahmad bin Madjid bin Muhammad bin 'Uman bin Fadl bin Duwaik bin Yusuf bin Hasan bin Husain bin Abi Ma'laq al-Sa'di bin Abi Raka'ib al-Najdi. But now the flow of family names does not matter. I have my father and grandfather in my bones. I have learned from them and with them. The world they lived in, the Red Sea, about which they composed navigational poems, has changed. It is no longer the world they and I knew.

I admired my father. A stern taskmaster, he taught me navigation. From him I learned about tides, sea currents, the look and changing shapes of islands on the route, the coasts and their landfalls, the different signs, mud, grass, animals, the fish and birds, that mark the nearness of land.

He taught me all he could about his little world which he knew so well that the pilots named one of the islands of the Red Sea after him. He once ventured beyond his world, to the island of Socotra in the Gulf of Aden, but was bewildered by the strange winds and currents that are part of *al Muhit*.

Al Muhit, the Encompassing, the encircling oceansea, that was the world I wanted to conquer by knowing it as my predecessors never did. And I came to know it all. The circle of my universe began at Sofala in East Africa, and went on to Mogadishu, to Aden, to Hormuz, around to Diu, to Chaul and to Calicut in India, and then to the region that stretches below the wind, that world of cinnamon and cloves that lies beyond Cape Comorin, and ends at Melaka.

I began to improve upon all branches of navigational science. In my pilot book, the *Fawa 'id*, I set down basic principles every pilot should know. He should be proficient in the theory of routes and latitude measurements. He has to be aware of landmarks and signs, and see to the wellbeing of the ship and the people in it. He has to know the compass, know when the Pole Star is at its lowest culmination, know the rising and the setting of the important stars, know the route he is sailing, know about the prevailing winds and the monsoons, and be skillful in the running of his ship.

I cannot bear to reread my *Fawa 'id* now. I had called it the book of profitable things concerning the first principles and rules of navigation. I wrote it for my fellow navigators and for posterity, so that my name would never be forgotten by those who traverse the Encompassing. I loved to write pilot books, and in the old days I used to spill words on paper with ease. I have more than twenty books that I still preserve in one of the large Martaban porcelain jars in the four corners of my living room. I had more than fifty, but I discovered that my friends would forget to return them. Some of the Rahmani publishers, who produce works for navigators to purchase and take to sea, have swindled me. They have copied some of them without paying me for a single one. But they have made me famous, and my name is on the lips of sailors all along the coasts of India, Africa, Persia, and Arabia.

But I no longer care now for either fame or money. I have written *rajaz* poems, poems called *qasidas*, a long poem about the coming of the Portuguese. And a book that lives by itself in one of the four jars in my house, a book of poems to the dawn.

That's the only book I now want to leave for posterity, not my elephant-like *Fawa 'id*. I now see that my pilot book, the work I thought was so great and encircling, is just a pause in the onward flow of time. The facts and observations I had set down in my *Fawa 'id* are obsolete now, as tasteless as stale rice. The *al Muhit*, no longer the Encompassing, has shrunk into the Bahr-i-Hind, the Indian Ocean. My nautical instruments will no longer do. The Portuguese have the astrolabe, and a vastly improved version of the compass. My instruments have now become primitive tools. My skills, my use of the *kamal*, my technique of measuring *'isba* and of taking finger latitude, have become obsolete, even though hundreds of pilots still use them. My fellow pilots do not yet realize that their world is about to come to an end. That the new science is a wedge of destruction. The word science, my friend João tells me, implies a way of precise knowledge.

My world, Usha, has been smashed. The only encompassing, encircling world I now remember is what your embracing arms told me without words. That the outer world, *samsāra*, always changes. What is lasting and real is the world of encompassing love.

Where am I. You have taken me to the faraway, and I need to get back to the world of time and place, to the world of facts, to the smell of this earth that Abdul disturbed when he watered and leveled the floor of this cave to set down my table for me to write our story.

Through the cave opening I can see some straggling boats swing in to land their catch. A boat with a carved square Portuguese stern has just made harbor. It must belong to Malik Gopi of Surat who admires things Portuguese and employs a Portuguese deserter to advise him on the build-ing of ships in the Portuguese manner. In the distance is Bandar-i-Turk, the section of Diu now termed *Vila dos Rumes* by the Portuguese. The three hulks that Malik Aiyaz thought would prevent the enemy ships from pen-etrating into Diu harbor are washed up on the fortresslet. The whole scene looks so peaceful that I can't bring myself to think that the furious battle of February the third ever took place.

I am also trying to forget what happened to me, Usha mine. I know what happened, but I see what happened as a blur.

Why, oh why, I look up at the sky and ask, silently. But unlike Malik Aiyaz I do not want simple answers.

João has a very simple answer. What will be, will be, he claims.

João has lost the faith he had in his Christian god. He lives from mo-ment to moment.

I just am, he says.

I want to find out who I am, I want to tell João, even though he's not here in this cave where I have begun writing this account. João is the only one to whom I have told a few fragments of my past. I did mention Usha casually once to João, and told him I wanted to write our story. Of late, he has drifted away from me, and seeks the company of Ishak Khan with whom he goes riding.

João is a very good polo player, Abdul tells me. João also practices shooting with Ottoman *tufengs*.

I am what I am because of Usha, I want to tell João. Before she came into my life I did not have a true self. I was a pilot. I used to consider my-self a poet. And I belonged to the Bedouin tribe of Qais 'Ailan.

What does that mean, I now ask. What is my true self I ask, looking at the sky above.

Usha is silent.

I must stop bringing in your name at every other moment, Usha, for it will distract me from the facts about the past I have to set down. I must try to becalm myself, and not swing around from fact to event to detail as I have been doing.

But I cannot, not yet.

Adrift on that great ocean, *samsāra*, I am trying to sail back into the past, against the onward flow of time, where to I do not know.

I am calming down.

It is always difficult to know where to begin a story of what happened in the past. In the first chapter of my *Fawa 'id* I ambitiously traced the onward history of navigation from Noah, the first builder of ships, and I kept tacking along, veering around, telling stories about places and people instead of traveling straight to the basic principles of the art of navigation.

I must write the way I used to sail, cutting a clean line of white through the water.

I hear the thunder of hoof beats above this cave.

It must be Malik Aiyaz.

TWO

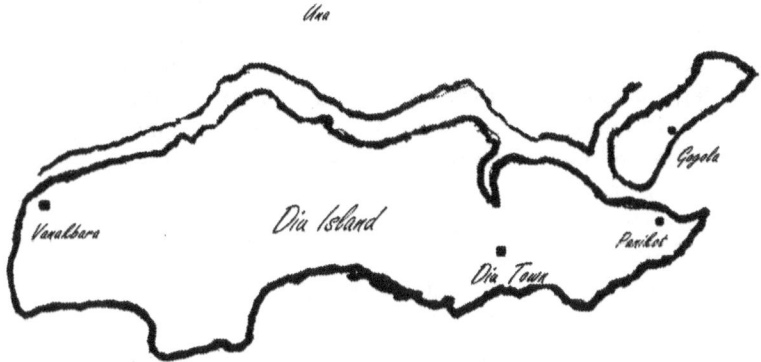

*M*ay 1509, next day
My house, Diu, NIGHT
I continue writing

It was Malik Aiyaz.

He had left his attendants, as usual, at my little house and, accompanied by Ishak Khan, his son, had ridden up to the blackrock promontory.

As I came up the steps of the cave I was greeted by an affectionate neigh from Rustum, Malik Aiyaz's Arabian charger, with his rippling black satin skin and the streak of auspicious white on his forehead. His breeding showed itself in the way he held his head, erect, and in the symmetrical build of his body, the muscles clearly defined. Rustum allowed me to stroke his neck.

I did not go to the couched camel tethered twenty yards away. Her skin was a golden brown, curried to smooth perfection, but she had an evil looking, perpetually chewing mouth. She had a different groom every time I saw her, for she kicked and maimed them so that they ran away after a week. She was a hybrid, a cross between a Bactrian camel and a dromedary. Ishak had paid two hundred *mahmudis* for her because of her extraordinary hump, flat and broad on which a saddle could be fastened. She would allow only Ishak to ride her.

Ishak was so huge that no horse could carry him. He felt cramped on the back of a two humped camel. Ishak loved eating and when a new eating place opened in Diu he would be the first to sample the food. His father would remonstrate with him about his eating habits.

I may not be following in your footsteps, Ishak Khan would tell his father, but I am imitating Sultan Begada.

Sultan Mahmud Begada, it was reported throughout Gujarat, had such an enormous appetite that he would eat a cupful of honey, a cup of butter and a hundred golden finger sized plantains for breakfast. Unlike Sultan Begada who was trim and wiry, Ishak was obese. But he was a powerful wrestler, and his father, Malik Aiyaz, had put him in charge of all the athletic events and entertainments that were staged in the city center.

Ishak resented the appointment.

I'd rather have Malik as my title, he told João, and be a commander of armies like Sultan Begada.

Alas, Ishak Khan complained to João, Gujarat has no enemies now and has reached the height of its power. She is at peace with all her neighbors. There are no wars left to fight on land. No enemies, only those sea pirates, the Portuguese.

With the help of Malik Gopi of Surat Ishak has got together a band of soldiers to practise shooting with Ottoman *tufengs*. Of late they have begun to use Portuguese arquebuses which some Portuguese deserters had sold to Malik Gopi. João is somehow involved in the conspiratorial world of Ishak, I don't know how. João teaches Portuguese. I did not know he was a man of action.

Ishak Khan and I exchanged salaams. He never used the customary embrace because he was so obese.

Greetings, Ishak Khan, I said. What new shows have you arranged for the citizens of Diu?

Ishak Khan is a born organizer. Last month he had brought in a tribe of acrobats from Bikaner, and they had put on a spectacular performance with their monkeys, and balancing acts, and the sword swallowing, and some excellent magic tricks. Ishak looked gloomy. He kept on popping salted pistachio nuts from a leaf cone into his mouth. The munching made him look even more dejected.

My father, Ishak Khan said petulantly, up there on the black promontory, insists on the performance of a play commissioned by Malik Gopi as tomorrow's show. I had arranged for a troupe to perform some *furusiya* trick riding on Arabian horses, to be followed by a shooting display with Portuguese arquebuses. But my father wants to have the play performed tomorrow night. A play written in Sanskrit which no one will understand. He has sent invitations to all the Diu villages, even to Vanakbara at the other end of Diu. The people will be bored.

Ishak was worked up. He popped a nut into his mouth. Suddenly he began to choke. His face turned red. I had to thump him on his huge back with both my fists until the pistachio lodged in the back of his throat flew out. Ishak nodded to me as a form of thanks, and sat down heavily on the hard black laterite. It must have hurt.

Why don't you come to a real entertainment, Ishak said. I've arranged a special show for my friends for the day after tomorrow. Come after the evening bell. I'll send Jan Mirza for you.

Ishak got up quickly, walked to the waiting camel and waddled on to her saddled back. She lumbered up, the forelegs first, then the hind quarters very slowly, and paced swiftly away.

Malik Aiyaz smiled at me as I walked up the blackrock promontory, and we exchanged a warm double embrace.

I saw what happened, he said. I didn't know whether to laugh at my son or feel sorry for him.

We sat down on the spongelike looking but hard black laterite as the low orangered sun deepened the shadows over the Bandar-i-Turk, the section where the foreigners lived. The Surati dhow had disembarked all its passengers, and the crew was hastily unloading some gaudy paraphernalia into a barge. The pieces looked like shining slabs of gold. One piece was a wooden throne. They were very light. The barge's waterline had not dropped at all.

Malik Aiyaz was in a distant mood. He had not glanced even once at the *sankalkot* nor had he cast his eye on the bridge to Bandar-i-Turk that the workmen were repairing. His eyes had crossed the treacherous Gulf of Cambay, as if wondering what was happening beyond its unpredictable tides and currents in Malik Gopi's Surat.

I know my friend's moods. Malik Aiyaz is no longer anxious about the past. He is worried about the future.

I am worried about the Portuguese, Malik Aiyaz said. My spies tell me Malik Gopi has been sending gifts of money and messages of friendship to them, in return for *cartazes* for his Melaka bound ships. He wants to make sure of Melakan trade.

My friend wanted to be reassured.

The Portuguese are like the Sankhodari pirates aren't they, Ahmadbhai, Malik Aiyaz said, just plunderers with ships and powerful guns. They will go away from our shores, won't they, Ahmadbhai, and allow us to resume our trading activities peacefully. Three or four of their ships visit the west coast just once every year. They will never establish themselves here, will they, Ahmadbhai.

He was deeply worried. I kept silent.

He paused for a long time gazing westwards.

I had once suggested that Malik Aiyaz place himself in the center of the Bahr-i-Hind so that he could see how the Portuguese ships and guns could menace its encircling ports. But Malik Aiyaz always looked at the distant Portuguese from a landsman's point of view.

I can destroy them easily on land, Malik Aiyaz said softly, but I can't fight them at sea.

I am Malik Aiyaz's personal *shahbandar*.

When I agreed to be his harbor master in 1509 my duties were quite simple. I was responsible for the day to day administration of Diu's ship traffic. And I had to see to it that his ships were always seaworthy. They had to be careened, drawn up on land, and tightly covered with woven palm leaves during the monsoon season when the seas were declared closed. It wasn't heavy work. I kept myself to myself most of the time, and refused to get involved in the doings of *samsāra*, a Sanskrit term my friend the pandit had explained to me.

I felt compelled, despite myself, to get involved in *samsāra*, when Malik Aiyaz, who became my friend, got worried because trading activities began to be disrupted all over the Bahr-i-Hind four years after the advent of the Portuguese. The traders and nakhodas who sailed on the Bahr-i-Hind began to be afraid of the Portuguese pirates who blockaded and disrupted their trading world. The customs revenues of Diu plunged as did those of the other port cities of the west coast of India. The volume of pepper and other spices imported from the Malabar Coast to Beirut and Alexandria had dropped so low that many Egyptian and Venetian traders were ruined. It was rumored that the Mamluk Sultan of Cairo had ordered an armada of war galleys to be assembled at Suez to drive the Portuguese pirates out of the Bahr-i-Hind.

I tried to reassure Malik Aiyaz.

There aren't too many of the Portuguese and their ships, I said softly. They only want to trade for pepper and spices.

Then I wondered if what I had said was true.

When I became his harbormaster I did tell Malik Aiyaz about the need to strengthen the sea defenses of Diu harbor. But at that time, in 1509, he had not heeded my suggestions. I had told him about the disturbances caused by the Portuguese ships and guns in Mozambique and in Mombasa in East Africa in 1498. But it was not possible for him to visualize what happened in those faraway portcities just as he and others on land could not understand how a few Portuguese ships could create panic along the coasts of southwest India. I discovered later that Malik Aiyaz had never sailed on the sea except once, when he had been brought from Jiddah as a young slave to Diu.

Like many others in our world, Malik Aiyaz had never seen the huge ships of the Portuguese nor had he ever heard the thunder of their powerful guns. He had seen only the Mamluk galleys that came occasionally from Suez through the Red Sea to sell siege guns and bombards for Diu and for Goa. The Portuguese confused him. He was aware of the Portuguese threat but was convinced that they were just pirates, not powerful enough to conquer his beloved Diu.

The victory at Chaul in 1508 made Malik Aiyaz think that his Diu was safe. The pirate ships were no longer a threat. They had been destroyed by the guns of the Mamluks. Their commander, Dom Lourenço de Almeida, had been killed. But he also became aware, Malik Aiyaz told me later, that his Diu needed better protection against these Portuguese pirates. Chaul, his military eye had noted, had an estuary bar at the entrance of the Kundalika river which formed an S curve that protected the port. Diu had no protective sandbar. The open approaches to Diu harbor, I told him, made it an easy target for any attacking seaforce.

The disastrous defeat one year later in February 1509 made Malik Aiyaz realize that the Mamluk war galleys and guns could not protect his Diu. Viceroy Almeida's refusal to accept the keys of Diu after his victory puzzled him till he came to the reassuring conclusion that the Portuguese were too few to establish themselves in his city. He resolved never to let the Portuguese establish themselves in his beloved Diu.

Help me understand, Ahmadji, Malik Aiyaz had said to me.

The pleading in his voice had moved me deeply. I could not remain aloof. I had to break out of my dark isolation and help my friend. And, as his *shahbandar*, I also had to understand the situation myself by talking to those who had taken part in both sea fights, especially the one at Chaul which I had not witnessed. So I went across the channel to Bandar-i-Turk, that section of Diu that Malik Aiyaz had set aside for *afaqis* and foreigners only.

I went there with my friend João who had a large number of acquaintances and drinking companions there. They were quite impressed when João told them I was the personal *shahbandar* of Malik Aiyaz. João and I accompanied them to the taverns which could be found only in this part of the city. João plied them with liquor and they relaxed and talked freely and boastfully about many things and, in a short time, I got a fairly complete, if confused, picture of what had happened at Chaul.

I took mental notes about what I heard from a wide variety of soldiers and sailors, Turks and Abyssinians and Mamluks and Persians who lived in Bandar-i-Turk and had participated in both battles. The Mamluk gunners that manned the Ottoman cannon told me that the guns in the cave openings were breech loaders, made of thin bars of wrought iron which got covered with rust during the monsoon. Put together with hoops and staves, they were obsolete and had exploded and needed to be replaced with new cannon made of bronze or cast iron that the Portuguese used. Smaller transportable cannon are far more effective than huge siege cannon, they said. The *sankalkot*, the Ottomans said, was not an adequate protection against any Portuguese attack by sea. Sturdy stockades and palisades of the kind constructed in Istanbul were needed for the defense of Diu, a port that was quite vulnerable to attack by sea, they said, unlike Goa which was well fortified and situated a few miles up the Mandovi river.

I asked them detailed questions about both battles wanting to find out why the Rumis, the term the Portuguese used for the coastal peoples of the Ottoman lands, had won the seafight at Chaul in 1508 but lost the battle at Diu in February 1509. I got vivid descriptions of the sea battle at Chaul from the Mamluk sailors and the Ottoman gunners so that I could clearly visualise the Mamluk galleys and the Ottoman guns battling the Portuguese naos at the entrance of the Kundalika river. I could easily imagine the tidal ebb and flow of the river that would control the movement of the ships. I could see the fishing stakes in the middle of the river that entrapped Dom Lourenço de Almeida's ship. I could even smell the smoke of the guns. I could create the Chaul sea battle in all its vivid detail for myself.

I also went with a shipbuilder to take a closer look at the new Mamluk war galleys. The builder at Suez, brought from Venice, had modified the Mediterranean transport vessels called *maonas* so that they could battle against the adverse winds and the heavy seas of the Bahr-i-Hind. He had equipped them with thirty oar banks instead of the usual twenty four, had fixed huge lateen sails at both stem and stern, and had placed a fortress-like castle at the stern end. My pilot's eye could see the *maonas* were not balanced, they had been constructed of wood that had not been properly seasoned, and they were not oceanworthy. The upper deck, which had to be low lying because of the need for oars, made them vulnerable to heavy seas. I asked the builder to show me the keels and discovered that the vessels were too flat bottomed to make swift progress in rough seas. I told João later that the Mamluk war galleys, unlike the Portuguese naos, were not ships for all seas and seasons.

Two Portuguese deserters that we met were so fascinated when João spoke to them in Castilian that they readily poured out everything that had happened at Chaul. They had jumped into the water from Dom Lourenço's ship and were saved because they announced loudly to their rescuers that they wanted to become Muslims. One of them had worked as Dom Lourenço's personal servant on board his ship. The other had waited at table and both were present when the war council had met on board the flagship.

The cheap liquor in the taverns loosened their tongues and, late into the night, they would quarrel among themselves as to who was to blame for the disaster. One blamed young Dom Lourenço for his recklessness, his foolhardiness. One should not wear armor on a ship, he maintained. The other one, the personal servant, faulted the older sea captains who had sailed away and left the young commander to his fate. I listened to them with my eyes closed. I could vividly enact the battle if I wanted to.

João suggested that Malik Aiyaz might want to interrogate them himself. Unfortunately the Portuguese deserters got killed in a brawl in a tavern with some of the Rumis on the very day we were to take them to Malik Aiyaz.

Fortunately I had jotted down detailed notes about the two battles and about the talks João and I had had with the deserters. I even jotted down the names of the Portuguese guns that the deserters referred to. I went to my office, wrote down two reports, and sent them to Malik Aiyaz presenting the situation as I saw it but not offering any advice about what needed to be done. I did suggest that because of the Portuguese threat there was a need for more announcements on the state of shipping on the Bahr-i-Hind.

Malik Aiyaz had not yet read my detailed reports about the two sea battles. I'll read them later, he told me. He was quite worried about his personal troubles.

I'm worried about my son Ishak also, Malik Aiyaz said. I talked to him during the ride from your house to the promontory. He is restless. The wars are all over, my son keeps repeating to me. I know he is involved in a conspiracy with Malik Gopi who is bribing him with gifts of opium and hashish. Ishak, who spends lavishly, is heavily in debt to Gopi. The band of cavalry that Malik Gopi and he have formed is really a band of assassins. I suspect that my son wants to have me assassinated to seize my malikdom. I have to send him to faraway Junagadh.

Ishak is a good organizer of entertainments, Malik Aiyaz continued. But he doesnt realize that I have to put on this performance tomorrow. Malik Gopi sent me a a letter signed by the Sultan himself, stating that the play had to be staged to convince people that the Sultan could defend Gujarat as a vital centre of trade from the Portuguese who really were harmless clowns.

People have to be made to realize that Gujarat is still the most powerful kingdom on the west coast. Foreign merchants and traders, said Malik Gopi's letter, who are easily scared away by any signs of trouble, must believe that Surat and Diu are safe centers for their trading ventures. And that Sultan Begada is the most powerful ruler on the west coast of India. That he can defend them and protect their ships and their goods.

Malik Gopi had craftily commissioned the nephew of the Hindu poet Udyaraja to transform a 1469 poem into a play. He wanted to glorify his portcity, Surat on the upper Tapi river, as a trading center safer than Diu with its *sankalkot*. There were two performances of this play in Surat fifteen days ago. Malik Gopi advised me to have a performance in Diu, before it goes on to Cambay, and then to Champaner to be staged before Sultan Begada himself.

It celebrates the tremendous power of the Sultan, Malik Gopi said.

That's shrewd of Malik Gopi, I told Malik Aiyaz. He's flattering his way even higher into the Sultan's favor.

Malik Gopi is a scoundrel of a Hindu. After he was elevated to a malikdom, he has sent a gift every month to Sultan Begada, Malik Aiyaz continued.

Malik Gopi's gifts are really weapons, said Malik Aiyaz. He wants to undermine my Diu and my influence with Sultan Begada, and is setting up both Surat and himself with the help of the Portuguese, on whom he lavishes bribes whenever he can to get *cartazes* for his ships. He has bribed a shipbuilder from Greece stationed in Goa to construct a ship in the Portuguese manner in Surat. It will be made of teak, not pine. And he has bribed some Portuguese deserters to sell him arquebuses.

I never did like Malik Gopi even when his business was based here in Diu, and before he moved his operations to Surat. He tells everyone he is a Brahmin, but he isn't. He's a bania, the cleverest of the *bania*traders in all Gujarat, a calculating machine. He can work out his own profits even before you've finished placing any business proposal before him.

Malik Gopi is a genius as businessman, João observes with reluctant admiration. His operations are as smooth as his depilatoried forearms.

As Malik Aiyaz's *shahbandar* I know that Malik Gopi has more ships than Malik Aiyaz, huge trading dhows for whom he obtains *cartazes* from tthe Portuguese to sail every season to faraway Melaka. Malik Gopi has now become the richest person in Gujarat.

I see money written all over his face, comments João, who is fascinated by the power of money. The most recent of the false gods of this world, he added.

True, very true, I tell João.

Malik Gopi's nose is acute angled, with a tip that throbs nervously when there is money talk in the air. There is money fever in his eyes that pierce you relentlessly in a business deal. His voice, strangely, is low and determined, rich with the magical promise of money that he spreads out like a rich Persian carpet in front of you.

But how will the performance of this play affect your standing with Sultan Begada. I asked Malik Aiyaz.

You don't understand our world, Ahmad. Don't you see, said Malik Aiyaz. If I refuse to have the play performed, Malik Gopi will report that I insulted the sultanate. If the play is performed, the Muslim religious leaders will criticise me because it is written by a Hindu and mentions Hindu gods and goddesses. The mahdawis who deeply resent the sultan's banishment of their Imam *Mahdi* will accuse us of undermining the Muslim faith. Malik Gopi has his secret agents everywhere, even among the mahdawis. My spies inform me that the mahdawis might deliberately provoke riots to make people believe the world will end soon as their Mahdi predicted. Ahmad, my friend, will you and your friends watch the crowd at tomorrow's performance and try to spot the troublemakers. The city patrol will be watching too.

I will, Malik Aiyaz, I assured him. My three friends and I will be there tomorrow for the play.

The captain of the guards will lead you towards the front of the stage, Malik Aiyaz added.

He did not need to thank me. We exchanged warm hand clasps, our fingers grasping the middle of our forearms. As he rode slowly away I lingered briefly on the promontory, and turned east hoping to get a glimpse of distant Girnar peak, fiftyfour miles from Diu, lit up by the setting sun, a landmark for pilots.

My friend the pandit has told me that one can see holy Girnar from here, but I never have.

It is a kind of *darshan*, he tells me, an auspicious moment of vision.

Like *nazar*, I told him, the glance that Rumi says, completes the act of knowing.

In the west I could see a few clouds, yellowish like the skin of a cow, and the sunset was red, an unusual purplish red.

Far out the waters crawled in crablike fashion.
My pilot sensibility was disturbed. I could smell the distant tufan.

Malik Gopi of Surat and Malik Aiyaz of Diu are rivals at the court of Sultan Begada. Both want to exercise power.

Malik Aiyaz is an army commander. The whole of Gujarat and beyond has heard about his exploits at the sieges of Junagadh and Champaner. His rise to power began on the day when he shot down the raven that had shat some purplish filth on Sultan Begada's head. It must have eaten the purple fruit of the jambool tree. The Sultan, with his personal escort, was on his way to Sarkhej to visit the tomb of Ahmad Khattu, his spiritual preceptor. He had taken shelter from the burning midday sun under a young banyan tree when a raven cawed twice.

Weh, oh woe, exclaimed everyone around the Sultan. The raven was considered an omen of evil tidings.

Only Aiyaz, who was a purchased slave brought from Circassia by the Turks and forced into Islam, had the presence of mind to snatch up his bow and bring down the illomened bird. The Sultan embraced Aiyaz, set him free, and appointed him to a command of a hundred men.

Aiyaz soon rose to become a nobleman, a Malik. He attained his malikdom at the storming of Champaner in 1485. He had advised that a huge cannon, purchased from a Mamluk galleycaptain at Diu, then hauled for over a month with great difficulty to Pawagadh, a clifflike fortress. The western gate of this fortress was then blown open. Malik Aiyaz with his men rushed furiously into the breach and fought their way to the roof of the huge main gate, opened it and let the Sultan's army pour into the interior. It was the end of the siege. Champaner, the mightiest of the Hindu Rajput strongholds, was doomed to fall. The battle continued for three days. At last, after the *jauhar*, that strange ceremony in which all the women and children ritually sacrificed themselves in the fire, after the Rajput men had cast aside all defensive armor, after they had bathed and purified themselves, they charged out of the bath through the palace gate, naked, sword in hand and fought till they were all slaughtered.

The Sultan voiced loud thanks to God. He proclaimed that the hero of the battle was Aiyaz, who was henceforth to be called Malik Aiyaz.

You can be the *malik* administrator of any province you want, said the Sultan, extravagantly generous in his favors.

Why don't you make Malik Aiyaz the governor of Diu, suggested Gopi craftily.

It will be an honor to oversee any part of your growing kingdom, said Malik Aiyaz.

Malik Aiyaz did wonders with Diu.

Before Malik Aiyaz took over, Diu had been just a minor port along the Gujarat coast, of no importance compared to Cambay and to Rander, the Navayat port on the Tapi River just above and opposite to Surat. Malik Aiyaz transformed Diu into a mercantile magnet. To Diu began to flow the riches of Africa and Arabia and Persia. They came in merchant ships, attracted by the convenient harbor that Malik Aiyaz caused to be deepened, and assured by the fact that it was monsoon safe.

At Diu they did not have to brave the shifting tides and currents in the Gulf of Cambay or the onward sweeping bore that twice a day dashes along the estuary. Also, Malik Aiyaz declared that for a period of five years custom duties would be minimal and that there would only be port and harbor taxes. He brought in all the merchants from the surrounding regions, and set them up in the city center that he organized and administered.

Diu's city center is like the wheel of a bullock cart with its eight radiating spokes.

Malik Aiyaz had formed his city center in a marvelous pattern. The control buildings, the courts, the police station, the customs office, the tax tribunal, the municipal office, were all at the end of the street spokes. The city center was the heart of Diu. Here on a raised dais Malik Aiyaz would administer justice once a week when he was in town. Anyone with a complaint could come and sound the bell next to the dais and cry out for redress.

News announcements about happenings in different parts of Gujarat would be made in the center at eight in the morning and at seven at night, the times when the bell was rung changing as the seasons changed.

The announcements in Malik Gopi's Surat never told of bad news. They were made occasionally in the evenings when the people congregated on the steps around the huge artificial lake called a tank, that Gopi was in the process of building on the outskirts of Surat beyond the Daman gate. They tell me it is a mile in circumference, shaped like a polygon, and it covers fifty eight acres of land. There are steps on all sides for the people to descend to the water, ten slopes for horses and two less elevated slopes for elephants.

Malik Gopi wanted to be regarded as a public benefactor. His announcements to the people told of the names of donors whom he had persuaded to raise public buildings. All around the lake are buildings of different shapes and sizes erected by the business community. Gopi has constructed an island in the middle of the lake where he has built a pleasure pavilion for his business acquaintances. There are no passageways to this island which can only be reached by the pleasure boats which the wealthy trader sheths maintain.

Someone asked Malik Gopi why he had not encouraged the building of mosques and temples at Gopitalao, as the lake began to be called.

I am a businessman, said Malik Gopi. My temples are warehouses and godowns. Money is my god. Business is my religion.

I am writing this account by the light of an oillamp that has not yet begun to flicker. The light is reflected on the four porcelain jars one of which contains my most precious possession. The sheets I have written on are weighted down under the beautiful conchshell from Sankodhara island, brown and intricately convoluted. I look at the large seashell into which Abdul has poured the liquor João got for me about a week ago.

It's been aged for five years, João had told me. Keep it for me. My wife does not allow me to drink at home. It's for you also, Ahmadbhai, if you need it.

I don't drink usually, but thought I wanted a drink today after my meeting with Malik Aiyaz and the memories of Usha. The cloud colors and the crablike waters have disturbed my inner being. Why, I do not know.

Abdul looked surprised when I asked him for the drink after I had had my bath. I ate a little of the rice and dhal he set before me.

Shall I get you some pickle, he asked, knowing my fondness for lemon pickle.

No, I said.

You should not drink if you don't eat, Abdul said gently.

I don't know what I would do without Abdul. He has been with me for so many years that he has become a part of me, ever since I found him lying unconscious next to the Well of Togetherness, his head all bloody, his left eye smashed in, on Chapora beach, in Anjuna, Goa. When he opened his right eye on the tenth day Abdul was surprised to find himself on the ship I was piloting from Chapora to Hormuz. My ship had set out from Diu, then sailed south to Chapora, celebrated for its skillful goldsmiths who built splendid thrones of silver and gold, ornamented with rubies and diamonds, for the installation ceremonies of neighboring rajahs and sultans. We had anchored overnight in Chapora so that I could pick up some gold ornaments for a businessman whose son was getting married in Hormuz.

High tide was late that afternoon and I had to hurry from Nakhoda Home, a resthouse for those pilots who had to anchor their ships overnight, to the built up platform under the banyan tree in the center of the village where the ancient letter writer with the flowing white beard sat.

He knew Persian and Arabic and several local languages. No one knew whether he was a Hindu or a Muslim or where he came from. He wrote and received letters for the whole village community, and knew and was trusted by everyone except the *afaqis*. Letters and packages and notes would be kept safely in the hollow of the banyan tree to be picked up after the old man left for the night. The package of bangles and necklaces, the businessman told me, would be kept there. I was about to leave, the old man said, giving me the package, it's getting dark. I am glad you waited, I told him, we have to leave early with the morning tide before the horse traffic begins.

Chapora handles the overflow of horse ships when the coves in the Mandovi river at Divar island are overcrowded. Horses landed in Goa were in great demand for the Bijapur mounted cavalry. That night it was so hot and sticky, and the smells of the many horse boats anchored alongside our ship were so overpowering that I couldn't fall asleep. My mouth was parched and I felt the need for a long cool drink of water. As I stepped out of Nakhoda Home, my nose checked the wind direction. I then walked slowly along Chapora beach past the customs house, past the giant banyan tree clamoring with crows, the exact center of the village, where letter writers sat on the built up parapet, a place where letters were written and sent and received, and where, for a brief moment, I felt pierced with loneliness, no family to write to, no one to receive letters from, a place where people met to exchange gossip and news, to a lookout tower with a platform erected by a Kadamba Hindu king to formally welcome ships and neighboring envoys. Behind it was a well whose water was always cool and sweet. People would come from all over Goa to drink its water and marvel at the well's location, only a hundred yards away from the edge of the salt sea. It was a favorite place for lovers to meet at night. They called it the Well of Togetherness. Small pots of water had been placed for wayfarers on the built up rim of the well. I rinsed my mouth and drank a long stream of water without touching my lips to the pot, when I heard a feeble moan. I found Abdul lying on the other side of the well, bleeding and unconscious.

When he opened his right eye on the tenth day we were nearing Hormuz in the Persian Gulf. I told Abdul I had to take him on board, else he would have bled to death. I could not abandon him at Chapora and there was no one I knew that I could leave him with in the early morning darkness. The ship had to sail. We could not miss the morning tide out of Chapora. Abdul did not leave me when we got to Hormuz. He stayed on as my friend and helper. And we have been together ever since. Except, except during the five years after Anegundi when Abdul was not allowed to enter Vijayanagar city and waited patiently for me in Kannanur in the house of my friend, Kotta Marakkar. Those were the five years from 1505 to 1509 when I was a wanderer on land and lacked a self and roamed through central India with my hakim.

Abdul was a man of few words. He gave me later, much later, bits of information that I had to put together about what had happened on the beach at Chapora. Abdul and the girl he loved had been attacked by a band of Hindu young men. There had been Hindu protests and disturbances because, Abdul told me, the Muslim superintendent of Chapora port, an *afaqi* from Turan, intensely disliked by both Hindus and Muslims, kept on raising taxes every year on houses and especially on the import of horses from the Red Sea and the Persian Gulf. The *afaqi* had been ordered by the Bijapur authorities to form a guild of Muslim horse traders in Chapora in order to supply purebred Arab horses for high ranking cavalry officers. So he arranged for the murder, one by one, of the landowners of the Hindu village. He then seized their lands for alleged nonpayment of taxes and distributed them among the merchants of the guild and the Muslim converts. The Hindu village was renamed Anjuna to mean guild. There were two horse ports in Goa, Bijapur's major outlet to the sea, Chapora and the main port on the Mandovi, Ela.

It was only in the second year that Abdul told me the real reason why he wouldn't go back to Anjuna to visit his old parents and his sister, Layla. He had been deeply involved with a Hindu girl, he said. They were students in the village school, he said. Abdul would slip away, he told me, through the window of the storage shed at the back of their two roomed house, whose iron bars he had loosened and could remove and replace, to meet the girl at night. Their parents did not know their secret. The ancient letter writer did, but disapproved of their meetings. It would cause trouble, he said. Why don't you finish school, he urged, I have plans for you. Abdul's sister, Layla, knew their secret, and the elder brother of the Hindu girl. They were planning on running away together and had arranged to meet at the Well of Togetherness. The Hindu gang, to which the elder brother belonged, had killed the girl because the family honor would be polluted by such a marriage, and no one would marry into the family. Then, afraid that the *afaqi* would avenge the death of a Muslim, they beat Abdul on the head with bamboos, smashing his left eye and leaving him in the jasmine bushes, telling him to leave Goa, warning him they would kill him if he ever came back to Chapora.

I cannot write, not yet, about those five empty years from 1505 to 1509 when I lived without Abdul and without Usha.

But I am glad I am now able to set down your name, Usha. For five years I couldn't. I couldn't say your name, even to myself. You belong to a world I have lost, one that I'm now trying to recover in these words set down on this paper.

Abdul is asleep now in the other room. His snores are loud, but reassuring. He must have had what I merely tasted, a supper of rice and dhal.

Tomorrow evening I'll let him go the city, and have his fill of *shish kabab* and *biryani*. He will go early in the morning to tell João's wife that João should be at the play tomorrow. I hope João won't be drunk. Abdul will then go to the pandit's who will be sitting in the fields looking at the sunrise. And finally he'll get to the house of the maulvi who'll be counting the ninetynine beads of his rosary on his verandah.

I just had a drink of water from the earthen pitcher that Abdul always places near my bed. First I rinse away the dryness from my mouth, and then I drink the cool, sweet water in long measured gulps. Why do I record such trivial things in such great detail. I don't know. But I feel I need to. As a pilot I always knew when I had to add an extra bonnet to the foresail even when there wasn't a following wind. I didn't know why but all my senses, my sense of smell especially, told me to.

The oil lamp has begun to sputter.

Good night, Usha.

THREE

*M*ay 1509
My house, Diu, NIGHT
What happened at the play

It's over, the play.

I wanted to set down every thing that happened as soon as I got back last night from Diu center. I asked Abdul to light another oillamp. But I felt too tired to write.

Why don't you go to sleep, Abdul suggested gently. It's not good for your eyes.

I was tired, but I knew I wouldn't be able to sleep. I wouldn't have been able to write either. For what had happened was too crowded with event and too immediate to set down in cold writing.

What's the ideal time to write about an event. Immediately, when the event is hot. Or after it has been cooled by time and filtered through memory. I don't know. Sometimes boiling well water, and then straining it through layers of fine Cambay mesh cloth, makes the water taste different. The water loses some of its salts, and tastes insipid. Unfiltered water is alive on the tongue, but can be a danger to one's health.

What has water to do with language, or taste with writing. My pen runs along this paper not in a straight line but making many swirls. To write is not like sailing a ship, though it may be. For one has to sail, as I may have to write, in different kinds of weather.

The weather.

That brings back to me my visit to the Diu promontory yesterday before I went to the play.

The seagulls circled and complained. There weren't as many of them as usual. As if they sensed that something was to happen, and had stayed away from the promontory. I sat on the black rock and allowed my senses to absorb the sky and the scene in front of me. There was a slight shade of dust in the faraway clouds which were higher than those of the previous day, and they looked quite yellowish like the skin of a cow. I sensed a disturbance inside me. The wind was not steady. My nose could tell of a sulphurlike warmth on the surface of the ocean that indicated to me that a tufan might be approaching. My mind assured me it wasn't the season for tufans on the west coast of India. The wind that blew was gentle and cool. But the reappearance of yesterday's deep purplish red clouds disturbed me profoundly. As if a tiny whirlwind, that had begun within me, wanted to whirl its way out. I wanted to stay to watch the cloud shapes and colors during sunset, but I didn't.

I would be late for the play.

I was.

I arrived at the city center a little before the intermission. The captain of the guards recognized me and led me to one side of the circular stage where a number of people who had come late were standing. I was surprised when Mustafa, Malik Gopi's consultant about the sea route to Melaka, greeted me.

You can join your friends during the intermission, said the captain of the guards, and left.

There they are, your friends, Mustafa said.

My friends were seated on a carpet in a group twenty yards from the front of the stage in a section reserved for the elite of Diu. I saw João quickly raise a thin flask of gold to his lips and then slide it with his left hand to someone on the adjacent carpet who turned his head to the right, then to the left, as if afraid he was being observed. I had never seen him before. He wore an elegant silk shirt worked with golden thread. Round his neck gleamed a circlet of diamonds. He had a black vertical streak on his forehead. I was sure he had provided João with a drink. I was worried.

There were Persian and Armenian nobles, and ambassadors from Egypt and Ethiopia. There were Muslim merchants and brokers, Gujarati trader *sheths* who belonged to the powerful world of trade and money. The Jain traders, who sat apart in a group, darted malicious side glances at me. One of the Jain Jhaveris glared at me.

Mustafa pointed to the pilot group seated in a corner to the far right.

You haven't missed anything important, Ahmadji, Mustafa said, except Gujarati folk songs and the usual comic exchanges between the *sutradhara* and the clown to keep the audience in good humor.

The play will begin now, announced the captain of the guards.

Our pilot group will meet tomorrow, said Mustafa hurriedly, to discuss what has happened on the Bahr-i-Hind after the arrival of the Portuguese. We would like your views about the matter. Can we come to your office at twelve noon.

Come to my house, I said.

Trade and shipping had been disrupted. The pilots wanted my help. I was the first pilot who had sailed with the Portuguese to India and I knew the Bahr-i-Hind like the salt toughened palm of my hand.

A weird cacophony arose from behind the red and gold double curtains that I had seen on the Surati boat. It lasted for some time, and then it stopped suddenly, and there was a hush of intense silence.

Two beautiful maidens stepped through the curtains, bowed to the audience, stepped back, and drew the curtains aside to allow a turbaned *shenai* player to enter and roam all round the stage playing on his black reed instrument. He delighted the crowd, teasing it with the notes of a popular Gujarati folk song, greeting the horn player, welcoming the two drummers, suddenly improvising on the melody for a while, then returning to the folk song, soaring finally into a wild crescendo that ended abruptly, as he sat down near the stage entrance.

A deep voice announced.

This work, the *Mahmudasuratranacharita*, is a small garland of flower offerings woven together for the mighty Mahmud Begada, Sultan of Gujarat, whose countenance terrifies all his enemies, especially the Portuguese.

The curtains then parted to reveal a procession of beautiful women from different parts of India. They streamed onto the stage arrayed in costumes of gorgeous color and design. They flowed from one end of the stage to the other, weaving intricate patterns of blue and gold and green and red. Their anklets sounded gracefully as they tiptoed, and ran, and danced, and then stopped all of a sudden, briefly, to allow the audience to appreciate the different color patterns. The girls were arrayed in their regional costumes, and seemed all ablaze with their gold and silver ornaments, all except a naked tribal girl covered all over with colorful beads that made music as she walked.

The circle of dancing women then parted leaving an open wedge at the apex of which was Sultan Mahmud Begada.

The actor who played the Sultan was dressed in tight pajamas and a long buttoned coat of the whitest silk. There was a simple gold crown on his forehead as he sat in royal dignity on a eight cornered throne. The maidens moved slowly toward and around him, their faces, eyes, eyebrows, hands and necks silently projecting stylized love for their lord and master.

The king greeted all his women.

Suddenly the tabla increased its rhythmic intensity.

The king stood up.

You, the king said, looking at the group of women on his right. The women gracefully receded, and left the stage one by one.

A woman, clad in the soft colors of the rainbow, was alone on the stage, her head and face veiled by her sari border ornamented with the *veena* and with peacocks. In one hand she held a lotus, while in the other was a bundle of palmleaf manuscripts.

You, repeated the king, his voice softening as she revealed her fair complexion and her ivory teeth. Who are you, may I know. I've never seen you before.

I am, the woman said, in a voice that rang clear through the center. I am Saraswati, goddess of wisdom and the arts.

I am most honored, said the Sultan, bowing to her, as they both moved in measure to the front of the stage.

Pray tell me, great goddess, why have you deigned to grace this humble court of mine with your auspicious presence.

A voice from the back translated the overelaborate Sanskrit into simple plain Gujarati.

My consort, Lord Brahma, has sent me to discover the secret of your power and wealth.

The Sultan walked away, pondered for a while, then came back to her.

My power has been granted to me by God. My wealth, he continued, does not consist of the gold and jewels in my treasury, but in the good name I have in the mouths of the people of Gujarat.

They call me Defender of the World and of the Faith, the Sultan said.

They call me Protector of the Faithful, the Sultan said.

There was a loud buzzing at the back of the center.

A voice shouted from the darkness.

You are a Hindu Sultan, said the voice.

You and Ishak Khan are traitors to Islam, proclaimed a second voice.

You murdered Imam Mahdi, shouted a third voice. The end of the world is at hand.

I turned and looked back. The shouters must have been the mahdawis who, the maulvi told me, believed the promised Mahdi had already appeared and the end of the world was in sight. They wanted to cause a riot and provoke a rebellion. The guards tried to locate the shouters. They couldn't. It was too dark.

Ishak stood up, and roared for silence.

Actor Sultan Mahmud Begada, at this point, cut short his stage speech and changed the tone of his voice.

Great goddess, please take up your residence in my court here, the actor sultan said hurriedly. You are cordially invited to a *darbar* that will be held here tomorrow evening.

The intermission now began.

My friends welcomed me warmly and made a place for me between João and the pandit who greeted me as usual with folded palms. Next to him sat the maulvi. João pretended to wipe the sweat of his face with a large towel, and managed to sneak a few swigs from another gold flask. His neighbor, the one with the black vertical streak on his forehead, had disappeared. The maulvi looked all around worried lest anyone was watching João take a drink. He gave João a drink of water from his *surai*. Then João stood up.

I have to stretch my legs, João said.

Don't, the maulvi said. He was worried about his friend. Don't go near the guards. They'll smell your breath.

I'll get some spiced gram, João said.

There's my friend, envoy Karim Khan, the maulvi told me. He has come from Kannanur to seek Malik Aiyaz's help to purchase horses for the cavalry of Bijapur. Horses, he tells me are in short supply now because of the disturbances caused by the Portuguese on the Bahr-i-Hind. Their price has gone up.

I drank some water in a long thin stream from the pandit's surai. The water was deliciously cool.

Isn't that the Hindu envoy from Vijayanagar that João is talking to, the one who was sitting next to him, the maulvi asked the pandit. Why didn't João introduce him to us.

I turned around. It was the one with the black vertical streak on his forehead who had sat next to João.

Karim Khan tells me, the maulvi said, that the Hindu envoy has also come to buy horses through Malik Gopi. And he wants to buy arquebuses for the Vijayanagar army.

The pandit was not listening. He was furious.

Look at that ugly black streak on his forehead, said the pandit. That proclaims him a *madhvin* from South India where Hinduism has been polluted by strange beliefs and practices. He calls himself VN to conceal his low caste. He asked me to take him to the Vishnu temple but I refused. He would have polluted the temple.

The pandit quivered with indignation.

The play is an abomination too, he said.

Calm down, I said.

João has changed. He has many friends in high places now, all because of Ishak. That is why he's not afraid that the guards would put him into prison for drinking. He used to be a school teacher, not well paid. Now he teaches Portuguese to pilots and envoys and merchants. Now he's a part of Ishak's world, ever since they discovered he was a teller of jokes, a good polo player, and knew how to handle an arquebus. Of late he has been neglecting us, his true friends, and, Abdul tells me, goes to the taverns in Bandar-i-Turk. He doesn't join us for the long talks and discussions the four of us used to have.

I saw one of the guards take João to Ishak's carpet and then to the back of the stage.

After a while João came back with four leaf cones of spiced gram.

Now, he said, let's talk about the play.

The pandit could not control his indignation. He gestured wildly, spilling some of the gram.

This play is an abomination, he repeated, looking all around, trying to whisper discreetly. That fellow has broken all the rules of the *Natyashashtra*. He shouldn't have mixed Hindu and Muslim matters, continued the pandit. He should not have used Muslim epithets like Commander of the Faithful, and Defender of the Faith. They lacerate my Hindu soul.

Sh, sh, hissed the maulvi. Can't you just relax and enjoy yourself. This is an entertainment for the people to forget their troubles.

That's just it, the pandit said, letting his voice rise.

I tried to restrain him. He wanted to leave immediately.

Don't, I said. Let's discuss this play tomorrow.

João began to talk to the maulvi, and soon had him laughing extravagantly at his jokes. João has a collection of jokes that he uses at just the right moment to make everyone laugh.

I got up to stretch my knees, and greeted some of the people I recognized.

João sneaked a couple of swigs from his flask.

The musicians came back on the stage.

The *shenai* began wailing in the cool night air. It greeted the audience as a friend, reached a high note, and then asked them what they wanted. It teased them, stretching and repeating the notes to call them back to their seats.

Come, come, come back, it sang, and the tabla took up the rhythm.

Come back, come back, have you forgotten us, the beats of the tabla insinuated.

Have you forgotten us, have you, have you, shrilled the *shenai*.

No no no, sounded the tabla, no no no.

Yes yes yes, went the shenai, yes, yes, yes.

The audience gradually picked up the dialogue between the shenai and the tabla, hurried to get their refreshments, and drifted back to their seats.

The *shenai* would throw out a musical phrase, and challenge the tabla to reproduce it rhythmically and melodically. After a time the tabla would take over, and challenge the *shenai* to a question answer exchange. Both times there would be an acceleration of rhythm till they arrived together at a breathtaking climax. Both instruments delivered their best, but neither wanted to assert its power over the other.

The audience was again being prepared.

The music began again, all four instruments letting themselves go and playing with abandon. The drums blended together, the shenai and the horn agreed with each other. A temporary truce was established.

Then came a swirl of princes and rajas, all dressed in different garbs and costumes. They wore the finest of cottons, brocades and silks. They wore turbans and kammerbunds into which the ceremonial short sword was slipped. All bowed in deep obeisance to Sultan Mahmud Begada who wore a magnificent crown and towered above them all on his eight cornered throne.

It was a celebration of the sultan's rise to power.

The first group to prostrate themselves were the conquered Rajputs, out of whose dominions the Sultan had formed the Gujarat state. The former Raval of Champaner testified that his city had been transformed by the building of mosques and public buildings in and all around Champaner.

The Prince of Malwa compared the Sultan to Mahmud of Ghazni, the destroyer of the Hindu temple of Somnath.

A village farmer thanked the Sultan for encouraging the planting of trees, the mango, the coconut, the fig, the date, all over Gujarat. For constructing and maintaining roads. For erecting resting places for the public good. Sultan Begada, he proclaimed, had transformed Gujarat into a paradise garden.

All now lavished extravagant praise on the Sultan. They compared him to Hindu gods and heroes:

in battle Mahmud is equal to Bhima

in benevolence he surpasses Karna

in sport

This is absolute heresy, shouted someone in the audience. It is a pollution of our faith.

Here is Mischief of the Last Days, shouted another. The end of the world is near.

A third person proclaimed, The Day of Judgement is at hand, as our traditions state.

This time the guards were ready. The mahdawis wanted to inflame the crowd into rebellion. The city patrol seized the three mahdawis and dragged them to jail.

The crowd was now getting restless.

A tall figure, dressed in white muslin, came before the actor sultan

I am Malik Gopi, the governor of Surat, Gujarat's safest trading center, this actor proclaimed. I am the malik of business. This magnificent crown studded with diamonds is presented to you, o great Sultan, because you have transformed Gujarat into the center of the world of trade.

The kings and rulers shouted their wahs.

Then they came forward with gifts that represented the trading world of Asia. The Samorin of Calicut came with a gift of the finest pepper. The ruler of Cochin brought ginger in a jeweled casket. The Sultan of Melaka presented mace and cloves. The Raja of Ceylon came with cinnamon. The Prince of Kashmir with two colorful embroidered shawls. The Lord of Nepal with gold and precious stones.

The crowd again began to grow restless. It was getting late. Tomorrow was bazaar day.

The King of Delhi was just about to present some heavily brocaded robes to the Sultan when suddenly a tiny creature, two feet high, pushed itself rudely through the crowd of rajas causing confusion among them. Some princes stumbled and fell. Then it stood unsteadily in the center of the stage, utterly bewildered, not knowing what it should do. It looked all around.

Everyone was surprised, those on the stage as well as those in the audience.

The director appeared most surprised of all. Trembling, he tiptoed cautiously toward the tiny creature. On its head it wore a monstrous black hat with a tall red horse plume.

Take care, take care, whispered the clown, who snatched a short sword from one of the rajahs, and tiptoed behind the director.

Take this, take this sword, the clown said, that creature may attack you.

A hush of silence.

The director pretended to be brave.

Who, who are you, the director barked.

No, no, no, said the clown. Ask it this question. What are you.

Let me see, the director said, bending low to the ground. He has feet, two feet.

Dirty white feet, the clown pointed out, they're smelly.

They held their noses.

Has the creature eyes, asked the director.

Only one eye, said the clown, in the center of its forehead. I shall blind it.

And the clown bravely pulled down the black hat over the creature's eye, and then over its ears and nose.

It has no neck, said the director.

Then, said the clown, it must be one of those neckless monsters from the west who has blundered into our world.

Ah, ah.

The director began trembling again, and went behind the clown on tiptoe.

Is it a human monster, the director asked the clown. Why don't you speak to it. You claim to know all the languages of the world.

But can it speak, asked the clown.

Wait, the director said, and gave the creature a tremendous whack on its horseplumed top with the flat of the sword.

Wão, não, tão, cão, pão, dão, mião.

The dwarf stumbled once or twice then ran in circles all over the stage screaming loudly as if it were about to die. All the sounds of pain appeared to come from the nose. It tore its hat off, flung it on the stage, and stood next to it. It had an innocent eye in a pale face, with which it stared at a world it had never seen before. It was confused. It didn't know where it was. Or what it should do.

It looked all around. Then it darted to the Samorin of Calicut to gaze at the gift of pepper, stared at the ginger and the mace, at the cloves and the cinnamon. The eye then opened greedily wide when it saw the gold and the precious stones.

The director bravely gave it another whack with the sword.

Wão, não, tão, cão, pão, dão, mião.

The clown stooped, bent his right ear towards the dwarf, and listened.

Ah, he said, it speaks Portuguese, which is always spoken through the nose.

The clown and the dwarf whispered furiously to each other.

Ah, said the clown. He tells me he has been sent.

By ship, the dwarf said. I come to your court as the envoy of the powerful Dom Manuel of Portugal, the dwarf says. Whose self conferred title, confirmed by the Pope at Rome is, King of Portugal and of the Algarves on this side and beyond the sea, in Africa Lord of Guinea, and of the Conquest, Navigation and Commerce of Ethiopia, Arabia, Persia and India.

That's ridiculous, said the director. No one here has heard of him.

And what gifts, oh great sahib, the clown asked the dwarf, have you brought from your great Lord for our magnificent Sultan.

The dwarf looked down sheepishly. He put both hands deep in his pockets and pulled them inside out. They were empty.

The audience roared with laughter.

What, no gifts. How dare you come empty handed to our Sultan. We have to send you back in your black ship, the clown and the director both said.

And they summoned the tribal girl who with one hand turned the dwarf upside down, stood him on his head, dumped his head in his black hat, and carried him off stage unceremoniously to the screaming delight of the audience.

The audience knew that the play was almost over. Many stood up wanting to be the first to leave the city center.

João, who was trying to manage another swig, nudged me with his elbow, and I saw that a messenger had been brought to Ishak's carpet. The audience was puzzled, amd wondered whether the messenger was part of the play.

On the stage the actor who played the King of Delhi finished presenting the heavily brocaded robes to the actor Sultan.

Then Ishak, accompanied by the messenger, lumbered on to the stage to make an announcement.

This messenger, he said, has just brought an important message from the royal court at Ahmedabad, that the King of Delhi, the real king, Ishak said, not this stage actor you see before you, has sent some presents in the way of friendship and kindness, to the royal court of the real Sultan Mahmud Begada.

Never before has the king of Delhi sent presents to a ruler of Gujarat, Ishak Khan proclaimed. It is an acknowledgment of the greatness and power of the kingdom of Gujarat.

There was an intense silence, followed by joyous acclamations everywhere, from the people on the stage and from the audience. The audience did not wait for the play to end. They were tired, tomorrow was another day and they began drifting out of Diu center.

I helped João to his feet, bade goodbye to the pandit and the maulvi, and went in search of Abdul. We reached João safely home. He wanted me to come in and have a drink and discuss the performance. But I was too tired, and João too drunk.

It had been a strange play. A *vidusaka* had once said that truth often walks hand in hand with fiction. What a clever flatterer Malik Gopi was. I wondered whether the audience had caught what the play presented, the mighty power of Sultan Begada and the clownish insignificance of the Portuguese threat.

FOUR

May 1509
My house at Diu, Night
Written after my nakhoda friends left

I am glad the nakhodas and pilots came to my house after I finished setting down what happened yesterday. The play had not convinced the pilots that the Portuguese were mere pirates and clowns who could be easily
driven away.

I knew why the pilots had come to see me. They had, each one, after
their seasonal return to Diu, come to my office to report to me as the *shahbandar*, and to tell me their human stories which I loved to listen to. Now
they wanted to consult with me as a group, and talk among themselves
about what was happening to their world. In 1498 they had dismissed
the Portuguese as just a bunch of pirates, too few to be a threat. In ten
years these pirates had caused confusion in the Gujarati world of trade
and shipping. I knew that some Diu traders were afraid of shipping their

goods to Hormuz and Aden. Many ships remained idle in Diu harbor during the sailing seasons. The pilots lost money for they were idle too. They
wanted to know if anything more could be done to drive the Portuguese
away. The pilots had done all they could. Requested rulers along the coast
to build fortresses and to set down *sankalkots* near river entrances as protection against these pirates.

The pilots also wanted my advice about problems of loyalty that presented itself soon after the arrival of the Portuguese. They knew I was
the first pilot accused of being a traitor to Islam because I had guided the
Portuguese to India. I had been denounced by the Jain traders who had
spread the rumor that I had stained the honor of their community. But
these pilots were too polite to ask a friend directly about what amounted
to an accusation. They were my friends, all five of them, but I had never
told any of them my story. Just as I had never told João about Usha and
Malindi and Vasco da Gama.

We knew each other, and the pilots knew our discussion would be
easy and free. They knew also they had to somehow help themselves. No
land power looked after their interests. Coastal chiefs would never fight
attackers that came by sea, pointing out that their soldiers and weapons
could only repel invasions from land. For no ruler, except the invisible
one above, could control that unstable element, the ocean sea, with its
monsoonal winds and its treacherous tides and sea currents. And then
came the Portuguese with their floating fortresses, huge ships that could
defy the blowing winds, and huge guns that could destroy ships from a
distance. And the Portuguese were already beginning to establish foot-
holds on promontories and islands in the south where they built *fortalezas*
to defend themselves from land and sea attack.

Samsāra, I was tempted to say, but the pilots were Muslim like me and
would not have understood that word that my pandit friend frequently
used in our discussions. I kept silent.

The west coast of India had been horrified by stories of the barbarianisms
of the Portuguese. As Malik Aiyaz's harbormaster I was aware of the news
fragments about Portuguese violence that traveled to Diu from ports on
the west coast and I knew, better than most of my friends, the situation
on the Bahr-i-Hind. But I could not put these fragments together to get a
complete picture. I could not, try as I might, discover what drove Portugal
into our waters. Was it just chance, or was it the desire to Christianise infidels and gentios. Was it a wild yearning to discover new worlds, or was
it a spirit of adventure. Or was it just greed for money, and the desire for
pepper and spices. Some merchants brought back news about the drop in
revenues at Beirut, and at Alexandria. The rulers lost customs revenue.

And it was difficult for some Venetian traders to buy pepper and spices in Cairo and transport them to Europe. All because of these Portuguese pirates.

Butchers, plunderers, the pilots called them.

The stern Vasco da Gama, whom I had met in 1498, had changed into a butcher in the course of four years. Infuriated because the *pardesi* Muslims had sacked the Portuguese factory in Calicut, he had exacted a hideous revenge. He lay in wait off Mount Eli for pilgrim ships returning from Jiddah. One large pilgrim ships carrying a number of *pardesi* Muslims, including women and children, was captured without a shot being fired. They offered no resistance, and handed over all the gold and jewelery they carried. The women stretched out their hands and their children towards Vasco da Gama who stood on the poop deck, imploring him to spare their lives. Vasco da Gama ordered his gunners to bombard the vessel and set it on fire so that everyone was burnt to death.

Viceroy Almeida, after the destruction of the Mamluk *maonas* here in Diu on February third this year, had celebrated his triumph in monstrous fashion. On their way back to Cochin his ships had dropped anchor in front of Muslim ports all along the west coast. The captured Rumis were hanged one by one from the yardarms, so that their dying yells could be heard by all the townspeople. Then their butchered limbs were stuffed into cannon, and fired over the towns which were splattered with fragments of human flesh and bone.

Armed Portuguese ships patrolled the entrances to the Persian Gulf and the Red Sea. No one knew what to do. Everyone was confused. I wondered if the Portuguese were confused too. Did they know what they were doing.

I have talked with João about Viceroy Almeida's utter inhumanity.

Do all Christian rulers act like this, I had asked him.

João had paused for a long time. It was a difficult question.

I cannot offer any excuses for the Portuguese barbarities, João had said. I can only tell you how they would justify them. Many Christians believe that the Muslim religion should be extirpated so that Christianity can flourish. Any method can be employed to serve this noble end. The Muslims, as you well know, also advocate *jihad* to establish Dar al Harb, the territory of Islam.

Consider also, Ahmadji, João had continued, this never usually uttered justification. The Portuguese, just a handful in this teeming sea world of many peoples, have been forced to use the tactics of terror to dominate this Islamic world in which, as Christians, they are not allowed to trade peacefully by the Muslims. Tell me, Ahmadji, what would you do if you

were a Christian. Would you courteously request your sworn enemies for
permission to trade, or would you display the power of your guns.

He paused.

Remind me, Ahmadji, some other time, to tell you my views about the
connection between religion and power.

I was about to say something about *samsāra*, but João sped on.

Ahmadji, my friend, said João, you have to understand power, the
politics of power, its language, its many languages. The Portuguese believe in *crueldade*. No, no, it doesn't just mean cruelty. It is an attitude towards one's enemies that insists on an utter lack of compassion. It is a
highminded virtue, some Portuguese say, that looks down with total dis-
dain on money and profit, and establishes a leader's reputation for ruthless vengeance that will always instill terror into one's enemies.

João, the pandit, the maulvi, and I have had long discussions on the rights
and the wrongs of exercising power over the oceansea.

The ocean, I maintained, like life itself, belongs to all people. By common human right the seas should be free and open to all navigators.

That may have been true in the past, said João. But has changed in our
time. It is true that the seas were open to all, but that had applied only to
the seas of Europe. And only, according to the church, for Christians. In
our time the boundaryless ocean, whose seas flow one into the other, has
become a newer form of space, and has been assigned to Portugal. Land
power is not enough.

That's ridiculous, said the maulvi. To pursue your argument, friend
João, the air above our heads, could, in the future, become a form of space
and would need to be controlled. Ridiculous, he snorted.

But, friend João, said the pandit, the churning ocean does not belong
to anyone. It is a manifestation of life energies, creative and destructive,
controlled by *jagad amba*, our universal mother. It is *samsāra*.

Please, my dear pandit, said João, some other time for your pauranic
observations.

The Portuguese have mighty ships and mighty guns, João continued,
and they claim sovereignty over the Asian seas by virtue of discovery and
conquest. No other rulers have the power to make such a claim. Do you
know the title that Dom Manuel assumed after Cabral returned from India. He titled himself Dom Manuel by the grace of God, King of Portugal
and of the Algarves on this side of the seas and on the far side, in Africa,
Lord of Guinea, and of the Conquest, Navigation and Commerce of Ethiopia, Arabia, Persia and India.

What a grandiose title, exclaimed the pandit. Arrogant too, he added.

Ah, my dear fellow, said the maulvi, teasing his Hindu friend, didn't the Hindu Samorin make claim to a similar title. You yourself told us that the title Samorin means lord of the mountainous seas, the Malayalam equivalent of which is *Kunnalakon*, king of the hills and the waves.

I opened my eyes and looked at my nakhoda friends.

They knew me quite well. They tolerated my long periods of silence. They knew I had been a good pilot. They also knew about my long fits of brooding, when I bent my head and shut my eyes. I would listen to their talk, but they could not tell whether I was asleep or not. I usually wasn't.

You somehow get people to confide in you, Ahmadji, Sinbad told me one day. But you yourself remain silent.

This time, after the shattering Diu disaster, they were in despair and wanted me to talk freely and advise them. That's why I invited them to my house, and not to my tiny office in Diu town. After all I knew the Bahr-i-Hind and had been deeply involved in the story of the Portuguese arrival in our peaceful Islamic trading world. My enemies, the Jain traders and associates of Sheth Chimanlal, have spread vicious rumors about this involvement.

That I had betrayed the secrets of the seasonal monsoons to the Portuguese.

That I had disclosed to them the sailing routes from the ports of East Africa to India and beyond.

That I had sold this information to Vasco da Gama. Had told him about Mount Eli, the landmark on the west coast of India, and told him how to get to Calicut.

That I was a drunkard.

And that the Portuguese had made me drunk in order to betray to them the secrets of the monsoon winds.

That I had drawn a seachart for the Portuguese that enabled their pilots to sail from Malindi to Calicut.

That I, a Muslim, had stained the Chimanlal family name and polluted the religious honor of the whole Jain community of Gujarat by running away with Usha.

That I was a traitor to Islam.

My friends had heard these rumors, but did not believe I was a traitor to Islam.

They respected my silence and did not question me about my past.

Pilots and nakhodas, said Mustafa the Yemeni, a fierce believer in tribal loyalty, belong to the ocean sea. They do not owe their allegiance to any land ruler except to the person who pays them for their services.

Mustafa is the master pilot of south east Asia whom everyone consulted about the seasonal sailings to Melaka. He was one of the few pilots who knew all about the prevailing winds there. He knew when the sailing seasons from Cochin and from Melaka would begin, when the winds would turn around, or die down suddenly in the straits before the ship reached Melaka. He was an expert on the straits of Melaka for he knew the shoals, the rocky headlands, the shifting currents that made the narrow gullet to Melaka so dangerous a passage. He was a special consultant for Malik Gopi who sent eight large trading ships to Melaka every season.

The arrival of the Portuguese ships in the Bahr-i-Hind had caused violent disagreements among the Muslim pilots. There were no long distance Hindu pilots, for the Hindus disliked the sea and considered it polluting.

The Portuguese are sworn enemies of our Muslim faith, some pilots maintained. We should not act as guides to their infidel ships with their powerful guns.

Mustafa disagreed.

I always offer my services as pilot to the highest bidder, Mustafa stated. I don't care whether the bidder is Hindu or Muslim. Or even Christian, he added. Money now has become a religion unto itself. Our friend, Ahmadji, used to pilot ships owned by Chimanlal Sheth, the Jain businessman. Now he works for a Muslim, Malik Aiyaz. As you all know, I work for Malik Gopi who is a Hindu. If the Portuguese want my services and offer me a great deal of money, why should I not act as their guide to Melaka and South Asia. There is no connection between *jihad* and trade.

Khalid al-Hamad, Mustafa's student, pointed out that the Portuguese now offered five times the regular amount to any pilot to guide any of their ships across the Bahr-i-Hind. I need the money for my family, Khalid said. Should I let my family starve. Too many pilots are now out of work. Religious leaders will not help me in my time of need.

There followed a long discussion on whether it was money that mattered or religion. Money, today, is a more powerful force than religion, Mustafa said. I was tempted to tell them then why I had to direct the Portuguese to Calicut. For me it was neither money nor religion. Perhaps it was the word of four letters, the noun verb Usha and I never uttered to each other. I had to escape from Malindi in 1497, I wanted to tell the pilots, or I would have been killed. But I didn't say anything. I bowed my head and listened, but did not offer any comments.

I had kept silent after I had returned to Diu in 1509 after an absence of eight long years. I had not explained my absence to anyone, nor had I told anyone why I had returned to Diu. But I couldn't stop ugly rumor from staining my name even though I was no longer a pilot. I had locked up my painful past deep within me. About my getting drunk, about the poisoned arrow, about the human storms I had weathered, about the beloved mouth that had dripped with her blood at Anegundi. My pilot friends trusted me. They needed no explanations. They accepted me and my long fits of brooding, and my silence. But after 1505 I could not accept my own self. I was haunted by the word *samsāra*.

My nakhoda friends had begun to drift in, one by one, an hour after twelve, when the sun was directly overhead. I welcomed each one with a warm embrace. Four of them looked sad, but tried not to display their sadness. Only Khalil al Hamad had a smile. All five were tired. They had to walk to my house from different parts of Diu. Mustafa had to walk all the way from Vanakbara. It took an hour for the group to assemble in a semicircle. One by one they took their places on the carpet in the front room. We sat in silence and, as pilots accustomed to the lonely watches of the night, we did not indulge in small talk. It was May, the seasonal end of their voyages. Their ships had been drawn up ashore, and careened. We had plenty of time.

Abdul had not returned yet. He had made coffee for me early this morning, and left for the Friday bazaar from which usually, at this time of the year, he gets provisions to last through the monsoon months.

June, July, and August are monsoon months when rain and winds lash the west coast. Diu harbor is shut down for incoming and outgoing traffic. And even inland trade slows down. Abdul stocks up before the rains come. He will buy rice, wheat, and other flours to make chappatis and rotlas, oil, vinegar, different kinds of dried beans and dhals, dried chillies, dried green mango slices to give the curry the right sourness, and two or three kinds of pickles that I like.

He had taken all the money I had in the secret covered hole in my back wall. It wasn't much. Abdul has been urging me to go to town to collect my monthly allowance as Malik Aiyaz's harbormaster. The last time I had gone to the Diu treasury some functionary had shouted at me. He was new, and did not recognize me. He had a huge fleshy hooked nose.

Don't you know, Hooknose had said, everything is in disorder after the Portuguese attack in February. It will take over a year for you to get your salary.

I walked slowly away.

I think that petty clerk in the treasury department has been appointed by Gobindlal Jhaveri, the Jain *shahbandar*, said Abdul. Why don't you complain to Malik Aiyaz.

You need the money, Abdul continued. The Jains have not forgotten what happened. They hate you because of the dishonor, they say, you have brought on the whole Jain community. They would have had you killed by now, if it had not been for your protector, Malik Aiyaz. His spies know everything that happens in Diu.

I can't bring myself to ask money from friends, I said.

Money, said Abdul with deliberate slowness, is money. One can't live without it in today's world. Your pilot guides don't bring in any money. You have no money saved, not even for your old age. You have this house, and this small piece of land around it, only because Malik Aiyaz gave it to you.

Abdul was right. It was because of Malik Aiyaz that I had a little money, and had stayed on in Diu. But I had needed more than just money when I came back to Diu in 1509 after my wanderings with my hakim. I had decided I would never go to sea and be a pilot again. I needed to heal myself. According to the hakim, I had to make my past present. So, for a month, in 1509, before Malik Aiyaz asked me to be his *shahbandar*, I again tried to write poetry as I had done in the past, but it didn't help me just as my hakim had predicted. I then tried to recapture my past by making sketches of the different kinds of ships that sail on the Indian Ocean. I wanted to see the world I had lived in before it changed forever.

I made sketches of all of the ships, the oceangoing deepsea voyagers, and the smaller boats that ventured up the Red Sea and up into the Persian Gulf, and those that sailed up the rivers and along the coasts of Africa, Arabia, Persia and western India.

My first sketch, I took a long time over it, was of the *kotia* of the west coast of India, queen of all the ships on the Bahr-i-Hind, with its sleek lines and delicate curves, graceful curved stem, with the parrot head motif. I then sketched her three sisters. The *battela*, with its open hull and its acute angled bowsprit, the *ganga*, with its crownlike stemcrest, the Mumbai *pattamar*, with its open hull, its elongated stemhead, its round stern, its bamboo bulwarks, the peculiar arrangement of its three masts, two raked forward, the third upright.

I then sketched the Arabian *baghla*, with its long stem surrounded with a plain knob, whose name is supposedly derived from the Arabic term for a she mule. And then the Persian *boom*, with its long raking stem and its sharp stern.

My sketches made me realize that our farflung oceanworld was inhabited by a family of ships. The lateen sails, the different stems either elongated or curved or upright, the mast that was always angled, made the ships cousins and brothers and sisters, all products of long established shipbuilding traditions. My fingers were driven to capture this world before it all vanished. The pen flew over the paper, like a ship on the sea with a following wind. The ship sketches multiplied. I also made sketch maps of the ports and *bandars* of the Bahr-i-Hind.

I knew I could go on and on making sketches of the small boats that crowded the ports and *bandars* of our world, the *houri*, the *machwa*, the *mashua*, the *khatira*, the *bedan*. Aren't these names musical. I wanted to cram my former world into the pages of a book which would grow as gigantic as my elephant like *Fawa'id*.

But I didn't.

The maulvi had once warned me against painting and painters.

Islam, he said, condemns image makers for they presume to imitate the Creator.

But my sketches were not presumptuous. I wanted to arrest time. God had created the world, and set it spinning in time. I wanted time to stop, and I did sketch after sketch after sketch noting down the different kinds of oars, of masts and sails, even of ropes and rope knots that are used. But I had to give up in despair. I wanted to end my collection with a sketch like the one I had done a long time ago so that Mian Mazlum could carve an ivory dhow for me to take back to Diu, but my fingers grew heavy and I couldn't. I ended with a sketch of a highflung, outstretched, butterfly winged Chinese fishing net, one of the many that dot the coast of South India. It is the only trace now of the former Chinese presence in India.

What could I do with all my sketches. I couldn't bring myself to tear them up. I would somehow use them, how, when, where, I didn't know. So I rolled up the sketches and maps, and placed them in one of the Martaban jars before going to see Malik Aiyaz who had sent for me.

I need someone whom I can trust, Malik Aiyaz had said in 1509, and who can advise me about my ships and anchorages. You told me, Malik Aiyaz continued, that you don't want to go to sea again. Why don't you be my *shahbandar*. You will get an official allowance for life.

I was silent.

It will stop my wanderings, I thought. I thought also of what my hakim had said.

They'll kill me, I told Malik Aiyaz, I shouldn't have come back to Diu.

Who, the Malik asked, surprised.

The Jains of Diu, I said, they'll have me killed.

Why, asked Malik Aiyaz, why will they kill you.

I was silent for a long while. Malik Aiyaz didn't realize, how could he, that his whys were two pronged. The answer to the first why was easy. I told the Malik why I had left Diu. But I couldn't explain to him why I had come back to Diu in 1509 when I didn't really know the answer myself.

Malik Aiyaz was not my friend at that time, just my employer. As his harbor master I was responsible for the ships that entered Diu port. The nakhodas had to report to my office when they returned to Diu. Only later did he become my friend and we would talk to each other about things. I gave him a few details about my leaving Diu with a young Jain girl. I didn't mention Usha by name, nor could I tell him our tragic story. Malik Aiyaz was determined to make his Diu the best trading center on the west coast by reducing customs duties. In 1509 he was not worried about the Portuguese who were not perceived as a threat to Gujarat but to the trade and shipping of the Kanara and Malabar coasts in the south

At that time in 1509 I did not want to and could not tell anyone the story of my life. I told Malik Aiyaz as little as possible. Perhaps he had heard the rumors that I was a traitor to Islam but did not want to hurt my feelings. I did not tell him about our sailing away to Malindi in the *Zephyr* in 1497, nor did I mention our return in Paulo da Gama's ship to Calicut on the west coast in 1498. I talked vaguely about her father's implacable hatred of me but did not give Malik Aiyaz all the details. Sheth Chimanlal had devoted himself exclusively to the making of money after Usha and I fled to Malindi in 1497. He became the wealthiest businessman in Diu. He also became a recluse.

Sheth Chimanlal has not taken a step out of his house for eight long years, Abdul told me.

I had to tell Malik Aiyaz about Sheth Chimanlal's fierce vow, despite the love he bore his fifteen year old daughter, to have us killed in order to wipe out the stain on the whole Jain community to which he belonged, because I, a Muslim, a friend whom he had trusted, had run away with his only daughter.

I don't know this Sheth Chimanlal, said Malik Aiyaz, but I will send a warning to the *shahbandar* of the Jain community. The whole community will be severely punished if anything happens to you.

Malik Aiyaz didn't wait for my reply. He was a man of action.

That's settled then, Ahmadji, he assured me, you'll begin tomorrow.

This had happened in late March, 1509, when the Portuguese were regarded as just a nuisance to trade and shipping by the Gujaratis. Two or three Portuguese ships would come every year to the ports of Kannanur, Calicut and Cochin in South India, load their ships with pepper and spices and return to Portugal.

I liked working for Malik Aiyaz. He became my friend and protector. He gave me a house that stood by itself, no neighbors, and that I liked very much because it was quite near the blackrock promontory from where I could look out at the spread of the Bahr-i-Hind.

In April that year I sent for Abdul, who I knew would wait patiently to hear from me at the house of my friend, Kotta Marakkar, in Kannanur.

In 1505 Abdul had left us, Usha and Layla and me, in Vijayanagar city and
gone to Bhatkal on the coast to sell a piece of *ponamhara* ambergris which
he had found on the sands of Lamu. We had spent all the money that
Paulo and his brother, Vasco da Gama, had rewarded me with for direct-
ing their ships across the Bahr-i-Hind from Malindi to Calicut. It wasn't
payment for my services but a token of gratitude. We needed money, especially to take care of the little one who would arrive soon. It would take
Abdul ten days to get back from Bhatkal on the coast to Vijayanagar city
where Usha and myna Yasmin and Layla and I would wait for him. I was
worried. Come and meet us at Kotta Marakkar's in Kannanur if anything
happens to us, I had told Abdul.

Abdul had gone to Bhatkal on the coast and sold the golden ambergris
there for a large sum of money, but the guards at the city gates would not
allow him to reenter Vijayanagar city. Perhaps because he was a Muslim.
He returned to the coast, sailed to Kannanur, and waited there for five
long years at Kotta Marakkar's.

I hadn't seen Abdul for five long years, and when he came to Diu in 1509
we double embraced and were silent for a while. Where is my sister, Layla,
he asked. Where is your wife. Strangely he never would pronounce Usha's
name. What happened at Vijayanagar, he asked me softly. I told him I was
so sure that the Jain assassins had killed both of them in Anegundi that
I didn't go back there to find out what happened. I couldn't speak any
South Indian language. And I couldn't go on to talk even to Abdul about
my despair. Abdul fell silent then and wouldn't look into my eyes knowing it would hurt me deeply to talk about what happened. I remember
wanting to ask him then why he couldn't say Usha's name but I didn't,
knowing he would tell me if he wanted to. We don't need to talk, Abdul
and I, we understand and trust each other.

Living again in Diu in 1509 I felt a kind of peace. I was no longer a
restless wanderer. No one tried to kill me. Abdul later told me that after
Sheth Chimanlal learnt I had returned he left Diu in disgust. The sheth
had gone to live in Patan, the Jain center in Gujarat with over a hundred
Jain temples.

The Jain traders and businessmen would avoid talking to me, and
would handle all their shipping through other nakhodas. Some of their
servants would taunt me at times, shouting drunkard, traitor, drunkard,
behind my back.

It didn't bother me. I did my work as Malik Aiyaz's *shahbandar*. I lived
by myself, to myself. I reread Rumi and Sa'di, whose poems I used to
recite to the bright stars during the lonely nights at the helm. Their comments on transiency and human suffering had always affected me deeply.

I often wondered whether their poems had sprung out of their own personal experiences or from just brooding about human pain.

Why, oh why, I had often wanted to ask my hakim during the five years we wandered from village to village. But I never did.

We didn't talk very much, and my hakim never asked directly for my help. But I was there when he needed assistance, for I was intrigued by the simple materials that he used to treat the sick and by the fact that he never accepted money for his servics. Onions and garlic bulbs that could be found in every village hut, leaves of the *neem* tree, rice*canji*, sesame seeds, these he would mash to make a poultice or else grind into a paste to apply to different parts of the body. I would accompany him when he went to the jungle to hunt for medicinal plants and herbs for more serious cases. I would assist him whenever a whole village needed to be treated for some illness or the other. And gradually I came to know some of the names of the medicines he used to treat his patients. What I disliked intensely was that I had to touch the patients to take their pulse. This distaste I concealed from my hakim. It's the beat of life itself, he told me.

One day during our third year together he suddenly looked into my eyes and said, Why don't you become a hakim. You have the right touch, he added.

I was quite shocked. He hadn't noticed my distaste, I thought.

Perhaps you'll become one after you cure your inner suffering that only you can cure. Write your suffering, and heal your shattered self first.

He didn't explain what he meant.

After my return to Diu in 1509 I had painful fits of brooding, especially at night. About what had happened to Usha and me. Why, oh why, I would often ask the sky above. I would try to compose poetry despite the warning of my hakim. And I would wake up the next morning, restless and confused as ever. I never could talk to people about what had happened to Usha and me, but I did like to listen to the stories other people told about themselves and their experiences. I would always remain silent. Perhaps my silence induced them to talk. Perhaps they sensed I was a willing ear. I would listen, patiently, to different versions of a single event from different people, and later put together, in my mind, what to me was the truth of the matter. The next day, alas, portions of my mental creation of the event would evaporate from my memory. But I never told what happened to me, even to my friends.

I had three true friends in Diu, João the convict exile who taught a Portuguese class in Diu, the maulvi, and the pandit. We came together as a discussion group . It had been announced at Diu center that a *bhikshu*, a Buddhist missionary, would give a series of four sermons on the Four Noble Truths of Buddhism. The first sermon would be on suffering. I was keenly interested, but I deliberately held back. I was so sure I wouldn't find the answer to my question, why, oh why, that I was reluctant to go to the center.

Despite my reluctance, my feet led me there. I had expected a large crowd of listeners eager to know why human beings suffer. The monk sat in a corner with his shaven head bowed. Four of us, strangers to each other, sat in a semi circle waiting to listen to the sermon. I sat at one end. João, the one on my right, I came to know his name later, whispered to me that the people of Diu were only interested in trade and in the making of money, not in truth.

The saffron robed monk raised his shaven head and stared at the tip of his nose. I was sure he was tremendously disappointed to see only four seekers after truth, but his face was impassive, his gaze fixed.

The sermon began.

Buddha, the great Physician who cures all suffering, has set down the Four Noble Truths. The first is, *Sabbe samsāra dukke*, the whole world is in pain. The most piercing form of such suffering is a passionate craving for a beloved who is no more.

That's all for now. Return to your homes, and meditate on the truth that the whole world is in pain. Meditate also on *impermanence* and on the *non self*. They will help you to understand the second truth about suffering, which is *tanha* or thirst.

Why, who, when, what. I was bursting with questions, but I didn't ask any. Nor did the maulvi who always invoked God as the fount of mercy and compassion and was never troubled by what it was all about.

The pandit spouted forth the word *Kāli* which made no sense to me.

Who is responsible for this suffering, João asked the monk, is it God.

There is no God, said the saffron robed monk in an even tone of voice.

About suffering, he said, staring not at João who had asked the question, but at me. If a man be wounded by a poisoned arrow, he said softly, would knowing about who shot the arrow and why be more helpful than the treatment of the wound.

He then relapsed into a deep silence and stared at the tip of his nose.

The sermon was a waste of time, except that it brought the four of us together. I felt sorry for my three companions who appeared to be confused, so I invited them to my house to talk about things, and to have some coffee. That's how we came to form a group for discussions. We became good friends. But we never did learn the Four Noble Truths. It was announced at Diu center next day that the monk had taken ship for Ceylon.

Perhaps because he realized that no one in Diu was really interested in the truths of Buddhism. Ceylon is already Buddhist, the pandit told us. Our *bhikhsu* should travel beyond the straits of Melaka to convert the island tribals who have not yet been touched by Hinduism.

Later, during one of our discussions on the spread of religions, the pandit said in a solemn tone, all religions spring into existence with an inbuilt missionary force that drives them all over the world.

Yes, yes, interrupted the maulvi, that's what drove Islam to India and beyond.

Hinduism, the pandit continued, ignoring the interruption, leapt across the black waters to the *suvarna*lands of south east Asia to convert the island tribes and create golden civilizations.

Didn't the Hindu missionaries follow in the wake of the traders, asked João.

The pandit was silent.

What about Buddhism, I asked.

That's not a religion, the pandit said, that's a cold system of ideas.

Did Hinduism impose the caste system on those faraway lands, asked João.

The pandit did not reply.

That's how our discussions proceeded, in erratic fashion, with many silences. But we always remained good friends. I usually remained silent and would listen to their voices.

Strangely, the voice of the monk had reminded me of my hakim's. The whole world is in pain, the Buddhist monk had said. The even tone of the monk's voice told me that the statement was not a complaint but a fact about life that the monk had willingly accepted.

If all are in pain, my cynic said to me, why should you, Ahmad ibn Madjid, be free of pain.

My hakim had said, return to Diu.

And I remember now the strange calm that descended on me when I set foot again on the soil of Diu, and looked at the coconut palms swaying with the seawind. Perhaps that was what I was looking for, peace.

You'll never find what you're looking for anywhere else but in Diu, my hakim had said. He had flung these words at me suddenly one day, back in 1508.

I didn't know I was looking for anything, I said to him. I shall continue to be your assistant and help you heal the wounds of people.

What about your own wound, my hakim said.

It was, now I think of it, the very last conversation we had had.

We were on the outskirts of Burhanpur in Central India. We had been travelling together for years. How many I do not care to remember, five maybe, because then I was living out of time, ever since he rescued me, bleeding and almost near death, from the ditch beyond Anegundi on the far outskirts of Vijayanagar in 1505.

The hakim had bound up my wounds, patched my torn clothes with his own hands, waited patiently for three months for my wounds to heal, and then said, come with me.

And I had accompanied him as his assistant, as we wandered through the hills and the valleys and the villages of Central India, through Raichur and the Doab, he never would enter cities, healing those who were sick, he never would accept any money, sleeping wherever we could find shelter, sometimes roaming around in jungles hunting for medicinal plants, talking only occasionally and briefly to each other. He didn't like to talk and was even more silent than I was, but would at times make cryptic statements that pierced my being.

I had mentioned a few random details about my involvement with Usha and Diu, about our voyage to the west coast in Paulo da Gama's ship, about the loss of our baby in Kannanur. But I never talked about what had happened at Anegundi. The hakim always looked straight into my eyes, but never asked me any questions about my past.

Only once did I ask him a question. That was in a village that had a severe attack of dysentery after a three day festival. Their stomachs were bloated. I helped my hakim prepare a paste of *hing* and dried ginger and coriander and neem tree leaves , which we smeared on the bellies of the villagers. We had continued working without stopping through the long hours of the night. I still didn't like to touch people.

I am exhausted, I told my hakim, I'm going to the hut to rest.

Go, he said softly. I'll treat the remaining patients.

I fell into a deep sleep, and the next thing I became aware of was his covering me with a cotton sheet against the chill of the early morning. He hadn't slept at all. I could hear the village cocks crowing. It was dawn. I opened my eyes and asked him a one word question that had often troubled me during our wanderings together.

Why.

My hakim had known immediately that I had meant, why did you become a wandering hakim.

It is a way out of *samsāra*, my hakim had said, an answer that still puzzles me.

You don't know that you're searching for something, my hakim had said. But you are.

We were resting under a banyan tree on the outskirts of Burhanpur. It was a hot premonsoon day. I was tired, sleepy. Sweat dripped from my forehead. My hakim looked his usual cool self. Strangely he never per-spired even at midday on the hottest of days.

I have to leave you, I heard my hakim say softly. I have to travel to the Himalayas to study the strange effects of the drug *datura* and why it has no effect on habitual drinkers of alcohol, and why the insane are not affected by it. I'll have to discard these clothes and learn how to discard the self I have accumulated all these five years, Ahmadbhai, all these years travelling with another self.

With you, he added softly.

Fare well, Ahmadbhai, my hakim said, you need to heal your self. It now has a protective scar. But your inner wound still needs healing. Only you can heal yourself.

He had never used my name before. Perhaps because a name, as he had once told me, confers a sense of self.

He stood up, took a few steps, turned around and looked at me. I wanted to stand up, but I couldn't. His eyes looked a little sad. My eyes were heavy.

Return to Diu, Ahmadbhai, he said.

And he walked away. He did not look back.

When I woke up I found a neat pile of clothes next to me and a white cotton bag full of medicinal herbs. My own clothes were torn and dirty. His fitted me, we were of the same size, so I picked up his bag and began walking towards Diu.

I walked all the way slowly, reluctantly, most reluctantly, to Diu. It took me a very long time, many months, avoiding towns and cities, stop-ping briefly in villages, trying to help the sick whenever I could. Try as I might, I found myself reluctant to touch my patients even to take their pulse. I'll never be a healer like you, I said aloud to my faraway hakim. I felt intensely alone.

I thought no one would recognize me, but one of the Diu nakhodas did, a former apprentice pilot. He must have told Malik Aiyaz who later sent for me. For a long time I had kept to myself. I did not want to see anyone, or talk to anyone. I lived in distant Una on the outskirts of Diu, near the tomb of Maulana Shams-ud-din, Malik Aiyaz's spiritual precep-tor. I avoided the sight of the sea, and went for long walks away from the coastline.

One day my feet took me to the blackrock promontory, where the salt tang of the sea breeze, the smell of the sea, the sails fluttering down below in the wind smote me. The coconut palms leaning towards the ocean sea led me to the Jain quarter of Diu along a path I had walked countless times a lifetime ago. Before I could reach her house I saw the kinsman, one of the Jain Jhaveris.

How's that you are alive, Jhaveri said. We thought you were surely dead. The assassins did not complete their job.

We never forget, Jhaveri spat out. We will get rid of you somehow.

The Jains did not kill me, Malik Aiyaz saw to that. I was calm. My being was quiet as a stone. Life had absolutely no meaning for me.

But Abdul was right. I had no money saved, not even for my old age. Or for Abdul, I thought. But I did not say anything to Abdul.

Abdul is worried about me. He usually never speaks at such length. He has never asked me for his wages. We have been together for too many years. He eats the same food I eat, though I have now become a vegetarian, and he loves to eat meat. We are brothers. I love him. But I cannot talk with him about what happened.

The pilots and nakhodas were in no hurry. They never complained about my silence and my brooding. We could take our time. They had had to walk from different sections of Diu. It took an hour for all of them to come to my house. Abdul would have immediately set forth *surais* of water and whatever food there was in our house for our guests, but he had gone to the Friday bazaar. I tried to get up to go into the kitchen to fetch a *surai* of cool water that Abdul would have offered first. But the pilots and the nakhodas courteously suggested I sit down with them. They had brought along their servants who served large slices of ruby red watermelon, of the near seedless variety, cultivated only in Vanakbara. The redbrown soil and the salt air there combine to produce large darkgreen yellow striped melons whose flesh is so tender and juicy, it melts in the mouth.

We sat in a circle, and ate without talking.

I looked at my five friends around me and, for a fleeting moment, I thought I could see not faces but a circle of the port cities of the Bahr-i-Hind, the whole of the Islamic trading world around me.

They were the best navigators of Diu, specialists in long distance sea routes. They needed no charts because they were familiar with every headland, every stretch of beach and every landmark, as they sailed in their ocean going, deep sea *dhows*, *baggalas*, *sambuks* and *kotias*.

Mustafa the Yemeni, who sat directly in front of me, was the most experienced pilot of them all. Tall and lean, his face pitted with smallpox, he is pleasant when his countenance relaxes into a smile. Today he looked quite troubled with his curved raven black beard. He was planning on taking his whole family on the *hajj* to Mecca and then to his home in Yemen.

Next to him on the right sat his friend and student, Khalid al-Hamad, an intense young man with a fierce mouth full of perfectly white teeth, a tiny untidy fringe of a beard, and a close cropped symmetrical moustache. He was enjoying the watermelon, and asked for a huge second slice. He was on the Diu to Aden back to Diu route.

The Portuguese, Khalid had assured me once, during a long talk in my office, will never be able to capture Aden.

I had agreed, silently. I knew Aden's geographical location.

The anchorage for Aden, Ma'alla Bay, shaped like a crescent, is protected by the precipitous sides of menacing brown black scarred mountains that plunge down to the sea. They defy any attack from the interior, and threaten to push any invader back into the sea.

Khalid al-Hamad, a passionate believer in Islam, proud of its great achievements, saw Aden in a religious context. He knew the world of the Red Sea and of the Persian Gulf, knew also that Aden and Hormuz were key cities in that region. Aden specially, Khalid maintained, even more than port Jiddah, is a major gateway that stands guard over our unfortified Holy Cities, Mecca and Medina. It controls the annual Hajj pilgrimage and the eastern trade through the Red Sea. It would be a shameful loss of Islamic honor for the Mamluks, the Ottomans and the tribal Yemenis, if they allow the infidel Christians to enter the Gulf of Aden. They have their dissensions but will unite to defend the Hijaz. The Sultan who captures and fortifies Aden will be acknowledged by all believers as a spiritual overlord and hailed as the Shadow of God on Earth.

For the Mamluks and the Ottomans to sail down the Red Sea to Jiddah to protect the Holy Cities and to conquer Aden will be very difficult, as you well know, Khalid, I said.

It was Khalid who then told me that the Mamluks with the reluctant help of the Ottomans had transformed Suez from the barren port with shoals and coral reefs that I had known some years ago to a dockyard where galleys were now built with timber and iron and copper hauled through the desert sands and brought from Alexandria and Cairo. He knew about the difficulties of sailing through the narrow coral reefed Gulf of Suez at the head of the Red Sea, but pointed out that Jiddah, the port for Mecca, was being transformed by the Mamluks into a station for galleys. A fortress, he said, would be built at Jiddah for added protection. And another armada will soon be sent to the Bahr-i-Hind.

Khalid had faith in the power of the Mamluks to defend the Hijaz. I had kept silent remembering what Malik Aiyaz had said.

To the left of Mustafa was his other pupil, Suleiman the stargazer. He was thin, with a *henna*dyed beard, a close trimmed black mustache, and discolored teeth because he incessantly chewed *pān*. He set down his melon slice and scratched the underside of his chin. Impatient, his elbows moving constantly, he could not restrain himself.

Don't you think, Ahmadji, that the Portuguese will never be able to pursue our ships in the crowded islands of the Maldives.

Mustafa glanced sideways at his pupil, but didn't say a word.

It was the venerable Sinbad, on my right, who uttered just one word. Eat.

Eating, in company, is a solemn occasion always, performed gracefully but quickly, without waste of time or talk. I couldn't see Sinbad's face, but I knew that no drop of melon juice would stain his white flowing beard.

Sinbad was the most senior of us all, a pilot who, like me, loved poetry, and a merchant who sailed and traded between Diu and Hormuz, the queen of the Persian Gulf, he said, to which and from which the riches of the world had flowed before the advent of the Portuguese.

No one can forget Sinbad, so named by his father, an Arab sheikh who loved to listen to the stories from the *Arabian Nights*. He looked magnificent with his white beard, his bushy eyebrows, his deepset black eyes and his aristocratic nose.

Isn't yours too romantic a name for a trader, he was asked.

I'm not a mere trader in commodities like the Jains of Diu, he told me. Like my namesake, I am a voyager. A poet too. I enjoy the making and spending of money. I don't worship money, but hasn't money now become the religion of our trading world.

He spends half the year in Diu, and the other half in Hormuz. He comes from Hormuz to Diu to arrange for the great quantity of merchandise that he buys here, chiefly textiles. He deals only in luxury goods that had a quick sale, catering to the nobility in Gujarat and in the Persian Gulf. He took advantage of Malik Aiyaz's customs proclamation. From Diu he exported silks from Masulipatam, shawls from Kashmir, Cambay quilts with silk linings, brocaded velvet, amber beads, cornelians, agates, ivory bracelets, plates of emeraldgreen jasper, scents from Navsari, and the most expensive *patolas*, woven for brides in Gujarat.

He would never transport Arabian and Persian horses although, during times of war, they fetched high prices at Goa from the Sultan of Bijapur, and at Bhatkal from the Raja of Vijayanagar. The risks, Sinbad said, were too great, and the insurance rates too high, the horse sailing season too short. And horses offended him as a poet, they made ships stink.

I asked him once why he preferred to live in Hormuz, a barren island of salt and sulphur, the hottest place in our world.

It is an important center, Sinbad said, where goods from the east and the west converge to be traded. It is hot, I know, but one can go to summer retreats on the Persian mainland. And one can beat the heat by lying in a marble bathtub with only the head above the water.

He insisted that he never suffered from the rash of prickly heat in Hormuz. He loves Hormuz. He has also popularized, all through Gujarat, the famous couplet about Hormuz,

If all the world were a ring
its jewel would be Hormuz

He is a handsome old man, Sinbad is. One who enjoys himself, untroubled by questions about life that torment me. I like him very much.

Unlike Sinbad, Saifuddin the Bohra does not deal in luxury items. He speaks Swahili very fluently, and is pilot and trader of the East African coast. He has teamed up with his friend, Behram the Parsi, who has an acute business sense, and a keen interest in new ways of shipbuilding.

Shipbuilding will be my family business, Behram told me once.

They make a good team and, I think, make a greater business profit than Sinbad.

Saifuddin carries coarse cotton cloths in bulk, *lungis* or wraparounds of different colors, a few silk pieces, spices of different varieties, grey, red, and yellow beads to Malindi, Mombasa and Kilwa, where local traders bid for his merchandise, which they take into the interior to sell at an exorbitant rate to the tribal peoples.

Behram and Saifuddin bring back gold, ivory, wax, and sometimes ambergris to Diu

It was Saifuddin who spoke after we had refreshed ourselves with the water of the green coconut, and after the carpet was cleared.

Thin, dark, with anxious eyes, Saifuddin said quietly but firmly, I am afraid I will no longer be able to trade at Malindi and Mombasa. Portuguese ships now patrol the coast of East Africa and are a threat to all the seaports there. What should I do, Ahmadji.

I had my head bent. My eyes were shut, though I knew Saifuddin had turned towards me with the question. I had been a pilot. I had thought I was a poet. But I have never really understood the world of trade and commerce.

It was Mustafa who replied to Saifuddin.

Saifuddin, my son, why don't you tell us about the situation along the coast of East Africa. Let each one of us state the dangers along his sea route. Then, perhaps, my friends, we can plan what can be done. Ahmadji can then advise us.

It was a logical way to proceed, Mustafa's. He wanted us to locate the trouble spots in the Bahr-i-Hind after the arrival of the Portuguese.

I knew my friends. Like me, they were too emotional, too confused to make plans.

There was a long silence.

Sinbad stroked his long white beard with his right hand to calm himself.

My friends, Sinbad said, what does it befit us to plan against the Portuguese. These are not human beings but ravenous wolves.

Another long silence.

Saifuddin then began to speak, slowly, deliberately, using the technique of *dharana*, keeping his eyes fixed on a stylized elephant figure on the carpet.

The Portuguese have established trading factories in the ports at Sofala, Kilwa and Mocambique, Saifuddin said. No one is allowed to trade at these ports unless he has a safeconduct pass, a *cartaz*. Ships from Cambay and Diu that carry Gujarati cloths and wraparounds are attacked and plundered. The Portuguese have discovered that the Africans will only exchange their gold for Gujarati cloths, not for cloth pieces from the west. We can exchange our textiles only for wax and ivory, but not for gold. The Portuguese carry away all the gold for themselves.

Why, why, I asked myself, Saifuddin said. Why have the Portuguese, those abandoned creatures, established themselves at Mocambique, and at Sofala and at Kilwa. I suddenly realized why. They need our Gujarati cloths and wraparounds to trade for Sofala gold.

Saifuddin paused, raised his eyes, and looked at each one of us in turn.

The Portuguese, Saifuddin continued with contempt, have come empty handed, like beggars, with no trade goods to sell. They have no money, no money at all. A little silver perhaps, and rods of copper. Some of our merchants have more money than all the Portuguese. Any one of our ships back from Mombasa after trading there could buy the goods and merchandise of three Portuguese ships.

What the Portuguese pirates have, Saifuddin continued, are guns and huge ships. They terrorize our ships, rob them of cloth which they then use to buy Sofala gold with which they pay for pepper and spices at Calicut and Cochin. What can I do, I ask again. And I have no answer. Behram, my Parsi friend, wants to build ships on the Portuguese model, and equip them with Ottoman guns.

Suleiman interrupted him.

The Portuguese have prohibited all ships carrying guns and Rumis and Habshi Muslims, he said. They have forbidden trading in spices also, which they now claim are a Portuguese royal monopoly. Even the ships that have a *cartaz* are subject to capture, and the crew together with the nakhoda are liable to death if they violate this law.

By what right have the Portuguese, Suleiman smashed his fist on the carpet again and again to stress each word, any claim to the Bahr-i-Hind. The ocean sea belongs to all of us.

My head was bent. My eyes were shut.

I thought of the discussion with my other friends about the ocean sea.

João had told me about the Portuguese claim of sovereignty over the ocean sea, a right conferred upon them by the Pope of Rome. It is a *bellum justissimum* for the Portuguese, João had said, a war most just, against infidel Islam. The Muslims, the Portuguese believed, had to be destroyed in an effort to acquire eternal glory. The Portuguese hated the Muslims. The Muslims considered the Christians to be infidel dogs. *Jihad*, a state of constant struggle, was essential for establishing the power of Islam.

I opened my eyes and looked at Suleiman.

Safe conduct passes, I wanted to tell him, had been used on the Bahr-i-Hind before the arrival of the Portuguese. But it wouldn't have helped Suleiman, such knowledge. He needed to pour out his rage. His chest heaved. He clenched his fists to control himself.

That word, *cartaz*, my friends, is a satanic word, Suleiman said. Two years ago my elder brother got a Portuguese safe conduct pass issued at Kannanur to carry pepper and rice and cloves to Diu. A Portuguese pirate, may he be boiled in oil, fired a cannon and ordered my brother's ship to come alongside. My brother went on board with his *cartaz*. That shaitan insisted that the signature was a forgery. He flung grappling irons onto my brother's ship. Then he tortured my brother to show them where the money and valuables were hidden. He plundered all the cargo, murdered my brother and all his crew, wrapped their bodies up in the sails, and with their guns bombarded and sank the ship to destroy the evidence. Some of the bodies were washed ashore at Maha'im, and in one bundle, miraculously, a youth was barely alive. Do you know what the Portuguese authorities did when the merchants of Kannanur complained. Viceroy Almeida deprived the pirate of his command, and sent him back to Lisbon supposedly in disgrace. The Portuguese are brutes, may God abandon them. There is no justice in their uncivilized world.

We all remained silent.

I looked all around. The smile on Khalid al-Hamad's face had disappeared. My friends had their heads bowed, their eyes were shut tight. They were in a state of despair, different from mine, not keenly personal, but piercingly felt all the same. That's why they had come to ask me what should be done. I could not just bend my head and brood about *samsāra*. My hakim was right. Perhaps the act of telling their stories may have begun the process of healing for my friends. I had to continue the process and provide them with some kind of hope, though I did not really have any hope to offer.

My friends, I said.

My voice, a little louder than usual, sounded quite false to my ears.

My friends, I said again, trying my best to sound a note of hope. We know how bleak the situation on the Bahr-i-Hind today is. We do not have guns, and we do not have huge ships. We are powerless. But we must not despair. We cannot fight them at sea unless the Mamluks and the Ottomans help us. Let us think of ways to trick the Portuguese.

But I had no real suggestions to offer them. I had no answer to my own questions about power. Is treachery ever justified. Can the powerless use any tactics to attack or defend themselves against those in power.

Suleiman the stargazer jumped in with the suggestion that the Maldives should be used as a port base for trade and as a refuge from the Portuguese shark ships.

We thought about this for a time.

The Maldives are an elongated garland of over a thousand islands off the west coast of India. The encircling reefs act as protective underwater walls with a few passages deep enough for large ships to enter. The treacherous coral reefs cause many shipwrecks. Portuguese sharkships would find it impossible to pursue any of our *sambuks* and *kotias* there.

Saifuddin this time was enthusiastic. Let us, he said, make the Maldives the center of our trading world from where our ships can set sail in different directions, to Hormuz and to Diu and to Melaka.

We all thought about his suggestion for some time. I knew it wouldn't work.

Sinbad too saw its disadvantages. Our ships, too, he knew, would be in danger.

The Maldives can be a good center on the sailing route to Melaka and back. But it simply will not do on the routes to Hormuz or to Aden, Mustafa said.

I counsel patience, Sinbad said.

But Saifuddin impatiently offered another suggestion. Why don't we hoist up a sail with that ugly bloodred cross on it when we sight a Portuguese ship, he suggested.

Even as he said it Saifuddin knew it would not work. Our sails and our ships were quite different.

Suleiman put forth the suggestion that we forge Portuguese *cartazes*. Vora is learning how to write Portuguese and will soon be able to prepare cartazes for our ships.

João had told me that Vora didn't know the abbreviations and contractions used in official Portuguese documents. An alert escrivão could easily detect that the *cartaz* had been forged.

I kept silent.

No, no, no, said Khalid. Let me counsel patience and offer hope. The Mamluk Sultan of Egypt, who has lost a great deal of money because of the drop in customs revenue and in the pilgrimage taxes at Jiddah, will send another huge fleet of galleys and *maonas* armed with Ottoman guns from Suez to protect the Holy Cities and to destroy the Portuguese ships. Let's wait for the Mamluk fleet.

How long will we have to wait.

No one knew.

I knew the Mamluk ships would take more than a year to assemble as a fleet, but I said nothing.

Mustafa didn't agree with Khalid.

I like Ahmadji's suggestion that we trick the Portuguese, said Mustafa. My employer, Malik Gopi, has accepted the fact that the Portuguese are now in the Bahr-i-Hind. But, greedy for money and open to bribery and corruption, the Portuguese are totally ignorant. They don't charge much for *cartazes* which we can afford to pay for because of the large profits we make. They don't know the language of business. They're only interested in buying pepper and some spices on the west coast. They are ignorant about other commodities like cinnamon from Ceylon and mace and cloves from Melaka and Southeast Asia. And they are ignorant of the seaports on other coasts.

They will learn fast, I thought, remembering the navigational instruments on board Vasco da Gama's *San Gabriel*, the maps and charts I had seen in his cabin, and their shooting of the sun at noon instead of fettering the stars like us.

We thought about our plight for a long time, but no one had anything to offer.

The meeting broke up.

My friends thanked me. They tried to smile but looked sad as they bade me goodbye.

In one of our discussions Sidi Ali had told me that Meditteranean war tactics used by the Mamluks and the Ottomans could not prevail on the Bahr-i-Hind which was an open not an inland sea. I hadn't told my friends that. That knowledge would only heighten their despair.

And Malik Aiyaz had told me that it would take a long time for a new

Mamluk fleet to be armed with new Ottoman guns. I wanted my friends to go back with a faint kind of hope. Malik Aiyaz had made me promise to keep the news a secret. He was afraid that traders would desert his Diu.

Just then there was a commotion in the compound. It was Vora who had come from Malik Gopi with an urgent message for Mustafa. One of their ships which was carrying a *cartaz* and a distant cousin of Mustafa had been sunk by the Portuguese off the island of Socotra.

As Diu's *shahbandar* who received reports and accounts from visitors and nakhodas about happenings on the Bahr-i-Hind I knew that the Islamic world around the Persian Gulf and the Red Sea was in confusion.

Amir Hussein, the admiral of the Mamluk fleet, had told me that there were disturbances about dynastic succession in Cairo, so that the Mamluk Sultan of Egypt had found it very difficult to put together a fighting force of ships and guns for an expedition against the Portuguese. The Mamluks had to redesign their *maonas* for the heavy monsoonal seas of the Bahr-i-Hind and they would have to ask the Ottomans to cast new cannon and train new ship gunners to attack the Portuguese.

According to Salman Rais, the Ottomans, rivals of the Mamluks, deliberately supplied the fleet with inferior artillery that was cast badly and cracked after two or three years. Guns of good quality were sent to defend the eastern Ottoman borders. The Mamluks cannot handle the new weapons of war, Salman Rais told me. They still rely on the sword and the lance and the horse, he said. Soon we Ottomans will vanquish the Mamluks.

The tribal Yemenis in the south were afraid that their control of the Hijaz would be lost. They refused to supply provisions for the Mamluk fleet. The Mamluks were forced to spend money and time building fortifications at Jiddah and at Kamaran.

Alas, bewailed Malik Aiyaz, there is no unity in our Muslim world.

Perhaps help would come, Malik Aiyaz told me, from Bijapuri Goa in the south of India. Many Mamluk workmen and armorers and shipbuilders, some of their gunners too, had managed to escape the Diu disaster and had made their way to the port city of Goa where the governor of the Sultan of Bijapur welcomed them. Goa had an armory and a shipyard. And teakwood in plentiful supply to construct ships in the Portuguese manner.

I could tell from his low voice that he didn't really believe that help would come from Goa. He was offering himself and me a faint hope that his Diu would be safe.

I stood at the gate and watched my friends leave. I tried to talk to Mustafa, but his eyes were full of despair. They had come to my house to ask questions about the Portuguese menace. They had come to seek my help. They knew I was the first pilot to encounter the Portuguese at Malindi. And they wanted me to provide them with a plan of action. What should we do about these pirates, they had asked, to whom should we be loyal.

I felt powerless. How, I asked myself again, how can those who have no power fight against those who have absolute power.

We could do nothing.

I wanted to say that perhaps the Portuguese were more than just pirates that had invaded our Bahr-i-Hind hunting for pepper and spices. But I myself was not sure of what the Portuguese really wanted and why they had come into our world. I wanted to say *samsāra* but did not. The Muslim pilots would not understand what this Sanskrit word meant. They were in despair. I was too.

FIVE

May, 1509
My house, Diu, Night
After my nakhoda friends left

After our guests had left I asked Abdul if I could have a bath.

It was refreshing to wash down and away the heat and the dust of the afternoon. I stepped on the stone slab, and with both hands lifted high the narrow necked onion shaped earthen pot that Abdul handed to me in the small enclosure of plantain trees next to the well. The cold water was refreshing. It gurgled out of the narrow mouth of the pot, splashed on to my head and streamed down my body. I closed my eyes and shivered as I waited for the next one which Abdul brought quickly. The dried red berries that Abdul had bought at the Friday bazaar rattled pleasantly in my hands, and the lather made me feel clean and in touch with the earth. The seventh pot washed away my exhaustion and I was ready to go to the blackrock promontory and write.

João came in just as I put on my loose flowing shirt. He was handsomely dressed. Tight white pyjamas, and a long buttoned up coat of black silkcotton. A blackred turban with a peak at its extreme right sat rakishly on his head. I welcomed him with a double embrace. His wife had daubed a little attar on his earlobes.

Where to, my friend, I asked João, surely you have not worn these magnificent clothes just to pay me a visit.

I knew it, I just knew it, João said. Ishak Khan was right. He said that you would forget, and I would have to fetch you for the entertainment.

I remembered the casual invitation Ishak had thrown out at the promontory. I thought he only meant to be polite. But he had gone out of his way to invite João whom, I thought, he disliked, and in the past usually ignored. Ishak must have given João money for his new clothes.

João felt highly flattered.

My wife bade me dress up for the occasion. The nobility of Diu, she said, will be there. She even hid the flask I usually slip into my under-pocket, and paid for the tonga that brought me here. But, this with João's throaty laugh, she does not know about this beloved fellow I hid on our compound wall.

And he pulled out a flask from under his wide waistband with a flourish.

Abdul hurried along with a tiny porcelain cup. But João shook his head.

My first drink of the day, he said, as he tilted the flask to his lips. Let's go. My wife gave me some money. Take Ahmadbhai to Axum's, she said.

João had *muta* 'married when he settled in Diu. Axum's is the most expensive Ethiopian restaurant in Diu, famous for its preparations heaped on a platter made of rice and teff flour which at the end of the meal one ate. The Habshi nobles flocked there. It was very difficult to get in.

Ishak Khan has spoken to the manager, João said.

I don't like eating meat now, I said, and I don't care for the vulgar entertainments Ishak enjoys and arranges for his followers. I have to go to the promontory to write.

So your secrets will be out at last, said João. At last I will know the story of Usha, and your mysterious past will be revealed. But all your secrets need not be set down today. The world and I have waited a long time. We can wait a few hours more.

He saw I was hurt.

All right, he said, all right. There's plenty of time before the show begins. We can have our meal after the show. My wife won't like it if I get in late again. I have to teach my Portuguese class early tomorrow.

I wondered why suddenly João was worried about what his wife thought about him. His *muta* 'marriage had been arranged by Ishak Khan to whom he owed a great deal of money.

But, Ahmad my friend, he continued, you will come with me, won't you, I need you at the entertainment. I swagger and joke with the others. But that's because I'm not sure of myself really. I am a good actor.

It was genuine, his need for me. The pleading tone told me so.

João is a born actor, a storyteller too. He can spin out stories, tell jokes and make people roar with laughter. He is a born teacher too. He spices his lessons with incidents from his past. I have heard almost all his stories. But I still admire the way he uses them in his classes.

The other day, to drive home some nautical terms, he told us how a pilot called Pedro Homem had illustrated the difference between starboard and larboard to Portuguese yokels who had never been on a ship before.

Pedro Homem tied a bundle of onions on the starboard side of the ship, and a bundle of garlic on the larboard. The orders shouted to the yokels were either, garlic side or onion side. Like a *vidusaka* João imitated the yokels, hurrying now to starboard, then stumbling on to larboard.

We howled with laughter.

Almost all of us have picked up some spoken Portuguese, except Vora, Malik Gopi's nephew. Vora has a thick Gujarati accent and cannot handle Portuguese nasals. But Malik Gopi, who paid for Vora's tuition, wanted him to learn how to write Portuguese for official and business correspondence.

I want Vora to learn how to write Portuguese *cartazes*, Malik Gopi said.

I do not know many of the abbreviations that are used in official correspondence, João told Malik Gopi, but I will give Vora special lessons in written Portuguese.

Vora is Malik Gopi's spy and agent, João whispered to me.

I have no gift for spoken language. I love the written form. I can follow written Portuguese now, but cannot speak it well, not as well as Sidi Ali, whom the Portuguese call *o torto*.

You're too self conscious, João tells me, you listen to yourself as you speak. You catch yourself mispronouncing words, and then you stop. One day you'll forget your selfconsciousness, and speak effortlessly.

João is right. I am not self conscious when I write. Or perhaps I am.

We neared the blackrock promontory. I had looked forward to an evening of undisturbed writing. Would the presence of João make me self conscious.

Where have my vulture doves gone, asked João.

It was very strange. There were no seagulls today on the stretch of black rock. I could hear the booming of the surf. A sudden premonition streamed into my being. My skin became tense, and the hair on my hands and forearms bristled, aware of forces outside of me. My eye felt constricted, and the high distant clouds appeared even more yellowish than they were yesterday. A strong smell of sulphur there was in the air, and my nose could sense the unusual warmth of the waters below. The winds from the west were light, but the waves did not sound low and continuous. Heavy swells broke intermittently on the shore, even though the tide was due to go out.

No, no, urged the cool voice of reason. Don't get involved. It doesn't concern you.

But fierce forces within me urged my feet toward Diu city.

Let's go, João, I shouted, dragging him down from the blackrock promontory.

What, where, why.

João was stunned. He had never seen me rush in this fashion.

I will explain as we hurry along, I said. The tufan will be on us tomorrow. I have to warn the people of Diu.

João sensed that I was compulsively driven. He followed without asking any further questions. I took a shortcut, an unused foot trail that went straight down to the outskirts of Diu town. It led through thorny bushes with bright berries, red, white, black, on them, and over thick clumps of cacti. I had to stop several times to catch my breath. João helped me over the mounds, steadied me and prevented me from running too fast. Just before we got to a stretch of flat black rocks that merges into one of the avenues that leads to Diu city center, João made me stop.

Look at you, he said. Look at both of us.

I looked at João.

João's turban was in his hands. His hair was disheveled. His white pyjamas were torn in a couple of places.

My friend, João said.

Both of us were breathing heavily.

I don't know where you are going in such a hurry, João said, but whoever you are going to speak to, believe me, will not understand what you say.

João stopped to remove the flask from his waistband. He took a swig of liquor.

Or worse, João continued, will not believe what you say. Haven't I told you, in class, that one needs to speak slowly and carefully in order to communicate with others. Not only in Portuguese. In any language.

He took another swig, then wiped his mouth and the mouth of the flask with the back of his hand.

Here, have some of this, João said.

He offered me his flask.

Without thinking, I took a quick swig. It burned my throat. I looked at João, and down at myself. My clothes were in disarray.

We rearranged our clothes, and I ran my fingers through my sparse hair. We both breathed a little easier when we heard the distant sound of the evening bell.

I have to get there soon, I told João, I have to get there before the announcer leaves the city center. He has to make an important announcement about the tufan.

All right, said João, all right. But don't let us run. We will get there before the announcements are over.

We got to the edge of the center just in time to hear the last two news items.

Malik Aiyaz has left Diu to visit the tomb of Maulana Shams-ud-din at Una.

That was the first announcement.

This year the monsoon will break on the eleventh of June, said the announcer. That was the second. God is great. Depart in peace.

I rushed to the platform.

People around the platform were beginning to drift away.

I shouted loudly, wait, wait.

The announcer was about to step down the platform.

I stumbled and fell on the steps, even as I again shouted, wait.

João held my arm, and helped me to my feet.

The announcer was surprised. I was out of breath.

A tufan, I shouted. There will be a tufan tomorrow. Everyone must be informed. Warning signals must be raised.

Immediately, I shouted.

I grabbed the announcer's arm and shook it.

Immediately, I shouted, there must be no delay.

The announcer recognized me.

All announcements prepared by the city office have been made, he told me. We have been repeating for the past week that the monsoon will begin on the eleventh of June.

No, no, a tufan will begin tomorrow, I shouted.

They didn't mention anything about a tufan, the announcer said, and turned to his companion. You brought in the weather announcement.

No, of course not, the assistant said, wrinkling his enormous hooked nose as if offended by a smell.

He whispered into the announcer's ear.

People crowded around us.

I could hear small cries of tufan, tufan. I shoved the announcer aside, so that his turban came off and he fell heavily on the steps. Then I rushed up onto the platform and sounded the bell four or five times. João held back the announcer and Hooknose. No police were around. More people gathered around the platform.

A tufan, I shouted. There will be a tufan tomorrow, one hour after the evening bell sounds. A tufan, I shouted again. Do not go fishing. Draw up your boats on the shore, as far as you can. Fasten all window coverings, and tie down your roofs with ropes.

The police overpowered João, and swarmed up on to the platform just as I was about to make an important announcement about the eye of the tufan.

I was dragged down. João was, too.

Go home, the announcer said loudly. Go home, all is well.

His bare head had hit the edge of the steps. It was bleeding, and his companion was trying to staunch the cut with a white turban.

Go home, the announcer repeated.

What you have heard are not official announcements, but those of a drunkard, Hooknose said. A well known drunkard and a traitor to Islam. There will be no tufan tomorrow.

Go in peace. All is well.

João and I were dragged to the city jail.

The announcer staggered into the *kotwal's* office, helped by Hooknose who groaned loudly, weh, oh woe. The announcer's head had stopped bleeding. But both, I noted, were good actors. One flourished a blood stained shirt, the other a bloodsoaked turban. Both flung their accusations at me, the announcer proclaiming that I had wanted to kill him, the companion displaying the shirt and the turban to the *kotwal*, who kept nodding his head vigorously.

I wondered what had happened to João, when in he walked with the superintendent of police. The superintendent ignored the *kotwal*, and bowed to me.

Let Ahmadbhai go, the superintendent told the kotwal.

He was from the north, tall and commanding.

You have to attend a performance at Mamalingams, the superintendent said. Ishak Khan is waiting for both of you.

I bowed in return.

My apologies, the superintendent said. He pointed to the *kotwal*. I'm sorry this imbecile detained you, and that you'll be late for the show.

I wanted to tell the superintendent to make an announcement about tomorow's tufan, but it would have been too late. Most people had left the center.

It wasn't the *kotwal's* fault, I said. He is not to blame.

Mirzasab, the superintendent bowed slightly towards João, has explained everything. My men will escort you to Mamalingams.

João and I rearranged our clothes. I patted my hair back. João set his turban in place, and we walked through some dark deserted streets, till we came to the entertainment district, brilliantly lighted, and crowded with people.

I know the way, João told the guards.

The street was broad, and rich with the smells of food. The *shish* balls of ground beef and the *shami* chunks of juicy lamb, both threaded on to skewers, were being prepared with a cumin cardamony, ginger garlicky marinade that dripped onto the smouldering coals and sent forth smells that quickened the appetite. Out from the tandoor ovens sunk neck deep into the pavement came hot red roast chicken spicily treated with yogurt masala. Inside the tandoor were leaf shaped *naan* breads.

In the old days I used to love spicy ground beef cooked with a lot of onions. I eat only vegetables now, like the Jains. But the smells of the food were maddening.

João wanted to hurry me to Mamalingams.

Ishak Khan will not like it if we miss the main show, he said.

A little worry crept into me. Why was João so concerned about Ishak. How and why had he got involved with Ishak. But I let the worry drift away. After all we were in Ishak's world here.

Ishak had created a spicy world of entertainment. Only rich nobles, envoys, Muslim merchant traders from overseas together with their families came to this place. They were all huge and fat. What need for exercise, they said, there are no enemies left to fight. The only sport they indulged in was wrestling. Diu was the one city, except for Hormuz perhaps, where one could taste the most delicious food in the world.

I told João of my urge to eat plain simple food.

No, he said, definitely no.

We were just about to pass Axum's. Two huge Habshi slaves stood guard at the entrance.

We will go to Axum's after the show, João said. He hurried me to Mamalingams at the head of the street.

This was the entertainment section. From here radiated the sidestreets where the courtesans and prostitutes, who came from all parts of Arabia and Africa and south east Asia, the land below the wind, plied their trade.

We arrived at Mamalingams just as the intermission was about to begin.

Servants and slaves rushed around bringing lights, and hookahs, and trays for Ishak and his guests who were sprawled on a great carpet of royal blue in semicircles of five or six facing the stage.

Ishak held the center with his group. After his first deep inhalation from the hookah he beckoned to João and me to join his group. João walked over and sat down next to Ishak. As an honored guest he was offered the second draw from the hookah. I watched João draw in the smoke without touching the pipe stem to his lips. I was amazed.

Ishak lumbered up from the carpet.

My friends, Ishak announced. Today we will really celebrate the power of Sultan Begada and the greatness of the mighty kingdom of Gujarat which the king of Delhi acknowledged yesterday. Alas, there are no more lands to conquer, there is nothing more to be done. Let us relax and enjoy ourselves.

What about the Portuguese, a voice asked.

Ha, ha, ha, laughed Ishak. Wait till you hear and smell the thunderous roar of the gun sent by my friend, Malik Gopi. .

I was about to join João when the younger son of Malik Aiyaz, Arselan Toghan, invited me to his group.

Toghan was a specialist in the world of narcotics. To him came all the dealers in ganja and opium for approval and permission, before they went to Ishak. Toghan sprinkled a few grains of *charas* onto the smouldering coals. Puffs and wisps of a delicate fragrance arose from the hookah as he inhaled deeply, twice luxuriously drinking in the smoke. His eyes began to relax and his nervousness fell away. He fell into a state of *kaif*, an Arabic word for the first degree of intoxication when the senses become lulled.

What's that you have in your *hookah*, Toghan, Ishak asked his brother.

Toghan didn't reply. João told me later that Toghan was furious with Ishak for ordering him to send Champa, Toghan's favorite courtesan, to the establishment of Malik Gopi. That Bania dog, Gopi, Toghan spat out the words. I'll kill him.

Ah, there you are Ahmadbhai, come and sit next to me, said Ishak. Tell me all about that tufan of yours.

The word tufan did not cause any disturbance here. The sea barely touched the world of these nobles who were in a drowsy state of *kaif*. They were content with themselves and the world they lived in. They wanted to enjoy life now that all wars had been fought. They had lost the vigor that had driven Sultan Begada to bring Gujarat into being.

Toghan's servant began to sprinkle Kashmiri *charas* on the hookahs.

I went and sat next to João.

How can you tell that there will be a tufan tomorrow, Ahmadji, asked Ishak.

My nose, my eyes, my skin, tell me, I wanted to say.

I don't know, I told Ishak Khan.

He knows, João defended me. But Ahmadbhai doesn't know how he knows.

I suppressed a powerful urge to get up, and shout to all around to beware of tomorrow's tufan. But I looked around at these indolent nobles, their lack of energy. And I remained silent.

The servants brought in swinging censers of burning sandalwood and incense. The air began to be filled with spicy Arabian odors.

Can you have an announcement made tomorrow, I asked Ishak Khan. It will be too late, otherwise.

Ishak turned to me, and then turned away. A servant whispered in his ear.

Ah, we're ready, Ishak said, and clapped his hands.

I'll tell my father, he said to me as the lights were removed and the stage lit up by a row of twelve candles at the back.

Malik Aiyaz is at Una, I said.

But Ishak was busy talking to the person on his right, the one from Surat, who had arranged the show, João later told me.

Let the show begin, said Ishak. It will be my reply to the Portuguese guns whom you all fear.

And he roared with laughter.

A middle aged man walked on to the stage. He had a round face with tiny eyes. On his head he wore a red cylindrical *fez* with a single black tassel. A pair of long moustachios that drooped almost to his chin gave him a sad look.

What amazed everyone was his huge potbelly, which stood out round and shone with oil. He slapped both his hands on it, in the manner of a wrestler sounding out his biceps. It was as if a taut drum had been played as an announcement for silence.

A slave boy took one of the lit candles to the front of the stage, placed a Sankheda lacquerware stool in the middle, handed the performer a hollow five foot bamboo.   Then the slave boy announced.

The great Humrumbum from Ghandubad cannot talk at all, but will make this distinguished audience hear the sounds of battle.

Humrumbum sat uncomfortably on the knee high stool and, holding the bamboo to his mouth, made several attempts to blow out the candle. He blew, he blew, and he blew, but did not succeed. He lumbered off the stool, and paced up and down, his face miming fury and disgust. He hit himself repeatedly on the mouth as if punishing it for its failure, and then opened it wide as if to shout, but no sounds came forth.

Let me use my other pair of lips, the slave boy supplied the words for Humrumbum.

Humrumbum pounded loudly on his belly.

He then threw off the loin wrapper hitched between his legs, turned his back, placed one foot on the stool positioned the five foot bamboo into his arse and with one loud fart blew out the candle. The spectators were stunned. A number of slave boys carried the lit candles around the stage and Humrumbum blew them out with uncanny accuracy. He followed this in the total darkness with the sounds of battle.

He first let off a deafening roar.

That's the sound of a siege gun, the slave boy said.   Humrumbum rushed to the other side of the stage and let fly a prolonged squeak which made everybody laugh.

That's a Portuguese gun, explained the slave boy.

I laughed and, for one wild moment, I could smell the stink of gun smoke and I thought the Portuguese were bombarding Diu again. The sounds were controlled. Some fart notes were high, others were low. Some were long drawn, others were short and staccato.

The siege gun won.

Humrumbum. What a name. What a musical instrument. What a cannon. What a parody.

Lights, shouted Ishak, roaring with laughter.

Incense, shouted Toghan.

There was no applause because everyone began to rush out to escape the deadly fumes and suffocating smells that filled the small theater. Ishak could not stop laughing, watching his guests hurrying away.

Wasn't that a marvelous show, Ishak asked João. The Portuguese will never set foot in Diu.

Perhaps we should have a show for the zenana ladies, he said to Humrumbum. And Ishak roared again with laughter.

João muttered his thanks, and we both hurried outside.

All real power had been drained out of Ishak and his friends, I thought.

It was a relief to breathe in the fresh night air.

João led me to Axum's.

I did not want to go in, hungry though I was. The fumes had made me nauseous. But João was most insistent. He, too, was hungry. I knew the liquor and the ganja and the *charas* would be bad for him on an empty stomach.

The two Habshi guards bowed deeply to João as we went inside.

The place was still crowded even though it was late, The other eating establishments had closed down for the night. We were shown to a quiet corner by the proprietor himself.   I know what you like, the proprietor said to João.

We sat in silence for a while, ignoring the noises and laughter at the other tables. João was in a strange mood. He loves to speculate about things, specially when he is on the very edge of being drunk. I kept thinking of Portuguese guns and ships and about the tufan. I felt a little unsteady.

The waiter came with our enjera platters, filled with spicy heapings of meats and vegetables. I broke off a piece of the enjera and scooped up some vegetables. João scooped up some meat, but he did not put it into his mouth. He set the piece down. He had not touched his drink.

Ahmad, my brother, João said. Sometime ago you had asked me about power and Vasco da Gama and justice, and the Portuguese use of the tactics of terror to survive on the Bahr-i-Hind. Could such tactics be justified, you asked.

I've thought deeply about all this, Ahmadji, João said, and I don't still know the answer.

He lifted his drink to his lips, but then set it down.

But your question made me consider other forms of power. The invisible power of love. The power in our day of business and the money flow. Human power displaced by mechanical power generated by guns. The power of religion, he continued.

But isn't that a spiritual power, I interrupted.

João paused for a long time.

Not always, João replied.

He took a long drink.

I have slowly come to realize, Ahmadji, that the beginnings of all religions are always pure. They lose their spiritual innocence when priests, popes and the *ulema* assume power over people. Ideals then harden into dogmas. I haven't worked it out yet, but power, religion, and conversion are somehow interconnected.

Remind me, one day, to tell you about the Tupinama of Brazil.

That was quite enigmatic. Who were the Tupinama. Where, what was Brazil. But I didn't interrupt João.

He gulped down the drink in front of him.

No, no, Ahmad my brother, don't say anything. Just listen.

I didn't say anything. João was teetering on the edge of being drunk. I'd have to take him home soon.

Eat a piece of enjera, I said.

Listen, Ahmadji. The arts of discussion and persuasion don't belong to the language of power. Religions speak languages that never usually allow them to talk to each other. Guns and towering ships employ a one way language. You have to use the same kind of language to reply to them. The Mamluks are in a state of *kaif*, their language is archaic like their guns and their ships.

I suddenly think of Saifuddin and the Maldives, and of the need to trick the Portuguese. I think of the Hindus and of how they have survived the onslaught and spread of Islam.

The drink has affected me. I cannot think straight.

But what about power.

Is the movement of power wavelike like that of *samsāra*.

Let's go, said João, suddenly. My wife will be waiting for me.

He finished his drink, I didn't. And when we got out of Axum's there was a single tongawallah at the stand.

One mahmudi, he told João, who agreed without bargaining at all.

That's twelve times the right price, I said.

Don't worry, João said. Ishak is paying for all this.

I wondered how and why.

Both of us were quiet as the tonga rattled along in the night. We were tired, and João was sleepy.

I hope my wife is fast asleep, he said, as we neared his place. He paused.

Why don't you come in for a drink, he said. The tongawallah will take you to your house later.

Surely, sab, said the tongawallah.

My wife is asleep, said João.

The servants were asleep, too, all except the one who came to the gate swinging a smouldering half coconut husk as a torchlight.

I wouldn't have gone in, of course. It was too late, but it was strange that João both wanted and did not want me to come in. He was worried. Usually we would spend long hours talking through the night.

I'd rather walk, I told João. The walk will clear my head.

I was afraid of snakes, but I wanted to think about things.

Goodnight. Tell your wife to make preparations for the tufan. I'll send Abdul to help you. I'll see you tomorrow in class.

The servant gave me the smouldering husk.

João and I parted with a double embrace.

I swung the smouldering husk till it burst into flame and lit the path as I walked to my house. The winds were soft and low. Insect sounds heightened the silence of the night. Occasionally there was an overpowering aroma from clumps of jasmine. Jasmine is called *rat ki rani*, queen of the night.

I didn't want to think about things.

I looked up at the stars above. The sky was dark blue, perfect for taking good *qiyas* measurements. There was no moon. The horizon was clean and distinct. And there was no following wind.

But what need have I to measure stellar altitudes. I have lost my bearings. I cannot take any measurements to guide me through my own life.

I looked up and recognized the *Sa 'd* stars, an inauspicious group of four stars with the fourth one inside the other three, in the shape of a tent. It is seldom used for latitude measurements, as it can only be seen on really dark nights.

I saw *Suha'il*, which João calls Canopus, the brightest star in the southern heavens, my favorite for determining latitude. I disdained using the Pole Star altitudes, except when training other navigators. In my *Fawa 'id* I refer to seventy simple methods for *qiyas* measurements, though I can boast that I know a hundred.

I disdained using the *kamal*, a two inch by one inch parallelogram of wood with a nineknot string inserted in its center. The string is held between the teeth with the *kamal* at such a distance from the eye that while the lower edge touches the horizon the upper edge just touches the star. The particular knot determines the latitude. I knew the *tirfa* distance traveled by my ship by using my pointing finger to determine the angle subtended by it against the horizon. I needed no instrument but the four fingers of my outstretched hand. I know I am boasting about my pilot skills. I proved it to the gentle Paulo da Gama. Perhaps he is in paradise now with Usha.

Fifteen long years ago, at the height of my piloting powers, I could sail my ship anywhere, in almost any season. The stars never failed me as guides. I remember now how Vasco da Gama and the Portuguese pilots would shoot the sun to take their bearings. And I realize that the finger measurements I used are no longer adequate. João tells me that degrees are used to determine exact measurements. Set down and printed, they can be transmitted to future navigators, not just to apprentice pilots. I still make use of my intuition and my senses and can not pass these along. I do not even have a son of my own.

Abdul was plaiting the leaves of a coconut frond by a simple oil light that had begun to splutter as I reached the porch. I was tired but not sleepy. My heart mind, is there such an organ, was exploding with thoughts, sensations, insights. Abdul sensed my state as I sat down on the top step of the porch. He knew I didn't want to talk.

I brought back the jar from the cave, Abdul said, the stool and the table too. I've roped down the roof. My friends helped me. But I do not have enough leaves plaited for the front or the back door.

Why don't you go to sleep, I said. There will be time tomorrow to do these things. I didn't thank him. It wasn't necessary.

Do keep a light, I told Abdul, I feel driven to write.

SIX

May 14, 1509
My house, Diu, NIGHT
I cannot fall asleep
I continue writing through the night

I was late for João's Portuguese class.

I had gone to the blackrock promontory convinced, more than ever, that the tufan would burst upon Diu and the upper west coast. I told Abdul about the eye of the storm. He would alert people near us. There would be a deceptive lull. The storm winds would die down for two hours, but then their fury would rekindle. He would then go on to João's house.

João pounced, greeting me as soon as I entered the classroom. He shut the folder that contained the water stained and burnt sheets of the Holy Bible. It had been salvaged from a Portuguese caravel washed ashore after the Diu battle. Abdul had spent more than a week helping João patch up the sheets.

Ah, come in Senhor Ahmad, come in, João said in Portuguese. You are late. You had to go to the promontory to check the approach of the tufan. We have been waiting for you. Senhor Vora will continue his recitation of the sacred poem he had to memorize for today. Vora scratched his left earlobe with his right hand, and smiled.

Vora from Surat is the worst of the students in our class. His pronunciation is worse than mine. He finds it impossible to produce gutturals and nasals. João would imitate Vora's pronunciation and the whole class would roar with laughter. I do it not to mock him, João told me, but to make Vora's ear realize how bad it sounds. Vora smiled, and automatically scratched his left earlobe with his right hand. I could see that he deeply resented João's mockery. Vora never forgets, Sidi Ali told me, he puts on a smile and accepts insults meekly, but is deeply vindictive. I would have warned João, but one day he suddenly stopped imitating

Vora after discovering that Vora's tuition was paid by Malik Gopi who was his maternal uncle.

I sat next to my friend whom the Portuguese nicknamed *o torto*, the cockeyed one, because he had a squint. He had acted as Malik Aiyaz's special envoy and had negotiated the terms of peace aboard Viceroy de Almeida's ship, the *Flor de la Mar*, after the Diu disaster. With his flowing gown of gold and silk brocade, his black sash of taffeta, his aristocratic gestures, Sidi Ali *o torto* impressed Dom Francisco de Almeida and the Portuguese captains.

His spoken Portuguese is much better than mine. After all he is a Muslim from Granada from where he had escaped in 1492, with some Jews who had been banished from Spain. The timbre of his speech is not colored by Gujarati or Arabic usage as ours is. He speaks with measured precision. He has no trouble with Portuguese nasals, and uses the right pronouns of address, the third person forms, not the second person forms we others almost invariably use.

Vora's recitation of the sacred poem in Portuguese sputtered to an end.

Very good, Senhor Vora. said João, very good, making his voice sound exactly like Vora's. The class roared with laughter.

Stop laughing, João said. Senhor Vora, you will repeat this exercise when our class meets for written Portuguese. Vora smiled, and scratched his left ear with his right hand.

Now, João continued, turning to Sidi Ali and me, we will have a change of procedure. I will not read from the *Biblia Sagrada* today. Instead, the class will ask questions. All of you know about the storm that Senhor Ahmad predicts will hit Diu.

A hum of excitement.

We want him to tell us about this storm. You will all ask questions in Portuguese, which Senhor Ahmad will answer in Portuguese.

When, when will the tufan start, burst out, in Gujarati, from the mouth of Raval of Varodra, whose family owned three trading ships.

Hold, said João.

Senhor Raval, haven't I drilled into you, time and time again, that no other language but Portuguese will be used in my class.

João was a very strict teacher. He insisted on our using only Portuguese in class. All our other languages, Gujarati, Persian, Arabic, were forbidden. I used to argue with him about this technique.

It's my method, João would say. The only way to learn how to swim is to dive into the water. Telling you about the technique of swimming wouldn't be of any help, would it. That's why I fling you into Portuguese. The intellect doesn't teach you how to absorb a new language.

João's method of teaching us Portuguese is, in a way, an adaptation of the memorization techniques used in our village schools to drive in the sacred writings, Muslim and Hindu, without understanding the meaning of the words. João does not accept what I firmly believe. That knowledge creeps into consciousness later, after memorization.

A great deal of it is mechanical. It doesn't last, João said. It is like teaching a parrot, he said, or a myna.

The word myna disturbed me greatly. João had never met Usha and I had not told him the story of our pet myna in Lamu, the one Usha had taught a few words to. The bird had become a part of Usha. Did they kill the little bird too in Anegundi.

Consider, João said, the problem of teaching a Hindu child the Qur 'an or of making a Muslim child learn the *Bhagavad Gita*. Is it just a language problem or does it involve religious beliefs. Are language and religion deeply interconnected. My problem is how to get all you students of Portuguese whose tongues.

João deliberately paused .

Whose tongues, he repeated, have been conditioned by other skies, by different beliefs and mouth makeups. Look at Arab jaws, at Gujarati throats, and at the spread of Persian lips. At times, I force myself to listen to language sounds divorced of any meaning. Arabic sounds are guttural, heavier than Persian ones. The sounds of Gujarati are light and nasal. Its tone inflections are infinite. The sounds of Portuguese are heavily nasal.

João paused again.

The mouth, like the mind, is a wonderful instrument, Ahmadbhai. Can a mind brought up on the Qu 'ran really understand Hindu scriptures.

He paused.

A mouth that's accustomed all its life to producing Arabic tongue sounds will naturally find it almost impossible to produce the sounds of Portuguese. But it can. That's why the drills, and the repetitions, and the readings from the Holy Bible. Which many of you complain about.

João was indeed a strict teacher. He taught us to recognize the sounds of Portuguese, but did not insist on our parroting his accent.

If you do that, João said, you will sound unnatural.

João spoke perfect Arabic and Persian. He would go to bazaars in disguise, and easily carry on a conversation in Gujarati, passing himself off as a Surati at times, and at others as a person from Junagadh in the north, so perfect was his imitation of regional accents.

It doesn't come naturally, João explained to me. I work hard at it. I learn about three hundred words a week of a new language. A new sound

I repeat several times a day. Whenever I converse with anybody in a language I am learning, I repeat their words inaudibly after them, and so learn the trick of pronunciation and emphasis.

I wish I had João's ability with languages. He has made me quite conscious of language and its connections with culture and religion.

I was nervous about answering questions about the tufan in Portuguese. The others were nervous, too, and took a long time to formulate their questions, whispering to each other.

Sidi Ali had no such difficulty, and when João looked at him, asked the first question.

Senhor Ahmad, what is a tufan.

I found it difficult to explain the word, whose meaning we all knew, in Portuguese. It is an Arabic word, João had told me, which will enter the language.

Senhor *o torto*, I said.

There was smothered laughter.

But I was quite serious and deliberate, and I spoke clearly and exactly.

A tufan, I do not know the Portuguese equivalent for this word. A tufan is a sudden storm whose snake coil winds whirl around with great fury, and cause great destruction of ships at sea and of houses on land.

When will the tufan begin, senhor Ahmad.

One hour after the evening bell sounds, senhor.

Has senhor Ahmad himself witnessed a tufan, asked one of the students from Cambay.

Yes, senhor. I predicted and then witnessed a tufan strike Kollam in South India some years ago. A coastal village, three miles south of Kollam, was completely destroyed.

I was beginning to feel more sure of myself as the second Ahmedabadi asked his question.

Have you, senhor Ahmadbhai, sorry, senhor Ahmad, experienced a tufan at sea.

Yes, I said. Yes senhor. My ship was once caught in a tufan off Socotra. I immediately reduced sail, and hove to on the garlicky tack under bare poles, till the ship could run free.

What should we do, asked Surati Vora.

Senhor Vora, I said, roofs of houses should be tied down. Ships and boats should be hauled up on to the shore. All house openings should be completely shut and protected. I wish, Senhor Vora, that you could send warnings to Dumas. The tufão will be quite severe over there. Ships from the Red Sea sailing towards Cambaya so late in the season could be shipwrecked at the entrance of the Tapi river.

I wasn't even aware I was speaking Portuguese.

I want to hurry home, and warn my wife, said the one who came from Champaner. We have a house about a mile inland. Will we be affected, senhor Ahmad.

Yes, senhor, I said.

He got up quickly, and made for the door.

I knew all of them wanted to leave soon, but I had to make an announcement. And it had to be made in Portuguese.

The eye of the storm, senhores, I said, beware of it.

They rose to their feet.

For two hours, after the storm strikes, there'll be a deceptive calm, I said. Beware. The storm will agitate itself immediately afterwards with even greater force.

It sounded pedantic, the words were heavy on my tongue.

The students crowded out of the room.

João congratulated me.

For the first time, João said. That was the first time you forgot your self, and let your self go in Portuguese.

By the time João and I got to the street the news had spread all over the city. Small knots of people gathered together, whispering furiously.

Cries of tufan filled the air.

It's just a rumor, said some.

It hasn't been announced, others said.

Malik Aiyaz has proclaimed that all public offices would be closed to prepare for the tufan, said another.

A few stared at João and me as we walked down the street. Along some of the sidestreets the shops were closing down.

João wanted to go to the jewelers' market, to buy a ring for his wife.

The goldsmiths and the silversmiths and the jewelery merchants will be the first to close down, I said.

Just before we reached the Avenue of Diamonds, as it was called, a messenger from Malik Aiyaz caught up with us.

Ahmad Sahib, he bowed down to me. Ahmad Sahib, he said, trying to catch his breath. Malik Aiyaz asks whether you will honor his abode with your presence.

I will go there immediately, I said.

Let's go, I said to João.

João wanted to go home. My wife will need my help, he said.

Abdul will go and help them. You know you'll only get in the way, I said.

It was true. João was as helpless as a baby when it came to doing things around the house. He can't even cook rice.

Malik Aiyaz was not in his administrative offices, nor was he at his official residence. He directed operations from a heavily protected pavilion that he had had built on the eastward slope of a hillock garden just outside his palace.

The guards directed us to the footpath.

Tiny rivulets of water trickled down the hillside. The Malik had a Persian gardener skilled in the layouts of gardens. There were roses and champaks, and clumps of jasmine growing on the slopes, even though it was the hot month of May.

The Muslims, said João, unlike the Hindus, know how to enjoy life. They have learned how to escape the heat and dust of the Indian plains.

I almost agreed with him. Then I thought of *baolis*, the underground stepwells that the Hindus and Jains had built especially in Gujarat, as a refuge from the searing heat. Cool they are, and comforting. Usha and I had held hands for the first time in a step well near Śatruñjaya, the only way then we could silently declare our togetherness.

I could not bring myself to mention step wells, even to João. They would stir up memories in me.

I plucked a tiny melon, the size of my palm, wiped off a touch of mud, cracked it in two with the edge of my palm, and shared it with João. We crunched it, skin and all, and then wiped off the dripping juices from our mouths. The circular climb to the pavilion didn't take too long.

How did you like my Persian melon, asked Malik Aiyaz. His lookout system was very efficient.

Sweet, and slightly tart, I said, and very delicious, just right for this May heat.

We exchanged embraces. Malik Aiyaz got down to business immediately.

I ordered all the government offices to be shut, Malik Aiyaz said. The kotwal sent me a message, and Rustum took just an hour to get here from Una. The port signals have been hoisted.

He took us to the center of the pavilion, where there was a detailed map of Diu engraved on an elevated angled slab of pure Sirohi steel. The revenue divisions were marked in different colors. It was a testimony to Malik Aiyaz's administrative skills.

I've sent messages to Vanakbara by the fastest of two bullock carriages, Malik Aiyaz said. The *kotwal* there will get it within the hour. Nagwa, Fudam, and Bhucharwada must have already got their warnings, including those about the eye of the storm. I also sent a message to Dungarwadi, to warn all the cultivators on that hill.

Dungarwadi was the highest point in Diu.

We sat down on the bench in front of the map of Diu.

What else can I do, Ahmadbhai, asked Malik Aiyaz. Your suggestion that more announcements be made about shipping on the Bahr-i-Hind is a good one.

You've done everything you could, I said.

What about your guns, asked João.

Thank you, Mirza Sahib, said Malik Aiyaz. Our gunners said that the new cannons from Suez would be very powerful and would need to be protected from the salt winds.

I hadn't mentioned it to Malik Aiyaz, but I think he knew. He knew that the Ottoman gunners had grown careless. The siege guns used for the defence of Diu were obsolete. He realized the guns were too huge and could not be placed on board the *kotias*. The Portuguese ships bristled all around with cannons. They were new, made of bronze and spoke the language of power. Malik Aiyaz had told me about the *manjaniks* of Champaner that spoke the old language of hurled stones during sieges.

I had suggested that Malik Aiyaz send a delegation to the Mamluks to buy more powerful guns.

They cant spare any, Malik Aiyaz told me. Sultan Begada far away in Champaner, does not realize the importance of cannon. Impossible, his advisers tell him, the Portuguese will not be able to drag their siege guns all the way to Champaner. The shipowners, here in Diu, do not want any change. New ships would have to be built in the Portuguese manner and fitted with guns. Gunners would have to be trained. Where would they begin. They were reluctant to invest in new ships to fight these seafaring vagabonds.

Malik Gopi had made a beginning by building a few ships with wide Portuguese sterns. Ship guns he wasn't able to get, as yet, or gunners to use them.

We were tired, all three of us, and we stretched out our legs and stared at the blue green sea. There was nothing else we could do to protect our worlds.

I'm tired, said Malik Aiyaz. Your tufan, like the Portuguese, will create a great deal of confusion in my world. I wish I could fling my whole world aside, and settle down in peace forever at Una, near the tomb of my spiritual protector, but I know I can't.

I knew what he meant. Diu was his child. He had used his power to bring it into being and he knew he was responsible for its welfare and could not abandon it.

I thought about João's ramblings about power yesterday. About the different forms of power in this our *samsāra*. Power and men of power, strangely, have always intrigued me. Me, who have never exercised power.

A force within man, they say. Very difficult, they also say, for people in power to abandon power. The rupture must be sudden. The pandit has talked about the renunciation both of *artha*, and of *kama* to liberate oneself from the snake coils of *samsāra*. He never mentions the immense difficulty involved.

I don't know how difficult it is. Usha's uncle surprised everybody when, in Śatruñjaya, he renounced *samsāra* and disappeared into the night to go to Vijayanagar and seek liberation in a Jain temple at Anegundi. It happens in the Muslim world too. Sultan Begada's friend abandoned his duties one day as an administrator when he saw a streak of white in his hair. He retired into the garden he had built near Ahmadabad, never stirred out of it, and is buried there.

Malik Aiyaz will never give up his malikdom, nor will João and I become ascetics.

Sitting on the bench with our legs stretched out, looking at *samsāra*, it was pleasant to dream of things that could have been.

I knew Malik Aiyaz was disappointed in his eldest son Ishak.

João wants to go back to Coimbra some day.

You will never go home, I tell him.

Yes, he says sadly, I never had a home, not even a house of my own. Perhaps all human beings are doomed to be homeless, João murmured.

My own dreams, they were simple. A simple house, like the one I have, with Usha beside me, cooking for me, sharing a life together. But that will never be.

I want to arrest time that, like *samsāra*, never stops moving. Like the faraway waves of the sea before us, murmuring, telling me of my homelessness.

João stood up.

I have to get back to my wife, he told us.

Malik Aiyaz said he had to reassure his womenfolk.

I had no one, except Abdul, to get back to.

João and I walked past the guards, past the platform in the middle of the empty city center. A solitary policeman stood on guard. I picked up Abdul who was at João's, helping them cover their roofs with plaited palm leaves, and we walked to our house.

I had to borrow some money, Abdul said. From the shethji in charge of the Friday bazaar. The sheth told me he knew João sab. I told him it would be repaid as soon as possible.

Abdul is right. I don't care about money, but I dont want Abdul to be embarrassed. I must go back to the pension office to get some mahmudis for Abdul and myself. Even though I don't like Hooknose.

Abdul had made our house windproof. There was no way the wind and the rain could invade it. Our house is built entirely of angled stone, cut to fit together compactly. The roof is overlaid with darkred Mangalore tiles, over which Abdul has laid down a triple layers of plaited coconut leaves. Noway, I reckoned, could the tufan enter my house.

It may enter the house of your being, my cynic whispered to me.

I'll be back soon, I told Abdul.

I had to go to my blackrock promontory. I wanted to look at the distant blue of the sea stretching to the west, and bathe my eyes in the peaceful green of the coconut palms that sway along the coastline.

Usha and I both loved the coconut tree.

If I am reborn, Usha would say, I would like to be a coconut palm. It's a coastal tree deeply rooted in sand and earth, and yet it does need the salt sea breeze and human sounds to be itself.

Ahmad mine, Usha would say, have you noticed how its long curved trunk stretches yearningly towards the sea and yet recurves back toward the land. Like the seagull, it belongs to the earth, and yet yearns to cast itself in the restless sea.

I know the coconut trees will survive the tufan. They will ride out the storm, bend dangerously with the winds, and almost never break. As I stood and watched and wondered, a rough seabreeze began, and the palm trees to my left rustled in the distance.

It was the beginning of the tufan.

It would gather full strength towards the hour of the evening bell. I was right about the tufan, even though I had mistimed it by a few hours. I was happy, and yet sad, sad about people who will not heed the warning about the eye of the storm. They will come out in the thick darkness to pick up fallen coconuts. They will not be prepared for the tufan's second onslaught.

I walked back to my house with great difficulty, buffeted by gusts of wind that blew so furiously I had to hold on to the trunks of trees and stumble along. It was only five in the evening, but the sky was coal dark with clouds. Not the elephant clouds of the monsoon, but jagged dark streamers that swept across the sky. Abdul had to hold on fast to the front door after he opened it to let me in. It was as if the storm wanted to invade our house. Abdul wanted to plug all the cracks through which the wind came whistling in.

Let it be, I said, as he tried to plug in a tiny hole in the west wall. It will tell me something.

I know, Abdul said, it will tell your ear about the movements of the tufan. And I remember what you once said about repairing sails.

Abdul doesn't forget. Like me, he keeps things deep within himself, and utters them only when he feels he needs to. We have been together so long that I sometimes think he knows what I am thinking.

He relit the oillamp that had blown out when I came in. The little jar of papers together with the writing materials were on the little teak table in the center of the room. The carpet had been rolled away, and a *satranji* set down under the table. My stool was placed just right. Abdul knew I wanted to write. He went into the kitchen.

I did want to write, but I felt disturbed, as if a coiling pressure that had begun within me would burst out of my insides. I thought I was going to fall ill, and I put my hand to my throat, and then felt my pulse. No fever, and my pulse was normal. Perhaps a drink would calm me. Abdul did not say anything but poured the drink in the smallest of cups, and then took back João's flask with him into the kitchen. I sipped the drink, set it down on the teak table, and walked to the jar that contained navigational manuscripts.

I picked up my father's treatise, and began to read his *al-Hijaziya* on the navigation of the Red Sea, but I could not read more than a couple of verses. It was very simple. One should only sail during the daylight hours never during the night, it said. The south flowing current towards *Bab el Mandab*, the Gate of Tears, it stated, is more powerful than the northflowing one, towards Suez.

I felt sad. Things change. The treatise had been written so long ago, before I was born perhaps. I was fourteen when my father died, but I cannot now remember his face, except for his deepset eyes, which could blaze with anger, and also be liquid black with tenderness. Where is he now. Will we meet again. He wrote a book, and produced a son. Is that why he was brought into existence. Is that why I was born. To write the navigational works I've written. To be one with Usha.

I replaced my father's navigational poem in the jar.

I walked around to the jar of Usha poems, took out the sheaf of papers, and looked at them. I didn't want to read them just yet. I know almost all of them by heart.

As I was about to place them back in the jar I caught sight of a scrap of paper stuck at the bottom. There were saltwater stains on it, and even though I unfolded it carefully, it broke into two pieces. I took them to the table next to the oillamp. The handwriting had faded. The salt had corroded the paper, and eaten up the words.

Except for one word. Consecrate.

My heart began to beat faster.

And then I knew.

Time was abolished. The pressure within me eased as memories released began to flow.

We were resting in each other's arms on the poop deck of the *Zephyr*. It was night. The sky was bright with stars. There was no moon. I had trimmed and angled the main sail, so that it caught the following wind that blew easy and free. The *Zephyr* sailed happily on towards Lamu, gently guided by Abdul at the tiller. Layla, Abdul's sister, was asleep in the cabin just under the poopdeck. She had at last persuaded Usha to eat some rice and vegetables, and I had coaxed Usha out of the dark, hot cabin. She had been seasick, but now, four nights out of Diu, we were at peace in each other's arms, stretched out against pillows on a green carpet.

We were silent, shy, savoring the first magic moments of being alone together. We had always talked guardedly, and secretly, always in the presence of others. Now intensely together, accompanied by the soft sounds of the waves, the sails flapping gently in the wind, we did not want to profane the silence of the night.

Usha breathed softly to me, By the wave of the sea.

By the light of the stars, I whispered.

And in unison we both said, By the beating of our hearts, let us consecrate our love.

We had created a poem.

> By the wave of the sea
> By the light of the stars
> By the beating of our hearts
> Let us consecrate our love.

Ours was a true marriage, witnessed by the waves, the winds, the stars above, and the beating of our hearts. Usha and I had abandoned family and relatives, friends and religions, and we belonged to each other, forever.

She must have jotted down our poem on this piece of paper, which managed to survive among my collection of poems. I placed the two pieces carefully within the jar, and sat down on the stool to write our past.

SEVEN

Late May, 1509
My house, Diu, Night
I write about how we left Diu in 1497
About how Usha and I sailed in the Zephyr
across the Bahr-i-Hind to Lamu

I know why I'm writing this.

I want to re-live the brief moments Usha and I were together. For I now, now, the tufan coiling within me, sense the past ebbing away from me, though memories can still flow back. It is as if our togetherness is slowly receding into the past, and evil rumor will stain our true story.

How does one make the past live again. Do memories flow as in a stream and always disappear.

Memory and love, the pandit once announced during one of our discussions on *rasa*, have always been *sandhī*ized. Bound together, he explained. *Smara*, the Sanskrit word for memory, is an epithet for the god of love. To remember is to transcend both space and time by stirring up the past, buried deep within one's being, in order to fuse it with the present. The Kashmiri philosopher, his name was

The pandit paused.

João frowned as the pandit then removed his turban, peered into its inner folds, scratched his head with his right hand, replaced his turban, and then slowly continued.

His name was Abhinavagupta, said the pandit, uses the opening scene of Act Five of the *Śākhuntala* to illustrate the primary role of memory in the experience of *rasa*.

The pandit then cleared his throat two or three times, and, as an illustration, began croaking out the song sung for King Dushyanta, when João clapped his hands to his ears and shouted,

Stop, my dear pandit, please stop. You cannot sing. You have no ear at all for music.

João, my impatient friend, yours is a limited ear. You are not capable of understanding our music, said the pandit.

And the discussion veered off into the differences between two kinds of music.

I never did get to know Kalidasa's views on memory. João told me, later, what a western thinker had said.

At certain moments I have been sorely tempted to confess to João what had happened in the past.

I remember, I would begin hesitantly.

The act of remembering, according to Plato, João would say, and then pause.

Who is Plato, I would deliberately interrupt him, and the momentary temptation to confess would pass.

Never mind who Plato is, João would state. The act of remembering is a form of love.

I do not know.

The venerable hakim, from whom I learnt not only medicine, but also the need for treating the whole man, told me, after he noticed my sad face and my fits of brooding in the first year when I was his apprentice in 1505, that I would forget only after I had excavated fragments of my buried past.

To merely remember the past, my hakim had continued, will prolong the silence which makes you look up at the sky and ask why, oh why. Your suffering springs out of a region where spoken words fail. Use the written voice. Writing is a form of action that takes place in the present. Only after you feel driven to write your past, my hakim said cryptically, will your past flow into your present so that the past will not be present to you.

Can my hakim, and my Plato João, and the Sanskrit writers, all three be right.

I do not know.

I feel compelled to write. I was sure the tufan would never enter my house. I was wrong. It has invaded my being just as my cynic said it would. It wants to burst out of me in words.

Usha, the world we lived in has changed. Its landscape is no longer the same. The Diu I live in now is no longer the Diu we both knew. A grey go-down has been built, they say, where your tiny lovely garden house used to be. I have not gone to see it.

A fortnight ago they announced in Diu center that inaugural ceremonies would be held for a new Jain temple built by your relative, Jhaveri, at Śatruñjaya, the mountain temple city you were unable to climb because your arm was hurt. I don't think that city of temples, that you and your father went to on a pilgrimage and took me along, perched high on Śatruñjaya hill, will ever change. Lamu, our bead pearl, has not changed, they say. I hope it never will. The Portuguese have bombarded Kilwa and Mombasa, and destroyed some of the landmarks I knew.

But Lamu, Lamu has been spared. Perhaps, dare I think so, to commemorate our oneness.

We lived our oneness the few days we spent in Lamu. I thought we would pour out our feelings for each other into words, and talk our togetherness, because we had never really talked to each other before that. We had only touched hands in a dark stepwell. I think of a time before language, when one needed only touch and eyetalk to communicate.

Lying in the twilight on the warm sands of Lamu beach we had no need for words. We would live in each other's arms, and watch the deep darkred sunset.

At times I'd ease away, fold my hands under my head, look up at the evening stars and think of the future.

And you'd say, don't worry, Ahmad mine, we're together now. We have all that we need.

And you would lean over me and kiss me lightly on the mouth, and then brush your lips over my forehead.

Ahmad, my dear, I want to wipe your worries away. And any bad luck that the goddess of destiny may have written on your brow.

I would smile.

You'll have to kiss my forehead over and over and over and over again, I said.

You'd be quiet and settle into the crook of my arm, and we'd look at the bluedark sky diamonded with stars.

I do not believe in fate. But I wonder about the rosary of events that took us to Lamu in 1498, and then tore us away. Why do I say rosary. The word is Christian, but the *rudraka* prayerbeads of some Hindus and Muslims can be called rosaries too.

I want to tell my own memorybeads.

Do you remember Usha, our days of utter peace as we sailed in the *Zephyr*, flew really, along the Bahr-i-Hind, till we dropped anchor at Lamu towards the end of March 1498. I go by the Christian reckoning of time, not the Muslim.

There are no instruments to measure time in heaven, provided there is such a place, João the cynic tells me.

In time. Out of time. I prefer space to time.

The *Zephyr* was more than a ship, it was our haven. How could I have known then in 1497 that I was building a home for us both.

The evening of our return from the family pilgrimage to Śatruñjaya, your father walked me to the gate in his usual courteous fashion. Did he want a respite from the crowd of relatives that had suddenly come to your house. All evening I heard whisperings and shrieks and giggles from the female quarters at the back.

And he said, in that gentle voice of his, when I thanked him for taking me on the pilgrimage,

I would like you to build a little ship as soon as possible for Usha and me to travel down the west coast, to see some of the temples and step wells she loves. I want to surprise her. You won't tell anyone, will you, especially Usha. It will be part of her dowry, he added.

I'm glad it was dark. For I would not have been able to look into his eyes. It hurt keenly, the word dowry, and all it implied, even though I thought I was prepared for what was inevitable, her marriage.

I waited for a day, though I didn't have to rest from our long journey to Śatruñjaya and back. And then, instead of paying the usual daily visit to your house, set about planning the construction of the little dhow. It would be my gift to you, an expression of the rising storm within me, that I could not release in language.

You loved art, and my ship would be a work of art that would speak to you of my love.

It was a thing of beauty, whose every curve flowed into a harmonious whole. On it I lavished my nakhoda knowledge. I went with the basic builder who, by custom, has to lay down the ship's foundations. We went to the Diu timberyards to choose the log of wood for the keel. Which always determines the ship's dimensions and construction.

It had to be of *aini* wood found only in the forests of the Western Ghats, a yellowish brown hard even grained wood that seasons well, and gets heavier and hardier under water. We found a superb baulk, smooth and unknotted, 27 feet long for a 25 foot keel. The ship's length would be 32 feet, the teak mast 28 feet high, and the three pieces of wood for the yard, each 11 feet, that could be fished and lashed together, and either stretched to 28 feet or else shortened to 24 feet.

For the long planks and strakes I did not want fresh teak which, strangely, sinks easily, but durable seasoned teak, which resists the boring shipworm, and the corrosive action of salt water, because the resinous fluids and oils gradually fill up the pores of the wood. For the yard and the various spars and blocks I insisted on Beypoori *poon*, a highly resilient wood that gives, at times of intense stress and wind pressure, when teak would crack.

I insisted also on light brown sweet tasting coir from the Laccadives. Seasoned for six months in seawater, this is the best coir for the yards and the shrouds, and for the caulking work. I walked for four hours along the roughest stretch of the Diu coastline, carefully marking the rounded boulders I needed for ballast. And I then went to the bazaar to choose the strongest smelling incense sticks which I placed on a stand in the *dabusa*. They would counteract the overpowering bilge smells.

I threw myself into a frenzy of work, wanting to blot out things I did not want to think about.

I took over, as a nakhoda should not, the construction of the ship even before the hull was finished. I supervised the stitching of each teak plank to its sister plank. No nails were used. Tails of stingray fish smoothened the holes after they were drilled. I painted a thick coating of tree gum on the lower hull that would be under water. And I lavished care on the caulking, so that the ship was watertight.

Abdul and I treated the hull beneath the waterline with oil to make it shipworm proof. We polished the upper hull till the teak shone a rich reddish brown. Before the sails were cut I had the light but close.woven Surati canvas dipped in hot incense.treated shark.oil and dried for three days in the midday sun. I had two main sails made. The spare one was stowed away in its bag under the deck.

I even experimented with a little triangular sail, which I attached to a pole that projected from the prow. I got this idea from the ramming spur that juts out from the prows of the Mamluk galleys. This headsail was for coastal sailing, so that the ship could slip into and up the many rivers along the west coast, when the winds grew fierce and the swells were heavy.

It was an ocean going vessel too that could take me to any port of the world I lived in.

Did I have any intimations about the future, our future. I only know the ship was an expression of my love for you. Why do I have no more use for the romantic images of Persian poetry. Our ship was also a farewell to the world I knew I would have to abandon.

It was this world I tried to spread out before your eyes as we lay stretched out, on the green carpet under the plaited palm leaf awning that protected us from the hot afternoon sun, the filtered sunlight woven into your soft black hair.

Most afternoons Abdul and I didn't have to wear the *Zephyr* around. For I could smell the changing winds as they blew down from the north.

When the wind shifted direction you would take the tiller. Layla had steered as best she could, rather uncertainly, for the five days when you were seasick. Abdul and I would shift the tackles, adjust the yard, maneuver and angle the mainsail to take full advantage of the fluctuating winds. You needed only a couple of hours of sailing to get the feel of the tiller and steady it. On the Bahr-i-Hind the winds in March are irregular and fitful. Most of the nakhodas prefer the regular seasonal winds, they would make use of the powerful *Rih al Kaws*, now called the southwest monsoon, for the voyage eastwards towards India. For the westward sailing they would use the gentler northeast monsoon.

I am still quite proud of the fact that I can sail anywhere in all kinds of weather. Except from the west coast of India during *al-ghalq*. Late June and all of July and a part of August constitutes the closed season when the monsoon churned waves beat so fiercely that it is impossible to venture outside the harbor.

I set the *Zephyr* on a course that curved ever so gently in an arc towards Mogadishu, helped by the currents that swing down toward the equator at this time of year.

There it was, my world, crowded with ships of all kinds. I did not need to describe in detail to Usha the ships that crisscrossed my world. Many a time as a child Usha would accompany her father who would set her on his shoulders so as not to dirty her feet in the brackish sand and the black slime of the waterfront, and watch his ships as they swung around the tip of Diu, and eased up past the sankalkot to the sounds of singing and of frenzied drumming, before anchoring at Diu bandar.

Sheth Chimanlal's ships were *kotias* made of Bulsar teak, all six of them of the same size and tonnage. Even at eight Usha could tell the name of each *kotia*. The ships of the Indian Ocean never had their names painted on them, unlike the ships of the Portuguese who, after the year 1500, insisted on identifying names for all ships before they would issue *cartazes*, but were known by the name of their owner, or by a holy name, like the *Triumph of Compassion*, or else by the name of the nakhoda, especially if he was well known.

That's uncle Ahmadji's *kotia*, Usha would say. That's the *Queen of the Night*, a name she had chosen herself.

No, her father would say, its mast is too tall. It's the *Flame of the Forest*.

Both ship were expected to arrive from Aden at the same time. Usha was right.

She recognized your ship, Ahmadbhai, when it was a mere speck in the distance, the father told me.

How did you know, Usha, her father would ask.

I don't really know how, father, Usha would say, turning her big black eyes toward me with a smile. I just know.

It was then, I remember, when I looked into her black liquid eyes, that I knew the present I would bring next time. It wouldn't be a jet black myna bird carved out of ebony that I had got for her this time, or the Persian halwas that I got especially for her from the time she was six. She preferred the ones that were not over sweet.

The next year, when she was nine, I gave her an exquisite ivory dhow. It was the first of the ships she began collecting.

My friend, Mian Mazlum, had carved it lovingly for me with his own hands. He was the best worker in ivory all along the East Coast of Africa, a master craftsman so famous for the finish and delicacy of his work that his workshop drew apprentices from Sofala, Kilwa, Mogadishu and Mombasa. The amirs and nobles of Malindi crowded his shop on the Lamu waterfront to place orders for coffers, all inlaid with ivory, for caskets to store jewels, cosmetic cases, bangles, ankle bracelets, all of pure ivory for their wives, and for ivory knobs to head canes and ivory scabbards to sheathe their daggers.

Mian Mazlum specialized in ivory miniature work. One year he had a travel chess set on display. It was a square box that could be carried in the palm of the hand. The square opened up into a fingernail thin board of ivory and ebony squares, beneath which were the chess pieces that stood thumbnail high when in play. Half of them were bluish white. The other half were tinged with a bluish green.

I wanted to present it to my friend, Sheth Chimanlal, but I didn't have the miticals to buy it.

Mian Mazlum saw the longing in my eyes.

Ahmadbhai, he said quietly, It has taken my workers and me two years to finish it to my satisfaction. It is destined for my patron, the Shirazi sheikh of Malindi, who protected me when I had arrived from India, and helped me set up shop in Lamu.

It was out of gratitude for his protector and friend that Mian Mazlum, every two or three years, fashioned the royal *siwas*, those manhigh trumpets of bronze and hollow ivory tusks curved like the new moon, used on ceremonial state occasions.

The entrance to Mian Mazlum's workshop and home was next to a neatly stacked pile of wood *borities*, red because of their heavy gums, near his neighbor's house. I found him looking at the work of one of his students who had just finished a royal *siwa*. Mian Mazlum welcomed me with an affectionate embrace, and bade me sit on the carpet.

What d'you think, Ahmadbhai, he asked.

The *siwa* curved in a delicate arc. The seamless bronze shone with a warm radiance. The ivory had been polished just right, so that its grain stood out distinct begging to be touched as it lay on the green carpet.

It is beautiful, I said.

Ah yes, said Mian Mazlum. He picked it up with both his hands. It balances well, but will it sound well.

I haven't tested it yet, said the apprentice, who had a cheerful face. His eyes smiled affectionately at his teacher.

Why don't you test it out, Kochama, asked Mian Mazlum. Today.

The *siwa* could not be sounded in the town even for testing. For its sounds were sacred, not to be heard except on ceremonial occasions. A narrow headland jutting out into the sea, two miles north of Shela, had been set aside for the royal trumpeter to practice on the *siwa*.

Kochama of the Kamba tribe is the best maker of *siwas* in my workshop. Next year his *siwas* will be as good as mine, said Mian Mazlum matter of factly.

The Kambas were famous for their honesty, their friendliness, their love of acrobatic dancing, the rhythmic drumbeats of their music, their pretty women who wore colorful beads, and, strangely, for their deadly archery. They smeared their arrowheads with a poison paste made by boiling a number of shrubs found only in the beautiful Machakos area where they live. The heart stops beating even before the harpoon shaped arrowhead is removed. Only the headman of the tribe has the secret ointment that acts as an antidote.

Two slaves came in with a heavy bundle, and I signaled to them to set it down on the carpet. Abdul had wrapped it carefully in gunnysacking.

What's this, what's this, Ahmadbhai, asked Mian Mazlum.

A gift, I said. A small gift for you.

Can I open it. Mian Mazlum was excited. Can I open it, now, can I.

He carefully cut through the layers of the gunnysack to expose a log of wood as long as the body of a four year old. It was covered with thick dust, and looked ordinary.

Ah, said Mian Mazlum. Ah, he repeated.

The surface of the log was mottled, slightly streaked with white, but the center was a deep black.

Don't tell me, Ahmadbhai. I know exactly where it comes from, Mian Mazlum said. It comes from the forests of South Kanara. It is the heart-wood of the ebony tree. I shall cut away the outer mottled layer, and make strips and planks of the inner wood.

He knelt down and touched the center of the log with his fingertips, as if it were a plate of celadon.

My friend, Kotta Marrakar of Kannanur, got it for me.

Look how heavy and even grained it is. It will stand a high polish. Yes, Mian Mazlum said, that's what I'll do. Last year I promised my wife a coffer of ebony inlaid with ivory for her clothes. Let me go in and tell her about this. You've never met my wife, have you, Ahmadbhai.

He parted the curtain and went into the inner rooms.

It was a strange question my friend had asked. In our world women do not meet men. Wives do not usually talk with their husbands' friends. I have often had my meals at Mian Mazlum's, but servants always served the food, never his wife. I've heard tell that his wife is very pretty, but I've never met her. There's some mystery about her. I've never asked my friend about it.

Mian Mazlum comes originally from Murshidabad in Bengal where, he told me, he learned the technique of ivory carving and polishing. It's strange, now I think about it. For all Indian workers in ivory are Hindu, never Muslim, according to the Hindu middlemen who would crowd Sheth Chimanlal's shop to bid for every load of ivory. Ivory is in great demand during the marriage season, and ivory bangles, I was told, had to form a part of every Hindu bride's dowry.

Mian Mazlum came back with two small cups of tar black coffee. The two slaves had gone back to the boat. Kochama had left to try out the sounds of the new *siwa*. The coffee, not too sweet, had been flavored with cardamon and ginger, with just a hint of clove and cinnamon. I sipped it slowly, allowing it to rest on my tongue.

This is the best coffee I've ever tasted, I said.

Ah, said Mian Mazlum, my wife prepared it with her own hands. There she is.

She had curved the edge of the curtain to frame her face, which was all one could see. The face was calm, the lower lip full, the eyes sad. Later, Mian Mazlum told me how they ran away from Bengal and that she missed her mother and that they had no children.

She asked her husband whether everything was all right.

Yes, Mian Mazlum said.

She smiled at both of us and withdrew into the inner chambers.

Now, said Mian Mazlum, Ahmadbhai, my friend, my family friend, what can I do for you.

Could you, I said, could you carve an ivory dhow, a little dhow, its keel could stretch from my elbow to the tip of my forefinger.

I would like it to be, the words came out in a rush, of pure white ivory, no wood to be used at all.

Ah, said Mian Mazlum, I know, you want it as a gift for your friend and patron, Sheth Chimanlal.

No, I said, I want it for his daughter, Usha. She is ten years old, I added hastily.

You don't want a mere toy, you want a work of art. I'll have to make a sketch before I start work on it, Mian Mazlum said.

Look at this, my friend, I said.

I placed a sketch before him. It was a sketch of a dhow with sleek lines, a white sail and a tall mast that I had seen anchored in Aden. I was sure Sheth Chimanlal would want such a dhow for his fleet of trading ships.

Mian Mazlum's eyes lingered over this sketch.

It was from this sketch that Mian Mazlum fashioned the exquisite ivory dhow that later I took back with me to Diu.

It's wonderful, Sheth Chimanlal said. Every detail is perfect.

It was. The green white ivory had a warm translucent tint, as if soaked in oil.   Aren't you going to thank Uncle Ahmad, Usha.

Usha didn't say a word. Was that the moment when she stopped calling me Uncle Ahmad.

She walked quietly away with her ship, and placed it on a shelf beside her favorite jasmine in the greenhouse. It was as though she had found a home for it.

Every year Mian Mazlum would fashion a tiny ship for me. I never paid him any miticals. Every year, Kotta Marakkar, my Kannanur friend, would send me a block of ebony. Mian Mazlum's wife, every time I visited Lamu, would serve us meals with her own hands. I was content and at peace. Life would drift on and on in this fashion. Life would never change. Every year I would give Usha a ship for her collection.

On the night I left my father and came away with you, Usha said, I went to the greenhouse and bade goodbye to my jasmine. The ships you gave me appeared black and white in the green darkness. I told them I would never see them again, and my jasmine rustled as if she understood.

Were you sad, Usha, I asked her, are you sad, at leaving Diu and your father, I asked.

She turned towards me, and placed two of her fingers on my lips.

Then she placed her small palm on my bare chest.

We have hurt him deeply, she said.

I could sense with her the beat of my heart. My eyes were shut. She knew what I felt. I had betrayed a friend and felt pierced with guilt.

It wasn't treachery but our need for oneness, she said softly.

Look, my Ahmad, she said, and her right hand curved across the night sky.

I thought I could see the stars move.

Usha drew up the coverlet over us both and, our hands folded under our heads, we listened for a while to the immense silence of the night.

The *Zephyr* moved easily on the flat sea with no pitch or roll, leaving just a little wake astern. A restful cooling breeze blew steadily from the east, and there were no sounds other than the occasional flap of the sail and the slow easy creaking of the mast and of the tiller.

Usha curled into the crook of my left arm and drifted into sleep.

We were two in one twice that night. I was afraid of bearing down on her and of hurting her. But she drew me down upon her in a fierce embrace, clasping the weight of my body as if wanting to absorb my whole being into hers. I shuddered with pleasure, and then eased away gently.

I want my mast again, she said, her hand searching for me, till I grew erect again.

I want my tiller, she said, guiding me into her. And we moved fiercely in unison, her eyes shut tight in rapture, her body arching upwards. And I had to put my hand gently across her mouth to muffle the fierce cry of abandonment when it came. She now lay asleep, and at peace.

I listened to the throbbing stars but they remained silent.

All day long the *Zephyr* had sailed steadily towards Mogadishu. There was very little sea traffic. For it was the wrong season to sail from India to Africa. It was the season when large numbers of flat bottomed boats would set out from Hormuz in Persia and from Dhofar on the Arabian coast to transport horses across the Bahr-i-Hind to the west coast of India. Their nakhodas wisely avoided sailing when the monsoon winds were strong and the sea was rough. They waited for what I called the horse season, the period of transition when the sea was usually calm. The winds would be erratic, so that the pilots had to quickly maneuver the sails to catch every fitful gust of wind that blew. The sea currents would be irregular so that the pilot would have to frequently adjust the tiller to make maximum use of the current flow. Horses are high strung animals and get seasick very easily. The sea swell is particularly heavy near the coast so that the boats have to turn around and sail upriver carefully, poop first, to coves where the land slopes down to the water.

Why do I describe this in such great detail. Because I am one of the few who appreciate the piloting skills of these horse nakhodas. I was eager to learn their piloting skills, but never could because I could never stand the strong smell of horse shit that sprang out of their clothes and clung to their very skin. Sitting on the banks of the Chapora river I would watch them let down the hinged door under the poop to disembark their horses. It was only when the wind direction shifted that I understood why the other pilots despised them. The stench was overpowering.

Abdul and I would check the wind direction and adjust the mainsail of the *Zephyr*, so as to veer off course when we saw the horse boats. Usha and Layla would not have been able to stand the overpowering stench that could make grown men faint. It was more difficult to avoid the few ships of trade heading towards Bhatkal and Kannanur. As a pilot I knew it was bad manners not to hail a sister ship, and ask the customary questions. Where have you come from. Where are you going. And to call down divine blessings. But I was worried lest Sheth Chimanlal somehow come to know which part of the world we were sailing to.

I was afraid for Usha. Usha loves her father. She trusts him completely. But does she, now, know what is churning within him

The father's love for his daughter must have turned into intense hate, directed towards both Usha and me. He had always been my protector and friend, gentle, courteous, generous with his money, a good man in his own way. But a marriage between a Jain girl of 15 and a 45 year old Muslim could never be accepted. The Jain community would never allow it. The honor of the Jain community, especially the sheth's kinsmen, the Jhaveris, would be so stained that marriages would be impossible to arrange for their sons and daughters. It would be a disaster.

I tried to understand my friend at the time, wondering about the different forces that drive us on. But I soon gave up. I have always found it difficult to understand human beings. It is easier to know the clean movement of ships, of winds, of currents, and of the different and the indifferent stars, so that one always has one's bearings and knows where one is. To understand other human beings one has to be involved with them. I have never tried to understand even myself.

I was married when I was seventeen but had to go almost immediately to sea. And when I came back the girl I had been married to, I couldn't really call her my wife, had died of smallpox. I have gone with prostitutes when my body found the urge unbearable, but I have never before got involved with any woman.

Now, with Usha breathing softly beside me, looking at the stars above, questions begin to vibrate within me. Why, my whole being clamors, but I refuse to consider that unanswerable question. Could we get married. Where could we stay. With Mian Mazlum and Ratna. How will Sheth Chimanlal react. I knew the first thing he would do. He would send out messages and agents everywhere on the Bahr-i-Hind to discover where we were. What would he do after that.

The stars, no longer disinterested, had no answer to that question.

The *Zephyr* sailed on peacefully towards Mogadishu, and we lost count of the days. Abdul would mention the things about the ship that he and I needed to take care of, and Layla would ask Usha about minor matters like food and the washing of clothes and the taking of baths. And they would at times sit in the shade, Layla drying and combing out Usha's long black hair.

Usha and I did not need to talk, especially in the nights. And I began to appreciate our Eastern wisdom of having the day begin after sunset, not after sunrise. The sun is not as sensitive a measurer of time as the moon is, so that when we saw the growing deepening crescent of the pale moon, I knew that we were moving into time again, and that the next day we'd be near Mogadishu.

The sea grew rough and the swells began to be heavy as we approached Mogadishu, not a port but a mere anchorage, a tiny curve in the Somal coastline with a breakwater as a shelter for ships. I had avoided the unbroken stretch of coast between Ras Hafun and Mogadishu with its white barren sunscorched sands.

Mogadishu was a landmark. The *Zephyr* would now keep in sight of land, and we would sail down the coast with Africa on the right. I did not want to hug the coastline because I wanted to avoid the big dhows that would, some of them, begin their voyage to Hormuz and Aden, before making the run to the west coast of India. But the *Zephyr* was a small light ship and the erratic winds of March could blow her far out to sea, so that it would be almost impossible to get back towards land again. Also, I wanted to take full advantage of the southern flow of the coastal current that sets in at this time of the year. March is a transitional month. The winds and the currents are both unpredictable. In March shipcontrol is very difficult.

Abdul and I had to lower the yard more than halfway down the mast as we rounded the coast off Mogadishu. The breeze sprang up and freshened. The mast creaked violently on its step, and jerked with the rolling. For two hours Abdul and I had to rush about to adjust the tackles, loosen the rigging, tighten some ropes, anxiously inspect the sails, and look helplessly when a seam of the mainsail came undone.

All for the good, said Abdul.

Layla was seasick in the *dabusa*, but Usha remained bravely at the tiller.

Lash me to it, she said, with a weak smile.
Then the wind died down, and the sea grew calm again.

We passed Merka and Barawa in the night, the ports of the Benadir, the Land of the Harbors, where a few trees can be seen along the coastline and the stunted savannah begins. Usha was still asleep in the *dabusa* when we went past Kisimayu, past Ras Kiamboni, past Kiunga, past a few elongated uninhabited islands that appeared to have been torn off the coast, past Kiwaiyu from whose islandtop I once saw the whole stretch of the Lamu archipelago.

Usha awoke in time to see Ndau, the smallest of the islands of the bluegreen archipelago. I was both happy and sad because Lamu was drawing near. The *Zephyr* sailed steady with the wind and the current, moving swiftly past the *mtepes* and the fishing boats and the double outrigger canoes that lazed near the coast. I did not need to ask Abdul to fling the chiplog into the sea to determine our speed. The yard had been mastheaded again. Lamu was an hour and a half away, and I knew I could time our arrival at Lamu harbor during the hour of twilight.

This night Usha and Layla and Abdul and I would sleep at Mian Mazlum's. He would be quite surprised.

Ah, Ahmadbhai, ah, he will say.

He is my friend, and will understand.

I told Usha about Ndau and the islands we would see, Pate and Manda and Lamu, their mangrovecovered sandbanks. I told her about the tall white sandhills of Lamu, the unique pillar tombs all along the coast, cool, limewashed, detached.

Usha as a little girl loved to listen to my stories. She would sit crosslegged with her chin on her proppedup right hand, and listen, eagereyed, to the stories I related to her father when I came back from my voyages, stories of the different places I had been to and the people I had seen.

I told her about the people of these four islands who were always called, strangely, no one knew why, the People of the Fire. Till a man from Siyu in the interior of Pate gave me this simple explanation. The name came from the common practice of burning the bush before the rains came in order to prepare the land for cultivation. It must have been a spectacular sight from the sea,

The *Zephyr* sailed smoothly along.

A few pale stars made their appearance in the cool evening sky. I sent Usha to the *dabusa* with Layla to pack her few belongings. Blackwraps, I suggested, would give them protection against the night wind that could arise at any time. Usha would understand the need for secrecy.

And then, just as we passed the southern tip of Pate, my nose knew. The hair on my wrists and forearms stood on end and I knew, even before the sail began to flap, that the wind would drop. The lightblue waters of Manda Bay were a distant disturbed yellow and red. It could have been the effect of the setting sun, but I smelt mud and silt, a drift of coral decay, and my nose whispered that the tide would turn, and the waters begin to swirl.

The *Zephyr* was fairly close to the shore, and three things conspired against her. The tidal drift from Manda Bay wanted to carry her out to sea. The southern flow of the coastal current ran into the northern making for a confusion of waters. And, strangely, the wind dropped. The *Zephyr*, confused, began to heel around. I swung the tiller hard to the right, but found it difficult to control her drift. Abdul bravely tried to maneuver the yard around, but the sagging sail dragged, and he did not have the strength to hold the yard in place singlehandedly.

Usha sensed at once that something was wrong, and rushed up and took the tiller.

She held on to it with all her might, while Abdul and I angled the mainsail so as to catch every gust of the erratic and fitful wind which would drop at times, then start blowing landwards, only to drop again, and after a while decide to blow towards the sea. It was hard work to swing the yard around.

Usha called Layla out of the *dabusa*, and set her to work controlling the foresail. She would shout directions to Layla in a clear voice. The foresail needed to catch every south blowing gust of wind. At times the tidal current and the wind would force the *Zephyr* away from the coast, and all of us would have to struggle to get her back towards land, so that we did not make any onward progress at all.

For an hour and a half we labored. Layla wanted to give up, and began to cry. But Usha would encourage her and somehow infuse enough strength into Layla, so that she did not let go of the foresail rope.

So involved were we in our zigzag sailing that we were almost run down by a large *boom*, beating its way up the coast with the help of the current and the southwind. The tidal current did not affect it at all.

Usha shouted a warning just in time. Abdul and I swung the sail sharply. And Layla, whom the sight of the oncoming ship had paralyzed, somehow clung to the foresail rope. And the *Zephyr* responded to the tiller, just managing to curve away from the *boom's* stem.

It was the *Sheikh Kitami* owned by Sheth Chimanlal sailing with a load of leopard skins and ivory to Suk in Socotra, where it would pick up a cargo of myrrh and frankincense before making use of the early monsoon for a fast run to Diu, and then go on to Melaka.

I knew its nakhoda. I knew he would recognize not our ship but my voice, so that when he shouted, Weh, do you need any help, shall I stop.

It was Abdul who replied,

No, may God's blessings go with you, Abdul said.

What kind of ship is that. Where do you come from. Which place are you going to, persisted the voice from on high.

The wind blew some syllables away.

-lindi, shouted Abdul, as we tried to make the *Zephyr* turn landwards.

But Layla, flustered, had let loose the foresail. Her black wrap blew away. And her long hair fluttered in the wind.

The *Zephyr* spun around.

Is one of your sailors a woman, asked the nakhoda disbelievingly.

Fortunately, the *Sheikh Kitami* sped on. A gust of wind filled in the *Zephyr*'s main sail, and we slipped along towards land, as night descended sudden and absolute. For twilight is brief in our eastern world.

We got to Lamu just past midnight. It was slow sailing because the coastal current was against us. But the wind blew soft and steady behind the *Zephyr*, not allowing the sail to take charge, but enough to make slow progress down the coast. The crescent moon provided sufficient light for me to steer by, for I knew every curve of that coast.

Usha and I stood with our arms around each other near the tiller, while the moon astern threw arabesque designs on the sail and on the deck. At the south end of the winding sea inlet, Shela offing, which the people of Lamu dignify by using the term *mto* meaning a special river, the tidal stream ran landward. And I could easily steer the *Zephyr* through the awkward turns of the Lamu river, with Abdul maneuvering the foresail. We sailed past the rock outcrops near Shela, left past Kishaka, the dangerous mangroveclump in the middle of the river, round its sandbank continuation. Till with yard lowered and mast bare, we anchored at the extreme right corner of Lamu harbor next to an Omani ship.

There were no people around. No lights were showing. I sent Abdul to Mian Mazlum's, who immediately took charge of everything without even uttering an ah.

Usha and Layla went to the women's quarters.

Abdul said he would sleep in the *Zephyr*.

I'll report the arrival of your ship tomorrow morning, whispered Mian Mazlum. The portmaster is my friend.

Ohe, Mian Mazlum, ohe, called his nextdoor neighbor, Yusuf. Is anything the matter.

No, no, said my friend, go to sleep.

Go to sleep, Ahmadbhai, Mian Mazlum said to me, we will talk tomorrow. Cover yourself, the night dew is heavy this month.

I lay in one corner of his sunken courtyard trying to calm myself, trying not to think, trying to listen only to the coconut palms overhead. Their low rustle kept being drowned by the clamorous insect noises of the African night.

EIGHT

*L*ate May 1509
My house, Diu, Night,
the tufan outside continues in the present,
my writing about the past continues too, about what happened
between the years 1505 and 1509, about the poems I wrote then,
the sketches I did of Usha and of the ships of the Bahr-i-Hind,
the arrival in Malindi of the Portuguese and their strange ships,
the rescue of the myna, Yasmin,
and about our togetherness

I must have fallen fast asleep after writing my account of our arrival in Lamu. When I opened my eyes it was dark. My left shoulder felt numb. I must have exposed it to the Lamu nightdew, I thought. But I was in my house in Diu, not in Mian Mazlum's sunken courtyard in Lamu. Abdul's hand was on my shoulder.

My head was resting on the writing table. The pen was still in my hand. The tufan had torn off the plaited fronds that covered a low opening in the kitchen wall, and the screaming wind brought in the rain. The cowdung washed floor was wet. Abdul had tried to patch up the hole without success. He wanted someone to hold the coir rope that he had fastened to the middle of a dried woven palm frond which he wanted to insert into the hole from the outside. It was pitch dark outside. Abdul would be drenched.

I got him to tie the cord to the middle of a split green frond, forced it through the small hole, pulled it tight when the leaves fanned out. Abdul stuffed in some coirhusks but the water kept trickling in. He could affix some more fronds on the outside later, when the winds calmed down for an hour or two.

Shall I remove the writing table, Abdul asked.

No, I said, I want to continue writing.

He filled the oillamp.
I want a drink, I said.
Of water, Abdul asked.
I shook my head.

He poured me a tiny drink from João's flask, and then took the flask to the kitchen. He wouldn't be able to sleep there, I realized, and I told him to spread his *satrangi* in the front room.

Go to sleep, I told him. It's not midnight yet.

His eyes were a little red.

I was not sleepy now.

I went to the Usha jar and touched it with both my hands. I felt the poems stream into me through my fingers. I remembered them all, all twenty four of them. Anchors they were, I thought, to preserve the past against the drift of time, hallowed spots I could always return to. I had written them between 1505 and 1509, during the years I had traveled with the venerable hakim, after the wounds of my body had healed, and he had told me how essential it was to write about, not just remember, the story of my past.

After the day's work had been done, and the last patient had left, the venerable hakim and I would have our evening meal. I would then go sit by the river or the local tank, where a poem would quicken within me, but not begin to assume form until I sat, at night, on my *satrangi*, with an oil lamp beside me.

The poem would begin as a word that would attract other words, and develop a rhythmic beat. It would take me a month to refine a poem, so that every word was just right. So that every syllable was liquid on my tongue. So that every pause sent forth echoes, and the poem rested complete on the page and in my memory.

It was painful, the process. Much easier to construct a ship. The words refused to come, at times. The line would stop, would refuse to proceed. I would be half asleep, vaguely aware of the venerable hakim removing the pen from my fingers, blowing out the oillamp, covering me with a sheet, and moving softly away.

And then, the very next day perhaps, the poem I thought would never be finished, would leap out of my pen on to the paper.

Should I set the poems down, now, in this my account. I went up to the jar again and, as I lifted out the sheaf of poems, I could hear the loud snores of Abdul warning me about something. Usually his snores were reassuring. Perhaps the tufan had entered Abdul too. The light on my table had not kept him awake. The paper sheets had yellowed slightly. Or was it merely the play of the light on the paper. Why do I want to read the poems when I can remember every word every line, of every poem. To read properly one has to distance oneself from the page. To recall one has to summon the poem up from the depths of one's own being.

I wanted to know whether I could place the poems into my story in prose.

I began to recall the poems in the order I had composed them. The first eight were *mathnavis*, and belonged together. A *mathnavi* can be a fairly long poem. but I made use of the shorter *mathnavi*form of sixteen couplets.

They were artificially spontaneous cries, outcries, cries of outrage, of raging anguish, of anguished despair. As a suffering lover, devastated by grief, I shed tears of blood. I wasted away, and became invisible to myself. The fires of my yearning could not be quenched by the billows of my weeping. My constant suffering, thus did I comfort myself, purified my heart, as gold is refined in the melting pot.

The next six were *mathnavis* also. Longer poems, like those of the Persian poets. In them I extravagantly bewailed not my personal plight, but the human condition itself. The heavens above, that prevented me from reaching heaven on earth. Fate, that compelled my lack of faith. The stars above, cruel and malign. Destiny, and the destination of mankind. All these I lamented.

Time was the enemy. The creator of time was a tyrant, cruelly exercising power over man, who had not asked to be, and did not know why he was created. Man, too, was cruel, and had created useless things like money, and useless conventions like arranged marriages. I bemoaned the inevitability of change. The sequence of poems ended thus,

Glad I am I haven't found the fount of eternal life,
Merciful it is that death is the end of life.

I felt passionately moved by my poems. Here was the I I was. I shut my eyes. I luxuriated in the final couplet.

Abdul began to snore loudly again as if commenting on my poems.
I came to myself.
I had to read the poems, not just remember them.
I began again.

I began to read them slowly. Deliberately. Looking at every word, pronouncing every line. Not allowing myself to be intoxicated by the rhythm. I began to feel a slow unease as I reread the first eight poems. An ache that began between my eyes mounted up my forehead as I slowly continued rereading the next six. I wanted to stop, but I forced myself to read the remaining poems carefully, not recite them.

They were *ghazals*, all of them.

A short love lyric, the *ghazal* presents a conversation between lovers. It is the most demanding of verse forms, with strict requirements about the rhyme scheme, and about the use of a common meter for all couplets. The metrical rules I had followed strictly. My ten *ghazals* were better love laments than the *mathnavis*. The I, what the pandit would term the *ahamkāra* or the superficial ego in Sanskrit, had been replaced with what I thought was my real self. I suddenly thought of the Buddhist term, the *non self*, which I had dismissed when the *bhiksu* mentioned it at the Diu city center. A poet, I thought, always needs a self in order to write.

The poems set down random fragments of our brief life together. The moment on Lamu beach when she told me she was with child. My last sight of her at Anegundi, her mouth dripping with blood. Our holding hands in the dark stepwell at Śatruñjaya. The night in Kannanur when she told me she had lost our baby. The visit to Gedi. The building of the *Zephyr*. The journey to Vijayanagar. The rescue and naming of Yasmin. The singing of the *Salve Rainha* aboard Paulo da Gama's ship. The way she combed her long black hair.

I read the *ghazals* very slowly, distancing my self from the words. The poems were ingenious, the rhymes were intricate, the rhythmic beat was always correct. And yet my ear began to sense a certain artificiality. The ache returned, I knew not why. Something was wrong, I knew not what. Till I read the last poem, *The Sands of Lamu*, a poem simple and direct. Not a great poem, but the emotion came through. The beat sounded natural like that of the human voice. It was a true poem.

It was written not in Persian, but in Gujarati.

I knew then.

What was wrong with the twenty three poems was that the language was one that I had not made my very own. Which language is mine.

That's a question. Should my answer be Arabic, the language of my youth. I have read a few Arabic poets. I can speak Arabic, but I do not use it very often now. It has grown rusty on my tongue.

Perhaps the answer is Persian, the language of my mind. Unlike Arabic, it does not have a holy book. It does have a national epic, Firdausi's *Shahnameh*. I know Persian poetry, have spent long nights at the tiller reciting to myself, softly, the poems of Sa'di of Shiraz, Rumi, Hafiz. I knew all these poets. I knew the great love stories they had composed.

The story of sculptor Farhad, who had to dig a tunnel through solid rock as a conduit for milk, if he wanted to win Princess Shirin, wife of the emperor, Khusrau. Farhad had almost completed this impossible task, when Khusrau sent him false tidings that Shirin was dead. Farhad then hurled himself down the mountainside in despair.

The Arabian desert legend, too, of the infatuation of Madjnun for the lovely Laila. The tribal hostility that kept them apart. His wasting away, and his wanderings through deserts and mountains. Till he became known as the madman of love, *madjnun*, the demented one. Few know his real name, Qais.

Both lovers have become symbols of absolute love.

Now I realized what was wrong with my poems.

Not my emotion, but my use of language that had stained the pure emotion. My sensibility had been deeply affected by the tyranny of literary convention. So that I fell back on stock phrases. I used the usual epithets and metaphors.

The cypress, never the coconutpalm, established my poetic landscape. The nightingale, not the myna or the bulbul, would sing in the bushes. The tulip, the rose and the eglantine made up the idiom of my *mathnavi*, never the jasmine. I tried once to write a poem titled, *The Sea of Love*, but could not because of the lack of a sea idiom and vocabulary in Persian. The sea images sounded artificial.

I loved words, could play tricks with them, pack double meanings into a phrase, use verbs that could be read as nouns. In the going jargon, I would be called a jeweler of intricate verbal images. I invented a *takhallus* for myself, a poetic penname which had to be flung into the final verse of a *ghazal*. I did not have a teacher to help me choose one. Nor did I have a circle of poet friends and poetry lovers to encourage me. No one to appreciate the ironic appropriateness of my *takhallus*. The awakened one.

Perhaps they would have responded to this couplet that took me five long nights to compose.

> Long black hair, long dark night, fireflies gleam,
>   it is dark, dark it is, come, dawn.
> Black rainclouds make longing intense. Tearpearls
>   gleam in the night, blind me, come, dawn.

What does this poem convey to me now.

The realization that I am no poet. That I have written just one poem, the Lamu one. Which no one will ever see. These verses before me, I cannot call them poems, will never enter this account. But I can ask questions about language. Does language change color under an alien sky. How long does it take to reroot itself in alien soil.

There is, said João during one of our group discussions, a profound inter-relation between language and religion.

The genius of Arabic, he stated, springs from its sacred book.

He paused. João's sharpest insights, as I have said, usually leap out of him when he is just beginning to get drunk.

I mean, João continued, the languages of great civilizations have always been rooted in the sacred.

The pandit, at this point, began to intone a verse in Sanskrit from the *Rigveda*, and João walked suddenly away.

Usha and I spoke to each other in Gujarati after we sailed away from Diu in the *Zephyr*.

A limited language Gujarati is, João says, a secular one, but highly absorbent.

He paused.

Because of the long Gujarat coastline and its many ports, its trade connections, it has always been porous to words connected with trade and business.

I suddenly thought of Usha's language. Her voice arose from a silence deep within her that reached out to animals, even to plants. Usha would talk to her jasmine. To her myna too.

What is the language of love. That was a word she never used as a verb, and only once before had she used it as a noun.

I must stop writing for a while. My language is confused, doesn't run straight. The syntax is twisted. I must calm myself, for my inner being is so flooded with her, that there is no space for words to issue from there, only a swirl of feelings. I will not set down my poems in this account, but I do want to set down here words that will make me see her again, as she was at Lamu.

One day, during my second year with the venerable hakim, instead of starting a new poem, I tried to do a sketch of Usha dressed in a patterned lightblue *kanga*, leaning against the white sand dunes of Lamu. The mangroves were green in the far distance. It was hot, and I was coming back from the well with a jug of water. The evening sun was low in the west.

I did the background with rapid strokes. It would be as easy as sketching seacharts on sand for my apprentice pilots. I found I could not even begin the sketch of Usha. I wanted to begin with her long eyelashes, but they turned stiff on the paper. Her eyes looked vacant, and I could not make them smile. I flicked my wrist to get the impish curl that always refused to be tamed by the brush, would always somehow escape from her hairparting, and settle on her forehead. But the ringlet didn't curl just right. The teeth, the third tooth from the right had been chipped when she bit into a hard almond. The fingers. The whorl of the left ear. The stick of charcoal was heavy in my leaden fingers. The paper was full of smudges.

I want her to live again, if only for a few moments. But even images now fail me. They can only capture just fragments of time past that vanish away.

I want to see Usha as just Usha. I want to see the way she talked, the way she smiled with her eyes, how she walked, not too fast, not too slow. To see her delicately rub her chin with her forefinger, when considering a problem. Suck a ripe mango without allowing a drop of juice to stain her fingers. Curl around a coconutpalm to whisper to it.

Ahmad ibn Madjid, wake up, wake up.
That's the voice of my cynic.
What did you expect, Ahmad my brother.
I only want to see my Usha again.
But the heart has no eyes.
Quiet, cynic, be quiet.

Why don't you make use of those sketches and maps you've bundled up in that Martaban jar, so that at least your reader can catch a glimpse, not of her but of the world you and she lived in, which, as you well know, will change.
Quiet, cynic, I am calm now.
Then go back and do the first sketch map now. Begin on the first page.
I will, soon.

I used to dream of her in the long dark nights after Anegundi, just before dawn. I would be trembling with happiness. We were to go away together, far far away. I was going to meet her soon at the entrance to the step well near Śatruñjaya. Near a lime washed pillar tomb that melted slowly into a coconutpalm. Near the altar of a Jain temple crowned with the white dome of a mosque.

I run towards her. A mist like river rises between us, but I don't care. Soon we will be together, and go away. Her eyes smile. I can almost touch her black hair, and then I wake up.

I do not dream of Usha now. She hasn't entered my dreams for over two years. Farhad wisely ended his sufferings at once by hurling himself down the mountainside. Or was Madjnun the wise one, whose torments made him sense at the end that his Laila was present everywhere he went, because she lived within him.

My hakim had said, write down the story of your past. I hadn't realized at that time how difficult it would be to write it. Our story, Usha's and mine, is not a mere *ghazal* but an extended *mathnavi*, a story intertwined with the stories of others, all of which I have to weave together in this account. But I do not yet have the figure which every weaver at his loom has to have in mind, even before he begins the weaving. Isn't Gujarat the home of textiles.

I sense a connection between our voyage from India to Africa, our arrival in Lamu, and the entry of the Portuguese into the Bahr-i-Hind, their arrival in Malindi. What the pattern is I don't know.

None of us had ever heard of the Portuguese intruders, who had blundered into East African waters. When Usha and I arrived in Lamu I was only worried that Sheth Chimanlal and his agents in East Africa would try to find us. I knew the sheth's chief agent at Mombasa, Gujarawala, who handled the ivory trade. Gujarawala would make inquiries all along the east coast of Africa and in two or three weeks he would find out where Usha and I were, and send a message to Diu. What would happen to us. Sheth Chimanal would surely let nothing happen to his beloved daughter, his only child. He would have me killed. I, who always knew my bearings, now could make no plans for the future.

Mian Mazlum and his wife, Ratna, took care of us. In the early morning after our arrival, he and Abdul took the *Zephyr* upstream to a small creek in the undulating lamu shamba, a long stretch of porous sands planted with tall coconut and stately mango trees, with somber baobabs, and occasional clumps of jasmine. Where he had a small house. He then reported the *Zephyr*'s arrival to the harbormaster, who made the clerk of the customs house note it down on his list.

Ratna took Usha to the tailor's for some clothes.

Kangas, two identical robes of gaily patterned cloth, one piece to be wrapped around the body, the other draped around the head and shoulders. Some had Arabic Swahili sayings printed on them, spicily clever, some of them, Usha told me. At social gatherings for women only, they would try to decide whose *kanga* was the best.

Buibuis, also, for Usha and Layla. A *buibui* makes a woman look like a shapeless shadow, but is a complete concealer. It is the swahili version of the Arabian *abaya*, a long black anklelength cloak with a hood. Ratna ordered a threepiece *buibui* for Usha, one with an attached hood that could be shaped and tied in different ways to give the head a distinct grace, and a long black yashmak, that veiled the face, and lent it mystery. There were slit openings for the eyes. The tailor also promised to have two boy outfits ready the next day for Usha and Layla.

Usha and Ratna and Layla, all three in *buibuis*, went to buy spices and provisions at a shop close by, while Mian Mazlum and I donkeyrode the two miles to his house in the shamba. Abdul had taken full charge there and prepared the house for our coming.

Before leaving Lamu town for the shamba house I took Usha and Layla, disguised as boys, for a walk through Lamu the next morning.

The previous night we had sat down to a family discussion about whether Usha and Layla should risk wearing disguise.

It won't work, said Mian Mazlum, it simply won't. Don't you agree, Ratna.

Yes, Ratna said, without looking at him.

Wives in our world never disagree with their husbands in public and never address them directly by name.

Do I have to explain, continued Mian Mazlum. One look at Layla.

He sputtered.

Ratna looked down with her sad eyes.

We smiled, Usha and I. And Layla, sitting behind the curtain, burst into a fit of giggles.

My friend was right. Layla had quite big breasts.

Ah, Ratna said, ah, not looking at her husband. You're referring to her long hair.

No, Mian Mazlum said, no.

And he looked at his wife, and she looked up, and they both laughed.

Look, Ahmadbhai, see how she makes fun of me, Mian Mazlum said.

They loved each other, and were deeply happy. Why Ratna, at times, looked sad, I didn't know.

What about my hair, Usha asked, shouldn't I have it cut.

She looked at Ratna, who didn't say anything. I glanced at Usha, and then stared at the carpet.

Her hair gleamed in the light, and flowed black and soft over her right shoulder.

I'll get a pair of scissors, said Mian Mazlum.

I did not say a word. I kept looking fiercely at the carpet.

They burst out laughing, Mian Mazlum the loudest of all.

No, Ahmadbhai, said Ratna, I won't cut Usha's hair. That would break your heart. Let me see what I can do for Usha and Layla.

And she took them both to the women's quarters.

Mian Mazlum knew I was worried.

Don't worry, Ahmadbhai, he said. I'll know if an outsider comes to Lamu asking questions. The harbormaster will inform me if any ship from Aden or Muscat gets in. And I've told my apprentices, especially Kochama, to keep their eyes open for strangers.

I wanted to give Mian Mazlum the little money I had for the clothes and the provisions. I wanted to offer him my thanks at least.

No, Mian Mazlum said, no words are needed. We are friends. What is mine is yours.

I smiled my thanks at him.

No one will disturb you at the Lamu shamba house, he said. The nearest neighbor is half a mile away. I'll send word immediately if a stranger is seen in Lamu. Lamu is too crowded a place for you and Usha.

The curtain was suddenly drawn aside, and Usha and Layla stepped into the room dressed as boys.

Usha's eyes sparkled mischievously like stars. She wore loose pyjamas, a long flowing *khamis* shirt with a black jacket at the top. Her long hair had disappeared. A white embroidered cap covered her head.

Poor Layla looked quite uncomfortable in her outfit. It was as if she had suddenly put on weight, and her jacket fitted tightly around her. She scratched her armpit and her forehead, the cap was tight there. She looked at Ratna, then at Mian Mazlum and me, burst into a fit of giggles, and ran into the inner rooms.

No one will mistake her for a boy, said Mian Mazlum.

She will be so disappointed, said Usha. She has been talking about how she will swagger around in the streets. Let's see if her disguise works for a day. Tomorrow, can we go see Lamu town.

Usha looked at me with her bright eyes.

The next day I woke up before dawn, and I went alone for a walk along Lamu beach, just beyond the north end of the harbor. The clean white dunes felt warm under my bare feet, as I walked to the water's edge, where the wet sand was cool and pleasant. The tide was out. High water, which in Swahili means the becoming full of the waters, would take place around noon today. The sun had not yet risen. Manda island was covered with a morning haze. Far out on my right I could barely make out the tip of the white pillar tomb off Shela point, a landmark visible far out to sea for sailors to determine their bearings.

I wanted to take my bearings for my future. Our future, my Usha, our bearings. For I no longer had a separate self.

Stop spouting mere words, poet ibn Madjid, my cynic said. You are a pilot. You have to steer through this treacherous *samsāra*.

.Yes, I must plan our future, oh cynic. I must, but I find I cannot. Before Usha entered my being, I was the pilot of my own life. I did not care for money or religion. Driven at times by my sense of daring, I would pilot ships to Aden, to Hormuz, to Maskat. Would sail against the wind to Colombo to pick up a special cargo of cinnamon and pearls during the pearldiving season. Make a sweeping arc across the Bahr-i-Hind to Kilwa to collect some gold bars. I could go anywhere I wanted to on the Bahr-i-Hind. Now I can't. I am no longer free.

I want to live out of time, but time and again I have to enter time again.

Wake up, Ahmadji, my cynic warned me. Stop spouting empty poetry. Wake up.

The pressures of money and of society now bear down heavily on me. We had very little money, Usha and I. Sheth Chimanlal had invested all the money I had saved in his trading ventures. I dared not ask him for any before Usha and I left Diu. I have to make money soon. The Arab and Persian traders will take me on as pilot. I can easily bypass the west coast of India, and sail direct to Melaka. But Usha, what will happen to Usha. Man can be a wanderer, woman requires a home. I could leave her with Ratna and Mian Mazlum for a while, or with Layla and Abdul. She needs a community. In our eastern world, a woman does not have a life of her own. In her youth, she belongs to her father. Later, to her husband. And in her old age, to her son, who has to look after her.

The Persian poets were right. Do what you will, they warned everyone, but do not fall in love. Love, say the guardians of Islam, undermines the very foundations of society.

I wrote the word love with the big toe of my right foot on the wet sand, and sadly watched the incoming wave cover the word, and slowly erase it on its way down to the sea. I could hear the distant chant of the muezzin summoning the faithful to prayer. Rays of light faintly streaked the sky. It was time to go back to take Usha and Layla for a walk through the town.

Layla jumped up and down as we set out. Usha held her hand tight to calm her down, as we walked along the curved waterfront.

It was midmorning. None of the shops were open. Some Bajun porters waited patiently outside the customshouse. The tide was out. No ship could make port yet. They would have to wait till noon. There were very few people on this street. Usha with deliberate steps, Layla, happy and carefree, walked ahead of me.

I wanted to take Usha beyond the south end. She would like the view of the Shela pillar tomb. The three of us stood on the small promontory,

Usha in the middle. We were looking towards Shela, admiring the erect beauty of this pillar tomb.

Layla scratched under her armpit.

It was getting hot. Her clothes were tight. The prickly heat season had begun. Usha pressed her finger into the center of my palm. She wanted to say something, but did not look at me. I wanted to tell Usha about the delicate Chinese porcelain plates, which we could not see, that decorated the pillar at the top. But Layla was restless.

Let's go, Layla said, I want to see the shops and the people and buy some sweets.

She jumped up and down like a little girl.

Calm down, said Usha. Let's go.

Usha looked at me.

Behind and parallel to the palmleaf riverfront, at a slight incline and packed with the houses and shops of the rich traders and businessmen, was the main street of Lamu. Narrow slanting lanes sloped down into it, like crooked fingers, from the top of Hedabu hill at the back of the town. The houses and the shops pushed against each other, their flat roofs almost touching, so as to protect the people crowding and jostling in the lanes below from the fierce sunlight. It wasn't bazaarday, and I'm glad it wasn't the evening hour, because people would have pushed against Usha and Layla. The shops along main street were open. But not many people were shopping. It was too early for the rich. The narrow lanes had people milling up and down.

I had never been up these lanes before.

Here, this one, Layla whispered to Usha.

It was Layla's day. She grabbed Usha's hand. I followed them up the lane above the customshouse. Only three people could walk abreast through it. I watched carefully. Usha tried her best to walk like a boy. Layla's broad hips made her walk awkwardly. I looked at the eyes of the people, and at the shopkeepers, but they were too busy selling and buying goods.

Layla had not been lucky in her choice of lanes. This was the lane for food and provisions. Women in *buibuis* bargained shrilly for meat and vegetables. Women slaves wearing dresses with horizontal colored stripes, under which they had on fringed pyjamas, accompanied them with baskets on their heads.

Beans, brinjals, cucumbers, melons of different kinds, all grown in the large vegetable gardens beyond the town walls, were on display. There were foodgrains in plenty, especially rice and millet. But no wheat, for wheat, an expensive grain, came from Cambay, and was only available on main street. Cumin, dried ginger, cloves, nutmeg, mace and cinnamon were imported from Calicut and Cochin and Melaka.

In one shop all these spices were cleverly displayed in small sacks between two pyramids, one of red chili powder, the other of yellow turmeric. There were plenty of fruits, oranges, lemons, limes, lowly bananas, the poor man's fruit, figs, and even a few Lamu mangoes. They would be in full season in midMay. Something in the soil, some say it is the wellwater, makes Lamu mangoes the sweetest of the ones all along the coast.

I almost stopped at a shop selling pickles and *achar*. The mango and the green chili pickles were tempting, but I had to keep up with Usha and Layla. They were about to reach the meat section. The smell of blood was thick all around, and black flies buzzed irritatingly everywhere. Raw slabs of naked cow flesh swayed heavily from curved iron hooks. The blood dripped softly on the sawdust sprinkled floor to show that the animal had been slaughtered that morning. The butcher's helper was using his chopper rhythmically, like a drummer, on lean beef pieces heaped on a wood block to mince the meat for *kheema*. Sheep flesh and mutton was available at the next stall.

I walked quickly up to Usha and caught her by the arm. She had turned her face away from the stalls. I thought for a moment she was about to vomit. Layla was used to such sights. She was not a vegetarian.

Let's go, Usha's eyes said. She controlled, and swallowed her revulsion. She looked quite pale. I myself, who have eaten meat all my life, felt a little sick.

A woman in a *buibui* patted Usha's chin, and lifted it up slightly.

What a pretty boy, she said.

We hurried down the lane.

It was a relief to get to main street, and walk back in the direction of Mian Mazlum's house. A coffeeseller, his brasspot set up on a charcoal brazier, clinked his tiny porcelain cups together to get my attention. But it was too hot, and I wanted to hurry along but Layla stopped. A woman in a *shiraa* brushed against her. Layla turned and stared, her finger was in her mouth.

Hey, stupid, what are you looking at, the woman shouted.

She stopped to adjust one of the two sticks that supported the colorful and all concealing tent canopy above her head.

Hey, stupid.

Usha hurriedly took Layla into the nearest shop, a cloth shop, to get away from the woman who wore the *shiraa*.

The shopkeeper didn't want them to go into the shop.

There's nothing for boys there, he said.

He was an importer of fine muslin, catering to the rich sheikhs and nobles who would visit Lamu for a holiday. His shop had a few readymade garments at the back, but specialized in exquisite closelywoven muslins of all varieties from India. He was by himself.

What can I show you, maharaj, he asked me.

Don't touch anything, he warned the boys as they went inside.

I would like to see some muslins, I said, pointing to the ones in front of him.

Let me show you some beautiful ones I have inside, he said. They're of the latest design, from Surat.

No, no, no, I said hastily. Thank you, I'd like to look at these ones.

Behind him, at the back of the shop, Layla had removed her cap. Ratna had plaited and fixed Layla's hair tight on top of her head.

I was afraid that the shopkeeper would turn around.

Layla was about to try on a transparent black rectangular shawl edged with gold strips when Usha took it away from her. No, no Layla, remember you are a boy, Usha said. She put Layla's cap on her head, and somehow made it fit.

I bought a green square piece of muslin, and gave it to Usha.

You can have this piece for a shawl, Usha told Layla as we left the shop.

At the corner of the third lane a man was selling *madafu*. He had a basketful of the green coconut.

I want some, I want some, said Layla. Her voice was shrill.

Some people, mostly men, turned and stared.

Usha caught Layla's arm, and we walked to the coconut seller stand. Coconut water would be cool and refreshing in the heat which was building up now. The *madafu* man had just sliced off the top of a tender coconut and was offering it to Layla, when she darted up the lane.

I want some sherbet, Layla said.

I walked quickly to the colddrink shop, and ordered some red sherbet. In her haste Layla spilled half of it on herself. The sherbetwala laughed.

You're a clumsy one, he said.

I was glad we were nearing Mian Mazlum's. One more lane, and Usha and Layla would be safe.

Just then, Mian Mazlum's neighbors, Yusuf and his son Salim, came along. They were on their way to their shop near the customshouse. We exchanged greetings and warm embraces, and asked the usual questions about their health and wellbeing. They noticed Usha and Layla, but were too polite to ask any questions about them.

I saw Layla tugging at Usha's hand. They went up the lane to a small confectioner's shop on the right. I wanted to follow, but politeness kept me back. I was glad I had given Usha some money to buy sweets.

I enquired politely about their *boriti* business.

Yusuf, a contractor, was the largest Lamu supplier of *borities*, iron hard mangrove poles cut exactly eight feet to be used as rafters, essential for the construction of houses and buildings all over Africa and treeless Arabia. That is why few large ships are seen on the East African coast.

Yusuf knew it was time to make polite inquiries about me. With old fashioned courtesy he asked, how was your voyage, Ahmadbhai, was the sea rough, which ship did you pilot this time.

I did not want to tell any lies and I was worried about Usha and Layla. I couldn't see them in the confectioner's shop. A *mukhadam* came running as fast as he could from the direction of the customshouse.

Yusuf *sab*, he said. He was breathless, he could hardly speak.

A ship has just come in from Mombasa with strange news.

He paused to take a breath and began coughing.

It couldn't be, no, I thought, it couldn't be. The tide must have come in earlier, an hour before noon.

Strange ships of a kind never seen before, the old man coughed again, have come, three of them, to Mozambique, big ones, with huge sails, no one knows from where.

Mukhadam sab, said Yusuf, patting him on the back, talk slowly.

A crowd gathered around us.

Some say they have come out of the sea of darkness, continued the *mukhadam*. They are Rumes, others say. Their skin is pinkogrey. They wear strange clothes and cannot speak our language.

Calm down, said Yusuf, is that all. They must have lost their way. There is nothing to worry about.

The crowd began to speculate wildly about these strangers but, like Yusuf, I wasn't worried. I wasn't even interested. I slipped away to look for Usha and Layla.

The two boys are at the back of the shop, said the confectioner. My five year old son wanted to show them his myna.

At the back I saw Usha standing near a small casuarina tree with a young myna cupped in her left hand, reassuring it gently with her right, and cooing to it. The yellow skin of the myna's right leg had been grazed. Its eyes were glazed with pain.

Usha applied some spit to the leg to quieten the bird. The myna struggled to free herself.

Usha gave me the little myna to hold.

Ask the shopkeeper if we can buy the myna, she said. Then she turned to Layla whose clothes were in disarray.

The little myna wasn't a beautiful bird. Its feathers were ruffled, its wings scraggly.

I went out to the front of the shop.

How much, I asked. The myna kept struggling to free itself. I gave the shopkeeper some money.

It's my son's bird, the shopkeeper said. He cries all the time. I bought the myna for him. From a Zanzibari sailor.

He'll kill it soon, I said. Look, its right leg is hurt.

I gave him some more money.

Usha had somehow rearranged Layla's clothes and turn Layla into a passable boy again. The five year old had disappeared. Usha took the myna from me, and we hurried on to Mian Mazlum's.

Later, on Lamu beach, Usha stroked the feathers of the myna and told me what happened at the confectioner's.

The myna beat its small wings in the dust trying to get away from the five year old. Its right leg had been tied with a string to the bench under the casuarina tree. The boy was about to grab it when the string broke and the bird had fluttered painfully on to a low hanging branch. Layla had climbed slowly up the scaly tree trunk. The myna couldn't fly. It tried to hop away but couldn't and dropped into Usha's hands. Layla lost her hold and slipped painfully down the broadtrunked tree, tearing her wet shirt.

Layla did rescue my little one, Usha told me on Lamu beach.

It will soon become a beautiful bird, Usha said. What shall I name her, my Ahmad.

The little myna was content to be next to Usha under our cotton covering. It chirruped as if asking a question.

Go to sleep, Usha told the myna, it's late.

Usha would talk to her and the little bird would at times cock her head to one side as if trying to understand what Usha was saying. The myna's eyes were a bright black ringed with yellow. It had a black head and a white patch on the wings. Its beak and legs were a bright yellow.

It was a week after the rescue, and her right leg had healed completely except for a brown scar caused by the tight string. Ratna's poultice of herbs from her vegetable garden at the back had done wonders.

What shall I name her, my Ahmad, asked Usha.

I don't know, I said.

The sun had set, the wind blew gentle and cool from the west, and we could hear the rustle of the coconut palms above us. From the bushes behind us came the faint evening smell of jasmine. African jasmine does not have the rich fragrance of *rat-ki-rani*.

Why don't you call her Yasmin, I said.

Come along, Yasmin, said Usha, it's time to go home.

For three weeks, my Usha, we had a home, a single syllable word, like another word of one syllable which we never uttered. For us home was a look, a smile, a soft kiss, the putting of food into each other's mouth when Layla and Abdul would go to Lamu for a visit, the picking up of seashells, tiny ones, a shell with a golden ring, the honey cowries edged with lilac, blue and light green and pink and turquoise shells, which you strung together into a necklace one night and wore the next day, your talking to Yasmin in the long hot afternoons while we waited for evening to come and night to fall, smoothing her feathers, they were becoming a glossy black, scratching her throat with the nail of your forefinger, gently rubbing her right leg, coaxing her patiently to speak, give up, Layla said, Abdul would shake his head, I waited anxiously, till one day Yasmin said, ush ush.

At that moment homeless Yasmin found her home.

That evening on the beach you told me Ratna's story. How Ratna ran away from home and from her mother, ran away with Mian Mazlum who was one of her father's apprentices, how they fled to Hindu Vijayanagar, thence to Bhatkal and on to Kannanur, from where they took a ship to Malindi. A Bengali Hindu, it took her a long time to get used to Muslim ways. She did it because of Mian Mazlum, and now she was content with him in Lamu, but sad because she missed her mother and they didn't have any children. Ratna is still a vegetarian, Usha said, a son would make Ratna's eyes gleam again.

Yasmin, Ratna and Mian Mazlum, and João, homeless creatures all, torn from home and yearning for a home. Usha and I too, we were wanderers, we did not belong, anywhere. We had no home, though I have said we did, for the *Zephyr*, the shamba house, Lamu beach, were not just places but states of being. Our togetherness, my I flowing into her I, and there was sense of peace.

But we knew at the time that our three weeks, was it only three, of utter happiness had to end. We were living in an unreal real world that couldn't last. When Ratna and Mian Mazlum came to visit us in Lamu and Ratna told Usha about the annual *mushaira* that would be held on the small maidan on top of Hedabu Hill on the night of the new moon, Usha looked at me.

Everyone will be there. The theme is love, said Ratna. It will be an exciting competition.

I hesitated, then I told Mian Mazlum we would come.

Come and have an evening meal, Ratna said, perhaps Layla's cooking does not agree with Usha, she whispered. Layla would coax Usha to eat and, many times of late, Usha would say, I'm not hungry. Layla prepared vegetarian meals. I didn't much care about what I ate, whether it was meat or vegetables. Abdul did his own cooking.

The Lamu *mushaira* began an hour after sunset. The crowd kept streaming up the hill. The sea breeze gentle and continuous blew away the heat and humidity of the day. The *shamiana*, anchored onto the maidan, swayed gently. The women of Lamu, the older ones in *buibuis*, the younger in colorful *kangas* but with veils and hoods removed, sat under the protection of the tent in the center of which a red carpet had been spread for the performers. When we arrived the *shamiana* was packed with women, and they had to open the tentflaps all around. Usha and Ratna, both in *buibuis*, sat at the edge of the outer circle of women. I was worried about Usha. The *buibui* would be stifling hot. The donkeyride to Lamu had made her feel sick so that she did not have any food at Ratna's except for a small cup of plain yoghurt. I suggested we not go to the *mushaira*. I would have been happy alone with her, but she wanted to go.

Mian Mazlum and I sat on the extreme right from where I could keep my eye on Usha, and at times look up at the stars. From beyond the town wall came the distant drum sounds of the Bajuns and the Bantus welcoming the birth of the new moon. Lamu's most respected poet, his beard was henna dyed, opened the proceedings by invoking blessings and then saying a few words of welcome. Tonight's *mushaira* is on the theme of love, only love poems will be presented to this distinguished audience. There will be a prize for the best poem.

Malindi's chief poet then rose slowly to his feet. There were murmurs from the crowd. And a few audible sighs from the women who were impatient. They wanted to hear the young handsome poets who had dressed up for the occasion recite their poems, addressed perhaps to their secret lovers in the audience. There was romance in the night air. All were eager for the competition to begin.

The *mushairachief* raised his hand for silence and the Malindi poet began. He looked old but his voice was surprisingly young and penetratingly clear like a caravan bell.

He sang about love, not about *ishq-i majazi*, human love, but pure *ishq-i haqiqi*, divine love. Heaven, he shut his eyes, has no *qibla* but love.

Wah, wah, said the crowd.

The goal of love, sang the Malindi poet, is the loss of the awareness of everything but God.

He made use of conventional images, wings to fly, the candle of the heart, the *tannur*oven of love. He cast a spell over the crowd, but I could not surrender my self to his words or voice.

I thought about Usha. How could I get some work and some money. Perhaps we could go to Kannanur and live in a remote village near my Mappila friend, Kotta Marrakar. The Muslim community would protect us. Would she be happy there, I asked the stars, and then looked for Usha. She was only a black dot on the outer edge of the *shamiana*.

Another voice suddenly shouted from the back.

Stop, wait, I have important news, it said.

It was Lamu's news crier. It took him some time to get to the *shamiana*.

The Christians are coming, he announced, the Christians, may God consign them to hell, are coming. They have huge swollen mouths. They are not Rumes. They do not have the books of the Law. When the Sheik of Mozambique asked for the Holy Book, the *nakhoda* chief said that it had been left behind.

The news crier paused to take a deep breath and, placing his right hand over his right cheek and his right ear, shouted.

All three ships are large. They have huge guns that can set fire to our ships. The harbor master warns all *nakhodas* to keep a sharp lookout when sailing towards Mombasa or Kilwa. That is all. I forgot. The harbormaster wants to know if anyone knows who or what or where is *Prastik Jan* the Christians are looking for. The council at Malindi wants to know.

The crowd became excited. Some people walked to get their women in order to leave. The lights of the *shamiana* fell slanting on the faces of a crowd of men. I thought, for a moment, I saw agent Gujarawala's face. But it couldn't be. Gujarawala wasn't interested in poetry at all. Sheth Chimanlal couldn't have sent word to his agent so quickly from Diu. It couldn't be. A strong smell of opium thickened the air. It took some time for the crowd to calm down and for the competition to begin again.

The poems, some chanted, others sung, were wildly applauded by different sections of the crowd. Each section cheered its poet and made him repeat some of his couplets. The poems sounded artificial to my ear. A Swahili poet bewailed his love torn insides. He did not know whether to blame his eye or his heart for his falling in love. The eye claimed it was the first and quarreled with the heart. Blame both those unreliables, went the refrain.

Wah, wah, cried the crowd, and then there was a commotion in the *shamiana*. A number of women in *buibuis* got up and crowded around the spot where Usha and Ratna were.

Water, water, a woman shouted.

I knew at once what had happened. Usha must have fainted. I rushed towards the *shamiana* stepping on some people. Mian Mazlum caught up with me just before the light fell on my face. Agent Gujarawala stared at me. Perhaps he hadn't recognized me.

Ratna will take care of everything, Mian Mazlum whispered fiercely, you will be seen. Ratna made Usha drink some water, and somehow we all managed to get back to Mian Mazlum's house.

Early next morning Usha and I went back to Lamu in a *mashua*.

Ahmad mine, Usha said, Ahmad my very own, she bent down and whispered, moving the tips of her fingers across my brow.

We were home, at peace, together, alone, on Lamu beach. It was nearing twilight time, and soon night would fall, black and sudden. It had been hot all day, but now a seabreeze blew high among the trees. Usha didn't want the *satrangi* under us, and today she hadn't brought Yasmin along. I stretched my bare feet lazily in the still warm sand. My head rested in Usha's lap. There were no stars yet in the late evening sky. I turned and looked at the distant horizon. There wasn't a cloud anywhere.

I shut my eyes. Usha was Usha again. We enjoyed our meals together and she had begun to like mango pickle, one of my favorites. Abdul had come back from a visit to the harbor master in Lamu town. When we were away he had found two large lumps of *ponamhara* ambergris, as round as ostrich eggs, washed up on our beach. It is used in the perfumery business. The Sheik of Malindi claims all the ambergris that is washed up on his shores. The nobles of the Sawahil have it placed in their oillamps to sweeten and scent the air in their homes. The harbor master entered Abdul's name in his book and granted him as finder a sum of money for one of the lumps. I didn't ask Abdul how much, nor what he did with the other lump. Abdul brought back halwah for Layla and Usha, a flowing white cotton shirt for me, a cap for himself and a letter from Mian Mazlum.

Many salaams, my friend began, and continued the traditional Swahili greeting which he did not invert, the sands on the shore are too few to express my feelings for you. Much news have I you for.

The letter continued in this fashion. I will not set down Mian Mazlum's letter with its Swahili colloquialisms and inversions in this account, but I'll summarize what he wrote. Mian Mazlum knew I was worried that Gujarawala, acting on orders of Sheth Chimanlal, would have me killed. But Gujarawala, according to my friend, had come to Lamu to order mangrove poles from Yusuf for a house he wanted to build. No enquiries were made by Gujarawala, said Yusuf, about you or your ship or about Usha. Gujarawala was at the *mushaira* because he was a friend of the chief poet.

Gujarawala had visited my place, wrote Mian Mazlum, to ask about

Kochama and to know whether his tribe could supply arrow poison for the Mombasan defence forces. Before leaving my place Gujarawala asked me about my shamba house. I was taken aback. I thought he knew you and Usha were staying there, But he only wanted to rent it for a friend.

May God the merciful, the compassionate, help you always and prevent harm from falling on thee, ended the letter.

It was a conventional ending. But Mian Mazlum meant it, I think.

He had written, Mian Mazlum mentioned it as an afterthought, to his friend the Sheik of Malindi asking whether I could be appointed as adviser in the shipping office. Kochama would bring me the news.

I was happy. It would solve the problem for Usha and me.

Ahmad, my very own, Usha whispered.

The tips of her fingers played softly on my brow.

You're so utterly at rest today that I wanted to let you sleep on. But it is late, Usha said, we have to get back to the house. Ratna told me not to be out too late. The night dews can be harmful, Ratna said.

I opened my eyes. The stars shone bright in the dark blue sky.

Don't look up at the stars, Ahmad mine, she said, and she shut my eyes with the tips of her fingers.

Wouldn't you like to live in Malindi, I asked.

Anywhere, Usha said, with you.

She paused.

And with Yasmin, I asked her.

We will no longer be two, my Ahmad, but three, Usha said softly. I carry our togetherness within me.

NINE

Mid-May, 1509
my house, Diu, Night
the tufan continues to lash the Gujarat coast and I furiously set down
what happened to Usha and me. I write about the poisoned arrow in
Lamu and our journey to Kilepwa and then to Gedi

I was in a twilight state. Part of me was in Lamu, my feelings aswirl, proud
and deeply anxious and deliriously happy. Part of me was in Diu, the pen
poised in my hand, wondering how I could set down my feelings about
our baby.

And then, through half asleep eyes, I sensed Abdul in front of the
table. He must have seen that I had stopped writing. There were split
palm fronds in his hand. He wanted to plug up the opening in the kitchen
wall before the tufan began again. I held the back door open for him and
stepped outside wanting to help him but he would not let me.

It was pitch dark. The torrential rains had stopped. The winds had
calmed down, though there were fitful breezes blowing. It was eerily quiet
except for the low continuous boom of the surf. Everything else was unnaturally still as if nature was in a state of breathless expectation. It wasn't
cold at all, the hair on my wrist and forearms was aware of an unusual
warmth funneling down from the sky above. The clouds had been washed
away, the sky was clear, and the stars shone bright.

Abdul came and stood by me. We heard human voices coming through
the silence of the night. A few lights began to move about in the darkness.
Some people swinging lighted coconut husks had ventured on the faraway shoreline below, hunting for fallen coconuts. I wanted to warn them,
but Abdul held me back.

There'll be snakes disturbed by the tufan, Abdul warned me. Those
fisherfolk, they won't listen to you.

Abdul refilled the oil lamp, and I sat down to write, but the words refused to come. I recalled the poem I had written about my feelings after the telling, when Usha said we would be three. Was the poem sentimental. Yes it was. Sincere, yes, but too full of my I. Usha told Ratna and Layla about the baby. I told Mian Mazlum who was happy for me, and then I told Abdul. He looked very happy and smiled at me.

I am happy you are happy, said Abdul. I am happy for your wife too.

Why dont you call Usha by her name now that she will be a mother, I asked Abdul. Layla always calls her Usha.

No, said Abdul, no.

It was strange. Abdul has a heart as soft as mulmul, as the poets would say, though his parchmentlike face makes him appear a little fierce. I knew Abdul would do anything for Usha. But he never would utter her name. I wondered why.

Layla pestered Abdul about buying her a red *kanga* which she wanted to choose herself. So they set out one morning from the shamba house with her on a donkey to go to Lamu. Usha made Layla wear a *buibui,* and I made Abdul put on the flowing white *khamis* he had bought for me. We wear clothes of the same size. His new cap made him look quite jaunty.

I was eager for news about my Malindi job, and I wanted to be alone with Usha. We could talk about our child, about names, whether we would give the little one a Jain name or a Muslim name, about where we would live in Malindi, I knew exactly where, a home by the edge of the sea at the extreme other end, away from the palace of the Sheik, next to the city wall. Today we would have a long lazy day together, for Layla and Abdul would come back only by nightfall.

I was in the backyard watching Usha wash one of my shirts using a few soap nuts when there was a banging on the front door.

It's Layla, Usha said.

Layla was screaming.

I opened the front door, and Layla rushed in, hysterical, screaming Usha, arrow, donkey, tearing at her hair. Her *buibui* was covered with dust and torn in a number of places.

Usha made her sit on the carpet and gave her a drink of cold water. I hurried out. Abdul was sitting on the porch steps. The cap wasn't on his head. His khamis was torn. He was breathing hard. Usha brought a small jar of water, and I carried it to Abdul.

He splashed some water on his face, rinsed out his mouth but did not drink any water. He shut his eyes waiting for his body to calm down. Abdul believes that cold water should not enter the stomach when the body is heated. I looked around, but could not see the donkey anywhere. Abdul must have been attacked and robbed.

The donkey is dead, said Abdul. Someone shot an arrow. At us. It missed Layla. It brushed past my *khamis*. It hit the donkey. On its right haunch. Layla tumbled into the dust. She began to scream. The man got down from the tree and ran away. I didn't see him. He did not rob us. The donkey is dead.

Abdul's words came fast. A robber must have attacked them, a tribal native newly come from the interior. No Muslim would dare attempt such a thing. The penalty for the first offence is the cutting off of the right hand. For the second offence, instant death.

We can pay Mian Mazlum for the donkey, Abdul said.

The donkey does not matter, I said.

Just then Kochama walked up the path. He must have come from Lamu in a boat.

I bring you salaams from my teacher, he said, and then he saw Abdul.

What happened, Kochama asked Abdul.

I told him about the attack, and what I thought had happened, but Kochama wouldn't dismiss it as a mere attempt at robbery.

No, he said, no. No tribal person would use a bow and arrow. A spear, yes, but not an arrow.

How long did it take for the donkey to die, Kochama asked Abdul.

Not long.

How long, Kochama persisted.

Almost immediately, said Abdul.

Ah, said Kochama, ah.

He turned to me. Let's go to the place, Ahmadbhai, I mean Ahmad ibn Madjid, sir, he said.

What's the use, I said. The robber must have fled by now.

The donkey lay by the side of the path. Kochama hunted around for the arrow but it wasn't there. Someone must have taken it away. I bent down and with a twig wanted to examine the wound.

I wanted to see how deep it was, but Kochama warned me not to touch the wound even with a stick.

The wound looked finger deep, the donkey had a tough hide. Its body was like a stone. Its muzzle was fiercely contorted as if the lips had been forcefully pulled back to display its teeth.

The arrow, said Kochama, its tip was poisoned.

He stared at the wound.

Kamba poison, Kochama said, dangerous even to smell.

I knew then we would have to abandon our Lamu house.

Tomorrow, I thought.

When we got back, Layla was whimpering in the kitchen. Usha had talked to her and managed to calm her down. But when Layla saw Abdul and Kochama and me sitting under the trees at the back of the house she grew hysterical again and screamed at Abdul.

Don't sit there outside, she screamed through the window at Abdul, they'll kill us all.

She began tearing her hair.

I want to go back to Chapora, home, to my home, home, she shouted at Abdul, now, now, now. They'll kill me, I'll die, die, I'll die.

I knew then we had to go this very evening, when the tide turned.

Kochama relayed the good news.

That I would be welcome as an adviser in the shipping office. Mian Mazlum said the Sheik wanted me to come to Malindi as soon as possible.

Let's leave, I told Abdul, for Malindi, this evening.

Abdul thought for a moment. The *Zephyr*, he said slowly, knowing I would be able to make sense of his words. In Malindi. Agent Gujarawala will know.

I knew what he meant. The east coast of Africa is a small world. Sheth Chimanlal's agents would discover the *Zephyr* in Malindi harbor, and find out where Usha and I were. They would use assassins to kill both of us.

Sheth Gujarawala has gone back to Mombasa, Kochama said, but he has agents in Malindi.

Kochama looked worried.

I asked about his father who had a clouding of the eyeball. I didn't know anything about this disease at that time in Lamu. Much much later, I helped the venerable hakim perform eye surgery many times in the villages of central India. I would get the instruments ready for my hakim, and, most reluctantly, I would hold firm the patient's head and hands, for there was no one else to help the hakim. But I would turn my face aside and never watched him operate. The patient would recover in two days.

Why don't you specialize in this operation, my hakim once asked me. In our sun scorched land many people suffer from this disease.

But I couldn't. I couldn't bear to touch the jellylike substance that is the eye. Even at that time, I disliked touching people. I even disliked taking their pulse.

You'll have to touch people to heal them, my hakim had said.

When will you bring your wife and children to Lamu, I asked Kochama.

Mian Mazlum had told me Kochama would be appointed the chief *siwa*maker of Malindi. He would have to leave the tribal village in the interior and settle down in Lamu.

That worries my father too, said Kochama. My uncle, my father's brother, and his sons are hungry for power, and want to take over the leadership of our tribe. You're too old, you're too weak, you'll be blind soon, they keep shouting at my father during our tribal council meetings, you want to continue the old ways that are dying, we want money, now, now, now.

They demand that we market our deadly arrow poison to other tribes and to the sheiks of Malindi and Mombasa. My father wants to follow our tribal customs which bid us use the poison only for hunting and for killing wild elephants, and forbid its use for the killing of human beings. The tribe is split into two rival factions.

From where I sat I could see Usha and Layla busy preparing the midday meal. We would eat outside just below the kitchen window. Dressed in a tightfitting blue kanga, Layla beckoned to us to come and eat. I was surprised but realized that Usha had given Layla one of her own kangas. Layla had calmed down.

My father refused to sell the poison to Gujarawala's agent when he came to Kilepwa, Kochama said, as we walked towards the kitchen. But I did see my uncle's son talking to the agent on the Malindi waterfront.

Layla was placing some cups of water on a stand. Kochama, fascinated, could not take his eyes off her. He stole glances at her all through the meal. Layla didn't bother to look at him.

I sat quiet all through the meal.

I was making connections in my mind piecing together the sequence of events that had led to the death of the donkey. Sheth Chimanlal must have sent a message about our disappearance by one of his swift boats from Diu to his agent in Hormuz. The nakhoda of the *Sheikh Kitami* must have reported to the Hormuz agent that he had seen a woman with long hair at the tiller near the Lamu coast. The news must have been relayed to Mombasa. Agent Gujarawala, who did not want to arouse the suspicions of my friend, Mian Mazlum, must have sent a spy to Kilepwa, where a Kamba archer belonging to the rival section, was hired to murder Usha and me. The killer thought that Layla was Usha, and mistook Abdul in his flowing new *khamis* for me.

We had to leave Lamu immediately, and hide the *Zephyr* so that we could escape in her from Malindi if we needed to, and trust the Sheik of Malindi to protect us from the agents of Sheth Chimanlal at least for the time being. Perhaps, after the baby, we would leave Malindi and go to my friend Kotta Marakkar in Kannanur.

I shook myself out of my brooding in order to make the necessary arrangements. I didn't allow us a walk on Lamu beach to bid it goodbye. The noonday sun would be too hot for Usha and this wasn't the time to be sentimental. The tide would flow seaward soon. We shut down the shamba house, got into the *Zephyr*, made our way to Lamu town, and anchored midstream in the riverbend near Mian Mazlum's house.

Mian Mazlum was shocked when I told him about Gujarawala.

Ah, he said loudly, ah.

Kochama suggested that we hide the *Zephyr* up a deserted creek near the Kamba settlement in Kilepwa.

My father, he will welcome you all to our house, Kochama said.

Kochama had eyes only for Layla who was quite aware of his interest in her. She never looked at him but kept playing with her hair and constantly adjusting her face veil when he was near.

Abdul never said a word.

I smiled and wondered what would happen to Layla. I knew that in Africa a son was not allowed to marry without his father's consent, especially if the girl was an outsider. I knew Abdul wanted to get his sister married but he didn't have any dowry money. Would Layla refuse to be a second wife.

From Kilepwa you can travel to Malindi by way of Gedi, said Mian Mazlum. The caretaker of the palace there is a friend of mine, perhaps you can spend the night there. Tomorrow I will start for Malindi, with Ratna. But not by boat, both of us get seasick easily.

Mian Mazlum knew I was in a hurry. The tide wouldn't wait for us. He walked with me to the boat where Kochama was waiting.

I have to deliver ivory bangles and necklaces to Bwana Mataka, Mian Mazlum said.

Bwana Mataka was one of the richest traders in Malindi, who never exploited the tribal peoples and had a reputation for honesty and fair dealing. He was one of the main suppliers of ivory and leopard skins and gum copal. I knew he owned many houses along the Malindi seafront.

I have to deliver them to him personally, said Mian Mazlum. I'll show them to you and Usha in Malindi. They're beautiful. For his new wife. She is a fourteen year old virgin, they say, has not become a woman yet. The Bwana lost his fourth wife a month ago. He has gone south to Mtwana la Jumbe to get married.

How old is Bwana Mataka, I asked.

Sixty five, said Mian Mazlum, but he has all his teeth. I stay in one of his houses when I go to Malindi, the one next to the wall beyond which rises the circular pillar.tomb. Come stay with us. Ratna never goes anywhere. Because of Usha she'll come to Malindi.

I embraced my friend.

I'll report your departure to the harbor master, he said as Kochama and I pushed off to the *Zephyr*.

We got to Kilepwa by late evening the next day after twenty four hours of continuous sailing. The current was with us, and I kept the *Zephyr* close to the coast allowing her to follow the curve of the bay between Ungwana and Mambrui. All along the way the boats we met, most of them struggling northward, shouted warnings at us.

The Christians, they have come to destroy all the cities along the coast.

Kilwa has been utterly destroyed.

Mozambique is completely burned down.

Don't go to Mombasa. Mombasa has been pillaged. The women have been raped, the children butchered.

I dismissed these outcries and warnings as just rumors. What could a handful of foreign vagabonds do, I thought to myself, as the *Zephyr* curved into the large mangrove fringed basin. We dropped anchor in a narrow Kilepwa side creek almost under the shadow of an octagonal pillar tomb quite close to the Kamba settlement. We could hear the beat of their drums.

There'll be a dance tonight, said Kochama.

He wanted to take all of us to his father's house, but Usha was exhausted and preferred to sleep in the *Zephyr*. The burning of incense would keep the mosquitoes away and, as Abdul pointed out, the pillar tomb would frighten away any intruders. Layla was eager to go, and Abdul had to go along though he didn't want to.

Come back early, I told Abdul, we have to leave early in the morning for Malindi.

Next morning we took a *mashua* to the northend of Mida creek and, as no donkeys were available, slowly walked the two miles to Gedi. Kochama did not accompany us.

I'll come in a few days, Kochama said.

He did not cast even one look at Layla. He smiled at us, but there was no happiness in his eyes. Usha and Layla were both tired and I was glad Mian Mazlum had told us about his caretaker friend. Abdul made all the necessary arrangements for meals. We rested all through the hot afternoon and in the evening I went for a walk through the central area of the town.

Usha couldn't have come with me even if she hadn't been tired. We had reentered the rigid world of social convention.

Gedi was one of the cleanest cities I've ever seen, almost unnaturally clean. Its buildings were whitewashed and they gleamed in the low afternoon sunlight justifying the city's name which means precious. The streets were broad and well planned and intersected each other at right angles so that one couldn't get lost here as one could in the mazes of Lamu town. The houses, each with its sunken courtyard, sat stiffly side by side conscious of forming a proper pattern. The whole town was circled by an irregular nine foot high black wall that tried to prevent this sterile world from being overwhelmed by the dark green outside. I couldn't see any coconut palms anywhere even though Gedi is only four miles from Watamu-on-the-sea.

I felt a sudden fear, I knew not why.

Ahmad mine, there's no water for your bath, Usha said when I got back. The wells here run dry in the evenings.

She had saved enough water for me to wash my face and my feet.

I won't eat with you today, she said, I ate two oranges.

I sat down. The lavender celadon plate had a thick layer of dust on it, I wiped it with my sleeve. Layla hadn't washed the plates, I thought.

Layla was exhausted but I saw her wash the plate before she went to sleep, Usha said as she served the meal. There's dust everywhere, she added, it's in the air. It settles on everything here.

The rim of my plate again had a very thin layer of dust. I couldn't eat the vegetables which Usha must have prepared with her own hands. Inspite of the spices they tasted like mud. Usha kept fanning me and coaxed me to eat. I called for Abdul.

Kochama's father asked me whether Layla could be his son's second wife. They would live in Lamu, Abdul said.

I drank some water. It was not refreshing but it tasted better than the food.

What did you tell him, I asked Abdul.

Abdul kept silent. I knew Abdul was worried. The responsibility for the marriage of his sister after their parents died fell on him.

Later, Abdul told me what happened in the Kamba tribal village in some detail.   My son, Kochama's father told Abdul, likes your sister very much. He will be rich. He will live in Lamu with Layla as his second wife.

Abdul told the father about the donkey and the arrow, and how frightened Layla was. Layla was summoned before the old man. He gave her an tiny ivory ball as a gift. It was perfectly round and smooth.

Don't be afraid of the arrow and its poison, the old man said, take this ivory ball. It contains a precious ointment worth a great deal of money.

Abdul told Layla about the offer of marriage.

No, said Layla in Gujarati, no, no, no. Kochama has thick black lips. And I don't want to be a second wife. And I don't have any friends here in Africa. And, she said, bowing her head, I want to go home to Chapora to my family.

But we don't have any family there, Abdul said.

Chapora is where I belong, Layla said, I still have a few friends there. She began to cry.

Abdul told Kochama's father that his sister had refused the offer of marriage, but didn't tell him why.

What an insulting gift, Layla said when she showed Usha the ivory ball. I am not a child. I can't even wear it.

I couldn't understand why Layla did not want to get married to Kochama. A good man, he could have provided her with a comfortable home and children.

It is not really his thick black lips, Usha told me. Layla is full of fears. The fear that all women experience, of leaving to become part of an unknown family. The fear of making another home especially in a place so far away that she will not be able to return home.

Where is home for us all, I thought.

And I moved closer to Usha and put my arm around her protectively.

She put her left arm around me.

Let's just hold each other close for a while, Usha said. There's something thick in the Gedi air. Yasmin refuses to utter a word and will not even hop around. There's something ready to pounce on living things. I can smell it. They tell me a whole tribe, men, women, children, and their sacred goddesses, many ages ago, were brutally murdered to make place for Gedi.

I held her close in my arms till she slowly drifted to sleep. I thought of the pillar tombs that dominated the Gedi landscape. It took me some time to fall into a dreamless sleep. I felt heavy and sluggish when I woke.

TEN

*M*ay 1509
My house, Diu, Night
the tufan continues in the present on the west coast of India,
my writing continues about our past, the journey from Gedi
and the arrival in Malindi in 1498

Halfway to Malindi we met groups of women with their attendant slaves hurrying on to Gedi.

The infidels are coming, the Feringhis are coming, the women warned us.

At the rest stop, five miles to Malindi, Abdul and I listened to various accounts of what had happened at Mozambique from people who were fleeing to the interior. And it was now possible, after setting aside gossip and wild rumor, for me to piece together details about the Portuguese arrival there. The report would help the sheik of Malindi when the strangers arrived there.

What Happened at Mozambique: my report for the sheik of Malindi

Seeing the three strange ships cast anchor out in the roadstead, the sheik of Mozambique sent some boats with trumpeters and drums to welcome these Turks as people of the faith, and to bid them enter Mozambique bay. The ships of the strangers furled their sails which had rectangular patches, the color of blood, on them. Then, taking soundings all the way, they cast anchor two bowshots away from the island, some distance away from four large *sambuks* from Kannanur anchored in the bay.

The chief captain paced up and down the deck. His right leg had a slight limp. He had fierce, overhanging eyebrows and black eyes, and a thick black moustache that drooped into a bushy squarecut black beard. He haughtily declined the sheikh's invitation to come ashore. So the sheik himself went to visit the ships, which were better built than ours, and with more decks.

Where are your bows, the strangers were asked.

The Turks were famous as mighty archers.

Some crossbows were brought up from the deck below, but they were of the plain kind, not the composite recurved crossbows used by the Turks.

Where is the holy book, they were asked.

They could not produce a copy of the Holy Qu'ran, and simply shrugged away the question.

Melons and cucumbers, which were in season, and madafus were immediately sent as refreshments. The strangers found it difficult to eat the fruit. Their gums were red and swollen over their teeth which were loose. I knew they suffered from scurvy. They had to be shown how to slice the top of a green madafu to drink the water, and eat the kernel which melted in the mouth. The sheik offered the chief captain a jar of date preserves, aromatized with cloves and cumin, which the strangers relished even though it was difficult for them to chew.

In turn they offered the sheik and his party some stale sweets.

From Madeira, they said.

The sheik of Mozambique politely pretended to place one of the sweets in his mouth, but spat it out discreetly when no one was looking.

Then there was an exchange of gifts. Hats, yellow wool jackets, brass mugs and colored beads were the gifts they presented to the sheik.

The sheik snorted with contempt.

I am an Arab sheik, he said to his people, all the time smiling graciously at the strangers, for the laws of hospitality insist on polite behavior. No one understood what the sheik had said.

These people think we are African blacks, and treat us like little children.

The problem was of language.

The strangers knew no Swahili, and only two of them knew some Arabic. Not however the Arabic of the Sawahil. Both parties used the language of grunts, headnods, signs, finger pointing, headshakes. Occasionally, an Arabic word would generate many vigorous headnods of understanding from one interpreter, who knew Moroccan Arabic. The other had lived in some place in Africa, which they called the Congo.

The strangers would nod their heads as though they had understood everything that was spoken, even though they hadn't. They asked many questions, pointing to the gold chains, the silver rings, and the rosary of black pearls around the sheik's neck. Then they brought up samples of cloves, pepper, ginger, from the hold.

Venezia, the strangers said, India.

Ah, said the Mozambicans, yes, yes. And they brought up some empty palmfrond baskets, used for packing spices imported from Cambay and Calicut.

In these, they said, and then they pointed across the sea.

The strangers danced with joy. They kissed and embraced each other. They were madly excited. Even the stern chief kaputan smiled, and showed his white teeth through his thick black moustache. Gold, silver, spices, lay spread out before them. They could be collected by the basketful. They wept for joy. God had answered their prayers. They would be rich beyond measure. The wealth of Ind was theirs. All the riches of the east would soon be in their hands.

Where is Prastic Jan, the chief captain asked through the interpreter.

The Mozambicans conferred among themselves.

What, who, was this. Was he a king.

Yes, he was a preste king.

Preste, preste, what was that.

The Mozanbicans went into a huddle again. Why create trouble. Let us humor our guests, and keep them happy.

Ah, they said, yes, yes. He resides there. And they pointed vaguely to the north up the coast. A king of many cities he is. Many merchants lived in his kingdom. He has huge, they stretched out their arms, ships.

The strangers again rejoiced greatly. But not as much as when they had heard about the gold and the spices.

The chief captain summoned the interpreter aside.

Malīm, the interpreter asked the sheik nasalizing the final vowel, malīm.

The Mozambicans could not understand what he meant. Till one of them went with an interpreter one deck down to where the tiller was. When they came up, all was clear.

Mu`allim, he told the others, a pilot.

Two mu`allim, the interpreter signaled with his fingers. One to find Preste João. The other for India. Thirty miticals each, in gold, would be paid for two pilots to show them the way.

Communication was now immediate. This language, the language of money leapt over all barriers. A long cloak, which we call a *cabaya*, dyed in red cochineal, would also be provided for each pilot. The chief captain glared fiercely at the waters of the bay. He stroked his moustache downward with finger and thumb. He was shrewd. He insisted that one of the pilots should always remain on board, if the other desired to go on land. All were satisfied.

Trouble arose when the Mozambican pilots, who had to live on board, informed the sheik that the strangers were kafirs, Christians, sworn enemies of the faith, worshipers of crucifixes, as the red emblems on their sails signified. They had cunningly encouraged the belief that they were Rumis. Water, a precious commodity, stored in cisterns, as there were no wells on Mozambique island, was immediately withheld. It had to be brought in barges from the mainland, and was in short supply. The water of the nearby islets was brackish. One of the pilots managed to escape when the accursed infidels, according to one report, instead of landing in Mozambique island, sailed to a thinly populated islet nearby, to perform their unholy rituals there.

At this point, the stories that Abdul and I heard, became confused.

There was fighting. Spears, bows and arrows, daggers and slings, were no match for bombards and firepower. The Feringhis sailed away. They returned to Mozambique after some days. They whipped the remaining pilot, and tortured him. They bombarded houses on the shore near the watering place, took all the water they wanted, and then destroyed the cistern. Two of the sheik's soldiers were killed. Two *mashuas* were captured and looted. Two prisoners taken. They sailed away when the winds were favorable.

End of the Mozambique report

Where did the strangers go, Abdul asked.

To Kilwa, some people said.

No, to Mafia, according to others.

They're now at Mombasa, we were told.

No, no, a late arrival at our rest stop assured us. They're already at Malindi.

Weh, oh woe, wailed the crowd at the rest stop, and they hurried along with their women to Gedi.

My pilot sensibility knew they couldn't have arrived in Malindi. At Mombasa, perhaps. The strong southern flow of the current would have forced the strangers back to Mozambique, and they could set sail and make headway, only when the north blowing winds grew more powerful. It would not be possible for them to make land at Kilwa because of the shoals and the strong offshore winds. They could now be in Mombasa. But they could not have reached Malindi.

I was right.

When we got to the mud and wattle houses of the African natives outside the town wall, we were told that the ships had not arrived at Malindi.

People were streaming out of Malindi's Gedi gate. Tribal Africans had to place their bows and arrows in custody in the guardhouse. Their belongings were searched, before they were allowed to enter Malindi. Their jungle liquor was confiscated.

The guards wanted to know if our party was from Mombasa. They asked searching questions. I told them about my appointment in the shipping office, and we were let in. Malindi was in an uproar. Main Street, which meanders through Malindi, but keeps more or less parallel to the seafront, was not as crowded as the crooked narrow side lanes where the bazaars were. People were buying provisions. The meat stalls were crowded. Fat tailed sheep were slaughtered every half hour. The jewelers and goldsmiths were shutting up their doors. The cloth shops and the tailoring booths were empty, as were the ones selling copper utensils.

Abdul knew a shortcut that bypassed the Cambay section where the Jain and Bania merchants lived, and we avoided the crowded lanes. He took us past vegetable gardens at the back of some houses to the south end of Malindi near the seafront.

Mian Mazlum and Ratna were waiting for us in a little house beyond the sea wall. It was part of a cluster of eight houses that belonged to Bwana Mataka. Because of his great wealth, his reputation, his munificence, he had donated a large sum of money towards the building of the mosque in the central marketplace as an act of piety, Bwana Mataka had been allowed to make a small opening in the sea wall, so that his wives and their children could walk down directly to the beach to take the air.

That stretch of white beach, with grains of sand that sparkled in the moonlight, led to a black rocky promontory. It had a small play area fenced off for children. The whole section made up the south end of the Malindi seafront. At the north end was the Sheik of Malindi's whitewashed palace built on a low hill to catch the soft breezes of the Indian ocean. Bwana Mataka's section with its eight houses was called Silversands. Two of his wives, we learned, had fled to Gedi.

I was glad we would be staying in the little guesthouse on the beach. Usha would be safe. Ratna took immediate charge of Usha, while Mian Mazlum and I refreshed ourselves with madafu, and then walked down to the waterfront. Mian Mazlum told me what he had learned. The three colleagues who would be working with me came to visit me at the guesthouse with gifts of welcome. There would be a formal welcome in the shipping office later, they said. I talked to each one of them.

The Malindi council had decided, unanimously, not to acknowledge the Arab Sheik of Mombasa as Sultan and had voted to refuse payment of the increased tribute demanded through agent Gujarawala.

The Sheik of Malindi, eighty years old, wanted to pay the tribute to Mombasa.

The Mombasan army was under the command of a Mamluk *amir* who imparted *furusiyya* training to the special bodyguards of the Mombasan sheik. These men could ride saddleless horses at a gallop. They could perform complicated lance exercises on horseback. They could mount and dismount lance in hand, tilt the lance in attack and retreat, and use it while holding the reins. They were proficient in archery, and in fencing on horseback. The small body of pike men were formidable fighters, well protected with polished shields, and well disciplined.

A huge cannon, made of two pieces bolted together, named *Istanbuli*, bought from the Turks and mounted on the wall of a small fortress over which rose a circular tapering pillartomb, protected the inner entrance to the deep harbor. The reefs and shoals in the curved channel up towards the northern point made the passage into the harbor tricky and dangerous. The Mombasans were not afraid of an attack from the sea nor, since theirs was an island city, did they fear a land attack from the wild tribes in the interior.

Mombasa, because of its far flung trade with Arabia and Persia, and India, had become the most powerful and the most prosperous of the East African coastal states. It had just issued its own coinage.

The forty year old regent listened respectfully to his father, whom he loved for his old fashioned Persian courtesy. He faithfully reported his father's words to a meeting of the council, to which I was invited to attend, and then he put forward his own views.

Submission and appeasement do work, the young sheik maintained. But they work only between individuals, not between nations.

For ten long years the Mombasans have bullied us, the regent stated.

Yes, said one of the younger members of the council. They are Arab bullies, not civilized people like us Persians.

The young sheik ignored the interruption.

We have been giving them money, the regent said. For what, he asked the council, why. They have done nothing for us, nothing at all. And now that Mombasan bully wants to issue his own coinage. Which will ruin our economy and our trade, and make us dependent on them.

The Mombasans have taken away our trade, he said. They have enticed our merchants away. They have levied taxes on goods we send through their port.

He banged his fist on the little table.

The payment of all tribute must be stopped, the sheik insisted. The

army, he meant the bodyguard of the Sheik, his father, would be expand-
ed. A tax would be levied on merchants and traders. Horses, now trained to
put on displays, would be trained for war. More archers would be recruited.
Additional guards would be posted to await the coming of the infidels.

The council, composed mainly of old men, most of them his father's
friends, reluctantly agreed. One old cynic asked if horsemen with bows
and arrows could be effective against ships with guns. His question was
brushed aside.

There were no ships in Malindi bay, except for two dhows just opposite
the custom house. I could tell they were from Cochin by the cut of their
sails, and the curve of their sterns. They had unloaded their merchandize,
and would hasten tomorrow to Lamu and ports north.

The sun was low in the west, and many people were handshading
their eyes wanting to claim the unique distinction of having been the first
to have spotted the stranger ships and to raise the alarm.

A sudden shout rang out from the top of the mast of one of the
dhows.

There they are, the voice shouted.

A crowd quickly gathered all along the waterfront. They pointed with
their fingers toward the setting sun.

There, said some.

Others shouted, I can see them, they are huge.

Mian Mazlum and I couldn't see any strange sails. The sun was quite
low on the horizon.

How many are there, a shrill voice asked.

I can't make out yet, cried the voice from the masttop.

Wait, wait, I can see them, they're three, no, four ships, two big, the
other two small.

The crowd grew excited. They had heard about three ships. The
fourth, where could it have come from.

The stranger ships wisely did not venture into the bay, but anchored
far out beyond the bar. They would not have known where the dangerous reefs were. Malindi is not as secure and protected an anchorage as
Mombasa. But they would be safe. My nose told me that the night winds
would be light.

The ships were a black blur against the rapidly sinking sun, and suddenly it was night.

Shouts and screams woke us early next morning.

The women of Bwana Mataka's household beat their breasts, and
wailed out their grief. Mian Mazlum and I went to the beach, where the

shouts were coming from. There were throngs of people, all shouting, all pointing to the ships. The fourth ship was one of the *sambuks* of Bwana Mataka. It had been captured by the brutal infidels. No one had any doubts about what had happened. The Christians had destroyed one of his two sambuks. They had seized all his goods, and had raped and murdered his young wife and her attendants. They were holding him a prisoner and a hostage.

They are barbarians, the crowd shouted, they do not know the law.

The young sheik welcomed me warmly in his office, and took me to the palace window which commanded a panoramic view of the harbor, and of the Malindi seafront. The black seawall curved to the right and ran on to Silversands. Down below us was the seagate with guards wide-awake and alert, though it was early in the morning. A flight of steps led down to rectangular whitewashed buildings on the seafront.

That's your office, Ahmad ibn Madjid, said the young sheik.

I liked the young sheik. He was dignified, not swayed by wild rumor. He knew what he wanted and he knew how to delegate power.

Your first job, Ahmadji, will be to find out what's really happened to Bwana Mataka and his wife, he said. Also, let me know the extent of our trade and shipping with Mombasa. Perhaps the state should get involved in matters of commerce, and not leave them to traders and merchants.

The stranger ships, out in the bay, looked calm and at peace in the morning light. From the middle of town came the cry of the muezzin summoning the people to the first prayer of the day. Malindi fell silent, except for the sea murmuring its own prayers down on the beach. I could see the pale glow of numerous lights on one of the stranger ships. From the distance came faint sounds of singing, low and deep, murmurs of peace, not cries of war. As if the sailors were chanting prayers of thanks and praise in unison. Perhaps they too were performing their early morning rituals.

There was no time for the formal welcome my colleagues had prepared for me at the shipping office.

I greeted my three colleagues, and allowed them to sprinkle a few drops of rose water on me, and then asked for the news dispatches sent by our agents and spies in Mombasa. The Mombasan spy network was more thorough and better organized than Malindi's. By now the Mombasans would have known the decision of the Malindi council not to pay the tribute.

Mian Mazlum had warned me that there might be a Mombasan spy in the shipping office. My colleagues wanted to discuss the arrangements that had been put together against the arrival of the Christian ships. But I told them I wanted to read the secret reports first.

It took them some time to collect the reports, for they were scattered on different tables in the office. I asked whether these were all the reports sent by our agents. Yes, they said. All, except for the ones that have been set aside as of no significance. I asked for that bundle also. There were papers scattered everywhere in the office, ship lists, names of nakhodas, customs payments, cargo manifests. I would have to introduce some kind of system here, but not today. The Sheik has asked me for details about our trade relations with Mombasa. About how many of our ships go to Mombasa. How many of their ships come to us. About the customs dues levied by them. I think the sheik wants to reduce our dealings with the Mombasans.

The three of you are experienced in these matters. Why don't the three of you discuss how we should prepare this statement, while I look at these reports, I told my colleagues.

It took me some time to read the various reports, and put them together.

Then I wrote down my own report. Two, really. A long one about what happened in Mombasa after the arrival of the stranger ships. It was meant for the eyes of our Sheik who would decide on some form of action, after reading it to the Malindi council. The other report, a brief one, was for the eyes of the Sheik only. About a strange rumor that I picked up from the discarded bundle of papers.

What happened at Mombasa.
My report based on the reports of our Malindi agents

The Mombasan council determined that they would trick the Christians and capture the three ships and their guns. The agents at Kilwa had supplied information about the Christian guns. The pilot who had escaped had said that each ship had guns and cannon, many of them stowed below deck and set up only when the enemy was sighted. And there were other firearms, he did not know how many. They also had crossbows, spears, half pikes, axes and swords.

It was therefore decided to use trickery not force. *Istanbuli*, the only cannon the Mombasans had, bought from the Ottomans, was hidden under cut green branches, so that it couldn't be seen from the channel. All ships had to remain moored in the harbor, and were under strict orders not to weigh anchor and sail away. All ship captains were ordered to dress their ships with gay flags and streamers. The auspicious green of welcome fluttered from the mast tops of every ship, even though the month of Ramadan had passed.

On the afternoon of the day after Friday, the Christian ships ventured slowly, cautiously, into the outer harbor of Mombasa, headed by the smallest of the three ships, which took soundings frequently. Deliberately, no boat was sent to greet them, or to challenge them.

Keep them guessing, suggested one adviser to the Sheik of Mombasa. The not knowing will make them tense. They'll experience relief when we welcome them.

At midnight, eighty Mombasans, twelve of them belonging to the bodyguard of the Sheik, crowded into a *mtepe*, and were rowed toward the Christian ships. They carried lit torches and flaming brands. They waved their daggers. Some brandished swords. They yelled and screamed, banged drums and played on trumpets as they approached. It was a chaos of sound.

Suddenly, a cannon thundered, and belched forth fire and smoke over the *mtepe*.

There was a sudden silence, except for the sounds of rowing. That too stopped.

No one was hurt.

The Mombasans realized then that a blank had been fired. It was a warning, not a challenge.

The voice of the chief kaputan roared into the night, shouting words in a language they could not understand.

Then came the interpreter's voice in Arabic.

Why have you come at this time, at midnight.

The Sultan of Mombasa greets the chief kaputan, and would like to welcome him, said the interpreter. Can we come and deliver the sultan's greetings. We could not come earlier. We had to perform our religious services.

Only four of you can come aboard, said the chief kaputan.

Four Mombasans, two nobles and two bodyguards, all with daggers in their waistbands, greeted the chief kaputan with salaams.

The two nobles conveyed the greetings of the Sultan in a formal speech in high Arabic, which the Portuguese interpreter found difficult to relay to his people. The two bodyguards, accompanied by the Mozambique pilot, wandered about on the deck, admiring the rigging and the fittings and pretending to ignore the four cannon, two on the bow, the other two on the stern. The four left after an hour.

Next day two men, dressed in long white robes, conveyed the Sultan's gifts. They wore four inch gold crosses on silver chains around their necks. The crosses, made overnight by goldsmiths, had been based on descriptions given by the nobles of the gold cross worn by the chief kaputan. The Sultan had also sent a fattailed sheep, a quantity of lemons and oranges, and sticks of sugarcane. Also, a thick ring of gold as a pledge of good faith.

No one would hurt a hair of their heads while they were in Mombasa. They would be supplied with all their needs.

Are you Christians, the two men were asked by the strangers.

Yes, they said.

They were forbidden to say anything else, the two men said. They pretended they could not speak Arabic.

The chief kaputan sent the Sultan a necklace of pink transparent coral beads, and said that he and his ships would enter Mombasa harbor the next day.

That same day four nobles of great distinction came to courteously escort two Christian nobles to Mombasa, so that they could approve the arrangements for the welcome ceremony.

The two Christians were greeted at the landing by a large crowd that accompanied them with loud acclamations and rejoicing, upto the gates of the Sultan's palace in the center of the city. They were led through four imposing ornamented doors, each guarded by a doorkeeper with a drawn sword, to the Sultan who received them graciously, and ordered that they should be shown the city, especially the Christian quarter.

They admired the clean whitewashed two storied houses, the gardens with fruit trees. They were taken to the supposedly Christian section of Mombasa, where a small group of South Indians lived. They were shown a cross that decorated the wall of a Christian house. They didn't look very closely, for they didn't notice that the cross had been freshly painted on the wall. They were given a paper with a cross on it, but were not allowed to talk to anyone. Then they were sent back with samples of pepper and cloves, and informed that they could load their ships with these items.

The Sultan of Mombasa and his council rejoiced greatly. All was set. They were ready to capture the ships as soon as they came into the inner harbor. They would then capture the guns. With these, Mombasa would conquer Malindi, dominate trade, and be masters of all the port cities of the Sawahil. All were tense. The excitement was almost unbearable.

On the morning of the next day, twenty Mombasans went to lead the ships in. A harbor pilot was sent to guide the small ship, which would not be too difficult to capture. The others boarded the kaputan's ship, after tying their *mtepe* to its stern. The chief kaputan stood on the top deck to direct operations. Sails were shaken out, anchors raised, but the sails did not catch the wind, and the ship would not respond. It began to drift toward some shoals and sandbanks. The pilot from Mozambique wailed out a warning. But the ship swung around and lurched against her sister ship that was following her. The chief kaputan bellowed an order to let go anchors. The captain of the other ship yelled at his men. Whistles were blown. The sailors rushed into action. There was much confusion everywhere.

One of the Mombasans thought that the plot was discovered. He panicked and led the scramble into the *mtepe*, which hastily cast off. They were able to pick up the two pilots, who managed to escape by flinging themselves over the side into the water.

The Mombasans thought that the Christians had somehow come to know what was intended. That it was just an accident was confirmed later, when they rescued one of the prisoners from Mozambique from the water. Both had been tortured till they revealed the Mombasan plan of action, about which the Christians had known nothing. Boiling oil had been allowed to fall drop by lingering drop on the bare skin of their inner thighs. They had been then bound hand and foot, and flung on deck. Both managed to throw themselves over the side. The one who had somehow freed his hands was rescued, the other drowned.

There was no time to lose. A direct attack was out of question, and the ships might decide to move out when the tide turned. The best divers in Mombasa were ordered to plunge into the water at midnight, and cut the anchor cables of two ships, but not that of the chief kaputan who would probably be on the lookout himself. The ships would surely run aground into shoals and be stranded.

The divers were expert, and swam under water like fish. They had managed to swarm up the side of the bigger ship in order to cut the rigging and had almost sawed through the anchor cable of the smaller ship when one of the Christian dogs, some said it was the one who had picked up the frangipani blossom in the city, raised the alarm. All the divers somehow managed to escape. The infidels stayed on for two more days hoping in vain to get a pilot to guide them. They departed in a hurry, abandoning a huge anchor from the chief kaputan's ship, which our divers hauled up and brought into port. It looked like a torture machine devised by an Ifrit from hell.

One of our agents added this note. Do not underestimate the cleverness of these accursed Christians, these men from Portugal.

End of the Mombasa report

I sealed the Mombasa report and set it aside.

Then I noted on another sheet of paper.

The following report by one of our agents was discarded by someone in this office. The Mombasans were, the report said, on the point of confiscating the cargo of all Malindi ships in their harbor, if the increased tribute was not paid. They postponed taking this action, because of the arrival of the Portuguese ships.

I folded the paper, sealed it with lac, and wrote
For the eyes of the Sheik of Malindi only.

I delivered both reports to the Sheik personally, just before he retired for his siesta.

I walked down the steps that led down to the seafront, and looked out at the bay that was covered by a shimmering haze of midday heat.

The stranger ships were a white blur in the distance. They would find it difficult to send a boat with a message to us today, as the tide was on its way out. The seafront was deserted. Shops and offices were shut. Everyone had gone home to rest in the dark cool of their inner rooms. away from the burning humid heat. Life in Malindi, and all along the Sawahil, begins before sunrise, goes on briskly till midday, slows to a stop, then begins again in the evening, and ends early in the night.

Abdul was waiting for me when I walked into my office. He had brought me some food.

She wanted to come, Abdul said. But Ratna had said she should not go out in the midday sun.

I was hungry. I finished the meal, and drank the cool water of the *madafu.*

She sent this one specially for you, Abdul said, slicing off the green top of the second madafu. This mulmul sheet too.

Go back when it is evening, I told Abdul. It's too hot to walk back now.

He let down the palm frond awning of the window in my office, so that it was dark and cool when I lay down on the carpet, and drew the mulmul sheet over my legs. Usha knew I liked a light covering even when it was hot. I closed my eyes, but my ears were awake, awake to the soft sounds of the outgoing tide and to the occasional clamor of the neighboring crows in the casuarina tree on the hillside.

Abdul woke me up, slowly raising the palmfrond covering to let in a warm breeze. People were up and about. Shops and offices were crowded again. The stranger ships had not drawn nearer. They rode at anchor in the distance, each ship flying a colored flag from its mast top. The young sheik had sent me a message, that he would like my presence at a meeting of the Malindi council. I splashed some water on my face.

The members of the council took their time to get to the palace after their midday siesta. They grumbled, because their *punkahwallas* who fanned them as they sat, were not allowed in the meeting hall today. The young sheik was impatient. One of his wives was a daughter of Bwana Mataka, who was the chief of the council and his principal adviser. He wanted to take action, but did not know what action to take. The regent would have liked to dismiss the council, and act on his own. But his father had instilled in him an awareness of the religious law of Islam which restricts the authority of the ruler.

The council did not know anything about fighting and war. They wanted to know when Bwana Mataka would be rescued. Why the delay. Why not surround the stranger ships, and kill the infidel dogs.

The young sheik asked a simple question.

Were they quite sure that Bwana Mataka was on one of the stranger ships.

The council fell silent.

He then read out my report of the happenings at Mombasa, and called for suggestions and comments. There were none.

What shall we do, someone asked.

The young sheik referred to my report and read out, once again, slowly and deliberately, the details about the cannons and the bombards carried by the stranger ships.

What we have to do, he said, is to do nothing. We have to wait for the Christians to make a move first.

He was about to dismiss the council, when a message was handed to him. It was from Bwana Mataka's chief assistant, with news about what happened when his two *sambuks* were returning to Malindi.

They had rounded a headland, and were sailing down the coast with the wind at the back when they saw strange ships bearing down on them with loud cries of *malemo, malemo*. The ship with the lateen sails overtook the *sambuk* in which Bwana Mataka and his young wife were, and captured it. It was laden with gold and jewels.

The other *sambuk*, loaded with provisions and some cloth, was able to escape and took refuge in a reef studded river mouth, where it could not be pursued by the Portuguese.

Weh, alas, wailed Bwana Mataka's son, who was one of the council members. He will be murdered. I told my father he shouldn't get married again.

Patience, the young sheik said, we will wait and see.

To me he said, we will talk about your second report tomorrow.

I had a refreshing bath at a well in the Silversands compound a hundred paces from the seafront. The water of Malindi is cooler, but not as sweet as that of Lamu. After our evening meal, Usha and Ratna, with Mian Mazlum and me in front as convention demands, went for a short stroll along the beach when it was dusk. When we got back, the children had gone home. We picked our way through the play area, past the bats and balls, toy bows and arrows, the stone horse, past the swings and slides and even a small merry go round, to the rocky promontory.

Why don't you and Usha go and sit on the rocks there, said Ratna, I want to have a talk with my husband about buying a house in Malindi.

She wanted us to be alone together, Usha said.

Usha leaned against my shoulder, and we held hands in the dark, silent, not knowing what to say. I had so many questions I wanted to ask. About how she was feeling. About the baby. About names. About the baby clothes she was making. But I didn't ask any. We sat in silence, holding hands, and looking at the bluedark sky and the bluedark sea. Till Ratna and Mian Mazlum came to take us back.

I woke up late next morning, an hour after the muezzin's call to prayer.

Usha and I had made love four times that night, and I felt relaxed and completely happy. Usha brought me a cup of hot black coffee.

Wait, she said, I'll be back.

I looked out of the window at the ships riding at anchor, the slanting morning sunlight accentuating the black of their hulls. Our room was bare. There were no ornamental plates on display in the wallniches. The walls were naked. No carpets hung from the protruding wallpegs. They were probably stored in coffers, to protect them from the increasing humidity. The monsoon would break soon.

But it felt like home.

Usha brought me another cup of coffee, and a brownflecked chapati on a bluegreen Chinese celadon plate.

That's beautiful, I said.

Celadon ware of exquisite design was always used to serve food in the households of the Sawahil nobles. A sign of wealth, it also indicated that the food contained no poison. It was believed that poison would make celadon crack.

It's exquisite, I said.

The chapati, Usha asked.

I looked at the chapati. It had an odd elongated shape.

I don't think it's exquisite, she laughed. Even though it is the first chapati I made with my own hands. Ratna is teaching me to cook. I'll learn how to cook meat for you, even though I will not be able to taste the dish.

No, I said, you won't. I'll become a vegetarian instead.

There were shouts from the beach. I could see a boat being lowered from one of the stranger ships.

All along the seafront people were clamoring and pointing to the boat. By the time I got to my office, the boat had reached close to the outer reefs. Then it withdrew, leaving someone behind on a sandbank. He began waving his arms.

The crowd was silent, then it shouted, Bwana Mataka, Bwana Mataka.

I immediately ordered a *parao* with two rowers who had to row against the tide to go to the sandbank. The sheik himself came down the steps. Bwana Mataka stepped out of the *parao*, carefully avoiding a puddle, holding his long white cloak, immaculately clean, away from the ground.

Tall, dignified, a black cap on his head, he had commanding eyes, black, piercing, Persian. Not a hair of his white oblong beard was out of place. His nose was not aquiline but slightly broad, hinting at an African strain in his ancestry.

The crowd welcomed him with acclamations of joy as the young sheik greeted him with a double embrace. I could see Bwana Mataka's long fingers and soft white palms. There was affection in his embrace of the young sheik.

The strangers will not harm us, said Bwana Mataka.

My son, I want a bath first, the Bwana stated calmly, not offering any explanations.

Later, after a leisurely bath, after eating a hearty meal, stretched out luxuriously on a couch covered with a white Isfahani carpet, wearing flowing white pyjamas, a white cloak thrown carelessly over his shoulders, a toothpick held between thumb and forefinger, he told us what happened. Only the young sheik and I were with him in the room. His friends and wellwishers, and some members of the council were made to wait in the anteroom.

Bwana Mataka's story

As soon as we saw the strange ships, we turned at once toward the rivermouth, he said. But the smaller stranger ship with the lateen sails raced ahead to our left, and cut us off. They were fully armed. Their crossbows were at the ready. The men were armed with swords and half pikes and swivel guns. We had nothing.

Not even, Bwana Mataka stopped and examined his fingers then continued, not even a toothpick to defend ourselves with.

The other *sambuk*, lightly loaded, veered around quickly, and managed to escape upriver.

Stop, they shouted, don't be afraid.

The voice of an interpreter cried out from one of the ships, we won't harm you.

I stood in front of the *dabusa* door with folded arms, prepared to die.

My men were terrified. They had never seen pirates like these before. They jumped into the water to escape. Strangely the strangers did not hurl down any weapons on our deck. Instead, they helped our men out of the water, and rescued those who got into trouble because of the swift river current.

The men from the small ship boarded my *sambuk*, but did not harm anyone. One of them wanted to enter the dabusa, but I stood firm near the door with my arms crossed. A halfpike was pointed at my chest, but I refused to step away. At that moment a nobleman, who came aboard, gave an order, and the half pike was withdrawn. He had a firm voice with a power all its own, which the interpreter could not convey.

May I ask, senhor, what is in that cabin. Do you have any guns, the nobleman asked me.

The largest of the three ships, with its banner flying from the mast top, now drew close by.

Paulo, roared a man with a black square beard, from its deck.

I could not understand what the man with the beard said. But Paulo, the nobleman in front of me, said *na da, na da*, which, I presume, meant no, no.

Paulo gently repeated his question to me, adding this time, does your cabin contain your holy book, your gold, your jewels, your most prized possession. We will not take anything from the cabin except guns, which we must confiscate.

Paulo's voice came from his heart. I knew instinctively I could trust him.

Yes, I told Paulo, my most prized possession is in there, my wife.

I opened the *dabusa* door, and out darted my unpierced pearl, my little Shirin. She clung to me tightly, and clasped me round the waist with her delicate arms.

I don't want to be inside there, she said looking pleadingly into my eyes. It's so dark there, I want to play in the sun.

She's a gazelle, my Shirin. She was dressed in pink silk. She wore the gold filigree bangles I had given her at the time of our marriage, but she didn't have a face veil on. An innocent, she wasn't afraid of the stares of the men around us. Her attendants covered from head to foot in *buibuis*, edged slowly out of the cabin.

May we inspect the cabin, senhor, asked Paulo.

They found no guns.

Thank you, senhor. Your wives can go in now, but your daughter can play on the deck. No one will harm her.

The interpreter translated these words most reluctantly. Then he whispered to Paulo, who looked at me as if he was sorry. Someone, perhaps another interpreter, whispered to the men around us. They burst out laughing. But one look from Paulo, and they fell quiet. Shirin laughed too, she didn't know why. She kept dancing all around me.

These Christians, they're ignorant. What do they know about the customs and conventions of our society. I stood firm and erect, with my arms crossed.

The gold and the jewels in the *dabusa* were untouched, and they tied my *sambuk* to Paulo's ship.

Paulo and I had long talks on the two nights, when the ships dropped anchor on the way to Malindi. My pilot showed them the way along the coast, but he was not a deep ocean pilot, and was not confident enough to guide them at night.

Paulo told me about the treachery of the Mombasans. We are looking for Preste Jan, he told me, a powerful Christian king who rules somewhere in Africa. I had never heard of such a king, even though I have often traveled deep into Africa for the purposes of trade.

We come in peace. We are on our way to India, to Calicut, Paulo said, to buy spices and load our ships. But we cannot find a pilot to guide us there.

All day I thought about what Paulo had said, and the next night I told him they would be welcome in Malindi.

I am the chief of the Malindi council, I said. Our young sheik, he is my soninlaw, has royal Persian blood in his veins.

Paulo did not seem impressed. But when I told him that, unlike the Sheik of Mombasa, you, my soninlaw, the Sheik of Malindi, are a man of honor who always keeps his word, Paulo listened very carefully.

The sheik will welcome you, I told Paulo. He will provide you with the best of pilots to take you across the Bahr-i-Hind to India.

Paulo conferred for a while with the black bearded chief kaputan, who came, that night, to visit my *sambuk*. He stood aloof. He had a slight limp, and did not take part in our conversation. He has an arrogant voice. He does not trust people, is restless and impatient. Who would believe it, that Paulo and Vasco da Gama are brothers. Paulo is the only one who can calm Vasco da Gama down. With soft words, Paulo convinced his younger brother that they should trust me, and that the three ships should put in at Malindi.

I wanted to be set down in Malindi in the morning after they dropped anchor here. But Vasco da Gama insisted on waiting for a day. He wanted to find out whether the Malindians would launch a treacherous attack on his ships. Paulo agreed to wait, but only because the next day was a special day for them, a holy day. Easter Sunday, he called it.

Let us offer prayers of peace and thanks, Bwana Mataka said. My son, did you hear them yesterday singing their prayers.

But your wife, is she safe. How did they treat her, interrupted the young sheik.

She's safe, my butterfly, completely safe. She loved to chatter to Paulo, who pretended to understand what she was saying.

She called him father, Bwana Mataka said.

And he laughed loudly.

Paulo wanted to send her with me, but brother Vasco would not agree. I promised my Shirin I would return this evening for her, and I told Paulo I would bring him word about the pilots.

End of Bwana Mataka's story

It was now an hour before midday.

The people in the anteroom were noisy and impatient to see Bwana Mataka. The sheik ordered his servants to admit only members of the council, one by one, to welcome the Bwana and pay him their respects. The sheik and I stood at the window looking at the Portuguese ships. There was a slight breeze, but the noonday glare was intense.

The young sheik was thinking out aloud.

Let's help them and make friends with them. Then we will not need to get together a fighting force. Our problems with Mombasa will be solved. I myself feel the need for a bath now.

He signaled to a servant, who let down the window awning.

Bwana Mataka, he announced to the noisy crowd, has to rest now. Early this evening he has to return to the ships.

He did not offer the council any explanations.

Ahmadji, he whispered to me, kindly arrange to have a boat ready for Bwana Mataka.

In the evening, when the tide turned, a low wide boat with eight rowers was ready at the landing dock next to the palace steps. Three plump, fat tailed sheep were dragged, reluctant and bleating, into the boat. The young sheik, wisely I thought, decided not to send any more gifts at this time. Servants from Bwana Mataka's household set down a coffer of clothes, and three large covered copper vessels of pungent smelling spicy food for the *sambuk* crew.

Bwana Mataka stepped into the barge with two packages of *halwah* gaily wrapped in red and blue Cambay muslin.

One is for my bulbul, he told us, my little princess, my Shirin. The other is for my friend Paulo, who will surely give it to his brother. Perhaps it will sweeten Vasco da Gama's tongue.

Just before Bwana Mataka gave the sheik a farewell embrace, I suggested that the three stranger ships cross the bar the next day, and anchor close to the seafront. A young nobleman and a distant cousin of the Sheik, both in ceremonial green cloaks, accompanied the Bwana. They returned a little before dark, for the tide was against them, bearing strange presents.

A drab brown woolen waistcoat. Two strings of coral beads of the kind tied around the necks of Malindi babies. Three polished brass washbasins. A strange three cornered hat which I've never seen before. Some bells of the kind tied round the necks of cows. And two pieces of striped cotton stuff of the type usually worn by African tribals.

Very strange presents to offer a sheik. No wonder the Mozambikan sheik had snorted his contempt. The Christians were either stupid or ignorant. Or else they wanted to insult the young sheik. Who wisely refused to jump to immediate conclusions.

Let's wait and see, Ahmadji, he said. Could you prepare a list of pilots who would be willing to sail to India.

The young sheik was a good organizer. He planned ahead.

I walked back in the dark along the seashore to Silversands. It would take me three weeks to establish order in the office. I had sent word through my colleagues to all available pilots to meet me in the office tomorrow. I had also arranged for a boat with a local pilot to direct the stranger ships to a place in the bay, where they could anchor safely.

One of my colleagues, Lambu, had stayed on to help me with the report about our trade and shipping relations with Mombasa.

I used to live there, Lambu said, in Mombasa, till smallpox took away my whole family. I have no one to go back to, he said, I can stay as late as you want.

I felt sorry for him. Another wanderer, I thought.

It's getting dark, Lambu said. Shall I accompany you to Silversands.

No, thank you, I said, walking down the steps to the seafront.

He stood, a tall, lonely figure, in the shadow of the town wall, when I left him. He lacked a home. I was touched, I liked his human concern.

Malindi would be home for Usha and me now. Mian Mazlum had taken Ratna and Usha to look at a house very close to Silversands. It needed to be repaired and whitewashed. Usha did not like it because it was not on the beach. She wanted me to take a look at it when I had the time.

I smiled, as I walked through the children's deserted playground, stopped near the stone horse, and placed my hand on its neck. Perhaps, perhaps my son would play here. We hadn't yet talked about a name for him. Him, I thought. Why not her.

Next morning, early, we dispatched a boat, with an auspicious green flag on its mast top, to a spot two bow lengths away, almost directly in front of the low blackrock promontory. I knew the place was safe and sheltered. Other ships could not anchor nearby. And the pilots of the stranger ships and the chief kaputan would appreciate the fact that their ships could easily cross the bar and escape, if there was any danger of attack.

They were shrewder than I realized. Just as our local pilot was setting forth, the chief kaputan's longboat entered the bay. They took frequent soundings and, our pilot said this with contempt, noted down the readings painstakingly on paper. They even, he said, set down every reef, every shoal, every sandbank, every protruding rock on the sketch they made of our bay.

I saw it with my own two eyes, our pilot said. A waste of time, he shook his head pityingly, to spend over two hours scratching this information on paper. They agreed that the place we had chosen was the best place to drop anchor.

I did not laugh.

My pilot sensibility was beginning to have a deep respect for the ship tactics of these strangers. Their ships were larger than ours, stronger. They had, though I had not seen them, cannons and bombards stowed out of sight in the hold and brought on deck only when needed. Some of their sails, unlike ours, were square and huge, and could perhaps generate more wind power. They carefully plotted their position on a chart.

They had fearlessly penetrated what Masudi calls the green sea of darkness beyond *al-Komr*, the white mountains, and entered our waters. They had penetrated our ocean world with their black ships. They had burst through the sea of shadows with its mad waves into al Muhit, the encompassing. What will happen, I asked myself. I can usually tell the approach of a tufan. Even on a day that is blue and clear except for three distant clouds. My eye notes the shades of color. My hair on my arms tingles, my nose detects an arrow like smell. A tufan is on its way.

Through the window of my office I could see the ships with their black hulls sail slowly, in a straight line, looking majestic, to anchor in our bay. They positioned themselves carefully. Any boat coming towards them would be in the line of their gunfire. Other ships, that had come from Aden and Maskat and Ormuz and had taken refuge in the bays nearby, had somehow received word that it was now safe to enter Malindi bay. They anchored on the left, opposite the palace, away from the Christian ships. Each ship was drummed into harbor, and greeted and welcomed with conches and trumpets. The bay was now full of ships. There was rejoicing on the waterfront, a festive air. People were happy and embraced each other. The nakhodas drifted into the office to register their ships. My three colleagues were kept busy.

Only five of the twenty nakhodas I had expected came to my office. They greeted me, each one of them, and then sat on the carpet around my low table. They all knew me, not personally, but by reputation. There was eagerness in their eyes, a little anxiety too. They knew what was expected of them but they wanted me to begin. I tried to explain the terms that would be offered.

The Christians, I began, need a pilot to guide them to Calicut. They will pay for his services.

When, when would they want to sail, asked the nakhoda on my right. His eyes were liquid black with excitement. I am sorry, I interrupted you, sir.

My friends, the nakhoda continued in a high pitched but pleasant voice, want me to speak for them. My only qualification is that I have read and reread, and I keep rereading your *Kitab al-Fawa`id*, the finest pilot book ever written for nakhodas. Though I don't understand the theory of navigation by stars.

Wah, wah, said the others, slapping their knees in appreciation of my pilot guide.

He meant it. I believed him. It wasn't just flattery.

Thank you, I said. We do not know when exactly they will sail, probably in a few days. Nor do we know how much they will pay.

We have agreed, all five of us, the young nakhoda said, that the pilot should be paid one hundred and fifty miticals for his services. Half here in Malindi, the other half in Calicut. We have taken two things into account. First, it is not the right season for sailing to India. Secondly.

The nakhoda went on and on. His name was Maimun ibn Khalil. He was young, not quite sure of himself. He was longwinded. He reminded me of myself at twentytwo. His explanations were elaborate. As a pilot I knew how dangerous a voyage it would be. The ships would reach Calicut towards the end of May, when low elephant clouds blacken the skies and fierce monsoon winds lash the Malabar coast, and the ports are declared *al-ghalq*.

His second observation shocked me considerably.

The religious teachers would condemn any pilot who dared to guide the infidel dogs to India. Such a pilot would be disloyal to all the merchants of Malindi, a betrayer of our faith, a traitor to Islam. I ask you, Ahmad ibn Madjid, sir, whether one's reputation will not be damaged so that no Muslim trader would make use of the services of that nakhoda.

Abdul came in at that moment. The sheik wanted to see me.

I thanked the five nakhodas.

I'll send for you later, I said.

The young sheik handed me a letter. The paper was of marbled blue and white, incense treated. The *tughra* at the top was a complex but lopsided monogram circle of deepgold.

The letter from the Sultan of Mombasa

His Royal Eminence, the great Lord and Emir, the magnificent Sultan of the powerful city kingdom of Mombasa, Lord of the Sawahil and all the cities therein, deign to greet you, our vassal, sheik of Malindi, from whom no tribute has as yet been received.

We inform you that the ships of the Christians, may they be curst to hell, fled from our royal city Mombasa, a name which signifies a place of war, before we could destroy them. They will seek refuge in your insignificant harbor, having escaped from our spacious anchorage where many vessels from Malindi are moored. No food, or water, or pilots, should be provided to these infidels. Punishment will be swift and dire.

This warning was written down in the month of April of the year of the world 1498, three years from the beginning of the tenth century of the Hegira.

End of the Sultan's letter

You notice, Ahmadji, the young sheik said, how the mighty Lord cannot yet handle the jargon of sultanship. The list of his titles doesn't sound pompously right. The Swahili name for his city is *Mvita*, which merely describes its location as a hidden place. Some calligraphist has hastily put together his *tughra*signature.

And the sultan has used the familiar you instead of the formal thou.

But, in the light of your second report, Ahmadji, the veiled threat in the references to punishment, and to the vessels of Malindi should be paid attention to.

I shall send word to our nakhodas to slip out of Mombasa harbor at night and escape, I said.

What of the warning, Ahmadji, what do you think, asked the young sheik. Don't you think we should defy this socalled Royal Eminence, this selfproclaimed Lord of the Sawahil. I did not say anything. People do not really want answers to some questions they ask. I knew the sheik had already made up his mind. The Malindi council would confirm his decision in the evening.

Through the window we could see the Christians busily repainting the hulls of their ships. Three colored flags fluttered gaily from their mast tops.

We must welcome our guests in a fitting manner, said the young sheik.

After the midday siesta, after the council meeting, word was sent round that there would be a grand reception for the visitors. The council responded enthusiastically to the young sheik's decision that the whole city, especially the waterfront, should display its welcome. The next two days were declared official holidays. No expense was spared. The shopkeepers contributed toward the decorations of their section of the city. Houses were whitewashed, streets were cleaned of rubbish, and sprinkled with water to keep down the dust. Merchants and traders assumed responsibility for the seafront. Cloths of gold and red and green hung down the black city walls facing the sea. Flags and banners and streamers began to appear everywhere. They flew from the palace tower, they flapped all around the city wall, large green ones flew from the tops of the pillar tombs at both ends of the seafront, they flew from the masttops of all the ships in the bay, carpets were laid out on the decks of ships and down their sides fluttered colorful cotton spreads.

Not to be outdone, the Christians spent all evening getting their ships ready. I noticed that they spent as much time tightening their rigging, repairing their sails and even testing the drop of their anchors, as they did on decorating their ships.

From my office window I had an artist's view of Malindi bay. Our ships on the left were a confused huddle of many bright colors. Black and geometrical cross blocks of red boldly dominated the other section of the bay. A boat carrying three fat tailed sheep, some plump hens, vegetables, and samples of cloves, cumin, ginger, cinnamon, and cardamon, moved slowly toward their section. The boat carried a message too.

Tomorrow the sheik would come in a *zavra* to meet the kaputan major.

Vasco da Gama sent back a terse reply. They could meet halfway, after dinner.

Bwana Mataka sent a note saying that the Christians ate their big hot meal an hour before noon.

The separate notes my colleagues had jotted down, when I put them together, revealed disturbing trends in Malindi trade and shipping. There was a steady drop in customs revenues. Many merchants had gradually deserted Malindi for Mombasa as their base of operations. The nakhodas and the names of their ships had been removed from the ship registers. Anchorage depths not adequate, the nakhodas had noted. Dredging needed, was one terse comment. The name Malindi is a mistake, one wit wrote, this port is no longer a deep channel.

No action had been taken. No one had informed the sheik. The nakhodas had been regulars, familiar with the soundings of the bay. Now they would just touch at Malindi for a day or two to pick up cargo and leave. For the hinterland of Malindi was rich in ivory and gum copal and leopard skins. Because of the reassuring presence of Bwana Mataka, the tribals from the *nyika* flocked to the neighbouring markets and fairs with their goods. The export trade of Malindi was still thriving.

Why was the sheik not informed that the bay needed dredging, I asked Lambu.

It was late in the evening, and he was helping me shut down the office, after we had received word that the sheik's barge was decorated and ready.

I didn't pay any attention at all to those comments from disgruntled nakhodas, Lambu said.

I knew it was Lambu who was in charge of keeping a list of nakhodas who brought in their ships to Malindi. Useless to blame anyone now, I thought, the whole system has to be changed.

We walked along the seafront, Lambu and I, toward Silversands. At the widest stretch of the shore mangrove poles, squared, polished, and unusually straight, were stacked together next to a deep hole in the sand.

For the entertainment the sheik has planned, Lambu explained.

Just before we reached the children's playarea, Lambu turned abruptly and, without saying goodbye, hurried away as if in sudden fright. It was quite dark now. I thought the stone horse moved slightly.

A black shadow detached itself, and, completely *cabaya* covered, came toward me. I awaited the poisoned arrow.

Usha, my heart cried out. My mind stopped. *Samsāra* roared away into the distance. And then there was only a distinct heartbeat waiting for time to stop.

It's Kochama, sir, I heard.

The world and my I came roaring back, flooding my being. I stood very still.

Mian Mazlum, my teacher, told me you would return this way, said Kochama.

I walked slowly, deliberately, to the horse. I was in a state of shock. Its cold stoneness steadied me. My voice wouldn't come back. I felt weak

Kochama went on talking, telling me about his father, about the house Mian Mazlum had rented for him in Lamu. He seemed to have forgotten all about Layla. He talked about his wife and his young son.

Perhaps my son will become a nakhoda, Kochama said.

Your boat, it is safe, he told me.

Thank you, I managed to bring out.

I had to come to Malindi, Kochama said. I have to get the *siwas* ready for the welcoming ceremony.

Usha was waiting for me.

As soon as I stepped inside, she sensed that something was wrong.

Have a warm bath, she said, you'll be able to sleep better.

No, I said.

She served me the meal with her own hands. I tried to lift the food to my mouth. Usha saw I could not, but she did not coax me to eat.

She lifted the bowl of water to my mouth.

Drink plenty of water, she said. I'll tell Ratna you're tired. She wanted to watch Yasmin perform her tricks. Mian Mazlum is busy polishing the ivory jewelry for Bwana Mataka. They will understand.

The night was humid. I found it difficult to breathe. Usha shut the door, and put out the light. And we lay face to face, naked, it was too hot for clothes, on the cotton carpet under a mulmul sheet.

She put her small arms around me, and drew my head down to her warm breasts. Breathe deep, Ahmad mine, close your eyes, we are together now, the three of us, at home.

Comfortable against her breasts, my eyes became aware of a blackness, this time warm and alive.

My mind tried to send forth three words towards her. Time. Death. Change. But I could not say the words.

She pressed my head between her warm yielding breasts. They released a faint fragrance of incense. I could hear her heart beating, repeating a single syllable over, and over, and over again like a *mantra*.

Gently she pushed my head down, so that my lips brushed on to her belly, smooth, curved ever so slightly.

Those mind words have no real power, Usha said. Listen, my Ahmad, can you hear what she is saying.

I listened. My ear lay gently on her belly.

Yes, I said.

But I could hear only the seabreeze blow, gentle, through the window.

No, I said quickly, no, my Usha.

Only in the fifth month, Ratna says, can one hear the heartbeat. The midwife says the babe will move only in the fourth month, Usha said softly. But tonight our togetherness stirs in my womb to tell you that all shall be well. She does not know any human language yet.

Usha was utterly exhausted. She fell asleep. I covered her with two cotton sheets, and went to the window. The wind blew soft and cool from the sea. The stars shone bright and alive in the heavens. I lowered the window awning a little.

Tomorrow would be a fine day.

It was.

It was a crisp and cool morning. Ratna brought two cups of coffee each, for Mian Mazlum and me, and we then walked down to the beach. The sun had not risen yet, the sand was cool under my feet. The stone-horse looked steadily at me with his open eyes. Usha was still asleep.

Let her rest, Ratna had said, she needs the rest.

Mian Mazlum and I walked past the play things scattered all over, the bats and balls, the toy bows and arrows, past the swings and the slides. The children would enjoy themselves today. It was a holiday for them too.

Malindi bay lay covered in a light mist. The houses, the ships, were halfasleep, waiting for the sun to stir them awake. We looked out in silence at the blue waters of the bay. The mist had begun to disappear.

The cry of the muezzin sounded loud and clear over town and bay, summoning the faithful to prayer, announcing that the day had begun.

We walked back. On the way Mian Mazlum showed me the house that was available for rent.

No, I said, definitely not.

We'll look for another house, Mian Mazlum said. Would you like to come with me to the mosque to pray, Ahmadbhai.

No, I said.

ELEVEN

*M*id-May 1509, my house, Diu, night,
the tufan rages outside,
I write furiously about Malindi in 1498,
about the ceremonies welcoming the Portuguese,
about my first look at their powerful ships,
and about what happened when the poisoned arrow struck my arm.

Mian Mazlum brought the news that the trader merchants were eager to welcome the newcomers but the religious leaders were opposed to the welcoming of the Christians.

Laza is their lot, the leaders said, blazing fire is what is reserved for them. Their chief quoted from *Surah* v. 58, if any one of you taketh them for his friends, he surely is one of them.

The areas near the mosques of the city were not decorated, and the flags on the pillar tombs nearby were ordered to be taken down. But they knew that Bwana Mataka, their benefactor, was a hostage. And they did not want to defy the young sheik who was immensely popular.

Let's wait till Friday, their religious leader said, I'll conduct the prayers and deliver the sermon myself.

Wait for the Friday oration, the followers were told.

They knew that they would not be able to influence the mood of the people.

Not today. Today everyone was wildly happy.

The men, dressed in their best clothes with bright colored handkerchiefs in their hands, went strolling through the streets of the city greeting and embracing their friends. The women wore their colorful *kangas* and their finest jewellery and went visiting the houses of their friends and relatives spending the day feasting and singing and gossiping.

There was singing in the streets, dancing too. Some of the tribals with paint streaks on their faces were allowed in the city to join the celebrations.

Children banged their toy drums and made squawking sounds on toy trumpets. They shrieked with joy in the wooden whirlabouts that were set up at every street corner. The sellers of madafus and the sherbet wallas did a brisk business.

The evening festivities were to be held all along the seafront. All Malindi would be on the beach. People poured out of the city gates onto the beach even before the rays of the evening sun had lost their sharp intensity. The beach was soon thick with the early comers and the guards found it difficult to control the people who wanted to view the royal barge. When a trumpet sounded they thronged the area near the palace to watch the young sheik ceremoniously descend the steps under his emerald green umbrella to get into the richly decorated barge.

All eyes were on the barge. Smooth planks had been laid across two wide flat bottomed boats to form a deck, with space left at the back and the front for the rowers who were hidden from view. As a boat it was inefficient. As a spectacle it was magnificent.

The deck planks too were hidden from view under a wide Shirazi carpet, bluegreen in color and bordered with gold. A couch with a covering of purple velvet and with red cushions had been placed on a dais. A slanting canopy with hangings that could be tilted around or removed, if need be, provided protection against the sun.

Two tall ivory tusks planted so that their tips touched each other at the top formed a stately entrance way.

The shrill sound of a trumpet announced that the sheik was about to step into the royal barge. The sheik waved greetings to the crowd. There was a roar of applause that began near the palace steps and continued like a rising wave all the way to Silversands. The whole beach resounded with acclamations of thunderous joy.

Just then the Christian bombards thundered forth a salvo.

I could see some Christian sailors climbing down the side of the chief kaputan's ship into their longboat. Then the second salvo was discharged, this time from the ship with lateen sails. The third salvo was fired moments later from the sister ship and I could see the chief kaputan, clad in black, descend slowly into the boat.

The crowd fell silent. Some observers then pointed out that the guns were firing blanks and that they were pointed seawards and not toward the town.

The young sheik, tall and erect, unshaken by the three salvos, stepped on to the dais and asked two of his friends to accompany him. I was glad he had heeded my advice not to overcrowd the barge. I turned to follow the city officials to the other boat that was to follow the barge.

The sheik called me by name and beckoned me to the dais. He then placed a gold chain round my neck, and made me sit on the carpet next to the notables. The officials shouted *wahs* of acclaim.

The sheik had not worn his royal insignia. His attire was just right for the summer heat, loose flowing pyjamas and a long shirt, both of ivory colored silk set off by a dark green jacket. He looked elegant and regal.

His companions wore heavy cloaks of red and of purple. Circles of sweat had already begun to appear on their necks.

The wind was gentle but not yet refreshingly cool, and the tilted canopy rustled softly. The ivory tusks did not move. They were firmly fixed on to the deck. The barge slowly made its way toward the Christian ships.

The chief kaputan's longboat moved swiftly towards us, so swiftly that the meeting would have taken place quite close to the shore. I saw the chief kaputan, his right foot placed on a boat plank, hold up his hand to slow his rowers down. Our barge drifted uncertainly towards them.

Two anchors were let drop when the barge reached the middle of the bay. The unanchored longboat, its stern shifting from side to side like the tail of a tiger about to pounce, leapt toward us. Its bow, covered all around with thick brown canvas, thrust its powerful snout through the water.

The two friends of the sheik, terrified, were about to jump into the water when I raised my right hand to reassure them. The longboat stopped suddenly a few feet away. I realized that Vasco da Gama was making his men practise tactics of boat control. The boat now lay parallel to the barge.

The chief kaputan and the young sheik greeted each other, the sheik with a courteous bow and a gracious salaam, the kaputan major, looking stern, stiffly inclining his head.

Will you very kindly honor my barge with your distinguished presence, the sheik said in highly formal Arabic.

Vasco da Gama's interpreter must have found this difficult to translate into Portuguese.

Before I left my country, stated Vasco da Gama, I swore an oath on the cross of the Order of the Knights of Christ, in the presence of my king, Emmanuel of Portugal, that I would never set foot on any foreign shore to greet any ruler until I had delivered his royal message to the ruler of Calicut.

Your king is both wise and prudent, said the sheik. But my little barge is not a foreign shore, he continued. It rides gently on the waters of this sea, that unstable element which God in his wisdom does not allow any man to rule. Besides, he said, dropping all formality of tone and speech, the barge will be more comfortable for our talks.

Vasco da Gama turned to someone who came and stood next to him. He wore a blue green cape lightly over his shoulders and a slanting black cap on his slightly bald head. He wore white pyjamas that, unlike ours, fit tightly on his legs. He had to be Paulo who had welcomed Bwana Mataka. Vasco da Gama talked excitedly to his brother. Paulo's voice was full of reassurance. He reminded me of Usha talking gently to Yasmin, calming her down when she was flustered.

The kaputan major wore leggings of black stretch material. Over a white shirt with long sleeves that were slashed, the slits revealing the contrasting black lining and a black steel plate. On his shoulders hung a long black cloak and on his head a four cornered black cap.

The Christians, I must now call them the Portuguese, wore clothes that I didn't have the exact words to describe. João it was who later provided me with a vocabulary for them. What I couldn't understand at the time was why they wore clothes that were so utterly inappropriate. The world of the monsoons with its heat and humidity requires garments that are loose, textures that can breathe, light colors that can repel the light of the sun, not black that absorbs it.

Paulo finally persuaded his brother to have the meeting on the barge. Vasco tried to get his elder brother to enter the barge before him, but Paulo would not. He stepped aside and helped his brother step into the barge.

Vasco da Gama, refusing the hand of the bargeman, stretched his right foot to climb onto the barge. I saw him wince slightly with pain. He helped Paulo across and they walked through the entrance way to the dais, Paulo stopping to admire the ivory tusks.

The sheik invited Vasco da Gama to sit on his couch, but the kaputan major declined the invitation and stood, legs apart, on the carpet. His feet were in tall boots laced at the side with the tops folded over. I could see a stain appear just below the back of his right knee under the black legging material.

The observant Paulo signaled to one of his men who unloosened the covered stern of the longboat where there was a curved chair which he carried to the dais. I noticed that under the stern cover, above which there flew the banner with a red cross in the middle, the Portuguese had concealed a gun mounted on a swivel. There was another one probably under the brown cover at the bow. The Portuguese went about well armed.

After the introductions the sheik courteously requested Paulo to sit on the carpet. Paulo tried to sit crosslegged like us, but his knees were too stiff. He gave up the effort and went and stood behind his brother's chair.

The sheik began by courteously enquiring about the kaputan major's wound, was it very painful.

What wound, said Vasco da Gama, I have a mere scratch.

I noticed the stain had spread. He was about to get up when Paulo pressed both his hands down gently on his shoulders. Paulo looked a little worried.

My brother, Paulo told the sheik, never complains. My brother and two of our mariners were attacked by some African natives and wounded with arrows. I have been using different ointments but their wounds will not heal.

Perhaps, I felt driven to speak, perhaps their arrow tips were dipped in poison.

The sheik consulted with one of his companions and told Paulo that he would send his own hakim to look at the wounds.

He is the best hakim in Malindi, the sheik said.

Vasco da Gama was growing impatient. His reddish face became redder. He stood up, legs apart, and addressed the sheik. His voice sounded harsh. He delivered a speech which the interpreter found difficult to translate for us.

My lord, the illustrious Dom Manuel, by the grace of God, King of Portugal and of the Algarves on this side and beyond the sea, in Africa Lord of Guinea, commanded me, Dom Vasco da Gama of Sines in Portugal, gentleman of the royal household, to undertake this long and perilous voyage to discover the seas and lands of India. For over eleven months now have we ventured through stormy seas never sailed before, encountered many tempests and braved many dangers to accomplish this great mission. We have arrived here despite the treachery of some evil rulers on the African coast.

We extend to thee greetings, oh Sheik of Malindi, and offer thee the hand of friendship, Vasco da Gama said.

The young sheik was overwhelmed by this torrent of words translated for him haltingly by the interpreter. He politely asked about a few things he could understand and was curious about.

Where is Portugal, the sheik enquired.

Vasco da Gama was taken aback, astonished that any civilized person did not know the whereabouts of his country. He looked down at the carpet, stroked his black beard, then turned his deep set, wide apart eyes to his brother.

Paulo pointed with his right hand towards the south.

Way way down, below Mombasa and Kilwa, past Mozambique, said Paulo softly, is the perilous cape of storms, which our former king renamed the Cape of Good Hope, beyond which, roughly eight thousand leagues up north, past the land of Guinea, lies my beloved Portugal.

I was filled with tremendous admiration for the Portuguese who had ventured across the green sea of darkness beyond Sofala in search of Ind.

What is the name of your king, asked the sheik. Could you write down his name for me.

Paulo wrote down Emmanuel on a piece of paper on which the interpreter scrawled a word in Arabic from right to left. The sheik tried to pronounce the name.

What does it mean, the sheik asked.

Emmanuel means God, he was told.

We were all horrified, a mere mortal assuming the name of the divine, what arrogance.

It had a powerful impact on the sheik, who wanted prosperity for his city and power for himself. The unjust domination of Mombasa had to be thrown off. These arrogant Portuguese with their mighty Sultan and their thunderous guns could help him.

Why did you not, the sheik asked Vasco da Gama, bombard Mombasa. At Mozambique your guns destroyed only their water cisterns.

The Mozambicans refused to give us water that God has given to all mankind. We come in peace, Paulo explained, seeking friendship. Our guns protect us against those who would destroy us. Our friend, Bwana Mataka, has told us how badly the Mombasans treated you.

My dear brother, Paulo, please let me interrupt.

Vasco da Gama got up from his chair and put his hand gently on his brother's shoulder.

He then turned to the sheik and proclaimed. My king, who is governor and administrator of the Order of the Knights of Christ, has many guns and bombards and many large ships, larger than the ones you see, that can dominate the vast seas of India. We will assist you against all your enemies.

The companions exclaimed *wahs* of rejoicing. Malindi would be safe from the attacks of Mombasa.

And how can we repay the assistance of the mighty Sultan of Portugal and help you in your voyage to Calicut. What you need shall be given to you, said the sheik.

Thank you, said Paulo, thank you for your hospitality and your welcome gifts of food. We would like to have our casks of water refilled everyday if possible. Some of our sick would like the oranges and lemons and even the sugar filled reeds you so kindly sent.

You mean the stalks of sugarcane, I said.

Thank you, sir, is that what they're called, said Paulo. They're very sweet, but very difficult to chew. Our gums have not healed. They are still swollen.

That's scurvy, I said.

At this point Vasco da Gama took over. He was businesslike.

We insist on paying for all the articles of food, Vasco da Gama stated. We will pay the fair price.

The sheik was about to speak when Vasco da Gama turned toward the three ships and raised his right hand clenched in a fist.

The chief kaputan turned around to the sheik and, with a slight bow of his head, continued.

In the name of the King of Portugal, we ask thee, great ruler of Malindi, to provide us with a pilot to guide us to Calicut. The customary payment will be made.

The sheik rose.

Here, to Malindi, the sheik said, come the best pilots of the Bahr-i-Hind. And here, on this barge, I have the most renowned of them all, Ahmad ibn Madjid, who is known as the lion of the ocean sea.

I stared down at the carpet, but stood up hastily when Paulo walked up to me to clasp my hand. I wanted to offer him a warm double embrace in the Muslim fashion, but felt a little awkward and offered him instead the distancing Hindu *namaste*, folding my hands together near my chest and bowing a little.

He is the right pilot to guide us to Calicut, said Paulo with a welcoming smile. Pray, sir, Senhor Ahmad, will you please guide our ships to Calicut.

Wait, said Vasco da Gama. When, sir pilot, will we see the Pole Star on our way from Malindi to Calicut.

My pilot sensibility resented Vasco da Gama's question which wanted to test my pilot skills. I realized that for him the sighting of the Pole Star was important as a guide. They relied on *al Jah* to take their bearings in the open sea.

I said matter of factly. On the fifth day out of Malindi on the route I chart to Calicut, the Pole Star will be seen.

Vasco da Gama, who had ignored me, cast his deepset eyes with their overhanging eyebrows on me.

The young sheik said hastily, we will get another pilot for you. Ahmad ibn Madjid is the controller of trade and shipping in Malindi. He cannot be your guide to Calicut. Ahmadji, tell them what has been arranged about the pilots.

Senhor Paulo, I said, there are five pilots who have offered their services, one of these will be your pilot. The charges will be one hundred and fifty miticals to take you safely to the Calicut roadstead. Calicut does not have a deep water harbor.

Vasco da Gama was indignant.

But but but, the kaputan said angrily, that is five times the price the pilots at Mozambique told us.

He paced up and down the dais. Paulo was more understanding.

Why, Ahmadji, Paulo asked, why is the price so high for us Portuguese.

I liked Paulo, I liked the gentle tone of his voice. To him I outlined the monsoonal system that regulates the sequential sailing patterns, the wind directions and the trade routes of the Bahr-i-Hind.

There are two sailing seasons from here to Calicut, I explained. *Musimu*, all through April, and *Demani* in August. You have missed the first season. If you begin your voyage now you will arrive in Calicut towards the end of May when the southwest monsoon has started. The clouds will be huge, black and laden with rain. The winds will blow continuously. And the seas will be extremely dangerous so that no ship can enter or leave harbor. That is why the charges are so high.

The young sheik was about to speak when we heard joyous shouts from the beach. The people waved their hands in greeting. Bwana Mataka's *sambuk* was curving its way towards the shore.

Vasco da Gama said. To mark the commencement of our friendship we have released Bwana Mataka and his ship with all his goods and valuables.

He was our honored guest, said Paulo. Would you, oh noble sheik, honor our ships with a visit.

The sheik thanked the two brothers for the release of Bwana Mataka.

Tomorrow evening, the sheik said, is the official ceremony to welcome you to Malindi. Your boat can draw up close to the seafront. You will not need to step on shore and so will not break your king's orders.

He turned to Paulo and said, We will send food for all the men of your ships tomorrow.

The sun was low in the west.

We cannot visit your ships today. But Ahmadji would like very much to row around and have a closer view of them.

I was eager to have a close look at the two larger ships. They loomed into view, huge, like black promontories, as the barge, its canopy removed, drew near. A few ships, larger than these, make the pilgrimage run to Aden and Jiddah, but they are stately, slow moving, like lazy queens ruling a world at peace.

These were packed with power. Their wood was not teak. But I could tell the wood had been seasoned. The lower hull, well caulked, had been recently covered with a double coat of tar. There were four runs of strong planking, fastened by nails not coir stitches, along the entire length of the upper hull reinforcing the decks and giving a sturdy curve to the ship.

The topmost plank at the edge of the upper deck prevented the waves from washing over it and the sailors from being swept overboard when the sea was rough. Other planks, extending horizontally through the side, supported the rigging for the foremast and the mainmast, both of which had basketlike constructions very near the top as lookouts. There was a bowsprit, much larger than the one I had fixed on the *Zephyr*, and a mast that rose out of a superstructure of two decks over the stern. Four masts on one ship. Its windpower would be tremendous with a monsoon wind at its back.

That projection that towers above us is the aftercastle, said Paulo, who had not departed with Vasco da Gama, but had courteously remained with us on the barge.

Forward, well beyond the stem, projected a high, flat forecastle. The military image was quite fitting for the castles could be used for both attack and defense. They made the ship stand higher in the water.

On the top of the mainmast flew a flag having seven castles as its border within which five shields were displayed, each one with five coins within, arranged *em aspa,* according to Paulo, in the form of a cross.

That's the royal coat of arms, Paulo said. It presents the seven Algarve cities that were captured and the five kings that were vanquished. The royal standard celebrates the birth and independence of our nation, said Paulo.

Why the five coins, I asked politely.

The coins in the center of the shield have to be counted twice, he explained. The thirty coins signify the blood money paid to Judas for the betrayal of Our Lord Jesus Christ. Some refer to the royal arms as the *Quinas*, because of the resemblance to the five of dice. For me they represent the five wounds of the Saviour, Our Lord Jesus Christ.

It didn't convey anything to me, but Paulo appeared much moved. He shut his eyes, with his right hand he touched his forehead, his chest and his two shoulders.

Paulo explained how the two large ships had been specially designed and built for this voyage. They had to navigate coastal waters like those of Mombasa and they also had to sail for long periods of time in the open sea. The sails, Paulo pointed out, were square on the main and the foremast, and triangular on the one that arose out of the aftercastle. I was profoundly interested in the cut of the furled sails, the sheik only politely so.

I didn't know it at that time but my *mu'allim* sensibility was deeply affected. For it was the moment that marked for me the advent of a new knowledge. I was suddenly equipped with a new pair of eyes that tried to look into the future.

Our barge swung toward the front of the kaputan major's ship. I estimated that the ship's beam was onethird its length. Its bow was curved, round, and it did not have a sharp keel. Its flatbottomness would allow it to maneuver up rivers to explore territory. On the high seas because of its square sail it could fly before the wind and outrun ours. Our ships can take all winds. They run best when the wind blows on the quarter.

The sheik looked up at the stem.

Up there hung a crude human figure with wings sprouting from its shoulders. It had been made of unseasoned wood, for the sea and the sal-twind had eaten into its body. It looked like a stone figure on the outside of a Hindu temple by the sea in South India. The Hindus and the Christians, unlike Muslims, bow down before idols.

Who is that creature, the sheik asked.

Is that the devil, one of the companions ventured to ask Paulo.

Paulo explained. He is San Gabriel, the angel who visited the Virgin Mary to announce the conception of the Savior. This ship sails under his special protection.

The interpreter found this almost impossible to translate.

In the discussion that followed while the barge was rowed to the *San Raphael*, Paulo's ship, the sheik's other companion, who was a *kazi*, said that the Christian Gabriel was Jibra'il, the medium of the revelation of the Qu'ran to the Prophet, may his name be forever blest.

Just before Paulo stepped on to the rope ladder to his ship, he was seized by a racking cough that lasted for a long time. He spat into the sea a glob of phlegm streaked I thought, it was twilight by then, with a little blood.

As the barge swung away aided by the tide the figure of Vasco da Gama could be seen standing on his poopdeck in black silhouette.

There were no people on the seafront as Abdul and I walked back to Silversands after I had seen to it that everything was in order for the reception tomorrow. The Malindi hakim had to be taken to the *San Raphael* early in the morning. Water arrangements had to be made.

You should have gone back, I told Abdul.

She asked me to wait for you, Abdul said.

In the distance a dimly lit lantern hung at the stern of the *San Gabriel*. Low sounds of singing drifted towards Silversands. It was a prayer song of supplication, but to whom or for what I could not tell. A couple of men were perched as lookouts on the railed basket platforms on the *San Gabriel* and the *San Raphael*.

Vasco da Gama was a shrewd commander.

I had a refreshing bath. Usha came and asked if she could be excused from serving me my food.

It won't happen again, Usha said.

It's Shirin, she said, she's been clinging to me ever since she came here. She won't talk to her attendants. Go away, she tells them, stamping her feet. The little one is frightened. She has told me everything about herself, shown me all her clothes and her jewellery. She misses her mother.

A shrill voice sounded outside, Usha, Usha.

Bwana Mataka wants to woo Shirin with gifts of ivory jewellery. Mian Mazlum and Ratna are with him. We will wait for you, my Ahmad.

The cries of Usha, Usha, grew shriller.

Layla served my meal. I ate a little rice with some pickle and yoghurt.

I stepped outside and walked to the little stone horse to drink in the night air. The night sky stretched on and on in an endless curve.

Layla was sitting outside Bwana Mataka's door with Yasmin on her shoulder when I returned.

Hullo Yasmin, I said, and tickled her throat with the nail of my forefinger. She pecked at it feebly. She looked sleepy, but cocked her head at once when she heard Usha sounds coming from inside.

Bwana Mataka's room was well ventilated. It had two windows, with white ant proof coffers of black wood edged with ivory. Ivory colored Persian carpets hanging from protruding wallpegs covered the niches in the walls where his treasures were stored.

Mian Mazlum was displaying the ivory pieces at a low oval table with cushions and pillows strewn carelessly all around the carpet. Bwana Mataka was holding out an ivory bracelet towards Shirin.

Look, my little one, isn't this beautiful, Bwana Mataka said. Let me put it on your lovely little hand.

Bwana Mataka was relaxed but looked old. His features were soft. His voice sounded sentimental. He was not the dignified person I had met at the palace.

The ivory pieces were all exquisitely carved. Necklaces, tiny pots to hold *kajal* to deepen the eyes. Others as containers for *mehndi* to color the soles of the feet purple. Anklets of many designs.

Come, my *beti*, my little one, my rosebud, the Bwana coaxed, give me your little hand.

No, no, no, said Shirin, turning to Usha and clinging to her.

Isn't it beautiful, Ratna asked Shirin.

No, no, no, Shirin said, I don't like it. I don't like any of those things. I don't like you, she sobbed, looking at Bwana Mataka and then burying her eyes in Usha's armpit.

They were too sophisticated, these ivory pieces, for Shirin. She was a child still, plucked out of her coastal home, dazed by her first experience of the sea, bewildered by her sudden marriage to an old man who could have been her grandfather.

Usha whispered into Shirin's ear.

Yes, yes, yes, cried Shirin. She laughed. She was happy. Where, where is it.

Yasmin, come, said Usha.

Yasmin flew into the room and perched on Usha's left shoulder.

Ush, ush, she said, and rubbed the side of her little head gently against Usha's cheek.

Shirin was delighted. She reached out to grab at Yasmin.

No, Usha caught her hand. No, she said firmly, no, you'll hurt Yasmin. No, or I'll take her away and she won't show you her tricks.

Ball, said Usha.

Ball, said Yasmin, and fearlessly hopped on to the table. Usha produced the ivory ball that Layla had rejected, and Yasmin began playing with it. She used her wings and her beak to roll the ball all over the table. A smart tap with her beak would send the ball rolling towards the edge, but it never got there, for Yasmin would deflect it.

Wah, wah, Usha would say, good girl. And she gave her a melon seed. Shirin danced around the table. We all joined Usha saying, wah, wah, at each clever move.

Ball, ball, Yasmin said as she rolled the ball towards Usha.

Ball, ball, said Usha as she rolled it back with her forefinger. It was great fun. We forgot we were adults and were children again, happy, sitting around the oval table. Yasmin was getting tired.

Sleep, Usha said and Yasmin hopped on to Usha's shoulder.

Yasmin would turn her head sideways.

Shirin began sobbing loudly.

Don't cry, my *beti*, Bwana Mataka said.

Let's go, said Ratna and led Usha and Shirin to the women's quarters.

The Bwana called Ratna back.

Give her this bracelet and make her wear it for tonight, he said.

He smiled at Mian Mazlum and me. There was a gleam in his eyes.

She is my pearl, Bwana Mataka said.

I have something for you and Usha, he continued. My house, the one you are now staying in, I shall allow you both to stay in it rent free for a year. Shirin loves Usha, they will be friends. Usha can be my Shirin's teacher. She is my bulbul, my unpierced pearl.

It was time to leave. Mian Mazlum stayed behind to store the ivory pieces. Usha and I, and our little one, would be together, at peace, for some time.

I thought of Shirin. Tonight would mark the end of her childhood. Ratna and Usha would have to prepare her for the marriage bed. I lay on our carpet and concentrated on the tip of my nose, refusing to let loose my imagination.

It was a long time before Usha came and lay down by my side.

She said, Shirin's attendants had to give her some sherbet laced with opium to calm her down.

We lay in each other's arms and Usha soon fell asleep. I lay awake for a very long time.

Next morning when Mian Mazlum and I were returning from the black promontory we heard screaming coming from the women's quarters.

No, no, no, the beach, I want Usha, I want Yasmin.

Shirin struggled with her attendants, broke free and ran towards us. Mian Mazlum stood still. After all she was his patron's wife. I ran and caught her hands.

The beach, the beach, Ahmadji, she said, I want to run along the beach and dip my toes in the water. I want Usha.

There were very few people on the beach.

Only for a short while, I said.

I told the attendants who were wailing and beating their foreheads to follow her. I wondered about last night.

Abdul walked with me to the office. I didn't ask him why. I knew what he would say. My Usha was worried about me. Halfway along the beach workers were setting up a long pole made up of sections tied together. It swayed slightly. Other workers were wetting down the sand to make it firm. Near the palace steps workmen were putting a platform together, the planking had been obtained from the nearby boatyard.

The city administrator and Lambu came into the office.

Two Portuguese boats have been sent, Lambu said, for provisions and water.

The administrator and I went to the landing. Huge empty barrels, some with broken staves, were being placed there, their insides smelled mouldy. They would be treated with vinegar, dried, and filled with clean water.

Don't these casks take up too much space, I asked the Portuguese supervisor.

Yes, he replied, but we need them. Some have to be repaired.

The administrator said he would make arrangements for them to buy provisions at the market price.

It was a very busy morning. The Malindi hakim with his assistant carrying his bag of medicines was dispatched in a canoe to the *San Raphael*. I told him to ask for Senhor Paulo. On my own initiative I sent some ship carpenters in one of the boats to build water tanks. They joined the planks together, stitched them with coir and caulked them with pitch in such a way that they were more water tight than the barrels. They were fitted below deck at the foot of the mainmast of the *San Raphael*. Later, watertanks were fitted into the *Berrio* but not into Vasco da Gama's *San Gabriel*.

They freed space, Paulo told me later, to take in more cargo.

Kochama came into my office with the royal *siwa* and placed it on the carpet. It had been well polished, the bronze sparkled, the ivory was mellow and transparent. Then Maimun ibn Khalil came in. He was the young pilot who had read my *Fawa 'id*.

The price will be paid, I told him, one hundred and fifty miticals. I didn't tell him that the sheik himself would pay half the amount. The sheik didn't want to haggle with Vasco da Gama. Maimun didn't look happy.

Do you want to be paid more, I asked.

No, Ahmadji, sir, he said, his eyes on the carpet. The other four pilots refuse to guide those Christian infidels to Calicut. They have been threatened. They are afraid for their families. Not even the sheik will be able to protect them. What's the use of money, the pilots told me, our lives will be in danger.

Piloting is a skill, I said. Pilots are professionals, loyal only to the oceansea.

We were both silent for a time.

What about you, I asked Maimun, are you afraid, are you willing to go with the Portuguese.

Ahmadji, he said, I don't know what to do. Forgive me, I have my wife and son here in Malindi. I will have another son soon, he added proudly. Could I let you know tomorrow evening. My wife's cousin told me he expects there will be trouble this Friday.

Forgive me, sir, Maimun said, they will label me a traitor. And he rushed out.

Mian Mazlum had told me that the religious leaders were not orthodox and that Malindi was not a religious town. It was a center for trade. It was through the medium of trade that Islam had come to the Sawahil. It was trade that had created the cities all along the coast. It was trade that created these pockets of civilization and culture, people who only wanted a certain amount of material comfort.

Of late, Mian Mazlum said, a fanatic preacher from Jiddah has denounced this desire for money as evil and demanded that the people return to their faith.

The sheik sent down a note to the office that the reception ceremony would begin a little late because it was a hot day. Bwana Mataka and I should accompany Vasco da Gama and Paulo when their boat made its way along the Malindi seafront so that the people could greet them.

Through the window poured in an overpowering aroma of *biryani* that made everyone around fiercely hungry. Three huge cauldrons were being loaded on to two boats. Baskets of oranges and lemons and figs and pieces of sugarcane were placed around the cauldrons to steady them. The captains and the officers of the ships would get special food cooked for the sheik and his family. The spiced rice and meat combination was for the sailors who had to be told not to eat the pieces of cardamon and cinnamon and the cloves in the rice. My colleagues had promised to take care of all the food arrangements.

I let down the awning in my office. Abdul had brought in a special plate of biryani sent from the sheik's kitchen. It had almonds and raisins, the rice grains were golden in color because of the saffron. Airy tissues of hammered silver, meant to be eaten, had been used as garnish. I could see the gleam of the ghee and the fat on the reddish brown chunks of meat and my hunger vanished.

I don't want it, I told Abdul.

I ate a little *dhal* and two chappatis.

The sheik has sent some clothes, Abdul said. It will be too hot for you to walk to Silversands and back. You can have a bath and change here.

I stretched myself out on the carpet.

A thunderous salvo awoke me. There was no time for a bath. I splashed some water on my face. The kaputan major was getting into his boat. A single trumpet sounded shrill and clear, and the old Sheik, clad in a velvet green cloak and seated in a chair of ivory and gold, was carried down the palace steps to the platform which was crowded with members of the city council and some city officials wearing garments of every color, except blue, the color of mourning, and the ceremonial green, worn only by the old Sheik and his son, the regent, who had on a cloak of green damask. Both sat on cushioned chairs under two royal umbrellas of crimson satin. The crowd greeted the old Sheik and his son with repeated roars of welcome. All the ships in Malindi harbor sounded their conches and beat on their drums as the Portuguese longboat drew near the steps and let down its anchors.

There was a solemn moment of silence disturbed only by the harsh cawing of the neighboring crows as the dignified *siwa* player, dressed in white with a loose black jacket, came with his sacred instrument on to the front of the stage. The *siwa* is from Persia, they say, and was brought by the first settlers here.

The musical welcoming of our guests was a strange blend of an invocation, to the spirits of the air, of a warning, to evil spirits and djinns to stay away, of joy, that our guests could come, sadness, for the inevitable departure, a pleading, to come again, and cries of benediction to wish them well. The *siwa* player drew all these moods out of this difficult instrument beginning with dark, solemn notes that seemed to spring out of the brown earth, and ending with notes that soared aloft happy to be released into infinite space. The people were quiet, the music stirred up their past and identified them with the sheik. It was their welcome too.

I shut my eyes. I must have drifted into a half sleep, for when Bwana Mataka touched my arm one of the members of the council was about to end his speech of official welcome in highly formal Arabic.

Never before in the history of mankind has the world witnessed such a covenant of love and friendship, and of concord and brotherhood. May it continue on into eternity.

Wah, wah, wah, the crowd shouted.

Isn't he a magnificent orator, said Lambu, one of my colleagues, he is truly a poet.

Vasco da Gama then rose from his chair and delivered an oration in sonorous Portuguese, announcing that the Sheik of Malindi would always have the protection of Dom Manuel, King of Portugal and of the Algarves on this side and beyond the sea, in Africa Lord of Guinea, on behalf of whom he, Vasco da Gama, swore eternal friendship between the two nations. It was a long speech. I missed most of it as Bwana Mataka and I slipped away to our boat.

We slowed our rowers and reached the back of the longboat at the end of the speech.

Not as many people as there were yesterday, said Bwana Mataka. Some members of the council have not come for the ceremony, though all the city officials are present.

He was right. The crowd was not as thick as yesterday's, perhaps because it was Friday. There was less excitement. Some women and even children seem to have stayed away. The merry go rounds and the whirlabouts weren't full at all. The sellers of madafus were quite busy and people crowded around the sherbet stalls. It was still quite hot.

There was prolonged applause at the end of the kaputan major's speech. All the people on the platform except the eighty year old sheik stood up, cried out their *wahs*, and waved their hands wildly. The sailors in the longboat yelled out wildly in Portuguese, and their cries were taken up by the three ships so that the whole bay shook with sound. Out of the silence that fell arose one prolonged note from the *siwa* to signify the end of the ceremony.

We'll have to go a little faster, I said to Paulo as the longboat began to make its way toward Silversands. The low sun began sinking in the west. The crowd was beginning to thin. Even the clowns running along the water's edge, jumping and somersaulting, couldn't keep them. Only when they heard the announcement about the *kabak*archery gourd game did the people stop leaving.

They crowded into a horseshoe formation around the tall pole near the top of which was a wooden circle. At the very top was a silver gourd with a pigeon inside. Horsemen on the gallop had to shoot at the target through the circle, break the gourd to make the pigeon fly away. The silver gourd and a robe of honor would be the prize.

The lance exercises with two small boys standing on saddleless horses gracefully twirling two lances in each hand at great speed were much appreciated by the crowd and by Paulo. Then came four marksmen at a furious gallop who tried to hit the target as they passed by the pole. Two were unlucky, their horses stumbled in the ploughedup sand. The third missed the target.

The fourth gave a superb display of skill. He had almost passed the pole when he suddenly leaned back, his head resting almost on his horse's rump, and shot his arrow hitting the gourd and breaking it so that the pigeon could escape. Everyone was astonished and the *wahs* were quite loud, but not prolonged for it was getting late.

Bwana Mataka and I thanked Paulo who thanked us and asked us to convey his thanks to the sheik and his father. Vasco da Gama stood aloof. He did not react at all to the gourd game. He stood at the prow, his right foot planted firmly, defiantly, on a boat plank. Paulo said that the hakim's ointment had drawn out some pain from the wounds. His brother felt better. We wanted to go back to our boat when Paulo requested us to remain for a while.

It's cool now, he said, the wind is refreshing, I'd like to be rowed along slowly to the end of the bay.

That's my group of houses, Bwana Mataka said, that's Silversands.

How is your lovely wife Shirin, asked Paulo.

Bwana Mataka was taken aback a little. In our world men don't usually enquire about other people's wives.

She's alright, he said.

A few children were still jumping around in the play area, their mothers kept calling out for them but they did not want to go back home.

Paulo became excited when the longboat drew opposite the blackrock promontory.

That, he said, is the perfect place to erect a *padrão*.

Yes, yes, Paulo, Vasco da Gama said, yes, coming up and putting his arm around his brother's shoulders. It will proclaim the glory of Portugal and of Christendom.

The interpreter could not explain what a *padrão* was. It is a pillar cross, he said.

Is it a pillar tomb, I asked, but he did not know what I meant.

Vasco da Gama turned to Bwana Mataka. We would like to build a landmark on that black promontory as a guide for sailors.

Paulo added in a courteous voice. We do not have the time to erect it now. Please enquire if the sheik would give us permission to build it.

Perhaps, Paulo said, perhaps we could have it built on our return from India.

Vasco da Gama shouted to his rowers, let's return to our ships.

It was João who, some years later in Diu, explained what *padrões* were, inscribed pillars surmounted by crosses, he said, and why his countrymen had to erect them on the shores of Africa and India. Not just landmarks, João said, but important announcements to inform the unknown Preste João that his Christian brethren were close at hand. And they confirmed to the whole world Portuguese claims to sovereignty over territorial lands and seas by virtue of discovery and exploration.

Christian arrogance, I began.

Patience, João said, as he paced up and down on the blackrock promontory in Diu, patience, Ahmadbhai. It will all become clear provided your Muslim mind accepts the assumptions of Christian theopolitics.

I had never heard the word before. I looked puzzled. João smiled. There was an ironic gleam in his eye.

The Holy Father in Rome, which is the center of the Christian world, he began, the Pope.

Who is the Pope, I interrupted.

The Pope, my friend, by virtue of his Apostolic Power, is the spiritual head of the whole world.

João made his voice sound both pompous and artificial.

In 1493, the Pope issued a bull, *Inter Caetera Divinae*, that drew a vertical line on a map of the world put together by the papal cartographer, a line that ran down from one pole to the other, dividing all worlds, the ones discovered and the ones to be discovered, between the kings of Portugal and Spain.

I was dumbfounded.

Everything west of the line was assigned to Spain, everything to the east belonged to Portugal. Both kings had to, the bull went on, and must, cause peoples dwelling in those islands and continents to accept the Christian religion.

I was bursting with a tumult of questions.

Don't, Ahmadji, don't ask the questions you want to ask, João said. I asked those very questions during the school debate we held in Coimbra in 1494 after the Treaty of Tordesillas was signed by Portugal and Spain. That's when I coined the term, theopolitics, Ahmadji, to project the new problem that arose in our Christian world, the conflict between religious and state power. No one understood what it meant then.

Neither António Louro, my debating opponent, nor the student assembly understood the questions that haunted me when I read the papal bull in 1493, questions which I opened the debate with.

Why, I asked the assembly, and there was an ominous silence.

By what right, I demanded loudly.

Who appointed the Pope the Great Divider of our world. Many, in the audience, gasped with horror. There was an uproar. I knew the question would shock them. One did not dare question the rights of the Church.

António was a good scholastic, he never asked questions. He spouted forth the usual jargon we both had learned, all about the line of demarcation, that the Church was a divine institution, that its task was to unite man with God, that it was founded upon a Rock, that the Pope held the keys of the kingdom.

António, the Prior announced, was the winner. Many students wanted the Prior to expel me from school. The students crowded on the stage to congratulate António. I was left to myself, quite sad but defiant, only Brother Clement said he was proud of me.

Power, I remember muttering to myself, as I walked down the stage, a one word answer to all those questions, power.

João stopped pacing up and down the blackrock promontory, bent down and stared for a long time at a weed that had managed to spring out of a crevice, but did not go on to talk about power.

Your world, Ahmadbhai, he continued, all of Ethiopia, Arabia, Persia and India, has been assigned to Portugal whose King Manuel has proclaimed himself Lord of the Conquest, Navigation, and Commerce of these lands. The papal bulls support this claim.

I can see a question trembling on your tongue, Ahmadji. What are bulls, you want to ask. They are papal *khutbahs*. Three papal bulls have proclaimed that the Portuguese, as crusaders, had to subjugate all Moors and *gentios* and had to convert them to the True Faith. No other nation could interfere with the Portuguese monopoly of commerce, and of discovery and conquest.   I opened my mouth to speak.

Try to understand, said João. Don't, don't ask useless questions using words like Christian arrogance. The word you need is power.

Consider this, said João, power tolerates no questions.

A *padrão*, with its seven foot high round pillar, with the coat of arms of Portugal carved into the wide square block at the top, with its two inscriptions in Portuguese and in Latin, displaying the name of the reigning king and that of the discoverer, with the day and year of the discovery, with an ascetically lean cross surmounting the whole and surveying the landscape, doesn't ask a question. A *padrao* announces that the surrounding territory discovered by order of the King of Portugal, belongs to the Portuguese.

Power, the power of ships and guns, has turned traders and merchants into conquerors. They have conveniently forgotten the quest for Preste João and the injunction to convert the people to the faith.

I was quite surprised. João was almost out of breath. He never usually talks at such length.

That day he had the faraway look of an exile gazing beyond the Bahr-i-Hind, trying to leap across the expanse of Africa, longing for a glimpse of home.

It took some time for our small boat to get back to the landing, the tide was against us.

I'll ask the sheik tomorrow about the setting up of *padrão*, said Bwana Mataka, we'll have to discuss it at a council meeting.

His servants were waiting to take him home. I went to my office where Abdul was waiting for me.

Abdul and I walked along the dark deserted beach towards Silver-sands which would be home for Abdul too, and for Layla.

Kochama leaves for his village tomorrow to get a second wife to live in Lamu, said Abdul.

Does Layla want to go back to Diu or to Chapora, I asked, is she happy here in Malindi.

Mian Mazlum's wife gave Layla a red *kanga* today, for the holiday, Abdul said. I hope to get her married someday. She is not fair skinned. She has no dowry.

It was a fact Abdul was stating, not a complaint.

We will get some dowry money for her, I told Abdul.

I could see a faint light through our window. Usha was waiting up for me.

I need a bath, I said to Abdul, a little hot water. Usha would arrange to have the water heated. A cold water bath at night can cause a chill, Usha had told me.

I'll be in soon, I told Abdul, and walked up to the little stone horse. A few white clouds raced along the night sky. The few stars that were out gleamed brightly as if they knew something but wanted to keep it a secret from me. Perhaps they knew I was tired but happy. I would write yet another pilot guide for the ports of Lamu and Malindi. I would be a consultant for the building of ships here in Malindi. I would make money to support Usha and our baby.

There was a rustle among the bats and balls and the toy bows and arrows a few yards away from the stone horse.

Come here, I said. A child probably, I thought. Not gone home yet, still wanting to play.

And then it stood up, monkey hunched, and there was a whiz and I felt a sharp sting in my upper right arm. It was just a toy arrow, it came off easily, I let it drop to the ground. The monkeylike creature loped towards me, then ran swiftly away like a rat.

Come here, I said, and tried to reach out to it with my right arm which began to feel heavy as lead.

And then I knew.

I rushed up to our room, lay down on the carpet and shut my eyes. The numbness crept slowly up my right arm to my shoulder and neck. My heart trembled, then felt tightly constricted. My mind was clear. Forehead sweaty. Eyes watering, throat dry, ears blocked, then clear.

From a great distance Usha repeating Ahmad mine, Ahmad, Ahmad mine, Ahmad, voice fading. Throat dry. Tried to say, don't come near. Tried, couldn't speak. Feet, legs getting cold, heavily sleepy. Tell Usha not to touch. Shut eyes for a moment.

Eyes stuck, then opened. A circle of faces staring, near, then far. Vinegar smell. Sounds clear. Usha crying, far, near. No. Ratna holding Usha back, no, no. Faces, Abdul, near, Mian Mazlum, Kochama, a swirl, strange face, far, Bwana Mataka, Layla, a blur, eyes stuck. Fingers, pulse. Slowing down, voice strange, cauterize. No, hakim, Kochama's voice, vinegar useless, too fast, nothing help.

No, said Usha, no, no, will suck the wound.

Open eyes. Cant. Stuck. Kochama's voice loud. Ratna screaming. Voices from the faraway. Shirin yelling, Usha in pain, Yasmin crying ball, ball.

TWELVE

Mid-May 1509, night, my house, Diu,
two tufans, one invades my house,
the other enters my being, fracturing my sense of time,
compelling time past to become time present.
I write furiously about the chanting of two mantras,
and about how Usha and Layla and Yasmin and Abdul and I found ourselves
on the San Raphael and about how the Portuguese ships set sail for Calicut

Abdul, Abdul.
   I woke up.
   I heard loud pounding on the back door against the screaming gusts
of wind, the rain driving furiously on the roof.
   Help, loud screams of pain, help, Abdul.
   Abdul put his ear to the kitchen door.
   They're Kharvas, two of them, I buy fish from them, he shouted.
   Shall I let them in, Abdul asked me.
   Yes, I said.
   My oil lamp was flickering. I must have been fast asleep. I lit a candle.
It spread a weak light on the papers on my table.
   Help, help.
   The voices became frantic, then sounded weak, distant against the
high pitched sweeping fury of the tufan. The screams were hysterical.
   The whole house will be flooded, Abdul said, I'll put your papers in
the jar.
   Open the door just a little for them to get in, I said.
   It would be difficult to shut the door. I went to help Abdul.
   Abdul undid the iron latch and the tufan burst howling in, dashing a
heavy body against me, forcing me back. Some pots crashed to the floor
in the total darkness.
   Push at the door, shouted Abdul.

I pushed forward with blind hands.

I'm dying, the woman screamed hysterically, help, I'm dead.

And she clung fiercely to me. Her fish smell was overpowering. I pushed her away, but she clung on, whimpering save me, I'm dying, her face sliding my knees. Save me, she screamed, and grabbed my knees tight. I almost fell over her, her fish smell was strong.

Abdul somehow managed to shut out the tufan.

Don't move, Abdul said.

He lit the candle on my table which threw off a weak yellow brown light.

Don't move, shouted Abdul to the man next to the door and he lit another candle. The man was stark naked. I could see the light of the candle reflected on his tar black gleaming skin. The woman pressed against my feet was naked too, a heaving mass of whimpering shadow down below.

Take your wife away, shouted Abdul.

Abdul was trying to light the kitchen oil lamp.

The woman began screaming again. No, she screamed, *nāg*, I'm dying. She was a mass of fright. She fainted away.

Abdul managed to get a wraparound for the man.

The Kharwas were the poorest of the poor. They owned just one body covering which they wore until it fell to pieces and they could wear it no more. Abdul and the fisherman carried the woman to the charpoy next to the table. The cowdung washed floor of the kitchen was soaking wet. I gave Abdul a *satrangi* to cover the woman.

What happened, I asked the man.

He looked at Abdul. He wouldn't look at me. Abdul had begun refilling my tablelamp with oil.

My wife, he said, following Abdul into the kitchen. Expecting a baby, he said. Tufan, he said. Gathering fallen coconuts, he said.

What happened, I asked.

The woman began to whimper again.

Nāg, the man said. Cobra bite, he said, avoiding my eye.

There was no medicine to treat cobra poison. It was too late to make incisions and to suck the wound. She would die soon.

And then the words of my venerable hakim flashed to mind.

There's no remedy for snake poison, my hakim had said sadly one day when we were searching for medicinal herbs in the Kanara forest. Sometimes the muttering of *mantras* proves effective. *Mantras* calm people down, and they recover. Very very few people die of snakebite, they die of snake shock.

Maybe it wasn't a cobra, I thought. They couldn't have seen it in this dark wet night.

I asked Abdul to ask the man. No, he hadn't seen the snake, but the place was a haunt of king cobras. The woman became agitated and sat up, perhaps the word cobra had excited her. Her husband pushed her down but she was uncontrollable.

Get me the oil lamp and hold down her feet, I told Abdul.

Above her left ankle there were small regular horseshoe teethmarks. I looked carefully for deep round fang punctures at the top, but there were none. There was no blood ooze, no swelling at all, no signs of paralysis. It was a nonpoisonous snake that had bit her.

Ask her if she feels any pain at all, I told Abdul, who told her husband who asked his wife.

No, Abdul told me, she doesn't.

Tell her she won't die, I said. I will cure her.

The woman was still moaning. Her eyes were wide open trying to understand what I had said. She wasn't sweating now.

I held out my pen and sprinkled some drops of black ink on the teeth marks and at the same time chanted the *mantra* that came to my mind.

Salve Rainha, mater misericordiae.

She looked at me with grateful eyes, shut them, and went to sleep almost immediately.

Shall I send them both away, Abdul asked.

The tufan was still raging outside. It would continue blowing for a long time.

No, I said, let them sleep here.

The kitchen floor was flooded wet so that all of us would have to crowd into the front room. I wasn't sleepy at all now, I wanted to write, I didn't have to tell Abdul that. He got my papers out, trimmed the oillamp, and rearranged the table so that I faced the wall and didn't have to look at them. The fish smell was quite faint now.

Pen in hand, I tried to hurl myself across the Bahr-i-Hind to reenter my past. I could see our little white home on Silversands. I could see Ratna and Mian Mazlum. Bwana Mtaka must be dead now. I wondered what had happened to Shirin, and to Kochama with his *siwa*. I can even see Yasmin perched delicately on Layla's shoulder.

Usha I cannot see.

I try to recall the sandal paste fragrance of her warm breasts. But the nose cannot remember the past. The faint fish smell in the room bound me to the present. Then I found myself hurled into the past. I was on board Paulo da Gama's *San Raphael*.

Usha never once complained about fish smells. The main deck of the *San Raphael*, the Portuguese called it the *conves*, was red with the blood and entrails of the sharks hauled in and butchered, then salted and hung up to sun dry.

It was on the next day at noon, four sailing days out of Malindi, that the fish smells hit everyone. The incense sticks did not help, and Usha vomited quietly in a basin in our little cabin, Paulo's really, crouched under a picture of a woman with large sad eyes holding her little son in her lap. Paulo would nod gently to the picture everytime he came into the cabin for his things.

Even the Portuguese could not stand the smell. So Paulo had all the half dried shark fish flung away. They ate fish on Fridays and days of fasting. No meat was allowed.

Christian fasting, João told me, was not rigorous at all. They could eat a limited amount and could drink water all day long. I knew that Muslim fasting during Ramazan, that month of burning, is very rigorous. It lasts from dawn to the moment when the sun sets. Not a morsel can be eaten, not even a drop of water can be sipped. Some strict observers do not swallow their own saliva.

On Fridays the Portuguese sailors were served what they called sardines, dug out of brine barrels, boiled, and treated with olive oil. I saw some sailors fling the sardines overboard and eat only the boiled beans.

They did not know how to cook shark. Boiled shark is tasteless. Fried shark flesh is tough and can only be chewed. The only way to cook shark is to curry it. Abdul prepared it for Layla and himself one Friday when no one was using the stand in the firebox. The curry was hot with red chillies and spices, and the gravy was thick.

Two of the sailors asked if they could taste the fish. The smell had quickened their appetite. It was quite pungent but tasty. But there was plenty of Malindi water in the watertank below. Abdul would prepare food for five of them everytime he was allowed to use the triangular stand in the open *fogão*. Its fire was lit in the early morning, carefully tended throughout the day, and put out in the late afternoon, after the pageboys had prepared dinner for the others, usually at midday.

Abdul made friends with the sailors on board the *San Raphael*. They would employ sign language and communicate in Gujarati and in Portuguese and make use of grunts and strange noises.

Abdul has begun to snore and I stopped writing for a while. His snoring has a rhythm of its own. Deep when he breathes out, a high fluttery tremble when he breathes in. I find it soothing at times, at other times a kind of a warning. Reassuring, except when the snoring stops for a while and I get a little worried, till it resumes its regular rhythm. My writing, its rhythms have become irregular, the language doesn't flow onward. Its rhythms have become choppy making my storyboat drift. I shuttle between the past and the present.

Abdul begins snoring again.

Write for her, sing for her, his snoring tells me.

Usha used to chant that *mantra* to me in Paulo's cabin. She believed that's why I recovered from the arrow poison.

Salve Rainha, Mater Misericordiae, I chanted again.

Usha would gently sing to me as I lay in Paulo's wooden bed in the dark of the cabin, rubbing my throbbing forehead firmly but tenderly with Ratna's balm and crooning over and over again, *Salve Rainha, mater misericordiae*.

The first few times I didn't know what she was chanting, the pain was too piercing. Kochama had warned me in Malindi about the savage headache caused by the poison and its antidote.

It will be almost unbearable, Kochama stated, it will begin every evening, sometimes early, sometimes late, and continue for about four hours. Just before the wound heals completely, Kochama warned me, you'll experience for seven days a final recurrence of forehead shattering pain that will leave you weak and helpless, until the poison has drained out of your system.

No liquor could be sold in Malindi, and they had to hunt around in the liquor dens of the town to get me the strongest of liquors, that of the coconutpalm. It was as clear as water, but the smell was disgusting. I had to pinch my nose shut before I could swallow it down. On board the *San Raphael* it took two *canadas* of wine for me to fall asleep, senseless.

Usha thought that it was the chanting that caused my headaches to diminish. Ratna's balm provided some relief. Usha disapproved of the Portuguese wine, but never complained about it. She would pour it into my cup and hold my head up while I drank the wine. She knew I needed it to go to sleep. I told her what Kochama had told me, that it would take time for the poison to drain in slow drops through the wound, that a second application of medicine would have no effect, and that only after all the poison had been drawn out of my system would the headaches disappear.

Abdul would clean the drained drops from the wound everyday with clothrags and fling them immediately overboard. I wouldn't allow Usha to clean my wound. It's dangerous, I said.

Her singing was soothing to my ears. Yasmin learnt to say, sal, sal. I could say the first line of the chant but did not know the language or where Usha had learned to sing it.

On the third evening out of Malindi I knew.

That was the day my headache began not at the usual time but later, an hour after sunset. Usha and I stood outside the cabin and looked down at the Portuguese crowded together for prayers on the *conves* and on the forecastle. Paulo, his head bowed, led the prayers. There was deep sincerity in his voice.

The Portuguese sailors, unwashed, unpurified, but all on their knees, prayed in different tones and voices as if they had never learned to pray together. Some sounded sleepy and tired. It was the end of a day. The *San Raphael* ran easy and free. Others hurriedly bawled out their responses. Someone snored loudly but was shaken awake to suppressed laughter.

On our ships the call for evening prayers, which have to be recited in the interval between the setting of the sun and the end of the day, is made by the muezzin. After ablution of hands and face and feet in water drawn up from the sea, the faithful stand facing Meccawards in orderly lines, with space between for the *sijda*prostration, to intone the set prayers.

I've never been able to pray, even in the midst of a storm at sea. Useless, I've always thought, to disturb that mysterious silence that lies beyond the stars. Communal prayers, they're not for me. But sometimes, somehow, at rare moments, something stirs deep within me, I know not why, when I hear prayer pouring out of the heart.

I sensed the headache approaching and turned to go into the cabin, but Usha held my arm, and such a moment came.

A voice ascended out of the ship and soared straight to the stars. The voice was clear, that of a young boy that could have been the voice of a young girl. For me it was the voice of innocence. Undisturbed by any hesitation or doubt, it sped on up with a complete faith that its prayer song would be heard.

I had heard it before as I walked home along the sands of Malindi, this prayer song of supplication. I have no ear for music, and it wasn't the music that moved me. It wasn't the words, I did not understand even one word. *Salve Rainha, mater misericordiae.* A tidal awareness flooded my being. I heard a profound cry beseeching deliverance from pain and suffering, a cry that surged into loud clamors for mercy and for a safe return home, all the sailors, the whole ship, repeating O three times before voices and song floated gently down to earth resting on the final syllable, ah. Then followed a moment of sacred silence. Far away in the west lingered the last dark red clouds of sunset. On the *conves* below a candle shone bravely like a star in the darkness.

I'll never experience such a moment again. I'm too sceptical, too bound to time to leap out of time.

Once, when I was young and all knowing, walking in the early morning on the mist covered sands of Kannanur bay, I heard the cry of a muezzin come ringing over the tops of the coconut palms hurling itself towards the sea. I couldn't see the minaretless mosque hidden by the luxuriant green tree waves inland. It didn't matter, for here in the south of India, mosque and temple and church grow out of the rich dark earth.

The summons to morning prayer, *Allahu akbar, la ilaha illa'llah*, made pride burn and glow within me. It was a powerful human cry that had to be heard, more commanding than trumpet or bell, the crier's voice lingering over the ah sounds, gliding over the liquid l's, pausing briefly at the r sound, then gathering power by merging the l with the ah and prolonging the final lah, till silence itself became resonant.

For me it was the cry of Islam that had issued out of Mecca and had traveled swiftly across burning desert sands, a cry then blown on monsoon winds to the hot wet fertile lands of India and beyond, to the islands of spice, and on to Melaka, the lands below the wind, lands teeming with gods and goddesses, too innumerable to count. It announced triumphantly to the whole world the majesty and the oneness of God, and the duty of all the people to propagate Islam. God is most great, there is no god but God.

I never was religious.

You're afraid of belief, João tells me. No, that's not true. You believe in mere words. You love sounds. Yours is the empty religion of a poet, says João.

Usha, I could have told him, was a believer. What she believed in, I do not know.

She grew into belief before my eyes as we sailed to Calicut on board the *San Raphael*. I saw her change. Her black eyes, they became softer. They had a strange tinge of blue I had never seen before, specially when she looked out over the sea. There was a faraway look in them except when they looked anxiously at me, helpless and in pain on Paulo's bed.

A tiny wrinkle began to form on her forehead. I thought it would disappear after I got well but it never went away. It wasn't a flaw, for strangely it heightened the glow on her face. I thought at times the glow was a sign of physical wellbeing, our baby growing within her, making her skin emit a faint radiance. I thought my throbs of forehead pain had distorted my vision.

Once, pretending to be asleep so that she could get some rest from her vigil at my bedside, I saw her through the cabin window gazing into the distance at the setting sun. From the *conves* below arose meaningless syllables chanted slowly, *te lu cis an te ter mi num*. A soft wind blew from the west playing with her unbound hair, the last light of the day brushing it, setting the shimmering strands afire. It lasted only a moment, this vision.

I held my breath.

Usha.

The cry sprang from deep within me, but I did not release it, my lips were pressed together. Mine wasn't a cry of pain. Perhaps it was a prayer.

Usha turned, looked at me through the window, and rushed in though she could not have heard my cry.

Ahmad mine, she said and placed her fingers on my brow.

It took me a very long time before I could bring myself to write down that word, prayer. Perhaps it was only a sob, not a cry. Just a belch, perhaps, released by my disturbed inner being. The arrow poison and the remedy, both could have shaken up my insides. Perhaps I was drunk at the time and my eyes were affected. Perhaps, perhaps it was Paulo who had led me to that moment.

Paulo was like some heavenly body that influences the tidal rhythms of the sea. All his men, the whole ship, moved to his bidding. He did not need the commanding voice of Vasco da Gama. Brother Paulo always spoke softly, except when he led the prayers.

His words sent ripples, I could almost see them, of affection and concern towards his men, they had a subtle power, a power the men didn't want to and couldn't resist. He gave himself completely to them, looking after them when they fell ill, treating their ulcers and sores with *unguentum apostolorum*, an ointment smelling of frankincense that, Paulo said, was made up of twelve ingredients in a white wax base. The sick would not allow the ship's barber surgeon, whose stock remedy was cupping and bleeding, to treat them. They wanted Paulo.

When the pilot, João de Coimbra, fell ill as we neared the west coast of India, Paulo spent many hours in the pilot's cabin ministering to his needs. He spent even more time looking after Rufião the *degredado*. Nobody knew his real name. Rufião kept groaning and cursing continuously, in great pain, his hands and feet were swollen, his gums were bleeding. The ship's clerk, João de Sa, pleaded with Paulo who had coughing attacks all through the night not to go down into the black foul smelling hold to which the foul mouthed *degredado* had been banished.

He is a human being, Paulo said.

Paulo gave Rufião his own share of oranges and lemons from Malindi and with his own hands spoonfed him with some of the honey he had in his medicine chest which was in his cabin.

To sweeten your tongue, Paulo said.

The time he didn't give to his men and his ship Paulo devoted to the saying of his prayers. He read these from a small book kept on a shelf next to the picture of that woman with a child in her lap. Paulo did not need the book, he said it was the Book of Hours, for he could recite the prayers by heart.

One day I found him at the start of the second watch which began approximately at sunset, just away from his cabin door kneeling and praying with his eyes shut.

I didn't want to disturb you, he said, I don't need the book.

He said his private prayers at regular hours three times a day, midway during the morning watch, just after the afternoon watch, the third after the night prayers were said and the *Salve Rainha* sung. The men took care never to disturb him at his prayers. A few whispered that he was a saint.

Nothing could disturb Paulo when he was rapt in prayer. Yasmin would fly up to him, perch on his shoulder, patiently wait for him to finish his prayers, then say pa pa, she couldn't manage the other two syllables of his name. Paulo would feed her a tidbit from one of his many pockets, scratch her throat gently with his forefinger and Yasmin would then fly back to Usha.

Usha felt deeply drawn to Paulo, she didn't know why.

He has never said a word to me, Usha told me, and, she continued, now I don't feel any need for language. In the first two days on board this ship, my Ahmad, when you were sweating and in great pain, and I was sure you were going to leave me, I would sit on the top step outside our cabin door when you fell asleep for a while, and cry in silence.

Language was of no use. I couldn't talk to Layla and I couldn't talk to Abdul about you. I would look up at the sky, but it was always fiercely white and empty. At night, like you, my Ahmad, I would look up at the cold stars. Did the twentyfour *tirthankaras*, full of compassionless compassion, makers of the ford that leads across the ocean of suffering, reside there as my uncle told me. No human cry could ever reach there.

Paulo would be at the bottom of the steps kneeling, praying, I slowly realized, for you. He would visit you five times every day, and bring the two *canadas* of wine. I could see the concern in his eyes for us both. He must have seen me looking up to the sky for help.

On the day you had a long fit of convulsions, and your forehead was on fire and I thought the end had come, till the fever broke and exhausted, you went to sleep, Paulo went into the cabin and came out with the picture he would always bow to and gave it to me without saying a word.

I didn't look at it, but a tear welled up and splashed on to the glass of the picture frame. I looked down and it seemed as if the woman with the child had shed a tear and had made my grief her very own. I felt strangely moved, Ahmad mine, I prayed to her without using words, knowing she would understand. I asked her to save you.

Never before had Usha talked to me at such length. Her voice had dropped low when she mentioned Paulo, and it began to hush down so that I almost didn't hear the last six words. She believed the woman in the picture had saved my life. She never talked about the picture again, never tried to convince me of its truth, knowing how very difficult it would be for me to accept the connections between her prayer and the picture and my recovery.

One day, when Layla was combing and brushing Usha's hair, just after the afternoon watch had been cried out by one of the ship's pages, having asked Paulo's permission, I brought the picture out of the cabin into the fierce sunlight to inspect it.

It was crudely painted. The colors were heavy, clumsy. The metallic dark blue of the gathers of her robe weighed heavily on the shoulders of the woman. The dull white of her tight head covering that framed her sad face and sorrowful eyes but allowed a few stray hair to escape bound her to the earth. There were two deep lines on her brow. Around the head was a thick band of purple that clashed with the intense black of the huge cross held by a naked loin clothed child who was held lightly by the mother whose fingers were long and delicate and tender.

The child did not look like a child. He had an unformed face. The artist had given him a muscular right arm, perhaps to hold on to the cross which towered above him. His tiny feet had holes in them painted red and on his head was a strange crown of twisted thorns or nails, I couldn't tell which.

He embraced his cross, which was rooted in the earth like a tree, but which leaned into his infant arms as if it was a toy that had hurt him so that he didn't want to play with it. Its name, written clearly at the top, was I N R I. One of the arms of the cross rested painfully on the shoulders of the mother who didn't feel her own pain but kept gazing with unutterable anguish at her child. The pain was too raw, not distanced by art.

The woman in this picture, Usha believed, had saved my life. I didn't understand how and why. Usha must have been weak and vulnerable. She had no one to turn to at the time. Layla, even Abdul, could not have sustained her. Perhaps the series of shocks she had received had disturbed her inner being, so that belief could enter there, the break with her father, our running away, the baby within her

It was Usha who had saved my life in Malindi as I lay dying in our room at Silversands.

When she heard Yasmin saying ball, ball, Usha rushed out and got the ivory ball, the gift that Kochama's father had given Layla, cracked it open, applied the ointment inside it to my arrow wound and saved my life. She never told me about what happened on that night. Kochama told me what happened, Abdul told me about it, Ratna too. Other details about what happened the next day and how I was taken to the *San Raphael* I got from Bwana Mataka and from Mian Mazlum.

Usha was just in time.

A few more moments, Kochama said, and the poison would have flooded the center of your being so that the ointment would not have had enough power to draw it out of your system. Everyone around my bed had given up all hope and they were surprised to see how quickly the antidote took effect. They saw me shake my head, open my eyes briefly, move my legs slightly. The color returned to your face, Kochama told me.

The Malindi hakim felt my pulse. A miracle, he said, it is beating, he has come back to life. Give him a vinegar wash, he told Abdul, and apply hot cloths to his feet. I'll set leeches to his wound tomorrow.

Kochama took charge.

No, he told the hakim, that won't do at all, the poison will kill the leeches. Ahmadji has to be made to sit up, then forty large pots of cold water have to be poured without stop on his head, Kochama told Abdul. Then let Ahmadji rest, but don't give him any food. I'll get him some jungle liquor to drink.

No liquor was allowed into Malindi. The religious leaders had issued strict orders that the gateguards had to inspect all packages of the tribals. Kochama, through friends, managed with great difficulty to get three small jars of strong smelly coconutpalm liquor. I don't recall drinking it that night, but I remember the beginning of a violent forehead pain. Ratna told me that I fainted and then fell into a deep sleep from which I awoke at midmorning the next day.

Usha sat near your bed the whole night and the whole day, Ratna said. She wouldn't talk even to me, though she smiled her thanks when I brought her some food. She didn't eat it but sipped some water. She wouldn't sleep, she wouldn't even cry. She had a bath and some yoghurt and went to sleep for a few hours after you woke up. When she awoke your headache had already begun and you had high fever.

I took her outside.

I'm afraid, Ratna, Usha said to me in a voice trembling with a pain she couldn't speak of. She looked up at the blue sky. I need help from somewhere. From above, she said. She was in despair. I grew worried about her, said Ratna. Think about the baby, look after yourself.

The spells of headache, the fits, the fever and the sweating must have worried Usha. I felt quite normal and well. My mind was alert all through the morning. And then, suddenly, out of nowhere, in the late afternoon the spasms would begin and I would roll on my bed helpless with pain.

Bwana Mataka sent me a basket of fruit, ripe apricots, figs that melted in the mouth, and oranges.

He had got an urgent message from the sheik, Ratna said, and would visit me later in the day.

Ah, Mian Mazlum said, ah, ah, ah, Ahmad my friend. He bent down and gave me a double embrace. Ahmad my friend, he kept on repeating, he didn't know what else to say.

I too remained silent. There was no need for words.

I have to go for the Friday service, he said after a while.

My colleagues came to greet me, Lambu wasn't with them. I began to feel sleepy. Ratna told the servants not to allow any visitors in.

It was only on Saturday morning after Usha had applied rose oil to my forehead that Mian Mazlum told me about the rioting and the disturbances that had taken place in Malindi on Friday.

The central mosque in the Malindi market place was packed with the faithful so that many had to take their places in the open courtyard under the noonday sun. The leaders rejoiced. The conditions were right. The humid heat would make it easier for the *khatib* to work on the passions of the people and set them on fire.

It was the preacher from Jiddah who recited the meridian prayers and also delivered the Friday oration from the second step of the *mimbar*. He had a powerful voice, penetrating even when reciting prayer, so that both prayers and sermon pierced through the walls of the mosque and could be heard all over the marketplace. Trained in Cairo, he had brought with him the Egyptian practice of holding a wooden sword in his hand whilst he delivered his exhortation from the pulpit.

He began with the traditional invocation putting great stress on the word Compassionate, pausing and prolonging the word, making it echo in the ears of the hearers. Praised be God, he proclaimed, praised be that God that hath guided us onto that path we could not have found.

I bear witness, the preacher said, that there is no deity but God. Fear God, o ye people, and fear the Day of Judgement. Let not Satan that great deceiver lead you astray.

And then, dramatically, he descended from the pulpit and sat on the floor of the mosque and said, Supplicate God.

He offered up a silent prayer.

The silence was intense. The people were spellbound as they offered their prayers in private. Not even a crow cawed.

The preacher then ascended the *mimbar* with the sword.

In the name of God, the Compassionate, the Merciful, he began again.

He recited prayers for the servant and apostle of God, for his family and for his companions and his descendants.

By this time his voice had climbed to its height and had reached a dramatic pitch. He had a perfect sense of timing. He knew when to pause, when exactly to hurl his words upward and onward. His voice burned with passion. His hearers lost their individual selves and became charged with the fervor of the *khatib's* own identity. He believed that God spoke through him and he hypnotized the worshippers.

O God, he prayed, aid Islam, and strengthen its pillars. Make infidelity to tremble. Destroy its might.

O God, he thundered, assist the forces of the Muslims, frustrate the infidels and the enemies of our religion near our shores. Invert their banners, and ruin their habitations and their ships. Give them and their wealth as booty to the Muslims. Praise be to God, the Lord of the beings of the whole world.

He ended the *khutbah*, raised the sword above his head, and descended from the pulpit to lead the worshippers in a two prostration prayer.

Trouble began as soon as the congregation streamed perspiring out of the mosque and into the market place. Knots of people gathered in lanes and at streetcorners, gesturing, talking excitedly about the sermon and about the Portuguese ships and about yesterday's celebration.

Angry voices exploded all around.

Attack the Portuguese ships. Don't give them food, those eaters of swine. No water, let them die of thirst, the infidels.

The voices were loud and insistent. They burst all around the marketplace like fireworks, but they lacked the power to fuse the people into a mob.

The knots broke up and reformed into other knots.

Let's go. Kill the Feringhis. Let us loot their ships.

From a roof top someone shouted, burn the ships, burn the ships.

It was catchy, this cry, the knots of people picked it up and it became a chant, it had a secret power. It happened to be just right, it had the right number of syllables, the right rhythm, and it was a call to action that forced everyone into motion. The knots formed into groups that formed currents so that the crowd streamed towards the sheik's palace chanting, burn the ships, burn the ships.

The shops along the lanes had been hastily shut. Some food stalls had a shutter or two open. The madafu vendors thought that business would be brisk because of the heat. Someone from the crowd grabbed a coconut and tried to run away with it but was caught by the coconut seller who threatened him with his sharp knife.

Save me, my brothers, save me, said the culprit.

Shouts of shame, shame, shame, filled the air.

The crowd gathered around the stall and began to tear it down.

Kill him, kill him, shouted voices from the rear, from those who couldn't see what was happening in front.

The vendor raised his long knife with his right hand and prepared to defend himself. Someone nearby picked up a coconut and smashed it on the side of his face, reddening the pile of green coconuts with splashes of blood. The left eye of the vendor popped out and hung greyishwhite, dangling out of the gaping red socket.

The ones around the smashed stall were horrified, but the crowd at the back pushed forcefully on, trampling the dying man.

To the ships, to the ships, they cried and picked up the coconuts to use as weapons.

Burn the ships, burn the ships, they roared as they smashed other madafu stalls and looted food shops and poured into the large courtyard of another mosque near the sheik's palace.

The crowd got confused here. People came running in from different lanes into the courtyard, but it had only one outlet that led to the seafront. Some rushed bravely out wanting to be the first to get to the beach but they were confronted by armed guards near the gate, only four of them, with lances and short swords, and the people, uncertain of themselves, backed into the packed courtyard, pushing against those that wanted to get through the outlet and on to the beach.

Confused rumors began to circulate.

That the old Sheik himself had come down the palace steps. That Mombasan ships had come to defend the Portuguese. That a Portuguese longboat was tied up near the steps with many guns and bombards. Fear gripped the crowd, they did not know what to do, they milled around aimlessly, talking, gesticulating, wanting to panic, wanting to disperse, waiting for someone to make the first move.

A voice suddenly shouted, kill the Banias, and the cry was taken up, kill the Banias, kill the Banias.

The crowd began to stream through the lanes that led to the Cambay quarter at the other end of Malindi where the rich Jain traders had their houses and their shops.

It was fiercely hot now and all the shops were shut and the perspiring crowd streamed through the empty lanes and the deserted streets holding on to their coconuts and brandishing sticks and pieces of wood from the smashed stalls, seeking desperately to vent their anger and their envy. Their way led back to the market place where they came across a lame pariah dog that had lifted one of its hind legs to urinate on a corner.

Unclean, unclean, they roared, kill the defiler, and, furious with rage, they rushed upon the dog and smashed it again and again with their sticks beating it into a pulp. Unaware that their sandals and the hems of their robes were sprayed with blood they rushed along into the courtyard.

They had to slow down here, for there were two lanes to the Cambay section. The shortcut led through a narrow diagonally twisting alley where some of the deep sea pilots lived. The other, a wider lane, curved right around another mosque and then ran into the shortcut to lead into a square that formed the entrance to the Bania quarter.

Let's go, yelled a self appointed leader, raising his heavy knobbed stick with both hands. Follow me, we'll loot their shops. And he plunged into the dark narrow alley.

The crowd split apart. About twenty people, in groups of two or three, stumbled bravely after him. The others, leaderless, ran halfheartedly around the mosque. It was as if the heat had drained all energy out of this group.

Cursing, yelling, grumbling, holding their weapons high above their heads, the twenty stumbled after their leader whose face was sweat red, inflamed with passion. He had the piercing eyes of a fanatic. He knew exactly what had to be done.

Halt, the fanatic cried, and stopped near a heavy newly carved Zanzibari door with four crude sambuks decorating its four corners, and waited for his followers to crowd around him, and then began thumping on the door with his thick club.

Open up, open up, Maimun ibn Khalil, open up.

The fanatic turned around and faced his followers who pushed and crowded eagerly around the door, their clothes completely sweat drenched.

My brothers, shouted the fanatic, this man, this Maimun, this money lover, is going to guide the ships of the enemies of our faith and show them the way to India and ruin the business and trade of us Muslims. He is a traitor to Islam.

Cries of outrage, *jihad*, may they be cursed to hell, those eaters of pork, those worshippers of crucifixes, *jihad*, come out, come down, you coward, you traitor, we know you are in there.

They pushed on the door, banged on it with their sticks, come out, break it down, set it on fire. Loud wails of women and children could be heard behind the door.

A small sidedoor opened and Maimun ibn Khalil, stooping low, squeezed himself through it.

Shut the door, Maimun cried. The door was banged shut. He turned to face the crowd that circled him armed with sticks, and then he began to shake all over. His knees trembled as he tried to stand up.

Friends, he pleaded, I will not guide the Portuguese to India.

Liar, shouted the fanatic.

Traitor, yelled the crowd.

Liar, shouted the fanatic again, and with a low swing of his club broke Maimun's right knee.

Traitor, the fanatic shouted, you won't be able to guide those infidels now.

Maimun collapsed in a heap, and the crowd roared, kill him, kill him.

The sidedoor burst open and a woman stumbled heavily out.

No, no, no, she screamed, and the crowd drew back.

She wore a red gown. She had not veiled herself. She was in an advanced state of pregnancy. She was Maimun's wife. She threw herself on Maimun and covered his body with her own.

A small bent figure, clad entirely in black, hopped out of the door and rushed towards the crowd, which drew further back. It was the wife's ninety year old grandmother.   Cowards, the grandmother screamed.

Jutting her pointed jaw forward and baring her naked gums, she glared at them with her glassy green eyes.

A witch with the evil eye, someone hissed, she can turn men into beasts. She has a black tongue. She spits forth poison.

May shaitan be your *ghassal ghasil*, the corpsewasher for all of you, she cursed the crowd.

Horrified at the idea of being handled by a washer of the dead, the crowd broke up and ran. The leader slunk away.

At the entrance to the Cambay quarter, Bwana Mataka had taken charge of the situation. Calm, cool, in loose shirt and pyjamas of pure white muslin, he stood with the city administrator in the shade of a high ledge of the entrance gateway and waited for the straggling groups, heat exhausted, drained of all frenzy, to drift into the square. He was dignified and greeted them as if he was their father. He welcomed them one and all.

My friends, my brothers, Bwana Mataka said, the administrator and I and our friends, the Bania traders, bid you welcome. Your throats must be burnt dry with thirst.

He made a signal and servants hurried out of the gateway with pots of sherbet prepared with cold water kept overnight in porous earthenware jars. He talked to the crowd as they gulped down the sherbet.

Drink as much as you want, my brothers, said Bwana Mataka, our Jain friends have provided plenty of cooling sherbet.

He told them about his recent adventures, immediately exciting the interest and curiosity of the crowd. The Portuguese, in his telling, became figures of fun. He described the strange clothes they wore, their odd head-gear.

Com esta, senhor, how are you, senhor, Bwana Mataka said in Portuguese, exaggerating the nasal twang of their language which made the whole crowd laugh. He exaggerated Vasco da Gama's peculiar limp because of the wound, and assumed the captain's haughty look.

What a clown, shabash, said the crowd.

D'you know that the Portuguese bathe their bodies only once in one year, yes only once, and they use both hands when eating their food, Bwana Mataka said.

And the crowd let forth a prolonged oh of mockhorror. Such barbarians, not knowing that the left hand is unclean and used for unclean purposes.

Yes, they were ignorant, these Portuguese. They had never seen a green coconut before. When a Portuguese sailor was offered a madafu, he did not know that the top had to be first sliced off to drink the water inside. He at once tried to bite off a piece and all his front teeth came off.

The crowd roared with laughter, and forgot why they had come there.

Bwana Mataka knew that this wasn't true, that he was exaggerating. It had been a stalk of sugarcane not a green madafu that the Portuguese sailor had bit into.

Our city administrator, he continued, is very shrewd. D'you know how much he charged the Feringhis for the food and water they bought from us.

Sh, sh, Bwana Mataka looked all around as if there could be a spy in the crowd, he made a thousand percent profit for our city, he whispered loudly.

Wah, wah, shouted the crowd, and they broke up and went back to their homes, there was still time left for the afternoon rest.

The city quietened down.

Bwana Mataka and the administrator went to the palace to reassure the old Sheik who had tried to walk down the palace steps to pacify his people. The young sheik had been kept informed of all that was happening and agents kept coming in with reports.

It was decided that criers would be sent to the different sections to announce a curfew.

A meeting of the city council was called. Bwana Mataka urged that the city gates be watched. Anyone trying to leave by the Gedi gate would be questioned. A messenger was sent to request the chief religious leader to attend the meeting and it was then discovered that he with two of his assistants, the ones who had incited the crowd, had fled Malindi.

For Mombasa, it was reported. It was clear that there was a Mombasan conspiracy to undermine the power of the sheik of Malindi.

Among those questioned at the Gedi gate was Lambu who wanted to leave with his servant boy and a few belongings. He offered one of the guards twenty miticals to let him through. He was arrested, his house searched, there were ashes in one corner where papers had been burnt. They dug up a small widenecked bottle with a few drops of the poison buried in the same corner.

The interrogation of Lambu in the prison near the sheik's palace did not last long. The police chief was an expert questioner. Lambu confessed even before they began to torture him. He told all.

Yes, I am a Mombasa agent.

No, I do not know the names of other agents here.

No, no, I am telling the truth, Lambu said, don't heat up that oil.

No, I have never met the religious chief.

No, I do not know any of his assistants.

Yes, yes, I received messages from Mombasa which I burnt.

Yes, I sent reports to Sheth Gujarawala. About the state of the harbor, about trade, about ships, their arrival, their destination, their cargo.

Yes, twice a month. Through my servants.

Yes, Sheth Gujarawala did supply the servants.

Yes, I met the sheth when he was here last month.

Yes, he had supplied me a servant boy.

Yes, he is a dwarf, a hunchback. Yes, he is a Kamba.

No, I don't recognize that bottle.

No, no, don't, don't dip that arrow in the bottle.

Yes, yes, yes, the bottle contains Kamba arrow poison.

I will tell all, yes, everything.

When the nakhoda of the *Sheikh Kitami* had dropped anchor at Hormuz, he had narrated the strange story of the woman with long hair he had seen at the tiller of a small sambuk just off the Sawahil near Manda. One of the agents of Sheth Chimanlal had then sent a brief message to the Jain shahbandar at Malindi and to Sheth Gujarawala in Mombasa, Kill Ahmad ibn Madjid.

Lambu was ordered to spy on my movements and get to know my habits. He had picked up a toy arrow near the stonehorse, given it to the dwarf, and told him where to lie in wait for me. The servant boy had told him later that the arrow tip had been poisoned.

Bwana Mataka, to whom the police chief had given the written report, told me that Lambu wanted to know how I was.

They will try again, soon, Lambu had told Bwana Mataka, tell my friend and his wife to leave Malindi at once. They will kill both of them.

I felt sorry for Lambu. He was a good man, but weak.

In the midst of this confusion in Malindi the Portuguese had been forgotten. The administrator, Bwana Mataka, and the sheik especially, were kept busy calming the fears of the people.

The old Sheik fell ill and hakims were summoned to his bedside. Rumors flew around. The old Sheik was near death. The Mombasan army was on the march. That's why the city gates were shut. Fights began in some quarters in the city. Old quarrels were renewed. Old grudges were settled. There was panic in the air.

The Portuguese sent in their longboat for food and water on Friday, and twice on Saturday, in the early morning and in the early afternoon. The gateguards sent them back, the administrator had not left any instructions.

The Portuguese asked for Bwana Mataka, but he wasn't available. They then asked for me and for a pilot, repeating *malemo, malemo*, for they could not say *mu'allim*.

The guards shook their heads. The palace gate was shut. No one could explain anything. The Portuguese left, quite bewildered.

Some sailors from two newly arrived Kannanur *sambuks* at anchor on the left of the bay waved to the longboat as it was slowly being rowed back. The Portuguese thought they'd be able to get some sort of explanation from them. But the sailors were *Khalassis* and *Kharwas* of the fisherman caste from South India. They had black matted hair on their naked chests, scraggly beards, and their hair was long and unkempt. They wore dirty wrap arounds. They could only speak Malayalam, not Arabic. Communication was only possible through gestures and grunts and gesticulations. The more daring of the Malayali seamen got into a small boat and accompanied the Portuguese.

The Malayalis were impressed by the towering height of the stranger ships. They admired the formidable masts. They looked closely at the guns and the bombards which they had never seen before. And they bowed down in front of a long oblong piece of cloth made of satin and silk, lavishly embroidered with threads of gold and silver, and red, blue and black, with figures painted on it, which the Portuguese displayed to them.

Mataji, mataji, they murmured fervently and, folding both hands in front of their faces, prostrated themselves on the deck, repeating mother, mother.

The Portuguese were tremendously excited.

Christãos, Christãos, they rejoiced. Hurriedly the Portuguese showed the Malayalis small crucifixes, holy pictures and holy books, but the Malayalis ignored these items and kept bowing to the cloth, saying *mataji*, wondering why these sailors used a different name for her.

The Portuguese were excited because they thought, as I later discovered, that they had found some of the fellow Christians they were looking for connected with Preste Jan. Paulo showed me the altar cloth one day after it had been used for an early morning religious service.

On it was the woman with the sorrowful eyes and the unutterable anguish on her face sitting, clad in a blue cloak, near the foot of a huge black cross rooted in the earth with I N R I on the top. Twelve men stood round about her. This cross wasn't a toy. It was an instrument of pain.

The child had turned into a man, whose corpse, gaunt and emaciated, had been taken down from the cross and placed in the encircling arms of his mother. The hands and feet had red woundholes in them, someone had stabbed him on the left side, a twisted crown of sharp thorns was stuck on his head. The dead son was past all pain. It was the mother who was suffering the agony.

This mother of sorrows had touched the hearts of these simple Malayali seamen and moved them to respond *mataji*, the *ji* signifying respect, *mata* their word for the mothergoddess whose mere glance would protect them from all harm.

The Portuguese were surprised when the seamen came again on Monday morning. Paulo allowed them on the *conves*. They prostrated themselves, and each one placed his offerings of five cloves and a handful of pepper corns. They were poor, they had no flowers to offer, only spices which they had brought from Malabar to sell, in front of *mataji*.

We were on board the *San Raphael*, Usha and I, that Monday morning but I didn't see the Malayalis present their gifts. Bwana Mataka had made all the arrangements. It was Bwana Mataka who, when the administrator and the *kazi* had been seized on Saturday as hostages by Vasco da Gama who sent word to the sheik that they would be released only after a pilot was provided, boldly went to the *San Gabriel* early Sunday morning to explain what had happened on Friday and to arrange for food and water, and a pilot. The food and water were sent immediately that Sunday afternoon.

The pilot was a problem.

Bwana Mataka and Mian Mazlum came to my bedside at Silversands to discuss the problem with me. Five other pilots had been summoned to the palace that Sunday and the sheik had offered them two hundred miticals to guide the Portuguese ships. But they all refused, they knew what had happened to Maimun ibn Khalil who would be lame for the rest of his life. It was not the right season for sailing, it was too dangerous, in every way.

I jokingly said that I wished I could go if only to earn two hundred miticals, I needed the money. I knew it was impossible. My weak smile took some effort. My headache was beginning.

Bwana Mataka started to say something, stopped, and suddenly looked at me with his piercing eyes.

It was then that he told me what Lambu had told him. They will hire assassins, Bwana Mataka said, somehow the Jains will kill you both.

Usha, our baby, I thought. The Jains avoid harming any form of life. That's why they never till the earth. They prefer trade and business. That's why some of them walk around with a piece of white cloth across their mouths lest they swallow living organisms.

That Sheth Chimanlal wanted to have me killed, I accepted. But to want to have his Usha killed, his only daughter whom he loved so much. That I could not understand. To injure others, Usha's uncle said once during one of his talks on the Jaina path of purification, is to injure oneself. One is bound tighter on the wheel of *samsāra*. Killing is justified only when performed on behalf of the whole community.

My headache began to intensify.

Why don't you go as their *mu`allim*, said Bwana Mataka. You are a professional pilot, a master of navigation, no one can consider you a traitor. You can guide the Portuguese ships during the day. At night they can use their own pilots.

Yes, yes, said Mian Mazlum. Kochama had told him not to worry about me. The toy arrow had barely scratched my arm, the ointment was so powerful that I would be well soon, in a few days.

My friend, there was concern in Mian Mazlum's voice, I don't want you to go, but Bwana Mataka is right, the Jains will kill you. Do not be worried about Usha. Ratna and I will take her to Lamu. We will send her to Kannanur after the baby is born.

The door was thrown open and Usha walked straight to my bedside followed by Ratna. They must have been listening at the door.

No, Usha said, no.

He is my husband, Usha said, slowly, distinctly. I cannot leave him. I shall go with him.

She looked at me. Her eyes became soft, then turned anxious. No one spoke.

My head clamored with objections.

It was impossible, couldn't be done, where would she sleep, the ships didn't have any *dabusas*, there'd be no privacy, where would we escape to, no money, the baby, we needed a home.

Usha became aware of the overwhelming ache between my eyes.

He has to drink his medicine, she said.

Bwana Mataka didn't say a word. He left just as Abdul brought in the foul smelling jungle liquor.

When I woke up on Monday morning I was surprised to find myself in Paulo's cabin on the *San Gabriel* with Usha asleep sitting on a little stool with her head next to mine on a cushion. Abdul wasn't there. He told me later what happened, when we were halfway to Calicut.

She did it all, Abdul said, wonder in his voice.

After I had passed out, Bwana Mataka had called all of them, even Abdul, for a meeting around the oval table in his room to decide what should be done. They asked Abdul first. He didn't say anything, just looked at Usha, and looked away.

Ratna, horrified, burst out, It can't be done. She is in too delicate a condition. Ratna stopped. She couldn't talk about such matters in front of men.

She tried to coax Usha.

Come with me, Ratna said, I'll take you to Lamu. You and your baby will be safe there.

Yes, my *beti*, my daughter, Mian Mazlum said gently, we will protect you from all harm.

Usha remained silent.

After a long wait Bwana Mataka said, I would like to keep Usha here for my Shirin. My unpierced pearl, my Shirin looks up to you as an elder sister. You will be well protected as a member of my household.

Bwana Mataka paused, then continued slowly, almost reluctantly. He did not look at Usha. I did not want to tell you this. The message sent was that both had to be killed. Even the sheik will not be able to protect her.

I have to go with my husband, said Usha.

It was decided that Bwana Mataka would go very early on Monday morning to the *San Raphael* to speak with Paulo who grasped the situation immediately. He and Bwana Mataka worked out all the details. An hour later, when it was still dark and Malindi still asleep, Usha and I would be rowed to the ship. They told no one, there were no farewells. Yasmin was left behind with Layla. Ratna clung to Usha without making a sound so that the servants would not awake. I do not know how Abdul managed to get me into the boat and row us to the *San Raphael* for I was fast asleep. They hoisted me on board and placed me on Paulo's bed.

Paulo sent a message to the *San Gabriel* and Vasco da Gama set the hostages free. The administrator arranged for provisions and water to be carried in *mtepes* to the Portuguese ships all through Monday.

The people were told that the Portuguese would leave on Tuesday afternoon or perhaps on Wednesday. No one was sure of the day or who their pilot would be, one of the rumors had it that a coastal guide would take them to Mogadishu where ocean pilots were available.

Bwana Mataka spent some time at the sheik's palace and went back to Silversands only after sunset. With the sheik's permission three hundred miticals were taken from the treasury as payment for my services, and Bwana Mataka added one hundred and fifty miticals of his own.

Mian Mazlum went to the bazaar, telling his friends he had to go back to Lamu, and bought baskets of oranges, lemons, figs and sugarcane. Ratna filled three little jars with honey and got together two bundles of parched rice. She pounded some herbs and prepared a balm for headaches. She also made a small bundle of cloves and cardamon as breath sweeteners. There was a packet of incense sticks for foul odors.

Layla had to look after Shirin who kept asking about Usha the whole day. She wanted to play with Yasmin who fluttered about restless, making complaining noises. Shirin was taken to the market and spent the whole day darting from shop to shop buying clothes and jewellery. Later, tired and drugged and weeping, the little one had to be taken to Bwana Mataka's bed. Abdul and Layla could begin packing our things hurriedly only after midnight when the servants were fast asleep. There were no farewells.

Abdul and Layla and Yasmin came to the *San Raphael* in the darkness of Tuesday morning.

It was Paulo who, moved deeply by our story, without any hesitation had told Bwana Mataka that he could take all four of us to Calicut on the *San Raphael*. We could use his cabin for the voyage. The sheik sent a message to assure Vasco da Gama that he would be welcome on his way back to Portugal. He urged him to visit Malindi again and agreed to accept a *padrão* made of white Lisbon limestone together with a *degredado* who could learn Swahili. Bwana Mataka said the landmark could be erected on the low promontory near Silversands when things became quiet again. In the meantime it would be kept hidden in the shipping office.

The departure was deliberately not announced, so that only a few people gathered on the seafront to watch the Portuguese ships leave late Tuesday afternoon.

All four of us, Yasmin too, remained out of sight in Paulo's cabin. The window was slightly open. The rhythmic chants of the sailors sounded loud and clear as they hoisted the heavy mainsail. The wind blew fair, the tide was favorable, the weighing of the anchors was timed just right, and the *San Raphael* got under way, pivoting a little, and then ran smooth and easy toward the east. We heard a few subdued shouts from the people on the shore as the three ships, the *San Raphael* leading, headed toward the open sea. The Portuguese sailors merely waved their hands. From the *sambuks* on the left arose a few cries of Krist, *mataji*, Krist, as farewell greetings to mataji.

From the *San Gabriel* came the thunder of their largest bombard, fired just once, an announcement perhaps to all Malindi that the Portuguese were departing. Or else it was Vasco da Gama's defiant proclamation of Portuguese power.

Yasmin, frightened, flew out through the window opening. Abdul tried to catch her. Layla began to cry. We dared not leave the cabin yet.

I hoped Yasmin would somehow fly back to Silversands.

Usha looked down but didn't say a word.

The *San Raphael* headed out to the open sea. There was a knock on the door. When we opened it there was Paulo with Yasmin sitting on his right shoulder.

He had been standing on the poop deck next to the pilot, João de Co-imbra, and Yasmin had, strangely, flown straight up in a state of panic, and landed on Paulo's outstretched arm as if asking for protection.

Paulo had calmed her down, stroking her feathers gently.

Ush, ush, said Yasmin, and flew through the cabin door home safe to Usha.

As a pilot, despite my not feeling well, I was eager to see for my self new modes of navigation they used.

Paulo took me to João de Coimbra who was shouting directions through an open hatch in the deck floor. Down below stood the helms-man at the tiller steering without being able to look at the open sea. He could see the lower part of the creaking mainmast, and could sense the pull of the sails only by watching the lift of the mainsail foot. In front of him, set for protection in a fixed wooden box, was the compass which we call a *huqqa*. On the box, also called a *huqqa*, stood a sandglass and next to it hung an unlit lantern. Up above, the sails were full but not taut, the San Raphael kept on its course eastward, the helmsman held the tiller steady glancing at times at the compass in front of him.

Bom, shouted João de Coimbra approvingly into the hatch below.

He then checked the ship's course on his own compass, fastened in its box on the poop deck. I looked at it with a cold eye, half expecting, half wanting to see a Mediterranean compass card with its sixteen *akhnan* based on the names of winds, a system we Indian Ocean sailors despise as limited and outdated. My headache was about to begin

The Portuguese could surely not have a better instrument, ours has thirtytwo rhumbs based not on the winds that are always uncertain and inconstant, except for the two monsoons, but on the rising and setting of the eternal stars, that we watch and that watch over us. Ours belongs to an ancient tradition, established for centuries, and unchangeable. It is an instrument we take for granted, the first one our apprentice pilots have to learn through practical experience so that they can check their course. We do not ever mention it in our books on navigation except to warn the inexperienced or careless helmsman about the errors and inaccuracies caused by using a poor lodestone or by slovenly magnetising or by an incorrect balancing of the *huqqa* that could lead to a corruption of the course.

I examined the compass card.

The Portuguese compass rose, cut out of thick paper, had thirtytwo points like ours, and the revolving magnetic needle, which they call *agulha de marear* and we *al-ibra*, was mounted over it. The patterns were different, the *akhnan* were not the same, the lines, they call them rhumbs, were in different colors, gold and green and red, at the top of the card was a stylized lily, on the right end was a tiny cross.

That cross at the east point, said Paulo, in Portugal shows us the direction of Jerusalem.

A ship boy gave João de Coimbra an oblong lodestone which Paulo called a *pedra de cevar* and which we know as *al-maghnatis*, the magic stone David used to kill Goliath, the stone which attracts iron and no other thing, the lodestone of fate according to Arab tradition, which I cannot believe in any longer, that holds the seven vast heavens above, and the earth too, in a state of suspension.

João de Coimbra began stroking the needle with its two steel blades, he used even strokes, avoiding the *samka* defect of poor magnetising, we warn our apprentice pilots about this defect, which causes the needle to swing to and fro, instead of pointing to true north. He was an experienced pilot.

After he finished stroking the needle, he asked me if the course of the San Raphael needed to be changed.

I turned and looked back at the white distant blur of Malindi bay. I shut my eyes, they felt warm, they hurt a little. I said that we should sail parallel to the coast, keeping a distance of six miles from it. The assistant shouted an order and I saw ten men, not the whole crew, rush to adjust the ropes fastened to the yard so that the square mainsail swung at an angle, just enough for the *San Raphael* to change direction and sail northeastward.

I looked up at the powerful spread of the slanting mainsail. The towering mast creaked on its step, the *San Raphael* moved onward slowly and deliberately. Our dhows, graceful and slim, could have outrun her easily. Our dhows, their sails like butterfly wings, can skim swiftly over the sea. But I know it takes all the members of our crew to undo the ropes, that are fastened inboard, in order to swing the curved yard and the lateen sail, from one side to the other when wearing the dhow around.

It is tiring work. Our sailors sing and dance, chant, clap their hands and stamp their feet when they have to masthead the yard. They throw themselves into their work, but it is brutal, exhausting. They have to expend all their energy, they grow old before their time so that in a few years they become skin and bone.

The ropes of the *San Raphael*, they call them shrouds, that held the mainmast in place, were fastened on the outer sides of the ship, and they had cleverly made a series of rope steps, called ratlines, to allow the sailors to reach the top. An ingenious wellplanned system of pulleys and tackles, braces and clews, allowed the Portuguese seamen to control the mainsail from the *conves*. They could lift the yard, swing it around, pull the corners and edges of the sail forward or upward without much effort. I had seen how it took only ten men to adjust what they called the running rigging to change the ship's direction. I could see the holes and ties at the foot of the mainsail for bonnets to be fastened so as to increase wind power.

I knew then I was reentering my old world in a new kind of ship guided by a new science of navigation.

There were two gunshots to signal a change of course. The *San Gabriel* and the *Berrio* confirmed the signal by corresponding gunshots, and then changed their course.

João de Coimbra asked me if the mainsail would have to be lowered at night.

No, I said, there were no reefs or shoals along the way. We would sail parallel to the coast for two days, shift eastnortheast for another two, and then turn boldly directly toward the east, and the southwest monsoon would speed us along the open sea to Calicut and to the west coast of India. The *San Raphael* settled to a steady lilt and dip and roll. My head began to hurt.

My headaches did become less intense as we sailed along towards Calicut. But I hadn't forgotten what Kochama had told me about the final burst of pain I would experience before the poison left my system. On the fifth night, after that axis of the revolving stars, the Pole Star, appeared low in the northern sky, and João de Coimbra greeted it from the poop deck as a long lost friend and guide, and Paulo embraced me saying I was a master *malemo*. I tried to go to sleep without the help of any wine.

But I couldn't. I lay awake a long time, my mouth, my tongue, were dry, my mind awhirl. My throat felt as if grains of sand had stuck to it. My body began to shake. I hurriedly drank the wine down without taking the trembling bottle away from my lips. It tasted sour and sharp and it washed away the scratchiness in my throat, but the hollow whirling in my stomach did not stop and my body stopped shaking only after I had finished the second bottle.

I must have looked worried. Kochama had not told us about such an after condition.

It is a *tanha*, Usha said.

It was a Sanskrit word her uncle had often used, a craving of your body, not of your being.

She was not worried. Abdul, whom Paulo treated as one of the crew, gave me his *canada* of wine. One *canada* was part of the daily rations given to every Portuguese sailor every morning. But they stopped Abdul's ration. Perhaps they discovered he did not drink. Perhaps Abdul thought three *canadas* would be bad for me. Sometimes, just before mealtime, I would feel an intense thirst. Abdul knew I wanted wine, but would bring me water to drink.

Usha was happy on the *San Gabriel*. I was worried about Usha and our baby, worried about whether she would be sick in the mornings and lose her appetite, but she did not even get seasick. Her cheeks filled out. It wasn't the sea air, Usha, but a warmth within you that nourished our baby too. It gave your cheeks that apricot color. The broken tooth, that impish curl, I can see them so clearly I could even sketch them on this paper instead of writing about them.

But how can words capture, even for myself, that mysterious beauty that slowly grew within you. Lying close to you on Paulo's narrow bed, I was aware of your new beauty, wanting to speak about it but not able to say anything, not to anyone.

We did talk about other things. About Ratna and Mian Mazlum, and how they both wanted a child, and how Mian Mazlum had no one to leave his money and property to, and how they didn't want to go back to India, Mian Mazlum would bequeath his property to the Lamu mosque. About Bwana Mataka and Shirin, and how he had arranged everything for us, and how Shirin was still an innocent, how she babbled to you about Bwana Mataka. He was too old, like a dried fig, Shirin said. He had tried and couldn't, and Shirin was still a virgin.

We talked about the *Zephyr*. It would probably be used by the Kambas. The trim little ship had been our home.

We ate our meals together in Paulo's cabin. Usha ate quite well. For our baby too, she said. We ate fruit and rice and pickle, and crisp salty fried rounds of rice dough, and honey and other delicacies that Ratna had packed.

Layla and Abdul would eat their rice with curried fish which Abdul would catch fresh from the sea and prepare at the *fogão* and share with some of the Portuguese sailors. Layla was happy. She had not liked Malindi, and was eager to get back to Diu. Yasmin was not as playful as she had been at Silversands. She had got attached to Layla.

She is a wise bird, Layla said, she knows things. She knows that I look after her.

Usha taught Yasmin to speak more words of just one syllable, she couldn't manage two. Ahmad, Usha would say, but Yasmin would only say Ah and stop. And she wouldn't respond to her full name Yasmin but only to Min which she pronounced clearly. Perhaps one needs two human lips to make the y sound, Usha said, it is difficult with a beak.

When Usha and I sat together on Paulo's bed, Yasmin would sit near the window and look out. At times Layla, her face covered with a veil, taught Yasmin a number of tricks and games with the ivory ball just outside Paulo's cabin door. A few Portuguese sailors would gather nearby to watch Yasmin playing with the ball.

Abdul laughed and joked with the sailors. He never learned Portuguese from them but, strangely, managed to teach his friends some pungent swear words in Gujarati. Abdul usually keeps himself to himself. I have never seen him as relaxed and happy as he was on the *San Raphael*.

Outwardly I was relaxed. But at night I would lie awake worrying about what would happen to us when we got to the west coast of India.

THIRTEEN

*M*id-May, 1509,
my house, Diu, Night,
the tufan outside my house has slowed down
but I continue to write furiously about João's inner tufan
his long confiteor to Brother Clement in Coimbra, and to me in Vanakbara

I had to stop writing for a while. I heard Abdul open the backdoor to let the fisherman and his wife out.

Shall I make some coffee, Abdul asked.

No, I said. Go back to sleep.

I needed some coffee, but it would be difficult for Abdul to light a fire. The firewood would be damp.

The sounds of the tufan outside had changed. I could hear low growls of thunder, and the wind howls now came as from a distance. My inner tufan has slowed down too. I felt quite exhausted as if the act of writing about the past, not just recalling it, had drained energy out of me. Writing is a form of action, my hakim had said. I am now aware of the many languages of the Bahr-i-Hind swirling within me together with the presence of a new language that has entered my being. The older languages, at peace with each other, belonged to my peaceful world. This new one has disturbed everything. I thought the new language was the one from beyond the seas that my friend João was teaching me.

João is a very good teacher. It was he who made me conscious of the many languages that swirl around the Bahr-i-Hind . And it was he who made me self conscious about my use of language. It is not just Gujarati, he said, nor is it just Portuguese, he said, it is the new language of science and power that has now entered the world of the Bahr-i-Hind and affected all the languages spoken there.

Perhaps that's why I'm tired. Summoning up the past on paper in a language that is changing is difficult. João did not have my problem when he recalled his past for me.

I am setting down all he told me about his Portuguese and his Christian past because our stories, his and mine, are somehow interconnected.

João and I were at the other end of Diu island, at Vanakbara, early this May. We were sitting by ourselves on a spur of black rocks that jutted into the sea, the wind blowing on our faces, looking at the swirl of the waves below, watching the reddish orange sun sinking slowly through a mass of dark blue clouds. Premonsoon cloud colors are always glorious, and I wanted to absorb them into my being.

João lifted his flask and took his first drink of the day.

He, also, kept looking across the sea towards the west.

Isn't it almost Angelus time, João said.

It wasn't a question. His voice was low, he sounded sad, I wondered what Angelus time was. He had already arranged for two heavy haunched women of the village for us for the night. He should be excited, I thought, but he was not. He was sad.

I have to recite my *Confiteor*, he said, though it may not cleanse my soul.

I didn't know what the word meant then. But I sensed that he wanted to talk. Not just to anyone, but to anyone who would listen and understand. He did not want to talk to himself.

Fierce streaks of purple shot through the orangetopped blue and black clouds. The sun was bloodred.

Suddenly João stood up, and spread his arms out wide.

Confiteor deo omnipotenti.

He hurled the Latin words with all his might toward the bloodred sun. The sea wind gusts carried them back and away.

I stood up startled. I wanted to help my friend.

João tried again.

Con, he began loudly, drawing out the syllable as if in pain. Then he suddenly stopped and sank down, clasped his arms around his raised knees, and bowed his head.

I thought he wanted to confess about his conspiratorial involvement with Ishak Khan and Malik Gopi and Hooknose. I knew João was in considerable debt to Malik Gopi. Ishak Khan wanted to get rid of his father with João's help. Abdul had heard rumors that João supplied Malik Gopi with information about foreigners who lived in Bandar-i-Turk in exchange for supplies of liquor. João didn't want to talk about any conspiracy he was involved in. He wanted to talk about his past not about the present.

I don't know what to believe in, João began. Or which god to talk to. There are so many now.

In the faraway days, when I was eight and innocent, no, ignorant, I would complete my daily duties in the monastery stable, grooming the Prior's horse, teaching his nephew, fat António, how to ride his pony. Then I would accompany Brother Clement who had to see to it that the great doors of the Coimbra cathedral of Santa Cruz were shut every night. We would listen to the *Salve Rainha*, he with his head bowed down, holding my hand, making me feel I belonged. I could sense his love for me.

May the Queen of Heaven always protect you, my child, Brother Clement prayed.

Go, little orphan, he would then say to me, rattling his bunch of keys aloud to signal that it was time for the people in the cathedral to leave. Go talk to our Blessed Lord. Tell him everything about yourself.

I would go slowly to the high altar crowded with playful cherubs, and kneel in front of the statue of Our Lord, say the *Pater Noster*, and tell all that had happened to me during the day in the cathedral school. How I had stolen some marmeladed bread from the refectory, I had pulled the hair of bully António and run away, how I had been the only one in class to know the Hebrew name for God, how I and bully António would begin the study of Greek tomorrow with a special tutor who had come from Bologna, how the teacher had pulled my ears because my first attempt to write Gothic letters was smudgy, how intensely lonely and jealous I felt when Antonio's mother, accompanied by her brother, our Prior, wearing a long white linen cassock, came to our classroom and the teacher praised António as the cleverest boy in the class, the one who always wore his dead mother's silver crucifix on his chest, how António had been given a box of sweets and how he had stuck his tongue out at me.

It was a relief to look up at Jesus and tell him my little woes. Jesus was my father.

Brother Clement, he had a huge hunch on his back, would tap my shoulder affectionately, make a small bow towards the tomb of our founder, Saint Teotonio, in the chapel on the right, and amble slowly down the central aisle.

It was time to leave. I would bow my head and make my act of faith.

I believe in one God, the Father Almighty, Creator of heaven and earth, João intoned.

João bowed his head and mumbled into his knees. A steady wind blew from the sea. The cloud colors kept changing every time I looked at them.

João took a long drink, paused for a while, then took another and lay back with fingers intertwined under his head, looking up at the deepblue sky.

A flight of crows cawed their way home to the huge pipal tree in the middle of Vanakbara village.

I do not recite the *Credo* now. João shut his eyes and continued. Though I can never ever forget the words. I stopped reciting it three years after they sent me to the College of Santa Barbara in Paris. Brother Clement urged me to go to the University of Salamanca, famous for its School of Civil and Canon Law. His brother lived in that city. But I didn't want to be a Doctor of Laws.

God is a mystery, said Brother Clement.

I wanted to unravel the mystery, João said. I wanted to woo the queen of sciences. I wanted to be a Doctor of Theology at the most famous university in all Christendom, the university of Paris.

Come with me, João, said the Prior. His voice was heavy, as if he had a pain in his chest.

I was surprised. He usually never took any notice of me, or talked to me or else would give me a cold look down his aquiline nose. He put his hand on my shoulder. He had become bent and frail. Brother Clement told me the Prior was only forty five. António, his nephew, had joined the Franciscan order in Loureiro after finishing school. I was a teacher in the cathedral school now. I began teaching even before I finished school. They all said I was the cleverest student they ever had, cleverer even than the teachers, they said.

I helped the Prior climb the three steps to his study. I had never been in there before.

João, my son, how long have you been with us.

Nineteen years, Reverend Prior, I said. Brother Clement told me I was brought here when I was one year old.

Ah, yes, said the Prior, draw near to me.

I drew up my stool near his stately mahogany chair, and looked into his eyes. They were troubled. He put his hand lightly on my head and turned my face towards the door.

My son, he said, and he paused for a while.

Did you know it was I who found you, the Prior continued, crying in the night on the front steps of the door of the cathedral the very year I came here from Braga as Prior.

Through my thick hair I could feel the weight of his gold ring topped with a single pearl.

For nineteen years I've watched you grow, the Prior said. Every year you grew in knowledge. I didn't believe it at first when they told me that you knew the grammar of Donatus by heart. By the age of nine you knew the *trivium* and parts of the *quadrivium*. You were much cleverer than your classmate, António, my sister's son who had to struggle through the seven liberal arts.

It was I who told the teacher to let you read Cicero. It was I who told that tutor from the University of Bologna to teach you Greek. Alas, he had to leave after two years. I ordered books for our monastery library, books by Virgil and Plato and Quintilian, the *Doctrinale*, the *Graecismus*, and that textbook of basic theology, the *Sententiae* of Peter Lombard, because I knew you would read them. I even ordered Arrian's *Ars Tactica* because you looked after my horse. I told Brother Clement to give you a pack of candles when I discovered you would go up the tower to read by moonlight.

Your mother was proud of you when I told her how brilliant you were in your studies, the Prior continued slowly.

I couldn't speak. I looked at the door. I never knew who my mother was.

No, my son, keep looking at the door. Do not turn your head to look at me and ask the question you want to ask. A mystery it will remain. My lips are sealed. She died last week.

I sat numb, Brother Clement.

The Prior took my hand in his. His fingers were delicate and slender. They looked like mine, especially the curve of the fingernails. But his touch was icy cold.

I've just discussed matters with my noble cousin, the Lord Bishop, the Prior continued. He has granted us his episcopal permission to dispatch you to the University of Paris.

His voice was no longer sad. The words were formal.

When I did my theological studies there I was a *cameriste*. I rented a large room, and my family paid for everything I wanted.

He stopped for a while. Then continued softly, I had a household servant. She prepared my meals and looked after all my needs.

He closed his eyes and sat brooding.

You, João, will be a *portionist*. I will be responsible for your room and board at the Colegio de Santa Barbara. Take your promotion exams every three months. It took me six years to become a *baccalaureus*. You'll be a doctor of theology before you're thirty. You're clever. Your Latin is correct and classical. Mine when I first arrived in Paris was full of flaws. I would use *ut* with the indicative, and at times interchange *quod* and *ut*, and the indicative and the subjunctive. Oh, it was hopeless. Did you know how many times the *lupus* fined me for not speaking Latin with my classmates during my first year.

He went on and on, Brother Clement, recalling his student days, telling me about the professors he came to know because of his illustrious family. They got him his appointment as Prior. His voice droned on and on for over an hour. Finally, he stood up.

I've arranged for you to go to Santa Barbara's college on October first, he said.

I was bursting with questions. But he had assumed, once again, that cold forbidding look. He didn't notice that I went out of his study intensely sad, oppressed, wondering about my mother.

Your eyes were wet the day I left Coimbra, Brother Clement, so as to get to Paris by October first when the term began. I molested you with my letters all through my first year in Paris, Brother Clement, letters I knew you would have to ask others to read to you. I boasted that I was excused from attending classes. I boasted that I passed the exams without even preparing for them. I wrote to you about my pilgrimage to the tomb of the Master of the Sentences in the church of Saint Marceau. For two years I isolated myself in the world of theology. I lived in libraries reading the great doctors of the church. Their world, wonderfully ordered, its patterns laid down by Aristotle and Aquinas, enclosed me. I felt safe as in a womb.

João paused. He did not know the sun had set and it was growing dark, for his eyes were shut tight. He wasn't in Vanakbara. He had traveled far into his past in faraway Portugal. He wasn't drunk, his mind was clear. He wasn't talking to me in Diu but confessing to Brother Clement in Coimbra.

I emerged in my third year at the Sorbonne, I had to. *Ecce venit molus*, my fellow students shouted in bad Latin, despising me for not drinking with them in the student inns, and for not joining in their street brawls and tavern games.

I didn't consider myself a mole, Brother Clement. I wasn't blind. I had to come forth. To attend lectures I was not interested in. I knew more than the twenty year old regents who had just finished their master's in philosophy. To attend disputations that were mere tournaments, abounding in hairsplitting trivialities about trivialities and in speculation about trifles. I despised the *determinatio* usually put forward by the master to a complex question. How I longed to hear the voice of St. Thomas

Aquinas, the angelic doctor who, it is said, never forgot anything he had heard or read. My fellow students envied me my extraordinary memory.

It was in 1494, at a crowded quodlibetal disputation held in that bastion of theology, the Sorbonne, during Lent, that I heard a voice I had never heard before, one that touched my being.

Let me recapture it for you, Brother Clement. For myself, too, João said, his eyes were shut tight.

I heard as in a dream the sounds of dawn on the edge of the Mediterranean urging me awake. The voice was warm. It spoke polished and elegant Latin as a living tongue. The consonants were open and created a sense of space. The undulating vowels made music. It talked about Virgil, Ovid, Horace, as our friends. The classics would rejuvenate this generation. It didn't preach. This teacher tried new strategies to lead his students to truth. Eloquence that celebrated the classics, adagia and colloquia and folk turns of phrase that put everyone at ease, humor and satire. Foolishness was praised to convince it of its own folly. It used the art of persuasion instead of cold argument.

Set aside the categories of Aristotle and the system of Aquinas, this teacher urged his students. Seek sustenance from the marvelous myths of Plato and the daring insights of Saint Augustine. Let me lead you through the double gateway of the classics and of Christ to true wisdom.

I, who had always taught myself, was drawn out of myself by this magic voice that promised me a new world. I emerged from a cave of shadows.

It is a composite voice I am trying to capture for you, Brother Clement.

That day in the Sorbonne aula I heard a clear voice that rang out above the thin spouting of the usual terms, *questio, utrum, sic proceditur, sed contra, nonsequitur, dicendum quod.*

The *quodlibetal* question posed by the master was a basic one.

Whether the will of God was the ground of all that is and of all that happens.

A *baccalaureus* rose and stated that God is omnipotent, and can do what He will.

The silence in the aula meant general acceptance.

And then this voice from the back of the hall calmly asked.

Can God, the all powerful, contradict Himself. Make black white. Undo the done. Unsight the seen. Make right wrong. Can He, the voice went on, make a man hate God. Could He have incarnated Himself in a fish or a wild boar.

There was uproar in the aula. Quarrels began. The master tried in vain to control the crowd.

I turned and looked at the one who had asked such devastating questions. He stood aloof above the fray. He looked so ordinary that I was disappointed. His face was a sickly white. The lips were thin, the eyes a watery blue, his northern blond hair struggled untidily out of the flat black cap on his head. His nose was aquiline like that of our Prior. He wore a white cassock. He was an Augustinian canon.

He was of our order, from a monastery at Steyn in Holland, older than most of us students, about twentyeight. No one knew his real name. Some called him Desiderius, others Gerhardt. He was also known as Erasmus. All three names, in Latin, Dutch, and Greek meant beloved. He was illegitimate, it was rumored. Impossible for him to get a benefice without a doctorate in divinity.

He was enrolled in the *Collegia Pauperum* at the College of Montaigu next door. We, Barbistes, would hurl taunts at our neighbors, the Capettes, so called because of their cassocks of dirty grey that crawled with lice. Cesspool, sewer, we held our noses and yelled obscenities across the street at the students of the College of Montaigu, the very cleft between the buttocks of Mother Theology.

The next time I met Erasmus was at another debate where the profound question was, *utrum* a prayer of ten minutes was as efficacious as ten one minute prayers.

Erasmus left in disgust, and five of us accompanied him out of the hall to the private lodgings he had taken in the new term.

On the way he poured scorn on the Paris theologians. They remind me of Epimenides of Greek legend who slept for fortyseven years. He, at least, woke up. Can there be horsiness without a horse. Was the sea salty when God made it. These theologasters talk quite confidently of hell as if they had been there. They speculate about what the boy Jesus discussed with the doctors in the temple. Surely, Erasmus said, it wasn't about the *primum mobile* or the *prima materia*.

Erasmus was at his sparkling best that day. It was a feast of talk for the five of us, hungry for wisdom. He had no food to offer us in his shabby quarters, or drink.

Drink of Helicon, but if you have to go to the Sorbonne, he warned, vomit up the draught.

He talked passionately about the need for a Platonic Academy in Paris. The range of his language matched the range of the topics he talked about, and the range of his reading. I discovered he had read even minor Latin writers, but could read Greek only in Latin translation.

I am an insomniac, he apologized. To my surprise he was able to cite Aquinas, Scotus and Lombard.

I am not a foe to scholasticism, he said, but I prefer the Fathers of the Church, Saint Jerome and Saint Augustine, to the great doctors.

Let us return, he pleaded, to the early sources of the Christian faith.

I thought we could study Greek together, and be friends.

We never did become friends. He craved fame and success. He charmed everyone, but did not make many close friends. He cultivated acquaintances that could further his career.

Erasmus did think I was clever. He asked me to read his own poems before he sent them to the printer. I didn't tell him he wasn't a good poet, though I wanted to. He had no time for me.

But he did change me, Brother Clement. He even changed the language I used to Ciceronian Latin. Erasmus opened for me the flood of new learning and of new books, no longer chained to library shelves, that swept across Europe after the discovery of printing. He charged me with a passion for Plato who accepted a world filled with contradictions, a passion for people like Ficino and for Pico della Mirandola. For Rome, for Venice.

I came to hate Paris. Erasmus filled me with wild dreams, impossible longings. For Florence, for faraway new exciting worlds of culture and learning.

But how could Erasmus ever have prepared me, how, tell me how, Brother Clement, for what happened to you, for what happened to me. How, when did it happen, why did it happen, what happened first, Brother Clement, were you murdered first, your head bloodred, smashed by that robber with a gold monstrance he wanted to steal as you shut the cathedral doors that night, or did your murder happen one week after the Prior collapsed in his study, clutching his chest.

I couldn't attend either funeral. I didn't care about missing the Prior's funeral, but I did want to say thank you and goodbye to you, Brother Clement. I was in Paris. They didn't send for me. They didn't even inform me about your brutal murder.

A month after the Prior's death the Bishop of Coimbra sent for me. He offered me his huge emerald ring to kiss.

It was, he solemnly proclaimed, the will of God on high.

He was curt.

No provision was made for you by my cousin, the Prior, in his will. Discontinue your studies immediately. Don't return to Paris. Never set foot in the Santa Cruz monastery again. You'll tutor the Gouvea children whose mother is the wife of Senhor Fernão Gomes, the administrator of

Mina House. He may get you a position in African Guinea later. The family lives in the Rossio, in Lisbon.

In a daze I got to Lisbon, Brother Clement. I found the house in the Rossio, I don't know how. Someone on high had smashed my mind with an invisible stone.

I can't hear you, Brother Clement. Who smashed your mind, you ask, what was his name.

No one told me, but I knew it was Will from on high.

Did it hurt, you ask, Brother Clement.

No, it didn't, there was no pain, but a cold numbness in me. My eyes, wide open, could actually see nothing. Its color was white. Nothing, what joy, made perfect sense. I could even feel nothing. I became a stone that smiled at nothing with joy. This stone taught the two children of Senhor Gouvea. This stone read the myths of Plato to their mother. This stone helped Senhor Gouvea, my old master, with his account books of the Guinea trade in the evenings, prepared his correspondence, made lists of the stores and trade goods sent to Guinea, and recorded the gold and ivory and slaves his ships brought back to Lisbon. The new discoveries in science and astronomical navigation that my master talked about meant nothing to me. I was dead.

She brought me back to painful life.

Where are you, Brother Clement, don't go away. Stay with me. Listen to me, Brother Clement, I have never confessed this to anyone.

I was the teacher of her two children. She was my teacher. For over a year she taught me. She taught me during siesta time in her warm bed without using any words. She embraced this cold untouched stone, ruffled my thick hair, shut my eyes with her warm fingers so that I cried with happiness, and then she drew me down on to her warm full breasts and gave me her nipples to suck. She took this hard stone, and then she eased it between her warm generous thighs.

In Elysium I was, in Paradise. During my throes of pleasure I would call her Helen, Venus. I would call her Eva, mother.

Then hell happened.

The door opened. He rushed in, the old man, with sword drawn. He wanted to pierce her first. I leapt from our bed, pushed away his trembling hand, and smashed his head with a candlestick. He crashed to the floor, his white hair bloodred. A hellish rage exploded within me. I was possessed. I shrieked with laughter and lifted the candlestick, and wanted to smash that red head over and over and over again.

She touched my arm, and looked at me.

I dropped the candlestick and fled, mad with fury, out the door, down the Rossio, into the blinding sunlight of siesta time, toward the harbor.

I didn't, I didn't, I shouted, facing the sea.

There was blood on my hands, and on my white shirt.

It was Will from on high, he did it. It was Will. It was Will.

They flung me into the harbor prison.

Where are you. It's dark, Brother Clement, I cannot see. I was an avenger. Don't go away. Tell Potiphar I'm sorry.

You've left me, Brother Clement. I'll tell him myself.

Potiphar.

Potiphar.

Potiphar.

The three syllables, repeated three times, resounded in the immense darkness of Diu. I sat up, reached out and touched João lightly.

Ah, there you are, Brother Clement, João said, opening his eyes.

Is it you, Ahmadbhai, João asked me, where am I. I cannot see anything.

It's time to go back to Vanakbara, I said.

It was pitch dark. The wind felt cold through my thin cotton shirt. It would be difficult to get back to Vanakbara village without a light. No stars had come out in the sky. Snakes would venture forth into the coolness now after the heat of the day.

Don't worry, Ahmadbhai, I'll finish the last of this jambool liquor and take you back, João told me.

João knew I was afraid of snakes.

He helped me down the rocks, gripped my arm firmly, and we began to walk along the seashore.

Let's not return by the shortcut through the berry bushes. Let's follow the line of the white sea foam, said João. There'll be no snakes by the edge of the sea.

It would be a long walk back to Vanakbara.

João walked confidently on the firm but wet sand, guiding me as if he could see in the dark. I stumbled one or two times, . His breath stank, but he wasn't drunk, as if the liquor had expended all its powers, arousing then casting forth the *djinns* of the past, freeing his being of anxieties. He was silent for a while.

Ahmadji, João then said, I talked for quite a long time, but I don't remember what I said. I thought I was confessing to Brother Clement. Did I tell you the story of my life.

No, I said. I knew he disliked talking about himself. You did mention a few names. You shouted for Potiphar. That was the last name you used.

João stopped suddenly and let go of my arm.

What did I say about him, he asked.

I didn't want to embarrass João. I didn't want him to know I knew.

I don't remember, I said. You were mumbling most of the time. Isn't Potiphar mentioned in the Qu 'ran.

Yes, yes, Surah 12, João said, and we began walking again. Potiphar is an *aziz ajiz*, a play on words, Ahmadbhai. He is a steward*aziz* who is impotent*ajiz*. Zuleikha, his wife, is mad with desire. In the Bible Potiphar is not a significant character.

João didn't mention Joseph, Potiphar's adopted son, according to the story in the Qu'ran.

What other names did I mention, asked João.

Oh, I said, that Plato you frequently refer to, and someone called Erasmus.

João stopped again.

Ah, Ahmadbhai, ah. Erasmus of Rotterdam was my teacher. He led me out of a cave into light, and bade me look beyond the horizon. Where is he now, I wonder. He would've been excited about these new cultures, these new civilizations. Old cultures for you, Ahmadbhai. New for people from the west. I could introduce him to new classics. To the Arabic classic, *Alf laila wa laila*, wherein he could have spent a thousand and one nights. To Persian *mathnavis* and *ghazals* and to Rumi, to the Bhagavad Gita in Sanskrit, to the plays of Kalidasa. I could have told him about other major religions. About the millions who worship Allah and whose holy book is the Qu 'ran. The complexity of Hinduism would've intrigued him. We could have explored the concept of the Brahman in the Upanishads the concept of the divine as *neti, neti*, not that, not that, all of which I do not yet understand. There's Jainism, there's Buddhism. The world teems with countless gods and goddesses.

João put his hand on my shoulder to steady himself.

We walked on. Our eyes adjusted to the darkness.

The world, your world, my world, the whole world, is changing, Ahmadbhai. In Paris in 1498, and then in Lisbon in 1499 after the return of Vasco da Gama from India, I became dimly aware of the powerful hum of new forces converging into and onto man, new sciences driving him blindingly through time.

When in 1500 I saw the Tupinamba, naked and innocent in their paradisal island named Vera Cruz by Pedro Alvares Cabral who raised the royal arms of Portugal as a sign of conquest during a mass celebrated there by

Frei Henrique, I knew that never again would their island be a virgin land. Never again would anyone call the Tupinamba innocent. A new power had invaded their land.

My language has become heavy, Ahmadbhai. I only wanted to trace for you how I arrived at the concept of change in our world. But my language is inadequate, it doesn't sound right, its syntax is rough, its vocabulary limited. I have not yet learned this new language. You'll have to learn it too.

No, Ahmadji, it is not just Portuguese but a new language of change.

Let me tell you my experiences in the cavernous hold of the *capitania*, the flagship of the fleet sent out to India for diplomacy and for trade, led by Pedro Alvares Cabral who was, I found out later, related to the Gouvea family.

They should have had me hanged. I wanted to die. I wanted to kill myself, but was terrified of the unknown.

On the 8th of March 1500, a day before the fleet sailed from Lisbon, they had me flung into another hell. Demons tortured me within and there were demons without, the stench, I was seasick, the lice, my own vomit, the cockroaches, the rats. I had been condemned to death. I now became a banished convict, a *degredado*.

One gets accustomed, Ahmadbhai, even to hell and to demons. I took a vow of silence, refusing to talk even to my fellow *degredado*, Affonso Ribeiro, who kept chattering away relaying gossip and bits of news. The sailors would yell murderer down at me when the hatch was opened. I refused to come out. I began to feel at peace in hell, even when the seas were stormy. I just wanted to ease quietly into death.

Frei Henrique would climb down the steps into hell.

Eat, João, he said softly, and would wait till I finished.

I didn't see his face.

Six weeks passed before I saw it. I had heard the anchors drop twice. A round reddish face, a small mouth, twinkling eyes, a small nose. He could've been an impish cherub just stepped down to greet me from the high altar in the Santa Cruz Cathedral, were it not for his fanlike ears sprouting with black hair.

Come forth, João Machado, Frei Henrique said, enter a new land, we need you.

Two sailors threw pails of water on me.

Frei Henrique told his assistant to take me to the admiral's cabin on the topmost deck. Frei Luís do Salvador pointed in silence to a painting. It was an image of *Nossa Senhora de Esperança*, Our Lady of Hope. I was then rowed to the landing site to help Master John.

I found Master John moving awkwardly among the strange instruments all around him. Hurry up, hurry up, Master John squeaked.

He was like a hen turning around and around, clucking, about to lay an egg.

It will be high noon soon, I have to shoot the sun. Write down what I tell you, Master John said. Exactly, exactly, no mistakes, no mistakes.

His forefinger pointed to a tree stump.

There were two books on the stump. One was an elementary textbook on astronomy which I had never bothered to read in school, the *Tractatus de Sphera* by John Holywood, a treatise based on Ptolemy's *Geographia*. The other was a notebook with a dedication on the front page. To my teacher, Avraham Zacut of Salamanca. It had a name and a title on the next page, Johanes Magister, with his degrees, *artium et medicinis bacalaureus*, and a list, astronomer, astrologer, personal physician and royal surgeon to Dom Manuel, mathematician, cosmographer.

A teacher Master John was, a scholar. I was impressed.

He limped. He had an infected leg wound that had developed from a neglected scratch. He spent a long time adjusting all his instruments. He was totally dedicated to his work.

The two pilots, some distance away, one the pilot of the *capitania*, the other the pilot of the nao, *El Rei*, commanded by Sancho de Tovar, would stroll up and Master John would adjust their instruments and patiently answer their questions, apologizing most obsequiously for being so knowledgeable.

I could hear the tone of contempt in their voices even though they did not call him a *marrano*. Master John's contempt for them blazed forth in his eyes, not in his voice. His was the silent language of the eyes all converted Jews were forced to use, part of their strategy for survival in our hostile Christian world.

It was only after they walked away that the contempt burst out of him.

Mindless fools, Master John spat forth. Lower than animals. Never, never will I become a *converso* like that Polish swine, that Gaspar da Gama.

He spat again, looked up at me, and then became aware that I had heard what he said. But I was harmless, just a *degredado*.

Who is Gaspar da Gama, I asked him.

He is a *lingua*, a translator, said Master John. He was brought back from India to Lisbon by Vasco da Gama who stood as his godfather and gave him not only his last name but the name of one of the magi. He is somewhere on one of these ships but I don't wish to talk to him. He knows Spanish and Arabic and some Indian languages. Senhor Cabral will use his services as an interpreter in India.

He spat out his contempt again.

But enough of him, Master John spat out.

Master John spat out his contempt again.

We have work to do.

Open the notebook to a blank page after a star diagram, said Master John.

He wanted to test me, I think.

Write down the date. Saturday, 25th April, 1500.

A Survey of the Southern Skies was written at the top of the star sketch. One set of stars looked like a cross. I read strange names. The guards. La Bosya. The pole antarctic.   Master John turned a pointer on an instrument that was suspended from a swivel thumb ring and held by a sailor.

Hurry up, he shouted, it is almost midday.

The sun's rays passed through both pinholes on the sight rule and cast a spot of light. He shouted, write this down. The height of the sun equals 56 degrees, shadow south. He referred to some tables in front of him.

Solar declination at noon for this day equals 17 degrees, he said. 90 degrees minus 56 degrees equals 34 degrees, the zenith distance of the sun. Minus 17 degrees declination, equals 17 degrees.

And then, wincing with pain as he stumbled in his hurry, Master John shouted to the pilots who were still looking at the sun through their instruments.

The *altura* is 17 degrees.

I signaled to Master John that he should rest. Very carefully, as if it was a sacred object, he took up the long flat book, the *Almanach Perpetuum* containing the sheets of tables prepared by his teacher, Avraham Zacut.

I wish I had his earlier work, *ha-Hibbur ha-Hagadol*, the Great Composition. The canons were clearer, the tables more detailed, he lamented.

Then he closely examined what I had written, nodding approvingly, and he sat down.

He told me their names as I carried his instruments very carefully, one by one, to the landing site. A marine astrolabe made of solid wood that hung on a tripod.

Astrolabe means star measurer, he told me.

A sphere with these capital letters C A D A T G slanting across it. That's the armillary sphere which represents the form and all the workings of the heavens and the earth and all the elements. Another one of the plane type. An astronomical astrolabe which Master John explained in great detail because he thought I had studied mathematics, a stereographic projection of the heavens with the star positions engraved at points on this pierced brass plate that turns above a stereographic projection of the observer's view of the sky as defined by a network of lines of equal altitude and lines of equal bearing.

Notice, he said, that round its margin are set the divisions of time and of the seasons which depend upon the rotation of the heavens and the yearly motion of the sun.

I kept nodding my head. I was quite impressed.

Master John continued his lesson. A quadrant, an hourglass, dividers. Then some strange tablets that had knotted strings subtending from them. Those are not scientific instruments but toys, exact copies of the *tabuas da India* which Vasco da Gama brought back to Lisbon, very laborious to use.

Rulers, charts made of parchment and rolled, some maps, instruments to know and to conquer the universe man lived in.

I entered a new world that day. From Master John I began to learn the new language of science and discovery.

And then, then, Ahmadbhai, I had a vision of innocence. I saw the Tupinamba.

They brought food for us, and water. Fruits of the earth which young women carried on their heads in woven baskets, their arms raised high, their breasts like apples. The men carried bows and arrows, like hunters not like soldiers. Their bodies were not covered with clothes, but had quarterings of color, red, black, bluish black, yellow, stains made of fruit juices and arranged in different patterns. The men wore diadems, bonnets, and mantles, skilfully made of brilliant colored feathers selected for uniformity of size and color. In their lower lips they had holes, made when they were young, through which labrets of white bone were placed. These ornaments did not prevent them from eating or drinking or talking. The women had long black hair and wore necklaces made of shells but no other ornaments. Each woman daubed color spots on the areas of the body she wanted to highlight.

The slits of the young women were high, closed, shaven of hair. A young mother, nursing her baby and sitting crosslegged, was given a piece of cloth to cover herself, she tied it under her breasts and used it to carry her baby. The men walked around and slept with their uncircumcized penises uncovered, the hair around there shaven and shaped like beards.

We Portuguese could not take our eyes off the round breasts and the pink slits of the young women. I too was a voyeur. Only the friars turned their backs and went away.

The Tupinamba were unconcerned. They did not know that they were naked and that they should be ashamed. I don't think they had words like privy parts and phrases like cover their shame in their language, or words like good or evil or sin. The language of innocence uses few words. I saw them touching each other, rubbing ears and noses, laughing, pointing, dancing.

They were the children of Paradise, Ahmadji.

They became thoughtful and opened their eyes wide when they saw the solemn procession led by boys swinging censers of incense, followed by five short black men dressed in heavy clothes as if they were unaccustomed to them and to the five caps they wore, followed by the friars chanting and intoning hymns of praise, and by Frei Henrique bearing the holy cross in front of him, and Senhor Cabral with two banners, the royal standard emblazoned with the royal arms, and the banner of the Order of Christ of which he was a knight, a red cross on a white ground, an emblem they had seen displayed on all the sails. The holy cross was planted near the altar that had been set up and decorated with red and gold hangings of silk and rich velvet. The two banners were placed on either side.

The other *degredados* and I did not pay much attention to the religious pomp and ceremony. They were fascinated by the multicolored macaws that squawked loudly in the trees above. *Terra de papagaios*, they said, the land of the parrots. I watched the Tupinamba men with their bows, arrows were not allowed, their bone ornaments, their feathercovered bodies, no women were allowed to be present because they would distract the mariners, watching the ceremony with great interest. They wanted very much to touch the golden vestments of the friars. The lit candles fascinated them, but the smell of incense puzzled them and made them clutch their noses tightly as if in disgust.

I wondered what they really thought. I am sure they thought we were pathetic womenless comic creatures who never had baths and who smelled bad, I could smell my own smell, and stared hungrily at their women's breasts and slits. We had been obviously sent here by our gods to learn the arts of language and of civilization from them. They were polite and understanding. They laid down their bows and knelt down, like us, when the Frei said Mass to celebrate the discovery of a new land. They raised their hands, like us, when the Gospel was recited and when the Host was elevated. They even wanted to partake of Communion, like us, but Frei Henrique would not allow it.

After the mass was over, the banners were sprinkled with holy water and blessed by Frei Henrique. The Tupinamba bowed their heads when Frei Henrique lifted the cross high above their heads, and shouted with joy when Senhor Cabral raised first the royal standard, then the banner of the Order of Christ, named the land *Terra da Vera Cruz*, and pronounced the solemn words that loudly bore witness that he was formally taking possession of the land in the name of his sovereign, Dom Manuel of Portugal. The royal standard was then planted in the ground. Pero Vaz da Caminha, the scrivener, recorded the act of possession on a document that was witnessed and signed by two officials of the crown.

Shouts of Viva Portugal, Viva Portugal, Viva Portugal, resounded through the island. For a moment the Tupinamba fell silent. Perhaps they could not pronounce the words. Perhaps they had a vague realization that the banners were emblems of power over them.

But soon they joined in the shouting and the celebration with whoops of joy. They blew horns and trumpets made of the leg bones of animals cased in wood. They stamped their feet, and leapt and danced around the royal standard, touching its soft velvet with their foreheads as if it were a sacred object.

Viva Portugal, they screamed.

For them it was some kind of unknown omen.

It was nearing noon now. Having removed his gold embroidered vestments, Frei Henrique took his seat on a high chair in front of the altar and addressed us all, including the Tupinamba, as children. His words were simple and sincere. His sermon, spoken in a deep but vibrant voice that everyone could hear, quite brief.

My children, the Frei said, let us rejoice, alleluia, on this auspicious day on which we have been resurrected into a new life. It is, appropriately, the season of Easter, a feast which we could not celebrate in a fitting manner on board our ships some days ago. There, yonder, and he pointed to his right, is the first land we sighted and named *Monte Pascoal*. In a few days we will celebrate the feastday of the Invention of the Cross, significantly here on a land which our commander has named *Terra da Vera Cruz*. I call to mind the prayer of Saint Francis from the New Testament. We adore Thee, O Christ, and we bless Thee, because by Thy Holy Cross you have redeemed the world. Bear in mind also, my children, that we were borne to this land in twelve ships like the twelve apostles. Truly, we have entered a second Eden.

He pointed to the Tupinamba who sat in a circle around the royal standard and they raised their bows in acknowledgment.

To you, oh Tupinamba, we bring the fruits of knowledge and of faith so that you can move out of your world of ignorance and innocence into our great world of civilization and culture with which we are blest. You do behave like true Christians even though you are not Christians, even though you do not understand our language. We will leave two Christians here, *degredados*, who will teach you our language, the language of Christians and who will soon learn your primitive tongue which has no script.

The Tupinamba raised their bows and shouted in acclaim as if they understood what he was saying.

The Frei turned to us.

I want to make you, my dear children of Portugal, aware of the great responsibility that has descended on us. It will be our mission to baptize these people make them Christians, and lead them to salvation in the name of our dear Lord Jesus Christ. Remember, these are not religious aliens, like the false Muslims and the perfidious Jews. These are human beings who belong to the stock of Adam but on the lowest level, unspoiled and in a state of nature as their lack of a language that we can understand and their lack of clothes proclaim. We have to embrace them with love.

One of the *degredados* sent forth an excited guffaw, but was immediately silenced.

Alleluia, let us now rejoice, said the Frei.

The Tupinamba were sad when the ceremonies came to an end, but Frei Henrique, whom they liked very much, somehow conveyed to them that there would be feasting and dancing and merrymaking. They were overjoyed and would not wait but began to leap and dance and play their wooden trumpets.

Viva Portugal, we shouted, and they joined us in shouting over and over again, Viva Portugal.

I didn't know, Ahmadji, why the Frei's sermon had such an impact on me that I can remember every word he said. Now, looking back, I know it made me realize that religion too can be a form of power. I haven't really thought about this. But let me continue my story.

Frei Henrique told Frei Luís do Salvador to lead me away, and we rowed ourselves back to the *capitania*. The tide was against us.

Why did we not wait for the celebration, I asked Frei Luís. I would have liked to see the dancing, and hear the singing, and join in the feasting.

I didn't say anything about the naked women.

Those are pagan rites, Frei Luís said.

He was a young man who looked old, with a body like a stick. His shoulders were thin, and so were his arms, so that it was an effort for him to handle the oars. His flesh clung to his bones as if it needed more than the protection of his brown cassock. All his energies were concentrated in his face. The three deeply furrowed lines on his brow, strange for a young man, were not parallel but converged to a point between his thick eyebrows. His eyes were fanatical.

The Tupinamba are primitives, Frei Luís do Salvador said. As Frei Henrique pointed out, they are closer to beasts than to men. Though why he wants us to love such people whose skin color is that of cooked quince, I cannot understand. It will be easy to Christianize them provided we govern them by fear, not love. They live on the level of the flesh and the sensations. You and I, we live on a higher plane, that of the mind.

He let his oar drop, and the little boat began to swing around.

Frei Henrique told me all about you, Frei Luís continued. How clever you were. About your studies in the Sorbonne. And how you were tempted by the devil and how you fell into the sins of the flesh. And how you smashed the skull of the old man.

The boat began to drift back toward the shore. I could not control it.

Did he die, I almost shrieked, did the old man die.

Listen, Frei Luís said. Don't worry about such trivial matters. The foolish old man, Senhor Gouvea, took a month to recover. I want you to consider apocalyptic matters.

First, let me tell you what Frei Henrique has decided about your future. Vasco da Gama, who carried letters for the Preste, was informed at Malindi on the eastern coast of Africa that the realm of Preste João was either a little way inland or far north in Ethiopia. You will be left in Mozambique where you will learn the language, and then search for the lands of Preste João. After you have accomplished your mission you will report to us in Malindi or in Calicut to which place we are sailing with a letter to the Samorin.

We were able to control the little boat now, and rowed our way slowly to the *capitania*.

And then, said Frei Luís. And then

He paused.

I want you to be my chief disciple, he said slowly.

I was shocked. I looked at his eyebrows which were completely white. He glared at me with his fanatical eyes. Then he tried to stand up in the little boat and tried to spread his arms wide as if to embrace the whole ocean. But he couldn't keep his balance, and fell back upon his seat.

Listen, Frei Luís do Salvador said to me. Your name is João, an apostolic name. You're well read, unlike Frei Henrique and the other friars. I don't have to explain things to you in detail. I'll be brief.

Listen, João, listen carefully. You, as my apostle, are going to be the first to know what the whole world soon will know. That I, I am the resurrected Saint Francis sent down to earth to transform the whole world.

I could see the fanatic sheen in his eyes.

Yes, João, I am the *renovator mundi*, prophesied by Joachim of Fiore, sent to set the new world ablaze with the light of the gospel. I carefully chose my own name, Luís do Salvador, for I knew I was the one to lead the world to salvation. I have a new vision to offer this world and you, João, will help me realize it. It's a new world out there waiting to be converted, crowded with Muslim infidels and perfidious Jews and countless gentiles with different beliefs and languages who, with us Christians, constitute all the races of mankind. St. Francis lived in simple times and in a small world, João.

Frei Luís kept on talking, at times to himself, at times to me. At times his voice dropped. He glared at me with his fanatical eyes and his thick eyebrows that were completely white.

I could see that he didn't see me. He stared straight through me at the distant horizon.

That's why the Rule of the Friars Minor is not at all effective today, he continued. It aimed at too simplistic a return to the early church. That's why the pointless conflict between the Spirituals and the Conventuals. And that's why all missionary efforts have failed. St. Francis believed, and Frei Henrique still believes, that his missionaries should be inflamed with love for Christ and for mankind, and they should burn with the fierce desire for martyrdom. Their desire to die for the faith, was really a form of suicide. And they failed, just as the Crusades failed. They lacked an ideology of mission, he said pompously.

But we, João, we, the Frei thundered suddenly.

I was startled by the unexpectedly loud voice.

We will be *viri spirituales*, Christian soldiers. These are not the last days, but the first days of the new millenium, which will end with the Last Judgement. The gospel can now be preached to all peoples and to all races in all the tongues of the world. I will create a new order, and there will be the new apostles that will go forth preaching to the new world. We will establish missionary colleges to learn the new languages and a new missionary method to preach to the idolatrous gentiles who will be converted with ease. And we will have the imperial power of Preste João behind us so that the Muslim leaders will be defeated, their lands taken.

Let me tell you, João, what I haven't told anyone yet. Your search for the kingdom of Preste João may be in vain. For it is I, I, Frei Luís do Salvador, who have discovered that the Preste is an emperor in India, not in Ethiopia. In the secret archives of the Vatican library I came across a page discarded from Poggio Bracciolini's life of Niccolo di Conti as too fantastic to be true. It was a brief description of how the Vijayanagar emperor with 72 kings under him would be bathed in diamonds that would be then donated to a temple. I shall go to Bhatkal and take the great western highway over the mountains to Vijayanagar where the mighty Preste resides.

Then, then, João, there will be the final conversion of the Jews. And then Christianity will flourish all over the world. Listen, João, we will translate the prophecies of Joachim of Fiore into reality, and create a world united in one faith.

Listen carefully, João, he continued. I am what I am. I am the Joachimite Messiah.

He was strangely silent after this, and did not talk to me or even look at me, when we were pulled up into the *capitania*, the flagship.

I descended into hell. My being was in a whirl. A madman obsessed with power.

Affonso Ribeiro was wild with excitement when he çame down into the hold a little later.

João, João, he shrieked, I'll be free, tonight will be my last night here. Tomorrow I'll be in Heaven. I'll fuck them, two, three, four, every night. I'll make them suck me. I'll fuck two at the same time. I'll use my big toe.

He stumbled towards me, his voice hoarse. I got the hot smell of lust and wine from his breath. He rambled on, incoherent, drunk.

It came out that the fleet carried 20 *degredados* who were to be landed at some places on the voyage to teach the natives about Christianity and to learn their language, and thus earn their pardon.

I smiled. Affonso Ribeiro would make an excellent teacher of Christian doctrine.

It also came out that the sailors of the *capitania* had demanded that I should be taken off the ship and left at Vera Cruz. Frei Henrique insisted that as I was educated I'd be of better use among the Muslims of India. He got his way. Frei Luís do Salvador insisted that I be trained to shoot an arquebus. Affonso Ribeiro would be left behind at Vera Cruz with another convict. They were ordered to learn the language.

I heard the thunder of the guns signaling our departure from Vera Cruz. My days passed in comfortable darkness. The sailors refused to allow me on deck except when I had to practice arquebus shooting even though Frei Henrique wanted me to help the pilot. He told me that a comet with a very long tail had appeared in the north, it was seen continuously for ten days. The sailors cursed me, called me Jonah, wanted me cast overboard.

A storm then began, and battered our ship continuously for over twenty days, the winds were so strong, the seas so wild and shattering, that four ships were lost as we were driven round the Cape of Good Hope. No one cursed me when I was called to help repair the tattered sails. It was after the storm subsided, as we limped our way to Mozambique, where, despite Frei Henrique, they abandoned me, that, famished and exhausted, crouched in the damp darkness of the hold, I felt the nightmare descend into me.

It wasn't the usual nightmare, Ahmadbhai. The vision didn't terrify me. I felt an intense chill within. I became a voyeur.

A man and a woman had slipped into a forbidden garden and the man was pointing to a shriveled tree that had only one monstrous apple, shiny and shaped like a star, hanging temptingly down. Shrieks of laughter issued from a background of darkness.

Wait, said the woman, that's not the tree of life we seek, that's what's left of the fatal tree of knowledge. Beware, the serpent may still lurk there.

Your serpent was a delusion. I'm hungry, said the man.

Ha, ha, ha, more shrieks of laughter, and then I realized that while I could hear the laughter the man and woman couldn't.

The man plucked the apple and ate of it.

I thought I heard the voice of Plato but I couldn't make out what he said.

Ohe, Ahmadji, ohe.

We heard shouts and cries.

There, there, I told João, pointing to flaming torches that appeared on our right.

Ohe, Ahmadji, ohe.

The headman of Vanakbara had sent some villagers to find us. They had taken the short cut.

João never continued the story of his strange nightmare. At Vanakbara he was his usual boisterous self as if he had freed himself from the burden of his past. I was deeply affected by his story which made me brood about change.

End of João's *confiteor.*

FOURTEEN

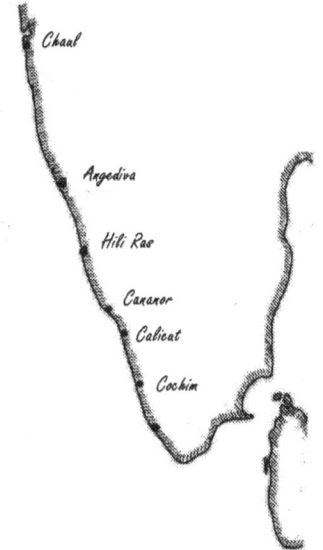

$\mathcal{M}$ay 1509, Diu, early morning, my house.
I woke up suddenly aware of an uncoiling within my being.
Not an unburdening like João's confiteor but a kind of relief
caused by the act of writing all through the night, perhaps.
I hurl my self back into the past, back to 1498 and onto
Paulo da Gama's ship, the *San Raphael*. I write about
how I made a rough outline of the Bahr-i-Hind for Paulo,
and how, impressed by the scientific knowledge of the Portuguese,
I pointed their ships towards Hili Ras on the west coast of India

I was flattered that the Portuguese pilots wanted to learn my piloting language.

You knew exactly when the Pole Star would be seen, they were impressed, Paulo said to me. My brother Vasco sent a message stating that the three pilots should meet to discuss navigational matters.

Could you, Ahmadji, accompany pilot João de Coimbra to the *San Gabriel* tomorrow, an hour after they take the sun at midday.

It was probably an order from Vasco da Gama that Paulo had changed into a request to me.

It won't be possible, I said.

João de Coimbra looked a little shocked.

Why, Ahmadji, Paulo asked, concern in his gentle eyes.

Because the *Rih al-Kaws*, which today is steady, will, after the noon hour tomorrow, blow hard and become inconsistent. I can smell the approach of the *Dabur* wind.

João de Coimbra looked at me disbelieving.

Paulo's faith in me took the form of a question.

When, Ahmadji, should the meeting of the pilots be held, Paulo asked.

I turned and faced the stern of the *San Raphael*, lifted my face, looked up at the ragged white clouds edged with blue racing eastwards, and smelt the wind.

Tomorrow morning, I said, three hours before noon, the monsoon wind will shift into a *shamar* whose slight breeze will create a flat sea with ripples. Then, three hours after midday, the sea will become boisterous. The *Rih al-Kaws* will blow again with renewed force. We may not be able to get back to the *San Raphael* that day.

João de Coimbra warned his helmsman about the strong wind. The sailors would have to trim the sails, and adjust bowlines and make everything secure.

I informed Abdul. He would look after Usha.

Take Abdul along, Usha said, and take some wine.

Abdul may be needed here, I said. And Paulo told me his brother Vasco would provide the wine.

Next morning, just before the *shamar* began, the *San Raphael* fired four gunshots to lower sails. The *San Gabriel* and the *Berrio* confirmed this signal. The three ships drew parallel to each other, boats were lowered, and the three pilots greeted each other on the poopdeck of Vasco da Gama's ship.

The *San Gabriel* was the flagship, the *capitania*, but for the voyage to Calicut Vasco da Gama had assigned that leading position to the *San Raphael* to honor his brother. Paulo did not accompany me. João de Coimbra introduced me to the dignified blackbearded Pero de Alenquer of the *San Gabriel*, an experienced pilot who had, before this voyage, sailed down the length of Africa to the Cape of Good Hope. Then Pero Escobar of the *Berrio*, busy adjusting his compass, greeted me.

All three pilots were full of questions. They wanted to learn everything they could about the world they had entered.

How did you know about the Pole Star, asked Pero de Alenquer, the night sky in this part of the world is crowded with stars.

João de Coimbra wanted to know how I could tell that the wind would drop. I couldn't smell anything, he said.

The pilot of the *Berrio* reminded me of Maimun ibn Khalil. He was not young but was eager to know everything, especially about my instruments. Where is your astrolabe, where are your charts, where is your compass, when will we get to India, where are your tables of the sun.

I did not know where to begin. I wished I had my *Fawa 'id* to read to them. There I began by stating that navigational theory could help determine the Qibla of Islam, and I then went on to present twelve useful things for my brother navigators and for all those seamen who would continue our seafaring traditions. That was easy for they spoke the language of navigation.

But these fervent seekers after knowledge used different terms. Our words were not translatable into theirs, even if I had had a dictionary. Our word *huqqa* was not an exact equivalent of their compass. The thirtytwo points on their compass rose were based, as João de Coimbra had explained, on wind directions. The thirtytwo *akhnan* on our compass card took their names from the prominent stars that rose and set on these rhumbs.

I felt moved, I know not why, to sing for them the names of all the important directional stars, *al-Jah* for the Pole Star, then going on from *al-farqadan* to *al-na`sh*, then on, in order, to the other stars till my voice came to rest on *suhail*.

Strangely, despite their interest in the Pole Star, they weren't curious about the other stars. They didn't want to listen to the jewel music of star names. They didn't want poetry but cold facts.   Pero de Alenquer waited till I finished my recitation of star names, and immediately rolled out a wide chart of prepared sheepskin that was well rubbed. The neck was clearly on the left.

What's the distance we have traveled from Malindi, Pero asked.

He had a ruler and a pair of dividers at the ready.

What's the distance between Malindi and Calicut, Pero Escobar broke in impatiently, what is the *altura* of Calicut.

Pero de Alenquer, annoyed, stroked the curved tip of his beard upward with his forefinger.

The interpreter pointed to a name with some numbers next to it freshly written on the chart.

Malindi, the interpreter said, three degrees and nine minutes south.

On the chart I saw the African coastline that ran southwards and did not turn towards the west as we Arabian pilots thought it did, but curved up at the tip northwards. Place names were written inland continuously round the African coasts most in tiny black and a few in large red letters. Malindi was written in red ink. To the west of Malindi was an open space with compass stars from which a network of *akhnans* extended to the uneven edge of the sheepskin. A black line ran up parallel to the coast and then proceeded diagonally into the open sea where it stopped.

Senhor Pero de Alenquer pricks his ship's position on this chart everyday, the interpreter said.

I could have sketched in, roughly, the west coast of India on the chart and made an approximate mark for Calicut. I could have told Pero de Alenquer the distance we had sailed from Malindi in *zam*. I could have easily told Pero Escobar the actual distance our ships would travel between Malindi and Calicut, easily because we were not negotiating the direct route across the Bahr-i-Hind but would sail the *dirat-al-iqtida* route which changes its bearing in midocean. For them to understand these terms they'd have to know the twelve *usul* principles of navigational theory.

Where, where should I begin my answers to their questions.

With distance, perhaps.

I tried to explain what *zam* meant.

A *zam*, I ventured boldly, is a measurement of distance sailed. One *zam* is one watch of three hours sailing, eight *zam* are sailed in one day. That's simple, I thought, easy to understand, but I was asked how many *zam* there were between Malindi and Calicut.

What they wanted to know was the *istilahi zam*, the theoretical distance between two places. But such knowledge for our pilots is useless. Variables such as the route taken, weather conditions, the build of the ship, the ocean currents, determine the exact *zam* sailed.

I then realized, for the first time as a pilot, that *zam* was not a unit of time, or of distance, as I had always, without question, accepted, but maybe, just maybe, of timedistance.

I tried again.

Eight *zam*, a day's sailing due north, raises the Pole Star one *isba'*. A *zam* is an angular measure of one eighth of an *isba'*, I told the three pilots.

What is an *isba'*, asked João de Coimbra.

My answer was simple. An *isba'* is divided into eight units of *zam*, I said.

All three stared at me. I was going around in circles. I felt dizzy. I realized that the terms of our language were so interconnected that no term could be used in isolation. To understand *zam* one had to know about *isba'*, and both terms needed the help of the *kamal*, while all three were used for *tirfa* measurement, and *tirfa* was linked up with *masafat* and *bashiyat*, and all terms had to be used for the art of *qiyas*, the measuring of stellar altitudes.

I fell silent.

They kept looking at me. A bad teacher, they must have thought.

I stared straight beyond them at the horizon. I didn't want to appear confused. The confusion was within me. I was experiencing swirls of insight. About language. That language is not just words but also music and meaning, and certain basic assumptions.

João Mirza, whom I was yet to know, would have liked these flashes of insight. I was also trying to solve the problem of immediate communication. Perhaps I would begin with our alphabet, and explain the simpler terms of our language.

The *mawasim* from Calicut, I began slowly, knowing they would be eager to note these sailing dates, when out of his cabin strode Vasco da Gama clad completely in black from head to foot, holding the suspension ring of a circular instrument in his right hand.

He stared all around, compressing his lips and fiercely contracting his black eyebrows as if trying to discover who I was. Then he gave a nod of recognition, and asked about his brother Paulo's cough. His lips and his eyes relaxed a little when I told him Senhor Paulo was well. He looked up and pointed at the sun. The three pilots picked up their instruments from the deck. It was nearing the time to shoot the sun.

The four circular instruments were heavy, perhaps to counteract the movements of the ship. They were made of polished metal that was not iron. There was not a speck of rust on them.

Vasco da Gama lifted up his instrument effortlessly. He did not limp at all, and was about to position it in front of his chest, when his eye fell on the unrolled chart. He raised his fierce eyebrows. He summoned Pero de Alenquer and spoke to him angrily.

Sigilo, Vasco da Gama shouted loudly, *sigilo*, at the chief pilot.

He summoned the interpreter who was standing next to me, shouted at him and sent him away from the poopdeck.

All four stared at me. Vasco da Gama stood erect and repeated *sigilo*.

The three pilots talked furiously among themselves.

I stood in the fierce sunlight wondering what had happened. João de Coimbra then led me by the arm to a cabin. He pointed to a jug of water on a grooved rack above a table. Next to it was a bottle of red wine enclosed in wickerwork. The water tasted stale. It must have been drawn from the barrels scrubbed with vinegar and filled at Malindi. Vasco da Gama had not allowed the Malindi carpenters to construct water tanks for the *San*

Gabriel. I had to pour half the wine into the water. The mixture was not refreshing but I drank it down. I felt dizzy. Perhaps I had been too long in the sun. Perhaps I was hungry. I sat down in Vasco da Gama's chair, ill at ease. I was an intruder in his world. His possessions surrounded me.

Staring down from on high was a picture shield of the royal coat of arms which I had seen on the flag waving triumphantly on the mainmast, and which, Paulo had told me, celebrates the victorious beginnings of Portugal as a nation. Beneath it, on a white cloth background, was the same deep red cross displayed so proudly on all the billowing sails. On the ledge were four large books. They were not prayer books but Portuguese *rahmanis*, navigational manuals. The one on the top had a picture of a sphere with a broad slanting band around it on its cover. The patterned deep red cross, each of its four corner ends elongated like a sharp curved blade, conveyed a sense of menace, unlike the simple black cross that now reminded me of an anchor in the arms of the child held by the sorrowing mother.

Did Vasco da Gama bow to this royal standard every time he entered his cabin, I wondered.

I poured some more wine into the mug.

To the right was a small table where rolled charts, dividers, rulers, hourglasses, spare compass needles were arranged in neat order. In the corner was a large tripod from which hung an astrolabe, a hand's length in diameter, with markings on its heavy wood, its pointer had been removed and lay on the ground. A slate board was propped against the wall with pieces of chalk to write down calculations.

The scientific instruments had been placed on three racks. The one at the bottom had a small sphere which rotated when I touched it. The second rack had astrolabes and quadrants, all made of metal. The third was crowded with compasses of different sizes and shapes.

I was amazed. I never knew so many kinds of compasses could be put to use on the ocean. Above the racks, fixed on the wall, was what looked like an ornament, but turned out to be a shiny locket containing a lodestone.

I have seen a few compasses and charts used by some Mediterranean pilots who traveled overland to Suez and sailed slowly to Jiddah and thence to Aden, but who rarely ventured on the Bahr-i-Hind. One of these pilots, years ago, loaned me the famous *Al-majist* of the Egyptian astronomer, Ptolemy.

I admired the astronomical speculations and read the mathematical calculations in Ptolemy's book. But I did not need their help to find my way across the Bahr-i-Hind. My whole being had its own tools, the nose, the eyes, my skin, my hands, my fingers, that allowed me to determine my position in my universe.

Mine was a knowledge that was not precise and scientific, an *'ilm* that resided deep within me. I felt a sudden shiver as if Vasco da Gama's instruments had deliberately sent a cold message against an invader. Your knowledge and your language will no longer do, Ahmad ibn Madjid, the message stated. Ours is the new language of science and power.

I rose from the chair and took a drink from the mug. A sudden wind gust made the *San Gabriel* roll a little and the sunshine burst through the cabin window on the left on to an open coffer the length of a human body, lined with blue cloth. I could scarcely see what was in it, for the glinting reflections dazzled my eyes.

It was Vasco da Gama's arms and armor, his helmet, the plates to protect his chest and back, knee guards, a lance, and a scabbarded sword with a golden hilt. Paulo's armor, which had been tranferred to João de Coimbra's cabin to provide more space for Usha and me, was not as precious to him as the medicine chest which Paulo carefully checked and refilled every day. Vasco da Gama's armor was polished to perfection as if ready for attack, anytime.

I made haste to step out of this concentrated world of science and power.

Another wind gust shook the *San Gabriel*.

I looked up at the wind rag fluttering near the foremast top.

The *Dabur* wind would blow from the south. The two wind gusts, clear early signals of windshift, had not disturbed anyone on the ships which maintained their parallel courses. Abdul would know. Perhaps he would tell Paulo. The pilots would have to hurry up with their observations of the sun so that we could get back to our ships. The wind would arrive suddenly, in full force, earlier than I had predicted.

The four shooters of the sun were intent on their work. Vasco da Gama's concentration was fierce. I could not interrupt them. The interpreter had been banished from the poopdeck. João de Coimbra and I would have to spend the night on the *San Gabriel*. Abdul and Layla would look after Usha, Paulo was there too, Usha would be safe.

I watched the four shooters at work, each in his allotted circle on the poopdeck. Their movements were deliberate and precise as if they had, all four of them, been taught in the same school for pilots.

Each one would hold up his astrolabe, turn it till a ray of sunlight shot through both pinholes, look at the pointer, and call out the reading to a clerk who chalked it down on a slate. João de Coimbra and Pero Escobar, not quite sure of themselves, had two sailors to help them and would, at times, consult a large book. Pero de Alenquer and Vasco da Gama were experts at shooting the sun.

To shoot the sun. What an image.

I rolled the phrase on my tongue though I didn't know what it meant or what they were measuring. I knew how to fetter the stars. How impossibly daring to shoot at that solitary sultan of the sky.

I looked up and was blinded. I looked down, and there, in front of my bedazzled eyes, was Vasco da Gama as a black magician, holding up a golden ring to propitiate his deity, with attendant worshippers in white taking part in the ritual that ended with a loud incantation of numbers. I shut my eyes.

How appropriate that Vasco da Gama chose to wear black, a color that could absorb heat and light.

Did it, I wondered, absorb power too from the sun.

We heard a fanfare of trumpets from the *San Raphael*, a second blare and a third, then a warning voice. Vasco da Gama, his eyes on his astrolabe, ignored the voice and continued looking at a page in an open book that had columns of numbers on it.

Only when he heard Paulo's shout did Vasco da Gama look up and immediately issue orders.

The interpreter appeared. Paulo wanted me and João de Coimbra to start back at once.

I told João de Coimbra we would need two extra oars.

Why, he asked, looking up, there isn't a cloud in the sky. We'll reach our ship in no time at all.

But he made Rufião, who was one of our boatmen, carry down the oars. Rufião carried them reluctantly, grumbling continuously to himself.

I took up an oar, wanting to get to the San Raphael as quickly as possible. But João de Coimbra, who took the tiller, forbade it.

That was no job for pilots, João de Coimbra said, there's no need to hurry.

It was a flat sea but a disturbed one. I could see small eddies of green and red below the surface. Rufião was still grumbling. We were more than halfway to the *San Raphael* and would soon be in the shadow of her stern, when there were yells of warning.

There was no time for João de Coimbra at the tiller to take action. The sudden swell dashed against the side of our boat and instantly swept it up high, so high that our heads were at anchor level. Down we slid into the trough of the sea, the four of us flung together in a heap inside the boat. The *Dabur* came on bringing with it a brief rain squall. Two oars were swept overboard. The boat spun around wildly in the confused sea.

João de Coimbra scrambled towards the tiller and discovered that the rudder had snapped free of its pintles.

I could see the *San Raphael* rolling and pitching, driven ahead of us by the *Dabur* wind which now began to blow at a steady pace. I managed to

tie one of the oars to the tiller, and the boat steadied somehow. João de Coimbra used the other oar to urge the boat onward. I tried to steer toward
the *San Raphael* that was now ahead of us. Grey and ghostlike, the ship
disappeared into the mist.

We would have to wait a long time to be rescued.

The sea was confused but not dangerous. The *San Raphael* would have
to make a wide turn and circle back against the wind to pick us up. I kept
pointing the prow straight so that the boat would not drift. The wind and
the set of the sea pushed it forward slowly. With one hand I pointed towards the left indicating that we should keep looking in that direction.
We kept on looking, João de Coimbra kept on rowing vigorously, but we
didn't seem to be going anywhere.

All of a sudden the *San Raphael* loomed directly in front of us, its stern
angled southeastwards.

It was, I knew at once, excellent seamanship.

João de Coimbra's assistant had shortened sail and, by maneuvering
the running rigging and by having the helmsman lean hard against the tiller, had thrown the ship across the wind so that, helped by the low broad
curve of its hull, it remained rolling and pitching but almost stationary,
hovering like a seagull, waiting for us.

We came along very slowly, João de Coimbra making frantic efforts
with his oar. Someone flung a rope from the ship. João de Coimbra lunged
out of the boat and caught it, but fell head first into the sea. He wasn't a
good swimmer or else he was tired, for he floundered helplessly for a
while.

Rufião, shouted Paulo from the *San Raphael*.

Grumbling, Rufião dived into the water and held the pilot till another
rope was thrown to them.

We were safe. Our boat was hauled up. João de Coimbra had cramps
in his right leg and had to be carried to his cabin. Abdul helped me to our
cabin. Usha bowed to the picture, and then turned to me.

That night Usha soothed my inner being. I couldn't explain to her why it
felt so torn apart. We lay together, side by side, in silence, for a long time.
She placed her hand on my heart and listened for a while. Then she took
my right hand and placed it on her bare belly. I sensed our togetherness
begin to move slowly within her. My fingers listened and became aware of
a slow rhythm, a musical beat, long short short long, long and a long. All
shall be well. All shall be well. All shall be well.

I fell into a sleep so deep that when I awoke, for a moment I did not
know where I was. Yet I had no anxieties, I was at peace. Usha was sleeping next to me.

I arose without disturbing her and stepped out of the cabin into the world I knew. The night was soft with stars.

Up north, above the horizon, the Pole Star shone warmly, sending rays of greeting to me and to all the other stars.

I liked talking to Paulo late into the night about the stars.

João de Coimbra tossed on his bed. He had developed a bad cold and had a high fever. Paulo applied Ratna's balm to his forehead, Usha said it would be cooling, and the pilot at last went to sleep. Paulo asked if he could use some of the balm for Rufioo, ill and restless, down in the hold.

When Paulo came back, we would sit on a carpet next to the pilot's chair. João had requested me and I had willingly agreed to relieve his assistant pilot for one watch. I didn't have to do anything. The *San Raphael* sailed along at a steady pace. The monsoon had yet to strengthen. The wind blew on the quarter. The huge square sail filled taut, and the *San Raphael* ran along steadily on the Bahr-i-Hind.

We sat in silence on the carpet, Paulo and I, listening to the unhurried flow of time, sensing also, when I looked up at the stars, the utter timelessness of things.

When I compose poetry the stars themselves recite it, I quoted the opening line of one of my own poems to Paulo.

I think Paulo understood its meaning without understanding the words. The interpreter was fast asleep in the pilot's chair and Paulo did not want to awaken him.

Paulo pointed to the Pole Star and said softly, *Stella Maris*. He made the four syllables sound like a prayer.

I thought of Usha, and pointed to a group of faint twinkling stars that hung like a cluster of grapes low in the sky, the constellation *Thurayya* whose quivering resembles the earrings of a young girl trembling for fear of separation from her beloved.

Paulo, still pointing to the *Stella Maris*, began to sing softly,

Ave Maris Stella
Dei Mater alma
Atque semper Virgo
Felix caeli porta

The interpreter awoke and joined him in the singing.

That's the star of the sea, said Paulo, the sailor's guiding star. The Virgin Mary in the picture is like that Pole Star.

I didn't understand everything Paulo said, but I now sensed what drew Usha to that picture. I'm not religious, but I remembered a passage from the *Qu'ran* my father used to recite. Allah it is who hath appointed for you the stars that ye guide yourselves thereby in the darkness of land and sea.

The stars never failed us as guides on the Bahr-i-Hind. We never relied on the blinding sun as Vasco da Gama and his pilots did. During the day we shielded ourselves from the sun's fierce rays and sailed by bearings alone. We waited patiently for the stars to come forth. I did not need the anchor that is the Pole Star to fix my bearings. I could coax any star in either hemisphere of the sky, northern or southern, to tell me the course I should set. I could sail anywhere on the Bahr-i-Hind. People called me, I would boast to myself silently, the nakhoda of nakhodas.

Why, why was I so confused on the *San Gabriel*.

Sigilo, Vasco da Gama had shouted, *sigilo*. Was that a curse he had flung at me.

I told Paulo what had happened and how flustered I had been, and I asked him what *sigilo* meant.

The interpreter laughed and Paulo laughed with him.

No, Ahmadji, he said, it is not a swear word, it means secret.

Paulo laughed again, affectionately.

My dear brother Vasco, he said, is haunted by the fear that our arch rival, Spain, will steal the secrets we Portuguese have so carefully collected, our maps and our *roteiros* in which sailing techniques and sailing directions are set down. He was quite outraged when Christopher Colom, that upstart who knows nothing about the science of sailing, happened to discover America and we Portuguese lost the national glory we had earned.

I was quite confused. Who was Colom and where was America.

So I changed the subject and asked Paulo when they would return to Portugal from Calicut.

We do not know when we will return, Paulo said.

We set forth from Lisbon, Ahmadji, on July 8, 1497. Today is the 14th of May 1498. For eleven months now we have ventured forth through dangerous seas never sailed before. We labored through violent storms before we could double the Cape of Storms. It was my brother's fierce determination, even more than the ocean winds and currents, that has driven our ships and our sailors onward.

With your help, Ahmadji, we will reach Calicut or Kannanur. We knew the names of these ports because, earlier, Pero de Covilhão, who spoke some Arabic, traveled in disguise to Calicut, overland, I think, and sent King Manuel a rough chart of the region and an account of the cloves and cinnamon, the pepper and spices, available there.

Paulo paused for a while, began to cough, then went on slowly.

Pero de Covilhão's letter is *sigilo*, Ahmadji, very few people know about it. It is one of our many secrets. Vasco tells me more voyages were made all the way down the African coast, after that of Bartolomeu Dias, but they were kept secret.

Don't tell anyone, my brother Vasco told me.

Knowledge can never be kept a secret, I told Vasco, Paulo said.

Paulo began to cough again, but went on bravely.

Knowledge has to flow across borders and boundaries.

Paulo sounded like a poet. The interpreter could not keep up with Paulo.

A violent fit of coughing attacked Paulo and would not go away. I became worried.

Take Senhor Paulo to the pilot's cabin, I told the interpreter.

It was getting towards the middle of the night when the dews are heavy and can cause chills and fever.

Abdul came up to the deck with a soft, lightly woven carpet.

She sent me, Abdul said.

I covered myself completely and closed my eyes.

I had to help Paulo get to Calicut. I would make a rough outline of the Bahr-i-Hind. I was not really worried any more about the Portuguese now. They would be just one more group of traders in the expanse of the Bahr-i-Hind.

The next morning I got the ship's carpenter to put together a six foot by nine foot oblong frame of wood. Abdul filled it with sifted dry sand three inches high, wetted it, and then tamped it smooth. He gave me a long thorn. Where Abdul got it from on board the ship I do not know. I used one of Usha's needles also.

Usha sat outside our cabin door stitching clothes for our baby. Yasmin nestled close to Layla who sat combing Usha's hair out, soft and black and long, after rubbing in a little sun warmed coconut oil.

With Abdul's thorn I made a rapid outline of the Bahr-i-Hind on the smooth wet sand. The East African coast, the stretch of the Sawahil, going toward Arabia, the gash that is the Red Sea, on to the Persian Gulf and to Persia, circling around Sind and going down the west coast of India, to the bulge of Gujarat, down to the Konkan, and to Malabar, on to that pearl drop, Ceylon, that hangs trembling from the southern tip of India.

With Usha's needle I wrote down the names of some of the seaports of my world.

The coastline of India looked desolate, so I put in some outstanding landmarks, Diu Head, Girnar, and then Hili Ras, the most prominent cape on the Malabar coast, which we were sailing towards. All the pilots knew this landmark, it was impossible to miss it.

The Bahr-i-Hind now looked wide and empty. There were no ships on it as if the monsoon had already begun.

I sketched in an outline of a sambuk riding on a few waves. I was tempted to write down the pole star altitudes next to every seaport, for I knew them all, but I put in only two. Four and a quarter *isba`* for Kannanur. Three and a quarter *isba`* for Calicut.

Vasco da Gama, I was sure, would appreciate these details about the Bahr-i-Hind.

He did.

Pero de Alenquer and Vasco climbed aboard after they had finished shooting the sun on the *San Gabriel* at midday. Vasco da Gama was worried about his brother. Furious when told that Paulo was not in his own cabin. He was on his way to João de Coimbra's, when his eagle eye fell on the chart.

He stopped suddenly then strode up to have a closer look at my world that now lay near his feet.

He beckoned to Pero de Alenquer who was checking the readings of the sun with the assistant pilot of the *San Raphael*.

Vasco da Gama stared at my outline for a long time, then he pointed his long forefinger and said loudly, questioningly, Portugal, Portugal.

Pero de Alenquer shook his head as if he didn't agree, but said nothing. Vasco da Gama pointed at me.

Ahmadji, said Pero de Alenquer, and then called Martin Afonso, the interpreter, who greeted me. By this time, because of Paulo, I knew the names of almost everyone on the *San Raphael*.

Vasco da Gama asked a number of questions.

Where is Portugal on this sketch.

I did not know.

Where is Hormuz.

I showed him the exact location.

Where is the kingdom of Preste João.

I did not know.

Where is Aden.

I showed Vasco where Aden was.

Vasco da Gama knew where Malindi was, and Mombasa, but had to be shown where Kannanur and Calicut were. He wanted to know the *alturas* for these ports and he frowned with his black eyebrows when he heard I could provide the altitudes only in *isba`* not in degrees.

He sent for the *escrivão*, João de Sa, who came with his pens and paper.

Use thicker paper, said Vasco da Gama, use parchment.

Then he started arguing with Pero de Alenquer, pointing to the chart, saying the word, Christøos, many times.

He got annoyed again when Padre Figueira interrupted them with a message. Paulo wanted to see his brother. He probably wanted Vasco da Gama to get back safely to the San Gabriel before nightfall.

Vasco da Gama hurried away to talk to his brother. Pero de Alenquer went with him.

João de Sa began to copy my outline carefully, noting down all the details, the interpreter helping him with the names.

Pero de Alenquer returned and said, Paulo has a high fever, Ahmadji, his forehead is burning. He is delirious.

Apply the balm, I said, it brought down my fever.

Vasco da Gama does not trust such remedies. The barber surgeon will apply cupping glasses to Paulo's head.

I shall remain on board all night, Vasco da Gama told me.

Vasco da Gama was much impressed with your outline, Ahmadji, said Pero de Alenquer. That's why he has ordered the *escrivão* to make five copies. It is the key, senhor Vasco told me, the key to the secrets of India.

Tell me, Ahmadji, how do you determine measurements.

With these my fingers, Senhor Pero.

Pero looked disbelievingly at my fingers.

My fellow navigators say I have a magic hand with magical fingers, I told Pero. With them I can calculate the altitude of any star in the sky. I do not need a *kamal*. The term *isba`*, which means a finger, is the angle subtended by a finger held at arms length against the horizon. My four fingers, the thumb is never taken into account, make an exact *dhubban*, the standard width of the measuring instrument. Apprentice pilots shake their head with amazement when they check my four fingers against certain stars, especially *aiyuq* and *suhail* with their *dhubban*s.

I was wildly excited. I couldn't help myself. I couldn't help boasting to a fellow pilot whom I could dazzle by charting the complete starstretch of the night sky I couldn't help boasting to an expert from the west the seventy different methods I knew of measuring star altitudes. I would show him how to fetter the stars, how to *abdal* the measurements of two stars of equal declination, how to. I stopped.

Pero de Alenquer, wide eyed with amazement, stared at me. He hadn't understood a word. The interpreter had left.

I stopped.

The voice of Vasco da Gama, loud and commanding, summoned Pero de Alenquer.

Martin Afonso brought me a bottle of wine. From Vasco da Gama, he said.

Abdul hastened to take it away.

The sun was sinking fast in the west, an orange red ball descending through stripes of deep blue clouds. It would be a clear night.

João de Sa had made one copy of my sketch.

I'll make other copies tomorrow, he said.

The *farol* lantern at the stern was lit. Vasco da Gama wanted everyone on board the San Raphael to pray for Paulo. The officers managed to get their men together in some kind of order on the *conves* and on the steps. They knelt down and Padre Figueira led the prayers.

I didn't understand the words. I knew they were praying for Paulo. I wanted to pray with them. But I couldn't. Something in their voices offended me. They were too demanding, too insistent. Vasco da Gama's voice was the loudest of all. It was as if he and his men were attacking a fortress and wanted to take it by storm. The prayers went on for a very long time.

I went up to the door of the cabin where Paulo lay, but did not go in and disturb him. I went to our cabin.

Usha was fast asleep. She hadn't eaten for two days. Stomach upset, she had told me and I deliberately stayed away from our cabin to allow her the privacy and sleep she needed. I didn't go in.

I told Abdul that the outline would be needed for tomorrow. He knew what to do. He would spread a cover over it to prevent it from drying out in the night. I shall sleep here, next to it, Abdul said.

I sat on the poop deck drinking the wine that Abdul had sparingly poured out for me, listening beyond the loud drone of the prayers to the deep silence above and to the sounds of the stars as they slowly began to emerge into the night. I had been like one possessed. I had to calm my self down if I wanted to show Pero the use of the *kamal*. It was an ideal night to take star readings, dark and clear.

There was no moonlight to blur the straight shine of the stars, no strong frontal wind, the sea was steady, the horizon was as straight as the edge of a knife. I would be calm. I would be patient. I would be a good teacher.

I never was able to teach Pero de Alenquer anything about my wondrous night world above that provided us with guidance below. The Portuguese pilots preferred to shoot the sun rather than to fetter the stars.

Your method is not precise, the pilots said, not scientific.

The Portuguese will never learn Arabic and they will never read my *Fawa`id* and learn the arts of stellar navigation. With their well constructed ships and their scientific instruments it was inevitable that they would find their way across the Bahr-i-Hind to Calicut. They did not really need me.

Vasco da Gama did take the *tabuas de India* back to Lisbon. At Calicut some pilots sold him *kamals* for silver coins, but they were never put to use. The only Portuguese pilot who was eager to learn the use of the *kamal* was João de Lisboa, the young assistant pilot of the San Raphael. I showed him the *kamal*reading when we reached four and a half *isba`* and he then changed the ship's bearing and the *San Raphael* headed east down that latitude towards Hili Ras which we sighted on May eighteenth 1498.

Vasco da Gama went wild with joy.

It was as if something hard within him had melted. Tears ran down his cheeks into his black beard. He hugged Paulo and they danced on the poop deck as if they were children again. Together they knelt down, and Paulo bowed his head in silent prayer.

Vasco da Gama gave loud thanks to God.

Viva Portugal, he proclaimed, viva, viva Portugal.

Viva Portugal, the whole ship shouted.

Vasco da Gama had come aboard the *San Raphael* to share with his brother the first glimpse of Ind. Paulo was much better, but he looked pale, and felt weak. João de Coimbra lay in bed, he had a deep pain in his chest. Rufião died suddenly. Abdul saw some sailors heave his canvas wrapped corpse from the stern one night. No prayers were said.

I could tell we were nearing the west coast of India. The bluegreen surface of the sea began to shade imperceptibly into a more intense blue, the shape of the wavelets, their curves, changed ever so slightly, changes of a kind most pilots would fail to notice. I wanted to make an announcement, but I waited.

I waited till the signs were unmistakable, yellow sea snakes squirming below the surface of the waters, a clear sign to every Indian pilot that the west coast is near, the birds flying past with their bald heads and their white stomachs, the star shaped seaweeds with tails drifting by.

The assistant pilot was interested in these signs of *isharat*. He made notes on a piece of paper. I found myself, I know not why, strangely reluctant to explain to him these indications of the nearness of the coast. I noticed he did not set down some of the signs.

I did tell Paulo that we would reach Calicut the next day.

Everyone on board the *San Raphael* was excited.

Bright eyed Yasmin knew somehow that land was near, she kept hopping around Layla wanting to play with her ball.

Layla began to fold clothes and pack our few possessions, even though I had told them that it would take two more days to get to Calicut.

Only Usha and I were calm.

Usha, at peace within, was at peace without.

Outwardly unmoved, I was deeply worried about what would happen after we arrived at Calicut. We surely couldn't go to Diu. We had no home. And we couldn't make any plans.

I told Usha we would go to Kannanur after landing in Calicut. My friend, Kotta Marakkar, would welcome us.

The Portuguese were not worried at all, especially after Vasco da Gama came aboard. They were miles away from home. They did not know what lay ahead. Vasco da Gama brought his power and confidence with him which, like a monsoon wind, swept into the men. It compelled them to fling their fears away. They looked ahead fearlessly at the future. Eager eyed they looked beyond the prow of the *San Raphael* for Hili Ras. Two men were perched on the lookouts above.

It was a heavy day. The skies were leaden, they hid the sun from view. The wind blew from the south west, but it was a premonsoon wind. The clouds did not smell of rain. They were not the dense dark blue elephant clouds of the Sanskrit poets.

Vasco da Gama was lucky, the monsoon this year was late. It would not be too difficult to find anchorage for the ships near Calicut. Far out towards the east there were thick masses of clouds. It was a time of transition.

I suggested that the sails be lowered a quarter of the way down the mast. The weather could change at any moment.

And then, then, there was a sudden onrush of unexpected wind that surprised me, a sudden parting of the cloud curtain ahead, and even though we could not see the sun, Hili Ras stood out, its peak sharp and distinct in the bright sunlight.

It was a shock. Was it an illusion. Everyone gasped.

And then the Portuguese went wild, cheering, dancing, shouting their joy, hugging each other, throwing their caps in the air, dancing with each other, shouting Viva Portugal, Viva Portugal.

Vasco da Gama did not order prayers to be said. He immediately ordered the ship's chart maker to make a panoramic sketch of the landmark on a sheet of paper. Then he ordered a barrel of wine to be rolled out on the *conves*. Bombards were fired and soon the other ships discharged their bombards, and the air was thick with smoke and rejoicing.

I stood alone on the poop deck staring at the familiar landmark that didn't look eight hundred and fifty feet high. I had never climbed to the top. It was a sanctuary for large monkeys. I wondered how many wanderers and exiles Hili Ras had welcomed down the centuries to India.

Paulo called out to me.

He came up and gave me a double embrace, and all the sailors greeted me shouting, Viva Senhor Ahmadji.

Vasco da Gama presented me with a hundred silver coins, and they all greeted me again with vivas.

He also sent me two bottles of wine, and he and the pilots invited me to join them in their celebrations.

But I didn't want to celebrate anything, and I didn't join them. I stood staring down in a daze at the sand outline I had sketched. I felt a piercing headache beginning, though it was just midmorning. Also, a sudden stab of guilt. Was I a traitor.

Why, why a traitor, a traitor to whom, asked my cynic.

I kept silent.

The Portuguese could easily have paid another pilot to guide them across the Bahr-i-Hind, my cynic observed.

You are not a traitor, he added.

Perhaps you have been the one chosen to witness the dawn of a new world of science and power. He said this rather solemnly.

I couldn't tell whether he wanted to make fun of me or make me laugh at myself.

I felt giddy.

Abdul wanted me to send back the two bottles of wine. But the sudden onrush of forehead shattering pain made me seize one of the bottles, put it to my lips, and empty it without stopping. I flung the bottle away and then started on the second bottle. Abdul, shocked, pulled it away from me.

Then, apparently, so Abdul tells me, I fell senseless into the world at my feet.

FIFTEEN

*D*iu, May 1509
My house, Night,
The tufan outside has stopped
But my writing continues

I woke up, sluggish, in the late afternoon, after a very long stretch of furious writing about our return voyage to Calicut. I couldn't continue the story of what happened after I fell senseless on the deck and after the four of us and the Portuguese got to Calicut. Why, I do not know. Perhaps I was too sleepy, too tired to continue. The force that drove me to write ebbed away for a while.

Through the window I could see the slanting shadows of the trees on the mud wall of my compound. The cardamon flavored hot coffee Abdul gave me was refreshing. It would make me perspire, then would cool me down. Later, Abdul would bring me some lime juice. He had tidied up the front room and put things back in their proper place.

It was as if the tufan had swept into Diu and departed in a hurry. Nothing had changed. Now I was aware of my inner tufan clamoring within me with its demands. Abdul must have placed my papers in one of the Martaban jars. There was no fish smell in the room, only a faint odor of the incense Abdul must have used. He had thrown open the front door, and through the open kitchen door I could hear my friends arguing.

Your friends are waiting to walk with you to the blackrock promontory, Abdul said.

He placed a small pot on the window sill.

To have a wash, Abdul said. The well water is cloudy after the rains. I've saved a little water for drinking and cooking.

I splashed a cupped palmful of water on my face. Not till tomorrow could I have a bath when the well water would run clear. Through the window came the warm fresh smell the earth always releases after the first rains.

João and the pandit, sitting on the built up parapet of the well and facing each other, were gesticulating and hurling words at each other.

Ra-sa, screeched the pandit.

Ka-thar-sis, yelled João, pounding his fist into his left palm at each syllable. Aristotle says, he continued. Then João saw me and stopped.

The pandit, who had his back to me, thought he had won the argument. He raised his right hand in triumph.

João moved away in disgust, then went and sat far away on the wall in the shade.

The maulvi, both hands clapped to his ears, came up to me.

Ahmadji, said the maulvi, they've been arguing like this for over an hour now.

João keeps on repeating the name Plato and the word change. Plato says, says João, that pure art is a waste of time.

That makes the pandit furious. Abhinavagupta says, screams the pandit.

I don't care what he said, João breaks in.

The maulvi was out of breath.

It was as if the tufan had invaded all three of my friends.

Abdul came out with the lime juice.

I took a glass to the pandit who was muttering away about the *vidusaka*. He was still talking to a João who wasn't there. The pandit's eyes were open. He was in a trance staring down the well.

I was afraid that the pandit might fall into the well. I touched him lightly on the shoulder, helped him off the parapet, and gave him the lime juice.

They had come to walk with me to the blackrock promontory. All three knew I would want to see what damage the tufan had done. I was in no mood to talk about the play. I felt I had to continue the sad story of what happened to Usha and me after the Portuguese ships had anchored near Calicut.

Let's enjoy our walk, I said.

But, Ahmadji, persisted the maulvi, I want to hear what you think about the play whose name I can't pronounce.

But, maulvisab, you didn't even listen to what I said about *rasa*, the pandit's voice became a little shrill.

João had just caught up with us and was about to say something. I interrupted him. I had to calm all of them down.

I will offer two brief comments, I said, placing myself between João and the pandit, and then we will remain silent until we get to the promontory. First, everyone enjoyed the play, the common people and the nobles. Second, and I raised two fingers. Then I paused, for I caught myself somehow imitating the pandit.

Yes everyone liked the play, agreed the maulvi, except panditji.

I did enjoy some of it, said the pandit, but it was definitely not art.

Plato said, shouted João.

I stopped him.

The play made me laugh, I said. The gorgeous costumes, they gladdened my eyes. The music, it delighted my ears. The play made me happy. For a little while it took me away from myself.

That's *katharsis*, muttered João.

But I did not stop.

The play also, I continued, told us about Sultan Begada's rise to power in Gujarat. It was also meant to reassure his audience by displaying the Portuguese as harmless clowns and ignorant vagabonds not pirates to be afraid of.

I wanted to tell them my thoughts about power and *samsāra*. But I didn't like the solemn tone of my voice and I didn't like explaining things.

So I stopped.

My friends had probably got tired of discussing the play. They accepted what I said. We walked on in silence.

Ah, said João, my tree, it's still there.

And he dashed off towards a large jambool tree. The ground beneath it was strewn with fallen jambools that looked like black pearls.

Stop, friend João.

The pandit ran on his spindly legs like a flustered hen. Stop, he said, and he prevented João from putting a jambool into his mouth.

Never, never eat any fruit after the first rains, the pandit said, shaking a finger from side to side, because somehow worms get into the fruit.

João looked disappointed. It was his favorite tree. Every time we went for a walk to the promontory he would pluck two large leaves, twist them into cones and collect the unbruised fallen jambools, and we would sit on the blackrock promontory and enjoy them.

We walked on in silence. There were no houses in this part of Diu. The leaves of the trees had been washed clean of dust, and they sparkled green in the evening sun. A light sea breeze made them rustle. As if they were murmuring thanks, I thought. There were twigs and branches all along the winding path.

Look Ahmadji, the tufan didn't bring your tree down, the maulvi said.

We stopped, all four of us, and looked at my gigantic baobab a hundred yards away. My friends were puzzled by my liking of the baobab which the Africans call the tree of a thousand years.

I can understand your love of the graceful coconut palm, the maulvi said, but I will never ever understand why you like that shapeless giant of a tree.

It was indeed shapeless. Its branches wandered in all directions, its trunk was short and thick, bulging out like a potbelly. I wondered why I was so drawn to the tree. It was a migrant. The seed must have floated across the Bahr-i-Hind from Africa or brought to the west coast of India by the Arab traders. It was rooted firmly in the soil of Diu now as if time itself had anchored there.

The sea gulls were back. They rose mewling from the black rocks and kept circling, sending prolonged complaints about us before they sped away. The orange sun descended slowly in the west. The clouds above drifted playfully like carefree balls of cotton. The sea was calm. It had made friends again with the gentle wind that kept changing the color of the waters from a distant darkblue to a blue and then to a deep green nearer the coast. Most of the boats had not ventured across the bar. One fisherman just beyond the *sankalkot* flung his net in a perfect circle for the last catch of the day.

At last, slowly, I turned my anxious eyes to the curved stretch of the swaying coconut palms along the coast. They were all there, not one coconut tree had fallen. They had bent and received the fury of the tufan, and now were as graceful and as enduring as ever. Usha and I always sensed the peace and calm they sent forth.

The tufan had come and gone, and nothing had changed. We looked out at the descending sun. The shadows lengthened over Bandar-i-Turk.

My roof was not damaged at all, Ahmadji, the maulvi said.

I slept through it all, said João. You, panditji, must have been muttering *mantras* asking for help all through the night.

João poked goodnatured fun at the pandit.

And you, Mirza sahib, must have snored your *mantras* to your great god, urrak, the pandit hit back.

They were good friends. Their quarrels were only edged with anger, and soon forgotten.

From Diu town came the clean sound of a bell.

I've never heard it so distinct before, said the maulvi.

Especially against the wind, I said, the air is quite dry.

The bell sounded again.

Two bells, that means that some important announcements will be made, said the pandit.

Let's go and listen to the news announcements, João said. Come along, panditji.

We didn't take the short cut, but the longer semicircular path. It would be twilight by the time we got to Diu center. Outside a small hut we saw a seated gathering, Hindus and Muslims, some in rags, others well dressed, watching a man sitting cross legged under a small coconut tree and staring straight ahead, monotonously sounding the one string of his onestringed drone. At moments he would throw out syllable notes from his mouth as if he were clearing his throat. A drummer next to him listened intently and tried out finger beats on his *dhol*, a one sided drum.

The pandit stopped and looked at them with openmouthed disgust.

They're waiting for it to get dark to begin their *bhajans*, the maulvi said, they're afraid.

Come along, panditji, João said, we have to hurry.

There. That. Those. The pandit sputtered. He couldn't continue. He turned fiercely to João who had taken his arm to lead him away.

Those people have abandoned the true *marg*. Instead of listening to prayers chanted by the temple priest in Sanskrit, the language of the gods, these thesepeople.

He sputtered again.

These people, he continued, listen to prayer songs sung by blind beggars who use salty village language, and they think they touch the divine.

Panditji, João said, don't be so sarcastic. Thesethese people, he sputtered, mimicking the pandit, are not allowed to enter temples.

But but but, the pandit said, how can they. That's their *karma*. They're not the twiceborn. They do not belong to the higher castes.

I was afraid we would now have the usual endless discussion between João and the pandit about the caste system that would take in kismet and *karma* and when it all began and why.

But this time it was the maulvi who, deliberately, interrupted the discussion.

When I was studying jurisprudence in a *madrasa* at Jaunpur, Ahmadji, the maulvi began in a deep voice, the religious leaders warned us about two new threats to Islamic society.

Sayyid Muhammad has gained too much influence over Sultan Begada who now takes his advice, not ours, they complained. The Sayyid's disciples proclaim that he is the long awaited Mahdi, the Deliverer, even though the Sayyid himself has not made his claim public.

João looked at the maulvi, quite puzzled.

Why are you telling us this, João asked. Everyone in Gujarat, even I, know that the Mahdi died four years ago up north in faraway Farrah.

The *mahdavis* have not forgotten, the maulvi said. I have been told that they are conspiring against the sultan whom they plan to murder one day.

Patience, João, I said, go on, maulvisab.

The second threat, the maulvi continued, was from the strange cults that call themselves *bhaktas*. They are heretics who have abandoned the orthodox path. They listen to Kabir, and indulge in senseless singing and dancing like the Bauls.

The maulvi turned hastily to me. Did you know, Ahmadji, that the word baul means the same as madjnun.

From Diu center came the clear sound of a third bell.

Let's hurry. said João, or we'll be late.

I wondered why João was so interested in news announcements. The twilight was deepening. It was the time of cowdust, as my hakim would say, a time when the cows come home from the fields just before the fall of night.

We got to Diu center just as the formulaic proclamations began.

The platform was an island of light in the middle of the center, and people thronged in front of it. It wasn't the same crowd that had attended the play. As our eyes got used to the darkness, I could recognize the faces of a few nakhodas. No coastal traders were present. All the students in our class were there except Sidi Ali o *torto*. João had told me the students also acted as envoys of the regions they came from. Some may be *barids*, he said, agents or spies.

There were a large number of overseas traders and merchants, a few government officials, merchants of frankincense, cornelian traders, owners of large workshops that manufactured ornaments of amethyst and coral, dealers in textiles, in damask and in colored velvets, dealers in carpets, dealers in bullion, moneychangers, ivory merchants. Here was the powerful world of business and money, anxious about the future of their trading investments.

There was silence after a trumpet sounded.

The chief announcer rose.

Malik Aiyaz, governor of Diu, has decided, in the interests of the mercantile community, to institute the practice of announcing what is happening and what has happened in the great world . Such announcements will be made twice a year. The first, before the *ghalq* season when the seas are declared closed. The second on Coconut Day, when the seas are declared open to all ships.

A great *shaitan*, as you all know, has descended upon us like a tufan and has imposed unjust *cartazes* to control our trade and the movement of our ships. You can then plan the arrival and departure of your ships, so that the trade flow is not blocked. With the combined power of the Mamluks and the Ottomans and the Samorin of Calicut, we shall sweep away these *shaitan* ships from the waters of the Bahr-i-Hind.

I was impressed by Malik Aiyaz's clever strategy.

The crowd murmured its approval.

First, we will tell you about the tufan.

Hooknose stepped forward.

The tufan has caused no damage to our Diu. The drunkard was absolutely wrong, Hooknose added. A few boats were damaged, some roofs were blown away and some trees blown down. Malik Aiyaz's palace was not damaged at all. Some fishermen report that a large *shaitan* ship was in distress off the coast at Dumas. May it be cursed to hell. May it suffer shipwreck.

That's enough, said the chief announcer.

The second announcer had a deep voice.

The trade situation in the Red Sea and the Persian Gulf has improved, and spices and drugs can flow again. Avoid using the port of Suk in Socotra. The Feringhi infidels have captured the fort, and lie in wait there for ships that set out from Jiddah and Aden.

The Mamluk sultan of Cairo, Kansuh-al-Ghawri, has sent word that the fortifications at Jiddah have now been completed. Bab-el-Mandab will be well defended. The Portuguese infidels will never be able to destroy our holy places.

Voices from the crowd asked. Where are the ships of the Mamluk fleet that survived the Diu battle. Has Amir Husain returned to Jiddah as its governor.

The whereabouts of Amir Husain cannot be disclosed at present for reasons of state, the announcer stated.

Has he gone to Goa, the voice persisted.

A few of our Mamluk and Turkish friends, who escaped from Diu with their ships, are now in Goa. About Amir Husain, we cannot tell you anything.

Another voice asked whether it was safe for ships to sail to Hormuz and to Aden.

Yes, definitely, the chief announcer said.

The deep voiced announcer continued.

From Melaka comes good news. The *bendahara*, Nina Chatu, reports that the Sultan of Melaka has collected over a thousand guns and that the bridge over the river has been heavily fortified so that no enemy ship can sail up river to bombard Melaka. No nakhodas should act as pilot guides for the Portuguese ships.

Karim, one of my nakhoda friends, who knew how unjustly I had been accused of treachery, of being drunk and of guiding the Portuguese to Calicut, shouted, that is impossible. The Portuguese can pay any nakhoda to guide their ships. The sea is open to all. Piloting is our profession. Nakhodas are not traitors. They should not be blamed.

That's very true, chorused the nakhoda group.

The chief announcer hastily rose up. No more questions will be allowed, he stated. I have another announcement to make.

He began to discuss matters with the huddle of announcers on the platform.

The pandit, restless, left before the announcement began.

The doings of *samsāra* do not interest me, the pandit said to me, and walked away.

Take care, panditji, I said.

Snakes are afraid of me, the pandit said.

I have only rumors to report, the announcer began matter of factly, they may be of interest to those who trade with and issue *hundis* to these regions.

It is said that Vira Narasimha, the king of Vijayanagar, and Yusuf Adil Khan, the Sabaio, the conqueror of Bijapur, are both ill.

About the Samorin of Calicut, a Hindu ruler but our ally, he is well, and has ordered many ships to be built and guns to be manufactured by some Portuguese deserters.

The Portuguese pirates have built forts and factories at Cochin and at Kannanur. It is reported that there is dissension among the Portuguese. May they be consigned to hell.

The crowd was now getting quite restless when the chief announcer rose up.

Two more news items, he said, of local interest. Those who caused disturbances during the play have been flogged and put in prison. They have confessed that they are *mahdavis*, secret followers of a corrupter of our orthodoxy whose execution was ordered by a *fatwa* before he escaped from Gujarat.

Secondly, the great mosque at Champaner has now been completed. The faithful are invited to go to pray there.

The crowd began to disperse before the last announcement.

No one wants to pray these days, said the maulvi sadly, not even on Fridays in the congregational mosques. They worship only the god of money and trade.

Sh, I said, and looked around to see if there were any religious leaders close by. That, maulvisab, could get you into trouble.

A few yards away, two of João's students were talking to him in whispers.

I'll see you tomorrow, Ahmadji, João said, and the three of them disappeared into the darkness of a sidestreet.

Karim and Suleiman came up to me.

I am glad you defended our profession, Karim, I said.

The profession is not what it used to be, Karim said.

The last of the lights on the platform was being handed down. Soon Diu center would be dark. The guards waited impatiently for the people to leave.

They have deliberately not told the truth about many things, Ahmadji, Suleiman said, about Hormuz and about Aden. Very few ships can get through to the Persian Gulf and the Red Sea. Drugs and spices have not been able to reach Cairo and Alexandria this year. The Diu administration doesn't want to frighten trade away and lose customs revenue. All traders are complaining. Prices have gone up in Egypt.

I wanted to ask him whether the Portuguese were aware of the system of dangerous winds and currents that swirl around below Socotra, but we saw a guard walking towards us.

Beware of Hooknose, Karim whispered quickly to me. He is Ishak Khan's agent, and he works as a spy for Malik Gopi.

Leave, the guard said, sternly.

The maulvi and I walked back along the same footpath that had brought us to Diu center.

Come along, maulvisab, said a group of people from his village. They were carrying a lantern.

Ahmadji and I will follow you, said the maulvi.

What times we are living in now, Ahmadji, the maulvi sounded very sad. Panditji is quite convinced that ours is the *kali yuga*. Perhaps the *mahdavis* are right in bewailing the mischief of the last days. You know about the vulgar shows Ishak Khan stages for his friends and followers. What times we live in, Ahmadji.

I remained silent.

I couldn't see maulvisab's face, but I could tell he was bursting with anger. Anger at himself.

Jaunpur, he said again, slowly. So far away.

It wasn't distance that he meant.

Ohe, maulvisab, come along, it's getting late, the people with the lantern called from some distance away.

I'm coming, the maulvi shouted.

It was quite dark where we were. The starlight just allowed me to make out where the footpath was.

I'm tired, Ahmadji, the maulvi said, let's sit down for a moment.

A tree rustled above our heads. The wind blew some leaves towards our feet.

No, no, I said, let's walk along slowly.

The maulvi placed his left arm on my shoulder and we walked on, slowly.

I could have followed Sayyid Muhammad Jaunpuri, maulvisab said, his voice dropping, I should have followed him. But I didn't.

Come, the Mahdi said, and a crowd of people followed him.

He didn't promise money or power but fellowship.

Ohe, maulvisab, come, come, it's very late.

Coming, maulvisab shouted to his friends.

The drumbeats became louder and faster. We walked on.

I was tempted to be a mahdavi, Ahmadji, but I was afraid. I became a maulvi instead, a teacher, he lamented.

The maulvi wanted to give me the lantern of his friends, but I knew their village was some distance away. The drum began to sound again, and I could see the light of a fire ahead.

I'll go to the *bhakta* group, I said, someone will give me a coconut husk there.

The crowd outside the hut had increased. There was a small fire to the right of the singer and the drummer. I looked around for a still smouldering coconut husk.

Come, brother, sit next to us, a voice said to me. The blind man is about to begin.

I am looking for a husk to light my way home, I said, still looking around.

Come, brother, sit down, another voice said, it is the famous singer that we all have been waiting for. He sings a few songs, two or three, but he repeats them and keeps on repeating them till all of us can sing them. The husks are on your right, he added.

I saw some coconut husks smouldering lightly on my right.

Come, a third voice said, sit down and listen.

I was tired, it was late. I didn't want to listen to some blind singer. I wanted to just take one husk from the pile, blow on it, and be on my way to set down the sad story of what happened to us in Kannanur. But to leave the group now would have been rude.

Just then the drone began. Undronelike it began to set forth different musical notes. The drum then started a beat that was sufficient unto itself. It did not say come, it did not say don't come. It began to create a world of rhythm for the singer to enter.

The singer burst in dramatically.

Oh blind ones, he sang.

Then he stopped. And the drone and the drum stopped. Now the silence became dramatic. The singer repeated his musical address to the whole gathering five times. And then went on

Listen, oh blind ones,
Shut your eyes and see.
Blind I may be, but I
Can see you in the dark
With the eyes of my heart.

The blind one repeated each phrase, each line. With each line his voice became softer. The silence grew louder. The crowd began to repeat the phrases, the lines, twice, three times, four times, five times. They got the whole song by heart. The singer repeated the song and made the crowd repeat it, till the music and the rhythm became part of its being, and every silence made the meaning of the words slowly sink into them, and the blind one still kept on repeating the song till the words and the music both melted away and the crowd was the song.

I was tempted to but refused to surrender my self. The song had lasted a long time, but it was as if it had only taken a moment. I wanted to know why. I began, in the João manner, with language. The blind one had started with *ulta* language. Shut, see.

The blind one began again. This mode was the same, but the language was less forceful. The rhythm, the beat, were not insistent. The silence was less vibrant. He sang in a clear voice.

A flame, then a flaming fire.
I have burnt my house to ashes
To be a seeker. Be warned,
Blind seekers. I will burn
The houses you sit in down.
Your eyes of logic cannot see
You sit in the house of *maya*.
I'll use the secret flame of

The blind man swept the crowd into the song. The crowd sang as one. They repeated the phrases till they could sing the whole song. They sang it without understanding the meaning of what they were singing. The last line stopped abruptly, the silence became vibrant, for the blind one did not release the unknown word. That didn't matter, for he had swept the song into the crowd.

I wanted to pierce the silence of that final line. I wanted to know why. The blind one had made use of *ulta* technique, upside down language. He had used silence too as echoing sound.

Language, rhythm, silence, meaning, the blind teacher had fused them all.

He began another song, this time with just a question.

What is the color of love, he sang.

He repeated the song question five times, promising but never giving the answer. Then his voice became soft, softer, more persuasive.

Oh, dear friends, he began, oh, dear friends, he repeated,
Oh, dear friends,
To be a man of knowledge
One needs to understand
Only one word
Love

The final word was sung softly. Then it became more soft, softer, as it was repeated, till the word wasn't heard at all, only silence could be heard.

This crowd did not become restless. I couldn't see their faces, but their voices told me that their hearts had been touched by wonder, without wanting to know what it meant. They did not look outward into the dark but inward into themselves. I was moved, my feelings were stirred.

The blind one began yet again, this time in a hushed voice

Blind ones,
The taint of *maya* is on your eyes
Only the touch of
Love will open them
And make you see
beyond
and beyond
and beyond

The song died into silence. Then it was quiet for a long time, except for the gentle wind that made the coconut tree rustle.

Tomorrow, the blind one said, we'll dance, we'll sing also, tomorrow.

He had used the word *kal* which signifies tomorrow, and also yesterday, time too, and death.

I couldn't understand my feelings as I walked home. I didn't want to sing. I didn't want to dance. I did and I didn't want to write. I only knew I had to listen to the blind one's songs tomorrow to see the beyond. I did not need a light to get home. There were faint streaks of light in the east, it was close to dawn.

I didn't feel tired at all.

Abdul, worried, was near the door, waiting, when I got back.

I want to write, I told Abdul.

Abdul placed my papers on the table.

Go to sleep, I told him as I sat down to write.

Once again I sensed in myself a strange reluctance to continue writing our story. It wasn't that I did not remember what happened after the Portuguese set the five of us, I include Yasmin, down at Elatur and we managed with great difficulty to get to Kannanur. But my pen refused to set down what happened there on paper. My venerable hakim had told me over and over again a long time ago to write my past. The act of writing will be healing, my hakim had said, your past will be present. But he hadn't warned me that the past would not flow out of me but spurt out in spasms. João had the gift of perfect recall. When driven by the urge to confess he would pour out his past in words. My hakim did not tell me how painfully difficult it would be for me to summon up and set down certain piercing moments. For I could easily recall everything that happened. I did not have to shut my eyes and see, as the blind one had urged.

João my teacher had been taught by Plato his teacher that to see is to know.

There are many ways of seeing, João had added, what you see depends on what you are at the time.

I shut my eyes, as the blind singer had advised, and tried to see with the eyes of my heart. But the pain was piercing.

Instead of re-living the past, just jot down cold facts about what happened at Kannanur and at Anegundi, my cynic suggested.

It was forehead shattering, my pain, at the sight of Mount Eli. At Malindi Kochama had warned me of its intensity and had said the pain would last for about seven days. I had a fit of shivering and a high fever that left me so helpless and weak that I could not speak and I was not able to guide the Portuguese ships to Calicut. They made their way down the coast to Elatur where they anchored on the fourth day. Abdul, knowing that the monsoon would burst on the coast soon, arranged to have a boat take the five of us to Kannanur. Vasco da Gama did not want me to leave because he wanted me to act as his guide in Calicut. But Paulo saw the helpless condition I was in and persuaded his brother to let me go. He gave Abdul ten gold coins as a farewell present.

Kochama was right. My headache disappeared on the seventh day when we arrived at Kannanur. My friend, Kotta Marakkar, arranged to have us land in the dead of night. A bullock cart was ready to take all four of us to one of my friend's houses near the foot of the ghats in a village a mile away.

Can we stay with you in Kannanur for a day or two, I asked my friend. Usha has not been feeling well. She is exhausted.

You are in great danger, friend Ahmadji, said Kotta Marakkar. The Jain community at Bhatkal has been told to keep a lookout for four persons with a myna bird, Kotta Marakkar told me. They know we are friends. We must not be seen together.

We went to Kotta Marakkar's house at the foot of the ghats and spent ten days without venturing out, except at night. One night Usha felt feverish and began vomiting violently. She was in great pain.

Get the midwife, Layla told Abdul and me.

The midwife, afraid of snakes, said she would come in the morning. When Abdul and I got back to the house from the village, I could hear no sounds of pain.

Layla opened the door, told Abdul to wait on the porch and took me in to Usha.

Usha lay in bed, covered with a cotton sheet. Her eyes were shut. I could see she was in great pain. She reached out for my hand.

Bend down, Ahmad mine, she whispered. I lost a great deal of blood. I have lost our baby.

I felt an explosion within me.

We remained silent for a very long time.

Then Usha opened her eyes and whispered, we do need a few words to share pain and accept it, my Ahmad. We have our togetherness. All will be well.

She fell asleep.

I waited by her bed till Layla came.

The next day my friend, Kotta Marakkar, advised us to leave Kannanur as soon as Usha had recovered. The Jain traders here are making enquiries about you. The rumor is that all five of you will be killed.

So we left Kannanur, the five of us, in 1499, and roamed all through South India, going from village to village, never feeling we belonged, searching for a home, avoiding coastal regions, avoiding towns and cities, avoiding places that had Jain communities, managing to stretch out the money given to me by Vasco and Paulo da Gama, Abdul and I working as laborers when work was available, Layla and Yasmin with her ivory ball staging small shows for village children and women who would provide us food and shelter for the night. Ball, Layla would say. And Yasmin would hop on to an ivory ball, steady herself, and then roll the ball towards Usha. Yasmin had grown into a beautiful bird with a yellow beak and with yellow round her eyes that set off the sheen of her black feathers.

The months drifted by and we were at peace, but without a home.

Till, one night, Usha whispered to me, I am with child again.

I was so shattered with joy that I didn't know what to say to Usha or what to do. I wanted to tell my joy to Abdul but he had already been told by Layla about the baby. I couldn't talk to Layla. I was restless, I couldn't stay in the hut, I wanted to go for a walk, but Abdul said two words, night and snakes.

So I paced up and down in the little hut.

Come and sit down, my Ahmad, Usha said. We cannot roam from village to village now. We will soon run out of money. The little one has to have a home. Let us go to Vijayanagar and then to the Anegundi Jain temple where my uncle said he would go for his renunciation of *samsāra*. He will help us.

It was a very long and a very slow journey. I was overjoyed with happiness. The uncle would help us, Abdul had some ambergris to sell. All would be well.

And then the assassins struck.

How, how, oh venerable hakim, how can I write about what happened at Anegundi when I cannot even talk or think about it. When you rescued me from the ditch beyond Anegundi I had no self. How, oh hakim, can one write about events that emptied me of a self. It is impossible to make that past present. I cannot.

I'm tired of writing. I want to sleep. I can hear the snoring of Abdul.

SIXTEEN

$\mathcal{D}$iu. May 1509, my house, night.
Written in a tremendous hurry despite my headache,
just before I left Diu in Gangaram's boat along with
João and Abdul and Gangu to bring back to Diu
the Portuguese captives shipwrecked at Dumas.
We had to wait a long time for João to come

I woke up just after midday. Malik Aiyaz had sent a messenger to my house with a horse for me.

But I wanted to walk not ride. I took a short cut. There were very few people on the hot city streets, and then it was cool along the avenue of stately mango trees that led to the palace. They provided shade but no fruit.

Malik Aiyaz loved mangoes. The best gardeners from Champaner could not coax these beautiful trees with dark green leaves to bear fruit. In early April the fragrance of the white mango blossoms was overpowering, but a week later they would turn black and fall off. Too salty the soil, too bitter, the gardeners explained. But they couldn't explain why melons and other fruit plants flourished in Diu.

Malik Aiyaz got his mangoes from Una on the river, his country home ten miles away. They were as juicy and as sweet as the ones from Halol near Champaner.

The guards at the palace door waved me on.

Malik Aiyaz was in his private room at the back. I passed through the thickcarpeted Hall of Public Audience. Then through the spacious dining hall lavishly decorated with colorful tapestries and damask hangings which would soon be taken down and stored during the monsoon months. The carpets of the dining hall had been rolled away and the bolsters and cushions for guests to recline on were piled next to the wall. The hangings smelled faintly of stale *ghee* and spices.

A long open corridor led to Malik Aiyaz's room.

I paused at a series of illustrations that had been removed from a book, framed in polished thick paper, and set up on ten trellised pillars in the middle of the corridor. They illustrated the ten episodes of the Laila Madjnun story. The sky colors were intensely blue. Gold pigment had been used lavishly in every illustration. The details of the animals, the rocks and the deserts Madjnun wandered through after his separation from his beloved Laila, were perfect. I admired the miniatures, all of them, every time I went to see Malik Aiyaz. Every time I felt powerfully drawn to the first one.

I paused before it.

Shiraz, the place. 1445, the year it was painted. The painter was not named. The scroll frame around the scene said it was the beginning of the Laila Madjnun story that has always moved me.

The illustration was set in a schoolroom. The central figure was an old teacher with a long stick in his hand, half asleep, teaching a group of young children. The pupils were talking noisily among themselves, their books lay everywhere on the carpet. No one paid any attention to the teacher. Only two, a boy and a girl, in the very front, were staring at a book on the carpet. The boy was pointing with a finger as if about to explain something to the little girl. The girl had just lifted her eyes from the book to look at him, as if about to ask a question. At that very moment the boy looked up. Their eyes touched. Time stopped. A shiver ran through me.

Outside Malik Aiyaz's door, leaning against a pillar, a man lay fast asleep.

The door burst open and someone ran out holding his palm tight against his mouth, and stumbled across the sleeping figure, and fell headlong, vomiting noisily and violently into the hot dust. Then he sat up, dazed.

João rushed out of the door to the fallen man who, trembling, was trying to keep down his vomit.

Don't say anything about me to Malik Aiyaz, João pleaded urgently to the man who was vomiting. And then João saw me and stopped.

A guard appeared out of nowhere and arrested the one who was still vomiting and took him away.

I went to help the man who had been so rudely wakened. His skin was like dark parchment. He smelled of the sea.

Come, Ahmadji, João said, as other guards appeared, Malik Aiyaz is waiting for you.

Come, have a mango drink, Malik Aiyaz said.

Sidi Ali *o torto* and Toghan sat on Malik Aiyaz's left, Ishak Khan on his right.

Sit down, Ahmadji, there, in front of me. Jan Mirza went and sat next to Ishak.

Go on, Ishak, Malik Aiyaz said.

Don't, said Ishak Khan. He set his drink down on the carpet.

Don't, Ishak repeated, don't send Sidi Ali *o torto* to Dumas. The Portuguese know him well. They won't talk freely in his presence. Send Mirzasab in disguise, Ishak Khan urged, he will be able to report their secret conversations.

Malik Aiyaz thought for a while. He turned his armlet as if turning Ishak's advice around in his mind. I sipped my drink. It was oversweet.

He may betray himself in spite of his disguise, Malik Aiyaz said, the Portuguese will come to know he is one of them.

How long is it since you left Portugal, Mirzasab, Sidi Ali *o torto* asked.

Twelve years, my friend, João said, twelve long years.

He speaks many languages, Sidi Ali informed Malik Aiyaz, he can speak Portuguese, Persian, Arabic.

Swahili, too, I added.

Can you speak the language of Castile, Malik Aiyaz asked João suddenly.

The question took João by surprise.

A little, he replied, just a little. Castilian is a near relative of Portuguese.

I wondered how Malik Aiyaz knew about Castilian.

A guard entered and was told to send Ghazi Mujli in.

He was the one who had vomited.

He cannot stand up, Maliksab, the guard said, he still feels giddy.

I will question him tomorrow, said Malik Aiyaz. Put him in prison, in a secluded cell. And don't allow anyone to speak to him.

The guard shut the door.

Let me question Ghazi Mujli tomorrow, Ishak Khan said.

No, no, said Malik Aiyaz. He stared down at the carpet for a time.

I have come to a decision, Malik Aiyaz said.

He was a little tense. He folded his arms across his chest and stared at each one of us in turn.

Malik Aiyaz continued.

We have a problem about the *Meri*, the pilgrim ship loaded with gold and jewelry that was captured by the Portuguese on its way back to Diu from the Red Sea. We cannot fight the Portuguese. They have large ships and powerful guns. We need to negotiate with the Portuguese who have taken the *Meri* to Cochin.

What we will offer them in exchange are the Portuguese captives from the *Santa Cruz* that was wrecked at Dumas during the tufan Ahmaji warned us about. Mirzasab, continued Malik Aiyaz, you will go as my official representative to Dumas. Take charge of the Portuguese captives there, and bring them here to Diu.

Ahmadji, continued Malik Aiyaz, you will accompany your friend to Dumas. Hooknose can go with them, Ishak Khan said, he knows Dumas well.

No, no, no, I said hastily.

Ishak looked at me, surprised.

I want Abdul, I explained.

That's settled, Malik Aiyaz said, the three of you will travel to Dumas by boat.

The guard was told to send in the boatman.

What's your name, Ishak Khan asked the boatman.

Gangaram, sir.

Ghazi Mujli, just before he rushed out, was telling us how he never even saw the tidal bore, and how cleverly you steered your boat across the treacherous waters of the Gulf of Cambay. How long did it take you, asked Ishak Khan.

Twenty eight hours, sir.

Impossible, said Ishak Khan.

The bore made it possible, sir.

It was a simple statement of fact.

We stared at Gangaram wonderingly, all of us.

Quite impossible, burst out of Ishak Khan, the bore is a destroyer.

Gangaram looked straight at Ishak. His eyes were quite steady, and white in a face burnt by the sun and the sea and the salt wind. He kept silent, as if reluctant to explain anything.

Have a mango drink, Gangaram, said Malik Aiyaz, it's very sweet.

No, maliksab, that's very kind of you. That sweet drink caused Ghazi Mujli's stomach to be upset. He is seasick still.

Ah, said Malik Aiyaz, I understand. Tell us, Gangaram, how the tufan helped.

Maliksab, the boatman explained, the tufan changed the flow of the water in the gulf, but only for one day. No tidal bores swept up the estuary that day. The swollen rivers rushed into the Gulf causing downstream currents that allowed the boat to reach Diu without going across to Gogha point.

Ghazi Mujli had been impressed by the quick passage to Diu, but none of Gangaram's listeners, not even Malik Aiyaz, realized the skill with which Gangaram must have avoided one sandbank after another and maneuvered his little boat across the continuous downflow of the currents.

Ishak Khan said, we should be able to get control of the Portuguese captives in two days.

Ishak Khan, I said, it will probably take Gangaram about four days to take us to Dumas.

Gangaram, we need to get to Dumas as soon as possible, Malik Aiyaz said, how long will it take.

He twisted his armlet, slowly considering the problem.

By the shortest and quickest route, Malik Aiyaz added, how long will it take.

Gangaram made some calculations on his fingers with his thumb.

The tidal wave rolls into the gulf twice a day, Gangaram said, we will have to go up the gulf to Piram island, that should take two days and a half, then we have to go to Suvali and then to Dumas. That will take a day and a half.

The maliksab is right, Gangaram added, looking at me, it will take four days. But we will have to set out immediately, this evening, just before sunset, to take advantage of the current and the east wind that blows at night.

I smiled.

I am not a malik, Gangaramji, just a boatman like you, I said.

The guard entered and was told to give Gangaram some food.

I don't eat meat, Gangaram began, and stopped.

Wait for Ahmadbhai outside the door, Malik Aiyaz told the boatman.

The three of you must leave today, Malik Aiyaz told João. Ishak Khan will give you a letter of authority. Sidi Ali will give you names of our people in Dumas and in Surat. Make your preparations and meet at Ahmadbhai's house.

Ahmadbhai, I want to talk to you before you go, Malik Aiyaz said.

After the four left, the Malik unclasped his armlet. A thin cord ran from it into a tiny hole in the carpet. Then he put on another armlet, an exact copy.

So that's why he kept turning the armlet, I thought.

Just a signaling device, Malik Aiyaz said, a form of protection too. Only a few people know about it.

He appeared slightly relaxed now.

I've had too much mango drink. I need to empty myself, Malik Aiyaz said, and went into a side room.

I shut my eyes and was worried about João's getting involved in a conspiracy with Ishak Khan and Ghazi Mulji.

Malik Aiyaz said, you've shut your eyes, Ahmadji. You must be wondering why I asked you to go to Dumas.

He had had a quick bath, and changed into pyjamas and a soft white muslin shirt that had been sprinkled with rose water. He eased himself down against a bolster, six feet away, his chin propped up on his left palm, and he massaged his armletless arm gently.

Relax, Ahmadji, Malik Aiyaz said.

He was telling himself to relax, I thought. His voice was tense. He wanted to talk.

I cannot trust anyone these days, Ahmadji, no one, especially Ishak, my eldest son. These days he lusts for power. He wants to have me assassinated, I think. Malik Gopi encourages him. One of my agents warned me about them.

Malik Gopi and Ishak Khan, the agent said, holding two fingers close together.

But the agent could offer me no proof, only suspicions. Ghazi Mujli, who is our Dumas agent, went first, according to my spies, to report to Ishak before coming here to give me the news about the shipwrecked Portuguese. I'll have Ghazi Mujli tortured tomorrow. Or I could bribe him. Malik Gopi must surely have bribed him.

Let Gangaram be sent to my place. Abdul will take care of him and make preparations for our departure.

Ah, yes, Malik Aiyaz said.

The guard was summoned, and orders were given efficiently.

But I could tell that my friend was brooding deeply, wanting to make sense of his own life. He wanted to talk, wanted to let the story of his life flow out of him.

Malik Aiyaz's story

I should be with the Begdo in Champaner, not here in Diu, Ahmadji. Malik Gopi is there in Champaner, that snake, poisoning the Sultan's ears, planning devious schemes to rake in revenues into the royal treasury. He and his accomplice, Malik Sarang, the Kiwam-ul-mulk, have raised taxes and imposed unjust tariffs after the Sultan appointed them chief administrators of his kingdom. Even the common people complain. That pig of a Brahmin, the people say of Malik Gopi. That Rajput bastard of a convert, they say of Malik Sarang, that damned Muslim infidel.

They do not care, these two. Gopi, through his dancing girls and courtesans, lavishes presents and gold ornaments from Melaka on the women of the Sultan's harem. They do not care, these two, about what is whispered about them at court. The nobles complained loudly to the Sultan's favorite son when Malik Gopi and Malik Sarang were made chief ministers. But they dare not complain to the Sultan himself.

For the Sultan now listens only to both his chief advisers who flatter him outrageously. Gopi especially. Gopi takes the Sultan to the royal treasury every month and displays the gold, the jewels, the precious stones, and all the gifts and tributes from the Rajput ranas that have been added to the treasury that month.

You are a mint unto yourself, the Sultan said to Malik Gopi in front of me. You produce more mahmudis than the mints of Champaner and of Ahmadabad combined.

And Gopi exploits the Sultan's fear of death and his turning to religion.

More mosques will be built at Sarkhej, Gopi tells the Sultan. A corridor will extend from the mausoleum we are building for you to the mausoleum of Sheikh Ahmad Khattu. Sarkhej will become the holiest of the Muslim shrines in all Gujarat, holier than Hindu Somnath and Jain Patan.

It will be, Malik Gopi concludes, faking awe in his voice, a sacred center of pilgrimage.

That wily Gopi, Ahmadji. The name, Gopi, is appropriate, after all. Like the Hindu god Krishna he has a retinue of dancing girls and courtesans.

Why this Hindu was given a Muslim title of Malik no one knows, continued Malik Aiyaz. And no one knows whether he is a treacherous Brahmin or a shrewd Bania. He brings Bania tactics of business and moneymaking to the world of politics and government. What a forked tongue he has, that Gopi, it drips both poison and honey.

The Sultan enjoys Gopi's honeyed flattery. He takes in a deep breath, raises both his hands and gives thanks to God for such a wonderful minister.

I am ready to renounce power. My advanced camp will be ready, the Sultan says, the one I will soon occupy after my life's march has been completed.

Our Sultan, he has changed, Ahmadji, the Sultan is not what he was. I do not, I cannot, understand why.

Malik Aiyaz fell silent for a while.

How old is Sultan Begada, I asked.

No, it's not that, Ahmadji. It's true he's sixty five. It is now his fifty first regnal year, but it's not that, not that. It's not his body, that's still strong. It's his spirit that has somehow grown old and weak. He does not have the ambitious drive to power that made him the mighty ruler of a vast kingdom.

Malik Aiyaz's voice sped on, charged with excitement. He sat up, his forehead had a slight gleam of sweat. He looked straight at me. He also looked beyond me.

You should have seen him in the days of his glory, Ahmadji. Tall, robust, imposing, born to be a commander of men. All were awestruck by his regal appearance. The penetrating eyes that at times turned mellow with compassion. The beard that cascaded to his girdle. The thick moustachios, always well groomed, that twisted and curled upwards and framed his indomitable face.

They hailed him as Mahmud of Ghazni. For he was a temple destroyer and a smasher of idols. He destroyed Dwarka, the Hindu holy center of pilgrimage. He demolished the Ranchhodji shrine on the island Shankoddar. He razed to the ground the famous Mahabala temples, hidden in a defile in the granite hills of Girnar where the women and children of Rao Mandalik had taken refuge.

Something in him drove him to be a conqueror.

What loyalty and heroism he inspired in all of us. In his soldiers, who were given interest free loans against their pay. In his faithful companions and amirs who rode along with him when he conquered Junagadh. They were his companions in the expeditions against Dwarka, Malwa, and Khandesh. Against Champaner, too. Ahmadji. I don't have to tell you what happened there. All Gujarat knows the story of the downfall of Pawagadh and the conquest of Champaner.

But let me tell you why I felt so drawn to Sultan Begada.

It wasn't because of the robe of honor he bestowed on me after the conquest of Champaner. It was because he became the father I never knew, Ahmadji. Even before I, a mere slave, shot down that ill omened raven, I felt drawn to him. It was his magnetic voice. At first, a compelling voice of authority.

Come, the Begdo would say to me, and we would talk about his aims as we rode together far ahead of the marching army to inspect the terrain and check the layout of the encampment.

Then it was the voice of friendship.

Come, he would say, and he would talk to me about his plans to establish justice and security and prosperity in his kingdom, how he wanted to make grain and food stuffs available at a cheap rate for all his people. How he wanted to lay out gardens in all regions, and plant different kinds of fruit trees all along the roads, make them free of robbers, and build caravanserais. So that Gujarat would be a paradise on earth.

And then, Ahmadji, his voice became a voice of genuine affection.

Come my friend, he would say to me, and we would go swimming together in the Sabarmati. We would practice sword fencing together, and listen together to ghazals and poetry recitations. We would even eat mangoes together, Ahmadji. Both of us love mangoes.

It's different now. Somehow things have changed, Ahmadji, they're no longer simple. I wish I could understand what's happening. We are close friends still, the Begdo and I. At Maha'im near Bombay he presented me with a robe of honor and a belt of gold after our glorious victory over the Portuguese at Chaul.

His voice, everyone says, I sense it too, now comes as from a great distance. What I mean is that he has different values now. He talks about the faraway. His voice has lost its tone of command. He no longer has the former passion he had to govern his kingdom. He has delegated authority to others. To Gopi, that bastard.

I have seen his eyes filled with tears and his countenance marked with grief as he recalls the names of his soldiers and of the sons of amirs who were killed in his former campaigns. No longer does he regard them as famous victories. He continually invokes the Mahdi of Jaunpur, Shah Alam the saint of Rasulabad, and, above all, Shaikh Ahmad Khattu of Sarkhej.

After Maha'im he went straight to Patan to get the blessings of Maulana Tajuddin Siwi.

The measure of my life is full, the Sultan told this holy man, pray for me.

I am confused, Ahmadji.

One is born, one lives, then one dies, that's all there is, it is kismet, fate, the stars.

I was a Christian slave. They brought me to India, circumcised me and made me a Muslim. I don't believe. In anything. Not in God, I say no prayers. Not in family continuity. My name, begun with me, will end with me. When I die I want to be buried in a simple grave in Una near the tomb of Shah Shams-ud-din. I've built no mausoleum for my bones to rest in, no mosque that will celebrate and perpetuate my name.

The only monument I have is this, this, and he struck the carpet twice with his right hand. My beloved Diu, which will always be coupled with my name.

End of Malik Aiyaz's story about Sultan Begada

The Malik was intensely moved. His eyes, I thought, were a little wet.

He rose abruptly and walked quickly to the small west window designed and placed so as to let in the low deepgold rays of the evening sun. He drew aside the heavy dark curtains that kept out the harsh glare of the afternoon. I followed him.

There, he said with pride, look.

I saw only a dazzling white stretch of desolate sand and jagged black rocks against which the darkgreen waves beat and swirled protectively, but I understood what he meant. That was his beloved Diu.

It will be evening soon, Malik Aiyaz said. Let me explain in some detail why I want you to accompany your friend to Dumas.

A Portuguese ship was wrecked by the tufan off the Dumas coast and the survivors have been captured. The Dumas *kotwal* has sent word to the chief of police in Gopi's Surat asking him what to do with the prisoners. The *kotwal* should have waited for orders from me for those are my prisoners. Dumas is under my jurisdiction as Admiral of the Sea.

I would like you and Jan Mirza to go to Dumas and bring those Portuguese captives here to Diu before Gopi uses them for his own purposes. I am sure Gopi will take the Portuguese prisoners to Surat and hold them there as hostages to bargain with the Portuguese for *cartazes*. He bribes the Portuguese officials all along the west coast to allow his huge ships crammed with Gujarati cloth and merchandise to sail to Melaka. He supplies the Portuguese with bits of information about the local trading routes and about some locations where they could set up their factories. The Portuguese don't realize what insignificant sums of money he doles out to them and the immense profits he makes, that Bania broker.

Our Sultan, long may he live, never ever defeated on land, now perched in isolation on Champaner, his eyes fixed on distant Sarkhej, does not realize how dangerous the Portuguese threat from the sea is.

The Portuguese are mere vagabonds, Malik Gopi tells the Sultan, who will ultimately go away.

Malik Gopi knows only that the Portuguese are a threat to his commercial ventures. He knows they won't disappear, and so he seeks to pacify them with a little money. What else can a Bania broker do. He knows nothing about swords and sea battles. A letter was sent, without my knowledge, to the Portuguese offering Diu as a trading base. What a crook that Gopi is.

That's why I want you to go with your friend Jan Mirza to Dumas. Send me reports. I want to know what has happened, what's happening, who's on my side, where the prisoners are, how many. I will send an armed galley to bring them to Diu, but it will take many days for the galley to get to Dumas.

Sidi Ali has told me you know sufficient Portuguese. You're the only one I trust, Ahmadji. I don't trust your friend and teacher, Jan Mirza, but I have to send him to Dumas. He has fallen into the coils of Malik Gopi and Ishak Khan.

Malik Aiyaz paused, and looked at me. My eyes were steady, and straight, but it took an effort.

The Malik looked away.

My spies tell me Jan Mirza spends money like water, on rich clothes and jewels and gold ornaments for his wife.

My temples began to throb.

And for drink which, as you know, is expensive and absolutely forbidden except on Bandar-i-Turk. I would like to find out what reports Mirzasab sends to Gopi.

That's why I want your help, Ahmadji my friend. Many Diu lives were saved because of the tufan warning you gave us. We were lucky to have you warn us. They were not so fortunate at Dumas and on the lower west coast. The tufan struck with full force there. Now I need your help. The mahdavis are no threat now. Those who disturbed the play are in prison. The head of their sect has fled to Palanpur.

But the Portuguese tufan is gathering strength and I need your help, Malik Aiyaz said. I couldn't bear to hear the pleading tone of the Malik's voice. My friend didn't have to beg.

I stood up.

Of course I will, Malikji, I said. But I wasn't a traitor and I wouldn't betray João.

Malik Aiyaz rose and gave me a double embrace. I'll send a messenger to your house immediately, he said, with some money and my seal.

Just outside the palace door, walking along the avenue of mango trees, I felt an ache in the back of my head.

Must be the sun, I thought, or the lack of sleep, or, perhaps, I had somehow twisted my neck while relaxing against the bolster.

Piram Island in the Gulf of Cambay
Night, Gangaram's small hut,
Very tired after the long boatride from Diu,
But I couldn't sleep
Some force within drove me to write

A strange headache this, a dull pressure at the back of my head, like the ones I suffered from after I was struck by the arrow in Malindi. It persisted all the way from Diu till we got to Gangaram's hut on Piram island.

My hakim had told me, soon after I became his helper, that headaches spring from the inside. From a sour stomach, he had said, for which I prescribe a cleansing decoction of neem leaves. The ones that arise from a disturbed heartmind, as do yours, need strange purges, confession, bouts of remembering, even a bout of crying.

You lock things up tight inside you. Never, never analyse your headaches, my hakim advised me.

But I couldn't help asking myself, why.

It wasn't the sun, of that I was sure.

It wasn't fear of the treacherous waters. I did trust boatman Gangaram, though anything could happen in the gulf of Cambay.

Perhaps it was being torn away after five years from Diu and a kind of peace troubled only by occasional stabs of memory. Perhaps the headache arose from my dark suspicions, confirmed by Malik Aiyaz, about my friend's involvement in the treacherous world of Ishak and Malik Gopi. The messenger, who had brought a bag with money and Malik Aiyaz's seal, had also brought a package for João from Ishak.

Abdul weighed it in the palm of his hand.

Opium, he said, thin strips of opium halwa.

My ache intensified.

I want a bath, I told Abdul. Then I remembered the cloudy well water.

Everything's packed, your papers too, Abdul said, and sent with Gangaram to the boat. Mirzasab said he would meet us at the boat. He had to talk to the envoy from Vijayanagar about horses.

Abdul brought me a glass of water. I thought the back of my head would explode.

I'll bring some food, said Abdul.

A drink, I want a drink, burst out of me.

Before Abdul could say anything I walked into the kitchen and quickly drank down the liquor that was left in the flask. Then I brushed the back of my hand across my lips. I couldn't taste a thing. I didn't look at Abdul. He didn't say anything.

Take the other flask, I told Abdul, and let's go.

It was by continual sipping, all through the night, from this other flask of jambul liquor, one that João had asked me to store safely in case he ever ran out of the stuff, that I decided to attack the strange headache.

All through the night, I sat on a plank, in Gangaram's boat, and gradually my temples tightened and my forehead also began to ache, so that my whole head became one throbbing blur of pain. A homeopathic clash of headaches sure to neutralize each other.

Like attacks and cures like, that's what you taught me, I said aloud to my hakim.

Where are you now, oh wanderer, where are you, I lamented.

Then I stood up and shouted, hakim, friend, wanderer, to the faint stars in the night sky.

Abdul's hand fell firmly on my shoulder to steady me.

Go to sleep, my friend, he said.

I woke up to the sounds of rushing water, almost falling off the narrow plank I had been sleeping on. I stood up, then I stumbled, and felt the boat wobble. Then it righted itself.

I looked up. The sunlight was dazzling.

Please sit down, Ahmadji sab, don't move, or the boat will upturn.

It was the calm voice of Gangaram.

He stood at the stern using an oar with a peculiar twisting motion to guide the boat as it sped along with the fast flowing current.

Ohe, father, what happened, came a voice from the bow.

It's alright, Gangu, Gangaram said. Keep a sharp lookout ahead, son, the sandbanks will get narrower.

I sat and looked, amazed, at the rushing scene as the boat sped along. It wasn't being rowed along at all. The tidal current, that swept along between two continuous irregular sandbanks, drove the boat onward. Father and son worked together. Gangaram used his oar effortlessly shifting the paddle sometimes to one side, sometimes to the other, to keep the boat in the center of the channel. Gangu stood tall at the bow, keeping watch, a long thick pole in hand, ready to shout warnings about the dangers ahead.

The tidal stream flowed easily and rapidly, but with hidden power. My feet on the bottom planking sensed the boat's vibrant tremble. Eddies swirled up near the sandbanks to the right and to the left. Gangu had to look out for shoals and for submerged reefs over which the water boiled up in little conical waves.

Ohe, father, warned Gangu.

The channel narrowed and the waters raced through with tremendous force.

Gangaram calmly raised his oar and held it almost horizontal, the paddle just below the surface of the running water. The boat responded immediately and veered towards the sandbank on the left.

Ohe, warned Gangu.

Take up an oar, son, said Gangaram.

We were moving dangerously close to the left edge, when I heard a roar of thunder as if a cannon had been discharged. I saw up ahead thick chunks of the left sandbank fall into the channel in quick succession, and set in motion menacing waves that swung the water flow towards the right bank. I braced myself for the blow. We would be overwhelmed. The waves would smash the left side of the boat. There was no time to warn João.

Gangaram and Gangu used their oars to counter this thrust. The prow was turned towards the oncoming waves, so that the boat spun around twice and, after a few unsteady moments, regained the center of the stream. The channel widened gradually and the boat moved swiftly along.

You can relax now, Ahmadji, Gangaram said, and move about.

It took me some time to calm down. I stood up and held on to the sailless mast just outside the small cabin made of woven strips of bamboo that formed the living space.

João was stretched out on a sideplank at the far end in the dark cabin, fast asleep. Abdul had started boiling water for coffee on a small earthenware chula. Outside, straight ahead, stretched the continuous sandbanks. They were a dark brown with coarse tufts of grey weeds at the top. There were no other boats in the channel.

I held on to the mast and an oppressive calm lay heavy on my eyes.

Don't stand in the sun, Ahmadji.

I stepped inside the cabin and sat on the narrow plank. Ahmad gave me some coffee and I asked him to get another cup for Gangaram. He put in an extra piece of gur in Gangaram's coffee to sweeten it. Gangu took Gangaram's place at the stern.

Abdul told me you're the most skillful navigator on the Bahr-i-Hind, Gangaram said, and that you know the Indian ocean as if it were the palm of your hand.

I haven't been to sea for ten long years now, Gangaram, I said, I don't think I'll ever be a nakhoda again.

I asked Gangaram why there were no other boats in the channel.

Too dangerous a passage, Gangaram said. The other boatmen prefer the outer passage along the Kathiawad coast. It's slower, safer, but takes longer. This passage through the sandbanks is quick. We will reach Piram island before nightfall. I took it because Malik Aiyaz wanted us to get to Dumas as soon as possible. Also, to teach my son Gangu a new route with new dangers.

Many years ago my boatman father was my guide through this passage which was broader then, and not as dangerous. My son Gangu will teach it to his son after I am gone, and so it goes, Ahmadji. That's samsāra. He said the word casually. Its many meanings did not trouble him. For him it meant an acceptance of life and of change.

I don't even have a son.

How, I almost asked. I must have looked quite puzzled. So Gangaram made the Gulf of Cambay vividly graphic for me. He placed my left hand, palm down, on a smooth worn plank.

Extend your thumb wide, he said, and keep the four fingers joined. There, there's the whole Gulf of Cambay. Your thumb tip is Diu. The inner thumb joint is Gogha from where the dangerous tides begin to roll. And that, he said, placing his finger nail on the curved stretch of skin between my thumb and my forefinger, that's the head of the Gulf of Cambay with two rivers, the Sabarmati to the left and the Mahi on the right. Up towards these two rivers the bore sweeps from the gulf and then down the rivers and on to the sea rushes the thick silt that continually forms and unforms shoals and sandbars and long sandbanks, and makes and unmakes ports. It was a vivid illustration of danger and change.

Then Gangaram told me about warning signs. Always check the color of the sandbanks, Ahmadji, he told me. If brown they are not dangerous. If black they have been recently formed and have to be avoided.

I could see the sandbank on our left slope down and taper into shoals. Our boat was carried along into the outer passage. In the distance I could see the Kathiawad coastline. The boat slowed down.

Time now to set up sail, Gangaram said. Father and son hoisted up the single sail which caught the wind and we headed up towards Gogha, Gangaram at the tiller.

It was slower sailing up the outer passage but we were much faster than the other boats which we overtook easily, all heading in one direction to Gogha. I got a keen appreciation of Gangaram's skills. A rope in his left hand allowed him to control the sail so that it swung about to catch every gust of the fickle wind. The tiller, and at times the steering paddle, enabled him to work the boat so as to take advantage of any strong current. He performed all this singlehandedly.

I could hear Gangu in the cabin making preparations for a fish curry. He had set Abdul at the prow with four fishing lines. Rice bubbled in a pot on the chula. Gangu moved a stone roller back and forth over a slate slab nicked with tiny grooves, that looked like a paliyo, a memorial stone, crushing the spices to form a thick orange paste. My nose picked up smells of red chillies, tamarind, ginger, garlic, onion, coriander and coconut. My stomach felt fiercely hungry.

We have to eat before it gets dark, Gangaram said.

It was one of the many facts of life on the Cambay gulf Gangaram had accepted. He began to talk about things, pausing for greetings along the way, addressing not the boatman but each boat we passed by its proper name. Boats have spirits, boats endure, Gangaram said, only their inhabitants change. Our boat was named the Maya. It had been used by his great grandfather and would be passed on to Gangu and to Gangu's son and on to the son's son.

The flow of time became visible for me.

Gangaram continued talking about the world he had lived in all his life, a world of water. His father had made him accompany him on this boat when he was a small boy. By now Gangaram had an intimate knowledge of the gulf. He knew every creek, every headland, every shifting channel. He knew the mood of every inlet, the tides to avoid, the currents he could make use of, the main routes, the short cuts.

It was backbreaking, the work of a Cambay boatman, carrying passengers and cargo from one place to another, never ending. But Gangaram never complained. He told me stories and legends, happy and sad, about Gogha and the Gulf, about a tribe of sailors called Gogharees who were part Muslim, part Koli, part Hindu, the ballad also of Mokheraji, the heroic Rajput Gohil chieftain who battled against the Muslim invaders, chanting the story at times, singing about what happened, using words I did not know but could somehow understand.

The food is ready, father, Gangu said.

The boats had all slowed down. The boatmen were busy preparing their evening meal before it got dark. It was simple, our meal, plain rice and fish curry.

That's all we can offer, Ahmadji, Gangaram said.

The curry was spicy hot. It set my tongue on fire, I had to keep on drinking water. But I couldn't stop eating. The fish flaked off the bones in tasty morsels. I even licked the curry off my fingers, and asked for a second helping of rice.

There's plenty, said Gangu, who was at the tiller. Another pot of rice was bubbling on the chula. After I had eaten my fill, Gangaram and I ate without talking, my tongue delightfully on fire, Abdul brought me a small cup.

What's it, I asked.

Pepper water, he said. It looked muddy.

Drink it, Abdul said.

I drank. The hotness vanished from my mouth and tongue.

How's João, I asked Abdul.

Still sleeping, he said, still seasick.

I sat near Gangaram and listened to him talk about his son. The slanting sun was no longer fierce. A cooling breeze blew up the gulf. Gangaram talked about how good a boatman Gangu he was. How good a son. How anxious his son was to get back to Dumas to know whether he was the father of another son. It would be his third.

How many sons do you have, Ahmadji, asked Gangaram. It was the usual question to ask, a polite way of showing human concern.

But I couldn't answer, and I didn't want to tell a lie. I stood up as though to ease a cramp in my legs and watched the slowly receding Kathiawad coastline.

We were slanting away from the other boats that were moving very slowly.

I thought you would steer parallel to the coastline, Gangaram, I said.

I want to avoid the thrust of the Shetrunji river current, he said, which, as you can see, is slowing down all the boats. We will swing out beyond the twelve fathom sounding. The wind and the swift currents there will carry us to Piram before the other boats get to Gogha, and before the sun sets. In that direction, he said, on a headland, one hundred and fifty feet above the sea, stands Gopnath temple, a white landmark. You cannot see it, it's too far away.

I could see a long line of white breakers. I felt a sudden stab within me.

Too much rice, I thought, eaten too quickly, gas in the stomach.

Gangaram liked talking about Piram too. Never once did he mention the dangerous bore, I asked him why.

A fact of Cambay life to be accepted, like samsāra, Gangaram said.

I thought the bore was a just a powerful rushing tide, I said.

No, said Gangaram, the bore begins as a rapid tidewave. When forced through a narrow passage it becomes as one possessed by a bhut. It turns into a gigantic roaring rushing crashing wall of water that smashes down everything in its path. You will be able to see it early tomorrow morning from the sandhill platform on the south western edge of Piram island.

Our boat picked up speed, the current drove it along in a curve towards Soshia. A steady wind filled our single sail.

I thought it would be good for João to feel the wind on his face. He tried to sit up on the sideplank when I stepped into the cabin shelter and called out to him.

My head is whirling, Ahmadbhai my friend, João groaned and lay down again, my stomach is churning, I want to vomit but there's nothing more to vomit, Abdul, Abdul, give me my opium halwa, I am dying, Ahmadbhai, dying.

I smiled at my friend. We'll get to Piram soon, I said.

Gangu was now at the tiller for the last stretch of the way. He made the boat swing in towards the Gohilwad coast so that we passed quite close to Soshia. And then it made a sudden arc, the sail hung limp for a while, the boat spun to the left, uncertain about its direction, but Gangu managed to steady it. Then the wind filled the sail, and the boat was swept onward towards Gogha.

Slow it down, Gangu, said Gangaram, you know how treacherous this channel is.

He seized an oar and the boat slowed.

I could sense the powerful surge of the current.

Gangu, we should move beyond the nulla, to the right, shouted Gangaram.

He told me why.

Midway up the channel between Piram and the coast was a sudden gap. Boatmen avoided it. The currents there were rapid, swirling, eddies rose unpredictably, and sucked boats into depths that had never been sounded. Mokheraji, the Cambay boatmen whisper as they approach Piram. They believe it is the secret abode of Mokheraji who in death became the guardian spirit of Piram. Save us, oh Mokheraji, all boatmen whisper joining their palms in an act of propitiation as they sprinkle an offering of pounded opium mixed with water on the waves. Gangu made the kusumba offering with João's opium just as we passed near the thirty foot high sandstone cliffs of Piram.

Gangu and Gangaram drew up the boat on the eastern shore of Piram on a sloping sandy beach next to two large stone elephants that appeared to welcome João and me as if we were victorious heroes returning from a battle.

A paliyo, a memorial stone to Mokheraji, had been set up between the elephants. No people came to greet us. I could not see any houses anywhere.

SEVENTEEN

*M*ay 1509, Gangaram's small hut
on Piram Island in the Gulf of Cambay
The evening just before we left Piram for Dumas
I felt tired and drained but my fingers felt compelled
to set down what happened that day

Early this morning Gangu took me to the sandhill platform on the south-western edge of Piram. He led me under stunted neem trees, past the collapsed richly carved pillars of a Hindu temple, and past the gateway and walls, some still standing, others propped up by sand dunes, of a fort that must have extended right across the island. Mokheraji's stronghold, surely.

I will not wait with you to see the bore, Gangu said. There's nothing there, Gangu told me, looking back at the broken gateway. I don't know why my father likes Piram so much.

Abdul will come later to fetch you. Gangu said, we have to catch the inflowing tide tonight to get to Dumas.

Gangaram was right.

The rounded sandhill platform on the southwestern edge of Piram commanded a spectacular view. The magical haze of the early morning bathed the gulf of Cambay with soft blues and with mysterious shades of green. The noises of birds feeding nearby, all along the Piram shoreline, the continuous murmurs of ebbtide, the near and the far, all mingled in me. Looking down from the platform, it was clear that the stone slabs and angular blocks of the fort walls had been cut from the reefs below. They appeared to be freshly cut, as if quarried just yesterday.

A poem about time began to stir inside me. Time past in time present.

I shut my eyes, listened, and waited, for a line, a word, to bubble up, but no sound came forth. Patiently I waited, my eyes still shut, the poem was struggling inside, but not even a syllable emerged from the silence within. Even my cynic, strangely, was silent.

I waited patiently.

When at last I opened my eyes the magic had vanished. The sun, low in the east, lit up the stretch of the Gohilwad coast. A flat bottomed boat was hurrying to Kuda point opposite. Higher up, northwest, eight miles away, was Gogha. What was quite strange to my eyes were the flat reefs and razor sharp ridges right in front of Kuda point that the ebb of the tide revealed. Perhaps the legend that Gangaram had told me was true, that Piram, in ancient times a part of the mainland, had been split apart by a gigantic earth demon.

Again I waited patiently. Instead of a poem there arose a swirl of insights from our many discussions about time and religion. For the maulvi, real time began only after the advent of the prophet, on whom be peace. Time is a noose, claimed the pandit, who would then spout forth views about *samsāric* time. João too confused the three of us when he stated that there was no time in heaven. Eternity, João maintained, had once descended into time to bisect time.

Suddenly, I heard a fierce cackling, and a whirring of wings. All the birds, the herons, the cranes, the seagulls, rose in one huge mass and with tremendous bellbeats of their wings fled in a mad dash towards the mainland.

What had caused this panic. I looked all around to find out. Everything was the same. The sounds of ebbtide had grown softer. Nothing had changed. The reefs were so clear I could have walked to Kuda point.

Then I heard prolonged wails from two conch shells on the opposite shore. They kept on sounding continuously, never stopping, so that the wailing seemed to be a prolonged lament for all mankind.

And then, then, there was a clap of thunder, a tremendous roar of sound.

And then I saw it. I saw the bore.

A perpendicular mountain of water appeared out of nowhere, a bluegreen wall that extended right across the gulf, and kept rolling along, bearing down on and sweeping away everything. Just in front of me, almost level with my eyes, was swept up the flat bottomed boat that the wall of water flung down in its fury, then smashed into tiny bits. Pieces of timber, fragments of people and of horses, I saw. Only for a moment. Then they vanished.

I stood up and shouted, *samsāra*, prolonging the three syllables. No human being heard my cry. I couldn't hear myself above the loud roar. I sat down.

Samsāra, I wailed, *samsāra*.

They welled up out of me, the three syllables, from a level deeper than where my poems had sprung from, from a space around the heart, where time stood still. They began as a hum of sonic power that had not yet coalesced into meaning.

The first, *sam*, began as a sibilant hiss, the sound a woman makes at the moment of absolute abandon, that shifted into a prolonged wail of surrender.

The second, *sā*, was a panting outbreath, a long open vowel that rose out of the channel of the throat and pulsed through my open lips.

The third, *ra*, was a short vowel, a hot spurt of sudden release, then a sudden end that made the after silence resonant.

Time whirled within me. A dam burst. My past flooded back.

Human beings try to imprison the past but cannot, my hakim had said late one night. It was the Aśvin full moon. We were walking back from a Bhavāi performance in a small village near Vadnagar in north Gujarat. We had been asked to visit the village by the headman whose daughter was afflicted by a wheezing cough. Her breathing was spasmodic.

Feel her forehead, my hakim said.

I did, but with my left hand, and with just the thumb and one finger.

He touched both her eyes gently, then looked at her tongue. And he felt her forehead with the four fingers of his right hand.

Come, he said. And he took me deep into the jungle at the outskirts of the village.

You have to touch people in order to be a healer, my hakim said softly. You will be one after your self has healed itself.

He stopped.

But one has to prepare one's self, he continued.

He stopped again.

He bent down and looked closely at a thick cluster of shrubs next to a large mound. Some of the plants were purple flowered. Others had white flowers. I bent down to pluck a purple flower.

No, no, no, my hakim warned me. Don't even touch it. That's *datura*.

There was awe in his voice.

It has strange powers, my hakim said. It is both a poison and a cure. Like the goddess Kali, it is a healer and a destroyer. It's good and it's evil.

The roots and leaves of the white flowered plants, dried and then smoked will cure coughing spasms, he continued.

All the parts of the purple plants, the leaves, flowers, seeds, roots, are highly poisonous. The seed powder can be infused into liquor distilled from Kashmiri grapes or Shirazi dates to render it maddeningly sweet and addicting. Thugs make use of the purple *datura* to drug their victims.

I didn't allow you to touch the purple *datura*, my hakim told me, because even its oozings are dangerous. It makes a person laugh for no reason. The senses become deranged, especially the *manas* which people wrongly refer to as the mind. Things in daylight appear dark, and often disconnected. It causes one to lose control over time. And there's no cure except the passing of time itself.

My hakim had never talked to me at such length, nor explained things in such detail. Why, I wondered. Carefully he collected twelve of the white flowered plants to treat the headman's daughter.

On our way back we stopped to rest at the edge of the village.

My hakim said, a plant of mystery *datura* is, found all over India. It has different names. The ascetics of Nepal claim to know its secrets. Perhaps I'll go to Nepal some day to learn their secrets but only after you have been treated

He never told me what he was treating me for.

The Brahmin headman, whose daughter the hakim had cured, had disapproved of our going to the play.

A waste of time, he had said, it's not a real *nātaka*, just a crude entertainment put together for the illiterate masses.

I had wanted to spend the night brooding over a poem that had begun to ferment within me, but the hakim suggested we go to the play.

It has been a busy five days for you without rest, he said. You're too tight, your self needs to unloosen. We'll leave if you don't like the play.

I didn't, at first.

We sat in a large courtyard with a garlanded image of the goddess Bhavāni in the corner. There was no stage, no scenery, a long piece of red cloth pretended to be the curtain. Two boys, who played the female roles, and eight men enacted everything. They provided the music, the narration, the different drum beats, the songs, the dances, the comments, and even explanations of certain events. It was a crazy mix of the comic, the pathetic, the vulgar, the ludicrous, the sentimental. I could make out three voices, one high pitched, one cracked, the third guttural. The instruments were simple, a trumpet, a small drum, and a long pipe that produced an irritating wail. The performance was primitive.

I looked at the hakim to signal to him that we should leave. But he kept looking straight ahead.

I looked all around. Everyone was drawn to this crude world, crudely put together in front of us. The little boys near me were fascinated by the sword play between the handsome hero and the villain who kept twirling his black mustache defiantly, with the fingers of his left hand.

Wah, wah, what technique, shabash, what a thrust, it was exciting, the little boys were ecstatic.

The women kept putting their sari ends to their eyes when the heroine sang a heartbreaking song of farewell to her dying hero as she was dragged away.

All will be well, the narrator assured the audience.

Do not fear, said the stage manager, his right hand uplifted.

The clown then jumped into the scene. He imitated the villain, striding like him, twirling his nonexistent mustache. He talked directly to the audience, commenting on the major characters, telling jokes, teasing them with riddles to which he would supply the answers. He exchanged words with the stage manager asking him barbed questions about some important village figures, the corrupt policeman who accepted bribes, the cheating goldsmith, the unscrupulous moneylender, even our Brahmin landlord. Everyone guffawed, even the little children, especially when the clown mimicked these characters.

The action was fast paced. The play somehow held together. It was what the pandit would call a *lilā*, a play full of play. The dialogue was racy. There was no script. The songs heightened feelings of sorrow and of joy. The dances were a riot of color and rejoicing, *mandala*circles around the invisible lovegod, acts of celebration and abandon, punctuated with handclaps and drumbeats and footstamping and singing.

The interludes were more than interludes. The comic story of the fashionable dandy involved in an intrigue with Mohanā, an enchanting temptress, parodied the main story. The theme of marriage was comicalized by having a child bridegroom carried off, screaming, in the triumphant arms of his elderly bride.

The clown, the hero's servant companion, was in almost every scene, swaggering around the courtyard when the hero wasn't there.

I am a mighty warrior, the clown proclaimed, making fierce grimaces that made the children scream with laughter.

You have no weapon, someone said.

Ah, my weapon is invisible, the clown said.

A maidservant ambled along swaying her ample haunches.

Ah, ah, aha, the clown said, clamping both hands between his legs as if in pain, tiptoeing behind her, grunting heavily.

Where is your weapon, a voice asked.

Here, the clown said.

From between his legs he produced a thick black knob of bamboo, and jerked it up and down.

With this, he said, I stab them.

And he thrust it forward.

Then I make them cry.

He jerked it back.

And I make them sigh, thrusting it forward again.

And I make them die.

And he ran off.

Everyone, even the women, roared with laughter.

It was, I began to realize, not just a play to be seen, but a whole world flung together to be experienced, one the audience was familiar with, peopled with their beliefs and fears, their hopes and their dreams, the gods and goddesses they prayed to, a universe they lived in and knew. So that when, at the end, the gods came down to punish the wicked, and to reward the good, everyone left happy and happily content.

It would be dawn soon. Another hard day awaited them. But all, finally, would be well.

I was eager to talk to the hakim about the performance as we walked back. But he was strangely quiet, lost in his own thoughts.

As we neared our hut, he said something that had nothing to do with what we had seen.

Some human beings try to imprison the past but cannot.

I didn't understand what he meant at the time. Now I do.

He meant that I clung to the past, afraid of letting go. Hence the poems, the pain, my fits of brooding. He meant that I lived on the plane of the past. I had locked what happened to Usha tight within my self. Had never spoken of it to anyone, not a word, not even to the hakim. He was my hakim too, without my knowing he was. That's why he wanted me to go to the play. It would take me out of my self. For the first time I had let go, and forgotten my past pain.

To forget is one way of healing, my hakim had said, to remember, too.

The past, released, came rolling on now like the bore, but without the pain, sweeping me to the time when it all began, my plunge into *samsāra* at Talaja. Before the plunge I had been uninvolved. I enjoyed the *lilā* of the human scene. Safe on the seashore I watched the waves sweep up to my bare feet.

I have to be careful of my use of image. The pandit would maintain that the plunge happens at the moment of birth. João would hasten to interrupt the pandit to prevent him from going on to talk about *karma* and rebirth. And João would then refer to his Plato, who had written that the human soul forgets its divine nature when it falls into time.

Looking back, I realize now that I was, even before Talaja, deeply involved in *samsāra*. I didn't know it at that time. I can see my two pasts now, the before Talaja past and the after Talaja. Let me set down what happened before Talaja, the slow sequence of events whose significance I did not understand then, that like a caterpillar has slowly climbed into my consciousness.

The Talaja story

At first, the casual telling by Sheth Chimanlal, whose ships I piloted and whose friend I slowly became, of stories about his motherless daughter whom he adored. About her bright black eyes that welcomed him home after a tiring day, the tiny fingers whose touch he loved, about the name he bestowed on her. That name was for me then just another name.

Usha is Sanskrit for dawn. My dawn, the father explained.

Her tiny smile when the sheth first brought the little one for me to see. What I saw was only the black smudge they rubbed on her right cheek to deflect the evil eye. How she began to talk when she was two, the father said it with pride, the tooth that was chipped when she was five, the year when she began to read. She could not go to school with other children because she was sickly as a child. So her uncle, her mother's brother, who conducted pilgrimages to Jain shrines in Gujarat, taught her to read and to sing devotional hymns. She would sing her favorite stavan with her head bent on her chest and with her eyes shut. Inner Lord, she sang, hear my song, carry me across the ocean of *samsāra*. Usha spent long hours reading the Jain holy books and would have long talks with her uncle about Jainism. When he was away, she began the practice of telling folk legends in simple Gujarati to all the women in the family, especially to her grandmother.

Sitting in the inner courtyard, the night air fragrant with jasmine, they all loved to listen to Usha singing *stavans*. The women then, wide eyed with wonder, listened to stories about how the Jain *Tirthankaras* showed the way to salvation across the ocean of *samsāra*. They listened patiently to the little one as she showed them a cloth painting of the wheel of human existence, and explained in simple language the Jain teaching about *karmic* bondage. They liked the story of monk Kalaka and were impressed by the section of the *Kalpasutra* that described the eight day Jaina ritual for acquiring forgiveness. But it was too cold a world, a world they were excluded from as women.

Unless, the holy books tell us, we are reborn as men, Usha told them.

So the little one told them instead folk tales that sprang out of the Indian earth.

She narrated descriptions of the spring, a season she loved, from the *Vasanta Vilasa*, a poem she loved. During that long period of rainrest, the monsoon, when time slows down, she told them of the mischievous pranks of the boy god Krishna, she told them the romantic story of the love of Radha and Krishna, and of their love meetings. She narrated a few episodes from that war epic, the *Mahabharata*, which didn't appeal to the women. They did like the *Ramayana* story of Rama's rescue of the chaste Sita, who had been abducted by the evil Ravana, with the help of Hanuman, the monkey god. At the end the forgiven husband ascended into heaven, and all was well.

But the little one stamped her little foot at the end of the story.

I don't think Sita was treated right, the little one said, and her grandmother agreed.

Sitting in his office where he checked his account books and where a pilgrimage cloth map of Śatruñjaya hung on the wall, the sheth and I could overhear the magic sound of his daughter's voice, quite different, he realized, from the other sound he so loved, the sound of his fingers counting gold coins.

So the sheth poured out vast sums of money into illustrated manuscripts for his Usha. He set aside a room next to his office where the finest scribes and the best illustrators from Patan, that center of Jain learning, made copies of Jain religious texts that had been preserved underground in certain temple libraries to prevent their destruction by the Muslim invaders. The manuscripts with their miniature paintings were works of art. They were the sheth's offerings to his daughter. With his own hands the sheth would thread a cord through the cinnabar spotted string holes of the manuscripts, and then enclose them in painted wooden covers called *patlis* for protection. After wrapping the book in the most expensive *patola* silk used only for marriage saris, the father would offer it to his Usha.

The sheth loved to see Usha's bright black eyes light up as she received the gift.

Not fitting at all, the uncle warned the father, not at all proper.

A few days before we left on the pilgrimage to Śatruñjaya the uncle came into the office looking quite tired. I offered to leave the office but the sheth wanted me to stay.

You shouldn't love so much, the uncle said to the sheth. You love money and you love your daughter. I love her too. She is the daughter of my dear sister.

The uncle walked about in the sheth's office, carefully avoiding stepping on the account books.

Love is a fetter, the uncle said.

I have to break my fetters, the uncle continued slowly, renounce my family and kin, and lead a wandering life of asceticism if I want to attain *moksha*.

Salvation or liberation, which one, the sheth asked.

Final liberation, the uncle said, from worldly existence. I'll leave you all after our pilgrimage to Śatruñjaya. I have to travel south to the Chandranath temple in Bhatkal to listen to the words of my teacher.

Isn't that a Digambara temple, asked the sheth.

At the stage of *diksha* Digambara or Swetambara doesn't matter, said the uncle.

For the rites of renunciation, the uncle continued, I will go to a small Jain shrine in Anegundi just outside Vijayanagar.

Slowly, without being aware of what was happening within me, I found myself bringing gifts from the faraway for little Usha.

Earlier, in this account, I did set down the offerings I made as Usha grew up. At first the Persian sweetmeats I brought every year for a friend's little daughter. Then the myna made of ebony, because I knew she loved plants and birds. Then I gave her that little ivory dhow carved by Mian Mazlum, because I noticed she waited with her father for his ships to come into harbor.

I didn't realize then, how could I, that it was for me she waited. She did stop calling me uncle after the gift of the ivory dhow. I did set that down earlier. What I did not realize then was that that was the exact moment when her inner being became porous wanting to absorb me.

My exact moment came much later, in Talaja. In Diu, for me, she was just like a daughter, a lovely part of my world. I became, I think, the whole world for her then. I looked at her sometimes looking at me. What I saw was only a little girl, eager eyed, legs folded under her, chin propped on her right hand, listening to the stories I told her father in his office about Hormuz and Lamu and Aden, stories about sailing the bluegreen sea, about storms and dangers.

More than to just my stories, she would be listening to my voice as it filtered into her. Her head, as she listened, was on her chest at times, bowed down, absorbing sounds.

No one was aware of what was happening. Not me, not her father, not the uncle.

The old grandmother sensed a change in her Usha. As Usha neared fifteen the discussions about her marriage grew urgent. The sheth told me everything. No one was good enough for his Usha. He confided to me the proposals that were received, the arguments, the rejections, the grandmother's arguings, her tears.

Usha remained calm. She simply refused to get married.

She began to live by herself in her greenhouse with her jasmine, and her ivory ships, and her books.

I felt sad for Usha, but it didn't affect me too much, the discussions about her marriage. I did suggest that Layla, Abdul's sister from Chapora, Goa, could be her companion. Abdul had told me that both their parents had died, and that Layla had gone to live with one of her friends because the *afaqi* had wanted her to work as a servant in his house till all the taxes had been paid.

I cant go to Goa to bring Layla to Diu, Abdul said. He sent a message and money to the ancient letter writer in Chapora who quickly arranged to have Layla sent to Diu. The *afaqi* seized the house and made it part of his estate.

She's a Muslim, her presence will pollute us all, the grandmother objected.

No, Usha said firmly. The Jain holy books do not accept pollution and the distinctions of caste.

The uncle agreed. We Jains adopted some of the beliefs and social practices of Hinduism, he said.

So Layla lived and cooked her meals in a little house away from the family, and looked after Usha.

I don't know whether it was the uncle, the grandmother, or Sheth Chimanlal who decided on the pilgrimage to Śatruṅjaya and the visit to Talaja.

It was still dark when we set out very early in the morning to climb the *tekri* of Talaja, a hill shaped like a cone.

It had rained heavily the day before we got into Talaja town, unseasonal showers towards the end of February with thunder roars and stabs of lightning. The towns people warned us not to ascend the hill. Go, after the lamp of Taluv Daitya is lit once again. The lamp had to be kept perpetually alit. Tomorrow would be propitious, they said. Else the god king in a rage wouldn't allow any visit to the other deities on the hill. Till the lamp was relit the wrath of the spirit of Taluv, who still ruled Talaja from his rocky eminence would descend on the town in the shape of rolling rocks and stones.

But the grandmother insisted, even though she was very tired. It had been a seven day journey from Diu by bullock cart. She refused to be carried up the hill in a *doli*. To be carried up the hill in a litter, the grandmother said, would be against the spirit of a true pilgrimage. And it is a propitious day, the grandmother maintained, the right one according to Usha's astrological chart.

So the family group set forth in the dark of the next morning. They were impatient to be the first to get to the top for *darshan* of the image of the *Tirthankara*. Usha held back to help her grandmother make the painful trudge up the hill.

The uncle, Sheth Chimanlal and I followed them. We kept twenty five feet away. The sheth soon felt tired. The uncle, who usually never broke silence, kept encouraging us, using small talk to make us forget the two hour long climb ahead. Yogic exercises had kept him in shape. We'll take a rest on the stone bench under a large tamarind tree, half way up, he said.

I asked why the Jains built their temples on mountain peaks inaccessible to ordinary men and women.

For human beings, the uncle said, access to the divine has always to be restricted. That is why man can visit temple cities briefly during the daytime hours, but cannot take any food or drink there. Or remain there after nightfall lest he disturb the divine solitude of the liberated ones who reside there in their world of eternal silence.

The sheth listened to every word.

It was a world the sheth yearned to enter, but did not want to, not just yet, he said.

In a few years, after I've made a little more money, he had told me once, after Usha, who is already fifteen, has married and settled down, after I become a grandfather, I shall abandon this world of business and money.

It was the uncle who had persuaded the sheth to begin the long process of liberation from karmic bondage by financing a family pilgrimage.

You will thus acquire *punya*merit, the uncle said.

So the sheth invested a great deal of money in this enterprise.

The grandmother, reluctant at first, agreed to accompany the party only if they proceeded to Śatruñjaya via Talaja.

Talaja is my birth village, she said.

Later, the sheth discovered why she wanted to go via Talaja. She wanted to arrange a match for Usha with one of the sons of a distant relative there.

You should come too, Ahmadji, the sheth said, you're like her second father. You could notice defects in him I might miss.

So I accompanied the party. I didn't really want to. I had brought in my ship into Diu harbor earlier than usual, and had looked forward to a long stretch of rest and quiet reading.

Do come, the sheth said, Usha will like it.

It was a strange way for me to travel, by bullock cart. I would have walked, but I was afraid of snakes. We had to travel by night. It was oppressively hot during the day. The up and down jolts and the side to side motion of the carriage on the unpaved uneven country roads made me sick, so sick that on the first day I had to get off in order to vomit.

Seasick, and on land, Ahmadji, the sheth laughed. You'll get used to it, he said.

Only the next morning could I, who have never been seasick in my life, laugh, weakly, at myself.

We walked up a winding path, the sheth looking down at his feet, holding on tightly to my arm, walking slowly. Then there it was, the tamarind with its million tiny leaves rustling continuously in the wind. It sprang precariously, at an angle, from a broad ledge that went curving around the hill.

It was dawn now, and the eastern rays of the sun lit up the whole hill. I joined a large group of pilgrims led by a guide. They couldn't tell I was a Muslim, my plain white shirt and loose white pyjamas allowed me to blend into the group. The guide poured out a nonstop stream of story and information that drew forth murmurs of awe and wonder.

Talaja, holy Talaja, he said, is the most ancient abode of the sacred in all Gujarat, older than Girnar, older even than Śatruñjaya. All deities have their home here in the caves, and abide together in peace.

I was deeply impressed.

The crowd was silent.

Then the guide began a series of stories. The story of the *Ghi no Kuo*, the well dug in order to be filled with ghee for the celebration of a marriage feast. The story of the *Hathi Kod* where elephants had been stabled. Cries of wah wah came from the crowd. No one asked how elephants could have reached there. He showed them the cave from where the *bhakti*mystic, Narasimha Mehta, used to travel through a secret tunnel to reach Gopnath many miles away. And finally, he led them to the *Chusio Pano*, a cave with a hole in the wall which when sucked produced a bubbling noise.

Magic, they said. They went into the cave to suck at the stone.

I did not enter the cave. I stood outside, aloof.

Perhaps a poem would bubble up.

The guide came up to me.

As a Muslim, sab, he said, you may want to visit that last cave. Just above the one covered with creepers of jasmine, a Muslim holy man made his home there last year, many people even Hindus go there to have his *darshan*.

How did he know I was a Muslim.

Your Arab nose, sab, he said.

I was tempted to visit the cave, but I heard them calling for me.

Most of our party were already half way up the flight of stone steps. Sheth Chimanlal and the uncle had started the climb and were about twenty steps ahead. I would catch up with them soon. I climbed up a few steps, and turned to look down at Talaja town on the right bank of the river that meandered along a perfectly level plain towards the gulf of Cambay. To the northwest there were low hills behind which rose the mountains of Śatruñjaya.

Then I heard a faraway voice from high up calling out my name, stretching it out, Ahmadji ii, Ahmadjiii i

Very faint, this cry for help.

I knew at once who it was, and I ran. I ran, keeping away from the stone steps, swerving to the left to avoid rocks and stones that came tumbling down just missing me. I ran, kicking off my sandals as I ran, between acacia bushes and thorny babul trees and stunted neems, and I saw Usha rolling down a bare slope of the hillside, rolling towards a dry nullah full of rocks and sharp stones. I ran, I flung myself down near the edge so that I caught her before she could fall into the dry rivulet. I caught her, and held her tight in my arms trying to calm her down. She was frightened, trembling, I could feel her heart beating, throbbing against my chest, I wanted to say her name, wanted to say Usha, but I couldn't, I was out of breath, she was, too.

We could only look into each other's eyes, and then, still trembling, she whispered, Ahmad mine, and fainted away.

And then the others came.

That was the magic moment of the plunge.

After that moment everything is a blank till the time when we got back to Diu. No, no, I do remember, as in a dream, the cool darkness at the bottom of the step well at Śatruñjaya where Usha and I touched hands. I wrote a poem about the touching.

But tell me, brother cynic, so charged a moment why did I forget so completely. And why does it leap now into my memory in such complete detail, tell me why, why. I have no one else to ask.

Calm down, my restless brother in love, calm down, said my cynic. Your being is swirling around trying to understand the mystery of love and *samsāra*. I can however tell you why everything was in a blur after that magic moment. Because, my brother, your entire world suddenly became Usha. The world outside her no longer existed for you. How then could you remember. What only you can do to complete the Talaja story is to put together the words of the uncle and Sheth Chimanlal and all that you overheard as you lay on the stretcher in a daze.

Usha, first.

Usha saved her grandmother, the uncle said.

Usha heard the rocks rumbling down the steps, heard the warning shouts from above, tried to drag the grandmother to the side. But the old woman stumbled and fell on the steps. One stone bounced above their heads.

The next one would have crashed into them, the sheth said, had not my Usha pushed her grandmother to one side into an acacia bush. Then Usha lost her balance and went rolling down the hillside.

They could not see Usha and me holding each other.

My clothes were in shreds. My arms and shoulders had been slashed by those thorny acacias and babuls. My sandalless feet were bloody, so that they had to carry me down to Talaja town on a stretcher.

The grandmother took one look at Usha first and then at me, they told me later, and collapsed. She had to stay behind at Talaja.

Usha refused to be left behind.

From the Palitana foothills, Śatruñjaya, that soaring city of temples and *tuks*, spread out on twin peaks and on the ridges between, appeared dazzlingly white and distant.

There, that's where I want to be, the uncle said, his voice full of a faint longing as if it had come descending from the peaks above.

The sheth arranged for litters to carry the whole party to the top. Usha and a female relative were left behind at the foot of the mountain. I didn't go.

Look after her, Ahmadji, the sheth said.

I do remember that day clearly, brother cynic, the day the party climbed to Śatruñjaya. That was when the touching happened, down at the bottom of the dark step well of a temple, where the female relative who was left with Usha was afraid to go and where there were many people performing their ablutions.

Our fingers touched.

We did not need words.

It was a moment of silence.

That night, after we returned to Palitana, after the evening meal that is always eaten before it is dark lest insects fall into the food, the uncle announced to the whole group his desire to be utterly free from karmic bondage.

You will never see me again, the uncle said, I renounce *saṃsāra*.

And he strode out of the lodging house into the darkness of the night.

Ahmadji.

A voice pierced my consciousness.

Ahmadji.

I knew it was Abdul even before I opened my eyes and saw the sun splashed gulf of Cambay.

Gangaram is waiting for us, said Abdul, we have to leave tonight for Dumas.

I have raced against time to set down this account. The words kept flowing out of my pen. Gangaram had said we had to catch the inflowing tide to get to Dumas.

EIGHTEEN

Late June, 1509
A cave like room on the hilltop at Pawagadh,
I write about what happened at Dumas and Surat
And what happened seventeen days after João and I
arrived in Champaner with Frei Louro and the Portuguese captives

João has left Champaner and gone away, I know not where. Abdul tells me the papers on which I have been writing my story have disappeared too.

He took all of them, Abdul said, Mirzasab took them two days ago when I went to Halol to buy mangoes. I was gone the whole day.

How do you know it was Mirzasab who took the papers, I asked Abdul.

I was worried that Malik Gopi had gotten João to steal my papers to find out if I had told Malik Aiyaz my suspicions about Ishak's conspiracy.

I know it was Jan Mirza, Abdul said, looking straight at me. I am sure.

Abdul held up a folder whose covers were tied with white ribbon.

Mirzasab took all your papers and left this folder in the box, Abdul said.

I recognized the folder. It contained the tattered sheets of the Biblia Sagrada which João used in order to teach us Portuguese. There was a note inside.

I have borrowed your papers to read, João's note said. Otherwise they would have been stolen. I will return them. Do read the Holy Bible, my friend. It will help you understand some things in times of your need, Your friend, J.

I flung the folder away.

Shall I throw out this folder, Abdul asked.

Yes, I said, it won't do me any good, tear it up.

Abdul looked at me.

No, I said, let it be in the box.

Why, why, I was devastated. Why, why did João take away my papers. Abdul was deeply worried, I could tell.

I met Vora walking down the hill when I was returning from the Champaner market, Abdul told me. He said he had gone to visit Kali Mata, but I don't believe him. He must have wanted to steal your papers.

I know Abdul knew it had shocked me deeply, inside, João's treachery. So deeply that it has taken me a whole day to force myself to write these words which leak reluctantly from my pen. Perhaps your pen has become rusty, my cynic, who is in pain too, says softly, not wanting to hurt me. The last time you wrote was in Gangaram's hut before we left Piram Island when you set down the magic moment at Talaja. You have not set down what happened at Dumas or at Surat. One has to keep on writing one's pain, Ahmadbhai. Write, your hakim suggested, tell the whole story.

Yes, yes, my brother. It's the middle of June now, and I haven't written for over seventeen days. That's a fact. But it does not explain why these words feel so heavy, why the rhythm creaks like a bullock cart. And why, I ask myself, why didn't I continue writing after we landed in Dumas and went to Surat at the end of May. No time, I could offer as an excuse, no time to set what happened down. But that's not really true. I was very tired at times but I could have found the time to write.

Perhaps you need the right surroundings, says my other, the cave at Diu promontory, the quiet of your home, no, no, your house, in faraway Diu. Or perhaps writing about what happened at Talaja drained everything that had meaning for you out of you. But didn't you, long ago, set down that you had to write the way you sailed, anywhere, in any kind of weather.

It's hot here on Pawagadh hilltop even at midmorning. A mid June pre monsoon heat, so that all court business, João had told me, ceases by late morning. From the cave like room where I write these words, high up on this isolated hill, I can see through the window the sun scorched Champaner plain way down below.

Before he disappeared from Champaner João told me that the amirs play polo down there on swift Arabian mares. The ladies of the Sat Manzil palace, João said, love to watch the handsome young amirs. In December it's time for falconry, and for hunting. To shoot down the tiger and the occasional wild elephant some use Portuguese arquebuses now, weapons more accurate than the Ottomani *tufeng*s. Malik Gopi had bribed some of the Portuguese to sell arquebuses to him, so João told me.

Ishak and the amirs should do army exercises and drills to prepare for the new challenge, João told me, not indulge in frivolous games and sexual spectacles. They will surely have to fight the Portuguese.

Why do I bring in João's name so often. I miss him. Abdul misses him too, and misses the stories he told us. I used to look forward to João's return from Champaner in the evening with the news and gossip of the day. He would imitate the amirs, exaggerate their walk and their pompous talk, and make us roar with laughter. And João would tell us jokes and stories about the Champaner court. Abdul's favorite story was about João's visit to the sultan's *haram*, the women's quarters that no man on pain of death could enter. The visit had been arranged by Malik Gopi. We had never visited a *haram*, Abdul and I. Abdul was so intrigued and fascinated with the story that João had to repeat it on three separate occasions. I can and will set down João's exact words. We were talking one day about houris and gardens and paradise when João said, I know why paradise on earth is a garden for the Persians. And he then went on to tell us the story of his visit to paradise.

There were houris in this paradise, Ahmadji, João had said, his eyes smiling, I couldn't see any of them, but they could see me sitting on a carpet in the middle of the room crowded with flowers and plants. I had been invited there by the queen mother to entertain the women who missed the excitements of Ahmadabad when the royal court moved to Champaner.

I kept them entertained for an hour and a half, João said, I made them laugh, I sang for them, I told them jokes, I even danced for them, a whirling dervish dance I had learned in Malindi. They were full of giggles and questions that they shot at me through the pierced screen *jalis* made of fragrant sandalwood. Strangely they wanted to know not about the doings of men but about women in the wide world outside.

The women of Burtukal, were they beautiful. As beautiful as the women of Persia and Hind. What did they wear. Dresses. What are those. No pyjamas. Shrieks of laughter.

Quiet, a deep voice said. How can he know. He is a mere man.

They also wanted to know about marriages, were they arranged, how many wives were allowed.

Only one.

There were screams of disbelief.

The questions would have gone on and on. But the chief eunuch raised his hand, it was time to stop. I ended by telling them three stories, one from the *Tutinama*, the tales of the wise parrot, the second from the *Thousand and One Nights*, and the third from Boccacio's *Decameron*, all about the wiles of women and how they deceive their husbands. There were squeals of laughter that took a long time to die down. Then the chief eunuch came with a message from the queen mother, Come again. And he gave me a green silk shawl filled with rubies and *mahmudi* coins and jewelry. Some of the necklaces had nestled between warm breasts, the beads were warm to my touch.

João paused awhile.

Alas, I've become a clown, Ahmadji, he said, now Malik Gopi's Champa and her group of women want me to perform for them.

João never did put on a show for Malik Gopi's women. He disappeared from Champaner.

Like Abdul, I miss João and his stories. I miss my papers too. They had become a part of me. João's treachery is like a wound that has begun to fester inside me. Nothing can stop my sense of rage and outrage, nothing. Yesterday evening as I walked to the dome shrine of Shah Sadan Pir at the top of Pawagadh I noted many medicinal plants that my hakim would have rejoiced in. But no poultice of herbs can draw this pain out of me.

I feel abandoned. João had been my pilot here in this world of intrigue. His piloting began as soon as we stepped out of the dangerous Gulf of Cambay. He took charge as soon as boatman Gangaram set us down in Dumas, Malik Aiyaz's territory, and then had to take us to Malik Gopi's Surat because the Portuguese captives had been transferred there. João knew exactly what had to be done. He became a marvelous actor and began wearing a distinctive turban with red, green and gold folds. Everyone in Champaner knew who he was. He fooled the other amirs, all the Portuguese hostages, even Frei António do Louro.

Unlike João I do not feel at home in this *samsāra* of court intrigue.

When João and I arrived at Surat from Dumas to take the Portuguese captives to Diu to Malik Aiyaz, we found Surat in a state of turmoil. Urged on by some trader merchants and goaded by yelling Muslim sailors, the Suratis wanted to set fire to the house in which the Portuguese captives had been lodged. During one attack Frei Louro went to the gate to address the mob and had to be rescued by João and by Malik Gopi's agent who announced that the prisoners would be taken immediately to Sultan Begada at Champaner as hostages.

Malik Gopi's agent explained everything, João told me later. The order to conduct the captives to Surat was signed by the Sultan, João said.

We left Surat for Champaner, João and I, the very next day with the prisoners and Frei Louro. Malik Gopi's agent accompanied us with an armed escort. João looked worried, and spent most of his time talking to Malik Gopi's agent whom he had apparently known in Diu. João told me that the Frei and he had been students in the Coimbra seminary. Frei Louro hasn't recognized me, João said, and suggested that we avoid using Portuguese when talking to each other. The prisoners thought that João and

I were the sultan's officers. They didn't know that we could understand Portuguese. They talked freely among themselves about the shipwreck and all that had happened to them. After overhearing the conversations between the prisoners and Frei Louro on the long journey from Surat to Champaner, and with the help of João, I was able to piece together what happened when the Portuguese were shipwrecked at Dumas.

The shipwreck of the *Santa Cruz*

Dom Afonso de Noronha, nephew of Afonso de Albuquerque, was in command of the *Santa Cruz* that was sailing to Cochin when a rich pilgrim trading ship, the *Meri*, returning from Jiddah, was captured. The *Meri* had no sailing permit and carried no guns even for defensive purposes. It surrendered without a fight. A Portuguese captain was put in command of the *Meri* along with twenty Portuguese. The Muslim captain of the *Meri* together with twenty merchant traders was transferred to the *Santa Cruz*. Both ships were making their slow way to Cochin on the west coast of India when the unexpected tufan I had predicted, separated the two ships, and the *Santa Cruz* was wrecked very near the coast of Dumas.

What happened at Dumas was not quite clear. A number of villagers gathered on the seashore and watched the wreck but were unable to offer any help. They saw the huge ship, tossed by the fierce waves, dash against a black reef that split the ship in two. The Muslim traders wisely did not leave the ship which began sinking. The Portuguese sailors in panic tried to save themselves by using planks to ride the waves to get to shore, but were drowned. Afonso de Noronha got himself lashed to a large plank and had the other end of the long rope tied to the mast. Then he flung himself into the tempest torn sea.

Don't, shouted the people on the shore in Gujarati, danger, don't.

The pilot of the *Santa Cruz* wanted to go to the rescue of his struggling captain who was being battered to death against the black reef, but he was forcibly restrained by the Muslim captain. It was high tide and that the waves were huge. The Portuguese sailors thought that the shouting villagers were urging the Muslim captain to kill the pilot. One of the mariners wanted to strike the Muslim captain with a piece of wood.

Wait, wait, Frei Louro shouted.

Frei Louro realized that the villagers and the Muslim sailors who were familiar with the coast wanted them to wait for low tide and for the storm to subside. He shouted at the mariners, grabbed the piece of wood, and managed to save the Muslim captain's life.

When the storm subsided the headman of Dumas, who had been appointed by Malik Aiyaz, imprisoned the rescued Portuguese and thereby saved them from the wrath of the villagers who wanted to kill them all after they were informed of the capture of the *Meri*. The tufan prevented the headman of Dumas from sending word to Malik Aiyaz. Malik Gopi's agent showed the headman the order that the Portuguese captives had to be sent to Surat and then to the sultan's court at Champaner.

The Portuguese sailors were quite bewildered on the long journey to Champaner. Many of them were from the north of Portugal, according to João. They were peasants flung into a strange world, João said. They had to eat strange foods, and they met strange people who spoke strange languages and whom they had to fight they knew not why. And they did not know why they had to sail to the island of Socotra and help build a fortress there, or why they had to leave the island and be seasick again in the *Santa Cruz* which had attacked and captured a ship sailing peacefully to India.

Cartaz, cartaz, the *Meri* had no *cartaz*, the prisoners were told.

These are cursed infidels, they were told, *mouros*.

It was the Frei who provided some answers to their many questions. João would move away to avoid listening when they made their confessions to Frei Louro. A sin, João said. I listened whenever I could and that is how we came to know what happened in Dumas and in Surat.

When we got to Champaner, João and I and Frei Louro were taken to the Pawagadh hilltop and lodged in three large adjoining rooms with vented domes that had been used as granaries. The Portuguese hostages were sent to the army camp at Hathikad just outside Champaner.

I am so confused, this my writing is also confused, and confusing, even to me. A fish on land, I am like. I know not where to begin, or whether to rebegin my story at the very beginning.

No I can't rebegin. I will continue my account.

One writes to understand the past, my hakim had once said. Whether one writes for others or for oneself I do not know, my hakim had added, looking into my eyes. Don't write poetry, he had often warned me. A poem is too thick a form, he lingered over this noun, to act as a cure. And then he walked away.

There will now be two meandering forms. Once, in Kannanur, the Portuguese call it Cannanore now after they built a *feitoria* there in 1503, an imp of a boy used a sharp knife to cut a long pink worm in half. I saw the two worm pieces, apparently unhurt, squirm their separate ways and disappear. I hope my two pieces will be whole some day.

Early this morning the shrill call to prayer of the muezzin came soaring up from one of the minarets of the Jami Masjid in Champaner down below. It was the time when João, before he disappeared, used to leave Pawagadh for his daily visit to Malik Gopi. Every morning Abdul would bring us two cups of coffee and everyday, without fail, João would suggest that I accompany him to Champaner town.

I would shake my head.

You're isolated up here in Pawagadh, Ahmadji, João would say. You should go down to Champaner and talk to people and get involved in the world of action. Don't brood about the past. You don't even write, now.

But I didn't want to get involved. As Malik Aiyaz's *shahbandar* I had performed my duty and sent a message to my friend in Diu asking what should be done about the Portuguese captives. It would take some time to get a reply.

Why don't you at least visit the sultan's *kitabkhana* near the Atak gate, João would say. The library has a complete collection of the Persian poets you love so much. When I was in Portugal I used to take refuge in that world of books, the library of the Santa Cruz monastery at Coimbra. That was a lifetime ago, João added, with a sigh.

But the sultan's library didn't tempt me to visit Champaner. I knew and still know the poems by heart, but now they seemed too distant from me, too full of vague complaint about fate and the stars. At times João would urge me to accompany Frei Louro who would go every other day to visit the Portuguese hostages at the army camp at Hathikad.

Four of them now want to become Muslims, João told me. The Frei is horrified. Do you want to talk to him. You will have to tell him that you know Portuguese.

I didn't. I didn't want to get involved in anything. I was a ship in a region of dead calm, unwilling to be moved by the waves of *samsāra*. I would see the Frei every morning after I inhaled the rich aroma of cardamon while I sipped my coffee. It would be cool outside and a light mist would cover the gray stones of the Kalimata temple. Frei António would have his arms outstretched, his eyes wide open and raised to the sky above, his back flat and tight against the curved jagged surface of the black outer wall of his cave room. A sudden bubble of memory about suffering arose within me, a picture of a black cross in the outstretched arms of an innocent child. It must have been very painful for the Frei despite the heavily patched brown gown he wore. Underneath, according to Abdul, he wore a shirt woven of horsehair.

The servants of the court, urged on by Malik Gopi, laugh at him and taunt him, João told me.

What are you, they ask, a *majzub*, a wandering mendicant, who is your *pir*teacher, did he hand you that patched cloak and make you his disciple. You smell strange, some say to him, why don't you have a bath. Why do you wear that gown, are you a eunuch, a *hijra*, what are you hiding under that patched *khirka*, is it holy, can we touch it. At times they gesture obscenely with their fingers but dare not hurt him. They're afraid of the Begdo.

I never disturbed the Frei. He was always far away, praying. I wondered whether he was trying to reach out to the beyond. Abdul would later prepare a fresh cup of coffee for the Frei. He takes an hour to finish praying, Abdul said. Abdul and the Frei have become friends. How they communicate with each other I don't know. Abdul doesn't know any Portuguese. I couldn't understand why Malik Gopi disliked the Frei so much.

The coffee will be ready soon, Abdul said.

Abdul had sensed that I did not want to follow the usual routine today. Every morning, after João left for Champaner, Abdul would get me another cup of coffee and I would follow my usual routine. I would sit next to a window overlooking a perpendicular precipice and stare at the Champaner plain down below and try not to brood about things. I would, on some days, go to a mountain ledge nearby after the sun had broken through the clouds, and I would stare at distant Halol, and at the ruined temples of Pawagadh down below. There, João pointed out, there is the palatial mansion of Malik Gopi. In the middle distance the white domes of the mosques stood out together with the royal citadel called the Jahanpanah. What I could not see from the ledge was the *Hathikad*, the army camp where the hostages were lodged.

Abdul would go down to Champaner when we needed provisions and bring back the gossip of the day which he would relay to me as I sat in the kitchen watching him prepare our evening meal which João isnt there to share with us now.

People are worried about what will happen after the Begdo passes away, Abdul said. He is sixty four years old now, gets ill frequently, and no one knows who his successor will be. He neglects his sultanic duties and spends his time in prayer at the tombs of saints.

Abdul also relayed to me the servants' gossip whispered in the royal court, that Malik Gopi was spending vast sums of money to purchase a number of dancing girls and courtesans who would entertain his *amir* friends.

João confirmed this news. Malik Gopi had become the richest trader merchant in all Gujarat after 1500. He would bribe the Portuguese captains so that they would issue *cartazes* for a trifling sum of money for his trading ships so that they could sail to Melaka. The Portuguese were quite ignorant, according to Malik Gopi. They had disrupted the trading world on the Bahr-i-Hind but did not know anything about the trading world that had Melaka as its center. And they did not know the sailing routes.

Malik Gopi has accumulated so much wealth and has become so rich, João said, he has gotten tired of the world of business and trade. He does not know what to do with his money and has turned to the world of power and pleasure.

He maintains a huge stable of courtesans, the amirs said with envy.

It definitely is a stable, Malik Gopi joked to João, all my friends like young mares, they prefer riding them only at night.

He maintained another establishment of courtesans at Surat to entertain foreign visitors and envoys. Together with Kiwam-ul-Mulk Sarang, that Rajput turned Muslim, Malik Gopi had become one of the most powerful nobles of the Muzaffarid court. Many of the *amirs* resented the growing influence of these two over the Begdo who entrusted all political and court matters to them.

I felt quite restless and empty after João disappeared with my papers. Today, I thought, after coffee, I would go to the library and take a look at the books there. Not at the books of the poets, the *Gulistan* of Sa'di, or the mathnavis of Rumi, or the *divan*collection of my favorite, Hafiz of Shiraz. Their poems, full of lament about fate and the stars, used to feed my soul in the past, before Usha came into my life. I felt today the need for another kind of sustenance. I wanted to look at the writings of the Arabic and the Persian historians. João had told me that the Sultan's library boasted a varied collection.

I walked down slowly to the Atak gate, past the ruins of the Jain temples, past the defaced Siva sculptures that surrounded the base of the ruined Lakulisa temple, past the catapults of black basalt that were used by the Rajputs to hurl stones during the 1484 Muslim siege of Pawagadh. I avoided the stone balls that lay strewn about, and made my way to the library. The librarian had to be summoned from a meeting he was attending. He welcomed me with an elaborate bow, and said that Jan Mirza, who was his special friend, had praised me as the nakhoda of nakhodas.

João has a special knack for making people believe he is their special friend.

You are a poet too, Jan Mirza told me, the librarian said. We do not have your *divan* of poems here, but we do have two of your sailing guides that Malik Aiyaz presented to the library. Abdul Karim Nimdihi, the official court historian from Persia, is here in the library. I think he would like to talk to you about the Diu sea battle.

Daroghasab, one of the library guards said.

Excuse me Ahmad ibn Madjid, I'll be back soon to show you the library.

João has had long discussions with this official court historian who has written flattering histories that celebrate the achievements of sultans. I survey events from the foot of the royal throne, Nimdihi had told João. The official history of Sultan Begada's reign upto the year 1505 was recorded in his *Tabaqat-i-Mahmudshahi*, copies of which were presented to foreign courts to proclaim the great achievements of the sultan. Nimdihi the historian could present defeats as victories and disasters as triumphs. The Diu sea battle was not considered a Portuguese victory but an event not worth recording for posterity. The Portuguese were, after all, wandering sea pirates, not a military power on land. They would be briefly mentioned in the second part of the official history that Abdul Karim Nimdihi was in the process of composing.

I had seen a copy of the *Tabaqat* which the librarian had allowed João to smuggle out past the library guards.

It's for Malik Gopi, João had whispered, for Champa, one of his women.

It was brilliant artwork, with its illuminations, its decorative drawings of gold and red rosettes, the impeccable calligraphy in cursive *naksh*, the medallion patterns in gold, the richly ornamented chapter headings, bronze in color, the border panels containing stems and scrolls. Just after the opening *Unwan*page was a portrait of the Sultan, regal looking, with fierce and commanding eyes, his long moustachios curving out right and left like the horns of a white bullock.

Like, João said, the arms of a person about to embrace.

I riffled through some pages and a miniature painting dropped out. It presented a naked courtesan enjoying herself with five young men, one was holding her, another had withrawn his erect penis from the open red lips of her yoni and was about to thrust it in again deep, the third was caressing her hips, the fourth nibbled at her ear, while the fifth held her waist. The five men looked eager, ready to change places, poised for their turn, their penises erect. The woman's body was curved, tense, waiting, her eyes shut.

Ah, João said, I know now why Malik Gopi wanted the book. He wants Champa, his favorite dancing girl, to see this picture, that's why. But why, why, hitting the palm of his left hand with his right fist, why, why, João asked, talking to himself, pacing around the room, why did Champa ask Vora to teach her some Portuguese words, and why does Malik Gopi want me to teach Champa how to pronounce words in Portuguese. It won't help her speak with Frei Louro.

He stopped pacing around the room. Then João turned to me.

It's a scene out of the *Kama Sutra* but done by a Muslim painter, João explained in a matter of fact voice and shut the book hurriedly.

The librarian came back and led me through the front courtyard.

This, he said, as he opened the door with a flourish, is my library. Isn't it magnificent.

Ah yes, I said and looked around, slowly. Yes, yes yes, the carpets are simply magnificent.

They weren't. They were gaudy with three fiery red roses in the center with borders of screaming yellow. Unlike João, I found it very dificult to put on an act. I was disappointed. There weren't too many books and manuscripts on the heavily varnished library shelves.

But the librarian was persistent. Ahmadsab, have you ever seen a library like this one, he asked me.

Never, never, I said, meaning exactly what I said.

Look at the polish of this wood, he said, a rich mahogany. Malik Gopi got the wood for this library all the way from Melaka in one of his merchant ships. It's white ant proof wood. My library will last for ever.

The *darogha* wasn't interested in books at all. For him the library was a showplace, meant to impress visitors, not an oasis for scholars. All the books were neatly bound, in handsome black leather, etched with lines of gold and green and red. Intricate medallions front and back decorated the centers of some covers. Some linings had an arabesque pattern, others were painted in gold and red designs, a few were laquered in the Persian mode.

The librarian flipped open the flap that covered the fore edge of a book whose cover was encrusted with rubies and amethysts to show me the burnished white of the paper which had gold dust sprinkled on it.

Feel this texture, he said, don't be afraid, it won't come off.

A library guard opened the front door.

Daroghasab, he said.

They want me again, Ahmadbhai, the librarian said. Why don't you look at the books in my collection. I'll be back soon.

It wasn't a very impressive collection. It wasn't even arranged properly. Books on medicine and philosophy, books of poetry, books on music and jurisprudence, were all flung together haphazardly. Only two piles were arranged with special care. On the right was a collection of religious books, books on mysticism, on *hadith* and tradition, and exegeses of the *Qu'ran*. One book was a miniature *Qu'ran* in a jewelled case meant to be worn as an amulet for protection against evil. Another was a *Qu'ran* with a jewelled cover. They were all presentation gifts made to Sultan Begada, that warrior who has now turned his feet toward religion.

The other pile consisted of books presented to the Muzaffarid court by different embassies, in which the histories of nations were set down.

There were thick gold covered histories of Mamluk Egypt and of the Otto-
mans. And there were histories that celebrated the Delhi Sultanate and the
Bahmani kingdom. There was no account of the kingdom of Vijayanagar.
Perhaps the Hindus capture time not in writing but in stone.

I searched for my own two books and discovered them at the bottom of a dusty pile of books of poetry. Sadly I blew off the thick dust that
lay on the paper cover of the first book. It was the *Qasida Makkiya* in one
hundred and seventy two verses which gave sailing directions to Jiddah
from Indian Ocean ports. It had been a workaday job for me, written for
money to please the Mamluk ruler of Jiddah. He must have had a number
of copies made.

When I opened the second book I felt my heart stop. It was the slim
Hawīya, my first born, the first pilot book into which I had poured all I
knew of navigational theory at that time, written when I thought I knew
everything about everything, an outpouring into verse, into one thousand and eighty two verses in the *rajaz* meter, of the first principles of the
knowledge of the seas. Somehow I had misplaced it, forgotten about it, so
that when I searched for it in order to write my *Fawa'id*, my elephant of
a book into which I've packed all I now know, I found I had lost it. But I
didn't care. For into my *Fawa'id*, meant not only for pilots but for all lovers
of the sea, my memory threw in lines and verses from my *Hawīya*. I knew
it by heart. I knew even the page numbers.

Here, here is a couplet about the stars,
My attention has been devoted to the shining of the stars
That when I am away from them, they ask after me.

Then here's another one, on page one hundred, there it is. About
change, and the betrayal of time which ends
Then the arrow struck us, separating us,
Is there a thing which time has not pierced.

The arrow. Strange that I had referred to an arrow then. And to time.
And to separation. I had composed my *Hawīya* long before I ever set foot
in Diu. Before, long before I met her, as Abdul would say. I paused, stared
at the open page, rememories crowded into me.

The librarian wants you, a voice at the back said.

I'll come back to you, I promised my *Hawīya*, soon, soon.

The librarian took me to the chamber of Abdul Karim Nimdihi who gave
me a double embrace of welcome.

Ahmad ibn Madjid, Abdul Karim Nimdihi said, we cant talk today.
You have been summoned to attend a ceremony at court. Perhaps you can
narrate for me tomorrow, the account of how we tricked the Feringhi so
cleverly that they believed they had won the sea battle at Diu.

He smiled broadly at me. But hurry, he said, do not keep our great Sultan waiting.

I bowed to him and walked swiftly out of the courtyard, and out the gateway towards the royal palace some distance away. I wondered what wild untruths Abdul Karim Nimdihi would spin out about the Diu sea battle.

I approached the palace courtyard where people assembled every Wednesday morning to get a *darshan* of the sultan, so that everyone would know he was well and the kingdom was safe. The sultan would show himself to his people from the *jharoka*, a window that faced the east and projected out of the wall face of the upper storey. Two silvered pilasters supported a gilded cupola that rested on perforated marble screens. Clad in immaculate white and radiant in the early sunlight the sultan would slowly raise his right hand. Women, of late, would hold up their sick babies for his blessing. *Jharokha darshan* it was called, a strange HinduMuslim ritual. Strangely appropriate, I thought.

The entrance to the palace was on the right.

One of the guards led me through a series of pavilions and through the spacious hall of public audience, told me to remove my sandals, and ushered me into a small crowded hall where a religious discussion was about to begin.

Sultan Mahmud Begada took two steps down the white marble dais, refused the help of his servants, waved away the golden slippers they wanted to place near his feet, refused the cushions they offered him, and sat down, cross legged, back straight, on a plain carpet with a rosary of black beads twined around his right hand. Suspended above his head, a *punkah* in the shape of a sail made of fine silk that had been dampened, began to move and fill the air with a rose scent. No, gestured the sultan, and the *punkah* stopped. The ceiling, I noticed, was made of marble, so white and pure that one could see the shadows of the birds flying overhead.

My fellow Muslims, the sultan began, members of the religious community that is our Islam, I have stepped down from this high seat in order to be one with you and listen, with you, to the words of our religious scholars, whom I have summoned here to decide upon an important religious matter, the conversion of nonMuslims into Muslims.

Four of the shipwrecked Portuguese captives, who are Christian infidels and who do not speak our language, have professed a desire to renounce their *dhimmi* status and turn their feet toward Islam. They are waiting outside for our decision. I have asked our religious scholars to speak, briefly, one by one, about the matter. I will then ascend the dais

and, as ruler of this state and as executor of the professed *shari'a*, will pronounce the divine law.

Six religious leaders clad in green and brown robes sat in two rows
facing each other. Their heads were turned sideways towards the sultan
who, head bent low, began counting the beads of his rosary. Around the
dais sat the amirs of the court, all dressed in white cotton. They wore no
ornaments, not even rings on their fingers. Kiwam-i-Mulk Sarang and Malik Gopi sat on either side of the Sultan. I was surprised to see Malik Aiyaz
on the extreme right of the semicircle, sitting erect, his hands extended
on his knees. Malik Aiyaz looked at me, he smiled. He wasn't dressed in
white, his eyes looked tired, he must have just ridden up on Rustum from
Diu. Behind him sat Sidi Ali *o torto*. At the side in a corner sat two scribes
to record the proceedings.

The sultan looked up and raised his hand. It was the signal to begin.

An *alim* rose to speak.

As the seniormost religious teacher in Ahmadabad, who knows about
the religious requirements of Islam, I shall present to you my thoughts
about conversion. I shall be brief. Listen carefully.

He paused.

Islam, he proclaimed, is a missionary religion.

He paused again.

I shut my eyes, I did not want to look at him. I did not want to look
at this short man, at his brown robe with a tattered hem that trailed along
the carpet, at his thick white moustache that flowed into his flowing white
beard that flowed down to a sharp point almost to his knees. People smiled
when he dramatically flung his beard across his left shoulder. His voice it
was that made one ignore what he looked like. It was a fanatical voice,
razor sharp, it shot out of a mind unclouded by doubt.

This is the mission of Islam, he said. To propagate the faith of the
prophet, may he be forever blest. And to establish the Muslim faith by
making people submit to Islam. By force, if necessary, a lawful method
of propagation during war and conquest. And, in times of peace, by the
sword of conviction, the awareness that Islam is a superior religion that has
generated the highest of civilizations. In our Islam all men are brothers.

He paused, looked at the Sultan as if for approval, then looked all
around him and satisfied, took his seat.

True, quite true, very true, said the tall *alim* opposite him who shot
up seven feet tall from the carpet. Suppressed laughter from all except the
Sultan.

He's from Sarkhej, whispered my neighbor.

But consider this, the tall one said fiercely, stretching out his voice.
These Portuguese infidels do not acknowledge the greatness of Islam.

These miserable feringhis know nothing about our military triumphs which are, as all of you well know, proofs that Islam is the true faith. They want to become Muslims only in order to escape the pains of imprisonment. Their hearts will remain hard with disbelief.

He paused. Then he suddenly thundered, they're uncircumcised dogs, prolonging the three words to convey his utter contempt.

Don't curse them, the Sultan said, after all they're people of the book.

The great Sultan is right, said the *alim* from Surat. These unbelievers will, in time, become believers. How can they, at present, have a change of heart. They're simply ignorant. The real change will occur not as a matter of personal belief but through social belonging and practice. The Islamic community with which the converts shall claim fellowship will change them. They will discover what it means to be a Muslim.

The Sultan raised his hand. Let the Christians be brought in before us, now, so that they can become aware of our Islamic community.

The *alim* from Diu rose next to address the gathering.

There were sudden sounds of disturbance outside the hall.

Anathema, a voice shouted. It was a word unknown to me.

A na the ma, the voice spaced out the four syllables in hysterical anguish. There were sounds of struggle, blows, a confusion of guards. Four Portuguese mariners, their left arms gripped by four guards, were led up to the Sultan. Their heads were bent down, they were unshaven.

Prostrate yourselves, they were ordered.

Outside the hall there were more struggles, and sounds of blows.

Anathema, the voice yelled out in despair, stretching the last syllable to a shriek. One of the mariners wanted to run back as if he understood what the word meant, but he was forcibly restrained.

Anathema. This time the syllables dropped heavily, one by one, into silence as if the voice had given up all hope.

It was Frei António. I was shocked. Never ever had I heard him raise his voice on our journey from Surat to Champaner. Two of the guards held his arms and dragged him along. The patched sleeves of his patched brown cloak were torn. One side of his face was covered with blood. The two guards tried to prop him up between them but he collapsed on to the carpet.

Bow to the great Sultan, a guard ordered.

The Frei did not bother to look at the Sultan. Scrambling on his knees toward the four mariners, he looked at them pleadingly as if trying to pierce their hearts. Tears ran down a face distorted with grief. He begged them. He entreated them.

In the name of the body of Our Lord Jesus Christ, in the name of the Virgin Mary and of all the saints, do not, do not, oh my Christian brothers, become Muslim infidels.

The hall was in an uproar. No one, except Sidi Ali and myself, could understand what he was saying. The guards began to drag the Frei away.

The Sultan raised his hand. Stop, he said, let him be.

I entreat all four of you by the passion and sufferings of Our Lord Jesus Christ, and by his five wounds. Do not, he pleaded, give up your faith. You will be flung into hell fire, he warned, you'll suffer eternal damnation. You will lose your immortal souls forever, he cried out in anguish. For all eternity.

Still on his knees, he flung his head back and then flung out both his arms. There was no black rock to support him now, and he collapsed on his back on to the carpet. He lay still, but his eyes were wide open.

Help him, the Sultan said.

Malik Gopi signaled to the guards to withdraw. The court physician bent over the Frei.

Is this the Christian holy man, the Sultan asked Malik Gopi, the one who risked his life at Dumas to save the Muslim captain of the *Meri*.

Yes, said Malik Gopi, he is the one. The one who mumbles throughout the day pretending he is praying, the one who pretends to fast not only during the Christian *Ramadan* but every day of the year. This is the one of whom it is said, though I don't believe it at all, not at all, Malik Gopi added, that he has never married, and has never had any children.

What a strange holy man, said the Sultan. Doesn't he know that an accumulation of semen within the body is harmful. Our holy men know that women and marriage are essential even for saints, for the fulfillment of life here on earth. The Sultan shook his head wonderingly. This one must be a holy *madjnun*. He must be fifty, the Sultan said, and has never had a woman. Impossible. I want to question him.

Sidi Ali and the court physician came up to the Sultan.

He fainted because of the heat, the physician said. He has had no food and no water for a whole day. No wonder he fainted. He's all right now.

Sidi Ali, said the Sultan, tell the holy man that I want him to talk to me later about his path to God. But ask him this question now. What happens when he feels an urgent stirring in his loins for a woman, what does he do then.

Uses his hand, said Malik Gopi. His thing must have dried up. Perhaps it needs to be sucked like a date.

All, except the Sultan, burst out laughing.

The Frei puzzled whispered to Sidi Ali who whispered back. Then the Frei looked at the Sultan.

I never, the Frei said to the Sultan, never think of women. Women don't affect me at all.

Impossible, snorted Malik Gopi, we shall see.

Let a basket of the choicest mangoes and melons be sent to the holy man's room, ordered the Sultan. And let him be given three *khil'ats*, two robes made of silk and one robe of taffeta.

No, no, no, no, protested the Frei as he was led away. I could not tell whether the no's referred to the robes or were addressed to the four sailors.

Let the discussion continue, the Sultan said.

The *alim* from Patan stood up. He looked very dignified and solemn but for the thin straggly gray beard.

I want to, he said, crossing his arms across his chest, I want to provide you with the true perspective on conversion. In the world of the desert out of which Islam has sprung, he stated, there were no problems. Whole tribes turned Muslim, conversion was just a matter of time. Here in India and beyond, Islam encountered peoples that are not of the book, and religions that do not acknowledge the oneness of God. He paused. So that you all can better understand the historic dimension of conversion,

The great Sultan warned us to be brief, so spare us your usual tedious ramble through history, interrupted the seniormost *alim*, looking at the Sultan, then looking all around him for approval. All of us here know what you're going to say.

The seniormost *alim* pounded the carpet with his fist to reinforce his points one by one.

First, you'll refer pompously to the Arab conversion of Sind. Then, you'll talk about Arab sailors and traders, and *mut'a* marriages, and the navayats, and mappillas on the West Coast. And then, you'll elaborate on how conversion in India ran headlong into the wall of the Hindu caste system. How mostly low caste Hindus have embraced Islam. Totally useless, these observations. What is important is that Islam will always go on being Islam.

Stop it, stop it, old man, shouted the *alim* from Patan, your understanding of conversion is limited. You are still living in the old world. Change is in the air. Conversion is now a slow process.

Both of them clenched their fists and glared at each other.

The *alim* from Surat then rose and addressed the Sultan.

Our enemies, he said, the enemies of Islam, offer three reasons why so many people now flock to our Islam. Merely to avoid paying the *jizyah*, the religious tax, they say maliciously. Secondly, to avoid the humiliation of a second class status in an Islamic state. And thirdly, to secure a high paying administrative position.

Our friends from Ahmedabad and from Patan, he continued, staring at them, are both wrong.

The two religious scholars glared furiously at him.

In their own way both are right, he said, as though to smoothen their feelings. They have not taken into account the strange influence of the many Muslim saints in India and the sanctity generated by their tombs that has converted so many to Islam. Consider the effect of holy Sarkhej, and the mausoleum of Sayyid Burhan-ud-din at Vatva, and the tomb of Imam Shah at Pirana.

Oh great Sultan, interrupted the Junagadh *alim*, this discussion is leading us nowhere. Let me ask this group an important practical question, should these unbelievers be circumcised before they're allowed to become Muslims.

The hall began to buzz loudly.

Ah, said the *alim* from Surat. He was young. His eyes, I thought, gleamed with mischief. He wanted to provoke the older scholars.

What if these four were women, would you have them circumcised, the young *alim* asked.

He didn't use the word *khitān*, the cutting of the foreskin, but *khifād*, the term for the excision of the clitoris.

I was shocked. There was a buzz of laughter and horror from the crowd.

The Sultan stood up. He looked quite tired, and a little annoyed. But he strode up and sat on his dais.

Listen to me, he said. His voice was surprisingly strong, as if his old self had decided to take command.

The sign of Islam will not be made on them yet. The Portuguese captives will not be circumcised.

Another buzz from the crowd. Malik Gopi and Kiwam-ul-Mulk Sarang both raised their hands for silence.

The four captives smell of stale sweat. Let them be given a bath and purified before they become Muslims.

All six scholars nodded their approval.

The holy man, too, should be made to have a bath. Let incense be wafted around him to purify him.

Let the ceremony of the proclamation of the faith be performed in public in a few days. The four will submit themselves to God.

I appreciated the Sultan's exact use of the verbal form, *aslama*, for the act of submission.

Let them utter the eight words of the confession of faith. The first time with their lips. Later the words will come from their hearts.

Let the four converts be given appropriate Muslim names by the youngest *alim* present here, you from Surat, in order to make them part of the community.

And let the four men grow beards and marry Muslim women who will teach them our language and the ways of Islam. Let robes be given to them, and money, and some land to set up house. Then let them appear before me one year from now.

You may go now, the meeting has ended, the Sultan said.

I shall rest now, said the Sultan, stepping down from the dais.

What about the hostages and the *Meri* captured by the Portuguese pirates and taken to Cochin, asked Kiwam-ul-Mulk Sarang.

I am tired, the Sultan said, just tired. Why should I bother about those wamdering sea pirates who have never won a battle on land. They will soon go away from our shores. God will punish them. You, Malik Gopi, and you, Kiwam-ul-Mulk Sarang, will take care of such matters. Hold a meeting today. Let the reports of our agents be put together. Take the advice of Malik Aiyaz in these matters. Get rid of those Portuguese pirates as soon as possible.

I wanted Sidi Ali and you to attend our meeting, said Malik Aiyaz to me, but he has to get back to Diu to attend to shipping matters.

Where is Jan Mirza, your friend, Malik Aiyaz asked as we walked towards the administration building where the meeting was to be held.

I don't know, I said, he disappeared from Champaner some days ago. I don't know where he went. He has vanished, I told Malik Aiyaz, trying to conceal the pain and anger in my voice.

He took all the pages of the story I was writing, I wanted to add. But I didn't. I found it difficult to control my voice. After Abdul gave me the news, it was as if my being had been stunned into silence again. It was painful to experience the slow return of feeling, the awareness of loss, even as I write these words.

I am sure Jan Mirza must escaped to Vijayanagar, Malik Aiyaz said. He is heavily in debt to Malik Gopi. My spies told me that Krishna Deva Raya, the Hindu king of Vijayanagar newly crowned this year, needs horses for his cavalry to defend his kingdom against his enemies. His agent ambassador was seen having long conversations with Jan Mirza a number of times. It was your friend who sent Ishak a message from Surat.

I was shocked. João had never told me that he had sent a message to Diu. I thought I knew my João. After all, we were friends.

What message did he send, I asked.

It wasn't a written message, Malik Aiyaz said. The Portuguese captives of the *Santa Cruz* will be sent to Champaner, the messenger had reported to Ishak, so that they could be under the protection of Malik Gopi.

Then, according to Ishak, the messenger whipped out a dagger. Ishak, sitting massively on the carpet and relaxed against a bolster, did a sudden wrestler's twist, and the dagger inflicted a cut on his shoulder. The bodyguards killed the messenger quickly.

Is Ishak all right, I asked.

Ishak's wound, Malik Aiyaz said sadly, will heal soon. Mine, Ahmadji, will never heal. I have lost the bravest of my three sons, my first born, who I was sure would continue the name that I single handedly have made for myself, a name famous not only in Gujarat but all over the Muslim world. Alas, alas. When I die, my name also will die.

It was Sidi Ali o torto who, later, told me what really happened. Ishak had not been in any danger. The messenger was not really an assassin. Ishak's agents had had the messenger murdered immediately after he had delivered the message so that Malik Aiyaz could not torture information out of him. They had also arranged to have Ghazi Mujli, the earlier messenger, killed in prison before he could reveal any of Ishak's secrets. When Malik Aiyaz came to know about all this he ordered Ishak banished immediately to Junagadh. Then he got the news about the capture of the *Meri* and left immediately with Sidi Ali for Champaner on his Arabian charger, Rustum.

Sidi Ali, as captain of Diu port, knew all about shipping along the west coast of India. He explained to me why Vijayanagar was eager and anxious to secure the services of João.

They are in desperate need of an interpreter who knows Portuguese well, Sidi Ali said, one who can negotiate with the Portuguese about horses. The Vijayanagaris need warhorses capable of bearing armored riders and their weapons to fight against their enemies, the Bijapuris and the Orissans. Horses for the Vijayanagar cavalry are in short supply because now Portuguese ships have disrupted the flow of traffic from the gulf ports. Traders have stopped shipping horses to Cannanore and to the Kanara port of Bhatkal. The Vijayanagar agent was sent to Diu to find out whether horses of the very best quality from Kacch and Sind were available.

I knew now why João was needed as an adviser in Vijayanagar. I knew the trade patterns that zigzagged along the Bahr-i-Hind. I knew the kind of boats the horse traders used, low, flatbottomed ones called *taforeas*. I knew that the Arab traders waited for the early monsoon when the breezes would blow soft and gentle so that the seaswell near the coast would not affect these delicate creatures. The shallow bay at Cannanore which did not have an estuary bar and the sandy slope at Bhatkal, were ideally suited for the disembarking of horses. Goa too, under the domination of Bijapur, had a safe harbor. Muslim Bijapur and Hindu Vijayanagar were rivals for the purchase of horses for their cavalry.

The meeting to decide what to do about the Portuguese was to be held in a magnificent round chamber in the administration building just outside the palace wall. I felt as I had felt after the meeting of the nakhodas, quite depressed, knowing that nothing could be done about the powerful Portuguese.

Malik Gopi had furnished the chamber with rich Persian carpets and with a circle of satin cushions and bolsters to lean on. The walls, the panels were made of Champaner sandalwood, had hangings of tie and dye fabrics in delicate colors of pale green and egg blue, and drapes of translucent Melakan silk embossed with floating sea dragons in red velvet. In the arcaded niches, let into the wall on different levels, were glass designs and, at eye level, rings made of bloodstone and jasper, small bowls of *babaghori* banded agate, vases of red cornelian from Ratanpur, and slender jars of green Chinese porcelain. The lighting was diffused. A concealed punkah released hints of jasmine that blended with the delicate aroma of sandalwood. Malik Gopi had created an aura of soft luxury that banished the fierce heat to the outside.

He had bathed and changed into a robe of translucent cotton, pale green and yellowblue, as if he had just descended from the wall into the circle. Malik Aiyaz had not changed his clothes, he had sprinkled some rosewater over himself to cover the smell of sweat. He stretched out his legs and relaxed against a bolster, but did not look as cool and as comfortable as Malik Gopi who seemed perfectly at home in this world of luxury he had created.

Let's begin, Malik Gopi said languidly.

Malik Aiyaz sat up straight, his back rigid against the bolster.

Gopi, he said, deliberately refusing to use the title conferred on Gopi by Sultan Begada. Gopi, he continued sharply, you had no right to remove the shipwrecked Portuguese from Dumas to Surat and transfer them to Champaner. I am the admiral of the west coast of Gujarat, and Dumas falls under my jurisdiction. Those captives belonged to me.

Relax, my dear Malik admiral, said the wily Malik Gopi, this chamber is not Diu harbor. You have no quarrel with me but with Almeida, that cruel Viceroy, that Portuguese barbarian, who bombarded your ships in Diu harbor and forced you to return the Portuguese sailors, the ones Amir Hussain had captured last year at Chaul and wanted to send to Mamluk Egypt. You insisted at that time, that was very prudent of you, Malik Aiyaz, that they had to be sent here to Champaner avoid an attack by Almeida.

He bent his right leg at the knee and began massaging his toes, one by one, glancing occasionally at Malik Aiyaz to see whether the barbed taunts had hit. I could see his skin, smooth and slightly yellow. Malik Aiyaz had told me that Gopi had his whole body massaged with coconut oil every day.

The shipwrecked Portuguese, Gopi said, do belong to you, Malik Aiyaz. I wanted to send them to Diu. But the tufan did not allow that and the sultan himself sent an order that they should be sent right away from Surat to Champaner.

Fetch me the order, Malik Gopi said to one of his scribes, show it to Malik Aiyaz.

Malik Aiyaz waved it away. It was well known that Kiwam-ul-Mulk Sarang and Malik Gopi had persuaded Sultan Begada to affix his official signature and his seal to several blank sheets of paper which they then used to execute their private schemes in the guise of royal commands. A very efficient method, Malik Gopi had assured the Sultan, we will use them only for the welfare of the state. Never for any religious edicts, Gopi had said.

Malik Aiyaz knew he had been outwitted. He remained silent.

What shall we do about the Portuguese and the hostages, Kiwam-ul-Mulk Sarang asked.

My dear Kiwam-ul-Mulk Sarang, said Malik Gopi, that question should be rightfully addressed to Malik Aiyaz. Who, after all, belongs to the world of action. Men of the sword, that's the category to which he belongs.

I detected an ironic heightening of tone in Gopi's voice.

He is one of the guardians of our state devoted to the arts of war. Whereas I, and Malik Gopi's voice dropped. I, he continued, am neither a man of the sword, alas, nor am I a man of the pen.

His voice dropped still lower.

I use strategies against my competitors in matters of trade, said Malik Gopi.

We could barely hear him.

My dear Gopi, said Kiwam-uk-Mulk Sarang, hastening to reassure his friend, you are above all categories, you are unique. But let's get back to our problem. What should be done, Malik Aiyaz, about the hostages and the Portuguese problem.

Malik Aiyaz, like the shrewd administrator that he was, paused for quite a while before he spoke.

I kept staring at them.

The Portuguese, Malik Aiyaz said, those dastardly Portuguese, have turned the ocean sea which we Muslims have always used for purposes of peaceful trade into a field of battle. They have to be defeated. They will be defeated. But we need time to plan tactics of action, not just of trade as Gopi suggests. The Portuguese, I've been told, have no goods to trade with nor do they have any money.

We need to learn, Ahmadji tells me, how to build new kinds of ships, how to shoot the sun, how to shift sails so as to catch the changing winds. Ahmadji has warned me that many things would have to be changed. All this will take time.

Ahmadji, how long will this take, asked Malik Gopi.

I dont know, I said.

Ahmadji, Malik Aiyaz addressed me, please tell us what you told me about guns and ships and sails.

I didn't want to get involved in any discussion. I didn't want to get involved at all. But my friend, Malik Aiyaz, did need my help. He must have read the reports on the two battles that I wrote for him. I had to convince the others of the need for change of tactics.

Wait, said Malik Gopi and signaled to his servants. I was offered a tray of green, clove studded triangles of *pān*. I bit into one. It exploded in my mouth, splashing the inside with honey and cardamon.

I speak only as a pilot, I said. I have talked with Jan Mirza and a few Portuguese deserters, with Mamluk sailors and fighters, and with some Ottoman gunners on the *Bandar-i-Turk* and have heard them describe in great detail our victory over the ships of Dom Lourenço de Almeida last year in March at Chaul. From the blackrock promontory where Straighthitter now rests, João, Malik Aiyaz and I watched the destruction of the *maonas* by Dom Francisco de Almeida's *naos*. Both events led me to warn Malik Aiyaz that the old order of attack and defence will not longer do.

Have another *pān*, Ahmadji, said Malik Gopi. It will make vivid your memories of the past.

I shut my eyes.

I wanted to be objective. I tried to be analytical. I tried to use the language of logic to explain things dispassionately to these three pillars of Gujarat. But I began to see visions. It was as if I was hallucinating, as if I had had hashish.

I saw João who I knew wasn't there.

João, I shouted. For there he was on the seashore talking to his friends who had astrolabes and compasses for faces. Their hands and arms were sections of cross staffs.

Look, shouted João, look there, Ahmadji.

He pointed seawards.

From a Portuguese ship lightning and thunder erupted into the sky as if heralding the monsoon and challenging a force of nature.

Ahmadji, Malik Aiyaz said. You've been silent for a long time. We are waiting, tell us what needs to be changed, Ahmadji.

I opened my eyes.

It's the *pān*, Malik Gopi said. The leaf was sent to me by the *shahbandar* of Melaka, Nina Chatu. Buddhists shamans eat it and go into a trance to relate the stories of their ancestral gods to their people. It has an explosive effect at first. Then it calms the consciousness and makes one see things clearly.

Malik Gopi was right. I could see the battle at Chaul now as a series of vivid images. I could picture the people, the ships, the estuary. the fishing stakes of the Kundalika river, the guns, the *maonas*. I would even be able to shift perspectives and tell the story of the battle from different angles.

Let me, I said to these three pillars of Gujarat, present an account of the battle. You can then decide what needs to be done.

The battle of Chaul

Six Portuguese ships ride at anchor, their sails lowered, in the curved Chaul roadstead, upriver. The black coating on their hulls has peeled, they need careening, they look weather beaten, exhausted. They've spent ten days patrolling the coast from Kannanur to Chaul, attacking any ship that does not carry a *cartaz*. Their commander, young Dom Lourenço de Almeida is determined to win all the glory he can, for his faith, for his father, for himself. Unarmed ships packed with rich trading goods, loaded with gold and jewelry, crowded with pilgrims returning from Jiddah, are their targets.

At Chaul the ships and sailors take a well earned rest. The Muslim port city, afraid of being sacked, has welcomed them. But Dom Lourenço takes no chances. The guns of three of the ships are at the ready, night and day, trained on the city. The sailors, relaxed and at ease, wander about in the bazaars buying trinkets, sampling the hot spicy foods. They drink the water of the tender coconut. It is March, the month of pigeons. The Portuguese eat the tender flesh of young green pigeons marinated with spices, then roasted on a spit. The vendors tell them that it is aphrodisiacal. On a high maidan near the harbor pigeon flying contests are in progress. It is early evening.

From the maidan they can see them coming, way out, beyond the bar, in single file and black against the low Western sun. Those surely are not the Mamluk ships they were warned about, but the ships of Afonso de Albuquerque. They're coming to the west coast of India after bombarding Hormuz, the sailors reassure themselves. They keep staring seawards. Two miles beyond the bar the sails can be clearly seen. Those are not our ships, says a veteran seaman, the red cross does not blaze on the sails. It is true. Half a mile from the bar the sea is as smooth as blue velvet. The strange ships lower their sails. The rowers take over. The oars rise and fall in unison. They are Mamluk *maonas*.

The *maonas* make their majestic way in double file across the bar of the S shaped Kundalika river mouth, trumpets blaring, red and green banners waving, scissor streamers flying. They are arrogant, the first Mamluk armada on the Bahr-i-Hind. Galeasses, the Portuguese call them. They're also called *bastardas*, hybrids, the invention of a Venetian renegade and an Ottoman galley maker, a combination of a rowing and a twodecked sailing ship designed primarily for war.

Made of oak and pine, then camel backed to Cairo, put together in rough shape in Suez, towed through the coral thick Gulf of Suez and through the rock studded gullet of the Red Sea, outfitted with oars and sails and equipped with guns and newly cast cannon at Jiddah, they've traveled down to Aden whose ruler Amir Hussain was compelled under pain of death to supply water, firewood and provisions. They then sailed, hugging the coast, across the ocean sea to Diu eager for their first encounter with those hated Portuguese infidels who, they had heard, were lurking, terrified, in Chaul.

There the Portuguese are, wild animals, trapped.

Let's attack at once and destroy them, says Amir Hussein. He's the *kapudan*. He stands on the bow of the *maona* next to ShipShatterer, with Salman Rais the Ottoman corsair at his side.

The *nao* of Lourenço de Almeida, in the middle of the river, its broadside vulnerable and exposed, is a tempting target. It cannot move, cannot weigh anchor, the sea breeze is too strong, the tidal flow too rapid. It has been caught unprepared. Its artillery is not primed for action. The Portuguese sailors hasten to board their ships. All is confusion.

Fire, fire, fire, orders Amir Hussein impatiently.

A cannonball thunders forth from ShipShatterer, soars in an arc over the *nao*, and smashes into a house on the river bank. The shot from Salman Rais's *maona* sputters, falls short.

Hang both those gunners, screams Amir Hussein.

Stop, stop, shouts Salman Rais.

The Portuguese are now ready, waiting for the galeasses to draw near, not wanting to waste any powder and ammunition which is in short supply.

Stop, shouts Salman Rais, and the *maonas* slow down, then stop. Oars are raised. Anchors drop. It will be night soon.

Useless to launch an attack now. It'll take too long to reload the cannon. They're trapped, Salman says, let's attack them in the morning.

No, no, no, says the *kapudan*. That's cowardly.

Amir Hussein wants to line up his *maonas*. He wants his fighters to use their powerful crossbows, board the ships, attack the Portuguese with short lances and swords, and redden the ships with infidel blood.

Salman Rais with great difficulty convinces his commander that it will be impossible for the *maonas* to position themselves for attack. It's high water, but they do not know the location of shoals and sandbanks.

Darkness falls. Only the distant rustle of the coconut palms and the ceaseless murmur of the onflowing tide dare to disturb the utter blackness of the night.

After a long while, slowly, human murmurs begin. Towards morning, sounds of prayer are heard, supplications rise up, the morning star listens. To the sounds of Latin, *Pater Noster, Ave Maria*. To the sounds of Arabic prayer just before dawn. *Allahu akbar, la ilaha illa'llah*.

Young Salman Rais cannot pray. He has to suppress the rage that seeks to burst out of him. Against the world in general. Against these contemptible Mamluks. Against Amir Hussein especially. Amir Hussein has had the second gunner, the renegade from Ragusa, secretly hanged and the corpse flung overboard last night. His own men hate him. He is a monster of cruelty.

That's why Sultan Kansuh-al-Ghawri banished him to the hell of Jiddah to build a fortress there to withstand the possible attack of the Portuguese infidels. That's why he was assigned a nonMamluk force that consisted of black African archers and Turkmans who could use handguns. Real Mamluks consider it beneath their dignity to fight with guns. They are cavalry soldiers and fight only with crossbows. That will surely doom the Mamluks. They and their Sultan do not realize that war on horseback is outmoded and that the crossbow, will no longer do against guns.

Look at Amir Hussein that Kurdi, as his men contemptuously call him. For the Kurds are a mountain people far from the sea. As an admiral our Kurdi is utterly stupid. He wants in this age of gunpowder and sail to bombard an enemy ship first and then use ramming and boarding tactics, and handtohand combat as in a land battle. Hasn't decided on a plan but wants to attack the Portuguese at the first light.

The Portuguese captains gather in council on the *capitania*, the flagship, to draw up their plans. They're trapped and they know it. A page brings in several cups of coffee.

Dom Lourenço enters the cabin. His face burns with excitement. Welcome crusaders, he greets all five of them including his former tutor and present adviser, Diego Pires. The cabin is luridly lit by four flaming torches. Welcome my fellow Lusitanians.

I am ready, he announces, my arms are ready for action.

He points to his sword and plate armour and helmet that lie polished and gleaming on a sidebench.

I am ready to vanquish the infidels, just as I was ready to sail to Hormuz and destroy it. All of you know how Afonso de Albuquerque deprived me of that honor. Let me, I entreat you, be the first to board the flagship and kill the leader of the Rumes.

The captains do not speak. They admire their young commander. He is their hero who, it is said, singlehandedly attacked and killed a crocodile, a monster sunning itself on the banks of a river in Ceylon, though they wonder about the plate armor he wears which is completely unsuitable for ship battle in the tropics.

Diego Pires breaks the silence. His voice is heavy with experience.

We're trapped, he observes. Those *maonas*, unlike the ships we're used to fighting here in India, are huge and armed with powerful guns and weapons. They are about 1500 strong, we are only 600.

But one Portuguese fighter, claims Dom Lourenço, equals more than 20 of the enemy.

We're Lusitanians as our commander has said, says the veteran who had recognized the enemy ships. We have to fight. But let's act prudently. Let's move out of this river trap and fight in the open sea, there we're sure to be victorious. We can sail through the southern outlet when the land wind and the tidal flow is in our favor. In the deep of the night.They'll dub us cowards, says the young commander. The Almeida family never runs away and you all now are part of the family and its honor.

Senhor Pires, my respected tutor, what do you advise.

Diego Pires begins by setting down on the table his sketch map of the Chaul estuary. There are only two ways to leave, he states. By the deeper and wider northern channel through which we and the Mamluks entered and which they now control. And by the narrow dangerous shallow outlet that swings around the steep promontory that descends in a sharp point into the river. This southern channel is usable only when the tide flows out.

The other captains refer to their notes and mark down on the sketch map the mudflats, the patches, the shoals that choke the middle of the estuary, they note down the tidal recordings, and the soundings especially for the least depth, the color of the water at different times of the day, the red rock of the sloping promontory. Two scribes make copies of the sketch map to be kept in an archive in Lisbon.

What a strategic promontory to build a fortress on, says one Portuguese captain, our cannons will be able to command the whole estuary.

Each captain has methodically noted down on his chart the number of their handguns and *espingardas* and *berços*, the bombards and cannons, where they are positioned on the ships, the position of their ships in the river, the half barrels of water on deck to drink from and the wet swabs to use in case of fire, the amount of gunpowder and projectiles available on each ship, and even the availability of urine buckets to swab down their guns. The Portuguese are well organized.

Don't begin till I give the signal, says the young commander.

The Portuguese dont know that there are fishing stakes submerged in the middle of the estuary, not visible during high tide. The *maonas* know only the tideless Meditteranean, they have no experience of shoals and sandbanks on the Bahr-i-Hind and its rivers.

ShipShatterer is ready. His elevation has been adjusted. His muzzle which points straight at the *capitania* gleams arrogant in the early morning sunlight. After all he has been cast in the newly built foundry next to the Cairo hippodrome, and was tested in the presence of Sultan Kansuh-al-Ghawri himself. He knows he is the finest of the six bronze pieces in the Mamluk fleet and he occupies the central position, flanked by three guns on either side, on the bow of Amir Hussein's *maona* which is being borne along by the incoming tide and the seabreeze. A hundred yards behind follow two *maonas*, behind them is a spread of three *maonas*. The formation speeds straight along like an arrow. A Calicut sambuk follows behind.

Fire, commands Amir Hussein.

Stop, wait, shouts Salman Rais, wait till they get into range.

Fire, fire, orders Amir Hussein furiously.

The thunder is deafening, thick blinding smoke covers the bow, the cannonball hurtles its way straight as if wanting to shatter the *capitania's* broadside, then it leaps up in a sudden arc and crashes down on a caravela anchored fifty yards behind, it plunges through the upper deck into a barrel of gunpowder. The ship explodes into flames.

Huzzas, loud groans, screams of victory, of anguish, trumpet blares, loud fanfares, voices yelling for help, the red cross flag on the mainmast of the caravela burns merrily in the wind, the *maona* banners rejoice.

The Portuguese are doomed. We're victorious, yells Amir Hussein to Salman Rais.

The five *maonas* swing wide to the right and to the left of Amir Hussein's ship. They form a line and with their prows pointing towards the Portuguese ships they discharge all their guns.

Loud huzzas, yells, shouts of victory.

The *maonas* cannot see what damage they have inflicted, for thick smoke blown by the seabreeze hides the Portuguese ships from view.

The Portuguese ships have not been greatly damaged by the cannonade. A few masts have been shattered. The mainmasts have been only grazed by balls of stone fired from castiron cannon that have lobbed harmlessly on to the upper decks. The rudder of Dom Lourenço's *nao* is cracked, but the sternpost has not been damaged. The carpenter and the caulkner get ready to repair it. The Portuguese bide their time, they wait for the gunsmoke to clear, they hold their fire, they have to conserve powder and shot. And they know that the *maona* guns need time to be prepared and loaded for the next cannonade.

The *maonas* march on in line, their prows aimed at the Portuguese ships, followed by a sambuk.

Wait, stop, shouts Salman Rais.

Why. Amir Hussein is furious.

The master gunner, an expert from Germany, in Dom Lourenço's *nao* angles a broadside cannon to the left and fires a crossbar shot at the *maonas*, which expands as it emerges, whirls dizzily along, and brings down the foremast top of Salman Rais's maona with its green crescent.

Slow down, else we'll move into point blank range of the Portuguese guns. Slow down, yells Salman Rais. Back away.

The *maonas* slow down, the oars go into reverse, they begin to row astern, awkwardly, but they manage to move out of range, slowly.

The oarless sambuk compelled by the tide and the wind cannot stop. Its nakhoda leans heavily on the tiller to angle the ship towards the shore. The Flemish gunner of the smallest of the caravelas on the extreme right, fires a shot through the porthole that flies low and skimming over the water and smashes into the lower hull of the sambuk, broadside, between wind and water, and makes it tilt to one side and drift wide towards the shore. Water rushes into the gaping hole. With their swivel guns, their *espingardas*, their *berços*, the Portuguese take careful aim at the escaping swimmers before they shoot. Some of the swimmers manage to make it to the shore.

Amir Hussein is beginning to realize that the Mediterranean mode of sea fighting will no longer do. But he refuses to allow that cowardly Salman Rais to teach him anything. He knows his *maonas* have to retreat and they back off towards the shore where they take up a defensive position and anchor, wide apart, stern first.

The Portuguese wait patiently for the tide to turn. They know it will, two hours before noon. Three of their ships venture cautiously toward the *maonas*.

It turns into a standoff fight, a prolonged one with few dramatic moments. Amir Hussein and Dom Lourenço, impatient, pace up and down on their ships. Both dislike ship killings from a distance. Its nonhuman. They prefer loud action, the clash of steel on steel, deeds of human glory.

The Flemish gunner fires an iron ball from a bronze cannon. It falls short. You fired when our ship dipped into the wave trough, the German master gunner comments sharply, you have to wait for the upswing of the wave.

A shot from a Turkish bronze gun travels steady and horizontal and smashes into the prow of a caravela damaging it and wounding a number of Portuguese.

The *maona* guns have the advantage. Anchored and level as if on land, they can shoot straight and hit the mark. The Portuguese have to take into account the nonstop up and down movement of their ships and the constant tidal flow. The mariners have to adjust the spritsail to counter the land breeze, and they cannot shoot recklessly for powder and cannonballs are limited. Their shots are erratic. Their ships have to keep out of range.

A Portuguese gunner fires a muzzle loader through a porthole and destroys the artillery platform of a *maona*.

A Turkish gun replies with a chain shot that brings down the foremast top of a Portuguese nao. Another lets loose a wildfire ball that explodes on the deck of a caravela.

It goes on and on in this manner, a four hour long drawn out duel of guns that will last till the tide turns and the wind shifts.

Guns, João had told me after the Diu battle, have become the major protagonists in battle now.

Human beings are slaves to guns now, I told my audience. Too many different kinds of guns have now sprung into existence. In the old days I used to be intoxicated with the poetry of ships on the Bahr-i-Hind. I was now intoxicated with the new poetry of guns and went on to talk about falcons and eagles and pelicans, and dogs and camels and lions, and vipers and *serpentinas*, the strange Portuguese names for their guns. The largest of the Portuguese guns is called the basilisk after a mythical monster. The Mamluks and the Ottomans give their siege cannon names like Thunderbolt and Exploder. So intoxicated was I with the music of gun names that I ventured to prophecy that guns would in the future outnumber human beings on earth.

Ahmad ibn Madjid, have another *pān*, Malik Gopi interrupted me.

Quite interesting. Very interesting, all this information about guns, interrupted Malik Gopi again. But will it help us solve the Portuguese problem.

Don't you see, Gopi, said Malik Aiyaz, what Ahmadji is implying is that we cannot fight the Portuguese. Not yet, not now. We do not have the ships. We do not have the latest guns. Our seamen are not trained, we have to learn new tactics. I thought the Mamluks had the latest weapons, that they would help us. I thought a coalition of three fleets would wipe out the Portuguese. But you know what happened at Diu.

I was at Champaner this February, said Kiwam-ul-Mulk Sarang. The report at court was that the event was of no importance. The Portuguese could not capture Diu. They fled away.

And I was in Surat, Malik Gopi said. What I still dont understand is why the Portuguese with their latest guns and ships were defeated in Chaul and successful at Diu. Was it a matter of luck.

I witnessed both battles, said Malik Aiyaz, I was at Diu. And I was at Chaul with our fustas. Let me continue Ahmadji's account, though mine will not be as vivid as his.

Have this *pān*, Malik Aiyaz, said Malik Gopi.

Malik Aiyaz's account of the end of the Chaul battle

We reached Chaul two hours before sunset just when the tide and the wind began to turn, and the Portuguese were retreating to the roadstead where their other ships were anchored. Salman Rais flag.signaled that we should enter the estuary by the southern channel. Don't attack, was his message, lie in wait for them. So we curved past the shoals and the fishing stakes and the mud patches and drew up our fustas, sixty four of them, on the beach under the shelter of the sloping promontory, and we waited.

Salman Rais sent a *catur* across the estuary to inform me that the Portuguese planned to leave after midnight, when exactly his spy on Dom Lourenço's *nao* didn't know. They would probably take the southern channel. We should be ready to intercept them, wrote Salman Rais. The *maonas* will be able to join in the attack only when the tide turns.

We drew up our plans carefully, determined not to allow any of the Portuguese ships to escape. We would capture Dom Lourenço's *nao* and seize its guns. The prows of our fustas were well armed with the newly cast bronze *berços* manufactured by the two Italian armourers who had deserted the Portuguese in 1505, and had established a gun foundry in Calicut. They had trained sixty of our men before the Samorin had them killed because they wanted to defect back to the Portuguese. Strangely, it's easier and quicker to train men how to shoot guns than it is to train soldiers how to use crossbows. The Zamorin had sent us seventy small guns.

At our war council the Chaul harbor master suggested that a couple of fustas with lit lanterns could be rowed across the channel as decoys to lure the escaping caravelas to the shore. The Portuguese wouldn't be stupid enough to fall for that trick, I thought. I thought then of the Diu fortresslet. It was the practice everywhere to use elephants to stretch a chain across a river as a barricade against the entrance of enemy ships.

Let's stretch a cable from the promontory end to the middle of the estuary, I said.

They didn't have a cable that long. We made do by stretching out thick ropes, and all the fishermen's nets we could collect, and three fustas fastened together end to end. It was hastily done and done in the dark.

Then we waited.

My men drew up some other plans. They wouldn't show them to me. You'll be quite surprised, Malik Aiyaz, they said. They wouldn't allow me to lead them in this battle. It's just a skirmish, they said, we'll easily capture the ships and the guns. The harbor master of Chaul took me to a spot half way up the sloping promontory with an excellent view of the southern channel and of part of the estuary. It was the spot fishermen used for lantern storm signals.

We waited.

The Portuguese, cleverly, did not weigh anchor when the wind and the tide turned around late at night. They began their move about two hours before sunrise when the darkness began to thin.

From my perch on the promontory I could see a caravela shape detach itself from a thick dark mass. No sounds of prayer or of trumpets disturbed the darkness, only the occasional flap of a sail as the caravela curved its way to the open sea.

Suddenly there was a blare of trumpets and conches, a terrifying din of cymbals, fanfares and a beating of many drums, that all converged from the right, to my surprise, on to the speeding caravela confusing the enemy. Our fustas, in two groups of three, had lain in wait amid the shoals and the mud patches. The first group, the suicide *ghazi*fustas, hurled themselves at the Portuguese ship which, taken by surprise, let loose all the broadside guns on its right destroying the three fustas and shattering them to pieces.

The other three fustas skilfully avoided the floating wrecks and the onflowing debris, and attacked the caravela using their *berços* to kill some of the gunners as they began to reload. Two of the men who were busy taking soundings were easily picked off. Some of our men lobbed wildfire metal pots on to the deck. Others, chosen for their muscle power, flung earth pots of soft soap and oil and quicklime to the other side of the caravela where the loaded cannon were. Grappling hooks with ropes attached were then tossed in order to swarm up the right side and on to the ship with loud yells and cries, and with oiled short pikes and swords. They would have captured the caravela had a barrel of gunpowder not exploded. All aboard, our men and the infidels, were killed. Pieces of the caravela washed up against the fishing net section of the barrier.

The other caravela close behind the first was attacked from the left by three suicide *ghazi*fustas that darted from the promontory shore. The same strategy was used. We wanted to capture the caravela and the guns. But this time it was one of the infidels who blew up the ship. We lost many warriors and almost all our fustas were sunk. But the caravela and all the Portuguese infidels were destroyed. Parts of burning wreckage and broken oars washed up against the fishing net barrier.

The Portuguese, I think, had by now become aware of our tactics. Two naos came sailing side by side but some yards apart, their broadside cannons blazing to the right and to the left. They delayed firing some of their guns this time so that the second wave of our fustas was also completely destroyed by their porthole cannon. The Portuguese rejoiced, they danced with joy on decks and poops. They did not see that they were heading straight towards the wreckage and the debris. It was then that our barrier fustas opened fire confusing the Portuguese, who had expected fire only from the sides not from straight ahead. Their *naos* got entangled in the nets and ropes. Four of our *caturs* managed during the confusion to slip inbetween and throw wildfire balls through their portholes. They fired *bāns* which are, as you know, rockets filled with fine gunpowder, well rammed, and tied to bamboo rods. The two naos, impelled by the current, burst through the barrier wreckage toward the open sea. Two hundred yards beyond the barrier they burst into flames.

The captains of the two remaining caravelas urged Dom Lourenço to make a run for it to the open sea in his *nao*. We'll follow, they said, the enemy fustas are in a state of panic and disorder. Never, said Dom Lourenço, never. I'll be the last one to get out of this trap. My honor forbids it.

By now the darkness had thinned considerably for the sun was just about to emerge from behind a hill. From the promontory I looked down at a chaotic blur of a scene. Fragments of wood, oar pieces, moans and screams and wails from bodies swirling around before being swept away, corpses caught in the torn fishing nets, pieces of smouldering wreckage. Impossible to describe, I lack the language for it. I could, of course, use scribal jargon and say, the river was red with blood. But that would be false, I could barely see the river through the rising mist and the smoke.

What a chaos.

The harbor master pointed to the north and we could see two maonas rowing against the current, approaching slowly through the rising river mist.

It's the time of counter current and change, the harbor master explained, when the forces of tide and wind are in a state of uncertain transition.

It was true. I looked down. The chaos and the debris and the human wreckage had begun to disappear. The tide wanted to cleanse away the disturbance wrought by man. Our fustas, their *berços* and guns overheated and misfiring, had backed up in disarray on the promontory beach. They watched the three Portuguese ships, using their spritsails, move toward the open sea. The two caravelas led the way. Behind loomed Dom Lourenço's *nao*.

The maonas were using their oars to make their slow way across the estuary. They began firing at the escaping enemy ships sailing in a straight line down the channel, their broadsides presenting a tempting target that kept moving at right angles to the prow guns.

I was sure one of the three ships would be hit, then our fustas would be able to swarm to the crippled ship to capture its guns. A number of shots were fired but none of them hit the mark. The shooting was erratic. The guns couldn't find the proper range. One of the shots soared over the ships and smashed down on one of our fustas.

The lead caravela was about fifty yards away from the barrier gap when I saw Dom Lourenço's nao swing to the right, then speed along suddenly aiming itself at the maonas, as if wanting to attack them head on. Then it began to wobble as if it had lost control of itself, it gyrated wildly two or three times, and came to a stop amid the circle of fishing stakes stuck in the middle of the estuary.

It happened so suddenly that no one knew what happened and why. Only later did we find out. A cannon ball from ShipShatterer had struck the rudder and the sternpost of Dom Lourenço's nao and splintered them to pieces. It had been a lucky shot.

The lead caravela could not be of help, and it could not stop or even slow down, it passed straight through the barrier gap. The second caravela managed somehow to slow down, and someone flung a rope to the *capitania* which was quickly wrapped tight around the mizzen mast.

The *maona* guns took a long time to get into position to train their prow cannon on the nao.

Six of our fustas took off from the promontory beach.

The harbor master showed me a short cut down the promontory to my canopied fusta that waited for me at the beach, guns at the ready, my men were well armed.

Hurry, hurry, I told my rowers who wanted to keep me and my fusta out of the range of the Portuguese and the maona guns. I wanted to get to the nao before that mad Amir Hussein, that *madjnun*, sent the nao with all its guns to the bottom of the estuary.

I could see the men of the caravela strain at the rope and pull with all their might to free the nao. The force of the tide was erratic. It would swirl and eddy and twist so that the caravela would heel at times, then sway from side to side as if eager to go. The nao wouldn't budge, it was stuck as if trapped between submerged rocks.

The caravela captain ordered his men to let down the ship's boat to rescue Dom Lourenço.

No, no, Dom Lourenço shouted. He appeared on the slanting poop helmetless, his dark brown curls in disarray, but he looked resplendent in full white plate armor on which the early morning sun shone.

No, he shouted again, save yourselves. I will be the last one to depart this ship.

At that moment a cannon ball struck the poop deck killing a number of men and flinging Dom Lourenço down the steps to the deck. His knees buckled under. Painfully he stumbled forward. Using both his hands to lift his heavy sword, he hacked twice at the rope to set the caravela free.

The maona guns kept shooting, endangering the lives of my men who were preparing to swarm up the slanting sides of the nao. I signaled the maona guns to stop firing.

I had given strict orders to my fustas not to hurl any fire balls through the portholes. They did throw pots of oil and soft soap on the deck but didn't use any *bāns*. Some of our men used short pikes greased in order to prevent the enemy from grabbing them.

Go with God, Dom Lourenço shouted to the caravela as it sped away.

Our men attacked bravely. They cut the nao's rigging with long handled sickles. They brought down the yard. Our crossbowmen shot with deadly accuracy so that they killed or wounded the Portuguese on the lower decks.

The young commander had waged fierce battle with his heavy sword which he wielded with both hands killing a number of my men until a shot from one of our *berços* struck him in the foot. A dozen Portuguese stationed themselves around Dom Lourenço to protect him.

Give me your word and surrender to Malik Aiyaz, one of my men shouted, or else you'll be captured by the Mamluks.

Never, said Dom Lourenço, even though he was in pain.

His soldiers set him down in a chair near the mainmast. Sword in hand he encouraged his men to fight.

My men didn't fire any more shots at Dom Lourenço for they knew I wanted to capture him alive. They would have attacked the soldiers around him with their swords and pikes had it not been for a Portuguese sharpshooter stationed on the crow's nest high up on top of the mainmast who, armed with a number of *berços* and handguns killed anyone who ventured near his commander.

Tell him to surrender, I shouted to my men from my fusta.

No, never, said Dom Lourenço.

I could see a maona shipboat approaching from the other side.

An Ottoman sharpshooter took aim at the crow's nest and wounded the Portuguese gunner in his right arm. Another shot grazed his right shoulder.

Yells and huzzas from the maona close by.

The Ottoman sharpshooter then took careful aim at Dom Lourenço and fired a shot that smashed the left side of his head and covered it with blood.

A shot from the crow's nest, the *gavea*, killed the *maona* sharpshooter instantly. We could see blood flowing down the right side of the Portuguese sharpshooter who continued to shoot killing more of the *maona* men despite being in great pain.

Tell Dom Lourenço to surrender, I shouted to my men.

Surrender to Malik Aiyaz, my men said, if Amir Hussein captures you and your men he will send you to the Sultan of Egypt, Kansuh-al-Ghawri.

We'll surrender to you, a spokesman said, provided all Portuguese lives are spared.

We agreed.

We have to take our commander to the lower deck, they said. When he comes up he will formally surrender to your Malik.

It was a strange request, for Dom Lourenço was clearly dying. But we agreed.

Four soldiers lifted the chair on which he sat and bore him down the steps, the fifth soldier carried his sword.

We never saw Dom Lourenço again.

His soldiers let his body down through a hole in the side of the ship. He didnt, they said, want his body, his helmet or his sword to be displayed before his enemies.

He was an infidel, Dom Lourenco was, but a heroic warrior.

End of the Chaul battle

Malik Aiyaz was much moved.

I could hear the emotion in his voice as it dropped at the end of his account.

Why did the heroic death of Dom Lourenço move him so, I wondered. I wondered if it moved the businessman, Malik Gopi.

I looked at Malik Gopi.

Gopi's eyes were wide open. He stuffed two triangles of Melakan *pan* into both sides of his mouth.

I have to relieve myself, said Malik Aiyaz, trying to suppress a yawn.

I'll come with you, said Kiwamul-mulk and they both left the room.

I know you think, Ahmadji, that I am just a businessman, said Malik Gopi, that my money has blinded me completely to other things. I used to be blinded by my own wealth. I made so much money I did not know what to do with it, or how to spend it. I couldn't fail. Everything I touched turned into gold. The eight ships I used for my Melaka ventures returned a thousandfold profit every year. I took pride in being one of the three people who control the vast realm of commerce on the Bahr-i-Hind with its three nodes, Surat, Melaka, and Ormuz. My Surat was the central node. One of my trading arms stretched to Melaka, the node governed by the *chetim* shahbandar, Nina Chatu. My other arm used to stretch to Hormuz where Sinbad's friend is in charge of the port. We are the three richest men in the world, we know the power of money. Malik Aiyaz with his Diu wants to be the fourth.

He paused.

Then, one day, Gopi continued, I decided to surrender my empire to my son, Amir Gopi, whom I had trained thoroughly in the techniques of business. I flung the papers sent by my spies and agents into boxes for storage. If you want it, Ahmadji, I will send you a jumble of material about the Portuguese. I have no use for it now.

I would like to read it, I said. The room was quiet, hushed, an occasional snore from Kiwam-ul-Mulk Sarang broke the silence. I am in the presence of a poet, I thought. I was fascinated.

Why why why, I asked myself, said Gopi. I got tired of making money, Ahmadji, very tired. I got sick of the world of trade, the sight of gold, the color of money. To what end, I thought, why be the slave of money. Let me become its master. I changed, I made it do my bidding. I made it feed the self I had starved all my life. I threw myself into the world of women and pleasure, into court intrigue and politics. I learned the art of controlling other human beings. I enjoyed myself. I enjoyed manipulating others. It was wonderful to control and outwit other human beings.

Then those miserable Portuguese beggars arrived. They came to hunt and steal, not to trade. They came, but didn't have any gold to pay for anything and had no trade goods to sell. The Portuguese have nothing. One of my Melakan trading vessels is worth more than all the ships that they send out to India.

Malik Aiyaz entered and Gopi's flow of words stopped suddenly.

Let's continue, Malik Aiyaz said. Let us, he said, listen to Ahmadji's account of the Diu battle.

We are tired, all of us, including Ahmadji, said Malik Gopi, it's getting too hot, we need to rest. Let's meet after the conversion ceremony. We agree that we cannot fight against the Portuguese. We have to use other weapons. I'll suggest other strategies we could use against the Portuguese. I'll tell the Sultan we'll send the report later.

A servant whispered in Sarang's ear.

I agree, Sarang said. I have to make arrangements for the conversion ceremony which will be held in a few days.

Malik Aiyaz reluctantly agreed.

NINETEEN

June, 1509
My room in the Makai Kothars granary, on Pawagadh hilltop
Written after my return from my visit to Champaner city
and João's letter to Frei António Louro and me

Abdul saw to it that I had my evening bath first and only after serving my evening meal, did he tell me that Frei António wanted to give me a packet.

Perhaps João has sent my papers back, I said to Abdul.

Yes, yes, that's it. I was happy. It would restore my faith in João.

Eat, Ahmadji, Abdul coaxed. And he served me with a tiny portion of mango pickle.

The Frei still doesn't know that you know Portuguese, Abdul said.

The Frei didn't know many things. That João had been his former classmate in Coimbra. That João had been a *degredado* who had turned Muslim. The Frei lived in his own world, with his faith and his prayers. The Portuguese hostages were confused. To them João was Jan Mirza, a Muslim teacher who, they didn't know why, had accompanied them from Surat to Champaner after the shipwreck at Dumas and the rescue and the riots in Surat. What they thought of me I do not know.

The Frei sent you this gift, said Abdul.

It was a robe made of gold brocade. Its mango patterned border had red and silver threads.

The Frei had another robe with him, Abdul continued, a green one with sequins that he gave me.

Abdul, usually a man of few words, now talks a great deal at mealtimes anticipating my replies and my reactions. I wondered why, and then realized he did it because João was not there. Abdul did it to keep me from talking and letting my food get cold. He would provide me with Champaner *khobor*, his Goan term for the news and gossip of the day. And he would stop as soon as I had finished my meal.

The Frei wants to sell the Sultan's gifts, Abdul said. It would be considered an insult to the Sultan if anyone else did it. But the Frei is a holy man. He wants to use the money to feed the poor. I was sent to the hostages at the *Hathikad* to fetch a friend for the Frei, Abdul continued, and Senhor Payo offered to come with me to visit the Frei. Yes, Ahmadbhai, Payo is here with the Frei. The Sultan was greatly concerned about the Frei's health.

Have they eaten, I asked.

Eat, Ahmadji, Abdul said. Yes, yes, Frei Louro and Payo Correia have eaten. Yes, yes, there's enough food for me.

A little more rice, Abdul said. Some buttermilk, he coaxed.

João had told us that the Portuguese hostages were finding it difficult to adjust to this food especially to the hot curry. They want bread, João said. There's no wheat grown in Gujarat. They'll have to get used to rice.

Payo Correia ate quite well, Abdul reported. The Frei ate very little. He stops eating as soon as his hunger is satisfied. The soldiers at the *Hathikad* camp crowd around to watch the Portuguese eating rice. They roar with laughter when they see them clutch the rice in their fists and push it into their mouths smearing their lips with the spicy curry. Like babies eating rice for the first time. Hot, hot, hot, the Portuguese say, sucking in air to cool their mouths and reaching out for water.

The women of the *haram*, continued Abdul, are dying to see the Portuguese eat their food. They keep on sending requests to the Sultan. But Kiwam-ul-mulk Sarang has advised against this. The women want to see the Frei too. Many many people want to see what a Christian holy man looks like.

The Portuguese have caused quite a stir in Champaner, I managed to bring out after a swallow of rice.

Please eat, Abdul said.

And he hurried on to tell me the *khobor* in Champaner.

The people in Champaner are deeply worried, Abdul said. About the Sultan, about his turning to religion, about the disturbances everywhere in Gujarat. The people believe he is no longer an effective ruler. What, they ask, will happen after the sultan dies. There are fears that something evil will happen, no one will say what. There will be the usual struggle for power. Who will be the Sultan, everyone asks. Some prefer Bahadur, the seven year old grandson, to his father, Prince Khalil Khan, the official successor. Questions are being asked about the successor. We need a strong Sultan, they say, not one who is just clement as his name, Khalil, states. He will be a mere puppet in the hands of Kiwam-ul-mulk Sarang and of Malik Gopi. The people dislike them both, they especially dislike Malik Gopi. He is not a Muslim, they say, he should not have been given such power in an Islamic land.

True, very true, I thought, pausing to lift a cucumber slice to my lips, then pushing away the *thali*.

The whole of Gujarat is in a state of turmoil.

The maulvi had talked to us in Diu about the Islamic rules of succession.

There are no established rules of succession, the maulvi had said. That's why there's bloodshed. That's why a Muslim ruler, once he occupies his throne, banishes his brothers or else has them killed. One of the Hormuz kings had the base of a redhot glowing bowl of burnished copper passed in front of the faces of his seven brothers, heavily bandaged except for the eyes. When the bandages were removed the faces were undamaged and their eyes were crystal clear, nothing was changed, but they were all blind.

Have some buttermilk, Abdul said, it's flavored with ginger and powdered cardamon. I'll tell you what was whispered in the bazaar today.

He set the buttermilk in front of me.

I took a sip.

Sultan Mahmud Begada, Abdul whispered, will be murdered.

Who, I asked, why, where.

The mahdawis, Abdul whispered. There's a rumor that an assassin has come all the way from Iran to do the killing. The mahdawis were outraged when their Mahdi was driven out of Gujarat on the orders of Sultan Begada. The vegetable seller from whom I bought some mangoes told me the mahdawis want vengeance. Have this mango slice.

No, I said, I feel full.

I wondered if it was true, what the maulvi had told João and me when he was in a bitter mood some time ago in Diu.

Take care, the maulvi had warned João and me, both of you are in danger.

Why, asked João, what have I done.

I live by myself, I said. I do not belong in this *samsāra*. I never ever want to get involved in anything.

You, Ahmadbhai, continued the maulvi, are hated by the Jain community, especially by the Jhaveris and the Chimanlal family. They may practise *ahimsa* and not kill any living thing. But they hire assassins to do their killing for the welfare of the community. And it's not a *pap* for them, a sin, as you, João, would say. Some people know that you, João, drink.

These be strange times, alas, the maulvi had sighed. How I wish I had followed Sayyid Muhammad Jaunpuri, the Mahdi, to Farah up in North India and had died with him there in 1505. His followers, the mahdawis, have lost the love he had for his people, his trust and faith. In less than five years the mahdawi movement has changed from a belief in love to a drive to power. It's not the people who have changed, but their leaders who have formed a secret band of assassins here in Gujarat to assume power.

I thought of João's belief that when religions lose the spiritual force of their beginnings they harden into churches and establish seats of power.

At first, the maulvi had said, the group consisted of dedicated believers who consider killing a sacred ritual act. For they never used poison or guns, only daggers.

That's nonsense, João had said, murder has no place in the Muslim tradition.

Only when it is justified, the maulvi had maintained, that's the true Islamic tradition. An unrighteous ruler has to be deposed by force or assassination. They do not call it murder but an execution, performed to free the community from an evil ruler.

I wondered what the true Islamic tradition was.

Alas, the maulvi had said, the mahdawi group has lost its idealism and become just a political sect. They have recruited people who are not even Muslims, and even Hindu thuggees. They give them hashish and promise them eternal happiness in paradise in the arms of houris.

Frei António and Senhor Payo Correia are waiting for you outside, Abdul said. Outside it had cooled down considerably. Clouds, black some of them, and grey, had gathered in the faraway west and I could smell the distant rain. The monsoon was late this year.

I greeted them both with a low bow. The Frei came up and gave me a double embrace in brotherly fashion.

My friend, the Frei said. He had bad breath.

Payo, taken aback on seeing the double embrace, did not offer me his hand.

Frei António took a small book from the inner pocket of his patched gown. It certainly wasn't my bundle of papers. It was the book of popular devotions he had read every day when we stopped for food and rest on our way from Dumas to Surat to Champaner. It was full of pretty pictures of virgins. It contained a series of short prayers. A *Book of Hours* it was called, so João had told me. The Frei then removed a thick packet and handed it to me. My hand shook a little with disappointment.

João told me to give you this packet to read, the Frei said in Portuguese.

I stared into his eyes without blinking.

Can you read Portuguese, the Frei asked.

I didn't reply.

I don't know why João asked me to show Ahmadji this letter, the Frei said to Payo. Perhaps Ahmadji will be able to read the passages that look like Portuguese but do not make any sense to me.

Can you read the Roman script, the Frei asked me.

I didn't reply. I didn't want to tell a lie.

He gave me the packet.

I'll go say my evening prayers, the Frei said. Come Payo.

It was a letter from João to Frei António. Louro

Frei António,

How strange to greet a ghost from a past I thought I had exorcized from my being and left behind in Coimbra so distant now in place, in time too. Has it changed at all, the Santa Cruz cathedral with its grey steps and its tall dark brown doors that Brother Clement always managed to open and close with ease. I was only twelve at that time.

It's the hinges and the balancing, Brother Clement would tell me when I asked him, you have to push the door at a certain point.

Do you remember Brother Clement, António. Perhaps you don't. He was the only one who didn't flatter you because you were the Prior's beloved nephew. He would reprimand you when you bullied the other boys. They would run away and you couldn't catch them because of that limp you were born with. And he would not eat the sweets that your mother would frequently send to the Cathedral for her brother the Prior who would have them distributed to all the priests. Brother Clement would give me some in secret.

How I used to envy you then, António. You had a rich mother, the Prior was your uncle, your future was assured, you would get a benefice. I, what was I, an orphan abandoned on the front steps of the Cathedral. The Prior knew who my mother was, but never told me who she was, even after she died. Poor I was, though I didn't know I was poor. Clever, yes I knew I was clever, but what good did that do me. Hungry, though then I didn't know what I was hungry for. I only knew I had an emptiness within me then, that I have never been able to fill.

I am writing this to you, sitting on a carpet, in the deep shade of a huge banyan tree, its branches spread so wide that it provides shade for our whole party of a hundred and fifty, not counting the horses, a welcome resting place on our way from Champaner to Vijayanagar. The midday sun is fierce, but it is cool here in the shade where I am sitting amid the twisted pillar roots that anchor this gigantic tree to earth, the sunlight filtered by the rustling palm wide banyan leaves.

I am reminded of the cathedral of Santa Cruz where I used to escape at times in the afternoons and lean against its gray pillars to watch the purified rays of sunlight stream through the stained glass windows. It is noisy all around me here under this tree, insects buzz, crows keep squawking incessantly above my head, people jabber to each other as they eat their meals, horses stamp and neigh, but I deliberately make myself deaf as I write and imagine myself in a dark Coimbra confessional talking to you.

How we two have changed, you and I. Yes, yes, I am a Muslim now. Does that horrify your Catholic soul. It should. Of course it should. Hellfire and damnation, that's what that preacher would have thundered at me, had he heard me recite the kalima, the Muslim Word. Do you remember that preacher, the one who came to Coimbra from Jerusalem to talk to us about the concept of mission "inter Saracenos et alios infideles."

Christianity is threatened today, the preacher thundered, and of all the threats none is as menacing as Islam. And he went on to shout out untruths and half-truths, about houris and the hundreds of wives that all infidels have, about the dangerous custom of having daily baths, and about the circling of a huge black stone as an act of worship, and about other demonic rites and prayers. He would always end by vehemently denouncing the prophet, may peace be on him, whose name he never could pronounce correctly.

He knew nothing, António. He was profoundly ignorant and misinterpreted everything about this religion that I have embraced and that fits me well like a well made garment in this part of the world. Why, you ask, why did you, João Machado, become Jan Mirza. I do not know, as my friend Ahmadji would say. I could offer any number of reasons, excuses perhaps, for becoming a Muslim. To save myself. No, not my soul, whatever that is, but my body. They would have killed me, those Arab Muslims in Mozambique when I was abandoned there as a degredado by Pedro Alvares Cabral had I not embraced Islam. At first I practiced taqiya without knowing I was practicing it. It is an accepted mode for Jewish conversos also. The word cannot be translated into Christian terms, it is more than just hypocrisy. It refers to the pretense of accepting beliefs to which one is secretly opposed. But one cannot abandon religion like a suit of clothes. I clung inwardly to Catholicism, while outwardly I was a practicing Muslim.

I studied Arabic, learned to speak it fluently, much better than the Mozambique Arabs who were mostly traders. I could handle both colloquial and educated Arabic. Gradually, a kind of fascination with the religion led me to memorize the Qu'ran. I even studied some hadiths which are records of deeds or words of the Prophet of Islam and of his companions. I began to appreciate Islam's cultural context. I studied the sacred texts in great detail. I came to be in great demand as a preacher, and was invited to Sofala to teach in its madrasa.

I became Jan Mirza, a Muslim teacher who was also considered a holy man. My disguise was perfect, my accent flawless. My skin turned a deep brown in the sun. No one could tell I was a Christian. No one knew I was Portuguese. I picked up Swahili and traveled slowly up the coast of East Africa, from Sofala to Malindi, then to Mogadishu, preaching to the people, teaching in madrasas, amazed at the new world and the new peoples, and the different religions I encountered.

I also set myself a challenge. I would fulfill my unspoken promise to Frei Henrique who had befriended me. I would discover the truth about Preste João.

Alas, Frei António, the truth was bleak, one that the King of Portugal, Dom Manuel, will not like. Nor will Frei Luís do Salvador. Did you know him, a fanatic friar who came to India with Frei Henrique in Senhor Cabral's fleet, fired with mad dreams of converting the whole world with the help of the mighty Preste João. I am sure that before he left Portugal Frei Luís had secret talks with King Manuel and his advisers who wanted to enlist the help of the Preste to destroy the infidels and capture both Jerusalem and the spice trade.

Frei Luís told me that Vasco da Gama, who had carried with him a letter for Preste João, was told at Malindi in 1498 that the Preste was a king of a faraway inland kingdom that could only be reached on camelback. That I discovered was not true at all. The story is a myth based on an anonymous letter, a story magnified by the Christian imagination for over three hundred years, that beyond the Muslim regions lay a Christian kingdom. That perhaps, provided the impetus that led to the exploration of new worlds.

Alas, António, Preste João is not a glorious descendant of the Magi. He is not the Emperor of the Indies. Nor does the tomb of the Apostle Saint Thomas lie in his land. Nor is he the possessor of infinite wealth. He is not a mighty Christian potentate with twelve kings under him whose empire lies beyond the Muslim lands. He is just the king of Ethiopia, his people call him Elati, the ruler of a land that lies along the shores of the Red Sea.

How can he be of any help to the Christian world, Frei António. Frei Luís thought the Preste would help conquer the infidels, and help convert the whole world to Christ. He didn't know that the Christians of Ethiopia are surrounded by hostile Muslims who fight with them continually. He didn't know that there are no Christians on the east coast of Africa. That there are just a handful of Christians, the Saint Thomas Christians, in South India, and that they are traders and pepper merchants, not fighters. Alas, António, alas, we have to give up the old dream of bringing about the conversion of all the peoples of the world.

I know from overhearing your talks with the Portuguese captives when Ahmadji and I were taking them from coastal Surat to Champaner that you too want to follow the Franciscan dream. In Socotra, you told them, it was easy. Hundreds clamored to be baptized in the church of Our Lady of Victory which had been a mosque that Afonso do Albuquerque had converted into a church in 1507. Here in Cambaya, you told the captives, among infidels and gentiles, conversion would be very difficult. You urged them to be strong in the faith, and set an example as good Christians.

No, no, it won't be easy, friend António, to convert the people here. Cambaya is not Socotra. The Socotrans, I was told by a Syrian Christian priest of the Saint Thomas Christians, had been converted centuries ago by the apostle Saint Thomas before he landed at Cranganore on the west coast of India. The Socotrans now practise a primitive form of Christianity polluted by pagan customs. Maybe that is why it was easy to convert them, don't you think.

Convert, is that the word I want.

How I wish I had your innocent faith, Frei António. You want to lead a new type of crusade, armed not with the sword but with trust in God. You want to imitate Christ, and live a life of poverty and suffering, and, if you merited it, endure martyrdom for the love of Christ.

Your words, António, your dreams, have disturbed my inner being. All along the way, after Ahmadji and I rescued you at Surat, I began to ask myself questions, one after the other. Who am I. A Catholic. A Muslim. Does a religion change a self. What about religions one merely studies, like Hinduism, Buddhism, Jainism, that I began to explore when I came to India. I find myself today in a world where different religions swirl by me and into me. What then am I, and who.

I do not know, as my friend Ahmadji would say.

An orphan, a traveller burdened with the baggage of the west who has wandered through the east not knowing what my self has discarded, what picked up. I want to be a wanderer again, Padre António, like I was before I stopped wandering and was muta' married and settled in Diu and got involved with Ishak Khan and Malik Gopi and lost my reputation as a holy man, and found I had to make money. I found myself in the coils of samsāra. I am so restless, so tired of my self, my selves. Isn't the self a Heraclitean flow, or is the self just a Buddhist Jaina illusion. I do not know, as you know who would say. I am all confused. It shows, doesn't it, in the way this letter keeps wandering and does not stay in focus.

Like my language, which also is strange. It is a strange Portuguese if you allow your ears to listen to it, with a rhythm and an idiom it has absorbed from other languages I know, Arabic and Persian and Gujarati, Swahili too, a mixture of languages. My friend, Ahmadji, uses this kind of language too, mating words together. There must be a connection between language and the self. Perhaps Ahmadji and I share a self.

But enough of that, that's staccato speculation. Ahmadji would not like that phrase. Too clever, he would say. Let me get back to questions about conversion. About which I've brooded so long, so often. Here, in India, can conversion be just an internal, a purely private matter. One cannot live, Why do I think of Saint Augustine, by oneself, to oneself. In isolation, like an outcast. Has there to be mass conversions, conversion of a whole community. Involving beliefs, customs, habits, practices. Can force be used....

Ahmadji, my friend, I had to break off this letter to Frei António because the whole caravan has to get ready to continue our journey towards Vijayanagar. It is evening now, the sun's rays slant through the rustling leaves. We will travel through the cool of the night and arrive at our next stop in the early morning. There I will write another letter to you, a long one, and comment on your unfinished account which I've borrowed and which I haven't finished reading and which disturbs me and excites me and makes me think and compels me to offer suggestions which you, I'm sure, will not like. I may also write to the Frei setting down my thoughts on conversion.

But there are more urgent matters I have to set down here before the regular horse courier for Champaner leaves. No explanations now. There's need for absolute secrecy. Malik Gopi's spies will, I am sure, read what I have written to the Frei who will be subjected to temptation. How, I do not know, but he will not succumb. Vora, I am sure, is one of Gopi's spies. They have a copy of Ishak's seal and will use it to reseal this letter.

The dotstobeputinravenshooterbegdoaljulfari threeinone to be dispatched by hooknoseprestekhorasani during the conversion ceremony. Remember your use of language, your technique of mating. The portuguese script hides Arabicgujarati sounds.

What a strange letter this is. I spent the rest of the day trying to decipher what João meant but without success.

The conversion ceremony will be held in the palace courtyard in Champaner.

TWENTY

*T*hird week of June, 1509,
Written in my room in the Makai Kothars, Pawagadh
After my return from the conversion ceremony in Champaner

The conversion ceremony of the four Portuguese captives was held in the palace courtyard down in Champaner where the people assembled every Wednesday for the royal *darshan*. The sultan's advisers had first suggested that it be conducted in the Hall of Public Audience. But that wouldn't hold many people, the Sultan observed. Then the advisers wanted him to sit high above the crowd in the pillared *jharokha* window.

There you'll be safe from danger, Malik Aiyaz said, there may be assassins in the crowd.

There, your face lit up by the morning sun, you'll radiate power and majesty, said Malik Gopi the flatterer.

Kiwam-ul-Mulk Sarang pointed out that the sultan would get a better view of the whole ceremony from the commanding window.

The sultan listened carefully but did not take their advice. I shall not be a sultan on that day, he said, nor will I act in my role as defender of the faith. On that day I will be just one of the faithful to welcome into our midst those who want to make their submission to God.

The *alim* of Champaner had stated that no formal ritual requirement had been set down in the sacred texts. The *kalima* had to be recited. It was the first of the five pillars of practice, a rejection of the false followed by an affirmation of the truth. There is no god but God. Muhammad is the Apostle of God. The sultan agreed. Would the people have to turn their faces in the direction of the *Ka'aba*. No, said the Champaner *alim*, a courtyard has no *mihrab* niche. It is not a place for offering prayer.

The sultan took an active part in planning the whole ceremony. It was to be simple but dignified. He refused to sit on a throne. Instead, a plain three foot high dais, carpetless and made of wood, was placed in the middle of the courtyard. The whole of Champaner was urged to come and bear witness. Special invitations were sent to the holy men of all faiths, Muslim and Hindu and Jain and Buddhist, and a special place was assigned to them near the sultan. Everyone, including the sultan, and his guards, would wear white garments of plain homespun cotton of the kind usually exported to Sofala and to Melaka. Malik Gopi and Malik Aiyaz undertook to provide the clothes for the whole assembly. The people would remove their footwear, purify themselves using the water in the two fountains outside the palace gate, change into new clothes to signify purity and simplicity and, directed by the sultan's guards, assemble in orderly fashion in the courtyard.

That will prevent weapons from being concealed and carried in. I will have my spies near the gate, said Malik Aiyaz. Anyone looking suspicious will be searched.

I will place some guards around the dais and among the crowd as added protection, Kiwam-ul-Mulk Sarang said.

Malik Aiyaz supplied me with all these details about the ceremony. I had told him that there would be an assassination attempt during the ceremony, though I didn't tell him from whom I got the information.

He wasn't surprised.

We are expecting something to happen, but we do not know when or how, Malik Aiyaz told me. We are taking all precautions, but it is impossible to distinguish the mahdavis from the other Muslims. I wish the Sultan would realize how difficult it is to protect him. Those who are good and innocent never believe anyone will harm them. One has to be extra careful.

I dislike ceremonies and I didn't want to go to this one which did not have any meaning for me, an unbeliever. I knew the four Portuguese captives wanted to become Muslims only because they wanted a more comfortable life. The sultan thought the ceremony would proclaim the triumph of Islam. I wonder what João, an unbeliever like me, would have said.

João's note confused me thoroughly. The letter to Frei António was written in Portuguese, and Surati Vora, Malik Gopi's spy, who was in our class, had surely read it, but it contained absolutely nothing about the assassination. In the note to me João had used the Roman script in which Portuguese is written. Frei Louro could read it but was not able to understand the words which released Arabic and Gujarati sounds that Surati Vora might be able to understand.

João didn't take any chances. He had cleverly concealed his message in the last three sentences with the two serpentine words that baffled me completely. I repeated them over, and over, and over again all through the night.

    dotstobeputinravenshooterbegdoaljulfari

and

    threeinone

and

    hooknoseprestekhorasani

Desperate, restless, my mind whirling, I tried and I tried. I broke up the two long words into separate words, divided the words into letters, into sounds, into sound combinations. The word begdo stood for Sultan Begada. And *hooknose* stood out. But who were *beputin* and *rasani*. To whom was the message dispatched. What about the art of mating. It didn't make any sense at all. My head kept churning. It was a very long night.

I was about to fall asleep when Abdul blew out the lamp. It was very early in the morning. Outside, even at the top of Pawagadh, it was still dark. Abdul said it was time for me to leave for the ceremony.

Frei António has said his prayers, and is waiting outside for you. I gave him some coffee, Abdul said, and he handed me a cup. Senhor Payo does not want to accompany the Frei.

We walked down in the cool darkness of the early morning, the Frei in his patched brown cloak, raising his eyes to the heavens, mumbling his prayers all the way downhill to Champaner. And I, equally desperate, repeating to myself the two words that coiled and uncoiled endlessly in my mind. Malik Aiyaz had wanted me to be in the courtyard before the crowd arrived. He was at the entrance gate before I got there, and had changed into a plain white shirt and pyjamas. I did too. Frei António refused. Malik Aiyaz offered to replace the patched cloak with new silk garments later. The Frei was stubborn. He shook his head vigorously. Malik Aiyaz took the Frei to the Sultan who, to my surprise, was sitting cross legged on the carpetless dais in the middle of the courtyard with his head bowed down. He had been the first to arrive for the ceremony, even before Malik Aiyaz.

The Sultan looked up.

This holy man does not need to dress in white, the sultan said, his inside is pure. And he bade the Frei sit next to him on the dais. The holy men should not be made to change clothes for this ceremony, he told Malik Aiyaz. The clothes they wear, like them, are holy and pure.

They formed a strange pair on the dais, the sultan dressed in white, his head bowed, his fingers counting the ninety nine beads of his rosary, and the Frei kneeling beside him, his neck stretched out, the silver crucifix on his chest, his hands folded in prayer, his eyes raised to the skies above.

Malik Aiyaz suggested we sit next to each other at the left edge of the dais so that both of us could see everyone who entered the courtyard which was soon crowded with people. The Sultan invited some of the common people to sit with him on the dais. From an adjacent courtyard beyond the wall arose the tantalizing smell of cooking. I looked around in vain for Hooknose. It was difficult to distinguish faces in that sea of white that surrounded me. The only spot of color was to the left a little beyond the open space in front of the sultan. The holy men sat there, a few clad in yellow. Many wore saffron robes. There were sadhus with ash smeared faces and chests. Others were dressed in white with face cloths across their mouths to prevent the swallowing of insects. They were Jain *munis*, five of them. And there were a large number of Muslim fakirs clad in rags, their hair tied in topknots.

My eyelids hung heavy over my eyes. I turned my head, made a great effort, and looked carefully at the sea of white, and then at the group of holy men. I was looking for Hooknose. I wondered why the *munis* had come. They were supposed to have abandoned this *samsāra*. Perhaps they had come for the feast after the ceremony. Something about the group disturbed me. One kept rubbing two fingers of his right hand with his thumb as if counting money or the beads of an imaginary rosary. The other *muni* kept constantly adjusting his face cloth as if it was too tight for him. I managed to keep my eyes open, and I tried to keep my mind open, even as I remembered as in a blur the two serpentine words

dotstobeputinravenshooterbegdoaljulfari

and

hooknoseprestekhorasani

wondering what message João meant to convey to me. So intent was I that I was not aware of it when the Champaner *alim* stood up on the sultan's right and began to speak. The ceremony had begun.

My brothers, he said loudly.

The crowd fell silent.

My fellow Muslims, he continued, we have gathered here to welcome four persons into our faith. Soon they will put away their former idols, and join Islam. Allah alone will be their God. The four have received instructions from four assistants who will help them recite the *kalima* and admit them to the faith. Each one will then announce to the whole assembly the Muslim name he has adopted. He will then become one with the community. The ceremony will end with a common meal to which the great Sultan has invited you all.

Let the four be brought in so that fellow Muslims can be witnesses.

Over my right shoulder I could see tears streaming continuously down the Frei's face as he looked toward the entrance gate watching the first Portuguese hostage accompanied by an assistant slowly walk down the path of certain damnation to recite the *kalima*.

They moved towards the dais.

The first one, I heard the Champaner *alim* say, will be helped in his recitation by a famous Khorasani *alim* who has recently arrived from Persia.

Everyone's eyes were focused on the hostage who began reciting the *kalima* garbling the unfamiliar words, mispronouncing them. The Sultan was leaning forward eager to bear witness to the first of the conversions. I kept looking at the Frei when suddenly one of the words of the *alim* hit me.

Khorasani.

The word struck me like a lightning bolt. My mind stopped whirling. I made the connections João wanted me to make. I put in the dots. Malik Aiyaz was the raven shooter. I was al julfari. I mated the words and remembered what Abdul had told me.

The Khorasani would assassinate the Begdo.

Stop, I yelled, stop, stop, the Khorasani is an assassin.

I jumped up and tried to run towards the sultan but I stumbled and fell. There were too many people in between. The guards rushed towards me. There was confusion everywhere.

The Khorasani snatched a dagger from the inner waistband of his loose trousers, and bounded on to the dais, his right arm raised to stab the sultan in the chest. It was about to descend when Frei António flung himself on the sultan, caught him in an tight embrace, and received the point of the dagger in the right side of his neck. The guards rushed toward the Sultan. The assassin was quickly dragged away.

Don't kill him, the sultan shouted. Help the Frei.

The ash brown cloak of the Frei was covered with blood.

Hooknose had to be nearby. I turned around, and then I saw two Jain *munis* run towards the dais. One of them stumbled, and then I saw the facecloth slip from the face of the one in front. It was Hooknose.

Look out, I yelled to Malik Aiyaz who avoided Hooknose's dagger blow by swerving suddenly to the side. I bent over Malik Aiyaz who sprawled on the ground and looked up at me. He wasn't hurt. Hooknose snarled viciously, then jumped towards me. The dagger hit the bone in my left shoulder and sent me sprawling on the dais.

Look out, Ahmadji, said Malik Aiyaz.

I turned and saw the other *muni* lift up his dagger. He was about to stab me straight in the heart. He couldn't have missed. Eyes, narrowed with hate and looking like arrow points, stared piercingly into mine.

Usha, I said softly and shut my eyes.

I waited for the dagger to descend. I was calm, I was at peace. She would be there waiting for me, and we'd be together again. I shut my eyes tight and waited for the dagger blow.

Usha, I said again.

When I opened my eyes, I couldn't see the dagger point. The *muni's* eyes looked softly at me. Tears had cleansed the hate away.

The *muni* was Usha's father.

I had to stop.

I had to stop writing this account and I went out of the room to look up at the distant stars, beyond the Kali Mata temple.

Too many confusions were whirling in and around me again. My feelings at the moment of recognition, re aroused by my re creation in language, were and were not the same as those at that actual moment of experience which is disappearing and yet exists for me as a blur of memory. João would have pounced on that last phrase. Vague, he would have said, pretentious. I wish he was here in Champaner. We would have talked about writing, and the process of memory, and whether language filters experience and purifies it. Talked also about the moment of composition and about my recurring problem. What's the best time to write about an experience.

I begin writing again.

I am calm again now as I re experience the moment of recognition. I was in a daze then, trying to compel my mind to stop thinking, feeling no pain though I could see drops of my blood on the dais, trying desperately to stop the jumbled swirl of feelings within me, which were like the people all around the courtyard, a sea of confusion, not knowing where to go or what to do.

I saw and heard things very distinctly.

Kill the Khorasani, kill the Jains, shouted the people in front, surging towards the dais.

The guards hurried the *munis* away. The Champaner *alim* raised his arms for silence, and from the dais Kiwam-ul-Mulk Sarang announced that the Sultan was not hurt. Go back, go home, he shouted, but the crowd did not listen. They kept milling around not knowing what to do. Then a voice shouted, look up, look there. The sultan, in simple white, his face radiantly lit up by the morning sun, stood in the *jharokha*, erect, motionless, his right hand raised high. Next to him stood Frei António with a white bandage around his neck. I heard the crowd shout with joy, Begdo, Begdo. Someone whispered into my ear. I tried to say something. The shouting grew distant.

It was then that I must have fainted.

Abdul told me that I had told Malik Aiyaz after they revived me that I didn't want to be taken to his Champaner house, but wanted to return to the top of Pawagadh. The physician had bandaged my shoulder wound. There was no poison on the dagger tip, he had said, it will take a few days to heal. Let him rest and give him plenty of fruit.

They carried me up in a *dhooli*.

Abdul hid away my papers for three days, and then on the fourth morning I discovered them on my table with my pen and the ink bottle. The tiedup folder with the torn *Biblia Sagrada* sheets lay next to my papers. João had said the sheets would help me understand, but what he did not say. The first page, sea water stained, was titled *The Song of Songs*. The first two lines had been underlined by João.

Beija-me, dando me o osculo da sua boca
Porque os tuas peitos são melhores do que o vinho.

Strange lines in a religious book, I thought, as I translated them.

Kiss me with the kisses of thy mouth
For thy love is better than wine.

There was João's note in the margin. To woo the Frei.

Cryptic, as usual.

Abdul brought coffee for me as he did every morning. I wanted spicy food. But Abdul would boil plain lentils and vegetables for me. It's good for you, he would say, good for your blood, and then coax me to eat with small helpings of lime pickle. Oranges, figs, and other delicacies would be brought up for me by the servants of Malik Aiyaz. Every day Abdul would go down to Champaner to inform the physician about my condition, and he would bring ointments and lotions for my wound. He would also bring messages, and the *khobor* of the day which he relayed to me in the evenings with my food.

Hooknose, Abdul told me, had confessed to conspiring with Ishak Khan and had had his right hand chopped off at the elbow, and had been banished to the island of Sankhodar. The Khorasani was tortured, but he wouldn't reveal the names of the fellow mahdawis in the conspiracy. He thundered forth a prophecy. That Champaner would become the abode of the tiger and the lion, that thorns would grow where flowers now blossomed, and that the winds of destruction would shatter its palaces and its buildings. Because of the sultan's wishes he wasn't put to death, but loaded with chains and taken to Cambay to await the first ship bound for Hormuz.

About Sheth Chimanlal Abdul could tell me only that he had been set free. I had sent a message through Abdul to the sultan to request that the sheth not be harmed in any way. The *munis* were questioned by Malik Aiyaz himself, but all three chose to remain silent. They are *munis*, the silent ones, said one of their followers. The sheth, the follower went on to explain, had experienced *vairāgya*, weariness with things of this world, and had been about to choose the path of *nivrtti*, of withdrawal from this *samsāra*, when he was informed of my arrival in Champaner.

The sheth was strongly advised not to seek vengeance, but hatred had lingered on till tears washed the hate away. He would have to return to Patan, undergo *posadha*, a period of rigorous fasting and penance, and then beg public forgiveness for all offences, intentional and unintentional. He could then perform his own funeral rites, and walk again the path of renunciation.

I thought suddenly of what my hakim had said, that I had to return to Diu to heal my self.

One has to pay one's debts before one dies, the pandit had solemnly said one day, staring vacantly at the tip of his nose, then turning it to João, to the maulvi and to me, when we were discussing the problem of death and the afterlife. Not just money, but *rrinn*, the pandit had emphasized, prolonging the r and n sounds, the debts to our ancestors and to the world we have been flung into.

I wanted to, but I didn't, ask the pandit whether he meant *samsāra*. I'm slowly realizing a now obvious truth that one must plunge into *samsāra* before one can renounce it, the truth that one cannot live with oneself, by oneself, for oneself.

Malik Aiyaz sent me a message that the Frei was lonely and would like my company in Malik Gopi's guesthouse. He himself would appreciate my advice in matters concerning the Portuguese.

Don't let the Frei know you know Portuguese, Malik Aiyaz said, messages might come from Cochin for the Frei.

The Frei had been taken to the guesthouse near the spacious compound of Malik Gopi's huge mansion in Champaner where he was recovering slowly. His stab wound wasn't deep but he had lost a great deal of blood. The patched and tattered cloak had been washed and repaired, and lined with light blue satin by one of the sultan's tailors so that it almost looked like new.

The Sultan would visit Frei Louro every morning after the Frei returned from the *Hathikad* where he went, the doctor had warned him not to, to say Mass for the Portuguese hostages. They didn't talk, the Sultan and the Frei. The Frei would kneel down and raise his eyes to the sky in prayer, while the Sultan would bow his head and count his prayer beads.

TWENTY-ONE

*M*onsoon months, 1509, Champaner,
Written in Malik Gopi's guesthouse

I feel very uncomfortable, I don't know why, in Malik Gopi's guesthouse,
so restless that it is difficult to sit down in one place and write. I pace up
and down. I go to the kitchen half where the familiar smells of Abdul's
cooking reassure me. I don't mind staring blankly at the tiny black iron
gate stuck in the five foot thick twenty two foot high wall covered with
glass fragments on the top that rises a few feet behind the kitchen entrance. The shrieks and giggles of Malik Gopi's women on the other side
worry me a little. Then I go to the front half. From the porch I can see the
edge of the royal library a quarter mile away and in the distance, against
the blue skyline, the soaring minars of the Jami Masjid from where the
adhan, the call for prayer, summons the faithful.

My nextdoor neighbor, Frei António, prays quite frequently on his
side of our common porch, both his arms outflung against the porch wall,
his eyes raised high to the heavens, the silver crucifix shining on his chest.
I have heard him pray and weep for the four Portuguese converts, and for
João for whom he prays passionately everyday.

Let my cousin João return to the Holy Faith soon, he entreats God on
his knees.

How João could be his cousin, I do not know. Nothing in this world of
things disturbs the Frei, except matters of belief. He never complains and
has never complained.

Except once, when he couldn't find his *Book of the Hours*.

It must have fallen out during the conversion ceremony, the Frei told
Payo. Or when my cloak had to be washed and repaired. How I wish I had
my breviary with me.

The Frei knows the book by heart, especially the *Hours* of the Virgin

Mary. But he would like to look at the pictures and meditate on their significance. He is greatly concerned about the welfare of his fellow prisoners who would have been comforted by the pictures of angels and of the Virgin Mary. Some days he brings one or two of them to the guesthouse to hear their confession.

Otherwise he lives in his own world. He feels at home anywhere.

I do not. My self is always acutely aware of my surroundings, and this guesthouse disturbs me. No, it's not the discomfort of my wound. That has almost healed now. Nor is it the prickly heat. It's something I can't put my finger on, a faint smell of stale perfume, a sense of being watched.

Abdul thinks it is because of the change in altitude. The air at Pawagadh is clearer, purer. And besides, the monsoon has arrived, Abdul says, so that it is stickier here down in Champaner city. Abdul is glad we have moved into Malik Gopi's magnificent guesthouse.

He loves it here, especially the clean kitchen with its brass utensils. He prepares food for Frei Louro and me, simple food, rice and dhal and vegetables. The Frei refuses to eat the rich oily preparations from Malik Gopi's kitchen, the sweetmeats made of cream and sugar. I dislike them too. So Abdul eats the food that is sent to us everyday. He shares it with Malik Gopi's servants who help him in the kitchen.

At times when the rains stop for a day or two, Abdul serves our meals on a floor covering on the front porch. Most of the time we eat our food in the front half sitting on the red floral pilecarpet strewn with embroidered cushions and with bolsters covered with dark green velvet. Abdul has taught the Frei how to eat rice without soiling the palm of his right hand. I tried to get the Frei to enjoy his simple food, but he is always in a hurry as if any kind of enjoyment is a *pāp*, a sin. He then goes to his room to pray.

I take a nap after the afternoon meal. That's when my discomfort slowly drifts away, and I drift slowly into sleep. I stare with distaste at the wall hangings, tightly stretched from floor to ceiling, crowded with violet rosettes that stand out against a ground of gold, covering every inch of wall space. At the corners hang four rectangular silk *patolas* that are usually used for wedding saris. They were dyed in the double ikat technique, of the kind Malik Gopi regularly exports to Melaka, each worth a thousand mahmudis. Then I look up at the ceiling which is a deepblue silk canopy studded with diamond stars, the Pole Star stands out bright among them. The first time I had looked up a memory of a distant time of peace when I lay trembling with happiness, waiting, had stirred within me then it ebbed away.

Why, why, I wonder. Why did Malik Gopi want such luxury for the Frei whom he disliked. My room was an exact replica of the Frei's, even the furnishings and hangings are the same. Malik Gopi's servants told

Abdul that their master always used the guesthouse to lavishly entertain ambassadors from Hormuz and Mamluk Egypt and distant Bahrein.

Don't you find it strange, Abdul asked me, that these hangings are crisp and fresh, and not mildewed in spite of the monsoon.

Tell me, I said.

Abdul had been greatly impressed, he wanted to talk.

It has been constructed of white ant proof wood from Melaka, Abdul explained. He took me all around the guesthouse. The brick walls, Abdul pointed out, even the wall space between your two rooms, are five feet deep all around, they are but they don't look fortresslike. The garden scenes painted on the outer wall with their fountains and waterfalls make this guesthouse appear to float up out of the ground. And there are no windows, the doors always seal tight, no moisture gets in. It's very cool and comfortable.

I agreed.

I didn't tell Abdul, but it was my inner I that did not feel at ease here. I would, when it didn't rain, leave in the early morning, and return in time for the afternoon meal with Frei António. I would wander about the broad avenues of Muslim Champaner and watch the city still in the process of being built.

The Bhils were busy digging circular wells in different parts of the city. Workmen were paving the broad avenue that led from the north palace gateway to the Hathikad. Mansions and manzils were being constructed for the amirs and the nobles. One of the master builders from Gilan in Persia, explained the layout of a manzil complex with its spiral water channels, its well laid gardens, its horse stables, the main building made of basalt blocks on the outside and bricks on the inside, the zenana houses built of beautiful yellowish Sankheda sandstone. Most impressive were the masjids which were being built everywhere. I watched the builders putting finishing touches to the Nagina masjid. Thin slabs of marble were being transformed into exquisite arabesque and silken filigree screens for its *jali* windows.

I had wanted this Hindu land, the sultan had said, transformed into a Muslim landscape crowded with mosques and madrasas and hamams. That's necessary for the process of conversion. I have fulfilled my duty to Islam.

The Sultan now was more interested in human beings than in buildings and matters of state, and spent most of his time with the Frei. He was anxious about the Frei's health especially about the persistent cough that had developed after the monsoon had set in. When he was told that the Frei had sometimes to say mass outside in the rain, the sultan arranged for a small house to be built in one day as a chapel for the hostages in Hathikad. The sultan's own hakim had to give a report on the Frei's condition.

The holy man's wound will heal in a few days. But, said the palace hakim, he does not eat proper food, that's why he is weak. He feels quite anxious, his heart is burdened with sadness. He needs someone to look after him. His nose, the hakim pointed out, is long and pointed, his complexion red and warm and moist. It is clear what that signifies.

But he is not married, the sultan said.

That explains it, said the palace hakim. The holy man must be given stimulating food, and he must be provided with a woman. Coitus, the hakim continued, keeps one physically and mentally healthy. The sperm, if retained for a long time in the body, releases vapors that give rise to anxiety and affect the heart.

Let the holy man practice coitus in a fragrant atmosphere, the hakim continued. The holy man should eat plenty of bananas, and cabbage and beans, and chick peas twice a day. The foul vapors inside his belly need to be expelled. I will provide some aphrodisiac if needed. His long nose tells me he'll not need it.

The Sultan consulted with his advisers about the Frei's condition.

The holy man has to be restored to health, the Sultan said. He saved my life. I want to make sure that the ailments of his body are cured. I want him to live for a very long time.

The Champaner *alim* announced that celibacy is condemned, and that the holy traditions state that when any servant of God marries, he perfects half of his religion.

But infidel priests are not allowed to marry, said the Sultan.

Malik Gopi said he would arrange some entertainment to make the Frei enjoy himself so as to heal his heart.

Malik Gopi, said the Sultan, why don't you arrange for courtesan Champa to comfort the holy man.

Malik Gopi remained silent.

The Champaner court knew about Champa, Toghan's beautiful courtesan, who was forced by Ishak Khan to go to the stable of Malik Gopi. That will settle all your debts, said Malik Gopi to Ishak.

I'll kill that Hindu, said Toghan.

I tried to send the Frei some courtesans, Malik Gopi said to the Sultan, but the Frei got furious and ran away.

Kiwam-ul-Mulk Sarang stated that he and Malik Gopi would arrange a ceremony to honor the Frei in the Hall of Public Audience.

Ahmad ibn Madjid, they tell me the Frei eats only the food that you provide, said Malik Gopi. Give him bananas and chick peas, and plenty of milk and honey. They will be sent from the royal kitchen.

Abdul was horrified when I told him what he had to cook for the Frei.

Chick peas are very nourishing, he cried out, but eating them every day will cause flatulence.

That stupid hakim, I said, believes that flatulence will cause an erection to occur, and that the Frei's penis will rise upward like his eyes toward the high heavens.

I was bitter, angry and disgusted, disgusted with myself, angry with the world, uncomfortable, I hadn't heard again from João, I missed my papers, I missed Diu and my blackrock promontory, and my house near the sea and the palm trees leaning toward the sea. I was bitterly angry with myself for not telling the Frei I knew Portuguese. And I found myself angry with the Frei too because he was so ignorant about the world. But I knew the Frei wasn't to blame. He was an innocent.

I wish I could talk with the Frei to find out what's it like to talk with innocence. I find myself now wanting to be with people, to listen to their voices. I miss my João, especially our talks on the blackrock promontory in Diu where he would let his imagination go.

Consider India and Ceylon, he had said.

His eyes gleamed, then he looked at the horizon.

I see Ceylon as a teardrop, no, no, a warm pearl, poised to drop, moist and cinnamoned, from the very tip of India, which I see as a hot juicy triangle, perfumed with rich spices, smooth and soft as sun warmed silk, its aroma maddening the senses so that all the peoples of the world are driven to enter her to assuage their desires.

At the Santa Cruz monastery in Coimbra they had told us about Alexander the Great's invasion of northwest India for plunder and gold. The Arabs and the Persians, armed with their beliefs and their goods, left behind their barren deserts, and traveled over land and sea to settle in India as traders, as conquerors, and then as rulers. And now, the Portuguese, driven by dreams and the power of new knowledge have arrived here, lured by the smell of spices and Christians.

He stopped abruptly, lost in his own thoughts, looking at the horizon.

I wanted him to continue. What will happen, what will happen, I asked.

I wish I knew, João said.

He was cryptic, as usual.

Abdul told me that Malik Gopi had sent me a wooden box which he had opened.

It was packed to the top with papers of all kinds, news reports, documents, lists, gossip, narrative accounts, that Malik Gopi's spies had sent him, not arranged in order but flung haphazardly together.

Malik Gopi kept himself well informed about all that happened in the major ports of both coasts. He had spies everywhere. He knew all that happened in Kannanur, Goa, Calicut, Bhatkal, Kollam, and even in the hinterlands of Pulicat and Negapatam from where the Chetim traders sent their ships and goods to Melaka and Pegu. He knew the world of fine textiles and diamonds and precious stones. His servants kept a record of the arrival and departure of trading ships, the interflow of inland goods, and the movement of commodities for the export trade. And he was an expert in the art of controlling the market.

Two years ago he bought up the year's output of Cambay cornelians because he came to know, even before his Melakan rival, Nina Chatu, that the King of Melaka's son wanted only cornelians for his wedding. Last year, Abdul was told, Gopi cornered all the roses in the Surat market for a week to celebrate Champa's birthday. As he himself had said, he was a trader king, one of the rulers of a vast maritime world.

It was this world of money and trade that Malik Gopi had given up. The papers were of no use to him now.

It took me a long time to rearrange the reports of Gopi's agents so that I could get a chronological view of the arrival of the Portuguese into our waters in 1498 and what happened thereafter. I myself had been a witness at the very moment when the three ships of Vasco da Gama had dropped anchor at Pantalayani twelve miles to the north of Calicut. But I was ill at that time because of the excessive drinking to reduce the pain of the arrow wound, and so I don't know what happened to the Portuguese at Calicut. Abdul arranged a boat for the five of us, I must not forget Yasmin, to be taken to Kannanur.

I remember João's image of India as a moist triangle but find I cannot accept João's image of the Portuguese entry into our world as a form of rape. After I read what Malik Gopi's Calicut agent had written about the behavior of the Portuguese in 1498, it was the first of the many narrative accounts in Gopi's box, I began to realize that the Portuguese when they first came were viewed as comic figures.

Not *vidushakas*, who always know they are *vidushakas*. But clowns strutting about on the stage of history, who later turned into embodiments of power.

Let me set down here the report, the title is mine, that the Tunisian agent sent to Malik Gopi in September 1498.

Christians and Spices
 A report on the arrival of the Portuguese in Calicut in the year 1498
 Written in Arabic by our man from Tunis in the year 904 Hegira and sent to
Malik Gopi, the chief merchant trader of Gujarat

My friend Al Masud was bargaining with a fishwife for a mess of
large blacktailed prawns that she had spread out on a plank on her basket,
when I saw the stranger step out of a fishing boat and walk awkwardly up the sandy beach at the mouth of the Elatur river. Children at once
surrounded him screaming and yelling, mimicking his limp. He waved
them away. He looked confused, his skin was greywhite, his black beard
unkempt, he looked like a ruffian, his nose red and bulbous, his clothes
strange and made of heavy woolen material. Fishwives began to scream
abuse at him. He was a bad omen. The fishermen in the boat pointed to
three strange ships anchored six miles away with thick red addition signs
on their sails. The man was obviously a foreigner. He looked lost, didn't
know what to do.

What fools, I said to Al Masud, where have the ships come from. Don't
they know that the southwest monsoon will hit the coast, and that their
ships need to be beached.

Al Masud was silent.

Then he shouted out in clear Castilian, the devil take thee. What has
brought thee here so far from home.

The foreigner appeared terrified.

We dispersed the crowd that surrounded him. And, either in gratitude or in fear, he blurted out a delayed reply.

Christians, he said, and spices.

He never expected Castilian to be spoken here in faraway Calicut.

We took him to our house where our temporary wives, as Tunisians
both of us were *muta'* married after we had arrived here as traders, cooked
the prawns for us for our midday meal.

The stranger was perspiring heavily.

He smells, my wife said, he should have a bath.

My friend, who knew more about the Mediterranean trading world
than I did, enquired whether he had been sent by the King of Castile, the
King of France or the Signoria of Venice.

Nã, nã, nã, nã, the stranger said. The King of Portugal wouldn't allow
that. The Church forbids it.

We laughed. Both of us knew how insignificant Portugal was among
the nations of Europe.

He told us that his name was Jan Nunez. He claimed proudly that
he was a *converso*, and said he also knew Arabic and Hebrew, and was an

official interpreter, a *lingua*. His Arabic was worse than that of a child just learning to speak the language.

We were polite however, and invited him to share our meal. We waited for him to wash his hands but he didn't. He bit into a prawn, then, horror of horrors, he spat it out. Too spicy he said, and we smiled at this searcher for spices who couldn't eat spicy food. We gave him wheat chapaties and honey, and when the tide turned in the evening, my friend went with him in a boat to the ships.

They welcomed me in their own strange manner, al Masud told me when he returned from his visit to their ships.

There was a human figure with wings sprouting from his shoulders carved in gold at the prow of the flagship they took me to.

It's Jibra' il the messenger of God, Jan Nunez said. That's the name of our ship, the São Gabriel in Portuguese. The other two are the São Raphael and the Berrio.

The captain major, black bearded, looking fierce and impatient, shouted two words, Christian and Preste, loudly at me, and then began asking questions even before anyone bade me welcome and asked me to sit down. Others, on the small deck, joined in, all speaking at the same time. What I heard was gibberish, nasal squeals from a people lacking in elementary courtesy and civility. They speak very fast through their noses, these Portuguese, like mules braying, and they call each other *senhor* instead of using proper names.

The captain major finally drove everyone from the deck except for the two *linguas*, Jan Nunez and Fernam Martins, and someone named Alvaro who never spoke but wrote notes on brown sheepskin. They had a pilot called Ahmad ibn Madjid who knew Arabic and Gujarati, but he was on another ship and was very ill, they told me. The four of us found it almost impossible to communicate. I knew a number of trade words in Castilian. The Arabic the two interpreters spoke was of a debased Moroccan variety. Using signs and gestures, along with mangled Arabic words not sentences, we agreed that I would help take the Portuguese to Calicut to meet the Samorin its ruler. The captain major thanked me, but distorted my name, al Masud, which sprang out of his black beard nasalized as Monçaide.

That's what my friend al Masud told me when he returned to Elatur from the ship Jibra' il. Fernam Martins and another messenger accompanied my friend, and the three of them left immediately by boat for Calicut seven miles away to the south. That's the last I saw of my friend, for the police flung me into prison. I think they were afraid I was a Portuguese spy. They released me a month after the Portuguese ships had sailed from Calicut in late August. al Masud, may God protect him from all harm and may I see him again soon, left with them for Portugal, so they told me.

For a long time I debated with myself as to whether I should send this account of the arrival and departure of these ridiculous Portuguese, put together from the many talks I had with my wife's family and with one of the royal guards, with the *mapillas* and the foreign resident Muslims, to Malik Gopi who pays me for news about the trade in spices and the arrival and departure of ships. He is in faraway Surat.

Send every bit of news, I had been told by Malik Gopi's agent. Write down everything.

I'll try to be brief. Perhaps the report will at least make Malik Gopi smile before he throws it away and forgets about it. Here then is the story of these ridiculous Portuguese. Perhaps they have sailed back to hell. May they never return.

The Samorin was attending a temple ceremony at Ponnani, twenty eight miles south of Calicut, when he got the news about the arrival of the Portuguese ships bearing gifts. The *kotwal* said the Samorin would receive the ambassadors of the King of Portugal as soon as he returned to Calicut. The Samorin loved receiving presents of gold and jewelry, especially from the rich traders and merchants of Hormuz and Aden, which he then would display proudly before visitors.

The harbor master told the Portuguese that the monsoon would set in soon and that the Calicut shoreline was not safe and advised them to proceed ten miles north up the coast, and drop anchor in front of the Pantalayani roadstead. The Portuguese pilots, suspicious, and afraid of being tricked, were reluctant to sail there. It was a plot, they thought. They were not afraid of the monsoon winds. They had after all, they stated this proudly, crossed the sea of darkness and rounded the Cape of Storms which we Arabs had never ventured to cross and were sure the Feringhis never would.

When the Portuguese realized that Calicut had an unprotected shoreline and wasn't monsoon safe, they sailed, reluctantly, guided by a local harbor pilot to Pantalayani. They did not heed the advice of the pilot and refused to drop anchor near a protective mudbank where the sea is smooth and they would have been safe from the swell of the surf and from where their ship boats could get to land with ease. Still suspicious, they ventured further up the coast. Only when their anchored ships were tossed about by the winds and by the waves did they seek the protection of the mudbank.

Fools, stupid idiots, come back, those on shore shouted in Malayālam, waving their arms wildly at the Portuguese who thought they were being welcomed and waved wildly back to the people.

Three days later the *kotwal*, with the king's factor and the guards, arrived at Pantalayani beach to escort them to Calicut by land. The Samorin would receive the embassy there.

One of the king's guards told me what happened.

It took a very long time for the Portuguese to disembark their men and goods at Pantalayani, to decorate the ship boats with flags and streamers, and to lower the bombards, which could not be fired because of the driving rain. The trumpets tried to announce the landing of the ambassador captain, but could only produce flatulent sounds. The monsoon season had already begun.

Serves them right, the *kotwal* said to the Samorin's factor in Malayālam.

The *kotwal* was angry because he had to dispatch an elephant to drag the ship boats to the shore. He paced up and down impatiently. Ambassador Vasacodagamama, they malayālamalized his name by vowelizing it, entered the hut arrogant and fierce, his heavy black garments dripping wet. He wiped his sweating brow, tried to stamp his feet to express his anger but only made squelching sounds with his drenched boots.

Like an irate bedraggled crow, the *kotwal* observed loudly.

It was not a dignified procession to Calicut by way of Elatur, the *kotwal* and the captain major sitting like drenched hens in their palanquins, the two factors walking alongside the coolies that carried the gifts and some of the goods, then the guards, the interpreters and the sailors, followed by a tumultuous jeering rabble.

After an uncomfortable night at Elatur town, they crossed the river in long narrow boats. It took four hours. A backwater channel took them toward Calicut. The captain major, he who had crossed the sea of darkness, appeared tired and sick. Perhaps it was the effect of the swinging swaying palanquin that had made him sick. The *kotwal* offered the ambassador a horse to ride to Calicut. But, as it did not have a saddle, Vasacodagamama felt insulted and refused. Afraid of being poisoned, he gulped down a drink offered by one of his men, reentered the palanquin, and they proceeded to Calicut.

On the way they were invited by some Hindu priests to visit a nearby temple. There was the figure of a bird with wings outspread on a pillar at the entrance. Three of the Portuguese sailors removed their caps and bowed their heads. Krist, Krist, Krist, the Portuguese shouted loudly as they entered the gateway and, following the example of the *kotwal* and the guards, they sounded the seven bells that hung on the main doorway.

Krist, Krist, they shouted again with joy when the priests, who were na-ked from the waist up and wore twined white threads that passed over the left shoulder and under the right arm, sprinkled water on them and applied an ashy paste on their foreheads and their arms.

Ma, amma, mata, the priests explained when the Portuguese stopped and pointed to a wall sculpture of a mother with large rounded breasts holding a child.

Ma ri a, Ma ri a, the Portuguese hailed this figure. All of them, including the captain major, dropped on their knees. *Nossa Senhora,* the captain said.

Mari, mariamma, the priests confirmed.

One of the sailors looked all around, and said something that sounded like *di a bo lo,* and all of them hastily rubbed their foreheads, their lips, and their chests with multiplication signs. The captain thought it was a church and wanted to visit the inner shrine. Krist, Krist, he said. But the priests refused to allow them in the dark *garbāgriha,* which I was not allowed to enter and which, the Hindus say, is the sacred womb of the temple.

Like me, three months ago when I had visited this Hindu temple, the Portuguese were horrified to see the frieze that ran along the outer wall. It presented upside down couples copulating unashamedly.

I don't know what the Portuguese visit to the temple signifies, but I'm writing everything down. All I know is that a temple is definitely not a mosque. There are two mosques in Calicut town, where our Muslim com-munity prays without distractions, perhaps those ignorant Portuguese thought the temple was some sort of Christian church where their long lost brothers worshiped.

The Samorin sent a nobleman with a thousand Nair guards to escort the embassy to the palace five miles from the Calicut roadstead. Did they want to rest, did they want to change their clothes, the Portuguese were asked.

Nã nã nã nã, the captain spoke rapidly through his nose. He walked proud and erect, even though he must have been tired, through the spa-cious palace courtyard and through four richly ornamented doors, all the guards had drawn swords, to the Samorin's audience chamber. Only the interpreter was allowed in with him.

I cannot report what happened in the audience chamber because my friend the guard was not a witness to the meeting. I have however man-aged to piece together what happened from the Calicut gossip I've picked up from Koka Pakki.

The Samorin apparently, wanting to impress this ambassador of a mighty king from a faroff country he knew nothing about, gave a mag-

nificent display of his wealth. Naked from the waist up like the priests, re-
clining on a richly decorated raised dais, he was clad in the finest of white
cotton muslin and he wore the finest ornaments he had, rings of gold and
bracelets made of diamonds, pearls the size of hazelnuts, the reddest of
rubies and the greenest of emeralds. A Nambudiri Brahmin priest told me
that this display of wealth indicated that the Samorin was no mere human
ruler but an agent of divine power, this signified by the triple white lines
on his chest, his shoulders, and his forehead.

About the meeting itself I cant say too much. The ambassador refused
to talk in front of the Arab and other merchants, and wanted to communicate to the Samorin in private. What they talked about I wont even speculate on. More intriguing for me as a student of languages is how they
managed to communicate with each other. Must have been quite comic,
I think.

The ambassador apparently brought two letters from his king, one in
Arabic, the other in Portuguese. I don't think the Samorin had them read
aloud to him. What my friend the guard told me, this he heard from the
kotwal, was the list of the strange Portuguese gifts that the *kotwal* and the
factor refused to present to the Samorin. It would be deadly insulting,
they both stated. Twelve pieces of *lambel* striped cotton, like the one we
in Tunis usually sell to East African negroes, twelve surcoats with scarlet
hoods, six hats, four strings of coral, six hand basins, a chest of sugar, two
casks of oil and two of honey.

No gold, no diamonds, sneered the king's factor.

Nã, nã, nã, nã, the Portuguese factor said.

Gold image, Jibra' il, the king's factor asked.

Nã, nã, nã, nã, was the reply. Wood.

How Vasacodagamama managed to endure the mocks and jeers of
the *kotwal* and the Samorin's factor I do not know and so cannot write
about. But the list was immediately made known to all Calicut by the rich
Arab traders who do not and still cannot see the Portuguese as I see them,
figures of fun. They told the Samorin that the worthless Portuguese had
brought worthless goods of worthless quality. The Portuguese were a de-
spicable lot, pirates not ambassadors, who would ruin Calicut and its rich
trade, and all revenues would be lost. Attack and destroy the ships, let
them not return, the Arab traders urged the Samorin, exterminate these
infidels, these evildoers, may God curse them.

The Samorin did not know what to do. He is a cautious ruler. He did
not want to lose trade revenues. He was also afraid of the guns and the
bombards that his *kotwal* had told him about. He wanted Calicut to be a
center for peaceful trade. Like the gentle Koka Pakki, the leader of the
mapillas, the Samorin had begun to resent the haughty ways and the cut-

throat trade practices of the rich foreign Arabs. Not of the ones from Tunisia. Our Tunis is not a rich country.

The Portuguese left after the monsoon towards the end of August without signing any treaty with the Samorin. If I were asked what they had accomplished by coming to Calicut thousands of miles from Portugal, I'd say that they accomplished nothing. They had found people that they believed, even after a three month stay, were strange Christians. They had sold their worthless goods at a loss since no one wanted to buy them and, since they had no gold or silver, they could only buy spices of inferior quality to take back to Portugal. What they took back were five hostages, why I do not know. My friend with the name they had portuguesized into Monçaide left with them, alas. Perhaps they had forced him to leave with them because they wanted to use his services.

My friend the guard told me that his last sight of the Portuguese was that of the black figure of Vasacodagamama standing erect at the stern of the Jibra' il with his right fist raised. His other hand rested on a cannon at his side. All the people in our boats jeered *shee, shee,* their expressions of contempt and shame. The five hostages were fishermen, naked except for wraparounds, the lowest of the low castes, whose mere sight, according to the caste Hindus, is polluting and who would pollute everyone on the ships.

I laughed too, my friend the guard said. Then, he continued, I remembered Vasacodagamama's raised fist and the cannon. What if they returned, I thought, and felt a stab of fear and stopped laughing.

End of Tunisian's account

I wish there was an account by one of the Portuguese sailors of their first visit to Calicut. Not Vasco da Gama's. As a man of action he wouldn't have the time to write it, and he couldn't have given an objective account. Not the interpreter's account, it would be distorted. Paulo's perhaps, but he wasn't present at the encounter between his brother and the Zamorin. Paulo was an honest man. His would be a truthful account and he might have told us exactly what happened in Calicut. Did they come all the way to search for Christians. Did they want to buy spices. Or were these handful of people driven by a desire for conquest.

What I am becoming aware of now after going through the papers in Malik Gopi's wooden box is the gradual change that took place not only in our world but in the Portuguese after 1498. I couldn't come to this truth earlier because I couldn't see the whole picture. Malik Gopi's papers provided me with an awareness of the disturbed trade patterns which I was not interested in. It took me some time to summarize the events and arrange them in chronological order in order to understand what happened during the years between 1505 and 1509 when I was with my hakim. I shall ignore the slanted comments and the prejudices of the accounts written by Malik Gopi's agents. I will also try to set aside my own prejudices, even though João said this cant be done.

CALICUT

September 13, 1500

Pedro Alvares Cabral, in whose armada João had sailed as a *degredado*, arrives in Calicut with six armed ships dressed with flags and banners. Bombards are fired to announce the arrival. The five fishermen, taken to Portugal by Vasco da Gama, former hostages, now dressed in Portuguese clothes, not wraparounds, and wearing stylish hats with feathers in them, are sent on shore with a letter to the Zamorin. The letter, unclean, was untouched and unread.

This letter, smuggled out for Koka Pakki who had to bribe the *kotwal* to get it, revealed that the Portuguese king was convinced that the Samorin was some kind of Christian. If it was the will of God, the letter said, they would meet one day. In the meantime they could embrace each other across the seas as brothers in religion and enter into an alliance against their common enemies. The language of the letters was, as João would say, grandiloquent and fake.

September 18, 1500

Cabral's uncivilized insistence on guarantees and his demands for hostages, an unheard of practice here, caused much confusion and ill feeling. Gifts of fine jewelry and of fine cloth were sent to the Samorin. Cabral and the Samorin met finally at a house near the shore but nothing was resolved. The Portuguese interpretation was not very effective. The Jew from Bijapuri Goa, who became a *converso* in Portugal and was renamed Gaspar da Gama after Vasco da Gama stood as his godfather, was distrusted by some of the Portuguese who did not want him as interpreter.

The Portuguese are quite ignorant. They have a lot to learn about Hindu taboos about inter dining and castes and pollution, and about the intricate mode of bargaining that traders use.

October, November, December, 1500

Aires Correa, the soft spoken factor, began negotiations. It took two months for the Portuguese to get permission to set up a factory, which they call a *feitoria*, in Calicut. They did not know anything about trade and trading practices. They did not know that they needed middlemen and brokers who know the market to act as agents for the buying and selling of goods. They were outbid everytime for the spices they wanted, because they did not have enough quickness or money or gold or knowledge of the market rates, or the language of brokers. They did not know the Indian practice of bargaining under a shawl, using hands and fingers and the touching of finger joints to signal secret agreed on rates. And, they expected the Samorin, oh what arrogance, oh what ignorance, to help them get pepper and spices at fair market rates. The Calicut ruler is not a trader.

They were sold pepper of poor quality because of the low prices they offered and could load only two of their ships after three months of waiting. They felt greatly rebuffed, and thought they were being cheated, and deliberately insulted, so that when they saw the Muslim traders busily loading their vessels and would set sail with their spices and cargo before them, they took violent action.

December 16, 1500
The Portuguese seized an Arab ship at anchor in the roadstead as it was being loaded with cargo and killed some sailors when they resisted.

A crowd in Calicut attacked the Portuguese factory in retaliation and killed Aires Correa and forty Portuguese. A few escaped to the ships. Two children of Aires Correa, playing in the house of Koka Pakki, a friend of the Portuguese, were saved by him.

Cabral indiscriminately attacked all boats he could find in the roadstead, firing against other ships and bombarding houses along the shore but not causing too much damage to them. Advised, it is reported, by Gaspar da Gama, the six ships set sail for Cochin in search of cargo.

COCHIN

January 9, 1501
Cabral's six ships, with a full load of pepper and other spices, stole away in the dark of the night after learning that the Calicut armada had set out to attack them and the Cochin Raja. They took with them the five Nayars they had on the ships as temporary hostages, and abandoned their own factor, Gil Barbosa, and thirty other Portuguese in Cochin to their fate.

January 15, 1501
Cabral sailed to Kannanur where the Kolathiri offered him as much cinnamon as he could load on his ships on credit. It was of the coarse kind, not good quality Ceylon cinnamon. The Portuguese did not realize this at the time.

What happened in the year 1501

Four Portuguese ships, according to unconfirmed rumors, came to Kannanur, committed two acts of piracy near Eli Mala, requested that spices be reserved for them, and left after four days for Cochin, where they could not obtain goods as they did not have any Sofala gold in their coffers. They returned to Kannanur to unload the cargo, which they had brought from Portugal and which the authorities reluctantly promised to sell, on to the rocky promontory that juts into the Bahr-i-Hind where they established a small *feitoria*. The ships took back with them pepper and dried ginger on credit. They were trading not war ships sent out to discover new areas for trade. One of them, commanded by Jan de Nova, may have gone to Colombo in Ceylon. Malik Gopi's Colombo buyer of cinnamon reported the sighting of a strange heart shaped rock inscription there.

The Zamorin sent his fleet towards Kannanur to attack the four ships.

Alas, how can bows and arrows prevail against mighty guns.

CALICUT

October 29, 1502

An armada of nineteen great ships commanded by black bearded Vasco da Gama arrives with bombards at the ready, not resting on the top decks but protruding through hinged gunports, a new armed mode not used on the *San Raphael* and the *San Gabriel*. The sails, main and lateen, were more efficiently arranged. The ships converged and met at Anjediva, then spread out along the coast to commit numerous acts of piracy.

At Calicut a ten year old Muslim girl was sent in a captured boat with a message to the Samorin signed by Vasco da Gama, Admiral.

Banish all foreign Arab traders from Calicut at once. Or else.

Never, was the Samorin's reply. Calicut is a free port open to all traders.

A relative recognized the little girl whose face had been badly burned. She was one of the few survivors of the *Princess of the Night* that was returning from Jiddah to Calicut with 300 pilgrims including fifteen wealthy merchants with their wives, children and babies carrying gold, jewels, diamonds and precious stones. Vasco da Gama, wanting to avenge the massacre of Aires Correa and the forty, and to teach the Calicut merchants a lesson in horror they would never forget, had boarded the vessel, robbed these people of all their belongings, then bombarded it at close range and set it on fire. No mercy was shown except to a few children who, they say, except for the badly burnt one, were taken to Portugal.

All the children were sprinkled with holy water, the ten year old whimpered in pain, I too.

November 1, 1502
Vasco da Gama bombarded the Calicut shore damaging houses, setting some on fire, and wounding a few people, mostly fishermen.

He seized those who had come in boats to his ships to sell fish and rice, about 800 in all. Some of these he hanged from the yards. Others were beheaded. He also cut off the noses, hands and ears of the rest, packed them in boats which were then allowed to drift ashore.

War to the death against all infidels, no mercy, was the message sent in the boats. And the word *RECONQUISTA*, capitalized, a word no one could understand.

COCHIN

November 3, 1502
Vasco da Gama left for Cochin. He left Calicut and its peoples in a state of shock.   The great Satan has come, the women wailed, beating their breasts, their hair dishevelled.   The Cochin Raja gave the Portuguese a warehouse that Vasco da Gama insisted had to be built near the shore and fortified with laterite. No bargaining, no brokers, all prices for pepper and spices were laid down by Vasco da Gama's factor. Rates were fixed for the merchants of Cochin and Kannanur.

The *cartaz* system was put into effect, no one knows what it implies.

In Kannanur, up the coast, the Kolathiri raja allowed a palisade to be built as protection for the *feitoria* across the neck of the promontory.

The armada sailed away in February, 1503.

Five vessels commanded by Sodre were left behind as a naval force to patrol the coast, to attack shipping and to defend Cochin against Calicut revenge. Instead, seeking plunder, they went to the mouth of the Red Sea on a piratical hunt, lying in wait for returning trading vessels to capture as prizes. A few ships were caught in a storm and wrecked.

Hostilities increased between the Raja of Cochin and the Samorin of Calicut. The Raja was fed up with the bullying tactics of his tyrannical overlord who would invade Cochin territory several times a year without any provocation, then draw back when it suited him. The Raja of Cochin did not have the right to mint money. He wasnt allowed to build a navy, and he wasnt permitted to roof his palace with tiles. This time the Raja defied the Samorin and retreated with his Portuguese friends to Vypeen, the holy island with the ceremonial sacred stone that the Zamorin and his armed fleet dare not attack.

COCHIN

1503/1504
In late August 1503 two Portuguese ships arrived and helped restore his territorial possessions to the Raja of Cochin. The Raja was, they say, so grateful that he sold all the pepper in Cochin he could collect to the captain major and allowed the Portuguese to construct a wooden fortress near the shore.

Afonso de Albuquerque, the captain's cousin brother, who arrived in the middle of September with three ships, had to help build the Cochin fortress.

Strange stories circulate among the workmen about the petty quarrels between the two cousins. That they divided the work in half and drew a line between the two parts of the fortress which they refused to cross. The walls of the fortress did not meet properly. A confusion of names too, two different names given by the cousins for the fortress. One named it *castelo manuel,* the other *castelo albuquerque.*

Both left in February 1504.

CANNANORE/*Kannanur*

1504
In the first week of September thirteen vessels, large ones to be used for both trade and war, anchored outside Cannanore, the Portuguese name for Kannanur.

Only the Kolathiri raja of Kannanur was honored with gifts and a letter of commendation.

Calicut was bombarded because it refused to surrender two Italian gunfounders who had deserted the Portuguese fleet. They manufactured a large number of guns for the Samorin's army, a thousand some say. Most of them misfired, and the rest were never used. The Nayar fighters considered it cowardly and beneath their dignity to use such unclean weapons.

Then Cranganore, a port town, was attacked and handed over to the Cochin Raja.

Before leaving for Portugal the thirteen ships broke up into groups, sailed to Pantalayini Kollam, to Ponnane, and to Dharmapatam, and attacked and burnt a number of merchant vessels loaded with trade goods about to sail for the Red Sea.

Those Portuguese who were wounded were taken to Cannanore and were treated in a warehouse that they term a hospital.

Some ships laden with cargo left before the monsoon began. Others remained behind.

The Portuguese presence is no longer seasonal. People all along the coast are now aware of two kinds of thunder, the new kind that erupts from ships frightens them even more than the kind that descends from the skies just before the monsoons.

1505
Francisco de Almeida arrived in Cochin as Viceroy with an armada of twenty two ships.

After 1505 there were no significant reports from Maik Gopi's agents except for lists and prices of various commodities which fluctuated wildly, especially the price of pepper and cinnamon with which the Portuguese loaded their ships. They did not know, I think, that other spices were available.

I am now beginning to see a pattern of significance in the dates and events I have set down. I see a progression in the number of the ships sent to India every year from 3 to 6, then to 19, then to 22. The ships used to come every year for trade, and return to Portugal. Now they come for trade and stay for war. Armed ships are left behind now. *Feitorias* and fortresses, *fortalezas* they are known as, are erected, in a pattern that I see as semicircular, beginning from Mozambique and Kilwa on the east coast of Africa, around to Socotra, and down to Cannanore, Anjediva, Calicut and Cochin, all along the lower west coast of India. The Portuguese have inserted themselves into our region. But, as I said before, they are a handful of people. They do have guns, however.

I wonder how João would interpret my summary if he was here to read it. The search for Christians perhaps drove the Portuguese ships.

Malik Gopi came to the guest house and sat down next to the wooden box of papers. Five women had accompanied him, heavily veiled, carrying small rolled up carpets and two brooms. They went around to the back of the house. I heard the kitchen door open. I didn't ask the Malik any questions, neither did I get up or even offer to get some water. Abdul must have gone to get some provisions. Frei António had gone to the *Hathikad* to say Mass for the prisoners.

The Malik wanted to see Frei António because he had just received a message that the two Portuguese mariners who had been left behind in Surat to recover from wounds they had received during the riots there, had arrived at Hathikad last night with some of the Portuguese cargo that had been recovered from the Dumas villagers. He particularly wanted to tell Frei António that the black convert from West Africa, preto Thomaz, wanted to become a Muslim.

I would have enjoyed watching the Frei's reactions to this news, the Malik told me.

Then the Malik gave me his other news. That the ceremony to honor Frei António and to thank him for saving the Sultan's life would be held in the palace in two days.

And Malik Gopi had a request.

This unworthy guesthouse will be secretly redecorated and refurnished in honor of the Frei on the day of the ceremony when both you and the Frei, and your servant, will be away. It will be my gift to him. Don't tell him about it. It will be a complete surprise when he comes back that night. And don't let your servant know about this.

I was immediately suspicious. Was this another of the Malik's wily tricks, and I looked straight at him, but his eyes were crystal clear.

The five women walked past the porch and Malik Gopi stood up to leave.

It began to rain.

Two of the women turned, glanced at us, and rearranged their veils.

I'm coming, Champa, the Malik said loudly. I have to go, he told me.

I gathered up my papers.

The monsoon began in earnest. The wind blew relentless, attacking Champaner city as if wanting to take it by storm, bringing down the temperature, bringing temporary relief from the heat, but making things humid and uncomfortable. It was prickly heat weather. The rain drove slanting, lashing against the walls of the guesthouse as if attacking them with arrows or iron pellets. It made strange hollow sounds, not like the reassuring monsoon sounds I usually heard in my Diu house near the promontory where the winds are always very fierce, these sounds appeared to come from a distance. My Diu house would leak at times, this guesthouse was monsoon proof.

I wanted to ask Abdul about these strange sounds. But he was dripping wet, he had just come in out of the rain through the kitchen door. Then I heard muffled voices. It was Frei António and a short black man, outside on the porch, both wet and bedraggled.

May I come in, asked preto Thomaz in broken Gujarati. He sneezed twice.

Mercy descend on you, I said.

Thomaz had a bad cold, a cough too.

Welcome, I said, enter.

They needed towels to dry themselves, and I asked Abdul to give preto Thomaz a pair of his pyjamas and one of his shirts. Abdul said he would prepare coffee for us all.

I went to the table where I had placed my papers.

I wasn't surprised to hear the broken Gujarati of the Portuguese. Frei António had the hostages come to the guesthouse in twos and threes to hear their confessions, they did not have any privacy at the *Hathikad*. They would try to talk to Abdul, tasting the food he offered them in his kitchen, telling him in sign language and using simple single Gujarati words about the tempting food that the converts brought for them to eat. The wives of two of the converts were specialists in the making of *jalebi*, a sweet that tasted of honey. They told the Frei how much they enjoyed *jalebi*. They made their confessions to him on our porch in Portuguese.

I could easily overhear what they confessed, but what they confessed I found utterly boring, cheating at cards, swearing, sexual fantasies, acts of masturbation, petty things really. Only once did I really listen carefully, when one of them confessed to killing one of the enemy in Socotra after the fort had surrendered.

He begged me for his life, the captive told the Frei, but I was hungry and dizzy with the heat, and I stabbed him with my pike.

It's not murder, the Frei said, this is a *bellum justissimum*, even though, as a son of Saint Francis, I'd rather have the infidels converted than killed. But the Church has decreed that all who kill in a just war are forgiven.

And he mumbled some words beneath his breath in another language, Latin, I think.

How strange, I thought, and then I thought of what the maulvi once told João and me, that all those who are slain while fulfilling their religious duty during a *jihad*, a holy war against unbelievers, will be taken straight to Paradise. João confirmed what the maulvi said. He quoted from the Qu'ran, *Surah 4. 76*, whoever fighteth on God's path whether he be slain or conquer, we will in the end give him a great reward. We had different attitudes towards war but we did not get into our usual heated discussion. I would have asked them not what kings and priests thought about war, but about what went through the minds of the ordinary soldier as he went to war and fought battles he knew nothing about.

I discovered that preto Thomaz was an African slave brought to Lisbon, converted to Christianity, and given his freedom and his baptismal name Thomaz, but no surname, he had no godfather. Everyone called him preto or black Thomaz. He wanted to turn Muslim now, and the Frei wanting desperately to make him change his mind had brought him to the guesthouse.

You'll lose your immortal soul, the Frei warned him, you'll go to hell.

It's my body I am worried about not my soul whatever that is. My body aches, I feel miserable. You shouldn't have made me walk in the rain, preto Thomaz whined. My nose runs, my behind too.

But think of your soul, the Frei was in desperate anguish, your most precious possession.

That's what you and the others tell me, Frei António. That's the kind of language you taught me in Lisbon making me unlearn the African terms I knew for the great spirit, so why should I not now learn new Muslim terms for the soul. And Frei António, I want to know whether the color of my soul is *preto*. I wasn't treated like a real Portuguese when I turned Christian in Portugal. Don't you think I became a Christian because I was promised freedom and because of the demanding needs of my body not of my soul. Won't my body be better treated because I become a Muslim here. I'll be married, they tell me, and I'll have a good life here on this earth. I won't have to wait for heaven.

He was completely distraught but his complaints were logical, I thought. Then he ran to the back calling for Abdul and clutching his behind.

Padre António was dumbfounded. He shook his head violently two or three times. Perhaps he was reminded of what João had said about the difficulties of conversion in his letter, the problems involved. I knew he wanted to talk to somebody, to tell them about his Franciscan dreams. He looked at me, his eyes full of despair. I was tempted to reveal to him that I knew Portuguese. I felt the urge, I know not why, to tell him about the two lines, but how would they help, from *The Song of Songs* that João had underlined and jotted down in the margin.

To woo the Frei, João's cryptic note had said.

Impulsively I copied the two lines on a piece of paper.

Beija-me, dando o osculo da sua boca
Porque os tuas peitos são melhores do que o vinho

Ahmadji, the Frei said, Ahmadji, and he rushed to my table and pointed to my papers.

To Frei Henrique, he shouted, but the word shouts were not directed at me, they were in Portuguese, to himself.

I gave him some sheets of paper, a pen, and a bottle of ink, and he sat down opposite me and bowed his head. It took a long time for him to begin writing.

Writing, I have now come to realize, is a medicine prescribed by my hakim for me.

I try to, but do not sound like João. My tone is heavy, not light and cryptic.

The July sun shone bright on the day of the ceremony to honor the Frei. Abdul had been invited to Halol by one of Malik Gopi's servants. They promised to be back after sunset. Like me, Abdul didn't believe that the guesthouse would be redecorated. But even Malik Gopi's gossipy servants did not know anything, except that there was lots of excitement and whispering in the women's quarters. It was said, Abdul told me, that Champa, Malik Gopi's favorite courtesan, had planned a Hindu spectacle more exotic than any Muslim entertainment.

Your papers, they're safe, Abdul said. Frei António's also.

I had placed in my inner pocket the scrap of paper with the two lines from *The Song of Songs* on it. Perhaps I could later pretend I found it and give it to the Frei before the ceremony.

As we stepped out of the guesthouse, the Frei and I, two large carts loaded with some covered merchandise came to a halt near the porch. So it isn't a trick, I thought. The guesthouse would have a different look when we got back. I accompanied the Frei to the *Hathikad*. I had wanted to go to the top of Pawagadh near Kali Mata to collect some tonic herbs for the Frei who looked weak and frail, but Abdul suggested I not overexert myself.

The Frei celebrated Mass on a small table in the large room that housed the hostages in the center of the *Hathikad*. It was a simple ceremony I attended, unlike the one I had witnessed on the *San Raphael*. There was no pomp, no candles, no smell of incense, the singing did not soar to the stars, and was unremarkable. The Frei had not changed his cloak. He made use of a misshapen earthenware cup that he raised with both his hands for all to see. And yet I was moved, moved by the voices uttering a prayer that was heartfelt, recited kneeling down. They were praying not for a successful voyage to the unknown, but to be restored to safety.

Amen, they all said in unison.

One of the hostages then placed a roughly hewn soapstone cross on the small table and the Frei, who began preaching a sermon, would turn and bow to it every time he uttered the name of the Lord Jesus Christ. The cross had four Portuguese names scratched on its arms.

I didn't at first pay too much attention to the Frei's sermon which was full of advice and pleas that they not succumb to the temptation of changing their religion. Then it struck me that the tone of his voice had changed. It had become softer. No longer was it a despairing voice that threatened dire punishment. It suggested that they, as ones born into Christianity, should understand those who were not so fortunate, and forgive them.

This morning, he said, marks a special occasion. Today I did not just read the dry Mass, the *missa sicca*, as on shipboard. Today, because Malik Gopi gave us permission to have wine made from the fermented juice of grapes, later the malik said we may be able to bake our own bread, we had a consecrated Mass. Soon, I am sure, we will be able to celebrate mass properly and you will be able to receive holy communion.

Let us now kneel down and thank our Lord Jesus Christ, and pray for Malik Gopi, our benefactor, who is a *gentio*, a Hindu not a Muslim. Let us also pray for the repose of the soul of André Fernandes, who was brought here as a prisoner from Chaul, died here, and was buried but did not receive a Christian burial. We pray also for two of our brethren who turned Muslim and who are now, they tell me, very ill, at death's door, they say. Perhaps they will make their confession before they die. Malik Gopi has promised to let me go to see them.

A simple meal was then served to all the hostages.

I had planned to take the Frei for a long walk to show him the sights of Islamic Champaner, the houses built of fragrant sandalwood so plentiful in the surrounding forest, the mosques with filigree screens, the well laid gardens planted with mangoes and grapes and pomegranates and bananas. Instead, I offered to accompany him to the dying converts, I wondered how and why they fell sick. Perhaps I could be of help. Just as we were setting out I got an urgent message asking me to come to a meeting.

You shouldn't have, Malik Aiyaz was saying to Malik Gopi as I entered the round chamber in the administration building. Kiwam-ul-Mulk Sarang was not present.

You shouldn't have sent a message to the Portuguese telling them we would be willing to exchange hostages, Malik Aiyaz said, his voice tense with controlled anger. You should have waited for our advice.

Malik Gopi appeared utterly relaxed, his legs stretched out, his head resting on his intertwined fingers against the bolster.

My dear Malik, you are a mighty warrior, Gopi said flatteringly, you are a master of battle strategy, but you know we cannot fight the Portuguese on the sea. You need to use the tactics of a trader, perhaps you need a *banya* mentality.

I was impressed by Gopi's verbal tactics. He was always soft spoken, and his sense of timing was impeccable. He knew when to pause, when to change his tone of voice, when to heighten it so that one was compelled to listen to what he said.

The Mamluk Sultan of Cairo will, I am sure, send more ships and guns to fight the Portuguese, Malik Aiyaz said, as he paced up and down the room. I sent him a request for help and suggested that the Muslim rulers in our world unite to crush the Portuguese. We do not need the Hindu Samorin. United, Malik Aiyaz proclaimed, we'll be victorious.

I was surprised to hear this. Malik Aiyaz, usually a practical man, surely he didn't believe such unity was possible. Surely he must have said it just to impress Gopi.

Are you quite quite sure, asked Gopi. They will never unite even against the common enemy of Islam.

True, very true. I thought of the fierce enmities between the Persian sheik of Malindi and the Arab ruler of Mombasa in East Africa in 1498, and of Vasco da Gama's escape from Mombasa. I thought of the petty quarrels of Calicut and Cochin and Kannanur, the three Hindu kingdoms in South India. I thought of how it was to the great advantage of the Portuguese that there were divisions in our ocean world. Our rulers fought among themselves, instead of uniting to fight against the Portuguese.

And of course you know, Aiyaz, Malik Gopi continued, that because of the Portuguese blockade, trade in the Red Sea and the Persian Gulf has collapsed and shipping is in disarray. My spies report that only one sixth of the annual supply of pepper and spices got through the last year. Even the revenues of Venice and of the Levant are down, I understand. I'm glad I told Amir, my son, to abandon the practice of sending ships to Aden and Hormuz. Now he sends them now only to Melaka and South Asia.

I shook my head slowly with reluctant admiration for Malik Gopi, and for his highly efficient spy network. He knows everything about trade and commerce in our world, but never reveals what he knows. He studies a problem, then proceeds to immediate action. That's why he is so rich. And so very powerful, even though he appears to be a mere trader, his power springs from money and organization.

But but but Gopi, we have our pride and our honor. We are nobles, we cannot beg the infidel Portuguese for peace.

Malik Aiyaz sat down heavily on a bolster.

Listen, Aiyaz, listen to what I have done. I have sent a flattering letter written by a deserter in high sounding Portuguese to the head of the *Estado da India* requesting *cartazes* to allow my ships to sail to Melaka, and offering money and help in the exchange of hostages.

Why, you ask, why stoop to such tactics. Because, my friend.

Malik Gopi stopped, sat up, scratched his big right toe, then he quickly stood up.

Because, he continued, that's the only way to fight them. Listen, Aiyaz, listen. Those Portuguese are moneyless fools who know absolutely nothing about trade, and have blundered into our world. But.

Malik Aiyaz was about to interrupt.

But these fools have mighty ships, Gopi continued, and powerful guns which we can't match, yet.

I never saw Malik Gopi so worked up before. He paced up and down on the carpet. Words came out of him in a rush.

We need to use tactics that will undermine their power. Take the *cartaz* situation. The *cartaz* gives the name of the ship, its size and weight, the ship captain's name and age, the commodities carried, the ports of embarkation and disembarkation, and the dates of arrival and departure, all items that can easily be changed if needed. The port captains can very easily be bribed. The fee charged for each ship is negligible, the port taxes are insignificant. I have merely to increase the prices for the goods I trade in to recover ten times the amount. Soon, Ahmadji, very soon, I'll be able to have *cartazes* forged very easily. My writer Vora, you know him Ahmadji, has already forged a number of *cartazes*.

Tell me, he turned to Aiyaz, what's the use of that useless thing you call honor, what's the point of questioning and denouncing the absolute power that some obscure Pope in Rome is supposed to have bestowed on the Portuguese king so that he makes the false claim that he is the rightful lord of the ocean sea and justifies his barbarous tactics. He may claim that grandiose title, but we, and Gopi paused, I, and he paused again, will be the real king of the trading world soon.

Money is power, he proclaimed, it will be more powerful than guns.

Malik Gopi was no longer Malik Gopi. He stopped pacing up and down, and sat on a bolster with his arms stretched straight up above his head. His eyes appeared glazed as if he was in a trance, his voice trembled, he began talking to himself not to us, about his vision of himself as a mover of the whole world which he held like a golden apple in his hands.

I'll make millions, he hissed, more money than what the Begdo has hidden away in his treasury at Pawagadh. With this money I'll hire Portuguese deserters, Ottoman renegades, and Safavid fighters, have mighty ships built, I'll have guns manufactured. Not the small number that the two Italian armourers made for the Samorin, nor the thousand guns that the Melakans have obtained from the Ottomans. I'll drive the Portuguese out of the Bahr-i-Hind.

Kiwam-ul-Mulk Sarang and the Sultan walked into the room, and Gopi reverted quick as a snake into Gopi again.

Both Maliks greeted the Sultan, who entered in a great hurry. Today the Sultan didn't want to concentrate on matters of the state. His face was flushed as if all his blood had swept up there, the tonic herbs on Pawagadh might have been useful, but I knew he had his own doctors.

I feel disturbed, the Sultan said, I know not why. I need the Frei to calm me down, he has *baraka*.

The Frei to me was just a very good man. I had never experienced *baraka* nor did I believe in it. The maulvi had said *baraka* was the invisible glow a holy man like the Mahdi radiates that soothes his followers and those around him.

Have you decided what has to be done about the Portuguese, the Sultan continued abruptly, his words coming in random bursts. Pay as much ransom as is needed to get the *Meri* and Ali Khan back. Where are the Portuguese headquarters on land. Let's decide these matters soon, I want to go and meditate with the Frei.

The Frei has gone to visit the sick converts, I said to the Sultan.

Ah.

He paused.

Malik Gopi, is it true that you offered the Portuguese permission to set up a factory in Diu, asked the Sultan.

Malik Aiyaz glared at Gopi.

I never commit myself to anything, ever, said Gopi. In my letter to them about the hostages I said that it would be to their advantage to set up a factory at Diu. I said that it might be possible for me to arrange it.

But but but Aiyaz said.

Aiyaz, you yourself offered, didn't you, Malik Gopi said, after the Diu battle, to surrender Diu to the Portuguese.

But that was just a trick, Aiyaz said. I knew Viceroy Almeida would refuse, he didn't have enough ships and men to hold Diu. And he had told Sidi Ali *o torto* he didn't want to acquire any territorial possessions in India.

And I, Gopi maintained, in my letter I suggested other places besides Diu for them to set up a factory, on Gogha or on Piram island. And in the letter I deliberately used a Gujarati word, *bakhar*, which is ambiguous, it means a sturdy house, but it could mean anything, a trading post or a factory or a small fortress. It will take time and discussion and bargaining to determine its meaning. Believe me, Aiyaz, the Portuguese know nothing about our land and its dangers. They do not know about the bore that sweeps up the Gulf of Cambay, they do not know that Gogha does not have an anchorage for their large ships, they do not know that Piram has a steep shoreline and is infested with snakes. We need to use what I told you about, the tactics of prolonged negotiations and delay, that's the only way to treat a bully.

The Sultan was impatient.

I have to go, he said, let me know what you both decide.

I want the Frei, the Sultan told Kiwam-ul-Mulk Sarang as they went out. Send for him.

My dear Aiyaz, I did not have the time to tell you everything, Gopi said. My spies inform me that all is not well in the Portuguese camp at Cochin. There are quarrels, dissensions, infighting.

What shall we do, asked Aiyaz.

I suggest, said Gopi, that it is not the time to send an ambassador to the Portuguese. Let us send two envoys who can also act as our spies. Let us send Sidi Ali *o torto* and Vora.

No no no said Aiyaz. We will send Sidi Ali and Ahmad ibn Madjid, they both know Portuguese and will keep us in touch with what goes on among the Portuguese. My agent in Cochin will help them.

We'll send them when the sea is declared open, towards the end of August, after Coconut Day, said Gopi.

Don't forget to come to this evening's ceremony to honor the Frei, Gopi told Aiyaz as he was leaving.

I want all the people to be seated before the Frei walks in, Malik Gopi said. They will welcome him with shouts of joy. The Sultan will be pleased. I'll send a messenger to Hathikad to summon the Frei and you to the Hall of Public Audience. Ahmadji, please see that the Frei doesn't lose himself in prayer. Please lead him into the Hall.

It was I who had to go to the houses of the converts to bring the Frei to the ceremony. The Sultan's messengers, four of them sent one by one at intervals, were told every time that the Frei was praying for the converts and that he would come to the Sultan soon, but he never did.

I had spent my time at the *Hathikad* watching the hostages at their lessons. Diego Correa, their leader, had divided them into groups. Those who knew how to read and write were split into two groups, the one headed by Payo Correa was learning Gujarati, the other, led by Antoo Nogueira, was studying Persian. Those hostages who were illiterate were being taught Portuguese. All were kept busy and had no time to brood on their troubles.

I was impressed. Soon the Portuguese would not need interpreters. I thought about Vasco da Gama and the furious energy these Portuguese had brought with them to India. They wanted to do things. They wanted to know new things. I thought of the obese Ishak who could wrestle but was no warrior. I thought of his companions, voyeurs stupefied with opium and with *charas*, enjoying the antics of a Humrumbum. They preferred playing polo to performing war exercises. They were all living in an unreal world of leisure and pleasure, not the world of action.

We waited for the Frei. When the Frei did not return, I knew I had to go to fetch the Frei. Most of the hostages, who had been invited to the ceremony, had already left. Payo Correa offered to come with me.

I found the Frei in the room where the two converts lay doubled up in pain on the floor, moaning and groaning, pummeling their huge bellies to force out the pain within. Everyone else had abandoned them, even their wives, they were afraid, they did not know what to do, the two looked as if they would die soon. Their eyes were gaunt and bloodshot, their cheeks hollow, their faces pale. They looked like skeletons, except for their bellies, rounded like drums. There was only a very old woman present who was grinding a medicinal paste of dry ginger, salt, and pepper. I was struck by a vague memory of what my hakim had once told me, and I told her to add a fistful of asafoetida and to throw in a palmful of cinnamon powder to the mixture, and then smear some of the paste on to their rounded bellies.

The Frei knelt down near them, praying continuously, reciting the rosary, placing his silver crucifix on their naked bellies, entreating God for mercy, wanting to save their souls, he would not give up. Confess your sins, he begged them, it's not too late to ask God for mercy.

Payo knew how important it was for all the hostages that the Frei not antagonize the Sultan by not going to the ceremony. He gestured to me to leave the room Perhaps he didn't want me to be a witness to Portuguese shortcomings. Perhaps he suspected that I was some kind of spy, and that somehow I did understand Portuguese. I don't know what he said to the Frei but it took a long time for both of them to come out of the room, Payo looking tired, the Frei looking quite weak and disheveled and crucifixless, sweating profusely. I don't think he had had anything to eat or drink the whole day.

The Sultan welcomed the Frei up the steps of the dais and bade him sit down next to him on the couch. He was not angry even though the whole assembly, which included the new ambassadors from Bengal, Vijayanagar and the envoy from Ceylon had greeted the Frei with feeble shouts of acclaim. They had had to wait a long time, and were restless, and soon it would be dark. The Frei sat with his head bowed.

The Sultan's orator delivered a *qasida*, a praise poem addressed not to the Frei but to the Sultan from whom he expected some remuneration. It was full of adulation expressed in grandiose hyperbole. The first verse, the *matla*, fell on cold ears, it did not arouse any interest in the listeners. The exordium, the *tashbīb*, fell flat. This orator was clearly no poet. The words, heavy, could not fly or make the listeners fly. The poem shuttled between extravagant praise for the great Sultan of awards and rewards for rewarding the Frei, and grudging praise for the Frei who had the good fortune to merit the Sultan's reward. The assembly began to murmur its disapproval, softly at first, then loudly, even before the poem ended. The Sultan raised his hand for silence.

Stop, stop, said the Sultan. Enough.

The second speaker, the Muslim ship captain, then spoke using simple words about how the Frei, whom he called his friend, had risked his own life to save him from certain death. He tried to tell the assembly what happened during the shipwreck but he couldn't. Words failed him. So moved was he by his recall of the incident that he stopped silent, then rushed towards the Frei with his arms spread out wide. The Frei stood up awkwardly and with great difficulty. Then the captain, tears in his eyes, double embraced him as his brother.

I was worried lest the Frei faint as he had done at the conversion ceremony. He sat down, his head was bowed. I think he was praying.

The Sultan stood up and announced that five robes of honor would be bestowed on the Frei.

I know he will never wear them, he will give them to the poor, the Sultan said. In honor of this holy man the robe money will be used to provide a feast for all the poor in and around Champaner.

Malik Gopi then got up and announced that everyone in the assembly was invited to a feast to honor the Frei in the next room. There were shouts of joy. The Sultan did not stay for the feast. He bade farewell to the new ambassadors and thanked Malik Gopi for arranging the ceremony.

Take care of the holy man, the Sultan told me.

Malik Gopi escorted the ambassadors and everyone hastened after them into the next room. I helped the Frei off the dais. He was very weak and he stumbled on the last step.

I feel faint, Ahmadji, he said, please get me some *agua*.

I signaled to a servant to get a tumbler of water. The Frei drank it in two choking gulps, then he began to cough.

More, he said.

No, I said, taking the tumbler away, that will be very bad for you. You haven't had any water the whole day and your whole body is parched and needs to absorb water slowly or else it will suffer a shock, you have to sip the water slowly.

I gave him the water and he took one sip, and stared hard at me.

But, Ahmadji, he said, you know Portuguese, I never knew you did, you speak Portuguese, you speak it well, can you write it too.

I don't know who was more surprised, he or me, that Portuguese had erupted out of my mouth. Some impulse led me to give him the scrap of paper from my pocket.

Surprised, he read the two lines aloud.

Beija-me, dando o osculo da sua boca

Porque os tuas peitos são melhores do que o vinho

These lines are from *The Song of Songs*, he said, do you want to know what they mean.

I said, João. And I stopped. I was flustered. Your cousin João, I said. I copied the lines. João said they were meant for you, I don't know why. To woo you, he wrote in his letter.

I'm glad João remembers the Bible, the Frei said.

Just then we heard shouts and cries from the direction of the palace gate. The Frei placed the paper in his inner pocket. One of the guards came dashing into the Hall, prostrated himself in front of the Frei, then rushed into the other room which soon began to resound with shouts of disbelieving laughter.

Jadu, they roared with laughter, magic.

Many of the disbelievers rushed outside the Hall of Audience.

Loud clamors of Frei, Frei, Frei, and of Louro, Louro, Louro, could be heard outside the palace gate.

A crowd had gathered outside the palace gate and demanded a *darshan*, their spokesman was a Hindu, of the Frei, the holy man who had just performed a miracle. The two converts who were at the point of death had been miraculously brought back to life. Their wives had confirmed this. They were now walking about, breathing, eating, as if nothing had happened to them, as if they had never been on the point of death. It was a miracle, they said, performed by the holy man and the crowd insisted that they should be allowed to see him now, at once, without delay.

Kiwam-ul-mulk Sarang went to the gate, and convinced the crowd that it was late, that the Sultan would be angry if he was disturbed, and that they would be able to have *darshan* of the holy man the following day.

The spokesman said he had brought with him the holy man's magic instrument that had performed the miracle. He was allowed to go to the Hall where he folded both his hands which he lifted to his forehead. He then slowly gave the Frei something wrapped up in soft white cotton. It was the silver crucifix.

I do not believe in miracles. I was still worried lest the Frei, who looked pale, faint. So I led him to the other room. Everyone had left except Malik Gopi who sat at a low square table entertaining the two ambassadors and the envoy from Ceylon.

Come, Frei Louro, Malik Gopi said, we heard about the miracle, and about your magic instrument. Perhaps we'll be able to test it soon.

His guests laughed uproariously. They were drunk.

Come, Ahmad ibn Madjid, said Gopi.

And he made us sit on either side of him. The table was loaded with rich aromatic food, shami kabab, honey roasted chicken, lamb biryani. Goblets of wine were kept out of sight under the table. Servants kept bringing more platters, parathas dripping with ghee, pickles of all kinds, jalebis, barfi, carrot halwa. The Frei kept his head bowed, he did not even look at the food. The rich smell made me feel a little nauseous.

Give the holy man some water, I said.

The Frei sipped the water without looking up.

I know both of you will not eat this rich food. I told them to prepare special dishes for both of you, Gopi said, dhal and plain rice and chappatis, and spicy chick peas.

Malik Gopi paused, raised his eyebrows, and looked slyly at his guests who burst out laughing. They drank from their goblets.

The servants will soon bring you your food, he said. In the meantime why don't you and the Frei try some jalebis.

It hit me then, a memory of how my hakim had treated a whole village in Raichur in Central India that had feasted for three consecutive days on jalebis and sweets to celebrate the festival of *Dassara*. On the fourth day their bellies were bloated with severe pain. *Hing* he had prescribed, a drug from faraway Iran, and pepper and salt and dry ginger, and the green leaves of the neem tree, mashed, then smeared on their bellies and, mixed with water, drunk as a concoction. It had worked.

You are a more than a hakim, you are a magician, the headman had said.

My hakim wouldn't accept any payment.

It wasn't a miracle at all but a miraculous purge. I was relieved, but I didn't have to tell anyone, even the Frei. I then remembered I too had not eaten the whole day. I was hungry, and I gulped down the rice, tasty basamati rice with its cumin fragrance, the dhal was hot and spicy, I didn't care for the chickpeas which the Frei ate with chappaties. He was hungry too. I had two tumblers of water and felt a little full, tired also, my feet began to feel strangely heavy. Malik Gopi offered me a *pān*, but I remembered what had happened and shook my head. I would not allow myself or the Frei to be tricked by Gopi. I turned towards the Frei to warn him not to accept the *pān*, and saw or thought I saw a servant drop a pinch of powder in the Frei's tumbler.

Don't drink that water, I warned the Frei.

So the Frei knows that you know Portuguese, said Gopi.

Why, Gopi asked me, why did you not want the Frei to drink that water.

I told him why.

Bring it here, immediately, he told the servant.

Look, Ahmadji, he said, there's nothing in this water.

He shouted at the servant. Throw it out, Gopi said. At once. Bring another tumbler.

Gopi turned the tumbler upside down, then filled it with water himself, and gave it to the Frei.

I felt thirsty, but refused Gopi's offer of a drink of water.

It was quite dark when we arrived at the guesthouse. Malik Gopi had insisted on accompanying us right up to the steps of the porch. I was sure Abdul would be there to greet us, but he wasn't.

Malik Gopi was about to leave when from behind Frei Louro's door we heard a voice calling out, a feminine voice so melodious it seemed to descend from above, the words melting into each other, the vowels prolonged.

Fre i. Frei Lou r o. Frei Anton io Louro. Son of Beatriz, countess of Porto. Nephew of the Prior of the Santa Cruz cathedral. Great missionary of Socotra a

The door opened and a flood of light, and a cloud of perfumed incense poured out. Soft music began to sound, a soft strumming on strings.

Welcome, oh holy man, I have come to grant you a foretaste of Paradise.

Come, oh holy saint, come to your well deserved reward.

Incense billowed out of the door, and wave after wave after wave of perfume and music.

The Frei was wonderstruck, I saw him move as in a daze slowly up the steps, and fling his arms out wide, then the incense filled room drew him in. Slowly the door shut.

Gopi squealed with delight, caught my arm and dragged me, I felt weak and strangely unsteady and helpless, to the back of the guesthouse. It was pitch dark. A gate screaked open.

A woman whispered, Gopi, and warm perfumed breasts dashed against me.

Champa, Gopi said.

I was pushed, and I stumbled and fell.

Abdul was there somehow.

Quiet, he said as he helped me up, or they'll kill us.

He led me into a cubicle in a pitch dark passageway between the rooms.

Don't shout, Abdul warned, whatever you see or hear, or they'll kill us.

I found myself staring through the transparent wall hangings into a brilliantly lit room, it was the Frei's room that had been rearranged.

The Frei was kneeling on a green carpet, his arms spread out wide, staring enraptured at a golden haired angel wrapped in a yellow silk garment, golden tipped white wings enfolded her, poised above him on a blue carpeted dais, as if she had just stepped out of the *Book of the Hours*. Incense and perfume filled the room that was alive with the sounds of music.

Hail, said the angel in Portuguese, *salve*.

Arise, and come, the feminine voice repeated. *Obsecro te.*

The Frei rose up slowly, uncertain and trembling, and he took one step forward, his arms outspread.

Come.

A seductive whisper.

Come gaze at thy reward.

A sudden release of perfume, then music and soft unearthly light. The white wings unfolded wide to reveal a pair of perfect breasts, high and round and earth brown and tipped with scarlet. A cloud of incense floated slowly up and veiled them. Below the dark navel and across the ample hips lay a shimmering scarf that concealed and deepened the mystery.

The Frei's open arms came together in a curve of yearning, and the front of his cloak billowed like a tent.

Come, make haste.

The Frei moved awkwardly forward.

The music stopped, the light dimmed, the voice trembled with passion.

Beija-me, dando o osculo da sua boca

Porque os tuas peitos são melhores do que vinho

To woo the Frei, I remembered.

A hush of intense silence.

Avaunt thee, Satan.

The Frei clutched at the tent with both hands, howled with outrage and then struck the dais with both hands, smashing it, and all the lights went out, and it was pitch dark and all was chaos and confusion, and there were screams of pain and hysterical laughter, and naked women and men came running out of the dark passageway, and Gopi's voice shouted Champa, and then an iron gate screeched loudly. Then the silence grew intense again.

TWENTY-TWO

*J*une, July, August
Monsoon months, 1509
Aiyaz's guesthouse, Champaner

I put together what happened on that day to Frei Louro in the guest house from what Abdul told me. He got the facts from Malik Gopi's servants, especially the women, who were given a feast to celebrate Champa's triumph.

Champa had arranged everything. It was she who thought up the plan for seducing the Frei.

The Sultan himself asked you to arrange a woman for the holy man who has never had a woman, she had told Gopi.

It was she who had thought immediately of the guesthouse. She and Malik Gopi had had it constructed four years ago to provide sexual entertainment for ambassadors and royal visitors. They named it the *House of Abandon*. The dark passageway between the two rooms with the transparent wall hangings on either side was a stroke of genius. It allowed Gopi and Champa to spy on the sexual embarrassments of their visitors, usually older men, who found it difficult to ride the young mares let loose into the guestrooms for their enjoyment.

At other times Champa would arrange live illustrations of *Kama Sutra* sexual positions in the two rooms, making use of acrobatic young girls from Malik Gopi's stable. Three handsome young noblemen, blindfolded, would then be led into the dark passageway. They would be joined by young courtesans who would slip through the iron gate in the compound wall. Champa and Gopi would join them in a wild night of voyeuring and changing partners and repeated couplings, no one knew who was who or whose, which would end just before dawn when a bell tinkled and the courtesans disappeared through the iron gate.

For the seduction of the Frei Champa had to summon forth all her powers of invention. It was challenging in many ways. She had to feed, and keep on feeding and exciting Gopi's demands for ever new sexual experiences. For some reason Malik Gopi had come to hate the Frei whose innocence he was determined to besmirch. But the Malik never showed his hatred openly. I think the Frei's goodness offended Gopi's reading of human nature, that man was basically evil and could easily be corrupted by money and women. Champa had to create a dramatic spectacle to show the Frei in the very act of succumbing to temptation.

It was a challenge for Champa too who did not accept the Muslim belief that sexual abstinence could lead to illness, physical or mental. As a courtesan trained in the art of Hindu erotics, as a worshipper of the great god Śiva, she had always been fascinated by the erotic powers of the ascetic. The Puranic myths, some of which the pandit had narrated to me, fascinated her. She knew about the tremendous control of the yogi who could draw his semen up to his spinal base and store its energies there. She knew that *tapas*, the intense heat generated by asceticism, charges the body with *kāma* and desire. She had been powerfully affected by stories of ascetics who had been seduced by courtesans and tempted by heavenly nymphs called *apsaras*. I suspect she was tempted to seduce the Frei herself. What would it be like for a holy man for the first time, she wondered aloud, and what would it be like with a holy man. But that would have been impossible. She knew Gopi and his fierce jealousy.

She planned every detail. She drew on erotic books and pictures which she got from the palace library. Then she studied the *Book of the Hours* which one of the servants stole from the Frei. The pictures of the Virgin did not interest her, but she was fascinated by the *apsara*like angels and knew, instinctively, that the Frei would be drawn to an angel temptress. The angel's folding wings were designed by Champa herself and stitched by her special tailor, carpenters made the special sloping dais, and the special effects, the incense, the perfume, the music, were handled by the one who staged spectacles for the palace ceremonies.

She called in Vora who called on João to provide the appropriate Portuguese words from the Bible. The words had to be pronounced correctly. João wasn't told everything, but he guessed that the seduction of the Frei had been planned.

You'll be killed if you reveal this to anyone, Vora, under orders from Gopi, told João. By assassins, Vora added. Perhaps that's why João escaped to Vijayanagar.

For Champa it was the triumph Malik Gopi said it was.

It was magnificent, Malik Gopi told Champa, both comic and erotic, an almost impossible combination. He paused. It was I who tricked

Ahmad ibn Madjid, let me tell you how. Instead of spiking the *pān* which I knew he would refuse, I told the kitchen to prepare the Frei's chickpeas with Melakan opium and to cook the dhal with *charas*. You know what happened.

Yes, yes, laughed Champa.

That courtesan, the one who tempted the Frei, was an excellent choice, said Gopi. I've never seen her before. Tell me her name, send her to me tomorrow night, her breasts were perfect.

Ah, said Champa, mischief in her eyes, they were. But you may not want her.

She told him her secret the next morning after their night of lovemaking.

That, she whispered in his ear as she nibbled on it, was neither man nor woman. That was an it. That was an impotent male who attained *nirvan* six months ago after the emasculation ritual, also called *nirvan*, when his soft penis and his balls, tightly tied in a bundle with string, were knifed off with two diagonal slashes. A tiny stick was then inserted into the opening.

The details of the operation did not horrify Malik Gopi, that voyeur. Something else shocked his Hindu sensibility.

But that's not Hindu *nirvan*, Malik Gopi protested. *Nirvana* is the experience of true liberation, of a second birth.

The *hijras* consider themselves reborn after the operation, said Champa. The ritual infuses them, they say, with the sacred power of *shakti*. That's why it is they who perform dances during marriage ceremonies to ensure fertility. That's why they're invited to homes where a male child is born.

Gopi was excited, and wanted to know where the operation was performed. I want to see it with my own eyes, he said.

I'll arrange it, Champa promised, I'll arrange an expedition to the main temple of the mother goddess, Bahuchara Mata, five miles north of Ahmadabad, where the *hijra* rite of passage is performed every six months.

Champa paused. Those perfect breasts were *māyic*, she said after a while. I fashioned them myself. Of earth, she said. I painted the nipples scarlet.

Ah, Gopi was delighted, I love that kind of *māyā*.

I wonder, said Champa when Gopi left, what it would be like with a holy man.

The Frei, Abdul and I now live in Malik Aiyaz's small guesthouse. It is crowded but we are content, and at peace. There is not much to do. The monsoon rains are intermittent, but very fierce on certain days when they storm across the parched land. This is the season when the earth cools down, stirs with new forms of life. It charges itself with secret energies. Strange insects, red, green, yellow, spring up out of the dust just for a day after the first rains, then they disappear. Nature takes command, urban man has to take a rest, and so do his constructions. The city quietens down. Champaner, surrounded by a silence made loud by the insect noises of the Indian night, is isolated. All activity at the palace, at the court, at the Hathikad army camp, comes to a stop. This is not the time for ambassadors to present their credentials. Visitors are few. The loud world of the Portuguese seems very far away. It's as if I've become deaf to the roar of *samsāra*.

Abdul has got his busy routine, he goes shopping, and cooks and serves food for the Frei and me. I feel relaxed as if my coiled being has unwound. Lazy too, I don't even feel the impulse to write. I have told my whole story, I tell myself, there's nothing more to tell. The cynic within me stirs but doesn't say anything. He has been quiet of late.

On days when it stops raining I go to the library. What I do there first is gently blow away the dust that has settled on my first born, my *Hawiya*, the first pilot book I wrote, but I do not open it, I do not need to. Then I turn the pages of a few books, but I don't pause to read even a page. These days I feel strangely dissatisfied, just as João implied he was, with the world of books, I don't know why. Even with the books of history I used to like to read. They always sing of success, never of failure or breakup. They're packed with praises of rulers and kings and dynasties. They glorify wars, but never mention battles lost. I no longer trust what they tell me.

I look up a book that tells the history of the mighty Bahmani kingdom that broke up into five separate states, Bijapur, Ahmadnagar, Bidar, Berar and Golconda, a decade after that great soldier statesman, Mahmud Gawan, was treacherously slain by order of his own Sultan. Mahmud Gawan had returned in triumph to Bidar, the Bahmani capital, after conquering Goa in 1472 and extending the western reaches of the Bahmani kingdom. I knew that Goa, where Abdul and Layla come from, which had been part of the Vijayanagara kingdom in South India, was a major outlet to the Indian Ocean. It was a port long coveted by the Bahmanis for the import of cavalry horses from Arabia and to promote international trade. I searched in vain through the pages of the official history. There was no mention at all of the death of the great Khwaja. It was as if Mahmud Gawan who had come from Gilan in Persia had never existed, and there naturally was no reference to the breakup of the Bahmani kingdom.

I don't bother to hunt in the library for the history of Vijayanagar, the great Hindu kingdom to which João has gone with my papers. Hindu Vijayanagar lies south of Muslim Bijapur, and both are constantly at war over the Doab, the land of the two rivers.

We Hindus don't believe in chronicles, the pandit had once told me. We don't write history but translate it into myth and fable. For we don't trust everyday time, he said solemnly staring at the tip of his nose, we seek a world of timeless truth beyond time.

I want just the simple truth, and I don't get that from history now.

What is truth, asks my cynic softly.

I get the strange feeling that many people before me have asked and have been asked this question, and it will surely be asked again.

Perhaps one has to be a poet to know the answer, I tell the cynic. Or a holy man.

The Frei has no questions. People look up to him as one who knows the answers. After the day of the miracle they came in crowds crying for *darshan*.

I am a sinner, he told the people in Portuguese, not a saint.

I didn't translate what the Frei said.

They would sit at his feet for hours asking questions about the future, asking what they should do. The Frei would try to answer every question very patiently. He did not have time to rest, or to pray with the Sultan. Abdul found it difficult to get the Frei to eat his food.

At times, Abdul told me, the Frei picks up a piece of chapatti with his fingers, and then forgets to put it in his mouth.

The Sultan was worried, and so was I. He decreed that the Frei would be available on only one day of the week for *darshan* and questions.

Only one day, but that's not enough, the Frei protested. That's not enough for me to affect their hearts or to convert them to

He stopped abruptly.

You have to be there with the holy man, Ahmadji, the Sultan told me. Look after the Frei.

The Frei spent the rest of the week praying, and talking to the Portuguese hostages. He advised them to get letters written, to send to their friends. He knew that Sidi Ali and I would sail to Cochin towards the end of August after the monsoon ended, and the seas were declared open.

He tried his best to learn how to speak Gujarati, but somehow couldn't. Something within him affected his tongue. His intonation was flat, the syntax so twisted that no one could understand what he was trying to say.

Malik Gopi has disappeared. Champa too. It was rumored, according to Abdul, that the sultan had banished them both because of the insult to the Frei. The servants said the master has gone to Surat. The courtesans believed he had gone to Ahmadabad, with Champa, gone they said, to escape from Toghan who it was rumored might have him assassinated.

Malik Aiyaz, Kiwam-ul-mulk Sarang and Sidi Ali discussed the negotiations to be entered with the Portuguese, the terms to be offered for the

exchange of prisoners and hostages, the compensation to be demanded
for the capture of the *Meri*. Should ours be an official embassy or should
we be sent as just negotiating envoys. Should *cartazes* be asked for the
Diu to Aden route. Malik Aiyaz was most indignant at first, then most
reluctantly he agreed to ask for the permits. Diu's customs collections had
dropped. The Sultan signed a gold embossed paper document that set
down the official credentials, the *crença*, of Sidi Ali as envoy. Outfits of
red silk and burnished velvet were prepared by the Sultan's own tailors
to give Sidi Ali a commanding dignified air that would impress the Portuguese who were fascinated by Oriental pomp. It was decided not to have
an entourage. I would be his assistant, and though Malik Aiyaz protested,
I insisted on wearing simple white cotton clothes.

Why not allow Frei Louro to accompany us, I suggested to Malik Aiyaz.

The Sultan will not agree, Kiwam-ul-mulk said, he's too valuable a
hostage.

Preto Thomaz has not yet completely recovered from his illness. He
had jaundice, which made his eyes and nails and urine yellow, and which
I treated by branding the sole of his right foot with a piece of red hot iron.
The shock to the whole body, my hakim had told me when I had asked
him how the cure worked, convulses the system and stirs up the yellow
poison which then drains through the open wound. It takes fifteen days
to heal completely.

The other hostages came to know about the cure and would come to
me for treatment of their minor ailments. A number of them fell ill because
of the change of food. They were not used to eating rice everyday, and the
damp rainy season is very trying for newcomers. I warned them about the
need to boil their drinking water to prevent cholera. It took me some time
to persuade them that blood letting, the usual Portuguese cure all, didn't
really work. Gradually they began to listen to my advice, and their health
improved.

I was most worried about the Frei who never looked after himself, but
was always concerned about the others. I knew a little about bonesetting,
and after I had set the bones of the Frei's right hand Abdul would see to
it that the bandages were changed every other day. The hand took some
time to heal. Abdul went up to Pawagadh and returned with tonic herbs
which I had him boil into a concoction for the Frei to drink. It didn't work.
The Frei continued to be sad and listless, brooding about things, lost at
times in his own thoughts, restless.

He needs something more than a tonic, Abdul said. He has a troubled
inside, he doesn't sleep much.

I asked the Frei what was troubling him.

Nothing, Ahmadji, he said, nothing you can help me with. I need another Frei to talk to. I need to confess.

You were tempted because of Champa, I said softly, it wasn't your fault.

That's not it, Frei Louro said. I need to talk to another friar, I wish I could go with you to Cochin. I can't talk to any of the other hostages here. It's a kind of confession I have to make about my loss of spiritual strength. I promise I will return here to Champaner as a hostage. Now I can't even write a letter, he tried to lift his right hand, to send to Cochin.

Why don't I write the letter for you, I said.

He showed me the letter he had been trying to write to his brothers in Loreto. It was four pages long, a messy scrawl of words and phrases that had been scratched out and rewritten, then scratched out again. He crumpled the pages with his left hand.

I can't write, Ahmadji, he told me, I have never been able to write. As soon as I do I have the feeling that my voice gets trapped. I see my words imprisoned on the page, my mind gets stuck, my fingers paralyzed.

Let me write the letter for you, I said.

We composed the letter in the dark silences of the long monsoon nights at a low table lit up by a single oil lamp. The Frei sat opposite me. He talked. I wrote. His voice was low, slow, full of pauses, hesitations. I found it difficult to capture his voice in writing. It was an immense strain for me to use the Frei's Biblical Portuguese with its Catholic terms that I was not familiar with. The letter was long and took a long time, for I had to ask the Frei to spell out some names and Latin words that I did not know.

To my dear brothers in Loreto
May the grace and love of Christ our Lord always help and assist you. And may your prayers assist me too.

I hurl my voice from Champaner here in India to you out there across the ocean-sea in faraway Portugal out of a deep despair. Not de profundis, my despair is not theological. I have full faith in God. My despair springs from my sleepless contemplation of the impossible Franciscan mission of salvation spread out before us today. Why impossible, you ask, my dear brothers, don't you trust divine providence. I realize how impossible it is to make you realize how impossible it is. Forgive me my brethren, forgive this my wordplay, a sign of the disturbance within me.

I have moved oceans away from you, thousands of miles in space, in time only three or is it four long years. But those measures of spacetime are totally inadequate. I have really traveled from ignorance to knowledge, an immeasurable chronotope, a quaint word my teacher of Greek put together. Only bonds of love and memory hold us close together, and it is love that drives me to reach out by telling you what now I know. I want to equip you with my terrible eyes so that you can see and know in the manner of Plato, as my cousin João used to say, and can then make the leap out of innocent Loreto into the world I now live in, and not remain the child Saint Paul mentioned to the Corinthians. I want to take you on the journey I took, and make you see face to face the caelum novum et terra nova of biblical prophecy.

The Frei paused for a long while, head bowed, brooding.

I asked him about certain words and phrases I had trouble with, especially the ones in Latin. He spelled them out for me.

Can I see what you've written, Ahmadji.

He stared at the paper for a long time.

I use a strange formal self conscious language, he said sadly, abstract and heavy with Latin. I don't ever talk like that, do I, Ahmadji. I wonder why my tongue when trapped on paper sounds so artificial. It's like the language I used to use in Loreto.

He paused.

It suddenly struck me that the tone of Frei Louro's voice sounded very much like that of João, his cousin. Did João know that Frei Louro was his cousin. I knew that Frei Louro's mother was the Prior's sister. Was João the Prior's illegitimate. My consciousness refused to release the word son trembling at its edge. Perhaps this wasn't the time to ask the Frei.

Let me continue, Ahmadji, said the Frei.

I don't know who or what led King Manuel of Portugal to order a small group of the three of us to come together in Loreto as pilgrim missionaries. Frei Henrique of Coimbra was our leader. And there was Frei Luís do Salvador who came from Lisbon with the news that the world had changed and that there was need to equip ourselves with a new vision in order to conquer the world for Christ. I was the third. We were told to keep ourselves ready to depart for new worlds. As you all know, Frei Henrique and Frei Luís do Salvador had to leave very soon for India in an armada of 12 ships commanded by Senhor Pedro Alvares Cabral. I was given the task of arranging for a selection of books of Christian doctrine, catechisms, missals, books of Hours, copies of the Flos Sanctorum, to be presented by our embassies to foreign rulers and kings. Frei Luís told me that King Manuel insisted on my obtaining The Book of the Destruction of Jerusalem, printed by Valentim Fernandes. It's for Preste João, the Emperor of the Indies, Frei Luís whispered, the Emperor will be our ally for a stupendous project.

I didn't want to collect books. I hungered to venture into the unknown, I wanted to be a martyr for Christ.

It was the letter from Frei Henrique sent from a new land that Senhor Cabral named Terra de Santa Cruz, the letter read out to all of us in Loreto in 1501, that made me realize how limited my language was and is to present a view of a new world.

In Loreto we lived in a Christian universe based on a Biblical geography. Based on a mappa mundi where Heaven and Earth came together, and all travel was a pilgrimage through space and time to Jerusalem, the sacred womb of our Christian world. Frei Henrique's letter from brazilwood land revealed to us in Loreto that newly discovered pagan space had to be made sacred. New lands had to be baptized with Christian names like Monte Pascual, new peoples like the Tupinamba were adams and eves. They were the new children of paradise that had to be civilized and made Christian.

Frei Henrique rejoiced because he found it easy to lead these children and lead them to Christianity. The Tupinamba were naked innocents, lacking the trappings of civilization. They had a spoken but not a written language which as you know is essential to embody our Christian truths. What we had to do to make the Tupinamba Christian in word and deed was to wean them from their barbaric customs like offering their wives and daughters to strangers and guests, and get them to discard their limited language and learn ours. They would not lose anything at all. They would gain Christianity and a new language. Frei Henrique rejoiced greatly. They would be taught by the two degredados left there. We have taken the first step, he wrote in his letter, to conquer the world for Christ.

I too set out with my band of four friars in 1506 to win the world for Christ. My missionary task, an official of King Manuel's court told me, would be to establish a monastery for the people of Socotra who had been made Christian by the holy apostle, Saint Thomas, before he set sail for India. Two centuries after the advent of Islam, we were told, these Christians had been oppressed by the invading Arab Muslims and then abandoned by the Chaldaean Church. Senhor Piteira, whose ship during a storm had taken shelter in Socotra and had wintered there in 1503, had extolled to our King Manuel of Portugal the advantages of a Christian Socotra as a strategic military base set near the Red Sea.

You will be the Guardião of the monastery responsible for the conversion of the whole of Socotra. Go as crusaders for Christ, the royal message ended.

Simple, we thought, like making them wear new clothes.

We set sail for Socotra in 1506 in an armada of 11 ships commanded by Tristão da Cunha with his cousin, Afonso de Albuquerque, as second in command with 5 ships.

Our missionary spirits leapt up when after our long and arduous voyage round the stormy Cape of Good Hope we beheld this wondrous island with its majestic cloud capped mountains, its green date palms, its silver white sands cut by clear flowing streams, and above all the aloes, the frankincense groves and the dark umbrella shaped dragon's blood trees that exuded drops of cinnabar. At last we were in the real East. We thought we had reached Paradise.

Then we saw an Arab fortress on the beach.

The ruthless massacre by our forces of the gunless Arab Fartakis, a few managed to flee to the mountains, who tried to defend their fort set above the portcity of Suk, and our inhuman treatment of Khwaja Ibrahim, their Sheik whose severed head dripping with blood was fastened to one of the four towers of the fortress shocked us friars greatly.

Why not spare their lives, I pleaded, why not show them true Christian mercy.

They refused to surrender, our captain Afonso de Albuquerque explained. This is Christian territory which our king ordered us to reclaim from the infidels for Christ.

One of our friars quoted from one of the Church Fathers. Only evangelization, he proclaimed, justifies the conquest and possession of a territory. Massacre, he continued, even of women and children, is permitted to frustrate the evil designs of an enemy.

I was greatly disturbed. I thought of Saint Francis and of what he would have said and done.

The celebrations that followed must have made me forget my doubts. We quickly converted the mosque in the fortress which we named after that vanquisher of Satan, São Miguel, into a church that we dedicated to Our Lady of Victory. We installed the portative organ we had brought from Lisbon, raised high a gilded altarpiece of the Virgin Mary for all to see, and then we rang the tower bell continuously to summon back the Socotran Christians who had fled from Suk. Carrying aloft my silver crucifix which my mother had given me I led a solemn procession with my friars, who were clad in gold vestments and swung censers of fragrant incense, from the gate of the fort to the church which was too small to accomodate all the Socotran Christians that had flocked there for the Mass of Thanksgiving that I celebrated.

A month later with the help of the Christians we rebuilt their church shaped like a synagogue, set on a hill overlooking Suk, and we dedicated it to their patron, Saint Thomas. The people crowded into the church for instruction in the faith after which they could receive the sacrament of baptism. They didn't know our language and I don't think they understood what we preached, but were overjoyed when we gave them gifts of food and clothes. Our hearts were filled with tremendous joy as we labored night and day in our vineyard, baptizing the people, teaching the casises, that's what they called their priests, our prayers in Portuguese and Latin. The people loved to sing hymns of devotion to our Lady which they sang in Socotri, a simple language which one of our friars who had a good ear for languages picked up. The Socotrans were very like children. They loved to kneel in front of the altarpiece of the Mother of God and sing these devotional songs with their hands folded in prayer.

In our innocent ignorance we friars thought that we could transform the whole of Socotra into a Christian land. Leaving my companions to take care of the Christians of Suk and to administer to the needs of our men in the encampment, I set forth boldly to preach to the Socotrans and to baptize them. Wearing my ash brown robe and a pair of leather sandals, armed only with my apostolic zeal and with a staff, accompanied by a casis and a Christian Socotran, I limped over and across the Haghier mountains through the dry river wadis rough with boulders to the other village towns. I thought the Christians would welcome me with open arms. They didn't. It took me some time to find out why.

They were afraid, they were too poor, they had been abandoned too long. Their religious ceremonies were performed in Aramaic, an ancient language no one, not even their cacises, now understood. They did not know how to read or write, they knew how to make the sign of the cross, they fasted on certain days but knew not why, they practiced circumcision like the Muslims. But they had somehow retained a primitive Christianity, these Greek survivors of shipwreck as they believed they were. Their women very fair, very beautiful, were all named Maria, the men, tawny and well shaped, all had Thomas as one of their names.

They lived in awe of their Muslim overlords who exacted forced labor from them, but wisely did not persecute them. They were not allowed to carry any weapons but were allowed to live in their own separate villages and to worship in their own churches which were strangely almost next door to the mosques. At times the Muslims would forcibly carry away their daughters, especially those that were fair with Grecian faces, marry them and force them to become Muslims. I found that the landless Socotran Christians were heavily dependent on the Fartaki Muslims for everything, especially for food which was scarce. They depended on them for dates and goats and sheep.

My visits to the distant village towns of Ras Momi, Kallensiya and Ghubba bore no fruit. The Christians stayed away from their churches. The Muslims had threatened them, they refused to give them food, they warned them that we Portuguese had come to enslave them.

Only at Hadibu, a town next to our encampment at Suk, did the Christians come in great numbers to listen to my preaching and they allowed themselves to be baptized. We gave them some clothes and dates as food gifts. We ourselves were running short of food.

Elated, I walked one day into the Hadibu mosque to make peace with the Muslim cacises. As soon as I entered a crowd of Muslims began yelling, waving their hands, pointing to my feet, threatening me. One of them grabbed my staff and would have hit me on the head, but was prevented by another Muslim who shouted at the others, then took me by the arm, led me to the entrance, bade me remove my sandals, and courteously led me back barefoot into the mosque. I was allowed to walk around. The mosque was severely bare except for a niche in the wall and some stairs leading up to a pulpit. I returned to Suk thoroughly ashamed of my ignorant behavior. I was exhausted after a month of wandering around and of accomplishing nothing. I slept for two days.

When I woke up I was shocked to learn that Afonso de Albuquerque had blown up the Hadibu mosque to avenge the insult to me. Ten Arab defenders were hanged in the public square, others had their noses and ears cut. I rushed to his headquarters set up in the fortress tower. The sheik's skull gleamed white in the fierce sunlight.

You cant go in, the guards said, capitāo-general Albuquerque is having a council meeting.

I stormed past the guards.

Stop the mad slaughter, I shouted to Albuquerque.

Come in, come in Guardião, Albuquerque said. He did not raise his voice. I had sent for you yesterday but was told you were asleep. You have come at the right time.

The killing must stop, I shouted.

Take a seat, Guardião. That one, that one on my right, next to João de Nova. Don't be afraid of his huge front teeth. They make him look arrogant. He is a very good fighter, but not as fierce to quarrel with words as these four.

He pointed to the four ship captains who glared down at the table in front of them.

Honorable captains, Albuquerque said. I have listened patiently to your arguments against my Hormuz campaign. What's the use, the four of you ask, of capturing that island city with our five ships and with just 500 men when we will not be able to hold it. Much better, since all these seas belong to Portugal, to do what we came to do, patrol the Arabian seacoast and plunder the enemy ships laden with rich treasure. We will gain both honor and glory for Christ and Portugal.

The four captains surprised, looked up expectantly at Albuquerque whose eyes had turned black, the centers intense red. He paced up and down in front of the table, then he turned to them. His voice changed, its tone became guttural as if it rose up from unknown depths within him, and it seemed to me that he grew taller, more commanding.

I know, Albuquerque said, I know exactly why you took up your commissions to sail the Indian seas.

Wealth and heroic adventure, burst through João da Nova's front teeth.

No, said Albuquerque, you joined in hopes of plunder. That was in the past. But now that Tristão da Cunha has departed for India, now as capitāo-general and sole commander of the Indian ocean seas up to Cambay. My mission is to conduct you to higher goals. First, get rid of the plunderer mentality. No longer will you be mere corsairs, you will be crusaders. The instructions of our king, whose full title is, by the grace of God, King of Portugal and the Algarves d'Aquem e d'Alem mar em Africa, Lord of Guinea and of the Conquest, Navigation and Commerce of Ethiopia, Arabia, Persia and India, are clear.

We have orders from King Manuel to establish bases in this part of the world and impose a naval blockade of the entrances to the Red Sea and the Persian Gulf in order to choke off all Muslim trade from Asia to the middle east and to Europe. Socotra was to be one of our bases, but as I have now come to realize it is too distant from the mainland, and Suk is not an all weather port. We are too weak to occupy the port city of Aden, semicircled by mountain walls. But we will conquer Hormuz and build a fort there. We will not be plunderers but conquerors. We will establish Portuguese rule in this part of the world. How, you ask. I do not know yet.

I shall be brief. I never explain matters and I do not propose to discuss my plans with you. Our king told me to consult with you, which I have done. Now is the time for action. I want you to get your ships repaired so that they are water tight. Your masts should be oiled and the spares in good condition. Tighten your cables and ropes, sew patches on sails and check the spares, fix any broken water barrels and get them filled, and check all crossbows and the shafts of lances. Above all see to it that your supplies of gunpowder are thoroughly dry. And be prepared to set sail on August 10th on our expedition to Hormuz. Start preparations immediately, today, now.

I want to consult with the Guardião, we have to talk.

He came and sat next to me in João da Nova's chair.

Guardião, he said softly, Frei Louro, he said, gazing into my eyes. About those Muslim infidels I massacred, how can I tell you I'm sorry for what I did when I'm not.

His voice had changed again. It now sounded as if it came through the grille of a confessional.

Senhor Albuquerque, I asked, do you want to make an act of confession.

No, burst out of him and he strode to the door, flung it wide open, looked to the left, then to the right, then sent the guards away.

I have enemies, he whispered to me, everywhere, here, in India, and in Portugal. I have to be very careful.

Listen, Frei Louro, about what you term massacres, that's just from your point of view which is that of a son of Saint Francis, with faith in man and in all embracing love. As you heard me tell the captains, I never explain. Nevertheless, I want you to consider this, from my viewpoint, as a leader with responsibility for my men and with royal duties to fulfill. The Muslim Fartakis on this island would have risen up and massacred us all after Tristão da Cunha and his ships left for India on August 1st. I had to make a harsh statement of absolute power. Which I immediately did. I had to. I terrified them into submission. No more explanations.

I sent for you to ask about a matter that troubles me greatly.

Is it a sin to act against the mad delusions of your own king that will lead his country to certain disaster.

Listen carefully, Frei, for I never repeat what I say.

Our king, Dom Manuel of Portugal, suffers from the obsession that the Holy Spirit has descended on him and, in these apocalyptic times, that divine design has ordained that he be the messiah emperor who will conquer Jerusalem, deliver the Holy Sepulcher, and establish a world united in one holy Catholic and apostolic faith. Many court flatterers encourage him in this messianic belief by pointing to telltale signs, his unnatural green white eyes and his unusual knee length arms, and above all to the miracle of his succeeding to the throne after five quick deaths, he being a distant sixth away from the throne.

And then there is one of your own order, Frei Luís do Salvador, an ardent believer of the teachings of Joachim of Fiore, who has filled the king's brain with his talk about the golden wealth of the Indies and the bringing together of all the Christian kings of Asia and the alliance with the wealthy emperor Preste João of the Indies in order to subjugate the foes of the Holy Faith. You are Emmanuel the fortunate, the mad Frei proclaims, the Promised One, the king of kings. You will reconquer Jerusalem with the help of Preste João of the Indies to whom I will go as your emissary.

I knew Frei Luís do Salvador's family. His mother whom he loved very much, who worked in the convent where her son was educated, and who thought he was destined to become a missionary in the new world, died suddenly when he was fifteen. His father, wanting to cure his son's delusions and crazy visions, wanted me to take him to fight in Morocco. But, driven by his dreams, he joined your order. They tell me he has traveled several times to India on a secret mission.

Your reign will witness the final conversion of the Jews, the Muslims and the Gentiles. You'll be the glorious uniter of all Christendom, Frei Luís da Salvador proclaimed to our king.

Listen Frei Louro, listen very carefully now. Albuquerque's voice grew more intense. King Manuel issues commands that are contradictory like the shifting crosswinds and unpredictable currents we encountered below the Cape of Good Hope. Conquer Jerusalem with the help of Preste João, orders the king. That fabled Preste we have not yet been able to contact. Dom Manuel wants me to attack the Mamluk kingdom of Egypt and Syria, and kill its ruler who, Frei Luis has convinced him, is the wicked sultan of biblical Babylon. Establish military bases, the king told me, in Socotra and especially in Aden. Impossible tasks. Little does he know, surrounded as he is by flatterers in Montemayor in faraway Portugal, about the new nonBiblical geography that we Portuguese discoverers have revealed to the world.

He has not learned, as I have, from the pilots and navigators of the Indian Ocean, and especially from pilot Omar whom we captured here at Suk, that Aden with its descending fortified walls and towering mountains is unconquerable. He does not realize that food supplies are very scarce at Socotra, and that the winds and crosscurrents make it impossible transform this island into a way station for *all seasons. And that the Persian Gulf and the Red Sea are just narrow gullets of water with swirling crosswinds and coral rocks and reefs that make it impossible for our caravels and naos to navigate to Bahrein in the Persian Gulf to obtain seedpearls, or to steer to Jiddah in the Red Sea, that port for infidel Mecca.*

Frei Louro, our faraway king has laid impossible tasks on me. My question which may appear strange to you is this, are kings divinely appointed, will I commit a mortal sin of disobedience against the king if I act instead in the interests of our glorious country, Portugal. These be turbulent times. I sense a powerful urge within me gathering power, the power of our Portugal.

He led me to the tower window and we both stared at a ship seemingly nailed to a horizon that shimmered in the hazy noonday sun.

That ship sailing beyond the horizon, can you see it, Frei. That's our ship of state in today's turbulent world, blown about by mad winds and erratic currents, drifting onward, pilotless and rudderless, into the future. I could continue my image, Frei Louro, but what's the use, you're no navigator. And I do not choose to explain myself. But consider this, our mad king who thinks he is in command in faraway Lisbon has no sense of a destination or a destiny. His gaze is fixed on a shifting map that confuses the new world with the old.

The people on that ship are also confused. The world picture has broken up. Our old social order is breaking up too. There are quarreling factions now. Each faction with its selfish perspectives owes allegiance only to itself. There are fidalgos who refuse to step into the new world and clamor for old time pomp and glory. There are the landless second generation nobility, greedy, their hands extended to grasp fame and fortune. There are the ignorant gente baixa. And then the traders from outside Portugal, estrangeiros. The merchant communities of the Genoese and the Florentines eager for profit, there are German financiers venturing money to make more money and to take our money away to their country, and Flemish and German gunners ready to sell their services to the highest bidder. Our ship alas is unequipped, our people have no skills, mercantile or military, and no materials with which to trade, and so our ship travels here and there erratically seeking it knows not what.

I will take over this ship of state, my patria, and transform it into the new Portugal, the ship of empire, proclaimed Albuquerque.

Yes, Frei Louro, that's what I'll do, that's what I have to do.

He paused for a while. Then he said, Thank you Frei, for it is you who have made me see what we both have to do.

I drew back, quite shocked. I had not said anything to him.

Albuquerque turned his eyes from the sea and stared deeply into mine. I could see his eyes turn completely red. And his voice changed again.

Both of us, he said, will be conquerors. You want to conquer the world for Christ with the sword of faith. I have to conquer the world and raise our Portugal aloft to glory. You want to use the language of love and human brotherhood. My guns and bombards will speak my language for me, that of thunder and power that will resound, Viva Portugal, Viva, Viva Portugal, all across the ocean seas from Hormuz to Cochin to Melaka. Impossible tasks, oh Frei my brother, yes, both our tasks are impossible. Do you realize how many infidels and gentios exist in our newly discovered world. Countless, pilot Omar told me, as countless as the sands on the seashore. The Indian Ocean is considered a vast Islamic lake which we Portuguese have to dominate and control. How, how, Frei Louro, how will you manage to convert them all and bring them to Christ. You don't have many friars do you, just as I have only a few soldiers and guns and ships.

But, it can be done, Frei Louro. I have big ships and I have guns. And I have some plans. Which I shall not explain to you now.

Patience, Frei Louro. I go to conquer Hormuz on August 10th, where do you go, Frei Louro.

Leave me now, Frei.

I left Albuquerque staring beyond the horizon at the oceansea.
Another madman, I thought, who believes that power and conquest, not love and martyrdom, will enable us to conquer the world for Christ.

Then, slowly, doubt and despair began to creep into me, my dear brothers in Loreto. Where will you go, Albuquerque had asked. I just didn't know.

I brooded about my failure in Socotra. I thought suddenly, I dont know why, of the miracle of the loaves and fishes. Then I reconsidered the interconnection between food and faith. Aren't both forms of sustenance, one for the body, the other for the spirit. I thought of our four Christians here in Champaner who have turned Muslim merely to enjoy a comfortable life. Could I really blame them. I thought of Albuquerque's strange views about the language of power. Could he be right. The Muslims here in Champaner refuse to listen to me. They dont understand and dont want to understand Portuguese, and I cannot speak Gujarati. Tristão de Ga, who is learning Gujarati, tells me that there are no terms in Gujarati for heaven, grace, cross. Everything's impossible. I never thought language would be so formidable a barrier.

Tell me what I should do, my dear brothers in Loreto. I need your prayers and your advice. I feel paralysed. After Albuquerque returned from Hormuz to Socotra with some food supplies that soon ran out, and after two of my friars died, I sailed to India to get help, and was shipwrecked off the Cambay coast. I don't know where I am. I still feel shipwrecked. Mine, unlike Albuquerque's, was the ship of faith. Help

I never did end the Friar's letter for him with the farewell salutation that he wanted.

May our Lord always assist you, as I desire he assist me.

Your dearest brother in Christ.

Louro

The Sultan summoned us both to the palace. Sidi Ali was quite ill and would not be able to travel to Cochin. The Sultan asked the Frei whether he was prepared to take a solemn oath that he would return from Cochin after the mission of the embassy was done.

What will you swear on, the Sultan asked.

By the holy cord around my waist and by this rosary and this holy cross, Frei Louro said, I promise I'll return to Champaner.

Will you keep them here in Champaner, asked the sultan.

The cord and the rosary I will, said Frei Louro, but not the silver cross which was given to me by my mother and which I want to look at on my deathbed.

Do not trust that Christian infidel, a courtier murmured.

He is a holy man, the Sultan said. I have faith in him. He will come back to us.

Never mind ending the letter, Frei Louro told me. I will make two copies of the letter and send one to Frei Henrique who will have several copies of the letter made in Cochin, that's in case of shipwreck, to send to Lisbon.

He smiled sadly.

TWENTY-THREE

*T*urushka Quarters, mid August 1509,
the evening after my arrival in Vijayanagar city
in the company of VN
I, João, am writing this account

I am in such turmoil that I don't know why I'm writing this, this account, this letter. Nor do I know who the I is who is writing this confession to you, Ahmadji, this cry for help.

This echoes the beginning of your account, doesn't it, Ahmadbhai. When you began your account you were confused, you did not know where to enter your past. Then as I read your story I watched it slowly turn into a voyage of discovery that has not yet ended.

But I do know what I have to do first. To return all your papers, here they are, Ahmadji. The Vijayanagar agents will deliver them to you in faraway Champaner together with this letter.

Also to say I'm sorry I took your papers.

When I took them my being was in a whirl, so that I didn't, and I still don't know why I didn't stop to consider what effect my taking of your papers would have on you. It was unforgivable, a sin against you. I think I took them because of many reasons. I envied you your calm of mind. I was also curious. I wanted to know the past out of which you sprang. Your past self which you've always hoarded tightly, and released only sparingly when we talked. I also wanted to know what you had written about my self, for I want to know if I have a true self.

I look down the corridors of my past, and consider its chronotopes. That's a strange word coined long ago for António Louro and me by our Greek teacher in the Santa Cruz monastery in Coimbra. The corridor image springs from the multi colonnaded Hazāra Rāma temple, wherein I spent six long hours yesterday dazed by its *apsaras* and its colossal magnificence.

Today, as I write, I am highly conscious of the military self I have assumed here in Vijayanagar, that of a man of action reputed to know all about horses and guns and war. I look back at my clown self that put on a performance for the sultan's *haram* women in Champaner. At the arrogant scholastic I was at the Sorbonne in Paris, a student of theology who knew everything about everything. At the stone I was, in the Lisbon Rossio, that had to be softened by a woman into human form. Then at my *degredado*self on Pedro Cabral's ship, at my *mirza*self wandering through East Africa and Arabia, with a back glance at my orphan innocence, lying on the steps of the Santa Cruz cathedral in Coimbra on Christmas Day, so so very distant in place and time. And I bewail my protean self that I fear is no self at all.

I also wanted to find out what you had written about the self I am thoroughly ashamed of now, the mask I put on in Diu and in Champaner, so difficult now to tear away.

I like to think, Ahmadbhai, that the true reason why I took away your papers before I left for Vijayanagar with VN was because I was sure Ishak and Malik Gopi would have had them stolen if I hadn't taken them. Malik Gopi had been informed that you were writing down things, and he and Ishak wanted to know if you had set down details for Malik Aiyaz about their treachery and mine. The day before I left for Vijayanagar with VN I saw Vora, who is Malik Gopi's chief agent and spy, as you know, reach out through the window grille of our Pawagadh house. Your papers were on the table. He was startled when he saw me come up the steps of the porch. What are you looking for, I asked Vora. Nothing, nothing *senhor*, Vora said, scratching his left ear with his right hand, I was looking for Abdul. What brings you to Pawagadh, Vora. In broken Portuguese Vora mumbled something about having come to visit the Kali Mata temple, and left hurriedly. Later Abdul told me never to trust Vora. He is a swindler, Abdul said, an assassin too, he conceals a dagger in his waistband. He is Ishak's friend.

Ishak, hungry for power, has hired an assassin to murder his father, Malik Aiyaz, who has his own circle of spies, and knows almost everything that is happening in Diu. Malik Aiyaz knew about Ghazi Mujli, and about Gopi's spy, whom Ishak had to stab to death on the pretext that the spy was an assassin, lest he reveal their conspiracies to Malik Aiyaz. But I don't think Malik Aiyaz knows about Ishak's involvement with Hooknose and the mahdavis.

You are, at times, a political innocent, my friend.

Not really, though. You do have a nose that twitches with suspicion. You did jot down in your account that I was somehow, you did not know how, involved in the conspiratorial world of Ishak and Malik Gopi. But you yourself wanted to be uninvolved. You didn't even want to know what is happening in the world you live in.

You're unaware that Champaner and Surat and Ahmadabad are places of conspiracy and political maneuvering. I am sure you did not know that Virappa Nāyaka, the Vijayanagar envoy to Gujarat, was also a spy. That he had been sent by his king to Diu to look at the defense setup of chains across Diu channel so that he could plan one for his horse port Bhatkal, sent also to buy guns from Portuguese deserters, and to get Arab purebreds for the Mahānavāmi celebrations to be held here in September. And to arrange for a regular supply of horses for the Vijayanagar cavalry. Sent also to outbid any offer made by that friend of our maulvi, Karim Khan, the envoy from Muslim Bijapur, for horses from Kacch and Sind.

Horses are now in very short supply after the advent of the Portuguese who have disrupted the regular flow of horse traffic from Arabia and Persia to Bhatkal and Goa, the two major horse trading ports of western India, as you well know. Why are horses so important, you ask, Ahmadji. Because the outcome of the war between Vijayanagar and Bijapur depends on swift cavalry forces now, not on elephants or on masses of foot soldiers that the Hindu South used to rely on in the past. Horses are essential. Guns, too.

What you perhaps do not know are the wily tricks of the Arab horse traders who had wanted to limit the number of horses shipped to India in order to drive prices sky high. They would never allow any mares to be imported for they did not want horses to be bred in India. And they forbade the bringing in of horse doctors, and of specialists in the rearing and feeding of horses. Horses in south India, where the climate is humid, are fed a heavy diet of cooked rice and pulses that these creatures of the desert are not accustomed to, so that many sicken and die. The Arab traders wanted the flow of horses to be continuous. The sailing season for horse transportation is limited. Horses cannot stand rough seas. They panic when there's lightning and thunder. The horse traders used to supply 10,000 war horses to Vijayanagara via Bhatkal, and to Bijapur via Goa for their armies every year.

At first they rejoiced because the advent of the Portuguese drove prices up. Now, with the flow down to a trickle, they curse the Portuguese and their thunderous guns. For though a purebred Arab now sells for over 1000 ashrafis, there are very few horses to sell.   Hindu Vijayanagar and Muslim Bijapur are now in fierce competition for the few Arabian horses that are landed in Gujarat. Both envoys have rejected the Kacchi horses as unsuitable for their cavalry forces. The Arab traders would prefer to sell their horses to their co-religionists at Goa, but Hindu Vijayanagar is so rich that it can pay any price that the traders demand. King Krishna Deva Raya takes horses dead or alive and pays a thousand pardaos each. He even pays for the ones that die at sea provided they bring him the tails as proof. Why pay for the tail, you ask. Because, Ahmadji, without a tail an Arabian horse cannot balance itself right and run swiftly. How's that you, João know such a lot about horses, your cynic asks.

Malik Aiyaz in Diu and Sultan Mahmud Begada in Champaner would make no commitments to either envoy. Sultan Begada, on the advice of Malik Aiyaz, has demanded payment not in gold coin but in diamonds from the fabulous mines of Golconda and Vajra Karur. That's why Virappa Nāyaka left Diu in haste. He suggested that I come with him to Vijayanagar where I would be safe from my enemies in Diu, from Ishak Khan and from Malik Gopi to whom I owe a great deal of money.

I can hear you, Ahmadbhai, though you are in faraway Champaner, ask me why, João, why, softly. You are keenly curious about things. You want to listen to other people's stories but you never tell them anything about yourself. You always remain silent, now you want answers to both whys.

Well, because I convinced Virappa Nāyaka I could train the Vijayanagara cavalry in the new technique of arquebus fighting so that they could vanquish the Bijapuri horse archers. That was after I discovered that the softspoken Virappa Nāyaka was not just an envoy. As cousin of King Krishna Deva Raya and one who sided with him in his struggle for the royal throne last year, he was appointed commander in chief of all the cavalry forces in the Vijayanagar kingdom. When I discovered he was keenly interested in horses and guns and war I set out to fascinate him.

I dazzled him. Not by using cold logic, but by zigzag flashes of insight, darting around from one topic to another to create the illusion that I knew everything about everything, especially about war.

I told him how guns had made the old modes of warfare by sword and lance and bow obsolete. Think of the Muslim invasion of Hindu India through the northwest, I said. That's a *nonsequitur*, Ahmadji. Why does my seminary Latin come back to me. Think of the Portuguese with their ships and cannons, I told him. I didn't elaborate, deliberately. I went on to talk about the use of elephants in war, how these huge docile creatures were not war animals, how they could not stand the to-them noxious smell of horses, so that it was difficult to get them in battle formation for attack or defence. I referred knowingly to Alexander the Great and to the *Ars Tactica* which the Prior gave me to read in Coimbra. I talked about Hannibal, and the use of elephants. I went on to talk about how bombards, like elephants, were unwieldy and could only be used as siege engines. I went on to dazzle him by talking impressively about guns and sails and gunpowder empires now forming about which, as you know, I know nothing.

But I did know a great deal about Ottoman tufengs and about arquebuses, which the Portuguese call *espingardas* and the Mamluks *bunduqs*. As a *degredado* I had been trained to handle an arquebus which the Portuguese nobility considered beneath their dignity to even touch. A chosen few of the *degredados* on Pedro Alvares Cabral's armada to India were made to practice shooting everyday. Except, of course, when the sea was rough. Frei Luís do Salvador insisted that I be trained too, telling the captain major that I had to be sent on a mission through Africa in quest of Preste João. I proved to be such a good shot that the Italian gun founder Pietro asked me to help him teach the other *degredados* how to shoot. I watched the gunners at practice firing cannons on the high seas, carefully noting the procedures they followed. I also learnt to shoot with the *tufeng* during my wanderings in East Africa and in Arabia.

I demonstrated both weapons at the Diu gun range to Virappa Nāyaka. The Portuguese arquebus is infinitely superior to the Ottoman *tufeng* which is a longer weapon and not as accurate. I could see that Virappa Nayaka grew quite excited. The black vertical streak on his forehead creased, the right corner of his thick lips trembled. But his voice remained calm. His eyes remained cold.

He began confiding in me. VN, that's what he wanted me to call him, told me that the three Italians who had sailed as armourers in Pedro Cabral's fleet had escaped from the Portuguese in Cochin to Calicut in 1501. They had planned to purchase precious stones and jewels in India, and return as rich men to Italy. One of them, Pietro the gunfounder, had been bribed away from Calicut to Vijayanagar, VN told me, with a diamond weighing 100 carats and worth 350 ducats.

Before I left for Diu, VN said, Pietro was in the process of setting up a foundry three miles outside the Vijayanagar city wall to manufacture guns and cannon for our army. Honawar would send us sulphur and saltpetre and a special kind of charcoal powder filtered through Cannanore wellwater. The other two deserters had already manufactured 500 pieces of ordnance for Calicut, but would soon defect to us in Vijayanagar to assist their friend and to train soldiers to handle guns.

Soon we'll have hundreds and thousands of guns for the Vijayanagar army to attack Bijapur and our enemies, VN said.

The corners of his lips trembled with excitement.

I also pretended to be greatly excited. But I kept discreetly quiet. I didn't tell VN that I had been trained by Pietro or that I was a Portuguese *degredado*.

That's perfect, I said. He gave me a broad smile.

It was now time to fling in the element of doubt.

But, I said.
And I paused.

But.

I paused again, wrinkling my eyebrows to look a little cynical.

You don't believe me, he said. Do you know how many troops we can mass together for a campaign.

I didn't say a word.

Eleven lakhs, he said, that is, eleven hundred thousand soldiers.

I pretended not to be impressed, though I was.

The whole of Portugal, I had been told when I was in Lisbon, was inhabited by just over one and a half million people.

What if a million outsiders from overseas invade your country, I asked VN.

Listen to what my guru, Sri Vyāsarāya, said. If every one in our land were to take a grain of sand, they could bury the Portuguese in sand.

But can you bury their guns.

VN ignored the question.

In addition, VN continued, in Vijayanagar city alone, my king, Krishna Deva Raya has 120 *ghattams* of elephants, that is 1200 trained beasts. He also has a force of 80,000 horse. On our war campaigns, when we march against our enemies, the Gajapatis of Orissa or the Bijapuri sultan, it is as if a whole city were in motion. An infinitude of people, VN said, an immense army made up also of spearmen, shield bearers, pikemen, lance bearers, swordsmen, and of water carriers, 12000 of them, 20,000 women of pleasure paid by the king, carts, camels, bullocks, chariots, so many only God could count them. My guru, Sri Vyāsarāya, has compared the Vijayanagara army on the move to the seething ocean, *samsāra sāgara*, he calls it, whose horizon is endless.

I looked straight into his cold eyes. I did believe VN, but I also knew that leaders deliberately exaggerate the size of their forces.

You don't believe me, VN said. Wait till you witness our Mahānavāmi festival.

It was time for a change of tactics. I had to resume control of the conversation.

You've forgotten what I told you earlier, I said softly, about the old mode of warfare. Thousands of foot soldiers, I said, will not prevail in this our present age of cavalry and guns and sails. What if your enemies come sailing across the ocean sea and attack you with cannons and guns.

Turushka Quarters
Vijayanagar
NIGHT

I have noted down place and time but have had to abandon setting down the date. The Hindu calendar here is based on phases of the moon. My body feels strange, my mind confused.

To steady my mind let me jot down the routine I follow here in Vijay-anagar.

Mornings Abolem my courtesan who looks after my needs brings me mango juice. Then I stroll through the streets of the city, getting crowded they tell me because of the approach of the Mahānavāmi celebrations. I want to get to know Hindu Vijayanagar but, unlike Muslim Diu with its minarets and domes, Vijayanagar with its dark and intricate temples and gods refuses to enter my being.

I walk to the House of Vision, the espionage center on the Turuttu canal road. The guards let me enter, and I walk up the stairs to my office which is next to VN's. In his office, on a royal blue Isfahani carpet presented to him by Shah Ismail of Persia, are set a low table made of polished ebony and two cushioned chairs. On the left wall is a white stretch of a sailcloth map that presents the expanse of VN's espionage world from Mombasa to Melaka. Spy names have been marked. In code, of course.

In my office I listen to *linguas* and interpreters who read aloud from folders that contain letters and news reports from a number of port cities of what you, Ahmadji, at the beginning of your account, termed Al-Muhit. I am gradually learning, in addition to the details of what I know from reading your account, all about what's happened and what's happening on the west coast of India after the arrival of the Portuguese. VN is anx-ious about the horse situation and wants to know all that can be done to increase cavalry supplies and develop trade.

I sit in my office, a red carpet under my table to rest my bare feet on, and I make copious but random notes about the port cities of the west coast, Kollam and Cochin and Calicut and Bhatkal and Kannanur, about the Muslim *afaqi* migrants that come from Khorasan, Turan and Gilan to Goa and proceed to the Bijapuri army and court, about the coastal trade in rice, the overseas trade from Melaka and Acheh in south east Asia, about spices and guns, and the ships that crowd the Indian seas. I am beginning to realize that this vast world we live in, what you, Ahmadji, call *samsāra*, is in a state of confusion, just like my mind is.

The folders with the Portuguese material that have been stolen or cop-ied by spy agents employed as servants by the Portuguese I have saved for later reading. I have to read them myself. No one else can, because not many know written Portuguese and not many can decipher the peculiar word abbreviations that are used. I vaguely sense that the Portuguese also are in a state of turmoil. There are a number of factions and there's a great deal of infighting.

VN knew about the quarrel about the naming of the first hastily constructed fortress at Cochin in 1503. Francisco de Albuquerque wanted to name it *Castelo Albuquerque* to honor his own family, while his cousin Afonso de Albuquerque wanted it to be called *Castelo Manuel* after the Portuguese king. Dom Francisco is a high ranked noble, a *fidalgo*, and belongs to the court faction, while Afonso de Albuquerque, a non noble of the second rank, is of the King's party. The cousins disagree violently about everything.

Factional infighting, according to Timmayya, will lead to the downfall of the Portuguese.

There is a letter from Timmayya to VN with the information that the Indian Ocean region has been divided by the Portuguese into three sections, each one under a separate naval commander. The first section stretches from Kilwa to Cambaya, the second from Cambaya to Colombo, while the third takes in the region upto Melaka and Acheh. No one is in overall control. According to Timmayya, this makes for confusion in the matter of decisions. There is no central command.

I am amazed at the number of letters, *mandados*, receipts, *regimentos* or instructions that the Vijayanagar agents on the west coast have been able to obtain through bribery and stealing, or by copying the Portuguese words exactly without knowing what they mean. There is no agreement among the Portuguese about why they have come to India. According to António Reál, captain of Cochin, in a letter he wrote to the king, we Portuguese should only trade in India and not concern ourselves with war. The *fidalgo* captains don't bother about matters of trade or conquest. They want to capture and plunder infidel ships which they think they have every right to do. Some regard themselves as crusaders.

The Portuguese send several copies, especially of letters and orders, by different ships to and from Lisbon. This they do because there have been a number of shipwrecks in the treacherous waters off Socotra, and off south east Africa, and off the Cape of Good Hope. The folders are full of Portuguese material. It will take me some time to read them all.

At noon it's time to return to my quarters, have another bath, and then go to the dining hall with Kasim Beg, the Bijapur envoy. He provides me with news and gossip.

Abolem now brings a bottle of liquor to my writing table, so it must be evening or night for, you may not know this, Ahmadji, I do not now drink during the day. Night's the only time I can write things down. Unlike you, Ahmadji, who can write anywhere, at any time. Abolem pours my usual drink, glances sideways at me with her liquid black eyes that never fail to send messages of invitation, and waits till I take two sips. I look at her with intense longing hoping that tonight she will come to my bed.

She shakes her head ever so slightly.

I had tossed and turned in the dark hours of last night, waiting for her to come to me. I want to tell her to come tonight.

But I didn't, I couldn't. We don't, Abolem and I, we can't, use words to communicate to each other. I can't speak the languages she speaks, Malayālam and Konkani.

A strong aroma of jasmine fills the room. It springs from Abolem's hair which she has coiled up her head into a bun and has wreathed with jasmine blossoms that speak to my body of a night of abandon to come. In the daytime Abolem usually wears tiny pink roses in her black hair. For the past two days she has worn no flowers at all, and has avoided me when my body needed her. My legs and back ache painfully after my visit to the Hazāra Rāma temple.

It's that time of the month for Abolem, Virappa Nayaka had explained, when she can't wear any flowers. They would all wither.

How's that you're so innocent, VN asked, smiling at me.

It took me some time to understand.

She can't, yet. It would be unclean. But you'll enjoy what she will do instead, Jan Mirza, Virappa Nāyaka had said, smiling again. You'll just have to be patient. I will send you a triple distilled liquor made of the finest Shirazi dates, he said. Sip it. Enjoy it.

I continue writing.

Strange, my mind clears as I begin to write. Strange, because I am not used to setting words down on paper. Spoken words shaped by the tongue and the mouth are warm and alive. When set down by hand on paper words become cold, distant. They move very slowly.

Our age of guns and sails.

I repeat the phrase, Ahmadbhai, for your ears this time.

Can one talk to two people at the same time. Yes, if one is setting talk down in writing. I am talking to faraway you in Champaner and also to Virappa Nāyaka here in Vijayanagar. You'll know when I switch.

What I wanted to convey to Virappa Nāyaka when we were in Diu is that the age of the crossbow is past and that the age of guns and sails has begun. I told him that the Mamluks of Egypt had relied on *furūsīya* horsemanship, and on exercises with sword and lance and bow. It was a matter of honor for them to reject guns and artillery, weapons assigned to the inferior janissaries, but eagerly accepted by the Ottoman Turks.

One can't go back, Ahmadbhai, you and I know that. We cant go back home, and mankind cannot go back in time.

I wanted to tell VN how the introduction of firearms would inevitably change the art of war. The crossbow, at present more efficient than the gun because a bowman can shoot five arrows to the gunner's one bullet, would have to be slowly abandoned as the art of gunnery improved. Arquebusiers would have to be trained to fight on horseback. New battle formations and tactics would be needed, and new ways to train soldiers. VN wouldn't understand. You would, Ahmadji. You've seen the change in the construction of ships and in the tactics of naval warfare used by the Portuguese at Diu.

What I wanted to make VN realize back in Diu was his immediate need for my services as trainer so that he would want to take me with him to Vijayanagar away from Ishak and Malik Gopi. He had a troop of North African horse archers that would have to be retrained as horse arquebusiers.

They'd be easy to retrain, VN had said. It takes a number of years to train a crossbowman, but should take only a few weeks to teach an arquebusier how to shoot.

True, very very true, I agreed. But the shooting has to be done on horseback. Have you ever fired a gun while riding a horse.

No, he said.

Let me show you an arquebus.

I showed him one of the twenty that Malik Gopi had bribed away from the Portuguese. It was 5 feet long and weighed 15 pounds. The stock was thick and carved from wood. The barrel, I said, had to be straight and smooth, its internal diameter had to be constant. I showed him the balls made of lead about three quarters of an inch in diameter that had to be stuffed into a slotted belt. I showed him the firing mechanism, the attached powder pan, and the long fuse that had been soaked in a solution of quicklime and saltpeter, then dried and fixed onto a trigger activated hook. The arquebusier would aim and pull the trigger which would make the glowing end descend smartly into the firing pan, and set off the powder charge. He would have to wait for some time before reloading his weapon.

I didn't explain the mechanism to VN. Instead I raised my weapon to eye level and sent a shot in the dead center of a target a hundred yards away. VN realized immediately that the stock of the arquebus had to rest upon the shoulder. The arquebus itself, which required the use of both hands, would be impossible to operate from horseback. How would the rider reload his weapon, and how would he control his horse who would be terrified by the smouldering fuse and the deafening noise, and how, I asked VN, would he ride in formation.

The arquebus can only be used by foot soldiers not by cavalry, is that what you are saying, Jan Mirza, VN asked me.

No, I said. But it will be later used from horseback.

I had to be cryptic. And I had to use discreet flattery, Ahmadji.

As the great commander in chief of the Vijayanagara cavalry, I said to Virappa Nayaka, you know that it is impossible to wage war in our day without using cavalry. What needs to be done is to reshape the stock and to shorten and lighten the barrel so that a horseman can handle the arquebus without difficulty. With just one hand. I know a great deal about firearms and, with the help of Pietro, the Italian armorer, I can devise a shorter, more effective arquebus. I will then retrain your cavalry to adopt new riding formations and tactics.

It was time after this to demonstrate my riding skills. He wouldn't have believed me otherwise. So I invited him to a polo game to be played the next evening on Diu maidan between Ishak's team and that of Malik Gopi, with four players on each side, one being a goalkeeper.

I was a tremendous success, Ahmadji.

I gave a superb display of horsemanship riding a mare that Ishak had loaned to me, controlling it with soft words and tongue clicks and with an indirect rein that left my right hand free. I played like a demon, riding short and standing at times in my stirrups, galloping, stopping, turning, swinging my polo rod with a wooden piece nailed on like a hammer. I hit the ball hard and accurately, showing off my skills by using cross shots, back shots, and under the neck shots. I hit the ball at a right angle to my horse's course by leaning forward and swinging the rod in front of the horse's nose. We played a halfhour game of two *chukkas* when night fell. I shot two goals.

I then astonished everyone by introducing a new ball that I proceeded to set on fire. It was made of the wood of the *palas* tree which grows only in the groves of Bengal and is known as the flame of the forest. It is a very light wood, and smoulders for a long time. A Rajput horseman and I took turns hitting the incandescent ball to each other, then chasing the ball, its sparks aflying, all over the polo field. It was an especially dark night and this *chukka* looked spectacular.

VN must have been dazzled. I left him abruptly that night, explaining nothing.

You must be amazed too, Ahmadji. You have questions, don't you, you want explanations. In your account you've complained of the many times when I was cryptic.

Well, since this is a confession, let me tell you about another self that I have never, though not deliberately, told you about. I too, like you, have a horror of baring my naked self to anyone. Even in writing. When I talk I can easily control my listeners' responses. In writing, this cold medium, it's difficult to manipulate the reader. But strangely, when I write, I am in control of myself. Writing assuages my sense of guilt.

Your writing, Ahmadji, your written account, is not a confession but an outpouring really. To Usha. Who lives just as you always dreamt you both would live, together, in a house of your own. Only, now, it is the house of your self. From where you can whisper the story of your life to her, who is both far and near, who lives inside you.

In that imagined confession to Brother Clement at Vanakbara that you recorded in your account, and that I felt compelled recently to reread, I observe my spineless self that avoided any mention of moments of action. Except that moment of fury when I smashed Senhor Gouvea's skull with a candlestick.

I note also that I didn't realize to whom I was making a confession at that time, to you or to Brother Clement. Just as an aside, were you aware that you, Ahmadji, used liturgical colors, the blue of heaven, penitential purple and sacrificial blood red, to describe that Vanakbara evening sky. I don't think you were. A true poet like you is deeply religious, Ahmadji. I trust that's cryptic enough.

When, why, did I change into a man of action. Into one who could shoot and ride and learn Arabic and Swahili and Persian and study the languages and absorb the wisdom of the East and become a Muslim who was tempted to go as a pilgrim to the holy cities but couldn't bring myself to violate the sacred, and so didn't go to those holy places. And Medina is a holy city, not the place of abomination where the shriveled mummy of the prophet, on him be peace, lies in a black stone coffin according to the Portuguese. What colossal ignorance befounds the Portuguese, Ahmadji. Didn't I touch on all this in my letter to Frei António Louro. You know me, Ahmadji, as a clown, a spinner of tales, so convincing as an actor performer that sometimes I become what I play. I am tired now of wearing masks that disguise what I am. But what am I, Ahmadji, and how can I confess if I don't know what I am.

I haven't confessed all, Ahmadji. You should ask me sternly, like a good father confessor, what about women. I shall be completely silent. For I want my self to remain a mystery that no one can resolve. Not even me. Just a *samsāric* thing, Ahmadji.

Perhaps I should now give you an answer to your second why. You asked why I agreed to come with VN to Vijayanagar.

I was in deep debt to Malik Gopi and Ishak. I was afraid I would be murdered by one of their agents. Then VN tempted me, Ahmadji.

Vijayanagar is not just the city of victory its name proclaims, VN said. Did you know it is a city of women.

I didn't believe VN when in Diu he regaled me with stories about the fabulous wealth of women of Vijayanagar. Many, he said, are richer than the nobles of the kingdom. He listed their cultural accomplishments as dancers and singers, storytellers and musicians, and skillful gamblers. They're the most beautiful, the most voluptuous women in the world, he told me. They're practitioners of the arts of love from the *Kama Sutra*. They evoke love from their patrons without ever loving them. They live near the royal center. When you, Jan Mirza, come to Vijayanagar, VN promised, I shall take you to the Avenue of the Courtesans. We will meet my favorite, Mohinī.

And he went on to describe what they wore. Diamonds in their noses and earlobes, rubies and garnets, gold bracelets on their upper arms, girdles of pearls and anklets of silver.

You won't believe it, he said.

I didn't.

Then he tried another tactic.

Muslim and Turushka women are kept as in a prison. In *harams*, VN said. By their men, he said. Even by the clothes they have to wear, black coverings from head to foot. Our Hindu women in the south enjoy a sense of freedom, he said. They're free to be their beautiful selves. They can choose anyone they want. They provide *bhoga*, enjoyment. And the men don't have to go prowling in the night.

VN paused.

For women and liquor, he said, looking straight into my eyes.

A faint suspicion had brushed my mind at that time in Diu that he had deliberately flung that pointed statement at me. I am now sure that he had known all along. Known all about my nocturnal visits across Diu channel. To brothels and taverns and hashish dens there in the *Vila dos Rumes*. I had to use a number of disguises. I used to pick up gossip and rumor from foreign visitors in these spots, and of course indulge myself. I had to report to Ishak and Malik Gopi, who paid me for my services, but not enough. I was in debt up to my ears.

My wife did not know anything about my nocturnal prowls in Diu. But she must have suspected things, and Ishak must have bribed her. After all, it was Ishak who had arranged for my *muta'* marriage. Virappa

Nāyaka came to know about my doings in Diu, my hunger for women, my involvement with Ishak and Malik Gopi, my debts. This soft spoken man had his spies even in Diu, and agents in all the ports of western India. He knew I was trapped.

So VN tempted me with freedom from all these problems.

Come with me, he said, come as my agent.

I wish Frei António do Louro were in front of me here in Vijayanagar. I would have knelt down to make my confession and said, Bless me Father for I have

But I haven't sinned, Ahmadji. It is my faith that has been greatly shaken by the Hinduism of the south as it had never been by Islam. I am terribly confused, my bewilderment reaching its peak the evening VN and I climbed up the thickly forested slopes of the ghats, and gazed down at the fantastic Vijayanagar landscape.

Bear with me, Ahmadbhai, mine's a confused story, a story of confusion, and of a whole world in confusion.

Very cleverly put, João. That's what your cynic would say, Ahmadji.

Ours had been a long tiring journey from Champaner by the landroute, sometimes in large groups of over a hundred persons, at other times just three or four, on foot at times, but mostly on horseback, skirting the main towns and cities so that we avoided going into Burhanpur and Gulbarga, and into Raichur and Mudgal. It would have been easier and quicker to go from Diu to Bhatkal by sea, had it not been for the monsoon and the Portuguese pirate ships prowling about, hunting for plunder, according to VN. The scouts of VN's spy network had made excellent arrangements along the secret mailbag dispatch route, so that we were well provided with horses and food and shelter, and we traveled along quite fast.

We didn't have too much to do all along the way. VN would spend many mornings writing brief messages, and replies to letters that he would send on by horse courier. I marveled at the way he kept in touch with everything happening in Vijayanagar.

You'll have an office next to mine in the House of Vision, he said, to prepare summaries of all the reports we have received from the west coast to submit to the king and his council. A group of translators, one who even knows Hebrew, will be at your disposal. You'll be the first who knows Portuguese well.

I had underestimated VN's shrewdness. He didn't want me for just my military skills.

Then VN told me he had received reports that the horse traffic to the west coast of India had completely stopped. No horse trader would take the risk of being attacked by the Portuguese ships. There are persistent rumors, he told me, up and down the coast, that the Mamluk Sultan of Cairo has equipped another fleet of *maonas* at Suez that is ready to sail on the Bahr-i-Hind to attack the Portuguese. Trade and customs revenues at Alexandria had dropped considerably.

One morning he was silent, didn't talk to me for a long time.

Bad news, he said, very bad news. The two gun founders at Calicut have been murdered, he said. They were unhappy. They wanted to return to the Portuguese. The five hundred guns they had made apparently didn't fire properly. The barrels burst. Pietro is waiting for me to return. He finds it difficult to get the materials he wants. He says he needs to establish a powder works and needs flowing water for this workshop. I'm sure you can help him with your knowledge of firearms.

Don't worry, I said. We can make do with *tufengs*.

Secretly I was glad. I didn't know anything about the manufacture of guns.

But I did practice shooting everyday with an arquebus on our way to Vijayanagar. I became a deadly shot.

I wrote just one letter on the way to Vijayanagar, to Frei Louro and to you under a huge banyan tree. I had to write to Frei Louro and I had to warn you about the conspiracy without Ishak and Vora realizing that the letter concealed a secret warning. I'm sure you broke the language code that I had to use not to betray myself. And I'm sure Ishak's group didn't. I am curious as to what happened. Did the temptation involve a woman. I'm sure it did, and I'm sure Frei Louro didn't succumb.

I have been brooding, Ahmadji, about matters that keep whirling about in my mind. About sex and sin, about the carefree naked women of the Tupinamba, and the teachings of our Catholic church, about our priests and chastity, and about Hindu temple priests who are allowed to marry, and Muslim holy men who can, too, and this tropical climate, warm and moist, that inflames the senses, and cries out for a minimum of clothes. After my journey to Vijayanagara, I see myself as a viator compelled to ask questions I have never questioned before.

Is sexual desire a sin, Ahmadji.

And what is sin, I ask myself that question now.

We talked all along the way, VN and I, from Diu to Vijayanagar, mostly in the cool of the early morning before sunrise, our horses ambling along together, and during cowdust time before sunset when the cattle are driven back. Strange, it was VN who talked most of the time. I didn't want to talk. I just listened. Like you, Ahmadji. I was merely a ear. He didn't talk about horses and guns and war. I had thought I was an excellent judge of character. VN, I thought, was primarily a man of action. I now find VN is unpredictable as perhaps a good master spy should be. He talked about matters I never expected this cold eyed administrator, this controller of courtesans, to talk about.

The talks began two days after we left Champaner. I had stopped to admire the clusters of fiery red berries that dotted the sides of the narrow valley through which we were riding.

Aren't they beautiful, I said.

I detest them, suddenly burst out of VN

I was shocked.

What he detested, it turned out, were his fellow Hindus of the north. They had treated him with contempt, looking down on him because of his darker shade of skin. He wasn't a Brahmin, though he could quote from the Vedas and the Upanishads, and he knew a little Sanskrit. But our pandit friend chose to ignore all this, and VN was not admitted into the inner sanctum of the Vishnu temple in Diu.

You belong to the Nāyar caste, the pandit said to VN, inflecting the last two words so that it became a statement as well as a question. It was really a pointed insult. The pandit, who has never traveled outside Gujarat, did not stay for an answer.

I remember, Ahmadji, how exasperated you and the maulvi would get when the pandit and I had our endless discussions about caste. But VN's observations did provide a different look at the caste system, a historical view from below, so to speak, at the Aryan invasion of the Dravidian south. There are more than four, VN insisted. And went on to talk at great length about mixed castes, about how the acquisition of land and money could make caste categories change in some regions, and about right and left hand castes in the south. It was confusing even for me. I had never heard of such castes before. He couldn't explain the origins of the caste system, and why it sprang into being only in India, and I won't bore you, but he did make me realize its bewildering complexity.

Is it different from social class, I asked VN. Is it connected with religious beliefs, I asked him.

Yes, yes, yes, he said fiercely.

What came through most forcefully was his terrible anger against the Brahmins of the north. I think if the pandit were here VN would have had him killed by his spy agents, so fierce was his anger.

Brahmanical society is absolutely tyrannical, VN proclaimed. It essentially is a power system. The Brahmin makes use of sacred texts in a language that the ordinary people cannot understand in order to impose rigid social patterns set by our karmic past that they maintain can never change, and that no one dare question. They use words like taboo, purification, ritual pollution, to terrify the common folk.

Only in the south do we have pure Dravidian Hinduism, VN maintained. It must remain unpolluted by Islam and by the Aryans. He continued on and on and on, venting his anger in this fashion for several days. Wouldn't talk about anything else.

VN's story

Then suddenly, one day, at cowdust time, the anger drained completely out of him, and his voice became soft, distant. He didn't let fall a word all through the night.

I dislike what I am doing, Jan Mirza, VN began the next morning. I never should have agreed to become one of the king's ministers. But my guru, who is also the king's guru, advised me to accept the office.

It will be a test, my guru said, to find out whether you want to remain involved in *samsāra*, in things of this world. I know you, VN, want to be one of my disciples. But first you have to fulfill your own *dharma*. The king and the kingdom of Vijayanagar need you. You are one of the few people the king can trust. Serve the king faithfully without complaining, for seven years.

Then my guru paused, said VN.

You'll also, my guru continued, promote devotion to Hanuman by building shrines and having images of this folk god so beloved by all our people carved on rocks and on temple walls. Hanuman is the protector of our city. Make Lord Hanuman your protector deity too.

Anxious, I waited for my guru to fix the day of my initiation rite to become one of his disciples before I left for Diu. But he didn't continue.

I will have served the king for exactly seven years at the end of August, Jan Mirza, when you and I return to Vijayanagar, VN said.

I wondered who Hanuman was.

VN's voice was barely a whisper, but my ear could detect the notes of sadness and longing, and apprehension, beneath the surface. The return to Vijayanagara would be a turning point in his life.

I couldn't talk about all this in Diu, VN said to me. There there was no one of equal status to talk to. Now I just have to talk to someone.

I was quite sure then that I wanted to renounce all worldly desires on my return to Vijayanagara, he continued. I wanted to abandon everything and, under the guidance of Sri Vyāsarāya, follow the *bhakti marg*, the path to salvation through loving devotion and surrender to Lord Vishnu. But I also sensed even then that my feet, the lowest level of my being, would compel me blindly to the courtesan colony in Vijayanagara, to the house of my Mohinī to surrender my self to her arms. How can I ever renounce her.

He paused for a while

Have you heard about *śakti*, VN asked me, the female cosmic force that is more powerful than that of the male. But then you don't know the Hinduism of the south.

I thought of Plato's two levels of being, the head above, and the senses below.

Listen, Jan Mirza, to the opening of a poem, VN said, it took me seven nights to compose.

He sat up straight on his horse, and recited four lines, his voice a-tremble.

Mohinī fair, Mohinī sweet
So enchanting to behold
With the *kinning kinning* of her feet
And the *fas fis* of her fold

I was puzzled. The four lines were ordinary, just sentimental. I didn't say a word, but I looked straight into VN's eyes. He stared through me. He must have thought I understood his dilemma.

As you know, Jan Mirza, he said, the *margs* are three. The other two are the *karma marg*, the path of uncomplaining fulfillment of the duties one is born to perform on this earth, a path I have followed faithfully for seven long years. The third is the *jnana marg*, the path of knowledge which I have also tried to follow, listening one day a week for two years to the words of my guru in the Madhva *math* where he instructs his disciples. After that I would hasten to the Avenue of the Courtesans to the arms of my Mohinī.

The end of VN's story

I won't bore you, Ahmadji, with a long account of what VN told me about the Hinduism of the south.

He took extraordinary delight in assuming the role of my guru, and from horseback he tossed out, morning and evening for several days, the insights he had obtained from Sri Vyāsarāya, his *jagatguru*. They sank, I don't know why, these random insights, into my very being. They were not the logical explanations that our pandit guru had inflicted on me in Diu. I had always rejected the pandit's words just as I had, in my Sorbonne years, gradually come to detest the *quodlibetal* questions and the methods of scholastic analysis that I had been offered.

VN would dart impatiently from topic to topic leaving me utterly confused and, despite myself, reluctantly convinced that the Hindus had asked questions that western man had never asked before. I would lie awake on my narrow cot in the loud silence of the dark Deccan nights, and ask myself questions that I knew VN would never be able to answer. About Reality, about the Brahman, about qualified reality that he termed *vishishta advaita*. I would step outside and, like you, Ahmadji, I would look up at the mysterious stars, and I would speculate on what lay beyond them. Maybe Usha has an answer. I remember, now, faintly, Brother Clement's acceptance of God as a mystery.

The path of *jnana*, of discriminative gnosis according to the Greeks, was not the one for VN. He didn't have the patience, VN said, to uncover the cause of suffering in this universe, and to track down the origins of *karma* and rebirth, in order to arrive at the state of liberation that is identity with the Brahman. But VN did want to show off, if only to just one pupil, his knowledge of the religious insights and speculations of the Hindu thinkers.

I was reluctant at first to think of them as theologians. In Coimbra and at the Sorbonne we had never heard of Hinduism or of Hindu theology. The gift of epiphanic revelation and of faith in the divine Word, had been bestowed exclusively on Christians, we thought. I look back now at the world of simple faith I had inhabited, a world created *ex nihilo* by a transcendent God, a world that sprang out of Genesis, dominated by Rome and the Christian west, disturbed just a little for me by Erasmus and Plato.

The Tupinamba first made me aware of simple human beings living beyond the Christian horizon. My faith was further shaken when I discovered the marvelous insights of Islam that also claimed to be a revelation, one later in time. The *Qu'ran*, Islam claimed, was the word of God set down in Arabic. I couldn't memorize the Christian Word, the Bible, it's too long. But I did memorize parts of the *Qu'ran* in Arabic, and as a Muslim preacher, I would quote from the Surahs most effectively. Islam provided wonderful insights, but it lacked speculative energy, I thought, and so couldn't generate a theology.

Hinduism now stuns and challenges me, Ahmadji, even though I do not understand it. How can I, when I don't know Sanskrit, the language of the gods, according to our pandit. I listened when VN spoke about the two main gods of Hinduism, Vishnu and Siva. I listened carefully when VN tried to explain its two main divisions, Vaishnavism and Saivism. I was absolutely fascinated when VN quoted his guru's Sanskrit to present *Dvaita* and *Advaita*, the two Hindu theological systems.

Dualism and monism one could term them, I think.

I could, of course, and I did, very easily repeat the Sanskrit VN had quoted to explain them, even seven days later. VN was quite impressed. I made him think I knew a little Sanskrit. I didn't.

And I must, Ahmadji. I must study Sanskrit, a language more difficult than Greek. How long it will take I do not know. It will be very difficult to master this language with its bewildering syntax, its profusion of adjectival compounds, its abhorrence of verbs and therefore of dramatic action. Only then will I be able to explore Hinduism's speculative systems, its insights into the two forms of Reality including the evolutive mode that my own guru, Plato, was perhaps not aware of, the stark difference between monism and monotheism, the several incarnations, not just one, of Lord Vishnu the Preserver to save mankind on earth. Christianity, for the first time now, has to confront the major religions of our world and come to terms with the truths of Hinduism, its most powerful challenger. Perhaps I have been destined to be a reconciler of religions. A preacher of ecumenism, to coin a term from the Greek. I feel a strong urge to return to the steps of the Santa Cruz cathedral in Coimbra and begin the study of Sanskrit and become, no, not a guru, but the teacher I've always wanted to be, a teacher perhaps to the western world. Perhaps I could return with Frei Louro.

My cynic, let me borrow him from you again, Ahmadji, asks. Who will listen to you, oh mighty reconciler. D'you want to be another Erasmus questioning the teacher in a Sorbonne aula. Whom will you teach and where. Could you teach here in India. Without knowing Sanskrit. Don't you think you'll have many problems when you return to Lisbon.

The questions bothered me all through the last days of the journey, and I was in a state of profound unease when VN and I climbed up a series of steep rocky ridges, and I stared at the fantastic Vijayanagar landscape.

My first look at Vijayanagar. I didn't really look at the landscape, Ahmadji. Plato and his word, perception, leapt into my consciousness. The landscape assaulted me, refusing to allow my eyes to tame it into any kind of order.

The sun was poised behind the black hills so that my eyes experienced vivid bursts of gray sandstone and of pink red granite, haphazard piles of massive boulders, some of them with dark fissures and bottomless crevices, and a tumult of giant stones of stupendous shapes. Some appeared to have just erupted out of the stubborn earth and were about to crash down at any moment. Others could have been hurled from the skies above, the architecture of nature challenging man the architect to equal this display of wild grandeur. On the far left, through a narrow gorge and a wilderness of rocks burst the gleaming Tunghabhadra, and rushed northeastwards.

You're looking down at Anegundi town that is just outside Vijayanagar city, VN said, the seed out of which Vijayanagar has sprung. There, to the west, is its fortified citadel built on rocky hills. We have come by one of the secret ways into Vijayanagar. Only the Golla tribe of herders in the hills beyond knows about this route. Some of them work in the royal stables. Anjanadri Hill, there in the distance on the other side, crowned with a walled temple, is called the bastion of Hanuman, the god of strength and courage, loved by all the people. It marks his birthplace. Shri Vyāsarāya, as I told you, has appointed me the official guardian of all the Hanuman temples in this region. I shall hold a ceremony to give thanks to my protector for bringing me safely back.

And VN folded his palms and bowed low in the direction of the Hanuman temple. In the far distance were a number of lookout posts perched on the summits of rocky ridges.

Anegundi. Anegundi, I repeated to myself. The name stirred something in me.

Anegundi town had circuits of formidable walls with massive protective gateways just wide enough for two bullock carts or one elephant to pass through. We entered the town by the north gateway. The guards, each one with a leather scourge in the right hand and a stick in the left, were also toll collectors. They monitored all movement into and out of the city. They questioned everyone. They registered all names. All persons who entered the city with goods to sell had to pay octroi duty. They greeted VN who knew them by name, and who told them I was one of his agents. They offered us glasses of mango juice.

Too sweet for me, VN said.

The two glasses of juice I had were cooling and very refreshing.

One of the guards whispered urgently into VN's ear.

Another guard took me to a small room up a flight of steps to mark the thumb of my right hand with invisible ink. The mark would be visible only when the thumb was dipped in water.

That's to identify you and allow you to pass through any of our city gates, VN said. We will have a flow of visitors because of the Mahānavāmi festival which will begin at the moment of the new moon, the first day of Aśvin. We have to be careful because of Muslim assassins.

He was disturbed but his face was impassive.

Pietro is dead, VN told me. Some Bijapuri spies told Pietro about what happened to his friends in Calicut. They bribed him with diamonds to escape with them to Goa. He couldn't be allowed to escape to Muslim territory. He was stabbed.

I noted his use of the passive voice, but didn't ask him by whom.

We walked down the main road of Anegundi to an open square.

Here, said VN, is the most sacred spot in Vijayanagar. Our holiest Hindu traditions spring out of Anegundi.

Anegundi. I had an excellent memory. But I couldn't remember where I had heard the name Anegundi.

An imposing Hindu temple complex occupied one corner of the square. VN pointed to an ancient Jain shrine with its rest house. Erected, he said, when Jainism flourished in the south. Its porch, hall, and court-yard with four freestanding pillars were massive, but severely plain, in contrast to the ornate Hindu temple with its towering gopurams.

A Jain ascetic from Gujarat has lived there in an underground cell for many years, VN said. He belongs to the Swetambara sect but has been ac-cepted by the Digambaras here. People bring food for him every day. He's now considered a very holy man. Never talks, never comes out of his cell except in the dark of the night. It's a penance for life imposed by his guru because he committed a sinful act of kindness by helping a woman on the very day of his initiation. His guru has since passed away, but this ascetic continues the penance to this day.

It intrigued me, this strange story, VN said, because without undergo-ing *diksha* he is considered holy by the people. It made me wonder wheth-er initiation is an absolutely necessary rite to enter any order. You can read the account, Jan Mirza, in the Anegundi police report for 1505.

VN walked ahead of me.

That's it, now I remember. Your account, Ahmadji, that's where I came across the word Anegundi. I link Anegundi with *diksha*, with Gujarat, with Jainism, and with your rescue from a ditch by your hakim. You didn't mention Usha. That ascetic could be Usha's uncle who, according to your account, vanished in Śatruñjaya. I will go see him. And I will get someone to translate the police report. At last you will know what happened to your Usha.

Diagonally across, some workmen were putting the finishing touches to a circular three stepped granite base with a hollowed center. Around the base were minute carvings of elephants and peacocks with spread out tail feathers and floral designs, all done elegantly and with great skill. On the ground lay a cross to be set up on the base. It wasn't the tall Latin cross with one bar longer than the other three. This cross was formed by the intersection in the center and at right angles of two bars equal in length. The three ends were pointed not flat.

That's very grotesque, VN said, pointing to the cross, it's unlike the delicate lotus designs on the granite pillars of our temples.

Those workers are Syrian Christians that have been brought from Mal-abar, VN told me. They will erect a church here. They are first setting up a pillar cross that will indicate the presence of a Christian church nearby. An installation ceremony will take place two days before the Mahānavāmi festival. It will be conducted by a priest who has been sent by the king of

Portugal. My agents inform me that he is white bearded. Looks and smells like a fat goat, they say. You'll meet him soon at a dinner meeting, VN told me.

I was surprised. Didn't know what to say. So I looked straight ahead at the granite base.

As a staunch Hindu I objected to the church very strongly, VN continued. I told my king that a foreign church would pollute these sacred surroundings.

But King Krishna Deva Raya said that all religions were welcome in Vijayanagar, and besides, it would be a goodwill gesture towards the Portuguese whose assistance we need for the supply of horses. Sri Vyāsarāya, my guru, agreed with the King.

Why don't you hold both ceremonies on the same day, I suggested idly, more to make conversation than as advice. The ceremony for Hanuman, your protector, and the installation ceremony of the church, if held on the same day, will demonstrate Vijayanagar tolerance of religions.

VN didn't reply.

I stared at the center of the cross. In the floral circle was an inscription in a language I could not decipher.

The headman of the Syrian Christians explained that the language was Pahlavi and meant, the love and passion of Christ saved the whole world.

It was a Persian cross. I knew some parts of Persia had been converted in the early days of Christianity.

That monstrous object, said VN, that ugly cross, will be erected in front of the first Christian church to be built in Hindu Vijayanagar. I am determined to make sure it will be the last. I shall personally be responsible for choosing the building materials for the church. You're right, Jan Mirza, VN said. Perhaps both ceremonies should be held on the same day. The people will then realize the tremendous difference between the two religions.

We walked through the south gateway of Anegundi that led down to the river. I could see an unending series of temples of different sizes, images of monkeys and half elephants and monstrous bulls, hooded cobra stones, groups of lingas sculpted on the rocks in different patterns, and sculptures carved on the huge boulders that flanked both sides of the Tungabhadra. Man the maker at work, I thought, trying to outrival nature.

We saw people ferried across the river in round basket boats, made of cane and covered with leather and rowed with paddles, that could carry twenty people, but couldn't sail straight across, so fierce were the river's swirls. The boats kept turning around. No toll was charged. Ascetics and

holy men, and all those who could pay, used the timber walkway supported on granite posts. VN pointed to an island upriver.

That's *Navā Vrindāvana*, he said, the site chosen for the resting places
of nine Madhva ascetics.

After the bridge crossing to Talarighat we stopped at the towering
Harishankha gateway. It had battlement designs at the top, and high
arched windows.

That, I said, is clearly an Islamic pattern.

Yes, alas, VN said, our Hindu culture of the south, is being slowly corrupted by Muslim influence. Even our king has adopted the outlandish
title, Sultan among Hindu Kings.

We walked on.

But, look, there's a Bagila Hanuman relief, VN said, that's Hanuman
of the gate. He is the guardian deity of turns and crossroads.

It was a strange sight. I saw a gigantic monkey in a heroic striding
pose. The long curved tail rose above his head. The face was in profile.
The right hand was lifted up denoting reassurance, while the left, placed
near the hip, held a flower with a long stem. A demonic creature crouched
for protection below the sturdy widespread legs. At the corner of another
crossroad VN showed me an image of Hanuman with folded palms in the
attitude of prayer. Yet another image depicted Hanuman flying through
the air carrying rocks.

Hanuman is the partial incarnation of Vayu the wind god, VN said
without offering any further explanation. I felt confused.

Our guides will take you to your quarters, VN said. Abolem the courtesan will take care of you and of all your needs. I have sent a message to
Kasim Beg, the Bijapuri envoy, who will be your next door neighbor. Cul-
tivate his friendship. It's important that you get to know him well and find
out what he is scheming. Rest for a few days. Familiarize yourself with the
streets and sights of Vijayanagar. Kasim Beg will help you. You'll have to
begin work in your office soon.

I am tired, VN said, but I have to perform my duties. I have to greet
my cousin the king, and tell him about the mission. I have to check all reports received in the House of Vision, my espionage center on the Turuttu
Canal road where you'll have an office. Then then I'll pay my respects to
my guru Shri Vyāsarāya, and then, I'll go to my Mohinī, and then offer my
devotions to Hanuman, my guardian deity.

Turushka Quarters

Is it night already
 I feel dazed.

I pour myself another drink. Where is my Abolem. My experience of time has become confused now. I can't remember what happened when. I cannot punctuate time past. Things now become clear only when I begin writing.

Just an observation about your story, Ahmadji. From one who, fascinated by the processes of language, believes language and the self are deeply interconnected.

You write in the oral mode. Your account demands to be read aloud for the rhythms of your self to be heard. I hope your readers will listen to the music of your account as they read it. Else they'll miss many of its meanings.

Kasim Beg, who lives next door to me in our spacious compound, has been telling me all about VN, that's how he's known even in Vijayanagar elite circles. In Diu I had thought, innocent that I was, that cold eyed VN did not know anything about anything.

Are you just pretending to be an innocent, Jan Mirza, Kasim Beg said. Didn't VN recruit you as some kind of agent. All of us envoys who live in this compound know that you are somehow connected with horses and guns and the Portuguese. Are we wrong. Didn't you know that VN is a master controller, in charge of the cavalry, of spies and agents, and of all the courtesans in the Vijayanagar kingdom. Don't you know that the taxes on all the courtesans of the kingdom go to pay for horses and for the maintenance of the espionage office. Haven't you yet realized how cold and efficient VN is. Beware of VN, Jan Mirza. He will do away with you once he has finished making use of you. He is ruthless.

VN is sentimental too, I thought to myself. Such people, I know, are incapable of love. They are dangerous.

I must be careful.

We were, Kasim Beg and I, the last two as usual in a corner of the dining hall that afternoon. The other envoys had left after dinner. As royal guests we ate royally. Our meals were always lavish. Kasim Beg's servant, Lonpal, who serves both of us during meals, had cleared the table.

Horses, spies and courtesans. Isn't that a strange grouping, I asked Kasim Beg.

I have this strange habit of imitating voices, Ahmad my brother, perhaps it's connected with my love of disguise. I tried to echo Kasim Beg's speech mode. And imitate his voice, which was distinctly Bijapuri.

Why João, you ask me, what good will it do you.

Well, I don't know, as you would say. A challenge it is. The Bijapuri voice is a fascinating blend of words and intonations from Persian and

Deccani and Urdu. At this point in my story, Ahmadbhai, I should go on to talk about the intonation blends in south India. But I am not you, and I will resist the temptation to digress, which you yield to so frequently in your account. I'll offer comments on your digressions later. Let me get back to Kasim Beg.

Kasim Beg, the Bijapuri ambassador to Vijayanagar, must have come to know about me from his first cousin, Karim Khan, our maulvi's friend, the envoy who had to return in haste from Diu to Bijapur to inform his Sultan about the demand of diamonds to buy horses.

Kasim Beg and I have become friends even though VN suggested I spy on him. He is here to gather information about horses and the Vijayana-gara cavalry. Actually everyone knows that every envoy in the compound is either a spy or an agent. Spying is a known fact here and in all capital cities. Secrets are almost impossible to keep. That's why VN isolates us all in a walled compound. Security is tight. Each house is looked after by a courtesan and her band of servants. No foreign servants are permitted to enter the compound. The houses are built of stone, each one in the mid-dle of a well kept garden. The water supply system here in Vijayanagara is excellent, almost as good, surprisingly, as the system in Champaner. Canals, irrigation channels, conduits and tanks are in abundance every-where, so that our compound is surrounded by water flowing in channels of cut stone. Every house is like a palace with its own earthen pipes and water supply. Every house has a identifying name on the entrance. I was assigned to Turushka Quarters because they thought I was Turkic. The one on my right, recently constructed and hidden behind bushes, is called PĀRASĪKA House.

PĀRASĪKA refers to the Portuguese, Kasim Beg told me.

I was intrigued.

I had casually asked Kasim Beg to show me Vijayanagar. The real Vijay-anagar, if you can, I had added jokingly.

We were sitting by ourselves in our usual corner of the dining room after finishing our meals. The others had all left. Kasim Beg signalled to his servant at the other end of the hall.

VN asked me to be your guide, Kasim Beg said. Why me of all the envoys, I don't know. Perhaps because we can both speak Persian. And I don't know what you mean by the real. For me the real is only what I want to see. For me the real is the material world of things that Allah in his in-finite wisdom has bestowed on us for our enjoyment to make life on this earth worth living. The Hindus call it *artha*. For me, Vijayanagar is now the seat of Hindu political power. Not so long ago the center of power used to be Bidar up north, the great capital of the Bahmani dynasty which, alas, after the murder of Khwaja Mahmud Gawan, lost both power and wealth, and broke up into five Bahmanid kingdoms that now fight each other instead of uniting against our common enemy, the Hindus.

Vijayanagar excites my envy. For it is the richest city in the world just waiting to be plundered by us Muslims. To it flow luxuries from everywhere, from Canton and Malaya in the east, and from Hormuz and Aden in the west. According to VN, the height of enjoyment, *bhoga*, can be experienced in this paradise city. Did you know that for Sufis paradise is a garden.

I knew that the word paradise was a transliteration of the Persian word *pairidaeza* which meant a walled garden. And I then remembered what Senhor Gouvea of Lisbon had promised me once, a long time ago. João, he had said, one day we will go to Venice, Europe's richest city, into which the wealth of the Indies flows.

A sheet of paper was placed before Kasim Beg.

Ah, he said, without looking up. You can clear the table.

A plate was removed from our table.

We bent our heads together to look at the map.

I have, said Kasim Beg, on this sheet of paper made a rough sketch of the northern section of Vijayanagar city. Here, on the lower left, is the royal center which can be visited only by special invitation. There to the right is the sacred area where most of the temples are concentrated. Below, here, stretches the irrigated valley and the residential zones. Here is our compound. This line, which curves gently from the west to the north east is the almost uncrossable Tungabhadra. Beyond its northern bank are granitic hills composed of piles of massive rounded boulders too steep to climb. Both are formidable barriers, Jan Mirza, between my Bijapur to the north and Vijayanagara to the south.

They think, Kasim Beg whispered to me, that no army can invade Vijayanagara from the north.

He bent his head lower, so that I could barely hear his whispering.

They do not know about the wide gap between the hills here, at Gangawati, and he placed a finger on a spot to the far east of Anegundi, that the Golla herders use to drive cattle into the city. Their headman, who works in the royal stables, is one of our agents. We have bribed him heavily. Our sultan plans to unite the five Muslim kingdoms and invade Vijayanagara, and seize its wealth. We need detailed information about what is happening on the west coast of India. Our soldiers and cavalry are much better fighters than the Hindus.

But we need more horses, we need more guns. We need detailed information about the west coast of India. And we need you. Rustam Khan, our leader, has heard about your skills with horses and guns and sends you an invitation to Bijapur to be a captain in his cavalry force.

The servant was clearing the last plate from the table when Kasim Beg looked up.

He stood up suddenly. The sketch map slipped out of his hands and fell to the floor. I picked it up.

You are not Lonpal, Kasim Beg shouted to the servant. Where is he. Why are you wearing his uniform.

VN suddenly appeared out of nowhere.

What happened, VN demanded.

Kasim Beg tried to explain, but he stuttered, incoherently.

Ah, ah, said VN impatiently. This servant is a spy. Summon the guards. Arrest this man. Have him tortured, he told the guards, and find out who he's working for. Don't worry, he told Kasim Beg.

He noticed the sketch map in my hand.

He took it, stared at it.

Interesting, he said. I like this map. Let me keep it for my collection. I am collecting maps of the Raichur Doab.

Jan Mirza, I came to see you really, VN continued. Soon we will go to meet my guru, Sri Vyāsarāya and visit Mohinī.

He left abruptly.

Kasim Beg was quite disturbed after VN left the dining hall. He was sure that the spy had been planted by VN himself.

VN will have that spy killed. We'll never see Lonpal again. Take care, Jan Mirza. VN is ruthlessly cruel, Kasim Beg told me. Don't fall into VN's trap. He'll kill you if you know his secrets, when he doesn't need your services. Have you noticed his eyes. Narrow, and cold like those of a fish. He won't have me killed. Not yet. As the Bijapur envoy I am protected. He dare not antagonize my Sultan.

He went off to talk to the manager of the dining hall about Lonpal.

Kasim Beg's words disturbed me greatly.

Kasim Beg did take me on a brief tour of Vijayanagar. He refused to go on foot. Too dirty the streets, he said, too narrow for horses. We will use litters.

So we were carried in dhoolies up a series of steps that sloped steeply to the top of Hemakuta Hill. And I looked down at the site of ancient Hampi. My eyes they were dazzled again. They were assaulted this time by a chaos of manmade objects. Temples, shrines, colonnades, columned halls, towered gateways, pavilions, images of colossal bulls, and of elephant trunked men with tusks and three arms and six hands, man lions, and Hanumans, men with monkey faces, all somehow not clashing but merging into the wilderness of boulders and fissures and giant stones I had first encountered at Anegundi. Bewildered, my eyes hunted for stays against such a confusion. They found only two. The towering Virupaksha temple to the north anchored on level ground. And a long broad chariot avenue flanked by buildings and structures.

Have you noticed, observed Kasim Beg, that walls surround everything everywhere in Vijayanagara. At times there are two concentric walls around temple complexes. The rulers live in fear of attack from the outside. This chaos all around us is contained by three circular walls and by formidable towered gateways that only open out, never in. Even at this height, at the top of Hemakuta hill, light does not dare penetrate the dark interior of the cave like buildings.

Hindu darkness, Kasim Beg added, awaiting Muslim light.

I thought of you know who, Ahmadji, and his myth of the cave, but didn't say anything. Kasim Beg was right. Where ever we went, to the top of Matanga Hill from where we could look down at the Venkateshwara temple, or to the Raghunatha temple at the top of Malyavanta Hill, I was aware of being confronted by the mysterious dark with a latent energy of its own, despite the fierce sunlight. The enclosures, the high walls, the towering fortifications everywhere made me feel like an imprisoned self.

I remember the two lines that VN had quoted from the *Katha Upanishad*. Human senses always open outward never inward, so that it is only the rare seeker after truth who looks into his dark interior landscape to discover his true self.

It was a relief to be taken through the bazaars and markets arranged in long colonnaded streets lined throughout with rows of houses and shops. Two thousand beasts of burden crowd into the city every week for the Friday bazaar with all kinds of merchandise, I was told. I could understand Kasim Beg's reluctance to take me to the market where they sold pigs and live poultry and dried sea fish.

But he did take me to the street of the roses, to the vegetable market, to shops where they sold all kinds of cloth including velvet and satin and watered silk and all varieties of saries including the expensive *ikat* ones. Shops where they sold provisions of all kinds including butter and milk and rice, and wheat, much in demand by Muslim soldiers. Then to the fruit sellers market where I saw the fruits they served to us during meals, white grapes, oranges, citrons, limes, pomegranates, jackfruit which I dislike, and mangoes which I love.

I want to shock you first, Jan Mirza, then surprise you, Kasim Beg told me.

He took me first to a poor section of the city to a small temple whose entrance gates were spattered with blood. The porch was red and slippery. A temple priest was slaughtering goats and buffaloes by cutting off their heads. Another priest carried the blood into the temple to smear it on the image of a goddess whose name Kasim Beg did not know. To propitiate her, Kasim explained. Reminded him of Bakri-id. I was indeed shocked. In Hinduism, I had thought, as in Catholicism, the act of sacrifice was symbolic. Murder in any form was forbidden. Then I noticed that the people who led the animals to the sacrificer were tribals. It was quite a shock. Perhaps I could ask VN's guru to explain the matter.

Kasim Beg's surprise for me was very pleasant. He took me to the Avenue of the Jewelers which he kept for the last, a long broad street which dealt only with precious stones and metals, and had just one outlet. Many rich merchants lived there. It was divided into three sections. The first, near the entrance, displayed the more common stones, cornelians from Cambay, zircons, tigers' eyes, and amethysts from the Malabar region. The third, near the dead end of the street, was where they sold precious stones, rubies and spinels and garnets, emeralds and jacinth and sapphires, seed-pearls, and glowing pearls of the finest water.

To this diamond bazaar, Kasim Beg said, come people from all parts of the world, merchants and *kelings* from the Coromandel and from Malaya, Tamil *nayakas*, courtesans from the south, traders from Persia and Arabia, and Jain businessmen from Gujarat to buy diamonds that sparkle with different gradations of color, the finest diamonds in the world.

Four diamonds, two as large as hen's eggs, the other two more than 25 mangelin seeds in weight, were kept on display. They could not be sold. They belonged rightfully to the King and had to be sent to the royal treasuries.

I was particularly intrigued by the section in the middle where the moneychangers sat on low stools under a broad porch, in six triple rows, with low tables covered with red velvet in front of them. Silver and gold coins of different sizes were stacked neatly on the tables.

Kasim Beg intoned a litany of their names and chanted their praises. That's the Egyptian ashrafi, he said, worth more than the rial and the mahmudi. The Portuguese call it the xeraphim. That's the Venetian ducat, made of gold. That's the Persian larin made of silver. There, that's the pratap made of gold. Nasalized into the pardão by the ignorant Portuguese. That's the cruzado, Jan Mirza.

I stood dazed. It was only midmorning but the dazzling sun was fierce.

I looked down and I could see, here, in front of me, all the moneys of the world, east and west, gold and silver, come swirling together, greeting each other like long lost acquaintances. This section should be a madhouse, I thought. I was wrong. It was solemnly quiet as in church when the Host is elevated for the congregation to behold in reverential awe.

I waited a while. I waited some more. Then I opened my eyes to a deep silence.

No words were exchanged in this place. The foreign merchant sat in front of the table, placed a coin in a salver, and pointed to the currency he wanted. The money changer would stare at the coin, pick it up, examine it minutely, then turn it over, and stare at it again coldly. At times he would weigh it in the palm of his hand, assay it Kasim Beg explained. At times if it were a gold piece, he would bite it between his back teeth. When completely satisfied he would place the coins he was prepared to offer in his own salver. There was an awed silence. Then the tinkle of coins.

The sacred service to the new god of money came to an end.

You look shocked, Kasim Beg said. All this money has dazzled your consciousness, and has left you speechless, hasn't it. Now you know why so many people flock to Vijayanagar, the richest city in the world.

VN had arranged a dinner meeting for all who were housed in the compound on the fourth day or was it the sixth of our arrival. It was quite hot and mango juice was served at all tables. I was very thirsty but Kasim Beg signaled to Lonpal, to take away the mango juice. He brought us two glasses of water instead.

I'll tell you why later, Kasim Beg said.

Many envoys had come specially for the Mahānavāmi festival. It was becoming difficult to walk in the streets. We had to introduce ourselves to the group by name and region, translators were provided. The applause was halfhearted, because everybody knew about everybody. But VN had insisted on introductions. He himself began with a startling announcement.

There's a rumor afloat, VN said, among the courtesans near the Royal Centre that one of you in this hall will be the target of an assassination attempt this year. We don't know when.

An angry buzz of disbelief.

That's why you need to introduce yourselves in order to know each other by sight. You also need to be careful, said VN.

I know, VN continued, that such happenings have never occurred in our well guarded city. Do not be afraid. The Tuluva dynasty always arranges things in a civilized manner even in a time of turmoil, such as ours is. The Saluva claimants to the royal throne have, as you know, departed in peace to settle in the distant citadel of Chandragiri.

Kasim Beg nudged me with his elbow.

That's the way to dispose of rivals, he whispered to me.

I wondered why Kasim Beg had begun to confide in me. I would never betray him. I'd suffer from guilt if I did. What did Kasim Beg want from me. I had nothing to offer. And why had he prevented me from having the mango juice that I enjoy so much.

I looked around the dining hall. Half of the glasses of mango juice had been emptied.

No wars of succession were fought, VN said, and Krishna Deva Raya has been anointed king of Vijayanagar by his *rajguru* Sri Vyāsarāya. Later, the guru told the king, at an auspicious time, you will be crowned emperor, the raya of Vijayanagar.

My cousin the king has asked me to place briefly before you, as our allies and neighbors, his vision of the new Vijayanagara empire that he wants to bring into being. His ambition is to reincorporate under the glorious Tuluva dynasty its former territories to the north, the south, the east and the west, and the lands at the periphery that were an integral part of the Vijayanagara kingdom during the First Dynasty of the Sangamas.

Guru Vyāsarāya has advised the king to bow down humbly before Lord Vishnu and proceed on a *digvijayan* for the maintenance of *varnāsrama dharma*. These three Sanskrit terms, which you do not need to understand, proclaim that the emperor should be not only a protector of Hindu religion and culture in the South but also one on whom rests the material prosperity and the spiritual welfare of the whole world.

I thought I heard a voice proclaim, Alleluia.

Impossible, I told myself. Who will use Greek in this Hindu land.

The annual Mahānavāmi ceremony, VN continued, which this year will be a simple one. After we conquer Orissa it will be celebrated with pomp and grandeur. It will then assume its universal significance and be a celebration of victory, and the glorious festival of a Hindu godking.

VN paused for a while.

VN's language fascinated me. I couldn't see VN's face from where I was sitting, next to Kasim Beg, but as I listened I could hear VN transform himself into a pompous spokesman for his king and for the kingdom. His voice sounded loud, and hollow.

Our first duty on our royal journey to godkinghood, VN continued, is to regain control, by using military force if necessary, over our former holdings and ports on the west coast, Bhatkal and Gersoppa and Kannanur, and especially to recover Goa, the port of horses, which was unjustly seized from us by the Bahmani leader, Khwaja Mahmud Gawan, in 1472. The Pārasīkans have temporarily disturbed the flow of horses to Bhatkal and to our kingdom. They are very few in number and have come from beyond the Sea of Darkness. Negotiations in this regard will be conducted by Timmaya, our loyal admiral of the west coast.

Our second duty will be to conquer and control Raichur and Mudgal and the Doab, the fertile land between two rivers. This territory will act as a bulwark against the enemy forces of the north, and will provide us with the resources we need to feed our people. We will take that disputed territory by force of arms if we encounter any resistance. This statement, to be conveyed by you to each one of your rulers, should be clearly understood by the rulers concerned. Be warned. No further messages will be dispatched. Steps should be taken to withdraw from these areas.

It's very hot today. All of you must be quite thirsty. I'll stop briefly to allow you to drink the fresh round of mango juice which is being served. I'll have a few sips of juice myself.

He sipped delicately from his glass.

That's clever, Kasim Beg whispered to me, he is drinking plain mango juice.

We drank our glasses of water.

That's a pointed reference to Bijapur, Kasim Beg whispered to me. I will have to inform our Sultan, Adil Khan, immediately about this threat. More horses will have to be purchased for our cavalry. We require more guns for the infantry, and cannon. Rasul Khan, the commander of the Bijapur cavalry, wants to know how much VN is paying you for your services.

I don't know, I said.

Rasul Khan is prepared to pay you double or even triple the amount in ashrafis if you come to Bijapur.

Kasim Beg paused and looked into my eyes.

One of the servants removed a dish from our table. It wasn't Lonpal.

We need to talk later, Kasim Beg said.

I had been stupid. I could have kicked myself if I could. I hadn't negotiated any terms before leaving Champaner. Why hadn't I thought of money. Because, Ahmadji, like you and unlike VN, I wasn't shrewd about things of this world. I thought of VN's speech, his political shrewdness, his deliberate avoidance of direct references to the Muslims as enemies, his use of political jargon, and above all his use of the passive voice.

It should not be thought, continued VN, this time using the smooth voice of a diplomat, that we are going to wage a Hindu *jihad*. All of you know that we employ a multitude of Muslim fighters in our armies. Ours will be a spiritual conquest of the South that will bring together under our ritual suzerainty all its Hindu peoples, the speakers of Tamil and of Telugu, the Kannadigas and the Malayalis.

The 75 *nayaka* chiefs, VN paused.

Alleluia, said a voice.

The 75 *nayaka* chiefs, continued VN, to whom lands will be assigned on *amaram*tenure, and whom we will arm with guns and horses.

Alleluia, proclaimed a voice again, Alleluia.

All the worshipers of Lord Vishnu and Lord Siva, together with their deities, their temple priests and their temple dancers. All the various local sects with their village deities and their mother goddesses. All these will be represented at the Mahānavāmi festival next year. Together with the people of other faiths, the Muslims, the Jains, and of late even the Christians. Our religious tolerance, he proclaimed, knows no bounds.

He paused, to let his weighty words sink in.

They did sink deep into my stomach. I felt nauseous.

Let us now proceed with the introductions, said VN.

He is a hypocrite, I told Kasim Beg.

The introductions followed a certain order. First, the ambassadors from Mamluk Egypt and Ottoman Turkey and Safavid Persia. Then those from Bijapur and Golconda and Orissa and Ceylon. Then the envoys from Cochin and Calicut and Kannanur and the lesser chiefs from the South and from those that bordered the kingdom. Then the newcomers. I introduced myself simply and briefly as Jan Mirza, world traveler. No one was interested.

Then came the turn of the Pārasīkan envoy who had been sitting next to VN in the center of the hall. He rose.

It was he who had uttered the Alleluia.

The hall fell silent. All eyes turned to a tall dignified figure who wore a chasuble with a golden shimmer. The velvet fabric had been woven with a silver weft and a golden woof which had the effect of a silk shot through with gold. Only bishops could afford such an expensive vestment. As an altar boy in the Santa Cruz Cathedral at Coimbra I knew about vestments, their names and what they signified. This two piled Italian chasuble had a perpendicular band that descended the whole length front and back with a short horizontal band at the top. This T-shaped cross was a proclamation of religious power. Over his shoulders he wore a golden shawl. Non liturgical, I thought.

He took his time. He turned slowly around to allow everyone in the hall to look at him. When he turned toward me, I thought I saw a bishop celebrating solemn high mass. I noticed his piercing eyes, his pink ears, and his coarse red lips. They sprang out of a face that was completely covered by a white bushy beard that descended from his strange eyebrows, they were completely white, to his thick white wavelike moustachios, then cascaded down to the middle of his chest. Three horizontals lined his forehead and merged into his thick eyebrows. His head was bald.

He bowed his head low to allow his assistant to place a golden circlet two inches wide and set with gems, jewels and pearls, on his brow. On top of this the assistant placed a triangular mitre, usually worn only by the pope, with a vertical band of gold, front and back. The envoy was then presented by his assistant with a golden staff topped with a golden cross. He held it aloft above his mitre for all to see. A negro convert from Guinea in Africa produced harsh music on a portative organ which he supported on a sling, using his right hand on the keyboard and the left for the bellows. He also sang in a loud voice. I could detect, with great difficulty after a time, the strains of the Alleluia.

I was astounded, Ahmadji. Even more so when this golden hybrid, this combination of pope and bishop and deacon, began to speak, slowly, carefully enunciating every syllable of every word.

Strange, Kasim Beg laughed. He's speaking Kannada.

I have come as an emissary from the two supreme powers of the western world. The Holy Pontiff in Rome, the head of Western Christendom, sends you all his papal blessings. Dom Manuel, by the grace of God, King of Portugal, and of the Algarve, Lord of Guinea, on this side of the sea and on the far side in Africa, and of the Conquest, Navigation, and Commerce of Ethiopia, Arabia, Persia and India, sends all of you his greetings.

He stopped a while. Once again the harsh strains of the Alleluia resounded through the dining hall.

I almost burst out laughing. But I stopped in time. The Kannada accents, distorted by Portuguese nasals, made me uneasy. The translators found the broken Kannada very difficult to translate. The process took a very long time.

The envoy then repeated the pompous greeting, this time using broken Telugu.

VN rose up, and whispered something into the pink ear of the Pārasīkan who nodded understandingly.

I wanted to make the announcement to you in four different languages, the envoy stated.

This time he spoke Portuguese.

But my colleague VN informs me that it will take too much time

I knew I had heard that voice before. Way, way back. Not in Portugal, but in a land distant in time.

And that there will be time in the future for me and my future disciples to go forth and speak to you people in different tongues about my visions.

Let me introduce myself, the envoy continued. My name is Frei Luísdosalvador.

The six syllables had suddenly rushed out of my mouth. And I began a fit of loud fake coughing.

Luís do Salvador, the Frei said.

The audience was puzzled, and looked from him to me, back to him. The Frei, also puzzled, stared at me. No one understood what I had said, not even Kasim Beg.

Are you alright, asked Kasim Beg. He thumped my back and handed me a cup of water.

Let me repeat my name, the Frei said. And also state my lofty mission.

The Alleluia resounded again.

My name is Frei Luís do Salvador, and my mission is, as my name proclaims, to bring salvation to the whole world, a world that will come to an apocalyptic end soon, as has been predicted in the Bible in the Apocalypse of John. Before that can happen, the enemies of our faith, those infidels and heretics, will have to be destroyed. All the peoples all over the world, the gentios, will have to be converted to Christianity. Before that they will have to renounce the worship of the monkey devil whose name I abhor and whose image is found throughout this land.

There were several gasps of horror. Everyone turned to stare at VN.

VN's face was impassive. His eyes deadly cold.

Three mighty powers will have to unite to establish a new order, in heaven and on earth. First, the Holy Pontiff in Rome, whom you could term the western *jagadguru*. Second, the King of Portugal, Dom Manuel the Fortunate, the Promised One. And third, your godking, significantly named Krishna *Deva* Raya, to whom I have come as an emissary from Portugal. Who doesn't realize as yet that he is the legendary Preste João of the Indies, whom the western world has sought for years in Africa and in Ethiopia, a mighty potentate and yet a humble priest, of infinite wealth, power and holiness, an emperor with 75 mighty kings, whom you call *nayakas*, under his rule. It will be my privilege to convince him that he is the Preste.

To his cousin brother, King Krishna Deva Raya of Vijayanagar, Dom Manuel, the Senhor of Portugal has dispatched through me, his emissary and delegated authority, fifteen of the finest Arabian horses in token of his friendship and his regard. Let them be deployed for the Mahānavāmi celebrations to be held next month. More relays of horses will soon arrive from the coast, from Bhatkal and from Kannanur.

I, I will be the new messiah, the new apostle of the east, who will bring about the union of all three mighty powers in order to destroy the Sultanate of Babylon and to recover Jerusalem. That will result in the conversion of the whole world to Christ. Like Dom Manuel, Senhor of Portugal, I am a man of destiny, having survived the Calicut massacre where four of my fellow Franciscans were killed by the infidels. Your king, Krishna Deva Raya, as a token of his high regard for me has presented me with this golden shawl and this golden cross.

He paused for a while. His words were translated by his assistant with a sharp nose, whose Kannada was quite fluent though I don't think the audience knew what Babylon and Jerusalem meant. They were impressed by the solemn tone of the Frei's voice.

The assistant's name, Kasim Beg whispered, is Balthazar.

I invite you all to my church that is being built in Anegundi where I will offer Mass and preach the new gospel of salvation. The service will be held two days before the Mahanavami ceremony.

He looked at the musician and raised his golden cross aloft above his mitre for all to see. This time the *Te Deum Laudamus* was played and sung loudly, harshly, African sounds distorting the Latin words.

I didn't know whether to laugh or cry, Ahmadji. I sat paralyzed. Memory hurled me into time past. Into a little boat, an oar in my hand, to the Tupinamba, to the Terra da Vera Cruz, to the mad dreams of a mad Frei who had perhaps heard them from a mad Portuguese king. Their mad dreams, would they, had they, come true. Would Dom Manuel somehow be a messianic emperor. And Frei Luis, would he now become the *renovator mundi*. And was Vijayanagar really the kingdom of Preste João who would help in the conversion of the whole world to Christianity. Impossible.

I sat dazed. Time itself stopped. I did not want to be moved at all. I wanted not to be. But Kasim Beg started time flowing again, hurling me back into time present, by whispering into my ear that VN was calling for me.

Take care, don't drink that mango juice, whispered KB fiercely.

I was still in a daze, Ahmadji. I barely heard VN asking me if I was rested now after our long journey from Champaner. He wanted to ride out very early next morning before sunrise to the big maidan to examine the horses brought by Frei Luís as a gift. We would then return to the House of Vision. VN had received an important news report from Honawar and Bhatkal on the west coast that he wanted me to look at. He also wanted from me a complete account of the horse situation on the west coast of India in order to bring his cavalry up to strength. News about Goa had disturbed him.

I took one sip of the mango juice that Abolem brings for me every morning and then remembered what Kasim Beg had said. I shook my head when Abolem offered me the second glass.

Abolem looked surprised.

Then VN and I rode at dawn through three successive fortress gateways, the guards waved us on after checking my thumb, to the big maidan three miles away. It was just off the great western highway between Bhatkal and Vijayanagar city. Horses imported from Hormuz and Dhofar would be landed upriver at Bhatkal at a cove with a sloping beach, properly fed and watered after their long sea passage, and then driven on a three day journey to the stables behind the maidan, to be trained. The best of them, the Arab purebreds, were reserved for the royal cavalry. A few would be sent as gifts to *nayaka*chiefs.

VN was proud of his maidan which had been modeled on the hippodrome in Cairo. But he lamented the fact that soon after the advent of the Portuguese in 1498 the number of horses had diminished considerably and the Vijayanagar cavalry was not up to strength.

The Portuguese have disrupted horse traffic. We need more horses to attack the Muslims of Bijapur, VN said. We need to recapture Goa from the Muslims.

You need guns too, I pointed out.

From the hillock overlooking the stadium I could see Muslim cavalrymen practicing tactical moves and field exercises to improve their horsemanship. Some were performing military exercises with lances and swords. At one end they were playing polo. Most spectacular was the game of *qabaq*, which involved the shooting of arrows at a gourd target at the top of a high pole from a moving horse.

Didn't you, Ahmadji, watch this archery game performed on the sea beach at Malindi in 1497. You wrote about this, Ahmadji, in your account which I had to reread.

VN had ridden out to the big maidan to select an Arab pureblood from the horses brought by Frei Luís as gifts from the King of Portugal. It would be the royal horse for the Mahānavāmi ceremony which would begin on the first day of the lunar month of Aśvin. It would carry the royal state umbrella and would have to be fully caparisoned. VN swiftly approved of the gilded bridles and saddlery of exquisite workmanship from Bankapur, trappings and coverings made of many colored velvet lined with damask and satin, and edged with brocade, and so profusely ornamented with gold and pearls and diamonds that VN said the horse would be worth more than a whole city in the kingdom.

Just outside the maidan some workers were being trained. They were taught how to plant rake stones in the ground to impede the passage of horses. And VN pointed out thin wires, almost invisible, strung along the ground against a cavalry attack. Horse trippers, he explained, to prevent the enemy from getting too close to a fortress wall during a siege.

I wasn't impressed. These strategies could no longer be used. Useless, I thought, against a cannon attack. Horses would give way to guns.

On the way back we overtook groups of people who were hurrying along.

Before the heat becomes unbearable, I asked.

No, VN said. They want to make sure that they'll be able to get into Vijayanagar city for the Mahānavāmi celebrations. All its thirteen entrance gates will be locked early this year. The guards have strict orders not to let anyone in or out except those with markings on their thumbs. Many will be turned away. We don't want too many visitors this year. And we dont want any disturbances.

After the gateway guards had checked my thumb I rode on to the House of Vision.

The Honawar news report was from Timmaya, the commander of the Vijayanagar fleet of vessels that was based in Honawar and patrolled the west coast of India between Goa and Kannanur. The fleet kept a sharp lookout for pirates, and protected Vijayanagar trading interests at sea. Horse boats heading for Goa and Chapora, especially those carrying Arab purebreds, were forced to change direction and sail instead to Bhatkal to unload their precious cargo. Before the coming of the Portuguese Vijayanagar had a powerful fleet. Twenty or thirty boats would lurk in the many inlets and bays of the Kanara coast, lying in wait for ships from Hormuz and Dhofar. Strung out at a distance of six miles in between they would use fire signals and converge when an enemy was sighted. They would then swarm on to the hapless vessel. Their archers were deadly accurate.

These tactics didn't work after the arrival of the Portuguese pirates with their round ships that rode high on the water and were armed with formidable guns and cannons. Nothing, but nothing, could prevail against these huge monsters that bore down relentlessly on Timmaya's helpless fustas and sambuks. Even chains strung along the entrances of rivers could not prevent the Portuguese boats from getting in to attack a port. Just one small Portuguese caravel, despite having its sides and yardarm and topmast bristling with enemy arrows, could blow seven *sambuks* out of the water with ease.

After the Diu disaster in February this year the Portuguese roamed up and down the coast creating chaos in the world of shipping. They disrupted the horse trade so that the horse merchants cut down the number of ships they sent to the west coast of India. Bijapur and Vijayanagar did not have enough horses for their cavalry units.

And these brutal corsairs, Timmaya noted, these Portuguese, have the temerity to brand me a corsair.

Timmaya did not consider himself a corsair. A descendant of the former rulers of Goa, Timmaya considered himself a protector of Goa and a defender of Hinduism. He had dedicated himself completely to avenge the savage conquest of Goa by Mahmud Gawan. He belonged to the Hindu nobility, having married a princess of Gersoppa. According to Kasim Beg, he knew every inch of the Konkan and Kanara coastline, its bays and inlets, the ebb and flow of its tides, the swirl of the winds and currents along the coast. He was a master of disguise and had a gift for languages. He could speak a Konkani accented Portuguese which he had learned from a deserter during monsoon seasons when his ships were idle.

Timmaya's letter to VN presented a plan of action.

Timmaya's letter to VN

Sir, wrote Timmaya to VN, we have to deceive the Portuguese who have big ships and mighty guns. Let us arm ourselves with the cunning wisdom of our political guru, Kautilya, on whose *Arthaśastra* you have based your administrative skills.

In 1506, as you know, our offer of an alliance of marriage between a Portuguese prince and a Vijayanagar princess was not accepted. What I now propose, Sir, is to lure the Portuguese into a trap by offering them the conquest of my beloved Goa as a bait. You know how devastated I was, sir, when my eldest brother, Chidambaram, was murdered by the *afaqi* tax and customs collector who then appropriated for himself our ancestral house near the Well of Togetherness and our family property along the banks of the Chapora river in Anjuna beyond the customs house. Our family had to leave for Gersoppa and I was sent to Honawar for my education and training. I vowed then I would return to Goa one day on a mission of vengeance and drive the hated invaders out of Goa. Forgive me, sir, for being so emotional, but I love my Goa, and I love my Anjuna, where I was born and where I played as a boy.

The *afaqi* still lives in my ancestral house which he has turned into a stronghold guarded by soldiers armed with tufengs. The people of Anjuna are intensely dissatisfied, even the Muslims and the Naiteas who have formed a small colony there. All fishermen have to have their boats registered and pay a yearly tax. All visitors to Anjuna have to pay an entry tax at the Customs house. Heavy customs duties are charged on horses which are then transported over the Bardez ghats to Bijapur. He even charges people for a drink of water from the Well of Togetherness. I write about this in detail, sir, because Chapora has now become an important port taking in the overflow horse trade of Ela. The *afaqi*, my spies tell me, has requested that a troop of Portuguese deserters armed with arquebuses be sent from the capital to quell disturbances here and to provide protection for the Arabian horses that are now landed in Ihrampur.

I shall present facts to you in the *Arthaśastra* mode though I will not make use of Kautilya's theory of the *mandala* circle of states involving friends and enemies and friends' enemies and enemies' friends. For ours, sir, is not a land based but a sea situation. Things and times have changed. Here are the facts. And I can provide a map if it is needed.

About the Portuguese: Neither our friends nor our foes, they are a new group in our region, limited to the Indian ocean world and to a few port cities on the west coast. Their ships come from Portugal just once every year. In 1505 they decided to establish *feitorias* and fortresses on the west coast for purposes of trade. Dom Francisco de Almeida was sent as viceroy. He attacked the ships in Diu harbor but shrewdly refused to land his troops there. The Portuguese lack troops and equipment, sir, and they dare not invade any territory beyond the coast. They may, I predict, be conquerors of land territory but will never be able to control or rule it. They are pirates and plunderers, sir, and have disrupted the horse trade.

The friends of the Portuguese are the ruler of Cochin and the Kolathiri ruler of Kannanur, an enemy of Calicut. The enemies of the Portuguese are the ruler of Calicut who is a Hindu, the Egyptian Mamluks whose revenues and power are on the decline, the rising Ottomans, and the Pardesi traders, whom the Portuguese call the Moors of Mecca, who want to regain their trading dominance.

About Bijapur: You are well aware of the situation there. Yusuf Khan, the present ruler, is ailing. His enemies say he is on his death bed. His successor, Adil Khan, is a fourteen year old youth. Kamal Khan has been appointed the regent of the kingdom. There are succession disturbances, quarrels between the Shias and the Sunnis, and rebellions on the northern borders of Bijapur. Armed forces have been summoned to the capital from everywhere especially from Belgaum, from Ponda on the eastern outskirts of Goa, and from Goa itself. There are very few forces left for the defense of Goa but there are many siege guns which cannot be hauled over land.

About Goa: a landlocked island completely circled by two wide navigable rivers, the Mandovi and the Zuari, connected on the eastern end by the shallow Comburjua backwater that separates the mainland from Goa island. An attack from the mainland would pose problems because the five channel crossings, used to register visitors and to collect customs duties, have been sown with crocodiles. Only the crossing at Benastarim is well fortified, it has a tall tower and a large cannon.

Goa on the Mandovi, together with Chapora, is the only significant west coast outlet for the horse trade, except for Chaul, for the five Bahmanid sultanates. The Rumi shipwrights and armourers who took refuge in Goa after the Diu disaster were reluctant to return to barren Suez after they realized the advantages of Goa as a seaport with its excellent shipyard. Teak, available in the Goa hinterland, would enable them to construct huge ships in the Portuguese manner to sail on the ocean sea. My spies inform me that a shipbuilder is prepared to come from Genoa to build ships of the Portuguese type. Four galleasses have been built but have not yet been equipped for battle. And they believe that sulphur and saltpeter can be mined in Goa to manufacture gunpowder. The Bijapuris would then, sir, dominate the horse trade and build up their cavalry force. We can't let such a thing happen.

My suggestion. I propose, sir, with your approval, of course, to write to Viceroy Almeida and advise the Portuguese to sail over the bar of the Mandovi river and capture defenseless Goa. It can be done without loss of men and ships.

My tactics are Kautilyan. Goa will then no longer be the port of horses for Bijapur. Their diminished cavalry forces will no longer be a threat to us.

In my letter to Viceroy Almeida I shall spell out the advantages of capturing Goa. It has a deep, monsoon safe harbor five miles up the Mandovi river. It is strategically poised in the center of the west coast of India, between Cambay and Colombo, so that the Portuguese will be able to control the sea traffic in the Indian ocean. And they will be isolated from the turmoil of the Malabar coast and the alliances and quarrels with the petty rulers there for pepper and trade. Goa has a large shipyard, and there is space for an arsenal near the river's edge to equip their ships. I will promise to help them with our sambuks. I am prepared to launch an attack against the *afaqi* of Chapora and then organize a revolt of the Hindus against the *afaqis* of Bardez.

Almeida will surely see the advantages of my plan of action and want to capture Goa.

For VN's eyes only. NOT to be sent to Viceroy Almeida

After the Portuguese conquer Goa for us, sir, and drive away the Muslims, our real Kautilyan plan can swing into action.

First, let us send envoys to them bearing gifts and presents. The Portuguese are quite poor, sir. They don't have enough money of their own to purchase pepper and spices to load their ships. They have to borrow from financiers and they have nothing except copper to offer by way of trade. We can bribe them easily. Let us send Viceroy Almeida a golden collar and a necklace of jewels, and many diamonds and precious stones. The Portuguese are greedy for gold and the *fidalgos* can easily be bribed.

Secondly, the Portuguese will not be able to administer the territory since they do not know the language of Goa, Konkani, and they know absolutely nothing about our revenue matters, and about customs duties and taxes that have to be collected. The Viceroy, it is rumored, is firmly against gaining territorial possessions because, he thinks, that that would weaken their strength. That's why he refused the offer of Diu when it surrendered. They will therefore have to farm out the territory to us at a very low rate to collect taxes. We shall pretend to consult with them about this, to our advantage.

Thirdly, sir, some time after the Portuguese have been lulled into a sense of security, it will be time for a Kautilyan masterstroke. You know, sir, that there are very few Muslims in Goa island. Most of them live in the city while others, like Naiteas, live near the mouths of rivers or near ford crossings. The majority of the people are Hindus. Both groups complain loudly about the exorbitant sums levied by the *afaqi* tax collectors. Taxes have been doubled. I will organize riots and incite rebellions in Goa and especially in Anjuna and in Chapora. The Hindus, and even some Muslims, hate the Bijapur administrator *afaqis*.

Finally, sir, we will attack Goa, drive out the Portuguese and the remaining Muslims, and Goa will once again belong to Hindu Vijayanagar. You, sir, I am sure, could be appointed governor, and I shall be delighted to be your assistant.

I request, sir, that I be appointed an administrator, or even a governor if you do not care for that office.

Turushka quarters

The next day perhaps, perhaps not, what day is it, Ahmadji.

Sometimes it gets dark before it gets dark.

I dream a lot now. I never used to before I came to Vijayanagar. Bizarre visions of the beyond. I float in the sea of time present, dimly aware of matters beyond the horizon.

I wish I could write them down, these visions, but I don't always remember them

I have now come to appreciate the cold act of setting words down. It steadies my mind.

Spoken words, I now realize, drift away in time. Memory cannot always summon back everything specially what has been spoken. Perhaps that's why you have set down your story in writing. Let me assure you, Ahmadji, your papers are safe.

Words written get anchored down.

Why do I use your pilot metaphors.

I used to, if you remember, have perfect recall. Now, after coming to Vijayanagar, I find I don't. My memory has been damaged. I have at times to reread your account to confirm certain things you noted.

I've just been hit by a brilliant idea.

You need a word that can bring the many pages of your account into focus for your reader. Why don't you use *samsāra* as the title of your as yet untitled account, Ahmadbhai.

Forgive me, my friend, but your word fascinates me. Perhaps you can combine it with the word for mirror, *mirat*, a favorite word of Persian historians, to get *Mirat-i-Samsāra* as a title.

I do sound pompous, don't I.

Of course I do, but doesn't my title sum up your account. And aren't you mirroring a whole world that is passing away. I shall make many random comments on your story in this letter. For isn't your story, oh wanderer, my story too, in a way.

Alas my friend, we cannot remain unpolluted by *samsāra*, can we. We have to plunge into this our world which, despite what our pandit friend in Diu maintains, is not a māyic world. We are political animals, as that ancient Greek philosopher, whose system with its rigid categories I so dislike, said. I think you want to dwell for ever in the cave of shadows, as my Plato said most men do. Your cave is your own past which you do not allow even your own self to enter.

Let me interrupt myself, Ahmadji.

I get tired of writing official reports for VN in the House of Vision, even though they do make me aware of the total situation. Here, Ahmadji, is a list of the places where the Portuguese have built their fortresses. Without any aim. Lacking an overall plan. You'll be interested. Kilwa, Socotra, Anjediva, Kannanur, Cochin, these form an arc around the perimeter of the Indian Ocean. The Portuguese have now had to dismantle the Anjediva and the Socotra fortresses that didn't have harbors where large vessels could winter safely and where the food supply was adequate. What Timmaya says is true. The Portuguese not only lack men and material but also a plan of action. Also, here is a dry sentence from Viceroy Almeida's letter to the King of Portugal. The more fortresses you build, wrote Almeida, the weaker your power will be, for your entire force rests on the sea.

But I want to write about human things, and not just be a channel of information. I want to talk to faraway you, Ahmadji, to tell you about your account. Your random broodings irritated me. Get on with Usha's story, I would exclaim impatiently as I read your account. I want to know what happened to her. But you never did hurry the pace of your story. Bit by bit you have put together your past world, and have been healing yourself in the process. No, not really, not completely. There's a gap you have not even attempted to fill.

There are many things I want to know. What happened to Usha, to your baby that she was carrying on the way back to India, did she lose the baby. You both left Diu in 1497, and you returned to Diu by yourself in 1509 when Malik Aiyaz appointed you his personal *shahbandar*. What did happen when the Portuguese ships brought you and Usha from Malindi to Calicut. Was the baby born, when, where. You mentioned Vijayanagar twice, and the year 1505, and a place beyond Anegundi where, bleeding and wounded in a ditch, you were rescued and treated by a hakim whom you accompanied and who advised you to return to Diu to be healed.

What happened to Usha and to you in Vijayanagar. An Anegundi mystery. Like the mystery of the Jain ascetic from Gujarat who ventures forth only at night. Could he be the uncle who vanished into the night at Śatruñjaya in Gujarat. I have told Balthazar to find out if he is Usha's uncle and I did mention the name of Sheth Chimanlal, her father. And I have told Balthazar to ask the ascetic about Usha by name. I would have gone to the Jain temple myself and to the police station, but I cannot speak Kannada. A police report for 1505, VN says, should be available at the police station. Balthazar will translate it for me.

About your story, Ahmadji, allow me to end with these comments. You demand too much of your reader. I, who am present in your story, find it very difficult to follow the sequence of events. You zigzag bewilderingly from the present to your many pasts, tangling up linear time.
I'm trying to understand. But I remain confused.

Don't be angry, Ahmadji, I wanted to offer you some suggestions. But I do want to mention Usha. I love her too, though I've never met her and you've never talked to me about her. She's there, everywhere, in you and your story, an invisible fragrance of jasmine.

A strong aroma of jasmine assailed my being. It was Abolem. She interrupted me as I was writing my account. Strange, she had neglected me ever since I had arrived, had neglected my needs.

This time she took away my pen. Then she took away my usual bottle of liquor, and placed another bottle and one small glass on this paper. It was late in the evening, time for my first drink of the day.

No no, Abolem, not yet, later, I wanted to tell her.

Abolem poured me a tiny drink and gave me a note from VN. It said, Abolem tells me you don't like mango juice. This is the thrice distilled Shirazi liquor I promised you. It's very strong. Have only three drinks a day.

The liquor was darkish brown, made of red grapes. Abolem waited till I took a sip. It was sweet, but made my tongue tingle. I took another sip.

I knew she was aware of my eyes watching her haunches swing slowly from side to side and up and down, as she walked slowly, awkwardly, out the door. Her legs were sturdy and muscular. There was a large gap between the first two toes of her right foot.

She came back, eyes looking down, an oil jar on one ample hip, and I knew she was aware that my eyes were on her breasts that yearned to burst out of her tight choli. It was as if a sculptured *apsara* had stepped down from one of the hundred Hazāra Rāma temple pillars. I was in a strange state. My body felt tired, and yet restless with desire. My thighs ached as did my calves, my neck was stiff. I looked at Abolem, and I wanted to, and I didn't want to.

I waited for Abolem.

She made me wait a long time.

I took two more sips of the Shirazi liquor.

It was getting unbearably long, the wait.

Let me write, I told myself. About what happened that morning.

We had walked around that morning looking at the temples and shrines of Vijayanagar, climbing up steep granite steps, looking up at the scenes of gods with their voluptuous full breasted goddesses carved on porches, staring at the dancing *apsaras* on the *mandapa* pillars. I had marveled at how the sculptors managed to transform stone into firm flesh one wanted to caress and fondle.

I had accompanied Frei Luís and Balthazar da Gama, his assistant and translator, an expert in jewels and precious stones, on this temple tour. VN wanted to learn more about Frei Luís and about the Portuguese from me. A guide had been provided by VN.

Frei Luís had wanted to be carried in a litter.

My head aches, Frei Luís had complained to VN. I feel tired ever since I came to Vijayanagar. My thighs also ache.

I felt tired too. It must be the monsoon heat. But I didn't complain to VN. My I felt strangely distant from my body at times

Frei Luís wore a dazzlingly golden shawl over his shoulders, a gift, VN said, from King Krishna Deva Raya. The other gift was a golden cross mounted on a long golden staff. VN had wanted the Frei to carry it with him as he walked through the streets of the city. But Frei Luis said it was too heavy. We passed a group of Muslim mourners carrying a corpse, wrapped up in a white shroud and strewn with flowers, on a bier made of four plain bamboo sticks.

The people will not know you if you do not walk through the city streets with the cross, VN had told Frei Luis. They have to know you and your Christian gods and your teachings. How else will you convert them. How else will they become your followers and disciples. Then they'll flock to the church we're building for you in Anegundi.

Let us go to Anegundi, Frei Luís said. I want to look at my church. Has the work been completed.

VN has told me not to take you to Anegundi, Balthazar said. According to VN, no sponsor should view an incomplete religious structure. That will be bad *darshan*.

People stood in groups at street corners and stared at the Frei in awe. At his foaming white beard, I thought. A few, led by one with a squeaky voice, began chanting *Krisn, Krisn*, as he walked past them. They followed the Frei, but kept at a respectable distance.

Maybe they will be some of my followers, the Frei said. VN told me some people want to know more about my religion. Do they think I'm Christ, the Frei asked Balthazar.

No, replied Balthazar in Portuguese. The golden shawl is an attribute of Lord Krishna.

One of their heathen gods, snorted the Frei.

The people folded their hands, and bowed low to the Frei as he passed.

The guide led us into a dimly lit temple where a group of visitors in long white wraparounds with black vertical streaks on their foreheads, some supporting themselves with long staffs, were staring in awe at an image carved on a rock. Their guide carried a flaming torch. It was the image of Hanuman meditating in the lotus position, a rosary in his hand, framed by a circle of 12 jumping monkeys. The guide looked like VN, I thought. But I wasn't sure. The visitors looked all alike to me in the fiery darkness.

This is the *Yantroddaraka* Hanuman, installed by Sri Vyāsarāya, said Balthazar. It is the only Hanuman shrine in Vijayanagar where rituals are conducted by the Madhvas.

Superstitious idolaters, these gentios, said Frei Luís to Balthazar in Portuguese. We will have to force open their ignorant eyes to Christianity just as your Jewish eyes were made to open wide to accept the truth.

I heard a note of concern in Frei Luís's voice.

Like a father's, I thought. As if Balthazar was his son.

It's too dark here, Frei Luís said. I can't see anything.

And he rushed out of the temple.

I shut my eyes tight, and in the double darkness I could see a blur of religions swirling madly together. I felt a little dizzy. Balthazar held on to my arm, and I opened my eyes.

For Frei Luís the truth was known only to Christians. All non Christian religions and cultures were the work of the devil. The Muslims, they were barbarous infidels. The Jews had to be converted and baptized before the world came to an end. The Hindus and the Buddhists and the Jains were all ignorant gentiles that had to be baptized and dragged into the orbit of Christianity.

The Frei was absolutely ignorant about Hinduism, had never heard its wonderful myths. Those stories, Ahmadji, that enable all religions to bring the far near and to translate the divine into human terms. The colossal rockcut Nandi, the bull of Siva, an image of utter peace and contentment, left him unmoved. The stone figure of Ganesh, the Lord Remover of obstacles, horrified him, for the Frei had never heard the story of how and why the human head had been cut off and replaced with an elephant head and trunk and one broken tusk by Lord Siva his father. The many armed figures with sacred icons in their hands were grotesque, bewildering. Human beings were created with only two arms, weren't they.

What infuriated him most, I know not why, was the carved profile of Hanuman the monkey god in a heroic pose on a gigantic wall panel. The Frei stood in front of it, glaring fiercely at it for a very long time.

Then he made an elaborate sign of the cross on himself. With the thumb of his right hand he made a cross on his forehead, then another cross on his lips, yet another on his breast, then he touched his right shoulder and then his left. He waved his arms wildly above his head, and hurled an imprecation in Latin, in a stentorian voice that could be heard throughout the square.

Adjuro te, spiritus nequissime, per Deum omnipotentem
Amen, I said.

Frei Luís turned and stared at me, surprised at my response.

The whole square fell silent.

Look, Frei Luís told us, just look at that devilish monkey man face. That's Satan incarnate. He is present everywhere. Here in Vijayanagar, I've been told, there are 732 representations of this devil ape that the gentios worship.

Can't you see, he asked Balthazar. Look carefully, look at that long tail that curves over the head. That's the evil serpent halo protecting him from all that's good and innocent.

And the Frei repeatedly urged Balthazar as a good Catholic to join him in cursing Hanuman. You too, he told me.

We didn't. The Madhva group looked puzzled. The mass of people around muttered to themselves. I could hear the squeaky voice distinctly but could not see him in the crowd. I was glad they could not understand what the Frei said.

Balthazar took the Frei by his arm and led him away.

He's a holy madman, Balthazar explained to the people in Kannada.

For them his madness is a form of divine possession, Balthazar told me.

The Frei turned and shook his raised fist at Hanuman's profile.

The group of Madhvas who had moved away, horrified, turned around to stare at us. Furious, they rushed up and wanted to attack us. One lifted up his staff.

Balthazar placed himself in front of the Frei, and flung out his arms to protect him.

Don't, came a shout like a gunshot.

The Madhvas moved hurriedly away. It sounded like VN, but I wasn't sure.

Our guide quickened his pace and led us away hastily. It turned out to be an exhausting tour. By midmorning the sun was unbearably hot. Frei Luís perspired heavily under his golden shawl. Balthazar and I in loose cotton shirts and wearing light sandals were more comfortable. Frei Luis with his heavy boots found it difficult to keep up with us. I wanted to be friendly, and tell him a few things that I knew about Hinduism. But the Frei snorted, and turned away from me when I pretended I was a Morisco who could speak Castilian.

Balthazar seemed quite interested, and full of questions. So we walked ahead, and I spun out for him a fictitious account of my adventures as a Morisco in Persia and all through India. Balthazar was fascinated.

At the end he asked sadly, have you ever found the home you have been seeking.

It was a disturbing question. Then I realized it had been directed not at me but at himself. He had become strangely quiet all through the tour.

I put together what I knew about him. His voice, it sprang out of the Levant, the gutturals betrayed this. His tendency to vowelize all words even those ending with consonants that he always released, implied that he knew some South Indian languages. His nose was Semitic, his skin was swarthy. The first name, his last name. Both provided clues.

Eureka, I found the answer. He had to be related to Gaspar da Gama, the *converso* thoroughly despised by the Jewish astronomer in Cabral's fleet. Balthazar's magian first name together with the pretentious of-the-house-of implied by *da* proclaimed him a converso who was a crypto. That's why this crypto converso was drawn to someone he believed was a crypto morisco.

Balthazar, like us, Ahmadji, is in search of a homeland. Caught between two religions, one he was forced to abandon, the other he was forced to adopt, he is an exile in search of a spiritual home unsure where or whether it exists.

Later he told me that he was the eldest son of Gaspar da Gama who, as a lingua and a negotiator, became totally committed to the Portuguese cause.

I found I was not able to practice *takiya*, Gaspar da Gama had told his eldest son. The strain of concealment would have driven me mad. Your mother, a pillar of strength, knew that I would have to act as advisor and interpreter for the Portuguese, for our family in Shingli Cranganore needed money. She understood our plight, the plight of our victim race in this cruel changing world which dooms us to be wanderers.

Remember, Gaspar da Gama told his son, we are go-betweens, forever doomed to serve under those in power. We have no place to call our own. We have to establish a reputation for loyalty and always remain faithful to those we serve.

Accept your tribulations, your mother said. Her face was lined with sorrow.

I read my prayer scroll every day, your mother lamented. The sounds of Hebrew bring me consolation in this wilderness.

It was one of the Hebrew scrolls saved after the expulsion of the Jews and the destruction of the synagogues in Portugal in 1497 and then brought to Calicut in one of Cabral's ships. Balthazar's mother had organized a collection of moneys from the community to purchase 13 scrolls of the Law for 4000 pardaos.

You, Gaspar had told his son, have to come to terms with the awful strain of *takiya* which I could not endure.

I want to escape, Balthazar said, but where, where in this world can I find a refuge. Perhaps you should go to Melaka where your brother works as a lapidary. The Portuguese will never get there, Gaspar da Gama had told his son.

Balthazar had to become a Catholic or else he would not have received a royal appointment as special assistant to Frei Luís who had been sent, as he himself had told me in the little boat at Santa Cruz, on a secret mission to the Vijayanagar court by King Manuel of Portugal. Balthazar didn't want to talk about Frei Luís, to whom he was loyal, and I didn't ask him any questions. One of the documents kept in the House of Vision was a copy of Balthazar's letter of appointment obtained by Timmaya.

Balthazar also acted as an agent broker for the purchase of jewels, diamonds and precious stones for the Portuguese fidalgos and the landless petty nobility whom he greatly despised. Pirates, he called them, plunderers. And added with contempt, leeches.

I knew what he meant. As younger sons who could inherit neither property nor title, they volunteered to go to India because they had no prospects in Portugal. They wanted to get rich in a hurry but had no skills and no education, and knew nothing at all about trade and commerce. They had nothing to sell except their fighting skills. The military expeditions to North Africa, still regarded as a holy war, were no longer profitable. And they didn't realize that their mode of fighting, with armor and sword and lance and pike was as obsolete as the code of chivalric honor which they lived by. As *gente limpa*, the clean ones, they refused to allow their honor to be soiled by the black smoke of gunpowder. That new mode of fighting they considered beneath their dignity. That was left to the *gente baixa*, the lower class.

Because they were never paid a regular salary and because they were allowed to carry back to Portugal duty-free goods in just one small liberty-chest, dignified by the high sounding name, *liberdades de India*, they were eager to get rich as quickly as possible. They rejoiced when their captains, disregarding orders to remain in port and protect the feitorias, set off on plundering expeditions to the mouths of the Red Sea and the Persian Gulf. It was a crusade on sea. After all infidel ships were lawful prizes to capture. They would get a small share of the loot which they could then convert to jewels and precious stones with the help of Balthazar.

We waited, Balthazar and I, for Frei Luís to catch up with us. The guide took us to places and sights that usually impressed visitors from foreign shores. To the *natya mandapa*, the hall where the *devadasis* practised the dance poses sculpted on its pillars. Through an open two storied gateway to the king's balance. I saw two tall columns and an exquisitely ornamented stone bar in the middle of which a swing was suspended from a stone loop. Used, Balthazar told me, to entertain the god by gently swinging his image on festival occasions. The king would, at times, be weighed in a balance against jewels and precious stones, which would then be gifted to a temple.

The guide took us next to a temple with five musical pillars that sounded different notes when struck. I tried to play the *Salve Rainha* using a small bamboo stick. I must not have played it right. Frei Luís couldn't or wouldn't recognize this hymn which I used to love in Coimbra.

You heard the *Salve Rainha*, Ahmadji, didn't you, sung on board Paulo's ship. You wrote that you and Usha were deeply moved by that prayer hymn that ends with a hush of sacred silence.

The guide then took us through endless streets and narrow byways to the small shrine of *Lajjā-Gauri*. The goddess, completely nude, was shown in the squatting position, with legs and thighs widely separated. Vermilion powder had been applied by childless women devotees to her breasts and to her vagina. Even I was shocked at this naked display. Balthazar said matter of factly that she was the folk goddess of fertility. Frei Luis stared in silence with fascinated horror. I don't think he had ever seen such a sight before. His pink ears turned a deep red.

Quite tired, I wanted to go back to Turushka quarters for a bath and then for dinner with Kasim Beg.

Just one more temple, the guide pleaded. I have to show Frei Luis this shrine. VN will be very angry if I don't.

And he hurried us through some dimly lit gopura passages, not bothering to stop at some facades with statues of voluptuous *apsaras* lit up by the full glare of the noonday sun, to the very end of a dark corridor. There, by the light of a flaming torch, we saw pillars hidden from the eyes of foreign visitors. *Mithuna* figures, our guide said. Copulating couples, the women, their eyes tightly shut, at the pinnacle of bliss and *bhoja*. And stonestill ascetics, their lingas erect, their eyes wide open, gazing at naked virgins but unmoved by erotic passion.

That's a form of penance and control, Balthazar said. That *apsara* with the parrot in her right hand is Mohinī, a manifestation of Lord Vishnu.

You must have been on a tour arranged by VN, said Kasim Beg to me at dinner. You look exhausted.

I felt so hot that unthinkingly I drank deep from a glass of mango juice. It was cooling and refreshing, sweeter than the juice Abolem brings me every morning.

Stop, stop, Kasim Beg said. Have you forgotten what I told you.

I am not as exhausted as Frei Luís was, I said. The Frei could hardly walk up the steps of Pārasīka House. I don't think he'll come for dinner.

All his needs will be taken care of by Mogrem, Kasim Beg said, all of them. It's been carefully planned by VN. My Xiumtem, your Abolem, and the Frei's Mogrem will begin with a penetrating oil massage that will search out and loosen the knots in his thighs and calves. Then the Frei will be given a hot bath assisted by those three *apsaras* who will contrive to splash themselves with water to make their cholis transparent. Some mango juice they'll give him, of the kind you're having. Some food. Then, when he is completely relaxed and sleepy, Mogrem will

Stop, I told Kasim Beg, don't tell me.

My mind knew what would happen to Frei Luís, but I stopped my leap to the visual.

I reached out for another sip of mango juice to steady myself.

Don't, Kasim Beg whispered fiercely, don't drink that. And he signaled to Lonpal to take away both the glasses of juice. He hadn't touched his at all.

Have you read the *Arthaśashtra*, Kasim Beg asked, Kautilya's treatise on the pursuit of wealth and power.

I hadn't.

Haven't you realized yet how devious VN is, Kasim Beg said. He has deliberately not punished Lonpal and allowed him to serve us to lull our suspicions. Don't you find yourself in a confused state. Doesn't your head spin. How many times since your arrival in Vijayanagar have you drunk mango juice.

He looked all around, then he stopped, as if he had to make up his mind about something.

I know from my Xiumtem who is friends with your Abolem that you drink two glasses of mango juice in the morning. It's the mango juice that makes your head spin, Kasim Beg explained.

I kept silent, though I was seething inside.

Quite true, I thought to myself. Before Vijayanagar and before mango juice I felt fine.

Into that mango juice, Kasim Beg explained carefully, the sap of the roots of the *unmatta* plant has been infused. VN has it given to all envoys when they come to Vijayanagara to get them addicted. It enables him to bring them slowly under control and make them do whatever he wants. The effects of *unmatta* are many, and quite unpredictable. It acts swiftly on the memory and on the will. The courtesans then proceed to soften the will with foot massage, and the person becomes weak and pliable. It takes many days for its effects to wear off. Different effects for different persons. VN knows that it will act as an aphrodisiac for Frei Luís. Has the Frei ever slept with a woman.

VN had told me that his holy man, Sri Vyāsarāya, has never touched a woman. And that Lord Hanuman always remained chaste. That's why wrestlers worship him as the god of strength.

I stood up abruptly.

You haven't touched your dinner, Kasim Beg said.

I smiled at Kasim Beg. Lonpal pointed to the food on the table. I smiled at Lonpal.

Then I walked out of the dining hall. With slow measured steps, as if I was a drunk trying to steady myself.

I was in a terrible rage. My head was whirling. I could taste my fury, ice cold and bitter in my mouth, as I walked out. Then I made a visual leap, not to the naked Frei Luis being kneaded by Mogrem, but to you, Ahmadji, standing stonestill before me.

Why, why, João, you ask me.

I don't know, I say.

Who, what, has made you so furious, João, you ask.

I don't know, Ahmadji, I say. This world, perhaps.

Ah, you say to me, that's *samsāra*, João.

Then you vanish mysteriously, Ahmadji. I try to will you back to stand again in front of me, but I am not able to.

I am quite calm now, but needled by that question of questions that has always tormented me. Who's responsible for it all.

I am, I tell myself.

Why, why.

For being so stupidly stupid. I should have known.

I'll never have mango juice again. That's why I am so confused. That's why there's this tufan within me, Ahmadji, that makes time whirl madly around. My body is aflame. It cannot stop desiring Abolem.

How many days will the effects of *unmatta* last, I ask myself.

I'll ask Balthazar, I tell myself.

Will he know.

How many times had Abolem given me mango juice. I try to count the number of days I've been in Vijayanagar, but can't.

Does Abolem know. Did she know.

Of course, she works for VN who must have told her to use the tactics of sexual delay.

The first time I had mango juice at the Anegundi gateway VN hadn't had any, had he. VN lured me to this paradise of flesh by telling me stories of beautiful courtesans. A clever snake, VN is, venomous, treacherous. He weakened the Frei first by exposing to him *apsaras*, and *Lajjā Gauri*, and *mithunas*, and then made this man of god succumb to soft yielding flesh.

It's a mortal sin.

Calm down, João, I tell myself. João, I say to myself, calm down.

I took a deep breath. I take a deep breath.

Is Frei Luís really a man of god, I ask myself. Is he capable of love and *bhakti*. Why, why do I not like him. He has an arrogant I.

So have you, João, I tell myself.

Aren't both of you innocent, driven mad by mango juice and by a world the Frei and you do not quite understand. And do you, do I, really believe now in mortal sin. And in *karma* too. D'you, João, do I, believe in reincarnation, and *advaita*, and *dvaita*, and in Jainism. Aren't there too many religions now. Too many deities. Who'll be able to reconcile them. Ahmadji, I vaguely recall your telling me about one who could. And where should I go to reconcile them all. Back to Coimbra, to the Santa Cruz monastery there where I was found on Christmas Day. Can one go home again. But where's home. I should ask Frei Louro. I will, but he's in Champaner now.

Calm down, João, I tell myself, calm down.

In my letter to Frei Louro that I sent to Champaner I had promised I'd write down my views about conversion. At that time I knew all the answers. Now I don't, I have only questions about conversion for him. I want him to reconsider with me the old medieval dream. Wasn't it a Franciscan dream, too.

Will it really be possible, António, to convert this strange new world with its innumerable peoples and beliefs, its multitude of languages and cultures and customs. I suddenly think of St. Thomas, that doubter of an apostle, who wanted to dip his finger into Christ's side before he would say, My Lord and my God. Because he lacked faith he was deliberately banished from the familiar Mediterranean world to the faraway. He had to preach to many different unbelievers in many different countries. How did he do that. He voyaged to Socotra and was martyred in South India.

My question to Frei António is this. How did Saint Thomas get to know the languages he used for preaching the gospel. How could the words convey Christian concepts like soul and resurrection. Didn't he have problems learning Socotri and Malayalam and Tamil, and teaching his disciples. Any other problems, you ask. A major problem about caste and its barriers. He must have somehow solved them, I wonder how, for there are many Syrian Christians, they are also called St. Thomas Christians, in Malabar.

Ahmadji, I must get rid of my man-of-action masks and return to Coimbra to my true self, to teach, to be a reconciler. When and if I do my first task will be to ask such questions to those Church authorities who want to send innocent missionaries armed only with the sword of faith to convert the gentiles. Perhaps I could convert the converters.

My beliefs, Ahmadji, and my verbs, oh they're both confused. I don't get them right.   A confusion of tenses marks a confusion about time. What does a confusion of beliefs mean.

Turushka Quarters

Never, never will I have mango juice again. How long will its effects last. I must ask Balthazar about *unmatta*. Maybe it's the same drug Brother Clement had used once in the Santa Cruz infirmary to treat madmen. Mandragora, he called it.

I'm glad I've come to like this Shirazi liquor made of dates.

Ahmadji, I still lose track of time present. My memory has been damaged. How wonderfully, Ahmadji, you controlled time past and time present in your account. Not like me, whose past is so dreary, whose present so confused, and whose future is uncertain.

I had to stop writing for a while, Ahmadji, couldn't continue. I want to make real for you yesterday's night of rapture, an experience my body will never forget. But when I tried to recreate the night for you on paper I couldn't. My mind went blank. Words wouldn't come.

Impossible, words told me, to convey the passionate immediacy of your night of abandon.

Must have been easier, Ahmadji, for you to make real the world of love in your account. After all, human love is an emotion, a flow in time. What I tried to but failed to convey to you is a world where the mind did not enter like a snake in a garden, the mindless world of the senses and of sensation. The mind needs language, so they say, to understand the human condition. But how can language convey the pure animal condition that we at times experience, a time when time stands still.

I give up.

My mind told my body to rise up from the mat when Abolem began the foot massage. It's not you, it's the *unmatta*, my mind said. I wanted Abolem to stop. But my body didn't listen, it lay helpless under Abolem's feet.

I'm confused, Ahmadji. I cannot give you up, Abolem.

Let me try again.

How, how can I convey to you my body's mindless rapture as I lay naked on that mat of cool green banana leaves, three twisted coir ropes dangling above me, flat on my stomach, warm coconut oil poured lightly from a warm palm on to my shoulder blades, warm oil dripping tantalizingly on the curve of my buttocks making them tingle, making me squeeze them together, the oil trickling teasingly lingeringly down the hollow of my spine, its slow flow spread all over by one big toe that danced so lightly, ever so lightly, ticklingly, all over my back, making it arch with delight, then skimming delicately, hoveringly, like a bee, like a feather, over my tense buttocks, the toenail scratching, caressing, but not entering their divide so that my whole body was aroused, my toes digging and straining and stretching against the banana leaves, my whole body waiting, wanting, poised to surrender, to melt into nonbeing, when the knotted ropes overhead creaked and my shoulders felt a burst of pain, a sudden blow from one bare foot that went on to knead the flesh below my shoulder blades, the heel of the other foot moving slowly down my spine, descending section by section by section to the base, insisting along the way that each section of the spine come alive before going to the other, the heel then circling the base, pressuring, then coaxing it to loosen the knot of pain, that little bird trapped there, coaxing it to climb up, and up, and up to my shoulders, then suddenly a double blow, both the heels digging deep, searching, probing the secret centers of my back, creating pain that became exquisite pleasure that turned into exquisite pain, then pleasure again, my body now an inert mass of sensation, turned effortlessly over and over and over by the two bare feet, my body limp, helpless, on its back, her feet dancing, dancing all over, the big toe barely grazing my erect nipples, descending to my body's aroused center, then a toegrasp, a toesqueeze, exquisite pleasurepain, a release then a tightening, a release, then rapture, exquisite death.

Then sleep.

The day following, I think.

I've stopped having the mango juice. But why do I still feel confused.

It takes time for the *unmatta* to release me from its grip

Kasim Beg has been repeatedly urging me to accept the offer of Rustum Khan, the leader of the Bijapur cavalry. He will even ride up to the outskirts of Anegundi, so anxious is he to meet you and take you to Bijapur, Kasim Beg tells me.

Go, João, go, you wanderer, go to Bijapur, I tell myself.

But I do need the services of Abolem.

Am I not her slave.

Can't I will myself to say no to her.

No, João, you can't.

My body needs her. It can't give Abolem up. My I won't.

You must be confused too, Ahmadji, my friend.

I am. A strange kind of confusion that befuddles my sense of time so that time eddies around madly sometimes. The confusion evaporates as and when I write. Have I said this before. Yes I have. It's a strange state, to experience confusion and sudden clarity at almost the same time. I don't get drunk now. Which is strange, not even at night. I am content with two sips of the Shirazi liquor Abolem brings me.

Virappa Nayaka had told me he had Abolem specially assigned to me from among the women provided for all important foreign visitors.

She will look after your needs, he had told me, all of them. I brought her, VN had said, from Mangalore on the west coast to Vijayanagara. She wanted to be a temple dancer, a *devadasi*. But the trainer took one look at her flat feet and trained her for toe dancing.

What's that, I had asked.

Impossible to describe, Virappa Nayaka had said, it can only be experienced.

The training was a torture, Abolem had told VN, that ended only after she was able to squeeze a thick section of bamboo between the first two toes of her right foot.

Now, Ahmadji, you know exactly what happened to me on that mat.

The rays of the evening sun lit up the back porch of the Madhva *math* VN took me to. Sri Vyāsarāya was sitting in the shadow of a granite pillar. A disciple, young, his eyes downcast, sat two steps below him, asking questions. The replies of the master were gentle, soothing. He did not use many words. Frequently he raised his right hand to say, without using words, do not fear.

VN wanted to interrupt their conversation. He had lost his usual calm. His face twitched a little. His eyes were not steady. His hands trembled slightly.

I am not used to waiting, VN said to me.

His voice became steady again. VN tried never to betray his feelings. He wanted his guru to tell him what should be done about the problem of horses and the Portuguese on the west coast. The war between Vijayana-gar and Bijapur could only be won by the side that, with the help of the Portuguese, had the superior cavalry, VN wanted to tell his guru.

My question to the guru would be simple. I wanted to know the dif-ference between the two theological systems, *advaita* and *dvaita*. I waited patiently. I felt disappointed because I could not see the guru's face which was hidden by the temple pillar. But I liked the tone of reassurance in his voice even though I could not hear what he was saying. It reminded me of someone faraway. Where are you now, Brother Clement.

That disciple's name is Purandara Dāsa, VN said. He's only twenty four, and they say he is the best composer of devotional songs in Kannada. Everyone in Vijaayanagar, even the courtesans, listen to his *padams* and sing them. He has become our guru's most trusted disciple. It's not fair, Jan Mirza. That's what I wanted to be. I should have been granted that honor.

The whine of resentment in VN's voice was unmistakable.

Then his voice changed.

Power, that's what I'll now seek, VN proclaimed. Did you know that I deliberately included the note that Timmaya had written for my eyes only in the letter sent to Almeida. The Viceroy will never trust Timmaya or make him a collector of revenues.

I will be appointed governor of Goa., VN shouted.

I was shocked.

VN noticed me staring at him.

To cover it up he began to chant the praises of his guru. He called him the teacher of kings and the king of teachers. So kingly, proclaimed VN, that King Krishna Deva Raya gave the guru a ceremonial bath pouring on his head basins, not of water but of gems and pearls that were then distrib-uted as gifts to temples. So full of love for his king and for Vijayanagar, VN said, that the guru agreed to mount the throne and act as king on the day the astrologers predicted would be fatal to the Raya because of a *kuhuyoga*, a conjunction of evil planets. So full of justice for all communities, VN insisted, that the Bijapuri sultan presented him with a drum on the back of a camel to honor him, and a green banner, a favorite Muslim color, as a token of his high regard.

VN's voice sounded hollow and false. Then it sounded sad.

My king has changed, VN lamented. My guru, too, VN said, a sudden change that came about after I left for Diu. He has withdrawn into himself. No longer does he use Sanskrit to preach to his disciples. He uses words very sparingly now, talks to people in Kannada, the homespun language of the people. He has even composed a few *padams* in Kannada. Most of the time he talks to people through his disciple.

To use language, Vyāsarāya had told Purandara Dāsa, is to remain trapped in the coils of *samsāra*. Only through song and through sound *śabda* can one leap back beyond the beyond to the very beginning.

The clear sounds of the *adhan*, the Muslim summons to the faithful to turn away from the everyday world to God, leapt to my consciousness. I also remembered you and Usha listening to the *Salve Rainha* on Senhor Paulo's ship. Way way back it was I as a child listening to this prayer hymn with Brother Clement holding my hand outside the Santa Cruz monastery.

I shut my eyes.

In the beginning was the word, I intoned.

I must have used Greek, though I was not aware of it.

The word, *logos*, then sprang out of me. I opened my eyes.

VN looked puzzled.

The Word had to be heard first, I told VN.

I was trying to make connections.

It was pure sound before it was written down in the Bible, I said loud-ly.

I was talking to myself.

VN, still puzzled, shook his head. Then he smiled, craftily. The mango juice, he must have thought. He left me to go to his guru near the granite pillar.

He came back after a while, greatly disappointed.

What should be done about the insults directed against Lord Hanu-man. Should the Frei Luís be killed, he had asked his guru.

The guru had raised his right hand. Does a protector need a protector, VN was asked.

VN had then asked about horses.

Don't fight each other over horses, he was told through Purandara

Dāsa, or the Pārasīkas will play one against the other.

VN then took me near the granite pillar, and I was allowed just the one question, the difference between *dvaita* and *advaita*, between dualism and monism.

Purandara Dāsa relayed the reply.

You are intelligent, I was told. But have not reached the level of understanding needed for those abstract concepts. This two image *padam* will speak to the present state of your being, your involvement with woman and with *samsāra*.

A flow in time, *dvaita* occurs when one is over or under a woman both aware of the you and the I.

That lightning moment out of time, *advaita* occurs when there's no two, just one

The next day or is it yesterday.

Abolem has just left my room. She had looked surprised when I had asked for the toedancing treatment not the other kind. I was feeling very tired. I wondered whether the doctor in Plato's *Symposium*, what was his name, would consider my want a wholesome force. Was Saint Paul right when he said that repeated satisfactions would extinguish sexual desire. The Abolem treatment was relaxing but not exciting, now. And strangely I couldn't go to sleep afterwards.

I've lost track of time, Ahmadji. That's why I cannot set down a time place month notation on this page. I don't drink any mango juice now. I am content with two or three sips of the dark brown liquor VN sent me. No *unmatta* in this, he said. Vijayanagar still bewilders me. I feel caught in the whirl of *samsāra*.

I am in a strange state, as if something within me is churning. No, it is not painful, but it causes vivid dreams that I forget as soon as I awake in the morning. All through the day I am haunted by visions and images. I can recall some words and events now, but have lost the power of total recall. *Unmatta*, I think, is being slowly purged out of my system.

I am glad, Ahmadji, I didn't send along this long letter together with the account you wrote in the mailbag dispatch to Diu. I will send both of them later to Cochin. VN's spy network reports that you and Frei António have already left Diu for Cochin to ask for the release of the *Meri* and its crew that the Portuguese hold hostage there. Frei António do Louro, according to the report, has left his sacred cord and his rosary with Sultan Begada of Gujarat as a guarantee that he will return to Diu even if the mission fails. Perhaps I should escape to Cochin from Vijayanagar but I don't know how to, without help. I don't know the language and I don't know the route to Cochin over the western ghats.

I should return your papers to you as soon as possible, Ahmadji. I have slowly come to realize they're a part of your being.

And I need to continue my dialogue with Frei Louro about conversion.

Frei Louro, you feel the urgent need to convert all the peoples of the world. There's no time to waste, you tell me. Let's hurry before this world comes to an end.

But, Frei Louro, wasn't the world supposed to end after the fall of the Roman empire.

I don't think the world will end soon, despite Joachim of Fiore. And, Frei Louro, perhaps real conversion is a slow process and not the lightning flash that fell on Saint Paul on the road to Damascus. I know the Biblical injunction to the eleven disciples. Go ye therefore and teach all nations, baptizing them in the name of the Father and of the Son, and of the Holy Spirit. Nations, as you know, is the biblical word for gentiles. Teaching the gentiles will require persuasion not force, and an awareness of the many different languages, cultures and customs in the world today. Perhaps the teacher will have to become a student before he can teach. We need the Saint Thomas mode not the earlier Pauline one. Nations have, maybe, some insights to offer us Christians.

Think about this, Frei Louro.

I have read almost all the Portuguese folders in the House of Vision. It's difficult to bring order and meaning to the jumble of information has been assembled by VN's spies and agents and is still pouring in. I have to impose my own order on the chaotic material before me. New letters, accounts, *mandados, regimentos,* reports from feitores of the fortalezas and from ship captains, from Genoese and Florentine merchants who finance some of the Portuguese trading ventures, letters to Lisbon and from Lisbon, innumerable letters of complaint and abuse from different factions of the nobility. One of the factions is led by Dom Francisco de Almeida, the other by Afonso de Albuquerque, virtually imprisoned in Kannanur in the house he lives in. Dom Francisco de Almeida offers all sorts of excuses and refuses to surrender his command to Albuquerque after his three year viceroyalty despite the instructions sent by King Manuel in Lisbon. I am trying to make logical sense of all this but cannot.

Let me make use of images instead of logic, Ahmadji. I sit in VN's office. I stare at the wall map of the Indian Ocean, and try to picture what has happened. The Portuguese have swept across the Indian seas like a tufan, that's your image, Ahmadji, creating confusion everywhere in this peaceful world of trade and commerce, and even of religion. I suddenly remember the Portuguese dwarf in the play, his tall black plumed hat slipping down his head and over his single eye, blundering around, buffeted by people. They were ignorant when they arrived, the Portuguese. Now their eyes are open, but they have problems of cognition, to use a word from my seminary days that now leaps to my mind They don't know what to see in the world they have entered. They need to understand it before they can act in it. Not only have they created confusion in this world, they themselves are confused.

I have a terrifying vision of Almeida as a one eyed giant, blundering around, bewildered. We thought, you and I and Malik Aiyaz, when we stood on the promontory a month after the Diu battle, that Almeida was a monster. He had ordered his ship cannon stuffed with the arms, heads and legs of the Mamluk and the Ottoman captives to be fired at every Muslim seaport so that the bloody fragments rained down on the coastal cities as the Portuguese armada returned from Diu to Cochin.

It turns out to be as much a personal as a political act of vengeance. According to the letters of those who know him well, Almeida changed completely after his son Lourenço, a brilliant jewel on whom the hopes of the father rested, was killed by the Mamluks and the Ottomans at Chaul. When the disaster was reported to the Viceroy in Cochin he was heard to grind his teeth and mutter, Who ate the cockerel must now taste the cock.

The Viceroy withdrew deep into himself, wouldn't talk to anyone, not to his friends nor to his subordinates. His energy drained out of him after the Diu victory. He refused to exercise power. He actually refused the gift of Diu when Malik Aiyaz offered to hand over the city to him after the battle. He refused to hand over command to Albuquerque convinced that it was Albuquerque who had deprived Lourenço of the glory of capturing Hormuz and who was responsible for his son's death. Perhaps that is why Almeida refused to honor the royal patent of King Manuel about the succession that Albuquerque presented to him in Cochin.

.Unmatta visions, Ahmadji, based on my reading of the Portuguese folders. Not all true at all, perhaps, but it makes Almeida human, not just an embodiment of Portuguese power. I wonder about Albuquerque, about whom I don't know too much. Except that his ship captains, disgusted because they were not allowed to plunder the rich trading ships returning to India from the Red Sea, deserted him at Hormuz, then sailed to India and sided with Viceroy Almeida who welcomed these rebels at Cochin instead of punishing them. Those letters of Albuquerque that I read were always addressed to some members of the royal council or to the king in Lisbon whose commands he always tried to follow. He never wrote about himself or about his only son who was illegitimate.

What a strange commander of men this Albuquerque. So difficult to understand. Doesn't confide in anyone. Loses his temper frequently. Keeps to himself. Unlikely, I venture, to be an embodiment of power in the Portuguese world. Shrewd, a fierce Catholic, who hates not Muslims but the Muslim religion. Perhaps I'll ask Frei Louro who sailed with him what he thought of Albuquerque as a commander in Socotra.

I again feel strange sensations within me, Ahmadji, the *unmatta* streaming through my body, and I experience strange visions. I remember a whirl of questions you asked in faraway Diu and the comments I made, especially about power. At that time I was full of clever answers and empty theories. About the power of power, about the language of power, about the power of politics and the politics of power. Clever statements, like the love of power and the power of love, sprang from my tongue. Did I ever make such a strange statement. At that time, Ahmadji, power for me was just a word to play with.

Now as I stare at VN's map of the Indian Ocean I have a vision of the ceaseless waves of the world that you call *samsāra*. I can actually see your abstract word now. Wave after wave after wave of power, and wave periods of time, surging and falling continuously, endlessly.

I've now become frighteningly aware of new forces of rapid change that have swept across our world. In the old days the pace was slow. Armies and pilgrims, beliefs and values, marched onward slowly traveling from one place to another, across land. Change was gradual. In our day man with his new ships, his guns, his new ideas and techniques, has crossed the seas to reach the ends of the earth. Countries have come together, peoples too, but not as brothers.

Forgive me Ahmadji, I got swept away. It must be the *unmatta*, or it could be my sudden awareness of what your *samsāra* really means. What a vivid image of the human condition and of the unstoppable flow of human existence your Sanskrit word projects. That is most terrifying. Human beings wandering, restless, homeless, forever in a state of exile, migrating from one place to another, trying to escape from *karma* and knowing that there is no escape from the doom of *karma*, searching for they know not what, generations living and dying, nations rising and falling, forever changing, experiencing endless motion, trapped in unnumbered existences, in a state of bondage, suffering from despair and disillusion.

Deliver me from this *unmatta* vision, Ahmadji my friend, my brother. Awaken me to the real, and tell me the answer to *samsāra*.

What's the use, Ahmadji. There is no answer to *samsāra*. I'm tempted to do what you did for ten long years. You kept everything locked up within you. Language, VN's guru maintains, traps one in the coils of *samsāra*. I'm tempted to ask about what happened to her whose name Abdul never would use. I'm human, and curious, and want to know, but, like you, shall keep a sacred silence.

Let me instead write not about human confusion but the state of confusion among the Portuguese. No one knows who's in charge of what. The threefold division of command does not seem to work. King Manuel and his court are too far away in Lisbon to exercise real control. Letters and orders to and from Portugal at times take over a year to arrive. The situation has changed by then and a different kind of action is necessary. Some believe that the system of *pareas* or payment of tribute from rulers along the rim of the Indian Ocean is sufficient acknowledgment of King Manuel's suzerainty. Conquest and sovereignty are not deemed necessary.

Others insist that *presas* or the capture of prizes is what they have sailed all the way to this part of the world for. Portugal is too small a country, they say, with too few people to exercise power overseas. All trade in the Indian ocean has been disrupted or slowed down as a result of the Portuguese arrival. I remember your account of the meeting of the pilots in your house at Diu and their bitter complaints. That gave me a vivid picture of the havoc the Portuguese wrought on trade and navigation in the Indian ocean. Traders everywhere, as one of the Portuguese feitores has observed, are timid by nature, especially the Gujaratis. Trade between Cambaya and the Red Sea and the Persian Gulf ports has almost come to a stop. The ships of Malik Gopi sail to Melaka and South east Asia only because he bribes the Portuguese ship captains who issue cartazes for his trading ships with large sums of money. It was his pilot, Mustafa, who told the Portuguese about the trade to that part of the world, but they haven't ventured there yet. They will. Ships sailing from South East Asian ports use the Maldive islands as stopover ports. They bypass the west coast of India, and sail directly to Aden and Suez avoiding Portuguese ships who do not take that route and are afraid of being shipwrecked in the maze of the Maldive islands.

The Portuguese, I note once again, are slowly trying to put together some plan of action. They have now made Cochin their naval base and administrative center. Their chief *feitoria* is headquartered there. The annual spice ships have their cargo loaded there, and they set sail on the homeward voyage to Lisbon from this port. Unlike Calicut, which is an open roadstead, Cochin has an excellent harbor, and is a good port of loading, though not as monsoon safe as Goa. Do I need to tell you this. No, but it will tell you that I'm disturbed, that I repeat myself, that I'm trying to regain my bearings in this strange world. The effects of *unmatta* have not disappeared.

Balthazar came to the House of Vision to inform me about what he had found out about the Anegundi ascetic.

I was preparing a short report for VN on the number of horses from Honawar and Bhatkal that would be available as royal gifts for the *nayakas* at the Mahānavāmi festival. Gifts are distributed to all Vijayanagar city officials to attend and celebrate the festival. VN gave me a large sum of money in *pardaos*. A royal gift, he said, to buy the clothes you will need for Mahānavāmi. You'll get a horse too.

The guards would not let Balthazar in to see me despite the marks on his thumb. They made him wait a long time before they took me down to the gate to meet Balthazar. It bothered him very much that they took so long. Why, he asked, why did they make me wait, there must be some reason. Balthazar trusted very few people.

A question of survival for our people, he said, we always have to be alert.

You have an office next to VN's, Balthazar asked as he stepped into my room. Is VN in his office now, he inquired anxiously, looking carefully around, even tapping on the walls.

No, I said. VN has gone to the new town of Hospet.

That's a league and a half away from the royal center, Balthazar said.

He spent some time going around the room looking at the boxes of folders on the shelves in my office, arranged according to the areas marked on the map in VN's office.

Can I look at some of these folders, Balthazar asked. Only the ones about the Jews of Shingli Cranganore.

No, I said.

I have much to tell you, Jan Mirza, Balthazar said.

Let me finish this Honawar report about the horses, and we will talk, I said.

Balthazar continued to walk around the room examining the labels of the boxes. I wondered whether I should tell Balthazar about the letter from Lisbon to Frei Luís that VN had shown me a couple of days ago.

No, I decided.

I had told VN I would finish the Honawar report today. I made myself comfortable and stretched my feet on the red carpet under my table.

Relax, I told Balthazar.

Balthazar felt at ease in my company. He sat opposite me, the table between us. He too stretched his feet on the carpet.

I didn't feel comfortable inside myself. I pretend but I don't really be- long, Ahmadji, to this world of intrigue.

A couple of days ago VN had looked straight into my eyes and had told me in a cold voice that the king and guru Vyāsarāya would both not be present for the Hanuman ceremonies that he, VN, had taken such great pains to arrange on Anjanadri hill, the birth site of Lord Hanuman. When asked whether his guru would attend, Purandara Dāsa had simply shaken his head. The king had been advised by the royal council not to move out of Hospet except during the ten days of Mahānavāmi when he could return to the palace with his retinue. There was the possibility of an assassination attempt.

VN had gone to Hospet to persuade the king of the absolute need to honor Lord Hanuman with his royal presence. He had prepared what he thought was a very convincing argument. Just as Krishna Deva Raya, like that ideal king of Hindu tradition, Lord Rama, had to honor the warrior goddess Durgā at the beginning of the Mahānavāmi ceremonies, so also had he, VN, to propitiate his guardian deity and to appease Lord Hanuman, the protector of the city, for the polluting imprecations hurled at him by Frei Luís do Salvador. Else disaster would surely befall. VN's voice had sounded calm and matter of fact, but I could tell that his inner being was seething with anger. He wasn't the VN I had known in Diu, in calm control of himself.

Even Mohinī, VN complained, had rejected his love and devotion. That's why he had not taken me to visit her. She had listened to the poem that had taken VN seven nights to compose on our journey from Champaner to Vijayanagar, but she had not responded to it with the delight he had expected. Mohinī had changed. She now neglected her clients, her servants had told VN, suddenly she began to despise wealth and spent most of her days listening to the devotional *padams* of Purandara Dāsa sung by her band of musicians. Mohinī had even composed a *bhakti* poem about her divine lover.

> It has gone with him, my heart.
> Come back, I beg, come back.
> It does not. Within him it stays
> and says, I am where I want to be.

VN felt abandoned. The Vijayanagar royal council had rejected his advice, and had advised that the king form an alliance with Bijapur to negotiate with the Portuguese over the matter of horses. Perhaps, VN told me, he should seriously consider Timmaya's suggestion and ask to be appointed governor of Goa. He felt desolate.

To the world outside VN tried never to reveal how he felt. But I could tell. His eyes, his voice, his gestures, all betrayed the turmoil within. But only to me, the outsider. No one else noticed. As spy master he had to be aloof. He had no real friends. On the days when we walked through the palace grounds in the royal center where the Mahānavāmi ceremonies would be held, he would occasionally, but without realizing it, let drop bits of information about himself, about Mohinī, about Lord Hanuman. It was his only way of unburdening. It did however enable me to put together pieces of his broken self in order to understand him.

His outward appearance was unchanged as we walked through the royal center. He told me about the elaborate arrangements that had been made for the ten day ceremonies. He showed me the platform on which the bejewelled throne would be placed to seat the image of the god and where the king would also sit so that both could be witnessed by the people and both could witness the processions, the dancers, the musicians, the jugglers, the wrestlers, the games and the displays. He showed me the temporary wooden pavilions that were being constructed to house the military governors, the *nayakas*. He showed me the section where, he said, I had been assigned a seat to witness the ceremonies as an honored guest. I would have to be dressed appropriately, of course. I asked where Frei Luís and Balthazar would sit. But he ignored the question with a snort of contempt.

He could not take me to the underground chambers of the royal palace to show me the royal treasuries, he said. But he could allow me to witness a display of military might that would dazzle Vijayanagar's friends and enemies. He did take me to the rehearsal parade of the twelve royal elephants caparisoned in crimson velvet fringed with gold, with silver bells attached. Led by their mahouts they walked majestically on the palace grounds, circled the throne platform once and returned to their palatial twelve domed stables. And he then showed me the lofty new state umbrella, made of embroidered velvet and damask, lavishly and gorgeously decorated with pearls and jewels and diamonds.

That's for the royal horse you saw at the hippodrome, the one on which the king will be sworn.

I repeated my question about Frei Luís.

He took me up a narrow flight of stairs to the top of the palace wall, looked around very carefully, then showed me a letter addressed to Frei Luís do Salvador. It had been intercepted by one of his agents and carefully slit open so that the Portuguese royal seal was intact. VN had had it translated, he told me, by a Portuguese *degredado* at Bhatkal. VN only wanted a confirmation of the translation from me.

Don't tell anyone about this letter, VN said.

It wasn't really a threat, but he had deliberately left the statement vague. I was worried. Worried about Balthazar and the Frei. About myself too. Perhaps I wasn't indispensable as a Portuguese translator any longer. What did Kasim Beg say would befall me when my services were not needed. Why can't I remember.

It was a brief *mandado*.

You, Frei Luís do Salvador, are ordered to return to Cochin and then to proceed to Lisbon. Vijayanagar, it has now been confirmed, is not the kingdom of Preste João. No more horses will be sent there as gifts. It was signed by the Secretary of the State at Lisbon in Portugal, António Carneiro.

Did you see the uncle, did you talk to him, I asked Balthazar after I finished the Honawar report.

Balthazar was silent. Then he sat up straight and removed two sheets of paper from one of his pockets.

He waited a while.

I cannot answer your questions, Balthazar said. What can I, I asked myself, say about a strange being who exists and does not exist. Instead, I thought to myself, let me write down a factual report for Jan Mirza. I tried to on this sheet of paper but couldn't.

He gave me the sheet. It was blank except for two words, *I* and *saw*, that were scratched out.

Let me tell you what happened.

Did you see the uncle, did you talk to him, you asked me, Jan Mirza. What I saw, no, what presented itself to my eyes, was a gray form clothed in darkness and total silence. I had waited four consecutive nights for him outside that secluded Jain temple and rest house.

He won't say a word to you, a disciple had told me.

He is just bones covered with skin, said another.

He will come tonight, a disciple said. He eats every fifth day now. He will achieve death by starvation, and gain liberation in less than a year.

And this disciple left a small earthen bowl of rice gruel next to a free-standing pillar in the middle of the courtyard. Then he left.

I waited on the other side of the pillar. It was the dark half of the moon just before Aśvin. Up in the sky a few stars shone bravely. Then a gray form emerged out of an underground cell, moved toward the pillar, slowly picked up the bowl, and turned to leave.

Wait, I shouted.

The bowl dropped and shattered in the darkness.

Wait, I said in Gujarati, did you know Sheth Chimanlal of Diu.

The figure moved away without looking back.

Wait, I said, wait. Did you know Usha. Usha, I repeated the two syllables loudly. Usha.

Startled, the figure hesitated for just a moment, turned briefly to look back, then stopped, as if deciding what to do. Suddenly the figure turned, and walked down the cell stairs into utter darkness and silence.

I listened in rapt silence to Balthazar. Then Balthazar gave me the other sheet of paper. It was the ten year old Anegundi police report translated by him from the Kannada for my benefit.

Read it later, Balthazar suggested, it's a fairly long report.

No, I said, Ahmadji is my friend, I am curious about what happened. I have to read it now and write to him.

And I jumped out of my chair. The carpet slid away from under my feet.

Ah, said Balthazar. And he tried to straighten the carpet on the other side.

Look, Balthazar said.

Underneath the carpet we discovered a stone slab that fitted snugly into an opening in the wooden floor wide enough for someone to hide himself and overhear what was said in the room.

I was quite shocked. I wanted to summon the guards.

Balthazar placed a finger on his lips to warn me not to speak.

On the blank sheet of paper he wrote, Let's write instead of talking. The guards must have concealed someone there when you went down to the gate to fetch me. That's what caused the delay.

VN has never trusted you.

Balthazar underlined the five words twice.

We talked in written language.

Frei Luís has not converted anyone to his faith here in Vijayanagar, Balthazar wrote. The crowds of people who followed the Frei through the streets were always led by one of VN's agents, an assassin with a squeaky voice. The Frei rejoices greatly. He has been led to believe that his mission is a tremendous success.

Why, I wrote.

VN wants the Portuguese to send more horses, wrote Balthazar.

Frei Luís has been recalled by the Portuguese king to Lisbon, I wrote. VN intercepted the letter of recall which I translated for him. Does Frei Luís know about his recall. Do you know.

No and No. Frei Luís will be a broken man if he has to leave for Cochin and Portugal without achieving his dream.

I'll give him the news after he celebrates the first mass here at Anegundi. It will be a kind of achievement for him. Let's talk about this later, I wrote.

With his right hand Balthazar took out a small packet from one of his many pockets and poured some ground pepper into the palm of his left hand. I knew immediately that he wanted to blow the powder into the crevices around the slab so that the spy would sneeze and betray his presence. But that, I knew, would alert VN.

NO, NO, NO, I wrote firmly and in capital letters.

I signaled to Balthazar and we rearranged the carpet exactly the way it had covered the stone slab.

Before leaving my office Balthazar asked for the same sheet of paper and wrote this down.

Will tell you more about *unmatta* later. Avoid it, it's a poison. Up in north India it is called *datura*.

As in a flash I remembered where I had come across the word *datura*.

Back at Turushka house I went straight to the pages of your account, Ahmadji, where your hakim told you about *datura*. It's all there, the information I needed from Balthazar, but scattered on different pages. That *datura* is an aphrodisiac, that it has different effects on different people. That the senses become deranged, that memory is damaged. that the sense of time is affected, that one experiences moments when reality melts into dream. Thugs infuse it into sugarcane juice to stupefy their victims.

What intrigued your hakim was that *datura* had little effect on jungle tribes who drank quite heavily and on people who were mad. How would it affect someone who has been drinking for a lifetime. I dont have to tell you who I mean, Ahmadji, it's me. VN, that snake, did not take any chances. He was sure Kasim Beg would inform me about the mango juice and its effects.

Abolem did inform VN that I had stopped drinking mango juice.

Why, VN asked me, it is not a poison, it contains only *unmatta*.

I had kept silent.

You'll like that special Shirazi liquor, a gift from the Persian ambassador, VN said.

I didn't believe VN but I wasn't worried. Two or three sips a day of the Shirazi would not harm anyone who drinks heavily.

I need to escape from VN and from Vijayanagar. But I had to read the police report before planning my move with Kasim Beg at dinner.

Am I doomed to be a wanderer all my life, Ahmadji.

The 1505 report of the police officer in charge of the Anegundi police station, written in Kannada and translated by Balthazar

I, the police officer in charge, cannot make complete sense of what happened here in Anegundi. But since, according to Vijayanagar law, every important event that occurs has to be recorded, I am submitting herewith the statements of some of the parties involved, my comments also, and the questions I asked. For I believe a murder took place and I leave it to the higher authorities to find out why what happened happened.

I recorded three statements about the murder.

First Statement, Layla's.

What's your name.

My name is Layla.

What's your religion.

Muslim.

Where are you from.

From Chapora in Goa, and from Diu in Gujarat. I worked as a servant companion to Usha and Ahmad ibn Majid.

Who and where is the fourth person in your party.

He is my brother, Abdul, who has gone to Bhatkal.

Why.

To sell a piece of ambergris because we need the money for expenses.

Were there any other persons staying in the resthouse.

No.

What happened on that night.

They hit me hard on the mouth, breaking some of my teeth. Don't shout, they warned me, or we'll kill you. They hit me hard again. Then they dragged me by the hair and burst into the room where Usha and Ahmadji were sleeping. They had thick bamboo sticks in their hands.

How many men were there.

Four.

Wait, how did you understand what they said. Do you speak Kannada.

No, they spoke Gujarati.

Continue.

I was gagged, then flung into one corner of the room. Two of them hit Ahmadji hard on the head. They gagged him, tied his hands and feet, forced his knees up to his chest, and bound him up. Usha began to scream, and the other two hit her hard on the shoulders. She screamed again. Stop that, one said, and struck her on the mouth. Blood dripped from her face on to her stomach which she tried to protect with both hands but couldn't. Her right shoulder was badly hurt.

Ahmadji opened his eyes and saw one of the men hit the knuckles of Usha's left hand which was on her stomach. Usha fainted. Ahmadji was bundled into a gunnysack.

Yasmin flew like an arrow towards both men. They tried to hit her. She flew to my shoulder for protection.

Wait, who is Yasmin.

Yasmin is Usha's pet myna.

Ah. Was Usha with child.

Yes.

When was the baby due.

In a week.

What happened then.

One man came up to me. He wanted to kill Yasmin who began to shriek.

No, the other man told him. We are Jains. It's a crime to kill any living thing. Let the bird be. Let us take up this bundle and hurry to the Anegundi gateway before the guards there change.

Then what happened.

I don't know. I fainted.

Second statement, the uncle's.

What's your name.

Have no name.

What's your religion.

Have no religion.

Where are you from.

It doesn't matter now.

Are you related to Usha.

Have no family, have no kin, have no self. Have renounced *samsāra*.

Note. I didn't ask him what *samsāra* was. Some religious nonsense, I imagine. I continued my questions.

What happened on that night.

He bent his head down on his chest, and was silent.

Then something I saw shocked me. Two drops fell on the ground.

Why are you crying, I asked.

It's the eyes, they are allowing tears to fall. She was my dear sister's daughter. I loved her. No, my former self loved her. Is she dead.

I didn't answer his question.

Note to the reader of this report. And to myself.

As a human being, not just a police officer writing this report, I didn't need to ask him any further questions. What a strange phrase he had used, my former self. As if his self had died. The uncle had managed to avoid using the word for the self, the word I, that we all use without thinking about it. Except once, when the I sprang out of him to link itself with the verb love. Strange. Makes me brood about things. Which, as a police officer, I don't want to. It could prevent me from acting effectively. After talking to the temple watchman, to the gateway guards, and to the four attackers whom I did arrest after they returned through the Anegundi gateway to

Vijayanagar, I was able to put together the account of what happened to them.

They had no money and the baby was due and Abdul had gone to Bhatkal to sell a piece of ambergris and Usha, exhausted after their long and difficult journey over the ghats from Calicut to Vijayanagar and afraid of being tracked down by her father's agents, went to the Jain temple at Anegundi to meet her uncle. He would not or could not see her. The uncle had to cut off all human ties before initiation. Had to be in a condition of absolute detachment. And he was then at the stage of concentrated meditation in preparation for the initiation rite. But he did perform an act of love, and sent them a large sum of gold *prataps* collected from Jain temple donors, and he did arrange to have Usha and her party stay for a few days in the temple rest house.

What happened happened on the very day of the initiation. The uncle, his meditation disturbed in the night by the screams, rushed to the rest house and saw Usha's face and stomach covered with blood.

The uncle's guru sternly condemned his disciple's act of love. It was a good action, the guru told the temple community, but it is an act that reinvolves one in the flow of *samsāra*, he said.

He forbade the initiation ceremony, and imposed a lifetime penance which the uncle fulfills to this day.

They had planned to leave for Bhatkal, according to Layla, after the baby was born.

Third statement, Jhaveri's.

What is your name.
Jhaveri of the Jain Jhaveris of Diu in Gujarat.
Did you kill Ahmadji.
No. Absolutely not. Jains are not permitted to kill any living creature. We were told by Gujarawala, one of the agents of Sheth Chimanlal who came from Malindi in Africa to Calicut, to hunt down a MuslimJain couple in order to wipe away the disgrace brought on the Jain community in Diu by that treacherous man whose name I will not pollute my lips by uttering.
We pushed him into a gunnysack, carried him through the gateway to the outskirts of Anegundi, and flung him into a ditch. The sack was untied. He was alive then, groaning with pain. We did not kill him.
The Anegundi police did not find the body, only a sack stained with blood. Where's the body.
I don't know. We did drag the heavy sack over stones to the ditch. But we did not kill him. He must have run away.

Did you bribe the guards at the Anegundi gateway.

Yes, we had to.

Did you hit Usha on the mouth so that blood was shed.

We had to, or else she would have awakened the temple watchman.

Do you feel any remorse about what you have done.

No. We acted as a group to remove the polluting stain on our community. Like Jain rulers, who have to wage war at times to defend their kingdom. We took the correct form of action to protect our brothers.

His eyes were clear with the conviction that he had committed no wrong.

End of the police report

Note attached by the police official

The temple authorities insisted that I make them leave Anegundi. Pollution, they stated, they should leave immediately. The girl is heavy with child and finds it difficult to walk, I told the authorities. She will give birth any day. That creature should die, they said. I felt sorry for them. The baby would die before they reached the coast. So I arranged for a litter, gave them some money, and from the top of the third fortress tower watched them leave for Bhatkal. Layla walked slowly on the left. Perched on the right side, the myna, its head cocked slightly, its beak open, appeared to be listening intently, to the one on the litter as if trying to reply to something. I wondered if the bird could speak.

The Anegundi police report had a powerful impact on me, why I knew not till I reentered your account, Ahmadji, and reread the story of your love, this time carefully noting and absorbing the details, how your love sprang from a region so deep within both of you that words could not penetrate there, and you only needed eye talk and touch. Your love for her uprooted your baobab self that detested change. You, Ahmadji, were able only much later to release your love into the written word. But she, your Usha, could never use that four letter verb word and say the unsayable. The second time I read your account I could sense beneath the flow of words her deep love for you, something you did not set down, a silent love that like the powerful force of nature it was, like a wave of the sea, as your poem said, like VN's *śakti*, slowly widened to include Paulo, and Layla, and the myna, and her acceptance of her baby's death in Kannanur, and

Abolem interrupted me with some food from the dining hall as I sat in my little garden in the shade. It was too late for dinner.

Some Shirazi, she asked.

I shook my head, but Abolem brought me a tiny cup of the Shirazi liquor. I took two sips and then brooded for a long while about what I, your friend, could write to you to heal your wound, Ahmadji. Perhaps your wound can now heal. Your hakim, who rescued you from the ditch beyond Anegundi, guessed but didn't know that it was the loss of Usha that had caused that inner wound. During the five long years of traveling with you he had suggested several ways of healing. Once he insisted that you accompany him to a play to make you forget your pain. He suggested that you write down your past. Not the poems that you did try to write. They prolong the pain, the hakim thought, and don't heal the wounded self. Clear clean writing would allow your past to be past and not be present, your hakim said, using wordplay that I liked very much. Your hakim then, I suspect, got tired of doctoring your self and told you, Return to Diu and heal yourself. But how could you heal your self, Ahmadji. You, who have never told anyone what happened, not me, not the hakim, not even your self. The return to Diu didn't help you at all, did it.

I feel a powerful urge to help you by composing a poem in celebration of Usha whose memory you have nourished and kept alive deep within you for ten long years now in the manner of Hafiz and Rumi. Alas, I am not a poet. Let me instead set down my deepest insight into the human condition to console you. Your inner wound is not raw now. It has, at this stage, developed a protective scar, as your hakim had said.

Life is

I hunted for words to complete the profound thought about life that had begun churning within me.

That's strange, I told myself. Words now, when I bid them come at a time of need, stubbornly don't come. Do words ever heal, my cynic asks. Don't lose faith in words, João, I tell myself. You are a teacher.

I tried again.

I wrote down, Life is

Again I had to stop. I found it strange that I couldn't go on.

I tried again.

Life is strange.

I found I could only set down those three words. After years of studying theology and exploring other religions and thinking about human existence, I could only bring forth a three word truism, Life is strange.

Then I began to laugh at what I had brought forth. I laughed, my stomach heaving slowly at first, then wildly. I laughed loudly, hysterically. Then I roared with laughter till tears came pouring down my face.

I stood up and yelled to the plants in the garden, Life is strange, announcing to them my stupendous discovery about life.

Kasim Beg, tired of waiting for me in the dining hall came to see me at Turushka quarters. Abolem brought him into the garden. I tried to stop laughing but couldn't.

What are you laughing at, asked Kasim Beg.

Then he noticed the tiny cup on the table and turned to Abolem, but she had left.

Must be the effect of the *unmatta*. What's that you are drinking, Kasim Beg asked me.

That's Shirazi liquor, I said. VN told me it was made of the sweetest Persian dates. I've had only two sips.

Kasim Beg was horrified. That liquor is more powerful than the *unmatta* in mango juice, he told me. My Xiumtem told me never to drink it. Its overpowering sweetness conceals the concentration of hashish and opium and *unmatta* infused into it. Two sips a day and you'll go mad in seven days.

That snake, I almost shouted, but didn't.

Kasim Beg brought me a glass of water, and I slowly calmed down.

Were you putting on an act for Abolem, Kasim Beg whispered to me.

An act. That was it. That, that would be my master stroke of deceit. I would act by acting. But I needed to plan my moves.

VN wants me to attend Frei Luís's celebration of the first mass at Anegundi, Kasim Beg said.

Let's not talk about it, I told Kasim Beg. Our conversation may be overheard here.

The next day Kasim Beg and I talked about our plans as we walked towards Anegundi.

The streets were crowded with people who had come specially for the Mahānavāmi festival, and took the opportunity to visit temples, and the images and shrines of their gods. There was a festive atmosphere everywhere. They enjoyed the fairs arranged by different trade guilds in different parts of the city, and took part in the many processions to their gods. The rich sprinkled each other with saffron water while the common people threw turmeric water and colored powder on their friends and relatives. They flocked to as many Hanuman shrines as they could, for Lord Hanuman was a popular deity whose appeal transcended caste and class. There were, as VN had told me, 732 representations of Hanuman. Carvings on boulders in the Tungabhadra, Hanuman reliefs on walls and gateways, images and sculptures of Hanuman striding vigorously, of Hanuman in an attitude of religious devotion, of Hanuman sitting on his tail, at many street intersections. I saw clusters of people gathered near the *Yantroddharaka* shrine. Kasim Beg kept looking back to see if anyone was following us. I didn't look back. I listened intently to voices around us in the street, but I didn't hear Squeaky.

Kasim Beg repeated what he had said yesterday. That VN had told him to attend the Frei's first mass in Vijayanagar to be celebrated at the Anegundi cross.

VN surely had some sinister plan in mind.

I am not a Christian, Kasim Beg had told VN. The Frei is an infidel.

That's why you should be present, VN had said, it will demonstrate that all religions are tolerated at Vijayanagar. Our king will send an official letter of recommendation to your Sultan about you. I myself, he continued, will first attend the church service even before I go to the Hanuman ceremonies with my gift offerings. I will also offer a magnificent cross studded with pearls and diamonds as a present for the church. It will be a donation from the king. You and Jan Mirza will help me present it to Frei Luís, VN had told Kasim Beg.

My nose twitched with suspicion. Like yours does at times, Ahmadji. With questions, too. Why had VN not told me about the presentation. Why would VN, who hated the Frei so much, want to honor the Christian god by attending mass first before going to the Hanuman celebrations that he himself had organized. And why would VN, who suspected that Kasim Beg planned some treachery but couldn't be killed because he was the Bijapur envoy, insist that Kasim Beg be present at an infidel ritual.

Something didn't smell right, I didn't know what. I was quite puzzled. Should I accept Rustum Khan's offer and escape with Kasim Beg to Bijapur.

Kasim Beg urged me to come to Bijapur.

Let me tell you how urgent it is that we escape as soon as possible. My Xiumtem heard from your Abolem the rumor that the Shirazi liquor you sip every day is heavily infused not only with *datura* but with *hashish*. It will destroy you slowly.

No, I thought, it couldn't be.

I could have left Vijayanagar some days ago, Kasim Beg told me, but Rustum Khan, the commander of our cavalry forces, insisted that I bring you along with me to Bijapur. A number of Portuguese sailors have fled from Cochin and Kannanur and deserted the Portuguese because they were not paid their salaries during the monsoon months. They have taken refuge in Bijapur. Some have turned Muslim. Rustum Khan would like to have them trained as horse arquebusiers by you. You're the only one who can speak their language, the only one who knows about guns and horses.

I'll train them, I told Kasim Beg. Tell your commander I'll teach his men how to fight on horseback. But I have decided to renounce fighting. I'll become an interpreter between armies.

It will be quite easy for both of us to escape from Vijayanagar, Kasim Beg continued. The markings on our thumbs will allow us to walk through the Anegundi gateway. The Golla headman, who works in the royal stables and whom we have bribed heavily, will keep horses ready for us a few miles away at Gangāvati. We can leave before Mahānavāmi, tomorrow or the next day, if you want to.

Yes, I said, that's it, we'll escape from Vijayanagar to Bijapur.

That will mark a beginning, I thought. I'll be able to get to the coast.

But there were others I had to think about.

What about Frei Luis and Balthazar, I asked Kasim Beg. I think VN wants to get rid of them. Frei Luís is of no use for him now. The Portuguese have discovered that Vijayanagar is not the kingdom of Preste João.

VN is very cunning, Kasim Beg said. He could easily have both the Frei and Balthazar murdered, but that would anger the Portuguese who might retaliate by selling horses exclusively to us Bijapuris.

Besides, Kasim Beg continued, there is no need for Frei Luís to be killed. The Frei's Mogrem tells my Xiumtem that the Frei is quite mad now. The *unmatta* has affected him and he loves drinking mango juice. Sometimes he demands toedancing twice a day. At other times he wont allow Mogrem to even touch him with her hands. On some days he allows Mogrem to brush his hair and comb his beard and is quite sane. On other days he lies completely naked on the bed, and screams *Con, Confi, Con,* gets up, then takes a whip and lashes himself fiercely on his buttocks till they bleed. Mogrem has told VN about this.

Very good, VN says, and smiles.

We can, you realize, Kasim Beg told me, leave Frei Luís to his fate here in Vijayanagar and ride to Bijapur tomorrow.

No, burst out of me.

I wondered why my no had been so emphatic. I didn't like Frei Luís. But he was a human being. He was also a fanatic with a dream, lost alas in a mad world he couldn't understand, and the daily dose of *unmatta* in mango juice was slowly driving him mad. The lashing on the buttocks betokened the punishment he inflicted on himself for his sins of the flesh that he wanted to tame but couldn't. And you easily can, Ahmadji, understand what the *con* sounds signify. You heard them on the Vanakbara promontory in Diu before I began reciting my long *confiteor* to you and to Brother Clement.

No, I couldn't abandon Frei Luís and Balthazar. I was sure VN would somehow have them killed. Perhaps they could escape with us and then go to Cochin. Kasim Beg would have to arrange it so that Frei Luís and Balthazar could escape to Bijapur with us after the celebration of the mass. I would refuse to go with him otherwise.

Karim Beg and I walked along the Turuttu canal road jostled by people who were anxious to visit as many shrines and temples as they could, and offer the gifts they had brought with them to their gods. People in gaily colored clothes bought flowers and flower garlands from street vendors to decorate the many images of Hanuman. The sellers of *pān* and of water squirts and powders of different colors did a brisk business. So did sellers of rice, to my surprise. They sold rice grains of different colors, red and green and yellow, in packets to the villagers who would place them as offerings next to Hanuman images. As a son of Vayu, the windgod, Hanuman preferred fruit and grain, offerings that sprang out of the earth.

Kasim Beg was not used to walking.

I wish we could be carried in dhoolies, he said.

But we could not make use of dhoolies. For five days before the beginning of the Mahānavāmi festival no litters were allowed in the sacred and royal centers of the city during the celebrations. Nor were any horses allowed. Kasim Beg and I walked along till we came to the Bagila Hanuman gateway. The monumental image of Hanuman had been freshly washed and painted in garish red and blue pigments. Flower garlands had been placed in front of the image. People looked up at the image in awe and prayed to Lord Hanuman for strength and courage and protection.

Kasim Beg's Muslim sensibility was disgusted with this display. Let's go, he said to me, turning his back on the image as a sign of his contempt. He wanted to leave immediately. I turned to warn him. These Hindus, he muttered. Out of the corner of my eye I saw someone in a white wrap-around staring at us. He had a green scarf wrapped round his throat.

Wait, I told Kasim Beg. I had to act. I walked up to a seller of garlands, bought the most colorful garland I could see, and laid it, with a low bow and with hands folded, near the foot of the Hanuman image. I turned round to look for the man with the green scarf, but he had disappeared.

We passed through the Harishanka gateway, and at Talarighat we crossed the bridge over the Tungabhadra and walked across the square. I wanted to look at the Jain temple with its rest house, and at its courtyard with the four freestanding pillars. I looked all around for the underground cell into which the uncle had disappeared but could not find the opening. We saw Frei Luís and Balthazar on the other side of the square standing behind the Persian cross that had been now placed neatly into the circular three stepped granite base with its carvings of elephants and flowers and peacocks with their tailspreads. It seemed somehow to be part of the Anegundi landscape. But it looked isolated there, and forlorn, as if its side arms were weak, incapable of an embrace. Its center however proclaimed its silent message about the love and passion of Christ.

I looked for the new church, but could only see a small thatched hut in the far corner. Rectangular trenches had been dug behind the cross as a foundation. Building materials were strewn haphazardly all around.

There were huge blocks of discolored limestone and irregular pieces of wood scattered everywhere. Frei Luís was talking animatedly to the Syrian Christian headman. The seven workers stood behind their headman in a semicircle. All eight wore short colored wraparounds which they called *mundus*. The headman had long hair tied up into a knot at the top, through which a shiny metal cross had been inserted.

Kasim Beg and I walked across the square to the Persian cross. Standing on its top step I began to experience the tableau below me with my *unmatta* eyes and ears.

The Syrian Christian headman was angrily replying to Frei Luís in Malayālam but he had to address his reply to Balthazar who did know the language and had to relay the reply in Portuguese to the Frei who of course didn't know Malayālam. The seven workers shook their heads up and down agreeing with what their headman had said. Like a Greek chorus, I thought. Frei Luis shouted at the headman in Portuguese complaining that they had not even begun the building of his church. The headman looked inquiringly at Balthazar. When Balthazar translated this accusation the headman looked skywards as if invoking God as his witness. He shouted to the sky, and then yelled at his workers who yelled back. Then the headman led Balthazar and Frei Luis to a large limestone block which he struck gently twice with his hammer. It broke in two. Very bad quality, Balthazar told Frei Luis, these stones will fall apart in less than a year, after the rains. Some of the logs of wood, to which the headman pointed, had already rotted. The church could not be built with this material that had been sent by VN. No explanations were necessary. The workmen now raised a clamor and pointed to the small thatched hut in the corner. They moaned loudly and beat their breasts. All eight of them have to sleep in that small hut, Balthazar explained. The headman muttered some words to Balthazar. They haven't been paid, Balthazar translated, they want to go back to Malabar.

Balthazar waved to Kasim Beg and me.

It was time to descend and enter the tableau. When I did, I had the strange feeling that I was inside the tableau and also outside it. My *unmatta* experience became both comic and tragic.

Consider, Ahmadji, the view from the outside. Consider the peoples on that stage in front of me. Syrian Christians, a Jewish converso, a Portuguese friar, a Turani *afaqi*, and my protean self. Consider also the religions professed, the languages heard. Malayālam, Latin, Portuguese, Persian, Hebrew, Swahili, Arabic. And the need for the crisscrossing of cultures. Don't you get a sense of comic confusion. I smiled to myself. I saw Frei Luís do Salvador as yet another confused clown like me, acting in a world full of confusion.

Are we all clowns on the stage of life and history, Ahmadji. You don't have to answer that question.

The Frei's voice dropped and I heard him whisper in Portuguese, What, what shall I do now, Balthazar, I have no church. Help me.

He was a child crying out to his mother.

Suddenly I saw him as a tragic figure. Consider another view, from the inside this time, Ahmadji. The Frei's eyes had been opened, and he could now both see and know. Perception is a form of pain, my Plato had said. The Frei's self had experienced a series of sudden shocks. He had at last realized that his church would never be built. That's why VN had not wanted the Frei to be taken to Anegundi by Balthazar. His missionary dream would never be fulfilled. Balthazar had earlier tried to warn him about VN and his treacherous ways, but the Frei had refused to accept such a bitter truth. He had been told about the effects of *unmatta*, but hadn't heeded the warnings about mango juice. Balthazar had repeatedly told him there were no followers or converts, but the Frei had pointed to the crowds and the acclamations in the streets, and didn't believe Balthazar.

António Carneiro, the Secretary of State, has written to say you may have to return to Lisbon and report to the king for consultations with the Royal Council, Balthazar told him.

That was a shock for the Frei who had met António Carneiro in Lisbon. Balthazar didn't reveal that Vijayanagar was definitely not the kingdom of Preste João. That would have shattered all the Frei's missionary illusions. Instead Balthazar told the Frei that the Portuguese delegation to the celebration of the first mass had arrived but had been detained at the Bhatkal gateway on the orders of VN. No one was allowed to enter the city. Not even the Florentine Corbinelli who had come with the delegation to buy diamonds with the help of Balthazar. The gold embroidered altarpieces, the red, white and gold liturgical vestments, the wine, the candles, the unleavened bread, the censers and the incense, the missals, and the new portative organ would not be available for the celebration. It would not be possible for the Frei to celebrate solemn high Mass with the pomp and splendor he wanted in order to impress his converts.

It was a devastating shock, this news, and it broke the Frei. He shut his eyes tight, as if he couldn't bear to look at the truth. His white head sank into his white beard.

What shall I do now, Balthazar, wailed the Frei.

Balthazar did not know what to say. He looked at me.

The Frei then turned to me whom he usually ignored.

What shall I do, Frei Luis asked me. I heard the despair in his voice and I couldn't bear his sufferings any longer. It was time to stop acting and to act.

I took him by the hand and slowly led him away from the group to the Persian cross. We stood in its shadow. His head was still bowed with grief.

We will not be overheard from here. I spoke softly but firmly. Not in Castilian, but in sophisticated Portuguese heard only in Lisbon.

Why don't we recite a simple *missa sicca*, a dry mass, Frei Luís do Salvador, I said, as we did on board ship on the long sea voyage from Lisbon instead of celebrating a *missa solemnis*, a solemn high mass.

The Frei stood silent for a long time, head bowed.

I could hear the distant sounds of drums approaching.

We cannot celebrate the offertory and the consecration rites of the Eucharistic sacrifice for we have no unleavened bread nor the wine of the grape. But we can recite the fore prayers of the mass at the foot of this cross which will be our altar. We can begin with the *Introibo ad altare Dei*, and say our Confiteors together.

The drumbeats became loud and insistent. It must be a procession, I thought, going to the Hindu temple across the square.

The Frei's head was still bowed. I thought he had not heard what I said.

I heard what you said, Jan Mirza, he said.

He sounded exhausted as if his voice had been traveling across a great distance in time.

Be patient with me, Jan Mirza. I just can't bear any more shocks. Did you study in a seminary. Tell me, how do you know these Latin terms of the mass. On what ship from Lisbon did you recite the *missa sicca*. Are you a priest, a priest in disguise. Will you hear my confession. Right now, here, in front of this cross.

The words came out in a rush, his body sagged and he would have collapsed on his knees if I hadn't caught him in an embrace.

I am not a priest. I am the João Machado you knew, the *degredado* on Cabral's ship.

The procession came into the square but did not proceed to the Hindu temple as I had expected it would.

I called out to Balthazar in sudden panic, VN must have sent them to attack us.

No, shouted Balthazar, the celebration is a preparation for tomorrow's feast.

They were a group of tribals sent by VN. They made a frightful din as they danced their way towards us with shouts and cries and drumbeats, and a clanging of cymbals. A hot smell of country liquor filled the air. The women carried baskets of vegetables and fruits and rice, and six earthen jars of rice liquor, and set them down near the thatched hut. The seven

Syrian Christian workers knew that the food baskets had been sent for tomorrow's feast and they clapped their hands and danced with joy. They rejoiced greatly when one of the women set down a basket filled with brightly colored new *mundus*.

Let's celebrate, the Syrian Christian headman cried. And he opened one of the liquor jars and passed it around. Even the women drank. Four tribal men carried the two plain litters made of flat pieces of aromatic sandalwood and placed them in the space cleared for the foundations of the church. Sheets of the finest cotton muslin, some white, others a faint yellow, were set down on the litters and, next to them, two jars of fragrant sandalwood oil.

The Syrian Christian headman, with a grin of joy on his face, told Balthazar that VN had sent a sum of money as payment for their work. Tomorrow, after the mass, all eight of them would carry the two litters filled with VN's gifts to the temple of Lord Hanuman on Anjanadri Hill for the celebrations. They would have a feast after their return. A second jar of liquor was then opened and everyone began to sing and dance.

Join us, they gestured.

Then they danced around the four of us. The women threw off their breast cloths to the wild acclamation of the whole group. They shouted obscenities accompanied by appropriate gestures. The women swung their breasts from side to side as they danced and the men moved their hips up and down in frantic abandon as they circled around us. Neither Kasim Beg nor I were affected by this crude display.

Balthazar was unmoved. The Frei however was visibly disturbed especially when one of the women stepped out of the circle, danced up to him and swung her breasts and her hips provocatively.

He jerked up straight, and tottered unsteadily on his feet.

I have to go back to Pārasīka House, he told Balthazar. Now, he said, at once. His voice was hoarse. His eyes looked dazed. He stumbled twice as he walked unsteadily towards the Talarighat bridge.

What happened, why. I was shocked. The change in the Frei was sudden.

Kasim Beg knew why. It's the *unmatta*, he said, and the mango juice. The Frei cannot control his body and what the Hindus call the body's *tanha*, its cravings. This is the time when his Mogrem gives him the toedancing treatment.

Balthazar, worried, said he would take a shortcut and see that the Frei got safely back to Pārasīka House.

I became quite worried about the Frei.

Kasim Beg reassured me. He'll he all right tomorrow morning, he said.

I had thought I would be able to have a long talk with the Frei and tell him everything. I would tell him about VN and his treacheries. I would tell him about our plans to escape from Vijayanagar after the *missa sicca,* and to send him to Cochin with Balthazar. I would tell him about Frei Louro and the converts in Champaner. And I would confess to him the whole story of my life. After all he was a priest like Frei Louro.

But, but, do I believe in sin. I do not know, Ahmadji. The telling would have to wait till the Frei and I reached Bijapur.

I told Kasim Beg I wanted to be by myself. So I walked alongside the rocky banks of the Tungabhadra towards Turushka House. At one point I stopped and stared at the fierce churning river. That's my river of life, I said to myself. Yours, Ahmadji, is *samsāra,* the ocean sea.

Stop it, I scolded myself. Don't make a fool of yourself again by imaging the meanings of life.

BIJAPUR
The Sultan's Palace
September 1509

Yes, Ahmadji, I am now not in Turushka House in Vijayanagar, but in Bijapur, writing this account in one of the inner rooms of the sultan's palace. But I don't know where I really am and I don't know what mask I am wearing. No, it's not the *unmatta.* That must have drained out of me completely during the long ride from Vijayanagar to Bijapur. It's some day in September 1509 I think, though I cant tell the time of day. You asked a long time ago, what's the best time to write. Immediately after the experience, or after the experience has been purified by distance and memory.

I used the word purified because I've been washing my hands twice every day, to remove the Anegundi stains that seem to discolor my fingers. The blood red Rossio stains, I remember, disappeared as soon as I was told that the old man whose head I had hit with a candlestick was well. Perhaps this act of writing will remove these invisible stains which may require more than just water.

Let me set down, immediately and exactly, what happened on my last day in Vijayanagar

Kasim Beg and I set out from our compound towards Anegundi in the morning. We did not carry anything with us so as not to arouse any suspicions. Even the money VN had given to me I left in Turushka House lest Abolem become suspicious.

That packet you gave me will be safe in the saddlebags of one of the horses waiting for us at Gangāvati, Kasim Beg told me. It was a flat packet, Ahmadji, and contained all our papers, yours and mine, the only treasure I took with me from Vijayanagara.

There were very few people on the streets, only those who could not make the arduous climb to the top of Anjanadri Hill. Kasim Beg and I were the first to arrive at Anegundi. The Persian Cross looked out serenely on a scene of quiet desolation. The place was empty. The two litters with their sheets of cotton muslin lay there untouched, and the two jars of sandalwood oil had not been opened. VN had apparently not yet sent any gifts to be taken to the Hanuman festival. The Syrian Christian headman sat moaning on a corner step in front of the hut with both hands on his bowed head. He had a tremendous hangover.

The empty scene did not shock Balthazar at all when he arrived with Frei Luís who staggered his way to the cross and sat down unsteadily on the first step. He wore his old ash brown cassock. Abolem had told him that his clothes and his golden shawl could not be found anywhere, according to Balthazar. The Frei's breath smelt strongly of Shirazi liquor. The Frei was in no condition to conduct an elaborate ceremony. The *missa sicca* would have to be brief. The Frei would have to recite the fore prayers at the foot of the cross hurriedly, with me as an altar boy. VN would then leave with his gifts for Lord Hanuman, and we could leave through the Anegundi gateway and go to Gangāvati. That's what Kasim Beg and I had planned.

There, Balthazar said, there is VN.

I did not recognize VN at first. He wore a long white wraparound, his chest and his arms were bare, he wore no jewelry, and on his forehead was a black vertical streak. He looked like a temple priest. He was not accompanied by a crowd of people, but by a man in a short white wraparound with a green scarf tied loosely around his neck carrying a cross mounted on a staff that shone and glittered in the morning sun. The staff was five feet high, its upper half was encrusted with red and green pearls, with turquoises, amethysts, cornelians, and a few diamonds. At the top of the staff was fixed a Latin cross, two golden pieces intersected at right angles. The lower piece was a foot longer than the other three bars which were of equal size. The cross appeared to be heavy. The man had to stoop a little.

Let's begin, VN said. They're waiting for my gifts at the Anjanadri festival.

But your gifts have not arrived, I pointed out.

They have, VN said.

He rushed down and looked at the two litters and at the jars of sandalwood oil. Then he ran to the hut. I had never seen him so agitated before.

Where are the bearers of the litters, VN snarled at the headman who had not moved from the corner step. VN was impatient. It took the workmen some time to wear their new mundus and emerge from their hut one by one. VN was very impatient. He made all eight of them line up behind the two litters. Two of them were assigned to carry the jars of sandalwood oil.

The man in the white *mundu* turned the heavy cross around and displayed it to the three of us proudly. Frei Luis and Kasim Beg were fascinated by the cross and could not take their eyes off it. I stared at the green scarf tied around the man's neck. It had come loose and I could see a thick black scar on the side of his throat. A stab wound, I thought, an assassin. I asked Balthazar in Castilian to ask the man a question, any question. I wanted to hear his voice. Balthazar asked the man if he could touch the precious stones. Nã, was the curt reply. I heard a nasal vowel. I also heard a faint squeak.

Balthazar walked up to the cross, and looked closely at the precious stones. He did not touch the cross.

It's a fake, he told me in Castilian. Those are not real precious stones, and the gold is highly polished brass.

Balthazar's words sent a shock through me. I was now sure that Frei Luís would be killed. But how, and why not use an assassin. why here, why in public, at Anegundi. I was quite puzzled. Why me as witness, why the litters and the sandalwood oil, and why the need for the presence of Kasim Beg. And how, how. I could see no weapon. It would be impossible for VN and his henchman to hide any weapon under their wraparounds.

VN rushed up to us. Let's hurry, he said.

Wait, I said. And I rushed down to the litters, and patted the sheets of white cotton, and put my hands under them. There was no dagger hidden there.

Hurry up, VN said. Don't disarrange those sheets. You'll pollute them.

His hands shook. His voice was hoarse. His eyes had a fanatic sheen.

Perhaps I had too suspicious a nose. Perhaps it was only the *unmatta* working within me. Perhaps VN was really excited about the Hanuman festival, and not about getting rid of Frei Luís today. We would be able to escape after the *missa sicca*.

I had carefully planned the tableau for the *missa sicca*. Frei Luis would stand at the foot of the Persian cross. I would be on his left.

Behind us, four paces away, would be VN with Balthazar standing on his left and Kasim Beg on the right. Two paces behind VN would be his assistant ready to hand over the cross to VN. I would make a signal after we recited the Confiteor, and VN would present the cross to Frei Luís. It would be quite an appropriate offering at a *missa sicca*.

Frei Luís and I genuflected together. I remained kneeling next to him with my eyes closed. I was once again an altar boy, serving mass in the Santa Cruz cathedral in Coimbra. Frei Luis made a valiant effort to stand erect but had to lean against me to steady himself.

He made the sign of the cross and recited the words of the blessing. *In nomine Patris et Filii and Spiritus Sancti, Amen.*

Introibo ad altare, he intoned slowly, then stopped. He couldn't go on to utter *Dei*, the *unmatta* had made him forget. I hurriedly completed the required response, *ad Deum qui laetificat juventutem meam.*

Confiteor, he said loudly, looking up at the sky, palms folded together. Once again he couldn't say *Deo*. *Confiteor*, he began again, but couldn't proceed. So I recited *Confiteor Deo omnipotenti*, and he repeated the words, and I led him through the whole prayer as if I was the priest and he was the altar boy. Both of us struck our breasts at the words, *mea culpa, mea culpa, mea maxima culpa*. We reached our *Amens* together. I got a faint smell of innocence, something I thought we both had lost forever.

Then I heard a triumphant shriek of two syllables, *Yāg* and *Nā*, the second syllable had an unmistakable squeak.

I pivoted sharply, and Frei Luis also turned around.

I saw Squeaky holding the crossless staff at a slant. VN had detached the cross from the staff and the cross turned into a dagger with a three bar hilt, the sharp point had been concealed in the lower piece. Squeaky thrust the staff into the Frei's stomach so that the Frei fell on his back on the steps. And VN plunged the crossdagger straight into the Frei's heart.

I kicked Squeaky viciously in the crotch, grabbed the bare staff from his hands, smashed VN's head with it, then plucked out the blood red dagger from the Frei's chest and plunged it deep, twice, into VN's chest. I stared at my fingers. They were red and wet with both bloods. I felt calm and then I found myself staring up at the sky. I could see nothing.

I didn't know what happened then, Ahmadji. I am still in a daze. Kasim Beg and Balthazar took charge of the situation. When I opened my eyes I found myself on a litter. I don't remember how we got to Gangāvati nor the journey to Bijapur. The tribals gave me a powerful narcotic made of jungle herbs and roots to put me to sleep.

I am writing this account in a hurry, Ahmadji, because I have to entrust the bundle of papers to one of Rustum Khan's agents who is leaving for Portuguese Cochin tonight. He'll give them to you or else to Frei Louro.

Before I part with your precious papers, Ahmadji, let me tidy up some loose ends in my account, for myself and for you. Let me tell you what happened.

Kasim Beg has been transferred for his own safety as the Bijapur envoy to distant Gaur in Bengal.

Balthazar has left Bijapur for Pulicat on the east coast of India from where he plans to sail to Melaka where his brother works as a lapidary.

Balthazar told me what happened before he left Bijapur. He had threatened Squeaky with death unless he confessed everything, which Squeaky did. We had to flee Anegundi in a hurry, Balthazar said. VN would be missed and they would come looking for him from Anjanadri hill. Squeaky had apparently pulled the staff from my hands and struck me hard on my left shoulder. I fell and hit my head on the stone steps and lost consciousness. VN's political plans, according to Balthazar, were to have both Frei Luís and Kasim Beg murdered on the same day at the same time. He then wanted to set afloat a rumor that the Frei had been assassinated by a Turushka. This news about the murder of Frei Luís, Portugal's special envoy, would, VN thought, destroy Portugal's relations with Bijapur. Horses would then be sold only to Vijayanagar and not to Bijapur. Vijayanagar cavalry would be more powerful than Bijapur's.

VN had other more sinister plans. The corpses of Frei Luís and of Kasim Beg were to be presented to Lord Hanuman as VN's gifts. They would be washed, anointed with fragrant sandalwood oil, shrouded in white and yellow cotton muslin, placed on the two litters, and carried by the Syrian Christians through the Anegundi gate to the temple of Hanuman on top of Anjanadri Hill, and offered as sacrificial gifts.

VN had been warned through Purandāra Dasa that sacrificial offerings were not appropriate for Lord Hanuman who was a nature god. But VN was adamant, and ranted wildly about pre-Vedic rituals and ancient human sacrifice and *purushamedha* and the significance of cleansing by blood. Squeaky, Balthazar told me, was sure that VN became literally mad at the end. And fiercely arrogant. VN wanted to be hailed by the people as the protector of a *maha*protector. He rejected the idea of any protection for himself. He wanted to lead the sacrificial procession to the top of Anjanadri Hill and announce triumphantly to all the people in the temple that he had singlehandedly expiated the offences against Lord Hanuman.

Balthazar did not kill Squeaky.

And so, goodbye for now, my friend. From a viator now driven by his need to learn Sanskrit and to return to the place where it all began for him, in Coimbra, an innocent one year old found by the Prior on Christmas Day on the steps of the Santa Cruz cathedral. Perhaps Frei Louro will come back to Portugal with me.

João, your friend.

TWENTY-FOUR

*W*ritten in Cochin
in the four sided two storied
Portuguese fortress lookout tower with a sweeping view of the Bahr-i-
Hind
Late October, 1509

You're wrong, João, quite wrong about what you wrote about my hakim
in your long account which I received yesterday in Cochin together with
my beloved papers. He didn't get tired of treating what troubled me. My
hakim knew I had to return to Diu for my inner healing to begin. He had
done all he could for me during the years we had spent together from
1505 to 1509, and he knew I had to heal myself. He suggested that I write
down my story, because he knew I could never talk to anyone about what
had happened to me. Thank you for trying to find out what happened at
Anegundi. Time paused like a comma, as I began to read the policeman's
report, an instant of hope, no mention of death, then the sentence of despair rebegan.

   Too too clever, said my cynic.

   I am writing this account here in Cochin which I know you have never
visited and which is no longer the minor port city that I used to know
when I was a pilot twelve years ago, but the trade rival of Calicut. There
are two Cochins now, *Cochin de baixo*, Portuguese Cochin, and *Cochin de
cima*, upper Cochin, the old city of Trimumpara Raja, five miles up river,
unchanged, but now bustling with different communities, Mappilas and
Jews and St. Thomas Christians, its bazaar, opposite the large tank in the
center of the city, now crowded with shops selling pepper and ginger, and
spices and other articles of trade that come from nearby Kollam and Cannanore, and from faraway Melaka. The Portuguese have stimulated the
commercial development of Cochin, and Cochin has become prosperous.
They have set up a small armory and established a shipyard where they

use teak and poon wood from the nearby forests to build caravelas, galleys and fustas. And they load their Lisbon bound ships with pepper and other commodities at this fast developing all weather port which has now become their major trading base.

Portuguese Cochin has been built on a low stretch of sand near the south entrance of the channel that leads to the deep water inner harbor. Unlike Calicut which is a shallow roadstead without a harbor nearby, Portuguese Cochin can accommodate a number of large ships. The fortress was originally built by the Albuquerque cousins in 1503. As a protection against Calicut invasions, the Albuquerques claimed, but they built it really to promote Portuguese interests. Its walls were made of double rows of coconut tree trunks packed in between with earth. It was rebuilt as a stone fortress by Viceroy Almeida in 1506. Outside the fort is located the *feitoria* with its large warehouses for storing merchandise, gunpowder and supplies of food. The settlement, planned by a Portuguese engineer, consists of neat rows of houses built with red laterite blocks with patios and roofs covered with woven palm tree leaves and cadjans.

From the two storied four sided lookout tower near the seafront I get a sweeping view of the Bahr-i-Hind. To my right, up on the Vypeen promontory of the Cochin river, are two huge bombards, mounted on a laterite bastion that commands the entrance channel. The bombards were left here by Afonso de Albuquerque when he built this fortress as a stern warning to the Samorin of Calicut that he should not attack Cochin again, and as a strong statement of Portuguese power. Frei Louro had arranged with António Reál, the Portuguese captain of the Cochin fortress, for both of us to lodge on the ground floor of the lookout tower. The *provedor* of the hospital provided us with beds, and sends us food from the hospital kitchen. I was asked to keep a lookout for strange ships. For there were rumors all along the west coast that another fleet of the Rumis would arrive from Suez to avenge the Diu disaster. I agreed to keep watch, though I knew it wasn't likely that the Rumis could build and equip another armada this year. Suez lacks timber and material for building ships.

I needed a quiet place in bustling Cochin to bethink myself, and to write down things. I clasped my papers to my chest to welcome them, and then reread, slowly, the painfully long meandering account of my past that you returned to me from Bijapur along with your long letter to me, a letter that wiped out any hope I may have had within me that she was somehow somewhere alive.

My prodigal son, I said to my papers, remembering the Biblical story Frei Louro used in one of his ship sermons. I wanted to embrace you too, João, my long lost brother, but my cynic warned me not to be sentimental.

I now realize why I missed my account so much when you took my papers away. It is, as you noted, a part of my very being, especially the telling of the time when our togetherness, hers and mine, began, at Talaja. It was quite strange, during the rereading of my own account, to remember the events of the past that pierced me at certain moments, and at the same time, to re-live the past cleansed of pain because of the distancing medium of words. My own past is, as you will realize, intertwined with the arrival of the Portuguese. It is also intertwined, somehow, with you and your adventures with VN and with the unfortunate Frei Luís do Salvador in Vijayanagar about which you wrote to me. With the world of Hinduism too.

I then reread my own account about Frei Louro and the conversion ceremony and the events that took place in Champaner, and how the Frei and I were sent by Sultan Begada to Cochin, an account you have not read yet. I splice the three narratives together, and I become aware, as you did when you read the news reports of Timmaya and Balthazar, that the Portuguese have swept like a tufan into our ocean world and created immense confusion everywhere.

My own state of mind is confused. But I will offer two observations that are now clear to me. First, the Portuguese will no longer be now driven by the mad quest for the kingdom of Preste João, and by their search for Christian kings to help them spread Christianity in this part of the world. Second, my re reading of the three accounts makes me somewhat aware of the Portuguese state of mind. Which, like mine, is confused. When I first saw the Portuguese ships at Malindi I could not tell whether they were pirates or traders. Usha and I and our unborn baby had to leave Malindi in a hurry in Paulo's ship to escape from the Jain assassins. We had to find a home and a community somewhere in India with Abdul and Layla. For five years from 1505 I traveled with my hakim and knew nothing about the doings of the Portuguese till I encountered them again in Diu in 1509.

When we saw the dwarf on the stage in Diu the Portuguese appeared to be barbaric clowns. The spy accounts obtained by Malik Aiyaz and by Malik Gopi, and the news reports of Timmaya and of Balthazar, now make me see the Portuguese as blundering savages, wandering across seas unknown, anchoring in strange ports, buying pepper and spices to take back to Portugal, planting feitorias and fortresses some of which they later abandon, firing their guns and cannons to demonstrate their power, cutting off ears and hands and noses to strike terror into people whose sheer numbers terrify them. They don't know how to act in this ocean world, to use your verb. They don't know why they have come here and what they want to do here, to trade or to plunder, or to conquer and rule.

I too don't know what to do with myself. My re-reading of our three accounts here in Cochin has left me in a sea of dead calm. Like the peace that descended on me at the sight of the coconut palms swaying with the sea wind on my return to Diu in 1509. That's when probably my healing began. I do not know whether it has ended. My inner tufan has calmed down a little. I have told my story and no longer feel driven to write. Writing has now become a daily habit. My being, no, my bowels, to use hakim language, don't feel comfortable unless I release a flow of words every day. My reading of the police official's report of what happened at Anegundi has created an aching hollow within me, a dead despair. I still do not know what happened to her and to the baby at the end. And I do not know whether I want to know.

Ah, warns my cynic, wordplay.

I only know that never again will she and I sit on the sands of Lamu and look up at the stars, and that she will never again brush my forehead with her lips and tell me we would be three.

Madjnun knew what happened to his Layla. He looked everywhere for her and then found Layla within himself. But that's poetry and I don't write poetry now. The hollow within me anchors down my being so that I do not know what I want to do or where I want to go. You, oh viator, now know, as you said in your account, that you have to go back to the place where it all began for you, back to the Santa Cruz cathedral where the Prior found you on Christmas Day on its front steps, back there to be born again.

That last phrase about being born again I've picked up from listening to the Sunday sermons of Frei Louro. Only now, after reading the last sentence of your account, do I understand what he meant. We have been flung together, the Frei and I, ever since you left Champaner. And we have become friends. We talk in Portuguese which has now, as you can tell, entered my language. The Frei talks to me about many things. His voice has changed, and become quite gentle and understanding. No longer does he refer contemptuously to Moors and gentiles. No longer does he want to convert the whole world. No, no, João, he doesn't want to convert me. I don't preach now, he told me, I talk to the people in church.

On the Portuguese *caravela* that brought us from Diu to Cochin I heard him tell the Portuguese sailors, during mass, that they should be born again. Impossible, I thought at that time, how can a man be born again when he is old. The Frei said the words were from the epistle according to John. He didn't explain what John meant, but talked about sin and a son of God and propitiation, which didn't make any sense to me, and went on to talk about love and sacrifice, and about why human beings should love one another. Frei Louro's words did make me somehow realize is that you, João, need to go back to Coimbra to heal yourself.

I wish I could help you heal, João. From my hakim I came to know how to cure some ailments of the body. Reluctantly, I think, for I would always shrink away from having to touch my patients.

As a healer you will have to touch people, my hakim had said, stressing the word touch.

Here in Cochin fort I accompany Frei Louro to the ramshackle warehouse that the Portuguese use as a hospital. The Frei cant do much for the sick and the injured. But he shows his love for them, and goes from bed to bed comforting them. In the mornings he brings them communion from the chapel of the hospital where he says mass. He listens to their confessions, recites the rosary with them, and sometimes kneels by the bedside, takes their hands into his, and prays with them and for them. I wish I could help them get well, Frei Louro laments.

I offered to help. I had brought with me a few bundles of dried herbs and plants that I had made use of in Champaner to treat the Portuguese hostages. I could get more medicines from the bazaar druggist in upper Cochin for the stomach disorders many suffer from because they haven't yet gotten used to our food and water. They complain about the hot spicy food prepared with heavy coconut oil instead of the olive oil they're used to. They dislike their daily diet of rice and bananas, and would prefer bread made of wheat flour not available here in the south and which only the rich *fidalgos* can afford. The water, which they don't boil, is the cause of the stomach *mordexi* that causes severe flux and kills in twenty four hours. And some of them are beginning to show signs of elephantiasis, a disease peculiar to these parts, that leads to a monstrous swelling of the legs and the genitals.

I could have helped them earlier, but the Portuguese doctor and the barber-surgeon disapproved strongly of bazaar medicines. The doctor has never encountered these illnesses in Portugal and does not understand what's wrong with his patients. He visits the hospital just once every week, and always complains that medicines are in short supply. The surgeon treats all patients whatever their illness by performing useless blood lettings, at times twice a day. They thought I was a spy, and that I would report their illegal trading activities which they conduct in the storehouse next to the chapel. They sell the food and medical supplies of the hospital for gems and precious stones. Frei Louro said he reported them to the superintendent, but apparently they are all in this business together.

There is corruption everywhere. Everyone wants to enrich himself. Everybody, from the highest to the lowest, wants to make money by whatever means and return to Portugal as quickly as possible. The king's trading interests are neglected except by the royal factor who is responsible for loading the Lisbon bound ships with pepper, ginger and other spices. Frei Louro and I noted how the captain of the caravela that brought us from

Diu to Cochin sold copper rods and returned from Diu with cotton goods at considerable profit for himself. The ship captains, who are *fidalgos* appointed by the king but who know nothing about sailing, say openly that they are here only for plunder and for prize money. They sell *cartazes* at exorbitant rates to Mappila traders. When questioned about maintaining the honor proper to *fidalgos*, they say proudly that they don't need to win honor because honor was born with them. But they do need money. Which is why they have come to this part of the world.

The Frei is quite worried about the effect of all this corruption on the *gente baixa*, ordinary people like the carpenters, the caulkers, the grumetes, the page boys. They go to him for confession, and he knows about their temptations and their sins. We must understand their situation, he says, not condemn them. They are underpaid, he explains, and not paid at all during the monsoon months when neither food nor clothing are provided. They suffer from *ociosidade*, idleness, during those three months of rain rest when they have nothing to do. No wonder they are tempted to sin, and live with the local women and father children. No wonder they become deserters, and steal arquebuses and sell them to get money.

No wonder they butcher cows for food, I added.

The killing of cows horrifies the Hindus and is forbidden by the Raja. Not knowing anything about Hinduism, the Portuguese could not understand why they couldn't eat beef when cows were so plentiful. Nor could they understand why the felling of a single coconut palm, that life sustaining tree, shocked everyone.

We talked about many matters in the dead of night, the Frei and I, he on a pallet in one corner of the room, and I on my bed in the opposite corner. There were stretches of silence between us when we would think aloud about things. At times I would ask him questions. About what he saw beyond the horizon.

I can't see that far into the future, the Frei said, and was silent.

We would listen to the ebb and flow of the waves.

About what happens when people move from one religion to another.

I used to think it was simple to change religious beliefs, the Frei said. But it isn't. The change is very difficult and doesn't involve just individuals, but language and families and the whole community. When Christianity began, Christians were encouraged to spread the faith.

And the Frei paused for a long time. His voice, sounding sad, trying to understand both sides of the problem, rose and fell like a sea wave.

Islam, I knew, also began as a missionary religion. It spread through India because of wandering sufi mystics and trading merchants. Holy men have always used the language of love and persuasion not of force to make people change their religion, I thought to myself. But that takes time. All churches slowly assume power, and then find they have to dominate their people.

There are more people in Gujarat than in the whole of Catholic Portugal, Frei Louro observed.

I knew what he meant.

Then he fell silent for a long time, and we both could hear the rustle of the coconut palms.

About whether he wanted to return, like João, to Lisbon.

I had told the Frei after I read your account about how you, João, wanted to go back to Coimbra to the Santa Cruz cathedral and begin again.

Frei Louro was silent for a long time. Then he inter knit his fingers and placed his hands under his head. He never uses a pillow.

I go to conquer the world for the state of Portugal. Not for its kings, they come and go, Albuquerque had told me in Socotra, Frei Louro said. Where do you go, Frei, Albuquerque had asked. me.

I didn't know then, Ahmadji, I do, now.

I have to go back to Loreto, Frei Louro continued, to acquaint my brothers with the true situation here. And to talk about the problems of conversion, especially the languages they'll have to learn and the cultures they'll have to understand. And I want to tell them in person, not in a letter, about the new world. One can't give up one's lifelong mission, Ahmadji, one has to change and continue.

But I will go back, the Frei said after a long silence, looking up at the ceiling. Perhaps I will return to Portugal accompanied by João as a prodigal son. I'll ask Albuquerque to request a royal pardon for João.

I have first to go back to Diu, the Frei continued. I swore to Sultan Begada and to Malik Aiyaz on my silver crucifix that I would return to Diu after the *Meri* mission here was accomplished.

Let me tell you, João, about the *Meri* mission that brought Frei Louro and me to Cochin.

As soon as we had arrived in Cochin after stopping briefly at Kannanur, Frei Louro went to see António Reál, the captain of Portuguese Cochin, to arrange for our accommodations and to hand over the packet of official correspondence that had been entrusted to him when we had anchored at Kannanur. Only the Frei had been allowed to disembark briefly at Kannanur to meet the imprisoned Afonso de Albuquerque who had requested a meeting with the Frei. I thought he wanted to make a confession, Frei Louro told me, but it wasn't that. Albuquerque only wanted to talk with me. But the captain of Kannanur, a friend of Almeida's, forbade the meeting. I was not able to see my friend, Kotta Marrakar. We spent the night on board the *caravela* and had to leave for Cochin with the morning tide.

I remembered the strange letter I wrote for the Frei about his talk with Albuquerque in Socotra. I wanted to ask him then what kind of a person Albuquerque was. But I didn't. Perhaps I'll ask him later who Caesar was.

I went to see Malik Aiyaz's agent in Cochin, who took me to the *Meri*. which had been drawn up by elephants and beached on Balghatty island in the river. Its cargo had been unloaded, the *Meri*'s nakhoda told me, and stolen by the Portuguese. Its crew had been placed under guard in a house in Upper Cochin. The nakhoda lived in his cabin with a bulbul in a cage for company. I noted that woodworm had begun to attack the ship's lower timbers and planking, and advised the nakhoda to have them scraped with sharkskin and treated with oil. The nakhoda complained that his crew were required to help in refitting Portuguese cargo ships that had to return to Lisbon. The *Meri*, in its present state, he said, is not seaworthy.

Frei Louro and I then went to Viceroy Almeida to request him to release the *Meri* and its crew in exchange for the Portuguese hostages in Champaner. We found him on the second floor of a corner tower of the fortress. He had locked himself in his office, refusing to talk to anyone. A crowd of officials and ship captains were waiting outside his front door. Frei Louro sent in the official letters from the Gujarat sultan and our *crença*, our credentials, through a page boy. But no message was sent back.

The Viceroy has become a hermit, António Reál said, he ignores everything now, even official business. He flings all official correspondence, into a large box, just outside his office door, unopened. He refuses to read letters addressed to him, even those by neighboring kings and rulers.

António Reál then drew Frei Louro aside, took him away from the crowd of fidalgos, and they talked for a long time.

The crowd of officials and ship captains ignored me. I wasn't attired in the colorful clothes of an envoy. My outfit consisted of my hakim's plain white cotton shirt and a pair of pyjamas. I even carried his simple bag of medicines. I didn't know any of them except António Reál. That the one with the horse face and the huge front teeth was João da Nova I knew because Albuquerque had described him thus in Frei Louro's letter to Loreto that I wrote for the Frei in Champaner. He had lost one of his front teeth, he looked ill, his clothes were shabby. The others ignored him. I stood silent to one side and listened to their voices rattling away in colloquial Portuguese.

I couldn't understand all they were talking about. I did recognize some words, diamonds, gems, rubies. The name Albuquerque was on everyone's lips, spat forth with contempt. I feel trapped here in Cochin doing nothing, one *fidalgo* said. There were many complaints voiced, especially about the lack of money. *Murmuração* was Frei Louro's word about the Portuguese tendency to always complain about things. We should have been near the mouths of the Persian Gulf and the Red Sea, hunting for prizes, capturing Muslim ships, not idle here in India involved in trade and spices, making money for the king, another said. I was quite surprised to find that two or three persons spoke Portuguese interspersed with Malayālam words. One of them, Diego Pereira, always addressed as *Senhor Malabar*, spoke Malayālam quite fluently. He had a paunch probably because he had gotten used to eating rice. He wore a richly embroidered Chinese silk *mundu* and shirt, and his lips were stained a dark red. He chewed betel. Like António Reál he had stood godfather for some Malayāli converts and both of them had made themselves quite at home in the trading world of Cochin.

That night Frei Louro came in very late. He said his prayers but didn't eat the evening meal that had been set aside for him.

I'll heat it for you, I said.

I'm not hungry, he said.

His voice sounded sad. He lay down on his pallet and was silent for a long time. I could not see his face in the dark. His voice told me he was disturbed, brooding about things. It wasn't a time to ask him questions.

Suddenly he broke his silence.

No one in Lisbon, Ahmadji, prepared us for such terrible shocks, the Frei said.

He was silent again.

The reason for the shock emerged slowly, jerkily, out of him.

As the seniormost of the missionary priests in Cochin because Frei Henrique had returned to Portugal, Frei Louro had to go to see a priest who had been sent to a village thirty miles in the interior to learn Malayālam and to convert its people to Christianity. He was a secular priest. Didn't belong to a religious order. No, not a Franciscan. The village elders had welcomed the holy man, and had provided a house for him. It took less than a month, Frei Louro said, for corruption to set in. Padre Antão stopped saying mass. That was just the beginning. Stopped saying his daily prayers. Started wearing *mundus*, and also wore a sacred thread across his bare chest like a high caste Hindu, spoke fluent Malayalam. Started drinking in secret. Three women did what the village elders told them to do, looked after all his needs.

I was shocked.

Come back to Cochin, I told Padre Antão, you're not a Hindu.

Why, he asked, I who never had a home in Lisbon and was forced to become a priest because I was the youngest son, have found myself here, they welcome me as a Brahmin, they have become my people.

Come back, I said, come back and confess your sins, and you will be forgiven.

Why, he asked, what sins.

I tried to persuade him to come back to Cochin with me.

I'll arrange to send you back home to Lisbon.

No, Padre Antão said, my home is here.

I felt sorry for him.

Write to me, I said, if you need my help.

I never expected a Catholic priest to turn Hindu. It was a terrible shock, Frei Louro told me. Antonio Reál wants to throw him in the *tronco*.

He kept silent for a long time.

I interknit the fingers of both my hands and set them under my head on the pillow, wanting to ask the Frei questions, many questions. I couldn't ask them. Frei Louro was too disturbed. So I didn't.

Let me hurl a question over the western ghats to you, João, my friend, in faraway Bijapur. I miss our Diu talks.

What's the question, Ahmadbhai, you ask me.

I do not know, João, I say.

You smile understandingly. To know the right question to ask, Ahmadji, is always difficult, you say.

João, I say, I want to understand encounters between peoples and between religions. I think of you and the Tupinamba in brazilwood land, of the Christian missionaries in the wilds of Socotra, of the Portuguese converts bewildered in Muslim Champaner. But my mouth cannot shape the question I want to ask you.

I shut my eyes and waited for a long time in the dark silence for João to speak to me from faraway Bijapur. But I could only hear the nearby rustle of the coconut palms and then, from the pallet nearby, a question sprang out of Frei Louro.

Did you know, Ahmadji, that João, who has turned Muslim, is my cousin.

Yes, I said, you had mentioned it when you prayed for your cousin to return to the holy faith up on Pavagadh in Champaner.

But João doesn't know he is my cousin, Frei Louro said. He is an orphan he thinks, the son of a nobody. In the cathedral school we used to tease him as João Ninguem, João Nobody. He is the son of my uncle the Prior and the young household servant, a distant cousin, who prepared his meals when he was a *cameriste* in Paris. They loved each other very much, and wanted to run away together. But she knew it would ruin him for life. The church and his family would disown him completely. They had no money and nowhere they could go to. The Prior wanted to acknowledge João as his son, but the cousin would not agree. Only his sister, my mother, knew their secret. Before my mother died she had me make a solemn promise that I would tell João who he was. I haven't done so, yet.

I won't write a letter, Frei Louro said. I'll embrace the prodigal when we meet and ask João for forgiveness.

Two days later Viceroy Almeida sent a message to Frei Louro saying he would see us both about the return of the *Meri* in exchange for the Portuguese hostages in Champaner.

We went to see the Viceroy, the Frei and I, and found him alone sitting in a low armchair with his back to a window that looked out on the Bahr-i-Hind. Sunlight fell directly through the window on a book in his hands, but his eyes were closed.

The room was large but ascetically bare. Huddled helplessly together in one corner stood a stack of tattered banners and streamers made of green and heavy white silk, and crumpled flags of red velvet and silver taffeta with Arabic and Persian inscriptions worked into them with golden threads. I had last seen them from the Diu promontory flying bravely with the land wind from the topmasts of the Egyptian maonas. And I had seen them shot down one by one when the wind turned around and the Portuguese guns launched their deadly attack. They were trophies of the Portuguese victory.

On a low table nearby were other trophies, Persian and Arabic books haphazardly piled together. Many were torn and water stained. Some were pilot guides, and on top of the pile was a copy of the *Almagest* which I was tempted to look at, but I picked up instead a book by Rumi whose poems I knew by heart. During those long lonely nights at the tiller, before Usha came into my life, Rumi's broodings about life and death and love used to sustain me.

Senhor Madjid can have that book if he wants to, Viceroy Almeida said. Those books and banners will be shipped to Lisbon, and then sent to the monastery at Tomar, he told Frei Louro. They will be placed in an alcove of the library as a memorial for Lourenço, my only son. No funeral prayers were recited for his soul, Frei Louro. Malik Aiyaz, the governor of Diu, who wants to be our ally now because he expects no help from the Mamluk Sultan, sent me a message saying that he tried to but could not recover my son's body from the Chaul river. My son's bones are interred there, far far from home.

The Viceroy remained silent for a long time. Frei Louro and I sat on a cushioned bench opposite him.

I looked at the Viceroy.

I had expected to see the cold hearted, bulging eyed monster who had ordered the limbs of the Diu prisoners stuffed into the mouths of cannons and fired high into the air, so that fragments of flesh and bone were spattered down on the Muslim port cities on the west coast.

Tomar is the headquarters of the military Order of Christ of which the Viceroy is a knight, Frei Louro had told me.

I liked Almeida, and I liked his voice, João. It was pitched low. It had come to accept things. It was a human voice, warm not impersonal. I also liked the slender fingers that held the small book in his hands.

That's one of the books of the Bible, Frei Louro whispered in my ear, the book of Job.

About the business of the *Meri* and the Portuguese hostages, the Viceroy said, that will have to wait until who's in command here in Cochin has been determined. The *Meri* may be allowed to return to Diu. Malik Aiyaz is our friend. We'll have to wait and see.

He talked to Frei Louro in this fashion, João, releasing odd comments, making abrupt statements, often letting his voice drop into a deep silence, as though he were weary of this world. He addressed all his remarks to Frei Louro.

If you want to make your confession, Ahmadji will leave the room, Frei Louro told the Viceroy.

I don't think the Viceroy realized that I knew Portuguese. Perhaps he just didn't care.

I don't have any sins to confess, Frei Louro, I do not care for power, said the Viceroy. My only folly is the loving of my only son whom I loved more than life itself. Is that a sin, Frei Louro. I will ask my family confessor about this when I return to Portugal and confront my king. I wish I had the patience of Job, he continued. In the book I am holding I read the words, The Lord gave him and the Lord hath taken him away. Then I have to stop reading, Frei Louro, I cannot proceed to read the words of Job after that.

Blessed be the name of the Lord, Frei Louro intoned. His will be done. That's what Job said.

I know those words of Job, the Viceroy said, but I can't bring myself to say them.

It was odd listening to their two voices, João. The Viceroy talked as if he wasn't used to talking. In sudden spurts. The Frei interjected soothing comments. Sometimes the Viceroy spoke so softly that I could not hear what he said. At times I could not understand his Portuguese. His remarks were often so disjointed, leaping from what happened during the battle at Chaul, to Albuquerque in Hormuz, to the Granada expeditions, to the return to Cochin after the Diu battle, that even Frei Louro could not follow the sequence of events.

Frei Louro told me later what the captains and *feitores* and *fidalgos* of Cochin said about the Viceroy to explain his isolation and his strange behavior. I'll try my best, João, in this account, to set down my version of the story of Francisco de Almeida. Malik Aiyaz had told me about the battle at Chaul and I remembered what Albuquerque had said to Frei Louro in the letter to Loreto that I wrote for him in Champaner. And I remember your summary of the reports sent by the Vijayanagar spies, especially by Timmaya.

What I write may not be the truth, João, but it will be a truthtry.

My Account of the Viceroy Almeida Story

I see the source of all confusion for both Albuquerque and for Almeida in King Manuel, driven by his impossible dreams of becoming the emperor of the East. Almeida, much against his will, was drawn into the king's schemes when Tristão da Cunha, a trading *fidalgo*, strongly recommended by the royal council to be the commander of the armada of 1505, suddenly lost his sight, the doctors couldn't tell why, on the eve of the fleet's departure from Lisbon. The departure could only be delayed for a few days, or else they would miss the monsoon winds.

A firm believer in omens, the king immediately appointed Francisco de Almeida as commander. Almeida, who was of noble birth, and who had been sent to France as an envoy, and who had fought valiantly in Granada, expected to be named Viceroy. The king flattered his commander. I give you power, Senhor Almeida, the king said, as though it were my own person, with the title of Viceroy of India, which in my days no other person will hold.

And then the king shrewdly decreed that the title of Viceroy would be bestowed on Almeida only after the fleet arrived at Kannanur. Almeida thought his appointment was permanent. He did not know that Albuquerque would be sent to India in the folloing year, 1506, with secret orders to take over as governor of the *Estado da India* in three years.

Perhaps Almeida had accepted the appointment to further the career of his only son, the brave and handsome twenty four year old Lourenço who had fought by his father's side at the siege of Granada, and who had been taught by his father the old fashioned virtues of chivalry. Of fighting hand to hand and lance to lance, and sword to sword, and not in the cowardly use of guns and artillery. The Viceroy provided his son with a tutor to teach him the new techniques of fighting at sea. And he made his son the *capitão mor* in charge of the caravelas that patrolled the west coast of India, while he himself directed state matters from the Portuguese headquarters in Cochin.

The son proved to be an exceptionally popular commander. His ships escorted cafilas, discovered Ceylon when a sudden storm drove his ships to Colombo, and defended Portuguese feitorias and fortalezas all along the coast. He acquired a tremendous reputation for courage and valour. He was loved by his men and hailed as a jewel of a son.

The news of his son's death at Chaul in 1508 was brought to the Viceroy as he sat looking out of a window of the Cochin fortress tower. Almeida didn't turn his head when the news was announced to him, nor did he ask the messenger any questions about how his son had died. He kept staring blankly at the waves of the sea for a long time.

Then he muttered, he who has eaten of the cockerel must eat of the cock. So softly did he utter these words, that only the page boy heard what the Viceroy said. Later the pageboy told the others.

That, João my friend, marks for me the exact moment of change in the Viceroy. A leap from boundless love to corrosive hate. It had happened to Sheth Chimanlal after he learned that Usha and I had left Diu and sailed away in the *Zephyr*. It happened to Almeida after the messenger told him about his son's death. His heart was immediately filled with bitter vengeance. Against life. Against certain people.

Against Albuquerque who, the Viceroy thought, had wrongfully usurped the glory of taking Hormuz that rightfully belonged to his jewel of a son. Albuquerque had to be punished. He was taken by ship to Kannanur and flung into prison there. Never, never would the usurper Albuquerque be allowed to succeed the Viceroy as governor of the *Estado da India*.

Against Malik Aiyaz and Diu. The father leapt from inactivity into furious action and took over as supreme commander of the armada in order to destroy Dabhol and to attack Diu to demonstrate to all the rulers of the seaports on the west coast his power and that of the Portuguese.

Against the Rumis, who had used cowardly cannon to destroy his son. An eye for an eye. The Rumi captives were stuffed into cannon and blown sky high so that no traces of them would be left for burial in any grave.

Vengeance is mine, proclaimed the Viceroy.

But the love for his son came swirling back. Like the love for his daughter that swirled back into Sheth Chimanlal when he heard me softly call her name. Love cleansed the father's heart of vengeance. Almeida changed the moment he stepped out of his ship on his return after the Diu victory to Cochin. He found that he now, he didn't know why, detested the sea, couldn't even look at it. He disliked talking about his son's death to others.

He could only look deep into himself. He tried to read the book of Job every day. Then found he couldn't recite the words, Thy will be done.

It may take a long time, but the love of his son will enable the father to finish reading that book and accept what happened.

End of the Almeida story

I feel a piercing isolation here in crowded Cochin, João my friend, keener than what I felt after you left Champaner and went away to Vijayanagar with VN.

Abdul left by boat for Bhatkal yesterday.

Frei Louro had got him a job as a helper in the hospital. But Abdul did not wait to be paid, he left as soon as he could.

João has written from Bijapur, I told Abdul.

I am sure she is alive, Abdul had said when I read to him what the police official had reported and what you, João, had written in your account.

The Anegundi police official did not state that she was dead, Abdul had insisted stubbornly, he saw her on the litter, the myna perched next to her, Layla on the other side. The three of them must have tried to go from Anegundi to Bhatkal to take a ship to Diu .

What about the baby, I asked Abdul. Wouldn't that make four.

Then I remembered what the police officer had written. The baby would die before they got to Bhatkal.

I don't know, Abdul said. She must be alive.

Who, I wanted to ask Abdul, who must be alive. But I didn't.

I wondered where the hope in Abdul sprang from.

They couldn't have gone to Goa, Abdul continued. Layla was terrified of the Hindu gang that roamed around Chapora in Anjuna attacking Muslims. After our parents died the *afaqi* tax and customs collector at Chapora insisted that Layla work as a servant in his house for non payment of taxes. She refused and stayed with some neighbors. She was glad when I sent for her to work for the Chimanlal family. No, no. She wouldn't go back to Chapora.

I remembered Layla's rejection of Kochama.

But Chapora was the only home she knew, I wanted to tell Abdul.

I will ask all the nakhodas at Bhatkal, one by one, whether they ever carried two women and a baby and a myna as passengers, Abdul continued. Some of the Bhatkal people may still remember myna Yasmin.

Does anyone ever remember what happened five long years ago, I wanted to ask Abdul.

But I didn't ask.

For I still remembered the brown scar on Yasmin's leg and the deep yellow round her eyes and the moment when she said, ush, ush.

Perhaps I'll ask Timmaya, Abdul said.

Abdul was persistent.

Cherian Marakkār, Kotta's younger brother, who lives in Bhatkal, will help me find them, Abdul said. The Marakkār family are skilled navigators well known up and down the west coast of India. I will find her.

Find whom, I wanted to ask Abdul, but didn't.

When I find her I will go to the street of the letter writers in Bhatkal city and have a letter written and sent to you addressed to Frei Louro.

You'll never find her, I wanted to say to Abdul, but I kept silent. Never have I seen Abdul so excited. Perhaps he has never experienced despair.

Frei Louro has promised to look after you here in Cochin till I get back, Abdul said. He says you are a good man.

Where will you go to find them, I wanted to ask Abdul, but didn't.

It's been over five years now, I wanted to say to Abdul, but didn't.

I felt sad when Abdul left for Bhatkal.

I have given up all hope, I wanted to tell Abdul.

From the day my hakim cut open the sack and rescued me from the ditch on the outskirts of Anegundi, I have drifted in and out of despair, never finding harbor.

My cynic stirred uneasily within me.

I stared out at the sea of life from the two storied four sided lookout tower. Wide and empty it was. I heard the murmur of the waves.

That's the Bahr-i-Hind, that's not life, my cynic scolded me, I thought you had stopped writing empty poetry.

Then I noticed a tiny shadow on the horizon. A lone fishing boat, probably, that shouldn't have ventured so far out, heading back to Cochin. I leaned out of the tower opening, and smelled the wind. The boat would have to make it back to harbor before noon, for the wind would turn around then, and the land breeze would begin.

I looked down at the seafront. Beyond the man high fortress walls, Chinese fishing nets, stretched out to dry on tall bamboo poles, were fluttering in the wind. They looked like large white butterflies trying to escape. A little beyond them on the left were coconut palms that swayed gracefully with the sea breeze.

I stared out at the sea. What sent a shock through me was that the shadow now had a topsail and behind it stretched a trail of ships. I ran up the steps of the tower and began waving the Portuguese flag vigorously from side to side, alerting the gunners on the Vypeen side of the river. They weren't Rumi galleasses, I was sure, for their prows rode high on the waves. But it clearly was an armada. I didn't know whether it was friendly or hostile. The sails were just a blur in the distance. The alarm had to be sounded.

The German bombardiers on Vypeen were efficient. They fired two shots to warn the people of Cochin. Blanks they were, but they sounded like thunder. Clouds of thick white smoke belched forth from the mouths of the two bombards. People from both Cochins ran towards the south bank where the brown sandbars formed a deep channel in the winding river.

The Frei and I could get a clear and spectacular view of the entry of the ships from the tower. The Portuguese rushed through the three gates of the fortress to look at the ships. They were a ragged, undisciplined crowd of men, looking rather comical, dressed for the heat not in breeches, but in red and blue cotton mundus wrapped loosely around their paunchy middles. Their woollen rat tailed caps didn't protect them against the sun. Quite bare from the waist up, their skins had been affected by the hot sun, and were splotched and pinkogrey.

The Portuguese crowd was excited and let forth tremendous cheers when the flagship at the head of the armada curved towards the Cochin harbor entrance. The huge bloodred cross on its billowing main sail made a statement of power, reinforced by two thunderous salvos from the guns of the flagship. The Vypeen gunners fired two more shots to welcome the new arrivals. All the ships of the fleet, lined one behind the other, the red cross on every sail, fired their guns one by one in exact sequence. A triumphal procession it was, a magnificent proclamation of pomp and power.

A sudden dread pierced my being. I had kept silent, I remembered, when Malik Aiyaz, wanting reassurance from his *shahbandar*, had observed that only three or four Portuguese trading ships came to the west coast every year, nothing to be afraid of.

The crowd on the river shore went mad with joy. They threw their rattailed caps high in the air. They hugged each other with cries of relief. They looked forward to real red wine from Portugal instead of the colorless local *urraca*. Some good food from home they would eat, and bread instead of tasteless rice. They would get letters from home. They would get news about their families. They would see some of their friends. No longer were they worried about the Rumes who would never dare attack such a huge armada.

From the fortress tower I gazed at the succession of ships bearing down on Cochin and a tumult of fears arose in me. I had sensed for a long time that my world was changing, but now, my eyes could actually see the terrifying specter of change. For reassurance I muttered the names of the types of ships that sail on the Bahr-i-Hind. *Dhow, Sambuk, Kotia, Baggala*. But the *mantra* didn't work. I had to chant the Portuguese names of the new ships, *nao, caravela, bergantin*, that bore down relentlessly towards the Cochin entrance. These ships were sturdier than those of Vasco da Gama that I had seen in 1498. The flagship was the only one with weapons on the upper deck. The others bristled with guns and cannons whose muzzles protruded menacingly from hinged gun ports in the lower decks. Frei Louro, who joined me at the top of the tower, counted the number of ships. There were twenty in all, and they sailed in a perfect line, one astern of the other.

The flagship was a *nau redondo*, a wide beamed round ship, with castles that towered at the fore and the rear. It made its way through the deep river channel and loomed threateningly like an armed fortress on the move. Its top deck was gaily decorated with cloths painted with the royal colors draped over the deck rails over which some swivel guns were placed. Flags and banners and scissored streamers fluttered in the wind on every topmast. The flag on the top of the *capitania* displayed the royal coat of arms. A larger and more colorful version of the royal standard had been placed on a velvet draped table on the top deck. It proclaimed that mighty Portugal was marching towards Cochin. The royal coat of arms, supported by an armillary sphere, had a border that consisted of eight castles that blazoned forth, Frei Louro told me, the capture of eight cities in the Algarve. There were five more shields in the centre. These five *quinas*, according to Paulo in 1498, proclaimed the defeat of the five Muslim kings.

On either side of the royal standard, next to two crimson banners, two persons stood stiffly at attention. The tall one on the left had a long face, a huge nose, and a broad white beard that flowed down to his waist. He was attired in plain black. The one on the right was quite short and paunchy, but his neck and his face were thrust forward as if to challenge anyone who stood in his path. He was dressed in green satin with a gold girdle around his waist, and a jaunty green beret on his head. His left hand was behind his back and he had a walking stick in his right hand instead of a sword.

The one in black is Afonso de Albuquerque, said Frei Louro. I don't know who the other one is. Must be a member of the royal council at Lisbon.

We later discovered that the one with the walking cane and the jaunty green beret was Dom Fernando Coutinho, one of the most powerful men in Portugal. He was the Marshal of the realm, a rank higher than that of Albuquerque, his uncle. He had been sent to the Indies by King Manuel with a single purpose, to destroy the heathen city of Calicut in order to demonstrate once and for all the power of Portugal. The Marshal and his fleet had stopped briefly at Kannanur, taken his uncle Albuquerque out of the prison where he had been detained, and sailed the very next morning for Cochin. The Marshal carried a walking cane just to show these cowardly Indios that he did not need a sword to be a destroyer.

There was no formal welcome. No one in Cochin had expected the Marshal's arrival. António Reál wanted to arrange a ceremonial procession the next day. The Marshal would disembark in the morning, and walk from the landing to the church under a golden canopy with his *fidalgos*, while the *Te Deum laudamus,* according to Frei Louro, would be sung by the church choir.

But the Marshal Dom Fernando Coutinho did not want to waste any time on empty ceremony. He was a man of action who had been given a mission to perform. The flagship and some caravelas would sail in the morning under his command, destroy the vermin of Calicut, and be back in Cochin the next day. The Marshal, who had never sailed out of Lisbon before, and who knew nothing about the handling of ships, thought the destruction of Calicut would be a very simple operation. He did not know anything about shifting coastal tides or changing winds or the great heat especially if one wore armor in the tropics. He did not know anything about the two monsoons. Neither did he care. He didn't even know that unwalled Calicut was just a roadstead not a port. Such trivialities did not bother him at all. What impelled him were lofty ideas about chivalry and honor. Before he set out from Lisbon he had announced proudly to the royal court that he would bring back the famous carved doors of the Samorin's palace as trophies of war.

It took Afonso de Albuquerque a number of days to persuade his nephew that the attack on Calicut should be put off till the new year. Albuquerque pointed out that it had been a sixmonthlong exhausting voyage from Lisbon. Many mariners were in agony. Their gums were swollen and had receded from their teeth. Others were so weak that they would find it difficult to even carry their weapons. Their joints ached. Lumps had appeared on their legs, and their sores had turned coal black. They suffered from scurvy, and from dysentery. The ships had to be careened, the sails had to be repaired, the timbers had to be treated for woodworm, the slackened ship ropes had to be tightened. Above all, the guns and cannons had to cleaned of rust, and more gunpowder had to be prepared. Albuquerque tried to explain the layout of the Calicut roadstead, where the land sloped up from the sea making landing from ships very difficult. The Marshal did not understand that they would have to use longboats and paraos to land, and would be vulnerable to attack when they disembarked.

The Zamorin has guns made for him by two renegade Italians, Albuquerque told the Marshal. Dom Fernando Coutinho did not care for such talk, but the information about the Zamorin's guns shook his confidence a little. He was surprised that the heathen savages of Calicut possessed guns. I am a knight, he told Albuquerque proudly, I have never made use of those cowardly weapons. But he agreed, reluctantly, to postpone the attack on Calicut to early January next year, 1510.

Neither the Marshal nor Albuquerque attended the simple farewell mass for the Viceroy who, in five days, left Cochin for Kannanur and then for Lisbon, accompanied by two cargo ships loaded with spices.

Dom Francisco de Almeida did not obey the royal instructions to step down as Viceroy, the Marshal told Albuquerque. He will be reprimanded in Lisbon by King Manuel.

Afonso de Albuquerque was then sworn in and installed as Captain General and Governor of the Indies in December 1509. The Marshal delivered into the hands of the new governor all the moneys and sealed letters and packets from Lisbon.

From different sources I have put together all this *khobor* about the Marshal and his arrival in Cochin. *Khobor*, that's the Konkani word Abdul uses sometimes for news and gossip. From my talks with Frei Louro who spends long hours consoling the patients who are homesick for Portugal. Also, from the conversations of patients I treat in the hospital, now so crowded with the sick and the wounded who beg me to treat them that I have no time, except during the night, to feel sorry for myself or to talk with Frei Louro. No time to write long accounts.

Strange, oh friend João in faraway Bijapur, I am now propelled by the need to write. If I do not write for a couple of days I feel strangely incomplete, as if my self had stopped flowing. The act of writing allows my voice to flow on to you, João, and to reach out to the faraway. I do write whenever I have the time, which I now consider a precious gift. For I spend almost all day in the hospital treating patients who keep asking for me.

What led me to offer my services to the hospital despite the opposition of some Portuguese doctors was the drawn face of Frei Louro who looked exhausted, but never complained about his lack of sleep, and about the long hours he put in as a helper at the hospital. I felt driven to help him in any way I could, though he never asked me directly for help.

Fred Louro told me there was an acute shortage of physicians from Portugal.

The patients are my children, Frei Louro said. They like you, Ahmadji, especially the *gente baixa*.

For me, at first, they were just people on whom I used what I had watched my hakim do. I would, with some distaste, place four fingers of my left hand on the forehead to check their temperature, and then take their pulse with my right. After a time, to my surprise, I didn't feel the distaste. It didn't bother me. It became a mere routine. I used bazaar medicines. I gave the patients plenty of the fruit in season, jambools and melons for scurvy. The salted meat, often rotten, that was provided on shipboard, had made them suffer from dysentery. I gave them a decoction of medicinal herbs, and persuaded them to have only rice *canji*, which they said was tasteless, for a week. I smiled at them, coaxed them with soothing sounds, and pointed to lemon pickle to eat with the *canji*. They were surprised when their health began to improve. They came to approve of my strange remedies, even the one for *mordexi*. I applied a red hot iron under the heel of the foot so that the patient screamed with pain. Many in the hospital considered the treatment barbarous, but the patients themselves thought the cure was magical. The cholera disappeared and they got well in three days. They spoke about me to their friends and *fidalgos*.

My reputation as a healer spread throughout the hospital, and my services were in great demand among the *gente baixa*. I came to know the personal names of my patients, and became a friend whom they could trust. They would shake hands with me, and bow to me with great formality, and call me Ahmad hakim, and take my hand and place it on their bodies to indicate where they were in pain. And they would freely indulge in gossip among themselves when I was present, so that I came to know what was happening in the Portuguese world.

I would listen to the *gente baixa* especially when they told me how much they missed their wives and children. I would listen to them, nodding my head at the appropriate time. They thought I knew some Portuguese, because I would greet them in the morning with a *bom dia*. And I used to say good night to my patients in Portuguese before I left the hospital. They all needed someone to tell their stories to.

Where were you yesterday, I missed you, Ahmad hakim, one of the patients who had a racking cough, asked me.

I had also to prepare a report on the Portuguese in Cochin for Malik Aiyaz, but didn't have the time to write it. My hakim would always treat a severe cough with a bitter decoction of neem leaves. I did prepare a decoction for my patient after I returned from Balghatty. He spat it out at first because it was too bitter. But he got used to it. I was no hakim. I considered myself just a ear into which they poured their wants and their woes.

The weeks of November and December 1509 sped fast along. So fast that I had no time to be aware of the flow of time. I lost my self in continuous work, traveling from one patient to another, so that I often had to gulp down my noon meal. After the meal I would continue working, and would drop down on my *satrangi* at midmight when the church bell rang once, and I would fall fast asleep as soon as my head hit the cushion pillow. My eyes opened only when I heard the church bells summon people for morning mass. Frei Louro would wake up before I did, say a silent prayer, spread a cotton sheet over me to protect me against the chill of the early morning, and then leave to say mass.

I felt a hollow peace within.

Then towards the end of December Afonso de Albuquerque sent for Frei Louro and me.

Why does the governor want to see me, I asked Frei Louro who accompanied me to the governor's office that was located in the corner tower. It was the same room that Viceroy Almeida had occupied. But everything on the second floor had changed.

Instead of confusion, here there was order. Instead of a crowd of people milling around and gossiping in the corridor there were three long benches with people waiting patiently to be summoned into the office by a secretary who sat at a table near the entrance door. Everyone who wanted to see the governor had to give his name to the secretary and then take his place on one of the benches.

Handsomely attired, three *fidalgos*, recently arrived, sat stiffly on a bench under the sign, *Fidalgos*. The second bench was crowded with the noisy *gente baixa* who had, according to Frei Louro, come to petition the governor, some about *quintaladas* which they had been promised, others to complain about their wages which had not been paid for three months. Leaning against the third bench and seated on the ground were four Naiteas looking uncomfortably out of place. They were Arabs who had intermarried with low caste Hindus and now made up a separate professional caste that had settled in the horse ports of western India and looked after horses imported into India. A Brahmin, wearing white cotton clothes, his head shaven, sat cross legged on the floor, his head bowed in deep meditation. Next to him a tall soldier stood stiffly at attention, a tight fitting cap on his head, an eight foot lance in his right hand, armored in a colorful jacket with slashes on the sides. I wanted to ask him if he didn't feel the heat, but I didn't.

That's the leader of the Swiss mercenaries, Frei Louro said.

A secretary opened the door to let Frei Louro and me into the office. The large box of official correspondence had been moved from the entrance to the center. It was now half empty. Three secretaries in three different corners of the office were busy writing down Albuquerque's replies to official letters from *visinhos*, the neighboring rulers, that had been addressed to but ignored by Viceroy Almeida. I wondered whether Timmaya's letter to

Almeida about the taking of Goa, written in Portuguese, had been picked up and read together with the plans to drive the Portuguese out of Goa. The official correspondence was picked out of the box and read aloud to the governor. Almost immediately Albuquerque would dictate his replies, without the slightest hesitation. He wore black leggings and moved from secretary to secretary as if he was dictating one continuous letter. Time, for him was precious, not to be wasted. He knew what he wanted to say and he said it.

When Frei Louro and I entered, Albuquerque did not stop what he was dictating to one of the secretaries.

Greetings from Cochin to you, Secretary General Carneiro in Lisbon, he dictated, rest assured that I shall take up your valuable suggestion that we send ships to Melaka, a suggestion that Viceroy Almeida chose to ignore.

Albuquerque removed the black cape he wore, turned and looked at us with his piercing eyes, and then pointed to some cushioned chairs placed around a small table near the fortress window. We were to sit there. Sunlight fell on a shining sheet of brown paper and an inkstand with a pen that had been placed on the table.

That's vellum, said Frei Louro. It lasts longer than paper.

He works late into the night, Frei Louro told me, dictating letters, reading official correspondence, planning every detail of the next day.

Albuquerque finished dictating his reply. End the letter, he told the secretary, with my customary greetings and thanks to the secretary general. Then he moved quickly to the other secretaries to sign two earlier letters, and went back to check the first letter carefully before signing it. He gave the three letters back to the secretaries and watched carefully as they sealed them.

He went to the door, opened it, looked to the right, then to the left, came back in, and asked the three secretaries to leave the office. Then he locked the door.

I looked around the office. All the trophies of the Diu victory had been removed. The royal coat of arms had been placed on the wall above the entrance. My eyes were drawn to the map of Kannanur on the left wall with its bay clearly marked and the fortified wall across the neck of the promontory that jutted into the sea. Then at the map of Cochin on the right wall. Both maps were full of vivid detail. The wind rose in the corner enabled the viewer to get his bearings, the soundings were neatly set down, the sandbars and shoals clearly indicated. Next to the map was a panoramic view of the Cochin coastline presenting an outline in green of its coves and beaches, the hills beyond in gray, and slanting place names perpendicular to the coast in black and red. A pilot could not have asked for more detail to identify the place.

Isn't that map wonderfully detailed, Senhor Ahmad, said Albuquerque in Portuguese, coming up behind me.

His voice, to my ears, was a continuation of Vasco da Gama's on the San Gabriel.

These wall maps have been prepared by my map maker, Senhor Francisco Rodrigues. Frei Louro has told me that you can speak Portuguese, and that you are the best navigator on the Bahr-i-Hind, Senhor Ahmad. That's why I sent for you. I want your help.

He turned suddenly to Frei Louro.

Welcome, Frei Louro, Albuquerque said. We meet again. I know what happened at the conversion ceremony at Champaner.

He could see that Frei Louro and I were both shocked, but he chose not to explain anything. He was like Malik Aiyaz and Malik Gopi, and like VN, with their spy networks. Did power always need a network of efficient spies, I wondered.

We walked, the three of us, to the long bench in the corner next to the fortress window.

I hope you now realize, Frei Louro, that your lofty mission to convert all the heathen of this world to Christianity is doomed to fail. When we met in Socotra I wanted to warn you that your band of priests would not succeed in converting the *gentios* because you lacked the power to impose your teachings on them. The church needs organization and the power of the state to spread its beliefs. It has to be borne along on the ship of state so that both can arrive at their goals. Albuquerque paced up and down, and paused.

At the time of our talk in Socotra, I was vaguely aware of my lofty mission. But I was confused by the confusing orders of a faraway king that takes over six months to get to me. He does not realize that the changing situation here demands that I always have to act quickly. He listens to his ignorant advisers and is afraid of delegating power to others lest it be snatched away from him. My subordinates in Socotra were too greedy and selfish to be of help. Now, Frei Louro, I know what needs to be done. I have no political scruples now here in Cochin as I had in Socotra.

He began pacing up and down again, then went to the fortress window and gazed out at the sea.

That, he said slowly and deliberately, that will be my empire of the sea.

I could see only the endless stretch of the Bahr-i-Hind.

I wondered what Albuquerque meant.

But I don't have time for explanations now, Albuquerque said abruptly.

Albuquerque turned suddenly and stared at me. Then he went to the door, unlocked it, talked briefly to one of the secretaries, came back, took me to the small sunlit table, and wrote GOA in bold letters on top of the vellum.

I want you, Senhor Ahmad, to help my chart maker, Senhor Francisco Rodrigues, prepare on this vellum sheet a large detailed map of the city of Goa and make notes and sketches of the Mandovi and its bar. The shifting of the tides and the soundings should be marked. I want the map mounted on the wall, Albuquerque told me. I have written to Malik Aiyaz stating that the *Meri* will be refitted and allowed to sail to Diu only after you perform this small service for us.

You will be paid according to what we pay Portuguese pilots, he continued. But the map must be prepared in about two weeks. A *fusta* will take both of you to Goa, and I will provide a guide who knows Goa quite well. The three of you will together produce a map that will enable me to know all I need to know about Goa.

I started to say something, but I was confused. Albuquerque had taken my acceptance for granted but had not told us why he needed a map of Goa. He was shrewd, he never revealed his plans to anyone.

The door opened and, to my surprise, a secretary let in the Brahmin who had sat cross legged outside on the floor.

Come in Senhor Timmaya, Albuquerque said. Let me introduce you to Senhor Ahmad and to Frei Louro. You were quite right about the current flowing north along the west coast at this time of the year, Timmaya, said Albuquerque in Portuguese. A *fusta* is ready for you and Senhor Ahmad and Senhor Francisco to leave Cochin tonight for Goa. We will provide you with the cannon you requested after you return from the survey of Goa.

Albuquerque looked meaningfully at Senhor Francisco who carefully began to take the maps down from the wall.

It will take us two days to get to Goa, Timmaya told the governor.

Timmaya's spoken Portuguese was good. I could detect the rhythm of Konkani in the way he spoke.

It was clear to me what had happened. Albuquerque had read the letter that Timmaya had told VN he would write to advise Almeida. to attack Goa. Did Timmaya know about VN's treachery and was Albuquerque aware of Timmaya's schemes for Goa after the Portuguese captured Goa. Why then did Albuquerque invite Timmaya. That was not clear.

The Swiss soldier was still standing at attention when Frei Louro and I left Albuquerque's office.

We will meet outside the hospital chapel when the midnight bell sounds, Timmaya said, and catch the north flowing current.

I knew the distance from Cochin to Goa, 200 miles.

TWENTY-FIVE

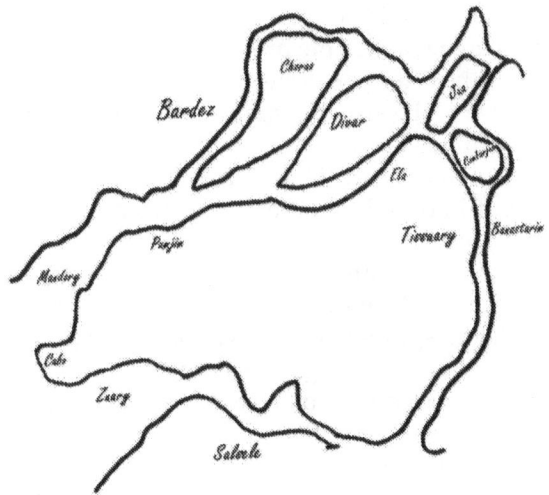

*M*id-January night, 1510
Portuguese Cochin
The hospital chapel
Written on the table Frei Louro uses to celebrate Mass

Chart maker Francisco and I returned to Cochin without Timmaya who left us on a moonless night off Chapora. The three of us had spent four tiring days surveying Goa island surrounded by the Mandovi and the Zuari rivers for Governor Albuquerque.

Timmaya and I never expected the survey to take so long. Pilots of sambuks and dhows on the Bahr-i-Hind do not require the help of any charts.

For us it was a matter of serving as apprentices to a pilot and then becoming familiar with the tidal rise and fall of a river, its shifting sandbanks, its soundings at different times of the day in order to determine the time for the crossing of the bar. No need to mark the shoals and reefs and sunken rocks on a chart.

Pilot Francisco jotted down whatever he observed or was told by both of us on pieces of brown paper which he would carefully place in a folder. He was full of questions, about tides and soundings at different spots on the river, and especially about Ottoman siege guns and bombards and their placement near bulwarks and walls. Governor Albuquerque wants to know everything about Goa, he told us.

Timmaya sang the praises of his beloved Goa. He told Francisco the legend of Lord Śiva's auspicious visit to Goa to bless the island and proclaimed that he, Timmaya, was the protector of Goa's remaining Śiva temples. He described the beauty of its beaches and of its women, the brilliant green of its rice fields, the swaying grace of its coconut palm groves, the sweet taste of its famous betel.

No need to take soundings of the Mandovi bar, they have not changed, Timmaya said. But I noticed that the sandbanks near the north promontory were turning black instead of being brown and, remembering what Gangaram, the Cambay boatman, had warned me about, I suggested we sound the bar with our heavily weighted fishing lines. Francisco made many notes. We had disguised ourselves as fishermen, and Timmaya presented two strings of freshly caught gleaming mackerel to the officials at the Ponjhe customs check point, so that they did not conduct an inspection of our boat. He had cleverly hidden the small berço that Francisco had brought along as a gift from Albuquerque under some nets.

We rowed slowly up the Mandovi and began fishing again at the widest part of the river in full view of the Bijapur sultan's imposing summer palace at Ponjhe. Poised high on the river's edge, with two arched entrances, it looked like a grey fortress, and was defended by pieces of huge siege artillery placed strategically around its bulwarks. Timmaya warned Francisco not to make any sketches of the place. Continue fishing, he said to Francisco, some palace guards may be on the lookout. We continued fishing, and taking soundings with our weighted lines.

How many guns are there around the palace, asked Francisco.

About fifteen, said Timmaya, enough to prevent any attack by sea.

Francisco asked whether the guns were made of wrought iron or bronze. A strange question.

Timmaya did not know.

How big are they, Francisco asked. What's their size.

They are huge, Timmaya said. The one I saw was twelve feet long.

They are probably old type hoop guns, unmovable, Francisco said. He smiled and looked pleased.

I wondered why Albuquerque would be interested in such matters. Then I remembered what happened in Diu to Straighthitter and what the Ottoman gunner had told me about guns and the monsoon winds. The best guns are the new bronze ones, they cost a lot of money, he had said. They do not rust, they are never sold to other rulers.

What about an attack by land, asked Francisco. Governor Albuquerque would want to know. And what about a sea attack up the other river, the Zuari.

The Zuari, Timmaya said, has begun to silt Large ships cannot sail up the river now.

Then he fell silent. And turned away, and went and sat at the other end of the boat.

I knew Timmaya would not want to talk about Mahmud Gawan's savage cavalry attack across the winding backwater channel connecting the two rivers in 1472 when Hindu Goa was invaded and conquered and became the main Bijapuri port for importing Arabian and Persian horses. Trade in horses became the chief source of income for the Bijapuri rulers. A toll in gold *prataps* was collected on all war horses which were imported by the thousands each year and sent over the Belgaum ghats to the capital.

What Timmaya resented so deeply that he couldn't talk about it was the desecration of the Hindu temples built by the former Kadamba rulers. His Hindu sensibility was horrified by the Muslim use of the skillfully cut stones and pillars of ancient Hindu temples to build a congregational mosque and a *hammam* and a public market place in Ela. I remembered what I had read in the history book at Champaner. The Muslims, according to the chronicler, did not want to use laterite bricks, the only building material available in Goa. So they used the stone of the destroyed temples in order to save money and time.

I spun out for Francisco many details about the five check points with guards and watch towers that the Bijapuris had erected to control the crossings from the mainland to Goa. Everyone who entered Goa had to be registered at one of these check points. At the main check point, Benastarim, a monstrous gun had been mounted on its well fortified tower. To make things interesting, I told Francisco about the shallow ford, where the water reached only to one's knees. It was sown with crocodiles who had been fed on criminals sentenced to death. They kept away trespassers and prevented the escape of slaves.

But Francisco was not interested in such exciting details, he wanted to know cold precise facts. He wanted to know the number of Muslims in

Goa and where exactly they lived besides Ela and Ponjhe. He wanted to see the backwater channel with his own eyes, he wanted to know the exact locations of the huge guns, he wanted to sketch the crossings. Albuquerque would want sketches of the guns and the bombards, if possible, and details about the fortifications, he said. He requires them to draw up his plans, Francisco told me.

It became clear that Albuquerque was Francisco's hero. He spoke with great pride and admiration of Albuquerque's piloting skills. Better than mine, he said, but I had my doubts. Senhor Albuquerque always makes it a point to calculate the position of a ship on the high seas, Francisco said, then he checks his readings with those of the ship's pilot.

I was surprised. Does he know how to shoot the sun, I asked Francisco, thinking of the commanding stride of Vasco da Gama clad all in black on the *San Raphael*. Albuquerque, for me, became a continuation of Vasco da Gama.

Of course, said Francisco. Senhor Albuquerque learnt the methods of warfare when he fought for nine years in Morocco. Unlike other *fidalgos* who still long for the old world of chivalry and individual combat, he made it a point to know all about the new methods of warfare, about military discipline and the Swiss style, about fortifications and mobile guns on wheeled carts, and how to deploy them for attack and defense, on land and on sea. He has a will of iron and has cultivated many skills. He could easily pilot a ship from Lisbon to Cochin, if needed. He wants me to make a detailed chart of the Red Sea, Francisco said, and especially of the port of Jiddah, the key to control the Red Sea, after we finish the Goa project.

I was quite impressed. Albuquerque must have some plan in mind to require a detailed survey of Goa. But surely he did not need such a survey just to attack Goa when the Portuguese had established *feitorias* at Cannanore and at Cochin where they had allies and where they loaded their homebound ships with pepper and spices. Frei Louro had heard some *fidalgos* and *feitores* state that the Portuguese were too few in number to establish trading bases anywhere else. And why, I thought, why make use of the services of Timmaya when Albuquerque surely knew from VN's letter that Timmaya was scheming to get Goa for himself. I was both intrigued by Albuquerque and puzzled by his tactics.

We continued rowing slowly up the Mandovi and only when we went past the deserted village of Raibandar, a small town overlooking the former harbor of the Vijayanagar rayas, did Timmaya consider it safe for us to use the weighted lines again and for Francisco to continue sketching.

Francisco made quick sketches of the city of Ela, which was six miles from Ponjhe, and formed a semi circle resting on the left bank of the river.

He sketched the fortifications in some detail. The fortress was a traditional one with mud walls that were too high in proportion to their thickness and shallow foundations. The walls were highly irregular, low in some places high in others, and had gaps that had not been repaired. It was surrounded by a dry ditch that was filled with water only during the monsoon months. From the river we could see the high towers, some palisades and the bulwarks, the sea entranceway that Francisco told me was like a *couraça*. The fortification reminded him of the oldstyle coastal Moroccan forts that the Portuguese had captured easily with their guns. Our German and Flemish gunners , with our new smaller guns, can easily batter down those fortifications.

Francisco made copious notes about the Mamluk ships in the dockyard, the half finished ships that were being built in the shipyard, the landing dock and stables for elephants, the arsenal, the customs house. He rejoiced when he discovered that the harbor soundings near Ela were never less than thirty feet at low tide.

Timmaya and I thought that that would mark the end of our survey of Goa. It had been a long and a tiring day. Francisco's folder was packed with pieces of paper. But young Francisco did not appear tired and did not want to stop.

He pulled out an empty folder.

Let's sail up the Zuari river, he said to Timmaya. I want to take some soundings and make some notes about the backwater channel and the Benastarim tower.

I knew Timmaya could not afford to antagonize Albuquerque who had promised him a Flemish berço made of bronze. I have to kill that Chapora *afaqi* before he escapes to Bijapur, Timmaya had told me.

Timmaya fell silent for a long while.

Then he agreed to sail up the Zuari. The tide is with us, Timmaya said. We can spend the night in the temple that celebrates Lord Śiva as the destroyer of demons. It will be a good omen for our cause. I have to discuss matters with the temple priest who will call a meeting of the local Hindus. I'll allow you one day to visit all the sites you want, in disguise. My boatman will accompany you. Your skin will have to be stained. I don't think Ahmadji should go with you.

I didn't go with Francisco the next day.

I spent a restless night in the dark inner chamber of the Śiva temple listening to fierce talk about the *afaqi* oppressors of Goa, listening also to the rattle of many weapons to attack the *afaqis*. Hatchets, daggers, and reaping hooks were brought all through the night and deposited in the adjoining room. Some would be sent to temples in Anjuna and in Bardez.

Timmaya left us just outside the Chapora river bar.

My boatman will take you safely to Cochin. There are disturbances now in Chapora and everywhere in Bardez, Timmaya told me. The Portuguese patrol the west coast and sometimes use horse boats for target practice. The horse traders don't know where to unload their horses. They have been warned not to sail up the Mandovi. Chapora now handles more boats than they can manage. Horse traders have to pay customs duties at the Chapora dock and then proceed to Ihrampur cove where they unload their horses near the Pir's *dargah* which is fortified. The Chapora *afaqi* fears an attack by the villagers of Anjuna and has posted guards armed with *tufengs* around my ancestral home which he occupies and has fortified with a wall.

Timmaya paused.

During my night walks along the beach in the old days when I used to stay the night at the Nakhoda Home for pilots, I would admire that imposing white washed house which stands on Chapora hill and overlooks the Well of Togetherness, and commands an excellent view of the river.

Tell Senhor Albuquerque that I'll come later to Cochin with some more news about Goa and about the horse traffic, Timmaya told Francisco.

A boat drew up alongside. Francisco handed over the *berço* with a pouch of bullets to Timmaya who handed it to the boatman and both disappeared into the moonless night.

I have been working day and night in the overcrowded Cochin hospital ever since my return from the survey of Goa, treating the sick and the wounded. And it is only now that I have the time to read João's second letter from Bijapur that was delivered to Frei Louro who handed it to me, and the energy now and the time to set down what has happened. I find myself slowly involved in the world of action so that I cannot find a stretch of free time to write. I am interrupted constantly, so that my writing is uneven, erratic. I have to write when I can.

I came back to find Cochin *de baixo* in a state of utter confusion after the return of the Portuguese led by Marshal Coutinho from their raid on Calicut on January 3. People gossiping in the bazaar shops in Upper Cochin regarded the attack a major defeat for the Portuguese who were no longer considered invincible.

The Portuguese were split into two factions. One group rejoiced, and maintained that the raid had taught the Samorin a severe lesson. Thatched fishermen's huts along the Calicut coast had been gunned and burnt down. The Samorin, warned about the raid, had fled inland. His palace had been attacked, its magnificent carved doors had been removed, and countless

Nair warriors had been killed. They praised the valor of the Marshal who had shed his blood for the honor of Portugal. Armed only with his walking stick and wearing a red skull cap, he had ignored Albuquerque's advice and, accompanied by Gaspar da Gama, the *lingua*, strutted heroically to the Samorin's palace five miles from the coast, had the carved doors removed as trophies to carry back to Lisbon, and then was attacked on his way back to the ships by the cowardly mob of Indios who had chopped off his legs.

The other faction thought the raid was a terrible disaster. They maintained that the Portuguese had come to India primarily to trade and make money not war. The royal trade in pepper and spices would be ruined. The Portuguese would lose their reputation as invincible fighters. Their disembarkation from the boats was totally disorganized and left them open to attack. The burning midday sun made the *fidalgos* shed their protective armor. Their shields could not protect them from deadly arrows, as they made their way back through narrow village lanes to the shore with their loot. Marshal Coutinho and Gaspar da Gama lost their lives during the retreat from the Samorin's palace, and Afonso de Albuquerque, despite being guarded by a formation of Swiss soldiers armed with pikes, was severely wounded in the left arm by a spear hurled over a palisade. It was a terrible disaster.

No one knows what to do, Ahmadji, Frei Louro said to me. Factions abound among us Portuguese. The *fidalgos*, proud of their ancestry, refuse to obey the orders of anyone they consider inferior.

The factors, who direct matters of trade, claim they were appointed directly by the Portuguese king and refuse to obey the orders of the governor general. The royal officials act in their own interest and are quite corrupt, wanting to become rich and return to Portugal. The ship captains want to attack pilgrim ships for plunder. No one is in charge. Governor Albuquerque is unable to issue any commands and is in great pain with a high fever. He delayed having his wound treated saying it was too minor a wound. His left arm is swollen with pus, his whole body aches, so that he finds it difficult to sign official documents placed before him. The doctor, recently arrived from Portugal in Marshal Coutinho's fleet, has never treated this kind of wound. He tried blood letting for two days and now the arm has turned septic. The doctor now wants to have the arm amputated, but Albuquerque will not allow it.

I must endure the pain, Albuquerque says, clenching his teeth, I have a great mission to fulfill. The Calicut raid has taught me an important lesson. The Portuguese should never venture far from the sea.

Albuquerque did not explain what he meant.

Albuquerque told me he feels destined to do great things for Portugal, Frei Louro said.

For the church too, Albuquerque had added. What you, Frei Louro, told me in Socotra forced me to reconsider many things and I now find our entry into the Indian Ocean not just a matter of trade but a further extension of the *reconquista*. We Portuguese have penetrated a world alien to us. Can we with our guns and our ships and our Christianity exercise control over this vast new world with its innumerable peoples and make it Christian. How.

He walked to the window and tried to lift his right arm to point to the vast expanse of the ocean, but the pain tore into him. Albuquerque bowed his head on his chest to hide his pain from me, Frei Louro told me.

I wanted, Albuquerque said, to gaze at our future.

Again, he did not explain what he meant.

Our doctors do not know the treatment for the poisons used in this part of the world, Albuquerque said, after a while.

I then told him about how you, Ahmadji, cured the flux of the Portuguese hostages in Champaner. I praised you as an excellent doctor who makes use of herbal medicines that the Portuguese doctors know nothing about. Albuquerque wants to see you, Ahmadji, in his office to talk about Goa. Perhaps you could examine his arm then.

I did examine Albuquerque's arm the next day.

Albuquerque could not talk at all. I slowly unwrapped the coarse cloth bandage the Portuguese doctor had used. The pain must have been piercing, but Albuquerque did not utter a sound. The bandage was filthy. Bits of putrid red flesh and yellow pus came unstuck. I could see the white of the bone. The wound smelled of rotting flesh.

Frei Louro couldn't stand the stench. He stepped back

I'll try to cure the wound, I told Frei Louro. I have never treated such a deep wound before. I'll have to consult the bazaar druggist in Upper Cochin.

I gave Albuquerque two opium pearls for the pain.

He clenched his teeth and nodded his head twice to thank me but did not utter a sound.

I had, a long time ago, watched my hakim cure a shoulder wound caused by a poison tipped tribal arrow by applying a poultice of many herbs. He never told me the names of the herbs which I helped him collect, and I wasn't interested in medicinal herbs then. I never thought of becoming a hakim.

You will become a hakim after your own cure, my hakim had said, not looking at me. It was the third or fourth time during our five years together that he had made this prediction.

I had kept my usual silence. I didn't ask my hakim the question that still bothers me. What was I suffering from. There was absolutely nothing wrong with me.

It's inside you, my hakim said. I can smell your suffering.

Remember, my hakim had added unexpectedly, medicinal plants can be found in every one of our villages.

Strange how the simple remedies my hakim had used in the villages we visited during the five years we were together have lodged in me. A paste of *methi* seeds to reduce swellings and inflammation, a roasted whole onion for jaundice, the milky juice of an unripe papaya for intestinal worms, ginger and garlic and tamarind for stomach upsets, the leaves of the *neem* and of the *jambul* pounded together in a mortar for headaches, hot steam baths at night before sleep for coughs and colds.

After my hakim left me outside Burhanpur, I had used some of those simple remedies on my village patients as I made my slow way to Diu. To my surprise my patients would get well. They flattered me. You have a magic touch, they told me.

I didn't. I didn't have my hakim's sensitive nose that allowed him to detect an illness just by its smell. Body smell often told him what the patient was suffering from. Too sweet, he would say after smelling a patient's urine that had been collected in a half coconut shell, and he would prescribe a bitter decoction from the bark of a neem tree as medicine. Your blood smells of jaggery, he would tell another patient. He would then ask me to smell the blood. I couldn't smell anything. Try again, he said, use your tongue. I was horrified and didn't. You give up everything, especially hope, too easily, he told me. But at that time I regarded myself as just a professional pilot who was returning to Diu, an assistant to a master hakim for five years, but never really a hakim myself.

The druggist in Upper Cochin wrinkled his nose, then stared right into my eyes as I walked up the broken steps through the unpainted front door into his shop.

Your body has an unusual smell, your eyes are yellow, he said, you have a severe case of jaundice. Do you feel giddy.

No, I said, I feel fine.

He thought I had come to see him as a patient. I didn't know Malayalam but he knew a little Konkani, and I told him in broken Konkani about the drugs and medicines I needed for the patients I was treating in the Portuguese hospital. He smiled and said he could supply them. Then I told him about Albuquerque's infected arm and how I had never treated a wound where the bone could be seen.

He said he would have to consult his teacher in another village.

Come back in three days, he said.

As I was leaving he called out to me, I'll give you a drug for your jaundice.

I'll eat a roasted onion, I told him.

That wont cure you, he said, that's a north Indian remedy.

But I didn't need a Hindu *vaid*. I was proud of my hakim and of the medical skills I had learned from him.

For five days after my return from surveying Goa and the Mandovi river I worked day and night treating my patients without stopping. I had told Francisco Rodrigues that I would assist him in the preparation of the maps and charts of Goa. But he didn't send for me. He didn't think too much of my navigational skills.

Your services as a doctor, Frei Louro had told me when I returned from the survey of Goa, are urgently needed.

It wasn't just a statement, I heard it as a plea.

Some of your former patients were asking for you, Frei Louro said.

Very few doctors from Portugal risked the voyage to India. The *fidalgos* refused to be treated by the local physicians, bazaar doctors they called them. The hospital was packed to overflowing with soldiers who had been wounded during the assault on Calicut. It was so crowded that the beds had to be removed and *satrangis* spread on the hospital floor for the patients. A *shamiana* was set up next to the hospital and even the lookout tower was put to use for patients.

Frei Louro had packed my writing materials and moved our meager possessions from the lookout tower to the hospital chapel where I am writing this account on a table he uses as an altar.

I miss the reassuring presence of Abdul but am learning to do without him. I miss the early cup of coffee he would bring to wake me up. He would have set up my writing materials on this table and removed them after I finished writing. Early in the morning now, when the first church bell sounds, Frei Louro uses the writing table to celebrate Mass in the hospital chapel. That's when my long workday begins. I go first to the fortress tower where I check on the condition of the patients there and treat urgent cases. Then my feet take me up the steps to the lookout window where the gentle wind freshens my being as I watch the coconut palms leaning towards the sea.

I then go to the big tent, the *shamiana*, where the *gente baixa* clamor to be examined first. Many wait for me near the entrance. Senhor Ahmadji, they call out. Senhor Doutor, come soon, I am dying, help me. I wait for them to go back to their *satrangis* before I begin treating them. I had been told not to go to the hospital which is reserved, Frei Louro tells me, only for fidalgos with war wounds who demand to be treated only by real doctors and barber surgeons from Portugal. A number of *fidalgos* who were with Marshal Coutinho had been wounded by arrows with poisoned tips during the retreat from the Samorin's palace in the interior.

They are in great pain, Frei Louro told me. Blood letting, twice a day, does not do the patients any good. Some are at the point of death.

I had watched my hakim apply leeches to arrow wounds. Leeches suck out the bad blood around the wound gently, my hakim had told me. Blood letting, even cupping, weakens the wounded patient.

I was feeling somewhat dizzy and wanted to rest, but I went to Balghatty island to the *Meri* to find out if there were any messages for me from Diu.

The nakhoda of the *Meri* had gone to Upper Cochin to hire some workers to repair the ship and make it seaworthy for the return to Diu.

He will be back soon, his assistant told me. Why don't you wait for him in the cabin.

I stepped into the cabin but the wild shrieks of the bulbul and the beating of its wings against the cage made me step back.

She misses the nakhoda, the assistant told me. He is lonely, too. He talks to his bulbul.

A name leapt into my mind, Abdul, that embodiment of hope, and made me ask the question I never would have asked otherwise.

Did you ever carry two women with a baby and a myna as passengers from Bhatkal, I asked the assistant. To Diu, I added.

No, he said.

I smiled to myself. It was just the answer I expected.

He was silent for a long time.

I've never seen a myna, he said.

It is a black bird, I said.

Does it look like a crow with yellow spots.

Yes, I said.

Many years ago, seven I think, when I was an apprentice pilot on a coastal boat, we took a woman and a baby and a bird that looked like a crow from Bhatkal to Goa.

One woman not two, I asked him in a rush. Was she young.

I only remember the strange bird, he said. The woman covered her face with a thick veil that slipped once. Her mouth was swollen, her right eye was bruised. She had lost all her front teeth and could only mumble. She paid us, that's why I remember her, with some gold *prataps* of Vijayanagar.

Did you take them to Goa.

Yes, he said. To Chapora.

The customs officer asked the woman some questions. You will have to see the *afaqi*, he told her and led her away to the white house on the hill.

I was puzzled and deeply troubled.

I'll have to send a letter to Abdul at Bhatkal, I told myself.

Just then the nakhoda returned, greeted his bulbul, and gave me a sealed message from Malik Aiyaz.

Malik Aiyaz's message

Don't trust Vora who hates Jan Mirza for making fun of his pronunciation in the Portuguese class. He never forgets. And Vora accuses Jan Mirza for not teaching him the official abbreviations so that the cartazes Vora had produced in the beginning were easily recognized as forgeries by the Portuguese ship captains. He has become an excellent forger of *cartazes* now.

And, Ahmadji, beware now of Mustafa who considers the Portuguese pirates deadly enemies of the faith and you, in particular, a traitor to Islam who has to be put to death for being the first pilot to guide the Portuguese ships to India. The Portuguese, despite the pleas for mercy of the women and children, and despite the *cartaz* prepared by Vora, gunned down and destroyed the pilgrim ship in which Mustafa's whole household was returning from the Hajj, after robbing the passengers of gold and jewelry. Mustafa has become a fanatic now and has sworn vengeance against the Portuguese, and against you as a traitor to Islam. He and his brother pilots now work for Amir Gopi, Malik Gopi's son, who now sends his ships only to Melaka and not to Aden or Hormuz, because of the Portuguese blockade of the Red Sea and the Persian Gulf with their huge ships armed with huge guns.

Toghan told the sultan about the intrigues of Malik Gopi and the attempt of Champa to seduce the holy Frei. Outraged, the Sultan has banished Gopi to Surat. His son, Amir Gopi, has made Mustafa his special pilot and consultant and, my spies tell me, will send him, with your student Vora as interpreter, to Bhatkal to make enquiries about the horse trade. There is more money now in the horse trade than in pepper and spices. Payment is now made only in diamonds and in gold coins. They will then go to Cochin to request the Portuguese officials for *cartazes* for three more trading ships to sail to Melaka. Mustafa has been told to bribe the Portuguese officials heavily. Bijapur and Vijayanagar both need horses to win the war between them.

Beware, Ahmadji, of hiring pilots recommended by Mustafa for the Melaka route and beware of sudden shipwreck. I know Mustafa and Amir Gopi are conspiring against you. They consider you a traitor to Islam because you are friends with the Portuguese. I shall let you know when I discover their schemes.

Malik Aiyaz

I felt sad after reading the letter. I liked Mustafa. I used to admire Mustafa's piloting skills and his detailed knowledge of the sailing route to Melaka. And he was a good man. The sudden shock of losing all the members of his family must have churned his being and filled him with a sense of helplessness because there was no way he could attack the Portuguese *shaitans*. And it must have led him to channel all his hatred towards the only one he could blame, me.

I have a growing feeling now, after the survey of Goa, that the Portuguese are more than just traders or pirates, that they have come to stay. Like João, let me translate my feeling into images, the black imposing figure of Vasco da Gama shooting the sun, Frei Louro and my talks with him, and his misgivings, the ominous and puzzling words and behavior of Albuquerque as he stared out of the fortress window at Socotra.

I wish I could have explained to Mustafa and to the other pilots when they had come to my house why I had to direct the Portuguese ships towards Eli Mala and Calicut. But my heart was heavy like a stone then and I could not break its silence and speak about our return to India. Perhaps the pilots would not have believed my story, even if I could have told it, that I had Usha with me and that she was carrying our baby, and that I felt powerless, tossed about by the waves of the ocean sea. Perhaps Mustafa will hire an assassin to kill me. I don't care really whether I live or die.

The Hindu druggist in Upper Cochin had consulted his teacher in the next village. He gave me an ointment he and his teacher had pounded from different herbs in a mortar.

First, he said, carefully scrape away the infection and the pus, use leeches around the wound, then use *urraka* liquor to cleanse the inside of the wound, the druggist said. The pain will be unbearable and the patient will scream and may have to be held down by your assistants. Apply the poultice and cover the wound with this large soft leaf which will draw out the pus. Never use a cloth bandage. The leaf should be changed every day, twice a day. The wound will heal in four or five days.

The druggist gave me a stack of twenty leaves and some stronger opium pills to dull the pain.

Only thick rice *canji* sprinkled with pepper and roasted cumin for three days, the druggist said as I was leaving the shop, no meat at all, and not a drop of water. The patient should have plenty of sleep and rest.

And here are pieces of snakeroot from the jungles of Java.

He looked deep into my eyes.

It will cure your jaundice and your giddiness in seven days. Your jaundice has become worse, he said, your skin and nails are yellow.

I mumbled a reply and paid him with the money Frei Louro had given me.

I hurried back to the hospital chapel to read João's letter again while I waited for Frei Louro to tell him about the treatment for Albuquerque's wound.

João's second letter from Bijapur
December 1509

Ahmadji, my fellow wanderer, I have to go home.

But, like you my friend, I don't know where home is. You wrote, in your account, that Julfar was your birthplace not your home. And I know you sensed peace in the *Zephyr* and in the Lamu shambahouse, but they were just anchorages for both of you, weren't they. Where are you sailing to, my friend, do you know. The voyage of my orphan self began on Christmas Day on the steps of the Santa Cruz cathedral in Coimbra where I now long to return. But is Coimbra really my home.

.You'll always be on *hejira*, our friend the maulvi told me one day, when I asked him if he knew where our home is

The maulvi was silent for a while. Then he added softly, Jan Mirza, you'll always be a wanderer across religions.

Alas, Ahmad my friend, do we have to keep on searching, are we doomed never to find home on earth.

I must stop this brooding about the several meanings of home, Ahmadji, just as you, forgive me, my friend, must stop brooding endlessly, wanting to understand *samsāra*. We must, both of us, act, really act. I have to go home, as I wrote when I began this letter. Perhaps home is a state of being not just a geographical place. Yet I feel driven to return to the place I started from, the steps of the Coimbra cathedral on Christmas day, and begin again. And study Sanskrit. And become a reconciler of religions, not a *jagatguru* like Vyāsarāya but a teacher to the western world. And now I can, Ahmadji. Now I can take the first step. I may be able to get to Chapora on the west coast where you rescued Abdul, the home to which Layla may have returned, and from there somehow I will get to Cochin and find a Portuguese ship that will take me to Lisbon.

The Chapora *afaqi*, afraid of being attacked by the Hindus and Muslims of Anjuna, has sent an urgent message to his father, Kamāl Khan, the acting regent of Bijapur, requesting that the six Portuguese deserters from

Cochin, armed with arquebuses, be sent to Chapora to protect him and the horse traffic and to escort him back to Bijapur. Bijapur needs horses for its cavalry. Chapora has become crowded, too many horses that are landed there and then sent over the Bardez Ghats to Bijapur. Very few horses are now landed on the Mandovi's horse ports. The road through the Belgaum ghats is not considered safe. Kamāl Khan, a close friend of the ailing sultan, wants me to leave Bijapur and accompany the six deserters to Chapora. Special arrangements have been made for *taforeas* laden with horses to land in Chapora. They would need protection, according to his son, the *afaqi* port commander. But Rustum Khan, the leader of the cavalry, wants me to stay on in Bijapur and train horse arquebusiers. Rustum Khan has become my special friend and warns me not to go to Chapora. They will kill you because you and I are of the party of the sultan. Kamāl Khan, the regent, is biding his time and will assume the sultanship as soon as the sultan dies and Ismail Adil Khan, the young prince, is assassinated. His son, the Chapora *afaqi*, will be next in the line of succession.

Ahmadji, I want to discard the Bijapuri mask that I have assumed here but find it very difficult to get rid of it in this our *samsāra* in which I still have to act.

Here at the royal court in Bijapur I put on a marvelous act. I pretend to be a happy go lucky fellow, friends with everybody. I cheer up the fourteen year old prince who is sad because the Sultan, his father, is very ill, and greatly troubled because he wants to assume the regentship. He and his mother, the wise queen *Bibi*, do not trust Kamāl Khan, the regent appointed by his father. His mother advises her brave young son to bide his time. Her brother, his uncle, tells him he lacks experience of war. The Bijapur army is too divided in its loyalties and too scattered on too many fronts to act effectively.

Young Ismail Khan has become my friend. He is wise beyond his years. Too many war fronts have to be maintained, he says. Vijayanagar is preparing to attack Raichur and the Doab. Orissa is poised on our northern borders. The Portuguese pirates prowl on the Bahr-i-Hind and attack the horseboats and our trading ships. Three of the Bahmanid states, envious of our prosperity because of Goa, are conspiring against us. All our enemies are waiting for my father to die before they attack us.

It's a period of instability for Bijapur, Ismail Khan tells me.

I can overhear you mutter *samsāra*, Ahmad my friend.

Actually it's a period of change for our whole world, the *samsāra* we live in.

I remember the exact moment long ago when the pandit flung out this Sanskrit term that fascinated you then and now fascinates me. *Samsāra.* The three syllable word erupted out of the pandit one evening when the sun was about to set and the three of us were waiting for you at Diu promontory. The pandit hurled the first syllable, *sam*, across the Bahr-i-Hind. *Sā*, he prolonged the second, and then quickly released the short syllable *ra*, so that I thought I heard the syllable drop into the water down below. One of its many meanings is the oceansea, the pandit proclaimed. He was perched on the black rock, his back straight, staring straight at the setting sun. I was afraid he might topple into the sea. It also means wandering, the pandit said, turning towards the maulvi and me. You walked up the slope just then, Ahmaadji, and the pandit flung the three syllable word at you. That was when it must have lodged within your being. I was in no mood for a discussion then, and the word meant nothing to me at the time

Now I think it does. After reading your account and after my many wanderings I have begun to see the word not in the abstract, as the unstoppable flow of human existence, as I wrote so pompously in my letter from Vijayanagar, but as a number of vivid images. I see you piloting the ship that is your self over the ocean waves. I see the rise and fall of the waves of countries and of civilizations. Your account makes me see the arrival of the Portuguese as a *tufan* that causes the rise and fall of the ocean waves. I see both of us as wanderers searching for home.

Forgive me Ahmadji. To see is to know, as my Plato taught me. Now I wonder what to see really means. Do you remember Rumi's *ghazal* wherein knowledge of the divine had to be completed by sight. The Persian word *nazar* and the Sanskrit word *darshan* both imply a glance. Perhaps one cannot understand *samsāra*, that fascinating word with its world of meanings. One is allowed only a glance.

Forgive me for dragging in my teacher Plato and for sounding so pompous.

Let me return to the Bijapur self I have assumed.

I talk to everyone here in Bijapur as I did in Diu and Champaner, I make jokes, I spin out amazing tales about my travels through Arabia and East Africa so that I make both factions, the Deccanis and the Afaqis, forget their rivalries and jealousies, and roar with laughter. They see me as a man of action, a skillful arquebusier, an excellent polo player, who often gives recitations of Persian *ghazals* to the applause of the afaqis who have immigrated to India from the Iranian plateau. I also compose odes in Dakhni, a colloquial mixture of local Muslim and Hindu tongues. Sometimes I sport a crimson turban with twelve peaks that proclaims I am somehow allied with the *kizilbash*, and the *afaqis* are impressed. At other times I wear a fashionable long black buttoned up coat in the Deccani style. No one knows to which faction I belong.

Both factions are curious about me and want to know why I have come to Bijapur.

To train horse arquebusiers, I say.

Being courtiers they don't understand and, teacher that I am, I have to explain the difference between an Ottoman tufeng and a Portuguese arquebus. I show them one of the six arquebuses that the six Portuguese deserters from Cochin brought with them to Bijapur.

The arquebus is shorter than the tufeng, an *afaqi* remarked.

I tell them how easy it is for riders to use a bow and a lance and a sword, and how difficult to handle firearms on horseback even if the armorer shortens them. The horse is terrified by the smouldering fuse, I said, and has to be slowly trained to accept it. The rider has to control his horse with one hand, then aim and shoot his arquebus with the other.

I don't have to explain anything to Rasul Khan, the leader of the Bijapur cavalry.

I will send you a letter, Ahmadji, as soon as my fate here in Bijapur has been decided.

Jan Mirza

I sent a letter to Abdul addressed to Cherian Marakkar in Bhatkal telling Abdul the cold facts that the assistant nakhoda of the *Meri* had told me about the woman with the thick veil and the baby and the black bird and the *prataps*, and that, seven years ago, he had taken them from Bhatkal to Chapora. I didn't use the word hope. I told Abdul that João had escaped from Vijayanagar and gone to Bijapur and might be sent to Chapora. João would like to go to Portuguese Cochin, perhaps Timmaya could help him.

Why don't you yourself, my cynic asked me, he stressed the word you, go to Chapora and find out about things and do something instead of. He stopped. I have to look after my patients, I told my cynic, they need me. That was not all true. Inside me lay the aching sense that it was all useless. I did hope against hope that Abdul would decide to go to Chapora to find his sister, Layla.

Let me know what you and Cherian Marakkar decide to do as soon as possible, in seven days.

Abdul would have to use the services of a Bhatkal letter writer to reply to my letter.

Frei Louro was impressed when I told him about the different stages of the treatment of Albuquerque's wound, according to the druggist.

I will inform Albuquerque, the Frei said. Perhaps the hospital can buy drugs and other medicines from the Hindu druggist.

I was worried. I can bring myself to touch human beings now, but not leeches, I told the Frei.

The Frei agreed to ask Albuquerque whether Francisco Rodrigues should help us when I cleaned his wound.

No, no, no need to. Albuquerque turned and looked at me with eyes that pierced me even though clouded with pain.

I looked at Albuquerque.

The pain will be unbearable, I said to the Frei.

I had never talked directly to Albuquerque.

I'll not utter a sound. I'll endure all pain, Albuquerque said. I'll even ask for a bed to be placed in my office for five days. I'll stop eating meat. I'll even give up horse riding.

He paused for a while.

Frei Louro had told me that Albuquerque still went riding around Portuguese Cochin every morning. Anyone of the *gente baixa* with a complaint could stop him and beg for justice.

But, Albuquerque continued, I will not, I just cannot rest in bed during the five days of treatment. There's work to be done.

He got up from his chair and strode towards the window, tried his best to push it open but could not. He came back.

Frei Louro, he said, I told you in Socotra that I have a mission to fulfill. I will not let a mere arm wound stop me. It is absolutely essential that my arm heal by the first week of February.

Isn't that when the coastal currents will begin to flow northward towards Honawar, Ahmadji, Albuquerque asked, turning to me.

Yes, *senhor*.

The two words jumped out of my mouth. Frei Louro stared at me wondering why I had broken my usual silence and addressed Albuquerque directly. I myself couldn't understand why they sprang out, these two words, from deep within me. Why, why, I wondered. Was it because of the *ji* of respect that Albuquerque had added to my name. Or was it because my inner me became sharply aware that Albuquerque was indeed the skillful pilot Francisco said he was and knew a great deal about the winds and currents that prevail on the Bahr-i-Hind, a knowledge only our best pilots would have. I wondered whether he planned to sail up the coast to Honavar. Or beyond, to attack Goa, perhaps. But surely Albuquerque was aware of Timmaya's plans. Frei Louro would not know the answers to these questions and I was deeply confused. What was Albuquerque planning.

The significance of that moment hit me much much later.

That moment, João, marks the beginning of a long confused process that ended with my seeing Albuquerque for what he really was.

Help me João, oh teacher and friend, for I am quite confused. Maybe we can help each other realize what your teacher Plato meant by seeing. The process of my seeing Albuquerque didn't proceed slowly, step by step. I experienced a tumult of insights, a flood of memories, a confusing clamor of doubts and questions, odd rememberings of what I had read in the books of history in the Champaner library and of what you wrote to me from Vijayanagar, recalls of the many talks I had had with you and with Frei Louro, my questions about power and your replies, Malik Aiyaz's telling of Sultan Begada's rapid rise to power and, above all, bits of the long letter I wrote for Frei Louro to his brothers in Loreto.

The malicious talk my ears overheard in the front room about Albuquerque's behavior and character made other images of Albuquerque appear and fade and loom again before my eyes. I saw Albuquerque at times with the eyes of Francisco Rodrigues. But I found it difficult to regard him as a hero. For I saw him everyday, twice a day, for five continuous days. I also saw Albuquerque with the compassionate eyes of a hakim, a patient in terrible pain, whose wound I had to treat.

And yet, my eyes saw Albuquerque, dare I tell you this, João my friend, turn into something more than just Albuquerque.

How, how can I expect you to see Albuquerque with my eyes, João. Do you remember what you told me a long time ago, that there are different ways of seeing. If you were here and I could talk to you face to face, perhaps my oral mode, as you put it in your letter, would make my words soar aloft to make you see Albuquerque the *Terribil*, as the *gente baixa* of Cochin call him with affectionate fear and awe. But you are far away beyond the western ghats and my cold words drop coldly on this cold paper. My hakim had suggested a long time ago that I treat my inner wound by writing out my pain. So I poured out our tragic story, Usha's and mine, on to paper without troubling myself at all about techniques of presentation that had tormented me as a poet when I strove to imitate Rumi and the Persian poets and wrote *ghazals* and *mathnavis* that did not ease my pain.

Now I need to write in order to make you and others see what is happening to our world. I need help. In your letter you said that this was a period of change for the whole world. Ten long years ago when Vasco da Gama and the Portuguese stood amazed at the sight of Hili Ras in the bright sunlight, my cynic had, mockingly perhaps, tossed out the wild idea that I may have been chosen to be the witness to the dawn of a new world of science and power. Perhaps I am also its recorder. Not a born writer, but one who has to painfully learn the art of writing. You had told me in your first letter from Bijapur that I zigzag bewilderingly between the past and the present and that I demand too much from my reader. You are right. Let me set down first a simple step by step account of what happened on those five continuous days, beginning with the events of the first day.

We went, Frei Louro and I, after he said mass, to Albuquerque's office. I stumbled twice on the way.

Are you ill, Ahmadji, Frei Louro asked me. He was worried. Your skin looks yellow.

I had just started taking the snakeroot drug.

The benches had been removed and four secretaries were busy in the four corners of the front room taking down the names of the early visitors who were all clamoring to see the governor. The Swiss soldier stood stiffly at attention, waiting patiently, aloof from the noisy crowd. The fifth secretary held the door open to let in servants who were carrying a heavy bed and a bedside table into the office. Some *fidalgos* wanted to rush in but were held back by the secretary who then shut the door.

No one will be allowed to see Governor Albuquerque for the next five days, the secretary announced loudly. Then he noticed Frei Louro and me and opened the door to let us in.

One of the fidalgos stretched out both arms to block our entry.

The padre can go in before me, but not this strangely dressed *gentio.*

Senhor Ahmad is a doctor, Frei Louro said to the *fidalgo,* who hastily stepped aside.

Let them come in, ordered Albuquerque.

I was wearing my hakim's white shirt and white pyjamas and, unlike the Portuguese doctors, I didn't have a servant but carried my own white cotton bag of drugs and herbs.

Come in, senhor hakim, said Albuquerque. Come in, Frei Louro.

Albuquerque was standing near the bed dictating a letter to the sixth secretary.

Inform the Raja of Vijayanagar of our plans, Albuquerque dictated. When his troops cross over the ghats and threaten Calicut by land, we Portuguese will attack Calicut by sea. We will then be able to supply Vijayanagar with enough horses to attack Goa. End with the usual salutations. I'll sign the letter later.

I must see the Swiss soldier later today. The Calicut disaster must not be repeated. Send him in when I ring the bell.

I washed my hands and, remembering the routine my hakim used to follow, I carefully arranged on the bedside table the items from his cotton bag in the order I would use them. First, the small scraper with its soft bendable thorns, then the bottle of clear distilled *urrak* , the best in Cochin the druggist had said, to cleanse the wound of pus, the jar of ointment that would soothe the inflammation and heal the wound, and the bundles of broad palm shaped leaves my hakim would always use, to draw out the pus, he told me, and pull the skin gap together. The packet of opium pearls I kept in my pocket.

Here are three letters that one of the secretaries gave me, Frei Louro said, these two are for you. He placed them on the table.

Frei Louro made Albuquerque sit on the bed before he removed the bandage. The stench released was overpowering. Frei Louro turned away but did not let go of Albuquerque's arm. I held the other arm and felt his forehead, but he had no fever. Then I took his pulse remembering what my hakim had told me. Its beat was steady as if it was under Albuquerque's control.

Would you like me to recite a prayer, asked Frei Louro.

Albuquerque shook his head.

I thought Albuquerque would surely yell when I dabbed the gaping wound thick with whitish yellow pus a number of times with an *urrak* soaked piece of cloth. I could sense his body tighten but he didn't utter a sound even when I began to use the scraper as gently as I could to dig out bits of stubborn pus. A few spots of pus required me to exert more force. Suddenly Albuquerque shot up from the bed. That's when I saw his whole body loosen up to express its unbearable pain. He shut his eyes tight and clenched his teeth, then, for several moments, quivered uncontrollably from head to foot. His forehead beaded with huge drops of sweat. We made him sit on the bed and I wiped his forehead with a heavy towel. After a time he stopped shivering and I took his pulse, its beat became steady once again. Francisco was right. Albuquerque had a will of iron.

I applied the ointment and bandaged the wound with the soft leaves using thin strips of banana trunks as strings. The bandages would have to be changed frequently today. I offered Albuquerque ten opium pearls strong enough to deaden the senses and the pain.

Will the opium put me to sleep, Albuquerque asked me.

Yes, I said.

I wont take them now but tonight, just before I go to sleep, he told me. There's work to be done.

Take me to the window, Albuquerque said to Frei Louro.

He took Frei Louro by the arm and they walked to the window. With great difficulty Albuquerque managed to push it open with Frei Louro's help. A sambuk with white full bellied sails was heading its way towards the open sea.

They went to the corner bench, and Albuquerque knelt down, and both of them made the sign of the cross and began to talk in whispers. I walked away. I did not want to overhear what they were saying. I knew it was an act of confession.

Looking through the open window I remembered vividly the ship of state drifting pilotless into the future that Albuquerque had made Frei Louro look at in Socotra, one that he wanted to transform into a ship of empire. His guns and ships would speak the language of thunder and power, he had said, and he planned to make himself the new Caesar of the Indies. I remember asking the Frei to spell the name but forgot to ask him who Caesar was. I was impressed by Albuquerque's magnificent overview of the situation on the Bahr-i-Hind and meant to tell the Frei about it but I forgot. It must have been because of the tremendous effort it had taken me to think and write in Portuguese.

I picked up the two letters from the table. The red lac seals on both letters had been broken and clumsily resealed. I wasn't worried. I had no secrets to hide.

The first was from Abdul.

A brief note to say how surprised he was to see Vora on the street of the letter writers in Bhatkal. Vora had introduced Abdul to one of the writers who wrote and sent letters for him. In Gujarati. Vora had, Abdul noted, kindly paid for the services of the letter writer I have used. Vora enquired about João, asked where he was because he wanted to thank his teacher of Portuguese, he told me, asked where you were. I did not tell him where you or João were. Vora then told me the sad news about the murder of his uncle, Malik Gopi, by Toghan because of Champa, and that he was now forging *cartazes* for Amir Gopi, who was now involved in the unclean horse trade because it had become very profitable, payment was made in diamonds and gold coins. Vora was proud of knowing Portuguese. He could speak broken Portuguese, but he had studied the script, and was now in great demand as a specialist in horseboat permits.

Cherian Marakkar has warned me not to go to Chapora. There are disturbances now in Anjuna and the whole of Bardez, he said. The Hindus strongly resent the unjust land taxes imposed by the *afaqis* many of whom want to escape with their families to Bijapur. You are a Muslim, he said, but I was insistent and he promised to help me.

Cherian introduced me to Timmaya who is preparing a small fleet to set sail to Chapora to attack the *afaqi* and to stir up riots in Bardez. Timmaya has promised to take me to Chapora when he gets his fleet together. Then I ran into Vora and offered to disguise myself as a *naitea* when he gets a special boatload of purebred Turani horses, worth a fortune in diamonds, to be sold in Chapora. Vora was prepared to write the appropriate *cartaz* for them.

If you come to Chapora to enquire about the woman and the black bird, leave a message for me with the old letter writer with a long white beard and with flowing locks of white hair who always sits on the built up parapet under the giant banyan tree, the center of the village from where all Chapora letters are written and sent and received. He knows Arabic and Persian, no one knows whether he is a Hindu or a Muslim. He will know where I am in Chapora. He used to write letters for our family and for the villager community. I did not take his advice a long time ago when I ran away from home, but I think he will understand.

Abdul, your faithful servant and your devoted friend

I was quite worried about Abdul. The news about Vora worried me deeply too. Why did Vora want to know where João was. Vora wasn't to be trusted. I was sure the letter writer would inform Vora about the contents of the letter sent to me.

The other was from Malik Aiyaz.

Malik Aiyaz's letter

Malik Gopi is dead, the letter began, assassinated by Toghan who had always bitterly resented Gopi's taking away of Champa. Ishak Khan will not be sent to Junagadh. His right leg was broken when he was thrown while playing polo from the Arabian mare I gave him.

Cleverly done by the Malik, I thought, that would solve his conspiracy problem. But I felt ashamed of myself for being so suspicious of my friend.

I have written again to Albuquerque informing him that no *maonas* now set sail from Suez and asking him to release the *Meri* and offering to pay an annual tribute they call *pareas* to the Portuguese which you and Frei Louro could negotiate. We have to pretend to be friends with the infidel Portuguese.

I am in despair, Ahmadji.

The state of Gujarat is in confusion, no one knows what to do. Our Sultan, on his deathbed, doesn't care for the world he himself has created. My desire for power, he told me, has been drained out of me by the approach of death. Gujarat faces threats from the Rajputs and from Mandu. The problem of sultanic succession has not yet been solved. My own desire is to save my Diu. But I can no longer expect the Mamluks to help me. All three Islamic powers, the Mamluks, the Ottomans and the Safavids, are too involved in their own quarrels. The Safavids are poised on the Ottoman border. The Ottoman Sultan is rumored to be on his deathbed. The Ottomans and the Mamluks are seriously considering abandoning the Bahr-i-Hind as a frontier and restricting themselves to the waters and lands of the eastern Mediterranean. They have to protect the Holy Cities, but realize that their *maonas* with their prow guns are useless, as you told me, on the open seas of the Bahr-i-Hind against the Portuguese war ships and their powerful broadside cannon.

I will send the gift of a young rhinoceros with its trainer as a gift to Albuquerque. A Portuguese deserter told me that such an animal has never been seen in Portugal.

What can I do, Ahmadji.

Malik Aiyaz

I heard the sound of a bell. The door opened and a secretary let in the Swiss soldier who entered and stood stiffly to attention.

I have heard Senhor Albuquerque's confession, Frei Louro said, coming up to me. I have to go to the hospital after dinner. Shall we leave.

No, I said, I'll eat later.

I could see Albuquerque coming towards me holding his left arm. Whitish pus oozed out of the bandage. I made him sit on the bed.

Can I talk to the soldier while you bandage my arm.

Yes, I said.

It wasn't a talk, it was a report. About the difficulties of the Swiss group who had to train Portuguese soldiers in the Swiss style of fighting. The soldier did not complain, did not waste any time, stated bare facts. The shortage of pikes. The frequent absences during training sessions. The many desertions. The resistance to drill discipline and the square formation.

Albuquerque listened quietly, never complaining even when I had to use the scraper . He asked the soldier just one question, did the other captains co-operate. We were told by the captains, the soldier said, that those on horseback do not mix with soldiers on foot.

I finished tying up the bandage and told Albuquerque not to move his left arm. A secretary came in with a steaming bowl of rice *canji* and a dish of roast pork. Albuquerque smiled when I checked the *canji* bowl with a spoon. The roast pork had to be taken away.

I'll be back in three hours, I said, to change your bandage again.

The front room was crowded when I left. I felt a little dizzy. Must be the *pitta* I thought. I must take more of that snakeroot medicine the druggist gave me.

When I came back Timmaya was leaving Albuquerque's office in a hurry looking a little dazed. The front room was empty. There was just one secretary, who let me in.

Come in, senhor hakim, come in and cast your pilot's eye on my world, said Albuquerque, making a half circle with his right arm.

I spun around, and found myself, as it were, anchored in the center of the Bahr-i-Hind, amazed, shocked, giddy.

Around me, on the three walls of the room hung maps, sailing charts and panoramic sketches of the port cities of my former world that Albuquerque now claimed as his own. Francisco Rodrigues had arranged them in an arc stretching from the east coast of Africa all the way to south east Asia. Sea charts and maps of Mozambique and Mombasa, of Malindi and Mogadishu, were on one wall, the coastlines in green, the place names in black except for that of Malindi, which was in red. I went up to the wall to examine the Malindi map. Wind directions and soundings were set down in great detail.

On the next wall I saw maps of Hormuz and Socotra island and Aden, together with an empty gash for the Red Sea, Aden at its opening, Jiddah at its center, Suez at its tip. What shook me deeply was the Portuguese flag in the exact center of Hormuz.

On the third wall was a detailed sea chart of the west coast of India, with the names Diu and Calicut, Cochin and Kannanur, in red, and Bhatkal and Honawar in black. The monsoon winds were clearly marked, as were some soundings along the coast, some rivers with their estuary bars and, amazing to my pilot's eye, the protective mud banks along the south coast known only to a few local pilots where a ship could take shelter during the monsoon. Far away to the right, beyond the vague outline of the Bay of Bengal, there was a long black arrow at whose tip was not a map but the place name, Melaka, in red. The Portuguese flag was to its right.

The flag shocked me deeply. It spoke to me not of pirates but of conquerors.

Ahmadji senhor, Francisco Rodrigues called out to me.

He was bent over Albuquerque's bed, straightening out a large roll of vellum.

Come, he said, and look at my work that I finished just yesterday.

It was a large detailed chart of Goa.

I was amazed, shocked.

It was a work of art, done with brush and pen, precise in its colorful detail. Francisco had set down everything about Goa that we had talked about and seen during out survey, the estuary bar of the river, Ponje, Raibandar, the city of Ela with its harbor soundings, the surrounding wall with its damaged portions, even Benasterim and the five towers that stood guard over the crossings from the mainland.

What shocked, no, stunned me was that the Portuguese flag had been placed in the dead center, between the Mandovi and the Zuari rivers.

Why, why, why, I asked myself again and again and again. I was going round and round. Why flags on some maps. Why on Hormuz in the Persian Gulf, a place his captains had made Albuquerque abandon after capturing it. Why the flag next to unknown and mapless Melaka, the world of Mustafa, at the far end of the world. On Goa island with its horse trade, I could understand, but surely Albuquerque must have been aware of Timmaya's schemes to make himself lord of Goa.

My mind spun round and round in a whirl trying to understand the mystery of the Portuguese maps of the Bahr-i-Hind, and the three flags. Why, why, why, I asked myself again. I remembered the crude sand outline I had done for Paulo da Gama. I remembered my ship sketches from which Mian Mazlum had fashioned the translucent green ivory *kotia* she so loved and suddenly had to abandon. But I never had needed to sketch maps of the major ports of the Bahr-i-Hind. I knew the details of my ocean world as I knew my salt toughened palm. My apprentices would listen to the sailing directions I gave them and would pass on the tradition to their apprentices. Mine was an inner knowledge shared with a few people. Here was a science that generated action and power.

Maps, my cynic said, are statements of possession.

True, I told him, and flags are announcements of power and domination.

The thunder of empire, my cynic muttered, perhaps to remind me of the words used by Albuquerque in the letter I wrote for the Frei.

Impossible, I said, quite impossible. What man can conquer the vast unstable sea with a handful of men and ships and guns.

Albuquerque, said my cynic.

But I wasn't convinced at all. I was in a daze. Nothing made sense. Everything was a blur.

I find it difficult to write.

I can't set down what happened in the simple step by step manner I had wanted to, João, my friend. Even after four days, as I write this in the hospital chapel, I can't remember exactly what happened after I saw the flags. I am still confused, giddy. The *pitta* has not yet drained out of me. My usual remedies like the whole roasted onion for jaundice don't work. The Cochin *vaid* told me that *unani* medicines spring from desert lands and at times do not work here in the south. A matter of water and moist soil, he said. I shall swallow my pride and be like my hakim who was always prepared to learn about new drugs. I shall make use of the Java snakeroot to stop this giddiness. It will take five days, the *vaid* had said. You will get very sick before you get better, he warned me.

I know I must have applied the ointment and bandaged Albuquerque's wound several times, how many I don't remember, I must have done it automatically as if being a hakim had now become second nature to me. As in a blur I can see the faceless people that flowed into the room, late that night, a carpenter, a caulker, a sailmaker, two gunpowder mixers, two arquebusiers, a cannon founder, why, why, I thought at the time, strange fish for a Governor to want to talk to when he was in pain.

I remember returning to the hospital chapel very late that night, terrified of snakes, quite surprised to find that Frei Louro was not asleep on his pallet. I felt tired, confused, giddy. I must have dropped off to sleep immediately for I didn't hear him come in.

When he woke me up the next morning Frei Louro looked as if he hadn't slept at all.

I have to say mass, he said.

He paced up and down the room.

I don't know what to do, he said. I have spoken to all our doctors in Cochin, Ahmadji, and no one is prepared to go there.

I did not understand.

Where, why. I must have looked totally confused, but Frei Louro was too disturbed to notice I was ill. Your eyes look yellow, he noted.

I got a letter from that Padre Antão I told you about, Frei Louro explained, the one who has yielded to the temptations of Hinduism. He begs on his knees for my help. There has been an outbreak of cholera in his village that many consider a form of divine punishment.

There is no doctor here, Padre Antão writes, my people are dying like flies. They look up to me for help. I cannot bear to see those who love me and whom I love suffer and die before my very eyes. I pray to God every day to take me in their stead. I am, alas, a sinner. You promised you would help me. Help my people, Frei Louro. send us a doctor from Cochin.

What should I do, Ahmadji. No doctor wants to go to that village. Too far, too dangerous, no money., the doctors say. The authorities are horrified. He is worse than a *renegado*, they say, he is a scandal to the Christian community. They want to fling him in the *tronco* and send him back to Lisbon.

After mass I will request Albuquerque for the services of a doctor, Frei Louro said.

I felt my own pulse, I felt my own forehead, I had a high fever.

I feel giddy all day now and I want to rest.

But I have to write. I feel driven to set down whatever I can remember even though my use of verbs is irregular, I slide between the past and the present. My skills as a hakim were, are, strangely, not affected by my jaundice and I treat a few patients in the hospital when I have the time. I bandage Albuquerque's wound several times a day during those four days when I spent practically the whole day from morning to night in the waiting room. And I had the strange feeling that all the captains and the whole of Portuguese Cochin had been summoned by Albuquerque to his office, though I couldn't see who through my half shut eyes. Was he making preparations for an expedition to recapture Hormuz. He must have some plan in mind.

What do I remember. Let me use Albuquerque as an anchor so as not to drift away from what really matters. Perhaps I really am both witness and recorder. João, teacher, bear with me.

People would come early in the morning to talk to Albuquerque, and the benches in the waiting room would be crowded even before the bell sounded for mass. They would stream past me into Albuquerque's office as I squeezed myself into the far corner of the waiting room, wanting to make myself invisible, head bowed, staring fiercely down at my feet, not wanting to brood about things, not wanting to listen to the insistent clamor of my self, not wanting to stare at the blurry faces of Albuquerque's visitors, looking up would make my head spin, listening instead to their voices, hearing almost all the languages spoken on the Bahr-i-Hind, throaty Arabic, the polite Persian of Safavid envoys sent to Albuquerque, the Surati Gujarati of Vora and of Mustafa who had glanced in my direction but did not recognize me and continued whispering the names of pilots who knew the sailing route to Melaka, the salty Konkani of some Naiteas, fast paced Malayalam, all spoken softly in the waiting room as if all the languages of the Bahr-i-Hind were aware of the presence of a loud nasal intruder that sounded harsh to my ears especially when it distorted our local names of places and people, listening to a mixture of Portuguese and Malayalam that sprang from the mouth of Senhor Malabar and from other Cochin factors sitting on the *fidalgo* benches, strange words like *duc* which I did not understand used by António Reál and the ship captains during a discussion about Goa and Albuquerque, and, strangest of all, the Portuguese word *murderer* whose meaning I understood but not why it had to be applied to Albuquerque.

Remember to ask Frei Louro about *duc* and *murderer*, I tell myself.

One of his secretaries would take me into the office when it was time to change Albuquerque's bandage, a time when visitors were not allowed in, a time when, usually, Albuquerque would be in deep conversation with Frei Louro. Why would Albuquerque, I wondered, consult a priest who detests war and fighting and had prevented a massacre at Socotra. I would be bandaging Albuquerque's wound as both of them sat on the bed talking but I did not listen to their talk, not because any sins were confessed, though Albuquerque would frequently be doing the confiding and the questioning while Frei Louro would throw in a few comments, but because I found myself, head bowed, changing the bandage and compelled to listen to the insistent clamors of my inner self.

I had thought my wounded self had healed but it hadn't. From out the aching hollow within me my inner tufan rebegan after the inevitable lull, piercing me again with despair, hurling out questions I cannot answer.

About what, asks my cynic.

All the questions that have always haunted me, the words that you always made me question.

Questions about what, my cynic asked, affecting his most innocent voice.

Stupid, shot out suddenly from the ache within me.

I looked up at the Frei and the governor sitting on the bed but they hadn't heard anything, they continued their conversation.

Sorry, I said to my cynic, I am not myself, but you know the words I mean, time that destroyer of the past, and suffering that afflicts the whole world, and home which I don't have, and change which I have always dreaded, and self, do I have one, and wavelike power which I detest, and

Ah, interrupted my cynic, all those swarm of whys that sting you. Do you have to know the answers to all these questions in order to live in this world.

I had no answer to his question, and fell into a brooding silence, perhaps it was the buzz of whys and not the jaundice that had made me giddy. I shut my eyes. And then, into my deep silence, there dropped a soothing voice and a strange statement.

The Muslims are our brothers.

I was startled. I finished bandaging the arm, raised my head, and listened.

The Muslims are our brothers, Frei Louro repeated softly, and stared, not at me but into Albuquerque's eyes. The Frei's voice had changed, it reminded me now of my hakim's. His Portuguese words dropped into my silent despair like balm on a wound.

The Muslims are hated infidels, said Albuquerque fiercely, they are our deadly enemies.

But one must love one's enemies, Frei Louro said. And he went on to speak softly about sacrifice and love and propitiation, the same words he had used in his sermon on the ship from Diu to Cochin, about why human beings should love and help one another, words I had heard before.

I turned to leave.

The wound has healed, I told Frei Louro. The bandage doesn't have to be changed for seven days. I feel very tired. I have to rest.`

You have offended Ahmadji, Frei Louro told Albuquerque. Don't you know he is a Muslim.

I don't hate the Muslims, I hate their worship of false gods. I hate their brutal conquest of my beloved Portugal, Albuquerque said to Frei Louro.

Hatred never heals wounds, Frei Louro said, why not look upon them as brothers and seek reconciliation with them since they far outnumber Christians in this part of the world.

Albuquerque strode to the window, pushed it open and stared at the wide open sea for a long time. Then he came back.

I may try that, he told Frei Louro, but just once, perhaps the gesture of peace will be more effective than the tactics of war.

Ahmadji *senhor*, Albuquerque then said softly, turning to me, you are not my enemy, you are a healer, you saved my life.

The door opened and a secretary entered with a letter that Albuquerque handed to Frei Louro who handed it to me. I stared at it. It had been clumsily resealed, it was from João.

Tell me, *senhor* Ahmadji, Albuquerque said as I placed the letter in my medicine bag, do you know how many Muslims there are in Goa.

The tone of his voice had become firm, businesslike.

I don't know, I said, no one knows.

Francisco had asked the same question, but had not been satisfied with Timmaya's reply. All I knew was that Hindu Goa had become a Bijapuri gateway, that Muslims from across the Bahr-i-Hind, Egyptian Mamluks, Persians, Turanis and Khorasanis, had settled in Ela and in Ponjhe, a few in Anjuna and Chapora. I knew that there had been a decline in the Hajj passenger traffic for Bijapuri Muslims because of the Portuguese prowlers in the Bahr-i-Hind. Bijapur had doubled the former land taxes imposed by Vijayanagar and the *afaqi* tax collectors had come to be regarded as tyrants.

My mind was confused. I can't remember what I said or whether I said anything about Goa to Albuquerque.

Tell me, Ahmadji, Albuquerque said, do the Hindus of Goa consider Muslims their oppressors.

My bag of medicines began to feel very heavy and I would have collapsed had I not clung to Frei Louro's arm.

You are ill, Ahmadji, said Albuquerque looking into my eyes.

He is very tired, Ahmadji needs to rest, Frei Louro said.

Albuquerque walked with us up to the door.

Frei Louro, he said, we need all our doctors for our expedition. But Ahmadji can go to that village to treat the cholera outbreak. I will arrange to pay him what we usually pay a Portuguese doctor.

Late that night I awoke in a state of pure happiness, undisturbed by any questions or doubts. I knew exactly what I had to do. I would set out for Chapora tomorrow. I did not want to disturb Frei Louro who was fast asleep on his pallet. So I lit a small candle. João's letter lay next to me. The Frei had offered to read it to me last night as I lay in bed trying my best to read the letter that I couldn't even hold in my trembling hands. I only remember vaguely that I had made up my mind about something just before I dropped off to sleep like a stone.

I began to read João's letter.

Bijapur, Sultan's palace compound, don't know the date

Greetings, Ahmadji, my friend.

I will probably leave Bijapur in a few days for Chapora. It will be the first stage of a viator's journey home. I wish I could take you home with me, Ahmadbhai, fellow wanderer, but I know your self will never rest until you find out exactly what happened to them. To all of them, I include Yasmin. Did you send Abdul to Bhatkal to find out. I am sure you didn't. You're terrified of knowing the truth, for to know what happened to them would prevent you from clinging to hope and could make you sink forever into despair.

I don't know what happened to them and I cant offer you any hope, but I can smell the faint fragrance of night jasmine that arises from your words about her, am I being sentimental, which makes me believe that all will be well. You have much more than just this four word sentence that I picked up somewhere in your account. You have her love which uprooted your being which then went on to widen, as I said, before Abolem interrupted me in Vijayanagar, into compassion for human pain and suffering. You were a witness to the exact moment when she changed, in Paulo da Gama's cabin where, despite what Plato said, you saw but did not know. Your former self, the one that absorbed Rumi and Hafiz, could easily respond to her unbound hair glimmering in the light of the setting sun. But it couldn't understand her chanting of the *mantra*, as you called it, the *Salve Rainha, Mater Misericordiae*. You were deeply moved by the picture of the child with the crown of thorns carrying the cross, and the mother with sorrowful eyes burdened with an inexpressible pain, but, you didn't know why, the picture didn't mean anything to you.

I have to stop, Ahmadji, for it would take me a long time to tell you the story of the woman and her child, and the story of mankind's redemption, a Catholic term you would not understand. Ahmadji, I don't want to convert you. What I do want you to realize is that love like Usha's can never die, it has to survive in some form.

I can do something to soothe your unbearable pain, Ahmadji. I can, when I get to Chapora, I don't know how long it will take and I don't know Konkani, make enquiries and find out if Layla ever returned to her home there. Didn't her parents have a house somewhere in Chapora. I have been told there is a platform under an ancient banyan tree where an old man and his writers sends and receives all letters in Chapora. I will send you another letter from Chapora as soon as I have any news about Layla.

Jan Mirza

I finished reading João's letter to find Frei Louro sitting up and staring at me, a lit candle near his pallet.

I will leave for Chapora today, I told Frei Louro.

He bowed his head and was silent for a long time.

I have to go to help Padre Antão, the Frei said softly. He sounded sad. His eyes were in deep shadow. The candlelight shone on his mother's silver crucifix which he held in his right hand.

I suddenly remembered what Albuquerque said to us at the door of his office. But I didn't want money.

I have to go to Chapora to find out about

Usha, Frei Louro said, I know, I read João's letter aloud to you last night. Your eyes were shut tight.

We both fell silent.

Will I ever see her, I asked the Frei.

I expected a no, I wanted him to say no, but he remained silent, head bowed.

Will she be what she was, I asked.

I don't know, he said. Her love will sustain you. And her pain, he added.

Emotions swirled up to my eyes but images began to crowd them out. The wrinkle of pain on Usha's forehead, the 24 Jain *tirthankaras* standing unmoved before the ocean of suffering, the woman with her child and her unutterable anguish who let fall a tear for Usha.

I bowed my head down on my chest as if to stare at my own pain, and I laughed as if I was mad.

Are you laughing or are you crying, asked Frei Louro. Is it the jaundice.

There was a loud pounding as if someone were trying to break the door down.

Frei Louro, Frei Louro, a voice yelled.

Frei Louro opened the door and a stranger hurled himself down at his feet.

Save my people, Frei Louro, they are dying, I love them. Save me, the stranger shouted, I want to confess my sins, and he clasped Frei Louro's knees tightly and wouldn't let go.

Come in, Padre Antão, come in and sit down, said Frei Louro. Don't shout or the soldiers on guard duty will come and take you to the *tronco*.

He had to drag Padre Antão inside and he made him sit on my bed while I hurriedly shut the door. The room stank of *feni*.

My people, the Padre kept repeating, they are dying, I love them. I couldn't bear to see them die any longer. So I rushed here in my boat to fetch the doctor you promised. Let's go to the doctor, Frei Louro. We have to hurry.

Shall I keep the door open, I asked Frei Louro. No, he said.

The whole room stank.

The candlelight made Padre Antão look like a *madjnuni*. He couldn't stay still, his body twitched. His hair was wild, uncombed and filthy. His feet were bare and smeared with mud. The dark red *mundu* he wore was torn and stained, the sacred thread was twisted out of shape across his shoulder. The tiny wooden cross that hung around his neck appeared stuck to his skin.

You promised to send a doctor to our village, Frei Louro, he said. My people are dying, I'll do anything, I love them, I'll confess my sins, I'll even go to Portugal. But send a doctor and save my people. I love them, he kept repeating.

But Albuquerque says no, Frei Louro said.

Padre Antão was drunk. He couldn't remain still. He stank of liquor. He began to weep.

I have to vomit, he told Frei Louro.

I watched them clutch each other and stagger out of the door. Then I hurried to my medicine shelf and poured a large dose of opium laced syrup into a cup of water. That would induce a two hour sleep.

I need a doctor, I need a doctor, the Padre kept repeating over and over again as Frei Louro and I made him sit on my bed.

Ahmadji is a doctor, Frei Louro said.

Then let's hurry, said the Padre, my boatman will be waiting. He tried to stand. Frei Louro had to hold him while I went to the medicine shelf and poured an extra measure of opium syrup into the cup. That would make him sleep for another hour.

H dropped on the bed like a stone and began to snore.

What shall I do, Ahmadji, asked Frei Louro.

I shall go with Padre Antão, I told Frei Louro, but only for a month. My hakim showed me how to treat a cholera epidemic. The Portuguese doctors would not know what to do. I'll go to Chapora after I return.

Frei Louro wetted a piece of cloth and wiped some vomit off the Padre's mouth.

I don't know why you're doing this, said Frei Louro.

It's because of the sermon, I said. He did not understand what I meant.

You're a good man, Ahmadji, the Frei said, I know it's not for money. Let me tell you what I can do to help you and my cousin João whom Albuquerque could use as a *lingua*. I have to go to Goa with Albuquerque, and I will go to Chapora to find out about things and to take João back with me to Lisbon.

Don't, please don't ask me any questions, Ahmadji, because I can't tell you why and how I will be in Goa, God forgive me, it would be a sin, it's part of a plan I can't talk about, may God forgive me.

It was time to act. I went to the altar table to remove my papers so that Frei Louro could say mass. I wished Abdul were here to pack them for me.

Don't take your papers, Frei Louro said. I have been to the village. There won't be a table in the hut. And you may not even time to write down things. I promise to look after them for you. I will leave a message for you with the Hindu druggist when you come back.

I went to the door, opened it a little, and stood waiting a long time for the faint light of dawn. I didn't want to think. Padre Antão would wake up soon. It would be time to go.

I went to the altar table and wrote down a twoword word, *Farewell*.

TWENTY-SIX

December 8, 1510, late at night
Cochin de baixo
In the hospital chapel that is no longer a hospital chapel

I am back in Portuguese Cochin and am writing this at what was the altar table by the light of a single candle. I set down these trivial details in order to anchor my self and to calm my turmoil down. It has been so long since I last wrote down things, some months ago, I think. I wanted to at times but never had the time, and I am again in such turmoil now that I don't know where to rebegin. With my departure with Padre Antão and the boatman to the faraway village with the cholera outbreak, far far from the roar of *samsāra*. Or with my return to the bazaar in the bustling center of Cochin *de cima* early this morning, listening to the murmur of the ocean waves. Frei Louro had promised to leave a message for me with the Hindu druggist there. The shop looked a little different. The front steps had been repaired and the door repainted.

The *vaid* gave me two letters which I read sitting on the first step. The first, a note from Frei Louro.

Ahmadji, Brother Pedro, who has been told by hospital patients what a good man you are, and who thinks you could be our first real convert, has stored your papers along with crucifixes and vestments and holy pictures and bibles brought on ships from Lisbon in the former hospital chapel. It is February 10, 1510, and I leave on Albuquerque's ship, the *Frol de la Mar*, for Suez and the Red Sea but will be back. *Frei Louro.*

The second was a letter from João.

Chapora, in one of the afaqi's houses
Ahmadbhai, my friend, where are you. With Frei Louro, in Portuguese Cochin, I hope. To whom the ancient letter writer who sits under

the huge banyan tree and whom you mentioned in your account of the rescue of Abdul told me my letter would be sent in a couple of days with the Kerala mail carrier. He stared at me and greeted me coldly at first in Persian mixed with Arabic which the interpreter could not understand. I didn't have to tell the ancient who I was. He knew. You are the *afaqi*'s protector, he said, brought from Bijapur to guard him and the wealth he has accumulated all these twenty five years.

I told him we were friends, Ahmadji, then he smiled and asked about Abdul.

Unjust taxes, the old man said, stroking his long white beard and ignoring the interpreter, The *afaqi* counts the ill gotten money that he stores in a strongbox every day. So that's how the *afaqi*, he never told me his name, spends his evenings.

I asked whether Layla had come back to Chapora.

No, he said, she would have come here to see me.

Where am I, I ask myself. In Chapora, on my way home to Coimbra, I remind myself. But is Coimbra where I was found on Christmas Day really my home, Ahmadji. Haven't I asked you this question before. Yes I have. We'll continue our talks about the problem of home when we meet again. But let me now anchor myself, to use your image, in time and place so that you can get my bearings. It's December 1510 but I do not know what day it is today. The Portuguese captured Ela on the Mandovi on the 25th of November. There is confusion everywhere, the interpreter tells me, but not yet in Bardez. Some *afaqis*, he says, have started sending their families to Bijapur.

I have just come back from a successful tax collecting expedition and am writing this letter in the house the *afaqi* has assigned to me, sitting next to a window overlooking the Chapora river. I can see, two hundred yards away to my left, the main entrance gate which I never usually use and, fifty yards below it, the boy with black curly hair and sad faraway eyes who always sits by himself on the built up rim of the well and at times says min, min, min, to the pots placed there. I wish I could talk to him but I do not know Konkani. I think this is the Well of Togetherness where you found Abdul lying wounded, and rescued him. It is a place I deliberately now avoid, I know not why.

I too want to be rescued, Ahmadji my friend. From Chapora, and from my self.

João, you actor, you have no self, my cynic tells me.

I feel the house that I live in is a prison. It stands next to a low fortress wall that runs right round the huge circular compound of the *afaqi*'s white palatial house that occupies the center. The six deserters live, each in his own house, all round the fortified wall so that the *afaqi* feels protected from outside attack. He has provided each one of them with a woman who looks after all their needs, so that they are quite happy and content. The *afaqi* was surprised to learn that I didn't want a woman. Do you want a young boy, he asked me with a knowing smile. No, no, I said, a little horrified. Food and water are left for me by a servant woman who comes when I am not there and whose face I have never seen. She wears a *burqa*.

I sit by the window and contemplate *samsāra* in the abstract like my teacher Plato who thought deeply about life and about the real, not about the meaning of his own life. Unlike you, Ahmadji, I am not driven by the need to set down my life and travels in writing. I am quite content to be by myself. I have finished with my need for women. And the *feni* liquor here is too raw for me. I do want to go home wherever that is.

I have no guard duties and am free to roam all over Anjuna, and have been temporarily provided with an interpreter who knows only Konkani and Gujarati, and who, I suspect, has to report all my movements to the *afaqi*. The *afaqi* has appointed me a kind of *shahbandar* in charge of the horse trade and traffic. Armed with my arquebus, I patrol the banks of the Chapora river up to the cove at Ihrampur, three miles away, where horses are finally landed, watered, fed and prepared for the difficult journey across the Bardez ghats to Bijapur. Wearing my *kizilbashi* red headdress with its twelve green peaks and armed with my arquebus, I present myself as a stern commanding figure who never opens his mouth and who accompanies the *afaqi* whenever a *taforea* of horses arrives here at the Chapora customs house to pay duties and taxes. The local people are in awe of me. I can see fear in their eyes. There's rebellion in the air. At times the six Portuguese deserters armed with their arquebuses march behind the *afaqi* and me to the customhouse. The land taxes of late are paid promptly now, the *afaqi* tells me.

Today I asked the *afaqi* whether he was afraid of a Portuguese attack on Chapora. No, he said, Portuguese ships are too huge to sail up this winding river. I was disappointed, I would have to somehow make my way to Ela or else to Portuguese Cochin to find a ship to get to Lisbon. I wish I knew Konkani. I asked the *afaqi* if he was worried about the Hindu landowners who at times refuse to pay taxes now.

Not any more. We *afaqis* are now well armed, he told me, and smiled.

He doesn't talk much, this *afaqi*, who speaks a kind of Persian Deccani, keeps to himself, is reluctant to answer questions, and doesn't appear to have too many friends. He and many of the Bardezi *afaqis* have sent their families with some of their possessions to Bijapur. His house is huge, a former Hindu palace, and he has a number of women servants who look after all his needs. Soldiers, some armed with *tufengs*, guard his house.

I felt sorry for him, a man with a huge house, not a home. He has a sour bitter voice as if he was born with a constricted throat. How long have you lived in Chapora, I asked him. Twenty five years, he said. Don't you feel lonely here, I wanted to ask him, but I didn't.

We had just returned from collecting land taxes from four Hindu landowners of Siolim, an adjoining village, whose tenants came armed with spades and reaping hooks, but were terrified of the strange head-dress I wore. *Kizilbash*, one of the tenants said. The *afaqi* sternly demanded payment of the overdue taxes. I didn't dismount nor did I utter a word. I placed a lead ball in my arquebus, cocked it, and fired one shot in the air to get everyone's attention. The tenants, frightened, stared at me with their mouths open. The landowner began complaining to the *afaqi* about the taxes. I waited for the gun to cool down, then I reloaded it, cocked it, took steady aim at a cock crowing defiantly on a gate a hundred yards away to the left, and shot it dead. The tenants fled. The four landowners hurried towards us with pouches heavy with coins which we poured into our saddle bags that rattled pleasantly as our horses galloped towards Chapora.

The *afaqi* was so overjoyed that something in him opened up and he began to talk continuously to me as we rode back. I didn't know you were such a good shot, he said. We should have no problems collecting taxes now, he said. The landowners are terrified and will bring the money to my door, he said. And I am expecting horseboats to arrive in a few weeks. I think I will double the customs duties on horses. We will then leave Chapora and return to Bijapur soon.

At the main entrance the guard took charge of our horses and we unloaded both our bags. I left my arquebus leaning against the gate. It was midday and I felt thirsty. The young boy who looked like a young girl was filling up the small pots kept on the built up rim of the well for thirsty travelers. Min, he would say as he filled each pot, min, min.

Ām will draw up some fresh cool water for us, the *afaqi* said, breathing rather hard and running his tongue wetly around his thick red lips.

Ahm. I thought of you immediately, Ahmadji, was that your pet name.

Ahm, is that the little one's name, the words rushed out of my mouth. The *afaqi* did not reply. He began running eagerly towards the little boy who looked quite pretty in his blue pyjamas and embroidered little vest. He couldn't have been more than six or seven years old. He had thick black curly hair and his eyes were appealingly sad.

Ahmadji, my friend, forgive me for leaping to conclusions. I put together your name and the story you wrote to me about in your letter about the woman, the baby and the bird that were brought to Chapora together, and I was so sure the little boy was your son that I rushed excitedly towards the well to ask the *afaqi*.

No, that's not his name, the *afaqi* explained, that's the name I gave him because I was told he loves eating mangoes that he sells when they are in season. I give him a ripe mango every day. Don't you know that in Konkani mangoes are called ām. The *afaqi* sounded quite irritated. The boy has not learnt to speak, he said, the only sound he utters is min, min.

So he couldn't be your son, Ahmadji. In a way I was glad. Whenever I came back from my morning rounds I would sit by my window, brood about *samsāra* and watch the little one draw up water from the eight foot deep well and pour it into the pots for thirsty travelers who would sometimes drop coins in a basin as payment. Min, min, min, he would mutter, and smile, perhaps his way of saying thank you. I couldn't look into his sad eyes. Perhaps that's why I would avoid going to the well. His sad eyes would lead me to the faraway, and I would feel profoundly moved, I know not why. A woman in a *burqa* would come to collect the coins and take him back.

Sad and disappointed because he wasn't the son I wanted to restore to you, I turned and walked back slowly to my horse and my arquebus. Then I saw the woman in a *burqa* walk through the gate. She did not greet me but walked swiftly past me. I picked up my arquebus and then I heard her scream loudly as she ran down towards the well. The child was trying to draw up water from the well, and the *afaqi*, standing behind him, was fondling him. His left hand caressed the black curls and then pinched one earlobe tightly, the right hand squeezed the child's buttocks and reached between the tiny legs to squeeze the boy's genitals. In pain and terrified of falling into the well, the child stood paralyzed, the woman in the *burqa* gave a piercing scream.

I felt outraged, horrified. I snatched up my arquebus, cocked it and took steady aim. I could have shot the *afaqi* between the eyes, I couldn't have missed, but the woman in the *burqa* came into my line of vision, and I lowered my arquebus. The *afaqi* looked at the woman, then glanced beyond her at me, and looked down. He lifted the child from the built up rim and placed him gently on the ground. Then he patted the child's head as if he was reassuring him. He spoke to the woman, I think he told her that he had saved the child, preventing him from falling into the well. I was just in time, the *afaqi* told me, he might have broken his head.

I remembered Sinbad, but I don't know what to believe, Ahmadji. I don't want the boy with his sad eyes to lose his innocence. I wish I could talk to the woman in the burqa, but I don't know Konkani. I am in a kind of shock, Ahmadji. I will write again. I have to rush this letter to the banyan tree before the mail carrier leaves.

Jan Mirza

I thanked the *vaid* for the message and for the snakeroot remedy from Java.

He looked into my eyes and paused, no jaundice, he said, that unusual smell your body had has gone, then he smiled at me, looking at the *mundu* I was wearing.

The *mundu* is very comfortable, I told him, remembering how hot and sticky it had been in the villages of the interior and how I quickly got accustomed to the comfort of the wraparound *mundu* and to the sad restful peace I experienced there. An odd kind of peace. I treated my patients from very early in the morning because I wanted to have time at night to write, but by night I would feel absolutely exhausted and I just wanted to stop, and brood and sleep, but the pain and the suffering, and then the love and gratefulness in the eyes of the villagers would make me go on right into the early morning, and I felt it wouldn't be right to brood about my own despair. It was a quiet, odd peace.

It is I who have to thank you, Ahmad *hakim*, the *vaid* said. The doctors now order many expensive drugs for the hospital from my shop, especially *hashish* to calm down patients in pain. My friend, Brother Pedro, bought a barrel of special wine made of Persian grapes from my cousin brother. For a special mass in the new church they have built in Portuguese Cochin to celebrate the conquest of Goa. You will find Brother Pedro there.

The news about Goa didn't shock me. It was an upsurge in the rise to power of the Portuguese. *Samsāra*, I said to myself, so that was why Albuquerque sent Francisco and me with Timmaya to survey Goa.

I turned to go.

Brother Pedro doesn't like *mundus*, he added.

I changed into my *hakim* clothes at the back of his shop.

Portuguese Cochin looked deserted. Eager for piracy and plunder, almost all the Portuguese, except for the royal factors, the sick and the wounded, must have joined Albuquerque's expedition to Suez and the Red Sea. The newly built chapel stood out white in the dazzling sunlight, a contrast to the red brown laterite houses with their palm covered roofs. It was sturdy, rectangular, the surface of its laterite walls had been plastered and then painted over with a white limestone mixture. The low pitched roof was covered with Mangalore tiles. A square tower from which hung a bell stood guard to the left of the entrance.

I shut my eyes tight before entering the empty chapel. When I opened them in the semi darkness inside, I could vaguely see someone struggling with a tall ladder in one hand and a framed picture in the other. A servant boy, I thought, and went to help him.

Holy Mother of God, a miracle, a voice boomed at me.

I was startled. The voice sprang out of a dwarf even shorter than the one I had seen on the Diu stage.

Our Lady of Sorrows has sent you, Ahmad hakim, and at just the right time.

Help me with this, he shouted, I am Brother Pedro. Frei Louro told me all about you, all about your papers which are safe in my keeping, and about what a good man you are. Ahmad hakim may be our very first genuine convert, I told the Frei. I was right, Ahmad hakim. Our Lady has summoned you to help me set up her picture in that niche up there on the wall for those other converts who cannot read or write.

I was puzzled and I almost burst our laughing at the thought of myself as a convert and as a messenger, but I controlled myself and placed the ladder next to the small niche and held it while Brother Pedro pulled himself up carefully, painfully, one step at a time. One or two steps of the ladder were loose.

Hand me that picture of Our Lady, he bellowed down to me. Take care, its glass has cracked.

I did. I felt sorry for him. He couldn't help shouting, must have been born with that overpowering voice.

He took a long time adjusting the picture frame in the niche, leaning to the left of the ladder, then to the right, turning and staring at the two high windows, one light green, the other light blue, on the opposite wall.

Stand a little further back, Ahmad hakim, he yelled to me, so that Our Lady can cast her eyes of compassion on you and pierce your infidel soul.

I strongly resented those words but kept quiet. He was ignorant, and he had my papers.

I don't know, I said, it's quite dark in this chapel. I can't see anything.

Ah, he snorted. I told the builder of this fortress chapel to set those two windows quite high, the green glass window and next to it the blue one, and I then told him where exactly to set the niche in the wall, do you know why.

He bent down and tried to whisper, but his voice sounded hoarse.

To shock *gentios.* into bowing down before our Lady and to make them believe in Our Holy Mother the Church. Most of them are low caste illiterate fishermen. For them words simply will not work, especially Portuguese words. I told them to come to the chapel door when the noon bell sounds, when the sunlight will stream through the windows and hit the cracked glass. Arrows of light reflected back from Our Lady in the niche will dazzle them. They will then prostrate themselves and make the sign of the cross that I taught them. That's the only way, Ahmad hakim, to convert such people.

He climbed down the ladder slowly, hesitatingly, afraid he might fall.

I was appalled. Perhaps all established religions resort to such tricks. In Diu João and I sometimes would talk about the tricks used by Hindu temple priests and Muslim fakirs and their accomplices to convince groups of people that their religion was the true one because it had endowed them with magical powers. What is true belief, João had asked once, but had never provided me with an answer.

Brother Pedro came up to me.

But that's not the way for you. I'll get a candle so that you can look at the picture and pray to Our Lady.

I smiled cynically to myself and looked up at the dark niche with my skeptical eyes.

And suddenly I remembered when it all began and where. It began when I was a boy, in Julfar. I remembered the niche in the Julfar mosque my father would take me for prayers after my mother died suddenly one night. They buried her the next day. I wasn't allowed to see her face. That's the *mihrab*, my father told me, that directs the congregation Meccawards. to pray. I would run and hold his hand and go eagerly with him to the mosque, has she gone to Mecca, will she come back with some incense, I would ask, when will she return, when, when. After a time I lost hope, I refused to go to the mosque, especially when my father was out at sea, and I was left to myself, I stopped asking when. I would wander alone on the seashore staring at the rise and fall of the waves. Why, oh why, I began to ask the stars above but I never did get an answer.

When at twelve or thirteen I was taken to sea to learn piloting, I asked my father how the exact direction of Mecca was determined at sea so that people on the ship could say their noontime prayers. He showed me how, but his answers did not satisfy me. What if a sudden storm arises, I asked, what if it isn't the right direction. God is great, my son, you have to have faith, my father would say. His answers did not satisfy me. That's when I stopped asking him questions. I began to withdraw into myself, and look up and ask why, oh why, but never could I find an answer. I began to read poetry.

Brother Pedro came back, lit the candle and placed it in the candlestick which had two tiny holes for sticks of incense.

The *vaid* offered this sandalwood candlestick and these sticks of incense, Brother Pedro said, as gifts for the new chapel. Why don't you place it in the niche, he shouted, handing me the candlestick, and let our Blessed Lady cast her sorrowful eyes on you.

The fragrance of sandalwood and incense mingled, and stirred memories within me, and a silent *mantra*. I remembered the words *darshan* and *nazar* and I felt a stab of panic. I wanted to run out of the chapel to avoid having to meet the gaze of those sorrowful eyes.

I'll hold the ladder, Brother Pedro shouted.

I mounted the first two steps keeping my eyes firmly down, placed my foot on the third step, and was holding the candlestick high when my foot slipped and a step broke and I had to look up to try to hold on to the niche and the candlelight made those eyes meet mine and I collapsed on to the floor.

I must have lost consciousness then.

When I came to, I found myself stretched out on Frei Louro's pallet in the hospital chapel that was no longer a hospital chapel. Beyond the lit candle I could see someone perched on the bed I used to sleep on, one of my former patients. He was fast asleep, snoring. I tried to sit up but could not. A pain in my ankle made me cry out. There was a strong medicine smell everywhere.

You sprained your ankle when you fell from the ladder, my former patient said. Brother Pedro caught you just in time or you would have broken your leg. It was he who carried you on his back all the way to this place. I have applied some liniment the doctor gave me to your ankle. He said you will feel no pain tomorrow. I have to go back to the hospital now, *senhor* hakim.

I ate some of the food that had been placed on the former altar table for me, then I hunted all around for my papers but could only find some blank sheets of paper on which I began to write down all that had happened to me that day. My hakim was right. I need to write down things. Writing for me now clarifies and orders the past so that I can make sense of it.

I hear the faraway midnight sound of the chapel bell and I feel, not a stab of panic but the turmoil that began when those sad eyes pierced mine and I collapsed, unconscious, with the candlestick, on to the chapel floor. Let me now set down what must have, I think, fused together at that exact moment. The incense and the sandalwood mingled to release the faint smell of a faraway love. I couldn't bring myself to chant the prayersong *mantra*, but I knew they were the eyes of *Mater Misericordiae*, the mother with a child who carried the huge black cross, the woman who had shed a tear for Usha, the woman to whom Usha had prayed without using words to save my life, more than ten long years ago, when we were on board Paulo da Gama's ship.

I had brought that same picture out of our cabin to examine it in the fierce sunlight. It wasn't a work of art, it had been crudely painted. The woman's face had been framed with a garish purple headband, the eight year old boy had the muscular forearm of an adult, his tiny feet had red nail holes, and a crown of thorns was perched on his head. It was the unutterable anguish in the mother's eyes that had caught my attention.

Yes, it was the very same picture. I was the very same person with the skeptical eyes. I hadn't changed. Why then did those eyes hit me so deeply. No, no, Brother Pedro, I don't believe in miracles, I am not religious, I still do not believe in prayer. And yet, somehow, that picture had managed to survive for over ten long years. Had it traveled all the way to Lisbon and back. It had survived Brother Paulo's death in faraway Portugal. Does it want to tell me something. An omen perhaps it is, about other survivors, somehow, somewhere.

No, no, that's impossible.

Let me not brood about this.

I shall stop writing and blow out the candle.

I fell into a deep sleep and woke up when I heard the distant chapel bell summoning the Portuguese to morning mass. I felt a strange peace.

On the altar table was a thick packet from Frei Louro. Brother Pedro must have come and left it there.

Saint Catherine's chapel
  Late December, 1510
  Ela, GOA
  I, Frei Louro, am writing this account

To Ahmadji in Cochin, via Brother Pedro, Chapel of Our Lady of Sorrows

I wanted to get someone to write this letter to you because it is difficult for me to write, as you know, and there is no priest here in Goa, not even my cousin João who was a seminarian and would have been able to understand the strange things I need to set down. I still remember the letter you wrote for me to my brother priests in Loreto. It was a clear presentation of our Franciscan dream when, full of faith, and hungry for martyrdom, our small band set out on our mission of salvation to conquer the world for Our Lord Jesus Christ. You set down clearly what happened at Socotra, my discussions with Albuquerque, my doubts, my protests, and his insistence on the use of violence and force. We had many talks, Albuquerque and I, and I thought I would be able to influence him, for basically he is a good man and a devout Catholic. And I had hoped his ship of state could sail peacefully along with our ship of faith.

But after the second conquest of Goa my hopes were shattered.

Albuquerque has changed completely, Ahmadji, he is not what he was. I don't know why even though I know the exact moment when the change happened. He has violent outbursts of temper now, the slightest disobedience infuriates him. The captains say Albuquerque has an ungovernable temper, according to Francisco, and is unfit to be a governor. Some say India is in greater peril from Albuquerque than from the Turks.

Ahmadji, I had to stop writing to hear some confessions.

I continue writing. Perhaps what I am writing is not a letter, but a Diário, a kind of confession made to you, Ahmadji.

I am sitting here in the chapel that Albuquerque built after his victory to honor St. Catherine, brooding about many things, weary of listening to Albuquerque's dreams of power and conquest, debating with myself as to whether I should give up the Franciscan dream, throw up my hands in despair, and return to Lisbon.

What should I do, Ahmadji.

But how can I expect you advise me when you don't know all that has happened since you left Cochin with Padre Antão many months ago. As father confessor and confidant to an Albuquerque deeply wounded in many ways after the Marshall's disastrous retreat from Calicut, I and Francisco Rodrigues knew about Albuquerque's plans for the capture of Goa but couldn't reveal them to you then because we were bound to secrecy. Now that it is all over, let me tell you what happened in my own erratic way.

Perhaps it will allow me to understand my own despair, this *diário*.

Or perhaps, you will then also be able to understand it, this my despair, and advise me.

An interruption, a noise at the back. They are unloading basalt blocks from a bullock cart to build an extension to this chapel. These are stones from a mosque that was demolished outside Ela city, the architect tells me. Such stones are not available in Goa.

Francisco and I accompanied Albuquerque on his flagship, the *Frol de la Mar*, at the head of an armada of 20 ships, 2 galleys and 1200 fighting men. Everyone was in a state of feverish excitement, for they thought it would be a glorious expedition to the Red Sea for piracy and plunder. Timmaya met us at the port of Mirjan, by chance everyone thought, but really the meeting was planned by Albuquerque to deliberately mislead his captains. Timmaya told them that all the Turushka troops in Goa had been summoned to Bijapur to put down the rebellions that broke out after the Sabaio's death. Goa was completely undefended, Timmaya pointed out. The wily Albuquerque deliberately kept silent during the discussion, only mentioning the fact that Goa was defended by a small force of Muslim inhabitants. It was unanimously decided that the whole armada would sail to Goa to capture and plunder the island instead of going to Suez.

We first bombarded and captured the Ponje palace fortress and then Ela surrendered peacefully without a shot being fired. All rejoiced when Albuquerque made his triumphal entry through the Sabaio's arch into Goa on March 1st, 1509, and was installed on a throne plated with gold by Goan goldsmiths, and studded with precious stones. Albuquerque wore a simple blue velvet cap on his head. The Adil Shahi captain and eight leading Muslim citizens presented him with the keys of the city. A large Muslim crowd gathered in the public square in front of the Adil Shahi palace and hailed him as Albuquerque the Great.

Albuquerque did listen to my advice as his father confessor, and generously offered peace and friendship to all the peoples of Goa, especially to the Muslims of the city. They are our brothers, I told him. He promised them freedom of worship. There would be no religious persecution, he announced. Mosques and temples would not be destroyed. Taxes were reduced and a mint would be established for new coinage in order to foster trade. Albuquerque was overjoyed, he never expected the Goan Muslims to be such loyal subjects. Muslims are our brothers, he proclaimed, and promised to inaugurate an era of peace. I too rejoiced, our Franciscan dream would be realized.

A month and a half later, to my horror, Albuquerque changed, he changed into Albuquerque the avenger when the Muslims of Goa who had taken an oath on the Qu'ran and had sworn total loyalty to the flag of Portugal conspired with the attacking army of the Hidalcão that had marched down the ghats from Bijapur to drive out the Portuguese. The rebels threw open some of the gates of the city, guided the Bijapuri cavalry in the middle of the night to the Passo Seco, and treacherously attacked the few Portuguese soldiers that guarded the river crossings. A few Hindus, afraid of antagonizing the Muslims of Ela, joined in the Bijapuri attack which was well timed.

Our Portuguese forces were ill prepared for the attack. Many suffered from fevers because the swamps near the city were unhealthy. Albuquerque had no time or stones to repair Ela's fortress walls of packed earth, and the fury of the early monsoon made it impossible for our ships to cross the bar. It was a complete disaster. We took to our ships, Ahmadji, but the ships could not clear the bar, and we rode out the monsoon, hungry and defenseless, our ships pitching helplessly in the Mandovi midstream in front of the Ponje palace fortress, our gunpowder damp, our guns coated with monsoon rust. We abandoned Goa in the middle of August when the fury of the monsoon subsided and our ships were at last able to cross the bar and sail towards Kannanur.

I was kept busy looking after the sick and consoling the dying.

But he came back. Albuquerque came back as a ruthless avenger. He could not bear the intolerable insult to Portugal. After all, the Muslims had sworn total loyalty to him as the embodiment of Portugal. He came back having commandeered the larger swifter naos and carracks that had recently arrived from Lisbon on the way to Melaka and were equipped with the newest cannon of cast bronze and were handled by well trained German and Flemish artillerymen, the *bombardeiros do mar*, powerful short cannon that could be fired through gun ports in the hull, guns against which the Mamluk galleys with their huge prow guns stood no chance at all.

On November 25, 1510, the feast day of Saint Catherine, Ela was stormed and taken. All Muslims in the city were slaughtered. Hindus whose lands had been taken over by the *afaqis* took part in the work of butchery all over Goa island, killing the escaping Muslims. The Turushka soldiers fled towards the mainland. Hundreds of soldiers and cavalrymen were killed. Albuquerque refused to listen when I urged him to show mercy to all the people of Goa. Why not convert them and make them all Christians.

Mercy to the *gentios*, those cowardly Hindus, yes, Albuquerque the avenger said. To the Muslims, never. We Portuguese must not forget what happened in the past, we need to take revenge. The Muslims, treacherous infidels, can never be trusted, they have to be exterminated.

How, I asked him, how can you get rid of people who are as countless, as Omar the pilot said in Socotra, as the sands on the seashore.

I don't know yet, Albuquerque said, but we now have the power to dominate the high seas, we have swift towering ships and powerful guns that can attack and get rid of these vermin in their own lairs, the Red Sea and the Persian Gulf.

How, I asked him.

Albuquerque suddenly became like one possessed. He looked at me with his black eyes, their centers a fiery red, and he kept staring beyond me without answering my question. That, Ahmadji, was the exact moment when, I was sure, he changed again. No longer was he just Albuquerque the avenger, he became Albuquerque the *Terribil*, the red eyed incarnation, so to speak, of Portuguese power, a man not just possessed but driven by some inner force. He had completely forgotten why we Portuguese had come to this part of the world.

The secretaries, terribly agitated, came to consult with me. After all, I was Albuquerque's father confessor. Albuquerque had his office set up in the Sabaio's former palace. There he behaved erratically, he would suddenly break off in the middle of a sentence while dictating a letter, they told me, he would talk to himself, wave his arms about, raise his right hand, an imperial gesture, toss out names like Alexander the Great, and his voice, they said, became deeper, as if it sprang from that inner force. He would shout loudly at his captains, something he had never done before, ordering them to refit their ships and have the sails repaired. Murderer, I overheard the captains say, grinding their teeth with rage. Hail Duke of Goa, they would mutter about him behind his back. A malicious rumor persisted that Albuquerque had secretly ascended the Sabaio's throne one night and proclaimed himself Caesar of the oceansea.

One of the secretaries secretly showed me a letter Albuquerque had dictated. in early December 1510, a letter to King Manuel informing the king that he had cleansed Goa of Muslims and liberated Goa from tyranny.

Sire, I burned the city and put everyone to the sword and for four days your men shed blood continuously. No matter where we found them, we did not spare the life of a single Muslim. We filled the mosques with them and then set them on fire. The peasants and the Hindu priests I ordered to be spared. We found that six thousand Muslim souls, male and female were dead, *Sire*, and many of their foot soldiers and archers had died. It was a very great deed, *Sire*, well fought and well accomplished. Apart from Goa being so great and important a place, until then no revenge had been taken for the treachery and wickedness of the Muslims towards Your Highness and your people.

I remain determined, *Sire*, not to allow a single Muslim to live in Goa nor enter the city, but only Hindus.

I am trying my best to understand the enigma that is Albuquerque who keeps changing in front of my very eyes. And I keep brooding about the devastating effect of power, it maddens both the conqueror and the conquered. I wonder whether one has to ruthlessly conquer a land in order to convert its people to Christianity.

What shall I do, Ahmadji.

Albuquerque talks to Francisco at times about his dreams of power and glory, but is now reluctant to talk to me. Actually, he has withdrawn into himself, is reluctant to confide in anyone. I have enemies everywhere, Albuquerque says.

These be military matters, Albuquerque tells me, matters that you, Frei Louro, cannot understand.

Sometimes he raves and rants, to use his secretary's phrase, about things that make no sense to me, tossing out fragments of comment and observation that I simply do not understand.

I do not understand Albuquerque, Ahmadji.

I wonder if I should ask his doctor to give him some *hashish*, the drug you, Ahmadji, told me about, to calm him down.

I need *hashish* too, Ahmadji. I am confused. In Socotra, we thought conversion would easily direct non believers to the truth. We didn't realize that they would find it difficult to discard the beliefs they were brought up on. The Portuguese architect, who recently placed a baptismal font in the chapel, was shocked to discover Hindu women, standing in front of the font, folding their hands and bowing their heads. The base of the font, he discovered, was a stone statue of a Hindu goddess with bare breasts which they were worshipping.

Christmas Day, 1510

At times, when or perhaps just because he finds no one else to talk to in his office, Albuquerque feels impelled to talk to me. In disorderly fragments that make no sense to me. I did suggest to Francisco that some *hashish* should be infused in the strong black coffee from Brazil that Albuquerque always drinks now in the morning. I don't know whether Francisco took my suggestion.

Patience, Frei Louro, Albuquerque tells me, pacing up and down his office, going occasionally to the window to gaze at the Mandovi streaming towards the open sea.

As a servant of the Church and as a man of peace, you find it difficult to understand the things of this world even though you are my father confessor. Listen, Frei Louro, listen very carefully.

The whole world is on the move and we, Portuguese, have to move with it.

Albuquerque paused for a long while. His voice sounded like an echo, a little pompous, as if it didn't quite belong to him.

We live today, we Portuguese, Albuquerque told me, poised on the turning point of history.

Albuquerque went again to the window and stared at the Mandovi. He was in a faraway mood that day. His voice came to my ears as if from a great distance.

I heard those two statements a long time ago, he said, when I was a ten year old page at the court of King Afonso. I was impressed, but they didn't make any sense to me, then, those words, that sprang from the lips of my history teacher who was telling our class about the turmoil raging all over Europe and *al Andalus* with our Portugal poised aloof on Europe's south western tip. Our beloved Portugal with its handful of people, has been pushed to the very end of Europe, our teacher told us, looking out of the classroom window. It is isolated now, alas, the poorest country in Europe.

The other students did not pay any attention to what he said. I was impressed, I didn't know why. He is almost blind, the other students said.

We have driven the Moors out of Portugal, our teacher said. Now we have to hurl ourselves beyond the edge of our *terra*. You all know what *terra* means. Now it will be *thalassa*, he continued, there is nowhere else to go.

I walked up to the window after class to ask him what *Thalassa* meant even though I knew he never ever answered questions. He pretends to be deaf, the students said

It is a Greek word. You will come to understand such things later, my teacher said.

Then our teacher added, those who are thickly involved in the processes of history are incapable of understanding its meaning and direction. Knowledge needs distance.

Here, now, in Goa, watching time itself streaming remorselessly by, in front of me, Frei Louro, Albuquerque pointed to the Mandovi in front of us, I sense that my teacher was staring through that classroom window at our Portuguese future.

One day, I was eleven years old at the time and eager to serve in the Moroccan campaigns, I stopped my teacher in the cathedral aisle, and announced quite proudly that I would leave shortly for Morocco and that I wanted to be a commander of men and lead my Portugal to greatness and glory.

My history teacher paused for a long time, then he bent down and stared hard into my eyes, you'll need to understand the meaning of the Moorish *conquista* and the Portuguese *reconquista* and the terrible problems of absolute power, he said, its blindness, its piercing emptiness. When you are a commander, remember that only divine power is absolute because it has complete knowledge.

He walked on, stopped abruptly, then turning, said to me, beware of revenge, revenge breeds only revenge.

I don't even know your name, he told me. I have to say my prayers now. He was a canon of the cathedral.

A month later, in the evening darkness of the cathedral, after the service of *tenebrae*, he stopped me and said, one has to be both detached and involved, one has to know first, then act. Beware. Never exercise absolute power as an act of revenge, it corrupts the soul of the avenger.

I never talked to him again, Frei Louro. He died suddenly one night and was buried the next day.

Albuquerque remained silent for a very long time. I thought he wanted me to leave.

Stay, Albuquerque said suddenly, stay Frei Louro, as I walked to the door. Your presence I find somehow quietening. As a priest, you know how to listen. Bear with me. He paused again. The questions you ask are always simple, you ask how, why, but like dagger thrusts, those words pierce deep into my past.

I did exercise absolute power in Socotra, as you know, Frei Louro. Here, in Goa, I was so outraged by their treachery that I ordered the Muslims butchered and ruthlessly massacred. For a while I was deliriously overjoyed, I saw myself as Caesar, the most powerful ruler of the whole wide world.

One day, suddenly, I felt blind and empty. And I thought in a flash of the words of my history teacher. I don't remember his name or his face, Frei Louro, but his strange words, which I did not understand at all at the time, now are beginning to make sense. Not absolute sense, Frei Louro, for his thoughts were disconnected, I had to put them together. My teacher was in his own way trying to prepare me for the Portuguese future. I am confused, Frei Louro. Let me try to talk about it to you. No, no, this is not a confession. Let me talk about my confusion to you. Then perhaps things will become clear and both of us will understand.

It was in Socotra that I first became aware of the problems of exercising power. I did talk to you about them, Frei Louro, but perhaps you were too preoccupied with your own problem, that of converting the Socotrans to Christianity. In the Cannanore jail, where I was flung by order of Viceroy Francisco de Almeida who, belonging as he did to the outmoded world of chivalric valor, used power tactics that failed miserably in the Indian Ocean, that I brooded over my problems that had become acute. Especially after I was rescued by the headstrong Marshal Coutinho who brought with him the letter appointing me not Viceroy, a title I deserved, but a lesser one, Captain General and Governor of India. The Marshal was totally blind to the real situation. You know what happened, Frei Louro.

I felt humiliated, torn apart, this way and that, by those commanders of limited vision who were blind or were blinded by what they saw in this vast new world. They did not understand this huge world spread around the ocean sea, and they did not know how to act in it. No need to tell you, Frei Louro, about the irritating behavior of the king's trading factors who have established themselves comfortably in Cochin, a place they now consider home, especially António Reál for whom all else except Cochin is wind, and who send back false reports and complaints about me and my actions to Lisbon.

Why should I bother about the stings of gnats and mosquitoes.

Albuquerque continued his story the next day.

What troubled me most and what still troubles me are the erratic poli-
cies of my faraway king, King Manuel, who, unsure of himself and of his
legitimacy, is afraid of relinquishing too much power to the commanders
he appoints. He has been woefully misled by ignorant advisers like Dom
Diego Lobo, the Baron of Alvito, for whom power translates into corsair
activity and the taking of prizes. King Manoel listens to the advice of different members of his royal council, men who have never traveled outside
Portugal and who are incapable of building a fortress or going to sea. They
don't realize that the situation in this part of the world keeps constantly
changing. That's why the king's commands to me are so confusing and
contradictory.

Take Aden, our king orders me in a letter that takes six months to get
from Lisbon to India. He knows it is the key to the Red Sea but he does
not know what I now know that Aden is well protected by mountain walls
that run down to the sea. We lack men and guns and ships, and long ladders, to take it.

Take Socotra, the king orders me next, not realizing how difficult it is
to get food and shelter there on that rocky island, unaware that contrary
winds and currents make Suk a hazardous base for the whole fleet to take
shelter in.

Take Anjediva, a minor fortified port near the west coast of India,
scrub land mostly, which we Portuguese took with great difficulty and
used as a watering place, then had to abandon for it proved to be a shallow roadstead.

A long silence. Albuquerque keeps pacing up and down his office,
staring into my face but not seeing me, trying to concentrate on his faraway plans.

Did you know, Frei Louro, that the King of France refers to Dom Manuel as the Grocer King. Albuquerque says this in a low voice.

Silence.

Destroy Calicut, the king orders the Marshal who rushed blindly to
board his ships to attack unfortified Calicut without realizing that it was
a mere roadstead not a port, and without drawing up a plan of attack.
You know what happened, Frei Louro. They brought back his corpse on a
stretcher instead of the gold and silver doors of the Samorin's palace that
he wanted to carry back with him to Lisbon.

Our king receives reports from António Reál and his factors who complain about what a unhealthy place Goa is, and advise him not to abandon
Cannanore and Cochin because of the pepper and dried ginger that can be
loaded there These men, like the Baron of Alvito, cannot see beyond their
noses. Little do they realize that we would be utterly dependent on the

goodwill of the rajas of the two ports if we hadn't taken Goa. Little do they know about the vast wealth and trade of India.

Just to teach Bijapur a lesson, take Goa, the king commands in the letter the Marshal gave me, without realizing Goa's strategic importance as an independent permanent base for our ships here on the west coast of India.

All the glorious wealth of Ind can now be ours, Frei Louro, not just a few cargo loads of pepper and ginger from Malabar and cinnamon from Ceylon, Albuquerque proclaimed as he walked up to the window and stared a long time at the Mandovi. I have to plan my strategies carefully, after collecting all the information I need about this new world that we have entered. Perhaps I will talk to you about my plans after I draw them up, I do need to talk to you and Francisco, there is no one else I can trust.

A long silence.

Our king had his impossible dreams, too, Frei Louro. He dreamt of an alliance with the mythical Preste João who would attack the Mamluks in the rear, he believed it would then be easy to capture Jerusalem, he even wanted to use workers from Madeira to divert the waters of the Nile and turn Egypt into a desert. The king now knows that all three dreams have to be abandoned.

Kings may come and kings may go, Frei Louro. But I have to realize my dream of our Portugal as an empire, as the *Estado da India*, that our king established in 1505.

Alas, Frei Louro, the ships the king sends to India are too few and are ill equipped and lack men and guns that can allow us to penetrate that Islamic lake, the Red Sea.

The king, who has had to rely on Italian investors and German merchant financiers, is reluctant to risk all the money that has been made by the sale of pepper and spices, Frei Louro, He is not sure whether to spend it on the fighting in Morocco or on the Indian enterprise. It is a problem for Portugal, Frei Louro. We Portuguese have the power. But the *Estado* needs money. We cannot spend it fighting the Muslims on the Bahr-i-Hind.

A long silence.

How many Muslims and *gentios* do you think, Frei Louro, there are in this part of the world.

The question shocked me into an uncomfortable silence. I thought of our Franciscan dream that brought us here.

Albuquerque's telling of his story to me, Ahmadji, is an act of confession for him, not a religious but a healing act.

But my head, Ahmadji, my head began to spin, how could it retain all these questions and fragments of information tossed out by this dreamer

of impossible dreams, this troubled visionary. A long time ago it was rumored that Albuquerque wanted to capture Mecca and exchange it for
Jerusalem.

No more, Albuquerque says suddenly, going to the window overlooking the Mandovi, send everyone out of the office. I have the glimmerings
of a plan.

There was no one else in the office except the two of us.

I was not able to see or talk to Albuquerque for the next two or three
weeks, Ahmadji. His waiting rooms, there were two of them, were always
crowded with people who came early in the morning wanting to meet
and talk with the governor, all kinds of people, all dressed in colorful costumes, speaking different languages. Many were distinguished and well
dressed visitors and envoys from abroad, welcomed and ushered into the
office by the chief secretary who informed me that Albuquerque had giv-
en strict orders not to admit anyone without his permission. Albuquerque
worked furiously, making use of twelve secretaries, dictating letters and
notes even on horseback when he went out to examine the defenses of Ela
which were being repaired. No one, the secretaries told me, except a few
linguas, we didn't have too many, no captains, and especially no factors
could be let into his office.

I sat patiently in the waiting room outside his office but Albuquerque
did not send for me.

Once it had become a Portuguese possession, Goa came to be regarded
as the center of the Bahr-i-Hind and the imperial seat of Portuguese power. Delegations and embassies streamed into Goa with offers of friendship
and with offerings of sites to the Portuguese to establish factories and invitations to establish fortresses The Sultan of Gujarat offered a site at Gogha
for a trading port. The Raja of Vijayanagara and the Sultan of Bijapur sent
envoys with rich gifts of golden ornaments and jewels. Both of them offered diamonds for all the horses landed in Goa. The Raja of Bankapur
dispatched four boxes of ornamental saddlery along with quilted tunics of
brocade and Mecca velvet for the Portuguese cavalry. Shah Ismail of Persia
sent ambassadors to Goa instead of sending them to Bijapur. Malik Aiyaz
sent a five year old rhinoceros together with its own trainer, Hussein. It
was a present for the King of Portugal to be sent to Lisbon.

All offerings had to be deposited in front of the throne on which the
royal shield of Portugal had been placed for everyone to bow in homage.
After which the delegations were escorted by a secretary to the office of
Albuquerque who welcomed them and spent some time talking to them,
after which presents were offered. I was struck by the fact that Albuquerque
spent a great deal of time talking with people who were not ambassadors

or delegates or envoys. He spent hours talking with caulkers and gunners, with mast makers and sail menders and people who belonged to the different trades. He spent days talking to traders and pilots. He wanted information about spices and trade routes. He let it be known through his secretaries that all sea pilots were welcome and that they would be paid generously for sea maps with trade routes marked on them. He wanted answers to many questions that I found strange, answers to questions about various spices and drugs and the timings of the monsoons that he made the secretaries take down carefully, and that he read, they told me, after midnight and slept for only four hours.

It was three weeks later when Francisco Rodrigues used the voice of despair in talking to me about Melaka, I did not know then where Melaka was, and about Albuquerque's Melaka scheme, that I myself fell into total despair.

Francisco felt even more disturbed than the secretaries of Albuquerque. He was actually in a state of near panic or he would never have talked to me about the weaknesses of his hero.

I have no one else to turn to, Frei Louro, Francisco told me. I cannot talk to Albuquerque's cousins and nephews who are the only ones our captain sometimes consults about his plans, or to Francesco Corbinelli, that Italian whom he has appointed factor of Goa.

Do you think our Governor, Francisco began suddenly, has become

He paused.

Come with me, Frei Louro, he said.

He took me through some narrow passages of the Sabaio's palace to a hidden well guarded room at the very end of a long winding corridor. The captain of the guards let us in. It was a spacious corner room with five large windows that let in the bright sunlight. A stately low semicircular chair had been placed like an anchor in the middle of the room.

Look, said Francisco,

I looked through the window at the silver blue Mandovi.

No, no, the wall, Francisco said. I turned and looked, and stood aghast confronting the wall.

There, before my eyes, stretching from one end of the huge wall to the other, like a wall painting in the Coimbra cathedral, was an immense map of the whole wide world.

There, there, Frei Louro, Francisco said, his right hand sweeping in an arc from the left to the right. That's the whole world that God has created and that we Portuguese have discovered in all its vastness and glory, a world that I, the royal cartographer, have put together from all the maps and charts of our voyagers to create another *Almagest* for Senhor Albuquerque. Do you know what the word means, Frei Louro.

No, I said.

It's the Arabic word for the greatest, used formerly for Ptolemy's work.

Genesis, I cried out, and was in despair, I knew not why.

Francisco sat down in the chair and was silent for a long time, but rather restless, staring at the map, shaking his head from side to side, lost perhaps, I thought, in admiration of the *Almagest* he had created for his commander. I too stared at the wall for a very long time trying to understand the huge map. It was totally confusing. I felt lost in this huge new world. I was no cartographer. I couldn't read the place names, many of them in black, a few in red. There were spiders' webs, and crisscross lines, and circles with strange arrows set on open spaces of blue which must have been the blue sea.

This wasn't the *geographica sacra* I had been shown in the seminary. I looked for Jerusalem, the center of the world, according to the *mappa mundi*, that statement of divine power over the world. I looked for the vertical line of demarcation that the Pope had drawn carving up the whole world between Portugal and Spain. But they weren't on this map.

All maps today are *sigilo*, Francisco told me, they have to be kept secret and not shown to anyone, for they are statements of royal power that proclaim ownership of new worlds discovered and to be discovered. Governor Albuquerque has given strict orders that anyone disobeying his orders would be flung into the *tronco*.

Francisco paused a long time.

I was highly reluctant to bring you here to this map room, Frei Louro, but I did, because you are his father confessor and I had to ask you a question I could ask no one else, a question that has tormented me for over a week.

Has Governor Albuquerque gone mad. The question burst out of him.

Bewildered, I stared at Francisco.

No, no, no, burst out of me. Governor Albuquerque is not mad. He is a dreamer of dreams, a visionary.

But this mad visionary will lead all our ships and all our men to total disaster.

How, I asked. I do not understand. He loves his Portugal.

Let me show you, said Francisco. Here we are.

He stood up, took me up to the map, and showed me where Goa was, the name was written in red.

Where is Portugal, I asked.

Here, he said, walking to the left to point to tiny Portugal perched precariously on the south west edge of Europe just above elephantlike

Africa. I could not believe my eyes, but I kept silent. I was no cartographer. Francisco could tell I was both shocked and puzzled.

Where is Socotra, I asked him.

There, he said, pointing to an island. And with a sinking feeling I remembered the site of our failure, the rocky island where we Franciscans made our first attempt to convert the Socotrans and failed miserably.

Francisco went on to point to the Red Sea and Aden, to the Persian Gulf and Hormuz, and to Diu in India. I asked him where Surat and Champaner were but he had never heard of these places. His forefinger then slid down the west coast of India, pointing out Cannanore, Calicut, and Cochin, resting finally on Ceylon. That's where cinnamon comes from, he told me.

Francisco went back and sat on the chair, facing the wall.

Frei Louro, he said, I am trying to calm myself down before I ask you that terrible question I do not want to ask about my hero, Is Albuquerque mad.

He asked the question softly, without raising his voice. Let me explain, he continued.

What I have shown you, on the left half of this map, is the spread of the world that we Portuguese are masters of with our huge ships and our powerful guns. It is a vast world, Frei Louro, the Bahr-i-Hind.

How many people inhabit this vast world, I asked Francisco. I didn't ask him the question that tormented me, would a handful of Franciscans be able to convert this vast world to Christianity. Instead I asked, what is the distance between Lisbon and Goa.

I couldn't tell you, Francisco said. Distance in the world of the sea is measured in time and not in miles. It takes four to six months to travel from Lisbon to Goa. An Arab pilot once calculated for me the distance from the Red Sea to Melaka in *zam*. It was about 3000 sea miles, perhaps he was wrong.

Where is Melaka, I asked, and he walked to the right and pointed to a place name in red at the extreme right corner of the map. There, he said, that's the place Albuquerque now wants to attack and conquer. He doesn't realize what that will involve. We will have to sail beyond the Bahr-i-Hind, through unknown and perilous seas with all our guns and our men and all our ships. The distance from Goa to Melaka, it seems to me, is greater than that between the Red Sea and Goa. It will be a total disaster for Portugal.

Suddenly the door was flung open and in strode the Governor accompanied by three people all dressed in flowing white shirts.

Francisco, Albuquerque shouted, I want you to show Abala and these traders from Nina Chatu your map of Melaka. Then he saw me, and stopped.

Francisco, the name exploded out of Albuquerque's mouth.

Sigilo, Albuquerque shouted.

Francisco wanted to say something, but Albuquerque shouted for the captain of the guards, take this man to the *tronco*.

I stepped forward.

No, no, Frei Louro. Don't explain anything. Francisco disobeyed my commands. I will talk to you later.

One of the guards led me out.

It took me a long time, Ahmadji, to come to know the plans of Albuquerque which, according to Francisco, he himself never wrote down but dictated to his secretaries to be sent to the king. I am not sure I know them all. Albuquerque understood his past, Portugal's too, but found it difficult to plan the future. He did once let fall the phrase, an empire of the sea, and he added, that's what I want to create for my Portugal. I cannot explain what he meant, but can only set down here some of his random remarks to me and to pilots and traders that I expect you, Ahmadji, to put together. You have made me conscious of my writing, but I am not sure I can put Albuquerque's master design together in this letter. Maybe as I write his plan will become clearer to me.

And, Ahmadji, I am beginning to realize that dreams of power and glory affect great leaders like Albuquerque in strange ways.

I feel more comfortable now, Ahmadji, as I set down words on paper. I cannot yet set down the despair I feel about conversion and Christianity. Perhaps I will be able to talk about my despair with João. Will our Franciscan dream never be realized.

Albuquerque armed himself with a knowledge of the world he had entered before he proceeded to act in it. He was no Vasco da Gama, who acted like a clown on the stage of history. He was not like Francisco de Almeida, who looked at the new world with medieval eyes of honor and chivalry. Unlike Marshal Coutinho he was not foolhardy. Albuquerque began with what his old history teacher had told him, our country's lack of money and its lack of manpower

The problem of money first. *Cartaz*, you know what that means, Ahmadji. We have to double the license fee we charge every trading ship on the Bahr-i-Hind, Albuquerque told me, for the seas rightfully belong to Portugal. He talked also about intra Asian trade, the coastal trade in food grains and other commodities, the trade from India to India, as he put it. We have to somehow control that trade, he said. He threw in the word, *cafilas*, which I knew meant ships sailing in a convoy, but I didn't understand why he used that word.

More important, Albuquerque said, is the horse trade which we will funnel to Goa.

All the *taforeas* from the Hadhramaut, from Hormuz, and from Dhofar, Albuquerque announced to the council of *feitores* and captains, should not be allowed to land in Chaul or Bhatkal. They must be issued *cartazes* to compel them to proceed to Goa where customs duties will have to be paid for every horse that is landed. Payment to be made only in gold and in diamonds, he said. To take them out of Goa across the ghats the Vijayanagar and Bijapur traders will have to pay another tax on every horse. All that money, Frei Louro, all that gold and diamonds, will go to swell our treasury.

The words rushed out of Albuquerque's mouth. Ahmadji, I have never seen him so excited.

The king will not have to invest in guns and ships and men to dominate the Bahr-i-Hind, Albuquerque told *feitor* Francisco Corbinelli and me.

We were facing the huge wall map, the three of us.

Malik Aiyaz has written that the Mamluks, afraid of an attack from the north, are not building any more galleys at Suez and therefore will no longer be a threat. We will set up a blockade and cut the Arab trade routes that run from India north through the Red Sea and the Persian Gulf to the cities of the Levant.

Do you think that we could patrol that area with just two *naos* and two or three galleys that will cruise between Aden and Hormuz, he asked us.

I don't think Albuquerque expected an answer from me.

I thought immediately of the two persons who could provide him with an answer. So I spoke to Albuquerque, first about Francisco, how he was agitated about the plans to attack and conquer Melaka, how he wanted me as father confessor to warn the governor that it would be a disaster for Portugal, how he was a hero worshiper. And I added that Francisco was preparing a *Roteiro*, a pilot guide about the Red Sea and the Persian Gulf.

I then told Albuquerque about João Machado and about the many languages of the Bahr-i-Hind that he spoke, and about what a wonderful *lingua* he would be, the best *lingua* of all, trustworthy and reliable. João, I said, could be of some help. I didn't tell him he was a *degredado*, perhaps I would, later.

Albuquerque listened carefully. I know about João, he said.

The door opened and a secretary came in with a *lingua* followed by two Arabs dressed in long white robes. Both were tall. One of them, his face pitted with small pox, had a curved black beard. He carried a roll of paper in his hand. The other had a tiny fringe of a beard and a closely cropped moustache.

These are the two pilots who are familiar with the trade route to Mela-ka, the secretary said. They have been sent by Malik Aiyaz.

I'll talk to you later about João Machado, said Albuquerque.

It was mid January before Albuquerque sent word that I should meet him in the map room. The guard let me in. I was surprised to see Francisco crouching near the right corner of the wall map staring at a paper on the floor, copying names on to the Melaka area that had been, to my surprise, whitewashed away.

Francisco looked up at me and smiled.

Our Governor is quite right, he told me. Our knowledge of the world is expanding. Our maps will have to change too. Do you know, Frei Louro, the number of islands in this part of the world.

He pointed to Melaka.

No, I said.

Thousands, Francisco said. Here, around Melaka, is a magical island world of spices. . Mustafa told me that all the spices and medicinal herbs in the world are available in these islands. That's what I am setting down on this map.

Have you forgotten our Christian enterprise, I wanted to ask, but didn't.

Who is Mustafa, I asked instead.

You saw him and his assistant come here with the Governor, Francisco said. He was the one with a curved black beard and a face pitted with small pox. Mustafa knows everything about Melaka and its trade, and is an expert pilot. He has promised to tell me about the seasonal reversal of the wind circulation in southeast Asia for my *Roteiro*. It is he who gave our Governor this Javanese nautical chart with the names of some of the islands around Melaka.

Listen, Frei Louro, listen to the music of these names.

Cloves from the Moluccas, nutmeg and mace from Banda, pepper from Sumatra and Sunda, sandalwood from Timor, camphor from Borneo, Sumatran gold, Burmese precious stones, Chinese silk and porcelain.

So fascinated was I by the magic world Francisco had conjured up that I didn't hear Albuquerque come in. We heard the sound of clapping, and there behind us stood Governor Albuquerque.

You have the soul of a poet, Francisco, said Albuquerque, but what is needed now is for me to put together a plan to channel all this wealth towards Portugal. Did you know that all trade and shipping in our world is in the hands of the Muslims.

We didn't say anything, Francisco and I. Albuquerque led me by the arm to the semicircular chair in the middle of the room.

Stand behind the Frei, Francisco, and let us gaze at our new world.

It was huge, this world. How could a handful of Franciscans preach the gospel of Jesus Christ to its millions, I wondered. And Albuquerque, like most of us Portuguese, had completely forgotten our Christian mission.

Let me place before you both my plan. Don't offer any comments, Albuquerque warned us. I want to think out my plan. Don't ask questions, don't even reply to the questions I ask.

Albuquerque had a strange way of thinking out his plans. He paced from one end of the wall map to the other, stopping briefly in front of Ceylon, then striding to the left to place the tip pf his finger on Aden and the Red Sea, shaking his head and muttering *não, não*, sliding his finger up to Hormuz that guarded the Persian Gulf. Yes, yes, he said, then he came back to us and pointed straight to Goa. That, he said, in a determined voice, that will be our chief naval and commercial base, Goa. And this, he said, striding to Melaka, this will be our second base, the key to all the spices and wealth of south east Asia and China and Japan. It is a city made for merchandise, I was told. Whoever is lord of Melaka, has his hand on the throat of Venice. Melaka has no fortress, Mustafa tells me, only a system of earthworks surrounded by a wooden stockade. We will build a real stone fortress which will command the straits. I will, he announced, name it *A Famosa*.

What do you think of my plan, Francisco, Albuquerque asked.

Francisco kept silent. I did, too.

I know it's not the complete plan I have in mind, Albuquerque said. We need to capture Aden as our third base. But we do not have the long ladders we require to attack its high walls. What do you think, Frei Louro.

I should have spoken about our Christian enterprise at that time, but it wouldn't have worked.

Speak, Francisco.

Speak, I encouraged Francisco.

Senhor Governor, Francisco said. What a magnificent vision, even though I only perceive it dimly. Never before has any commander, not even the mighty Alexander who led his army across the deserts and mountains to India, conceived such a plan. What a plan, the creation of a seaborne empire. Never has the world seen an empire of the sea.

But, Francisco continued, can it be realized.

Yes, yes, yes, Albuquerque almost shouted. He was excited, then his voice dropped, and he sounded sad.

I wish I knew the name of my history teacher. It was he who drove into me this dream of mastering the sea. It is my destiny, Albuquerque said, to leap out beyond *terra* to conquer *thalassa*.

He strode to the map and began pacing up and down.

I am a pilot, Francisco said, but I still do not understand.

Albuquerque said, most reluctantly, let me explain my plan. We will not conquer territories but build fortresses and factories in strategic sea ports, Hormuz, Goa, and Melaka, which we will use as bases to dominate and regulate all trade and shipping in the Indian Ocean. All ships will be charged taxes and customs duties. For these seas, as you well know, Frei Louro, have been assigned to Portugal by the Pope. We will free the seas from Muslim shipping and from the tyranny of the Muslims. Not Venice, but our Lisbon will be the commercial center of the world. And Portugal with its *Estado da India* will be the most powerful state the world has ever seen.

He stood in the center stretching out both arms as if embracing the whole world in front of him and proclaimed, we will create a *thalassocracy*.

What's the use of conquering the whole world, I wanted to ask, but I didn't.

Albuquerque turned to us.

Francisco, he said, you and Mustafa will be the chief pilots of the fleet that will sail across the Asian seas to Melaka. Review with him the annual alternation of the monsoonal winds and find out the best timings to sail to Melaka and to return to Cochin.

Send a message immediately to Timmaya. Inform him that Bardez can be conquered later. He will be appointed our *tanadar mor*, the chief collector of revenues and land taxes for us.

Frei Louro, we will need João Machado as a *lingua* for our vast enterprise. You will have to go to Chapora to bring him back to the fold, and to us. He may have to return to Lisbon for a royal pardon.

Ahmadji, I need your help. If João helps us as a *lingua*, he will be forgiven. I am sure Albuquerque will write a letter to the king requesting a royal pardon for João and he will be able to return to Coimbra. Will you take me to Chapora. I need to ask João for forgiveness, tell him he is my cousin, and help him get home.

Your brother, Frei Louro

I have to go, to Chapora, can no longer postpone going there.

Why, oh why, asks my cynic with an air of innocence.

I have to know, I reply.

Know what, he asks.

I have to get my bearings in order to know where I am. I cannot be adrift, alone, on the ocean that is *samsāra* A word haunts me, panditji's, *rrinn*, the debt we all owe to those who have gone before us and to those living in the world around us.

I have to act, as João would say.

I haven't heard from Abdul, I am sure he will come to Chapora.

I'll go to Brother Pedro and ask him to add these papers to the ones he is keeping for me and request him to send a note to Frei Louro asking the Frei to meet me in Chapora either at the Well of Togetherness or under the banyan tree. Also to arrange for a boatman to take me from Portuguese Cochin to Chapora. The out flowing tide will make it difficult stop in Goa and pick up the Frei at Ela. It will be quicker for Frei Louro to cross the Mandovi and ride across Bardez to Chapora. I hope he still remembers the *Ars Tactica* and how João in Coimbra taught him how to ride a horse, or else he will have to get to Chapora in a bullock cart. I remember how sick I was on the way to Talaja.

Nakhoda Home, Chapora
   End of January
   Midnight

I know why I am writing this.

Why, oh why, my cynic teases me, making me smile.

He was not quite sure of why I was writing, sitting uncomfortably on a narrow window seat, my knees up, a flat board resting on my thighs, two candles perched behind me casting shadows on the ancient letter writer's paper tablet I am writing on and listening to the murmur of the Chapora river, waiting patiently for the boatman who brought me here from *Cochin de baixo* to take me away at dawn.

They have all come together here in Chapora, my cynic continues softly, sadly, the ones who love you and the ones you love. We stole out of Abdul's house in the dead of night through the storage shed, you did remember to replace the iron bars in the window, but you could not whisper to each one of them the twoword word that you have now come to love, perhaps because they were fast asleep.

I let them sleep peacefully, I tell my cynic, you need to rest too.

Why do you keep shifting tenses, asks my cynic, then he drops into silence.

João Machado, a lit candle on a table above his head, lies stretched out on his bed next to the window, his arquebus by his right side, the *kizilbash* with its twelve green peaks on the left of his pillow. His eyes are shut and he is at peace with himself, restless no longer, ready to go back home to Coimbra. On the bench, next to the window through which João contemplated *samsāra*, Frei Louro leans, snoring, against the wall, his arms curled protectively around little Ahm who nestles lovingly on his chest, both keeping vigil at João's bedside. Abdul lies across the threshold of the next room, guarding Layla who is asleep in the far corner on a torn sheet, still wearing her *burqa*, Yasmin is next to her.

We, the cynic and I, stole past all of them, Yasmin opened then shut one eye, and we slipped through the window of the storage shed and walked down to *Nakhoda Home* where I go to my room, quickly light the two candles and begin writing on this paper tablet as there is not much time left.

I am strangely at peace, the turmoil of yesterday seems both far and near, as if time itself has come to a stop, and past and present are one. The blind one in Diu sang about *kal*, that signifies tomorrow and yesterday, time and death. It was a word that I couldn't understand at that time. I now do. And my hakim told me that I lived in a prison on the plane of the past. I no longer do. I am living out of time and, my cynic is right, it is affecting the tenses I use. I don't feel driven to write, but write I must about what happened yesterday to complete my account before dawn. Where should I begin.

With Abdul surely, that embodiment of hope and action.

It was Abdul who brought all of us together and, dare I say it, rescued me. Unlike me, it was Abdul who rushed from *Cochin de baixo* to Bhatkal to make enquiries without, I am ashamed to write this, asking me for any money. When he got my letter about the boatman and the woman with the veil and the black bird, Abdul hurried to Vora who had his boatload of Turani horses ready and was waiting for Timmaya who was preparing to set sail for Chapora. Timmaya's plans to stir up riots against the *afaqis* of Bardez changed when Albuquerque summoned him to be the *tanadar mor* of Goa, and he set sail with his small fleet and his *berço* to Ela instead.

I'll come to Chapora later to kill the *afaqi* with my *berço*, Timmaya told Abdul. Why don't you go with Vora to Chapora. The *afaqi*, I am told, has a protector who lives in the house your parents used to live in. He is armed with an arquebus.

Cherian Marakkar gave me some money, Abdul told me later, and warned me never to trust that viper, Vora. The boatload of horses, Cherian said, have been stained to look like purebreds from Turan. Vora wants to swindle the *afaqi*. He is a professional assassin.

Abdul never hesitated. Unlike me, who would have lingered on in Bhatkal to brood about the worthwhileness of action in this our *samsāra*, he rushed to Vora and somehow persuaded him to set sail the next day.

Disguised as an Arab trader, Vora with his fake *cartaz* traveled on the upper deck of the horseboat, while Abdul, as a *naitea,* endured three days of slow sailing, amid the smells and the horseshit of the hold. Our boats, mine from *Cochin de baixo* and Abdul's from Bhatkal, happened to anchor at Chapora on the same moonless night. The landing was not crowded with boats. Many *afaqi* had left for Bijapur after the Portuguese took Goa.

Afraid of snakes, I did not venture out that night, but walked on the sand to *Nakhoda Home* almost next door and was given my usual room with a narrow window seat and a view of the river. At the break of dawn I would meet the old letter writer, and wait on the platform under the banyan tree for Frei Louro to arrive from Ela and take him to João.

I had no paper to write on, and I did not feel the usual overpowering urge to write. So I sat on the window seat and looked out at the river I couldn't see, and listened to its murmur, and spent the long night brooding, in a half daze.

A strange brooding, it was. Not the heavy kind I would indulge in before setting down some words of the poems I used to write that my hakim did not approve of. But light eruptions, syllables, smells of sickness, that bubbled their way up out of my being. Single words and sentence fragments they were, that had haunted me in the past. Death, and time, those destroyers. The forms of power I always detested, the power of organized religion. The power of science, and of guns, and of money, the newest of the gods according to Malik Gopi. *Dukke.* The simple word home that tells me we all are orphans here in this world. The word change that had terrified me into making sure that my world would not pass away to be forgotten. Non self, and the word *tanha.*

Strangely, like my hakim, I seldom feel thirsty now. I do not keep looking up at the sky and asking ask why, oh why. And I do not want to put my words or my world together or even desire to understand my world. I keep wandering now in the world of words. I remember my hakim telling me that his wanderings were a way out of *samsāra,* an answer that no longer puzzles me when I remember the deep inner peace I felt in the villages I visited with Padre Antão to treat my patients and my utter exhaustion at the end of the day as if I no longer had a self.

I must have dropped off to sleep.

I suddenly awoke to the tidal rhythm of the Chapora river rushing towards the ocean sea, muttering *sam-sā-ra,* continuously repeating the three syllables that taunt me saying, to escape is not to understand.

João, who really knows, told me it is impossible to understand *samsāra* I was permitted just one glance, and I did hear its roar when I was on Piram island in the gulf of Cambay, and I was terrified. It was João who knew that *samsāra* was the unstoppable flow of human existence, doomed by *karma*, human beings as wanderers, restless, homeless, endlessly search-ing for what they know not, waves of power surging and falling continu-ously, generations living and dying, he explained to me, nations rising and falling, forever changing, in a state of bondage, suffering from despair and disillusion.

João uses his mind to explain *samsāra*. Mine is a vision that terrifies me. I have to use images, the Bahr-i-Hind thundering with tufans, its waves rising and falling, responding to challenges, its winds and ceaseless cur-rents, the peoples that arrive on the ocean sea and then go back, like the Chinese, the traders and the civilizations that have sailed on its waters, the Mamluks and the Gujarat sultans that do not know they will soon disappear, the new arrivals, the arrogant Ottomans and the Safavids, and the Portuguese, who came as clowns and now are conquerors, and who, Frei Louro tells me, want to create a floating empire of the sea. Perhaps I should warn Albuquerque of the inevitable decline and fall that awaits him and the Portuguese. Perhaps I should warn him not to hire Mustafa as a pilot for his ship *Frol de la Mar* for he seeks revenge and will surely wreck it in the treacherous currents of the narrow straits of Melaka. Perhaps I should plunge into action like Abdul. What should I do. I do not know.

I look up from my window seat. There's the morning star

I have to go to meet Frei Louro under the banyan tree. We will both go to João.

Abdul, unlike me, did not or could not wait when his horseboat anchored in Chapora. In spite having just one eye, he was able to see in the dark. A message was sent to the *afaqi* about the arrival of the Turani horses. As soon as the horseboat was tied up, and all were asleep, Abdul lowered himself into the water, and rushed barefoot through the dark, past the Well of Togetherness, to his former home.

I wanted to climb in through the open window of the front room, but I didn't, Abdul told me, I had no weapon, not even a kitchen knife. I calmed myself down, and decided to remove the iron bars, and quietly enter through the window of the storage shed at the back.

How I wish I had the time to ask, when Abdul was telling me the story of his encounter with João, if his past still lived in him. It might have evoked memories in him of the Hindu girl he loved, that question, and hurt him.

He continued his story.

Abdul stepped cautiously across the side threshold into the front room. A candle stump threw its weak light on the bed on which someone lay, covered from head to toe with a white sheet. It had to be the *afaqi's* protector. On the left of the pillow was a tall spiked plant. On the right, alongside the sleeper, lay what Abdul thought was a thick bamboo stick.

He walked up to the bed, bent over and was about to grab the bamboo when a soft voice spoke from a dark corner, *ki khobor*, Abdul. A knife gleamed in the dark.

Abdul whirled around, flung out his arms, rushed to the corner, and clasped the speaker to himself in a mad embrace. He knew it was João.

Those iron bars made a noise when you removed them. Don't shoot, Abdul, said João, laughing loudly, pretending to be terrified. He dropped the kitchen knife.

Abdul dropped the arquebus, and they embraced fiercely again There was no need for words.

I have to pause here. For me, it was a shock, their embrace. I thought I knew them both. Neither João nor Abdul could tell me about the feelings that raced through them at the time, and there was no time later to ask questions. João was my friend, I know him. But Abdul who always uses words sparingly, how can he be a mystery to me after the many years we have spent together. Was he, is he, capable of hope or despair, I don't know. I never, but never, expected them to embrace like long lost brothers. I am sure I never would or could have embraced anyone like that. A word began to haunt me, *madjnuni*. And something Usha had said, a long long time ago.

I will not let myself brood. I have to hurry to complete this account before dawn.

Abdul warned João about Vora, told him that Vora would be disguised as an Arab horse trader, and that he was a professional assassin. Told him also about the boatload of fake Turani horses, and that payment had to be made only in diamonds, and that they wanted to leave with the outgoing tide.

João told Abdul that the *afaqi* had sent all the members of his household in a procession, the guards with their *tufengs*, and the Portuguese deserters with their arquebuses, to Ihrampur to wait for him there. All of them would leave for Bijapur with the Turani horses. João had to stay behind to protect the *afaqi* with his arquebus.

Abdul shrewdly asked about the woman with the *burqa*, did she too leave for Ihrampur. João didn't know. Neither did he know anything about a black bird. João told Abdul about little Ahm. No, João added, I made sure he wasn't Ahmadji's son. Then he told Abdul the story about the mango and how Ahm was named by the *afaqi*, Abdul didn't believe the *afaqi's* story. He was outraged by the *afaqi's* strange behavior at the well. João told Abdul that Ahm was a beautiful boy but couldn't speak, and would cry but could never shed tears, and only say *min min min* very fast and that he filled up pots of water on the rim of the Well of Togetherness. Abdul was troubled. *Min*, he said, that's just part of a word, not a word. Was the little one taken to Ihrampur, Abdul asked. João didn't know.

João and Abdul did not sleep at all that night. Nor did they talk. Abdul sat by the window trying to put things together, waiting for dawn.

The next morning João and Abdul saw the *afaqi*, a little pouch in his hand, walk out the front door of his house almost dragging little Ahm down the steps. Ahm appeared very reluctant to go to the well.

Maybe he too is an orphan, said João, maybe he doesn't have a home.

The boy was restless and kept looking up towards the house.

Maybe he is looking for the woman in the *burqa* who sometimes accompanies him, João said, putting on his slotted belt and taking up his arquebus.

The *afaqi* kept dangling the little pouch in front of the boy to coax him down the steps.

That's the pouch with the mango in it that the *afaqi* usually gives him. I'll ask the *afaqi* about the woman with the *burqa*, said João.

Come along, Abdul.

They walked through the front door, and João put on his *kizilbash*.

I'll meet you near the well, Abdul said suddenly, I have to find out about something. And he turned and rushed back into his house.

When João came to the entrance gate, the *afaqi* was still struggling with the little boy.

João reminded the *afaqi* about the fake Turani horses as they walked towards the well, and the *afaqi* kept dangling the little pouch in front of the boy whose eyes were swollen with the tears he could not shed.

Why don't you leave the boy here with me, said João, as he took up his position with his arquebus near the well to protect the *afaqi*.

He may run away, the *afaqi* said.

Don't play with this pouch, the *afaqi* said, it is heavy. And he gave the little pouch to the boy who laughed and kept twirling and dangling it all the time, saying *min min min* like a bird pecking at a seed. Hand in hand, both of them walked past the well towards the horseboat where Vora, disguised as an Arab horsetrader, was standing some distance away from a magnificent horse that had a streak of auspicious white on its forehead and a *naitea* attendant.

That's when we arrived at the gate, Frei Louro and I. The Frei had been saying his morning prayers kneeling on the platform under the banyan tree, the ancient letter writer had not come there yet, when I arrived and took the Frei to see João. Abdul, to our great astonishment, walked out of the front door of the *afaqi*'s house and came running down the steps. The three of us came together at the entrance gate, and we walked down towards the well.

We witnessed all that happened.

The *afaqi* circled around the restless horse with little Ahm who was so fascinated by the swishing of the black tail that he refused to accompany the *afaqi* to the water's edge. The *afaqi* ran down, wetted both his hands, came back and began to rub the white streak on the forehead of the horse with the palm of his right hand. The palm turned white.

The *naitea* started shouting, and waving his hands.

The horse, excited, tried to rear up on its hind legs, but couldn't because of the soft sand. It snorted and neighed loudly.

Little Ahm, frightened, ran up towards the well swinging his little pouch, crying *min min min*. He saw us, strangers, near his well, so he turned to the right to hide behind the coconut tree, but stumbled on a stone, fell down and hurt his knee. The pouch went flying from his hand into the jasmine bushes

The *afaqi* went running after the little boy, but did not stop to pick him up, even though the little one's left knee was bleeding. He ran to the jasmine bushes, bent down to pick up the pouch, and pulled at its strings to open it.

Just then the Arab horsetrader shouted a command to the *naitea* who ran up to the *afaqi* and stabbed him twice in the back and once on the side when he fell.

The open pouch went flying into the trunk of the coconut tree, and a shower of diamonds burst out glittering into the jasmine bushes.

João cocked his arquebus and shot the *naitea* dead.

The Arab horsetrader turned around and wanted to run to the horseboat when João shouted, Vora.

Shocked on hearing his name, Vora spun around, and his right hand darted to his left ear.

Stop, hold up your hands, Vora, and walk up towards the well, very very slowly, João said in Gujarati, loading his arquebus, cocking it, and taking aim at Vora's heart.

Taken aback at first by the shot that killed the *naitea*, the Frei and Abdul ran down to the well to help.

Abdul rushed to little Ahm, picked him up, and carried him to safety behind the coconut tree.

The Frei ran to the *afaqi* who lay on his side, groaning and gasping for breath. He ran to the well and raced back with a pot of water.

A scream pierced the air.

It made João swing around with his arquebus. He saw the woman in the *burqa* on the front steps of the *afaqi's* house, and he turned back again towards Vora.

Quick as a snake, Vora had reached out for a dagger behind his back below his left ear, and ran up behind Frei Louro.

I'll kill the Frei, Vora said to João in Gujarati, if you don't drop the arquebus.

Vora was completely hidden by the Frei's broad back.

Behind them I could see Abdul with a kitchen knife emerge from behind the coconut tree. João could see him too.

João stepped to one side, then took slow aim, not wanting to hurt his cousin. Vora threw his dagger so quickly and with such force that it penetrated deep into João's chest.

Abdul rushed out from behind the coconut tree and stabbed Vora with the kitchen knife that he had gone back to pick up in João's room.

Standing next to the Well of Togetherness, I sensed I was not quite myself as I saw all that happened, as if with one eye open and the other shut, wanting to move and not wanting to move, as if I was on Piram island in the Gulf of Cambay, looking at wave after wave after wave of action, watching a *samsāra* of my own.

It was a *nazar*, a glance that hit my being not my mind.

My eyes looked up at the sky as usual, but I did not ask it any question.

The woman in the *burqa* limped slowly down the steps to the well, a black bird perched awkwardly on her right shoulder.

I knew it was Yasmin. I looked at Abdul and at the little one who said *min min min*, and I tried to put things together.

Vora and the *naitea* lay dead down below.

Frei Louro managed with difficulty to help João to the side of the well to give him a drink of water.

João shook his head. He made a great effort to keep both eyes open.

I wanted, selfishly, to ask João a question about *samsāra*, but I didn't. João was in great pain. He shut his eyes.

Frei Louro knelt and bent his head down to hear João's confession, and I moved away from them to one side. But João was too weak, he couldn't speak. Blood trickled slowly out of his mouth

Frei Louro whispered to João that he was not an orphan but the Prior's only son. He then tried to embrace his cousin, but João's eyes were shut tight. A weak smile played on João's face that was streaked with blood.

He sacrificed his life for me, the Frei lamented.

He stood up, sprinkled water over his cousin's body, made the sign of the cross, and said a short prayer in Latin that I had often heard in the hospital. *Requiescat in pace.*

The Frei and I walked to the coconut tree.

Abdul was not able to console the little one. *Min min min* complained little Ahm as Abdul carried him struggling to me. *Min min min,* the little one cried.

He is your father, Abdul said in Konkani, wanting to place my son in my arms.

Little Ahm slipped away from me and ran to Frei Louro who lifted him up and wrapped his arms tight around him. The little one buried his tear swollen face into the Frei's broad shoulder for love and protection.

Abdul walked to the well to drink some water.

We heard the happy squawks of Yasmin when she saw little Ahm who stretched out both his hands to her. Layla, who hadn't removed her *burqa,* set Yasmin down on the rim of the well. *Min,* said little Ahm welcoming Yasmin with a smile, prolonging the syllable into a musical wave of affection and tenderness. *Min,* he stretched out the second syllable into a wave-like question, where have you been, I missed you. The third *min,* I almost couldn't hear it, was soft as a teardrop, an expression of the melting love he felt for her.

I was deeply moved. It was as if squawking Yasmin had brought us all together, me and little Ahm, Abdul and Layla, the cousins Frei Louro and João who was resting in peace, in order to tell us something that she wanted to but could not express. Restless, Yasmin paced awkwardly up and down along the rim of the well, squawking, avoiding the pots, at times pecking angrily at them, avoiding Layla who was trying to calm her down by scratching her throat gently with her forefinger. Little Ahm, tired, his eyes swollen with unshed tears, fell fast asleep on Frei Louro's broad shoulder.

I listened to Yasmin's loud squawks and to the weak flapping of her wings. I saw the brown scar on her right leg, and the faded yellow of her beak and around her black eyes. And I felt a deep sense of absence, and in a rush I asked Abdul if he still missed

Then I stopped, I did not complete the question, I did not want to hurt him.

There was a loud silence.

Usha, Abdul said suddenly, then added softly, I do.

Yasmin cocked her head to one side.

Abdul stared at the bushes of jasmine.

That was where they were sitting, his Usha and he, in the jasmine bushes, when the gang killed his Usha and smashed the side of his head with a bamboo. That's why Abdul would never address my Usha by her name.

Yasmin stopped her pacing and her squawking, cocked her head to one side, and listened intently.

Usha, Abdul said in a low voice. The two syllables arose from deep within him.

There was a loud silence

Ush loves Ahm, Yasmin said.

The words were soft but had a low hum of power.

And then Yasmin fell silent, as if she had said all that she had to say. She never spoke again.

I wanted to stop at this moment to calm the turmoil in my being. I knew what I wanted to do when Yasmin uttered those three syllables. I would break my fetters and disappear like the uncle at Śatruṇjaya to become an ascetic and end my *dukke*, my *tanha* and the clamors of my self by attaining *moksha*.

But now, now, as I look back and am writing about, not just experiencing, that moment of truth and love, I feel compelled to understand and translate the meaning of what happened at the well before I step into the boat at dawn to become a wandering hakim. I now reject the three selfish my.s and want not just to liberate my self but to pay the *rrinn* I owe, the debt to all my readers by completing the writing of this account, and by the unredeemable encompassing love that your embracing arms taught me, my Usha, a love, João told me, that widened into compassion for all human beings in this our *samsāra*.

Abdul it was, that man of action, who did what had to be done, while I sat dazed on the edge of the Well of Togetherness and stared at the flow of the Chapora river.

He arranged for the removal of the bodies of Vora and the *afagi*.

Three *naiteas* carried João, his *kizilbash* and his arquebus back to the house. The fourth *naitea* was sent to the ancient letter writer who arranged for two corpse washers to lay out João's body on his bed with the arquebus along his right side and the *kizilbash* on the left of his pillow.

Frei Louro carried little Ahm, who was still fast asleep, to the house with Yasmin perched in drooping silence on his other shoulder.

I smiled at the strange sight.

The fifth *naitea* was sent to *Nakhoda Home* with some prataps to fetch food that Layla would serve in the house.

Abdul listened patiently to portions of her story that Layla sobbed out to him, calmed her down, and led her, still in a *burqa*, to the coconut tree where she helped him pick up the diamonds that were scattered in the jasmine bushes. They placed them carefully in the pouch.

Abdul and I then went to the banyan tree where the ancient letter writer greeted Abdul warmly, welcomed me, and arranged for a simple meal of curry and rice to be served to both of us.

Then Abdul told us what happened after Anegundi.

The Jain assassins had hit Layla hard on the mouth, breaking her teeth to keep her quiet, and it was only with great difficulty that Abdul could understand the Konkani she mumbled.

She died, Abdul said, not looking at me, two days after they placed her on a stretcher and left Anegundi for Bhatkal. She died on the way while giving birth, and Layla gave some *prataps* to the priest of a Hindu temple to say the appropriate prayers and to perform the funeral rites.

From Bhatkal a boatman took Layla and the baby and Yasmin to Chapora. There the customs authorities took them straight to the *afaqi* who seized all the *prataps* Layla had with her for the unpaid house taxes. Layla was forced to work as a servant in the *afaqi*'s house with strict orders not to leave the compound, and she lived for some years in a small room with little Ahm and Yasmin. She always wore a *burqa* to hide her face, and no one knew she had come back to Chapora. Layla refused to go to Ihrampur without little Ahm. She protected him fiercely and frustrated the evil designs of the *afaqi*.

Abdul had his suspicions about the *afaqi*. When João and he saw the *afaqi* emerge dragging the little boy, he rushed back into the house, picked up the knife João had dropped, ran up and entered through the back door of the *afaqi*'s house, where he found Layla with her hands and feet bound and her mouth gagged. He freed her, calmed her, and rushed down to the Well of Togetherness to help us.

I'm glad you have come home, Abdul my son, said the ancient letter writer. You'll be able to take my place here under this banyan tree as I had planned.

Abdul went up to him, bowed down, and placed the old man's hands on his own head.

I didn't tell you, Ahmadbhai, may I call you that now, that for five years when I was away from you at Bhatkal, I went to school. I can read and write now, Abdul said.

Abdul knew that, as *tanadar mor*, Timmaya would arrange to give him back his house where he could live with his sister. Layla would never remove her *burqa* and she would never be married, but she would be happy. Abdul would be the next letter writer for the village of Anjuna.

Abdul gave the pouch of diamonds to the ancient letter writer to distribute among the villagers as compensation for the unjust taxes the *afaqi* had levied. Layla would receive some to make up for the *prataps* the *afaqi* had seized from her.

All would be well.

Frei Louro arrived at that moment with little Ahm still fast asleep on his shoulder. He wanted to tell all of us the heroic story of his cousin, but realized, sadly, that no one would understand his Portuguese. He fell silent.

João wished to return home to Coimbra by Christmas, I told Frei Louro sadly.

The Frei fell silent for a while.

Then he spoke softly. My cousin's last wish will be granted. His body will be taken from here to Goa and shipped to Lisbon. I will see to it that his bones are laid to rest on Christmas day in the vault of the Santa Cruz cathedral in Coimbra.

We all fell silent.

Little Ahm woke up and looked all around for Yasmin. *Min min min,* he cried, *min min min.* He clung to Frei Louro. Two tears suddenly rolled down Ahm's face.

The ancient letter writer offered him a ripe mango but Ahm refused, he would only accept it from Frei Louro.

Everyone looked at little Ahm, then they turned and looked at me.

He misses Yasmin, Abdul said. Layla and I will take care of him. Yasmin will be with us.

Little Ahm can come with me, said Frei Louro. You can't take him with you as a wandering hakim, Ahmadbhai. Let him go with João and me to Coimbra. He will be educated in the seminary there.

I felt a powerful surge of love and I wanted to take my son from Frei Louro and hold him in my arms, if only for a moment, I wanted to feel his little heart beating against mine.

Maybe my son would be a pilot.

My cynic stirred within me and wanted to protest, but didn't.

But my son wouldn't come to me.

I sent a message to the boatman to come to *Nakhoda Home* at dawn. Then I asked the ancient letter writer for a paper tablet, some ink and a pen, and we walked slowly to Abdul's house. Frei Louro carried little Ahm, fast asleep, on his broad shoulder. Layla had cleaned up the house and put it in order. Frei Louro wanted to keep vigil at João's bedside, and little Ahm wouldn't let go of the Frei. We were all tired, and they soon fell asleep.

But I couldn't, I didn't want to.

I sat by the window looking at the calm flow of the Chapora river and tried to put things together.

Ush loves Ahm.

I looked at João lying peacefully asleep on the bed, hoping he would tell me something about the beyond.

Only a cryptic silence.

Ush loves Ahm.

Two ush.es, one Abdul's, the other mine.

Two Ahm.s, the little one and me.

The verb was that unsayable word we never used, Usha and I, when we talked to each other.

Why, oh why, did she have Yasmin use that verb.

Because, João my teacher whispers to me before leaving for the beyond, she is not talking to you but is transmitting a message, using the grammar of the absolute, where tenses, past, present and future blend, she loved you, she loves you, she will always love you, and she will go with you wherever you go.

I remembered then.

Laila and Madjnun, their story.

I remembered how on the *San Raphael* Usha could not get Yasmin to pronounce my full name, Yasmin could only say its first syllable.

Then it hit me, what the police official saw from the Anegundi tower as the three of them started for Bhatkal, Yasmin, at Usha's side, cocking her head and listening intently to those three syllables which Usha must have repeated for two days. She died soon after. Little Ahm was yet to be born. Yasmin's Ahm is, dare I say it, me, an Ahmad that includes and continues my Ahm.

Thank you, João, my friend. No more explaining.

I rose and I walked down to *Nakhoda Home* and began completing the writing of my account on this paper tablet. I did not bid farewell to any of them, not even to little Ahm, though my heart was heavy, for the twoword word could not express all that I wanted to express.

This account will. Though who will read it I do not know. Frei Louro will probably put it together with the other papers, take them with him to Lisbon, and place all of them in the dark vault of the Santa Cruz cathedral in Coimbra with João's bones. Will it ever see the light of day. I do not know. My writerly self, is there such a thing, which I will soon discard, would like it to be read.

Then it must have a title, my cynic says sadly, for he knows he cannot come with me.

João suggested, a long time ago, I should title it *Mirat-i-Samsāra*. My story does present a mirror of the world I lived in, its mad upheavals, the power struggles, the rise and fall of empires, the loud clash of civilizations, of cultures and of religions at the turn of our century. The same kind of struggles must have taken place five hundred years ago, and will be repeated, like the endless waves of the sea, again and again, and maybe, after another five hundred years from now, the roar of *samsāra*, alas, will be heard again and the mad struggles for power will rebegin.

I see the morning star. I hear the strong rush of the outgoing tide. I have to end, it's time to go.

But maybe, João, just maybe, our story, Usha's and mine, will somehow be heard above the roar of *samsāra*. Once I thought that love, unlike power, was weak. In Lamu, I wrote the word love on the sand and sadly watched the incoming waves wash it away. When I asked you about power, you once made a cryptic play on words, the love of power and the power of love. It was you who told me later in a letter about the silent power of love. A force of nature it was, you said, a tufan that uprooted my baobab self. It is, and you quoted the first line of the poem Usha and I composed, four nights out of Diu, on the *Zephyr*, a wave of the sea that can encompass the whole world. It is a word, I realized today, that takes one beyond time. Like the single syllable *kal*, it belongs to the language of the absolute.

My title will be *Love and Samsāra*.

I see the light of dawn. It's time. Let me say a prayer. O Pilot of the universe, take me ho

Coimbra, Portugal Christmas Day, 1512

Today my cousin João's bones, placed in a casket, were deposited in the vault of the Santa Cruz cathedral. It was a simple ceremony. I held a lit candle and said a short prayer. I could sense your presence, Ahmadji. Your papers, together with this short note, I placed in a whiteantproof sealed wooden box from Melaka, and I set it next to João. At Mozambique, on my way back to Lisbon, I heard the rumor that Albuquerque and his ship, the *Frol de la Mar*, were both lost in the treacherous straits of Melaka on his way to Goa. *Samsāra*, Ahmadji. I will return to Cochin next year as Commissary to continue our Franciscan mission.Where are you, Ahmadji. Allah, isn't that the Arabic for God, be with you.

Your brother in Christ, Frei Louro.

www.ingramcontent.com/pod-product-compliance
Lightning Source LLC
Chambersburg PA
CBHW021956050726
47498CB00001BA/44